W9-AZG-386

INK
EXCHANGE

INK EXCHANGE

melissa marr

HARPER TEEN

An Imprint of HarperCollins*Publishers*

Teen
Fiction
Marr

Ink Exchange
Copyright © 2008 by Melissa Marr
Tattoo image copyright © 2007 by Paul Roe and Melissa Marr

www.harperteen.com

Library of Congress Cataloging-in-Publication Data
Marr, Melissa.
  Ink exchange / Melissa Marr. — 1st ed.
     p.   cm.
  Summary: Seventeen-year-old Leslie wants a tattoo as a way of
reclaiming control of herself and her body, but the eerie image she
selects draws her into the dangerous Dark Court of the faeries,
where she draws on inner strength to make a horrible choice.
  ISBN 978-0-06-121468-4 (trade bdg.)
  ISBN 978-0-06-121469-1 (lib. bdg.)
  [1. Fairies—Fiction. 2. Tattooing—Fiction. 3. Kings, queens,
rulers, etc.—Fiction. 4. Self-realization—Fiction. 5. Fantasy.]
I. Title.
PZ7.M34788Ink 2008   2007040106
[Fic]—dc22   CIP
                                                        AC

1 2 3 4 5 6 7 8 9 10
❖
First Edition

To all the people who've been in the abyss and found
(or are finding) a way to reach solid ground—
you're proof that the seemingly impossible can happen.

And to A.S., who shared his shadows with me—
I hope you found what you needed.

ACKNOWLEDGMENTS

The past year plus has seen *Wicked Lovely* (my first book) go from revision to being on shelves—and *Ink Exchange* go from concept to completion. This was daunting, but the warm encouragement I've received has made it possible. To everyone at HarperCollins US and HarperCollins UK; to my publishers abroad (especially Franziska at Carlsen in Germany); to librarians, booksellers, readers, parents, journalists, teachers, and the folks at the fansite (especially Maria); to my amazing financial manager, Peggy Hileman; and to the innumerable others I've met online and in person: I've been humbled by your kindness and support. Thank you, all.

Special thanks go to Clare Dunkle, who has touched my heart first with her novels and then in the past year with her wisdom. It's been a privilege.

My agent, Rachel Vater, makes chaos look like order. Whether you're talking me down, keeping me company as I wander, or flashing those pretty fangs, I am ever grateful.

My two passionate editors, Anne Hoppe and Nick Lake, continue to exceed expectations. Your insights, notes, and hours of chatting have made the text clearer and closer to the ideals I strive to reach.

Kelsey Defatte read the very earliest versions of this manuscript. Craig Thrush read through my conflict scenes. I am indebted to you both. And I am extremely indebted to Jeaniene Frost for hours of talking, revision letters to rival editors' letters, and so many epiphany-stirring observations. Thanks, J.

My tattoo artist, Paul Roe, read the tattoo sequences and answered innumerable questions on the minutiae of the art and its history. For this, for decorating my skin, and for all the rest, you have been essential to me.

Some rare people have given me their affection through years of chaos and calm—Dawn Kobel, Carly Chandler, Kelly Kincy, Rachael Morgan, Craig Thrush, and most of all, Cheryl and Dave Lafferty. Thank you for keeping me steady. Words can't cover what you mean to me.

None of the rest of this would've meant a thing if it weren't for the people who enrich every aspect of my life—my parents, children, and spouse. I'm fairly certain I exist only because you are beside me.

—June 2007

PROLOGUE

FALL

Irial watched the girl stroll up the street: she was a bundle of terror and fury. He stayed in the shadows of the alley outside the tattoo parlor, but his gaze didn't waver from her as he finished his cigarette.

He stepped out just as she passed.

Her pulse beat too fast under her skin when she saw him. She straightened her shoulders—not fleeing or backing away, bold despite the shadows that clung to her—and motioned to his arm where his name and lineage were spelled out in an ogham inscription surrounded by spirals and knots that morphed into stylized hounds. "That's gorgeous. Rabbit's work?"

He nodded and walked the remaining few steps to the tattoo parlor. The girl kept pace with him.

"I'm thinking of getting something soon. I just don't know what yet." She looked defiant as she said this. When he didn't reply, she added, "I'm Leslie."

"Irial." He watched her struggle and fail to find more
words, to make him want to notice her. She was starving for
something. If he took mortals for playthings, she'd be good
fun, but he was here for business, not collecting trinkets, so
he kept silent as he opened the door of Pins and Needles
for her.

Inside the tattoo shop, Leslie wandered away to talk to a
dark-haired girl who was watching them warily. There were
others in the shop, but only the dark-haired girl mattered.
Because he'd made the curse that had bound summer so
many centuries ago, Irial knew exactly who she was: the
missing Summer Queen, the problem. She would change
everything.

And soon.

Irial had felt it the moment Keenan had chosen her, had
stolen her mortality. It was why Irial had come to Rabbit:
change was coming. Now that the Summer King would be
unbound—and able to strike out at those who'd trapped
him—true war was a possibility for the first time in centuries. Unfortunately, so was too much order.

"Spare a moment, Rabbit?" Irial asked, but it was a formality more than a question. Rabbit might not be wholly
fey, but he wouldn't turn down the king of the Dark Court,
not now, not ever.

"Come on back," Rabbit said.

Irial trailed his hands over one of the steel-framed jew-
elry cabinets as he passed, well aware that Leslie's attention

was still on him. He closed the door and handed Rabbit the brown glass vials—blood and tears of the Dark Court. "I need the ink exchanges to work sooner than we'd planned. We're out of time."

"The fey might"—Rabbit paused and rephrased it—"it could kill them, and the mortals aren't recovering well."

"So find a way to make it work. *Now*." Irial tried a smile, softening his expression as he rarely did for the dark fey.

Then he faded to invisibility and followed Rabbit back into the main room of the shop. Unhealthy curiosity made him pause beside Leslie. The others were gone, but she stood looking at the flash on the wall, lesser images than what Rabbit could draw on her skin given a chance.

"Dream of me, Leslie," Irial whispered, letting his wings wrap around them both, enclosing them. Maybe the girl would get strong enough to withstand an ink exchange with one of the chosen faeries. If not, he could always give her to one of the weaker fey. It seemed a shame to waste a lovely broken toy.

CHAPTER 1

EARLY THE FOLLOWING YEAR

Leslie slipped into her school uniform and got ready as quickly as she could. She closed her bedroom door softly, staying quiet so she could get out of the house before her father woke. Being retired wasn't good for him. He'd been a decent father before—before Mom left, before he'd fallen into a bottle, before he'd started taking trips to Atlantic City and gods knew where else.

She headed to the kitchen, where she found her brother, Ren, at the table, pipe in hand. Wearing nothing but a pair of ratty jeans, his blond hair loose around his face, he seemed relaxed and friendly. Sometimes he even was.

He looked up and offered a cherubic smile. "Want a hit?"

She shook her head and opened the cupboard, looking for a tolerably clean cup. *None.* She pulled a can of soda from the meat drawer in the fridge. After Ren had doped a bottle—and thereby doped her—she'd learned to drink only from still-sealed containers.

Ren watched her, content in his chemical cloud, smiling in a perversely angelic way. When he was friendly and just smoking pot, it was a good day. Ren-on-Pot wasn't a problem: pot just made him mellow. It was Ren-on-Anything-Else that was unpredictable.

"There's chips over there if you want some breakfast." He pointed to a mostly empty bag of corn chips on the counter.

"Thanks." She grabbed a couple and opened the freezer to get the toaster waffles she'd hidden. They were gone. She opened the cupboard and pulled out a box of the only type of cereal her brother didn't eat—granola. It was nasty, but his pilfering stopped at the healthy stuff, so she stocked up on it.

She poured her cereal.

"No milk left," Ren mumbled, eyes closed.

Sighing softly, Leslie sat down with her bowl of dry granola. *No fights. No troubles.* Being home always made her feel like she was walking on a high wire, waiting for a gust of wind to knock her to the ground.

The kitchen smelled strongly of weed. She remembered when she used to wake up to the scent of eggs and bacon, when Dad would brew fresh coffee, when things were normal. It hadn't been like that for more than a year.

Ren plunked his bare feet on the kitchen table. It was covered with junk—news circulars, bills to pay, dirty dishes, and a mostly empty bottle of bourbon.

While she ate, she opened the important bills—electric and water. With relief, she saw that Dad had actually paid ahead on both of them. He did that when he had a good run of luck at the tables or a few sober days: sent extra on the big bills so it wouldn't be a hassle later. It didn't help for groceries or the cable bill, which was overdue again, but she could usually cover those when she had to.

Not this time, though. She'd finally decided to go through with it, to get a tattoo. She'd been wanting one for a while but hadn't felt ready. In the last few months, she'd become near obsessed with it. Waiting wasn't the answer, not anymore. She thought about that act far too often—marking her body, reclaiming it as her own, a step she needed to take to make herself whole again.

Now I just need to find the right image.

With what she hoped was a friendly smile, she asked Ren, "Do you have any money for cable?"

He shrugged. "Maybe. What's it worth to you?"

"I'm not bargaining. I just want to know if you can cover cable this month."

He took a long hit off his pipe and exhaled into her face. "Not if you're going to be a bitch about it. I have expenses. If you can't do a guy a favor now and then, make nice with my friends"—he shrugged—"you pay it."

"You know what? I don't need cable." She walked over to the trash and dropped the bill in the can, fighting back the sickness in her throat at the mention of *making nice* with his friends, wishing that someone in her family cared about what happened to her.

If Mom hadn't taken off . . .

But she had. She'd bailed and left Leslie behind to deal with her brother and father. "It'll be better this way, baby," she'd said. It wasn't. Leslie wasn't sure if she'd want to talk to her mom anymore—not that it mattered. She had no contact information at all.

Leslie shook her head. Thinking about that wouldn't help her cope with her current reality. She started to walk past Ren, but he stood up and grabbed her for a hug. She was stiff in his arms.

"What? Are you on the rag again?" He laughed, amused by his crass joke, amused by her anger.

"Never mind, Ren. Just forget I—"

"I'll pay the bill. Relax." He let go of her, and as soon as he let his arm drop, she stepped away, hoping the scent of pot and cigarettes wouldn't cling to her too obviously. Sometimes she suspected that Father Meyers knew exactly how much things had changed for her, but she still didn't want to walk into school reeking.

She put on her fake smile and murmured, "Thanks, Ren."

"I'll take care of it. You just remember it next time I

need you to come out with me. You're a good distraction when I need credit." He looked at her calculatingly.

She didn't reply. There wasn't an answer that would help. If she said no, he'd be a prick, but she wasn't saying yes. After what his druggie friends did—*what* he *let them do*—she wasn't going anywhere near them again.

Instead of rehashing that argument, she went and grabbed the bill out of the trash. "Thanks for taking care of it."

She handed it to him. Right now, it didn't matter if he did it or not: she couldn't pay the cable bill and get ink, and really, she didn't watch cable enough to justify paying for it. Mostly, she paid it because she was embarrassed by the idea of anyone finding out that her family *couldn't* pay a bill, as if by keeping it normal as long as possible maybe it'd get normal. It kept her from facing the inevitable pity and whispers if everyone found out how lame her father had become since Mom left, if they found out just how low her brother had gotten.

By fall she'd be in college, escaped from here, away from them. *Just like Mom did—escape.* Sometimes she wondered if her mother had been escaping something she didn't want Leslie to know about. If so, her mother's leaving made more sense—but her leaving Leslie behind made less sense. *It doesn't matter.* Leslie had already sent out her first-choice applications and applied for a bunch of scholarships. *That's what matters—getting a plan and getting out.* Next year she'd be safe, in a new city, in a new life.

But that didn't stop the wave of terror she felt as Ren lifted his bourbon in a silent salute.

Without another word, she grabbed her bag.

"Catch you later, sis," Ren called, before he turned his attention to packing another bowl.

No. You won't.

By the time Leslie walked up the steps to Bishop O'Connell High School, her fears were safely tucked back in their box. She'd gotten better at watching for the warning signs—the tense calls that meant Ren was in trouble again, the strangers in the house. She worked extra if there were too many warning signs. She'd put locks on her bedroom door. She didn't drink out of open bottles. Her safeguards didn't undo what was, but they helped avoid what could be.

"Leslie! Hold up," Aislinn called out from behind her.

Leslie stopped and waited, schooling her face to be bland and calm, not that it mattered: Aislinn had been lost in her own world lately. A few months ago, she'd hooked up with the all-too-yummy Seth. They'd been practically dating anyhow, so that wasn't so weird. What was weird was that Aislinn had simultaneously developed a very intense relationship with another guy, Keenan. Somehow neither guy seemed to object to the other.

The guys who'd walked Aislinn to school stood watching her from across the street while she caught up to Leslie. Keenan and Niall, his uncle, didn't move from their post, seeming far too serious—and apparently oblivious to the number of people watching them like they were members of the Living Zombies. Leslie wondered if Niall played an instrument. He was sexier than any of the Zombies. If he played or sang too . . . he'd be halfway to success just by looking so delicious. He had a mysterious aura, plus he was a couple years older than Leslie and Aislinn—a college sophomore maybe. Add that oddly sexy responsibility thing—he was one of Keenan's guardians, an uncle, but still young—and he seemed like a perfect package, one she was staring at again.

When he smiled and waved, Leslie had to force herself not to go toward him. She always felt like that when he looked at her. There was an illogical urge to run toward him, like something was coiled too tightly inside her and the only way to ease the tension was to go to him. She didn't. She wasn't about to make a fool of herself over a guy who hadn't shown any genuine interest. *Maybe he would, though.* So far, their only contact had been under the watchful eye of Keenan or Aislinn, and that was usually interrupted by Aislinn's flimsy excuses to go somewhere away from Niall.

Aislinn put her hand on Leslie's arm. "Come on."

And, like they had so often, they walked away from Niall.

Leslie turned her attention to Aislinn. "Wow. Rianne said you were crazy tan, but I didn't believe it."

Aislinn's perpetually pale skin was perfectly tan, as if she'd been living on a beach, as tan as Keenan always was. It hadn't been that way on Friday. Aislinn bit down on her lip—a nervous habit that usually meant she was feeling cornered. "It's some winter thing—SAD, they called it—so I needed to get some sunlight."

"Right." Leslie tried to keep the doubt out of her voice and failed. Aislinn didn't seem depressed at all—or to have reason *to* be depressed lately. In fact, she seemed like she'd become rather flush with money and attention. A few times when Leslie had seen her out with Keenan, both of them had been wearing matching twisted golden necklaces that fit snugly around their throats. The clothes that Aislinn wore, the new winter coats, the chauffeurs, and—let's not forget—Seth's being cool with all of it. *Depressed? Yeah, right.*

"Did you go over the reading for Lit?" Aislinn pulled open the door and they joined the throng of people in the halls.

"We had a dinner thing out of town, so I didn't finish." Leslie gave an exaggerated eye roll. "Ren even dressed with all the required pieces of clothing."

They both continued to steer the conversation away from topics they didn't want to address. Leslie lied easily, but Aislinn seemed determined to direct the conversation toward neutral subjects. Eventually, she glanced behind her—as if there were someone there—and made another random topic switch: "Are you still working over at Verlaine's?"

Leslie looked: there wasn't anyone there. "Sure. It drives Dad mad that I wait tables, and you know, gives me a good excuse if I need to explain my weird hours."

Leslie didn't admit that she *had* to work or that her father didn't have a clue what she did for money. She wasn't sure her father knew she had a job or that she paid the bills. He might have thought Ren was doing it, although he probably didn't realize Ren was dealing—*or selling me*—to get his money. Talking about money, home, and Ren was so not the sort of conversation she wanted to have, so she took a turn shifting the topic. With a conspiratorial grin, she looped her arm around Aislinn's waist and assumed the facade she adopted with her friends. "So, let's talk about Keenan's sexy uncle. What's the scoop on him? Is he seeing anyone?"

"Niall? He's just . . . he's not, but . . ." Aislinn frowned. "You don't want to mess with him. There's prettier . . . I mean, better . . ."

"I doubt that, sweetie. Your vision's clouded by staring at Seth too long." Leslie patted Aislinn's arm. "Niall's top shelf."

His face was as beautiful as Keenan's but in a different way: Niall's had character. One long scar ran from his temple to the corner of his mouth, and he wasn't shy about it. His hair was cut so short that there was no chance of anything detracting from the beauty of that jagged line.

And his body . . . *wow.* He was all sinew and length, moving like he had been training in some long-lost martial art since birth. Leslie couldn't figure why anyone would notice Keenan when Niall was around. Keenan was attractive enough, with his unnatural green eyes, perfect body, and sandy-blond hair. He was gorgeous, but he moved in a way that always made Leslie think he wasn't quite meant for civilization. He frightened her. Niall, on the other hand, was luscious and seemed sweet—kind in a way that Keenan wasn't.

Leslie prompted, "So relationships . . ."

"He doesn't, umm, do relationships." Aislinn spoke softly. "Anyhow, he's too old."

Leslie let it drop for the moment. Although Aislinn was spending much of her time "not-dating" Keenan, she kept her school friends separate from Keenan's crowd as much as possible. When they did intersect, Aislinn clung to Leslie like an extra limb, giving no opportunities for Leslie to have conversations with anyone who hung around Keenan—most especially Niall. For a moment, Leslie wondered if she'd be so intrigued by Niall if it weren't for Aislinn's playing keep-away. The more Aislinn acted as an obstacle, the more Leslie wanted nearer Niall. An older guy with a drool-worthy body and seemingly no bad habits to speak of *and* somehow forbidden: how could that not be appealing?

But Aislinn's plate was overfilled with Seth and Keenan, so maybe she just wasn't getting it. *Or maybe she knows something.* Leslie forced that thought away: if Aislinn had a legitimate reason to think Niall was bad news, she'd say something. They might be in the middle of this weird dance of secrecy, but they were still friends.

"Les!" Rianne shoved through the crowd with her usual exuberance. "Did I miss seeing the dessert tray?"

"Just two of the tasty treats today . . ." Leslie linked her arm through Rianne's as they made their way toward their lockers. Rianne was reliably good at keeping things light.

"So dark-and-pierced wasn't on duty?" Rianne flashed a wicked grin at Aislinn, who blushed predictably.

"No Seth. Today was blond-and-moody along with scarred-and-sexy." Leslie winked at Aislinn, enjoying the brief moments of normalcy, of smiling. Rianne brought that in her wake, and Leslie was ever grateful for it. They stopped in front of Aislinn's locker, and Leslie added, "Our little dessert hoarder was just going to tell me when we're all going out dancing."

"No, not—" Aislinn started.

"Sooner or later, you're going to need to share the wealth, Ash. We're feeling deprived. Weakened." Rianne sighed and leaned heavily on Leslie. "I'm feeling faint with it."

And for a moment, Leslie saw a look of longing pass over Aislinn's face, but then Aislinn caught her watching.

Aislinn's face turned impassive. "Sometimes I wish I could . . . I just don't think it's a good idea."

Rianne opened her mouth to respond, but Leslie shook her head. "Give us a sec, Ri. I'll catch up."

After Rianne left, Leslie caught Aislinn's gaze. "I wish we weren't doing this. . . ." She gestured between them.

"What do you mean?" Aislinn grew so still and silent in the din of the hall, it was like the noise around them vanished for an instant.

"Lying." Leslie sighed. "I miss us being real friends, Ash. I'm not going to encroach on your scene, but it'd be nice to be straight-up again. I miss you."

"I'm not lying. I . . . can't lie." She stared beyond Leslie for a moment, scowling at someone.

Leslie didn't turn to see who it was. "You're not being honest, either. If you don't want me around . . ." She shrugged. "Whatever."

Aislinn grabbed her arms and held her close. Although she tried, Leslie actually *couldn't* pull away.

A jerk passing in the hall called, "Dykes."

Leslie tensed, torn between the once-instantaneous urge to flip him off and the still-new fear of conflict.

The bell rang. Lockers slammed. Aislinn finally said, "I just don't want to see you get hurt. There's . . . people and things . . . and . . ."

"Sweetie, I doubt they're any worse than what—" She stopped herself, unable to say the sentences that would follow. Her heart thunked at the thought of saying those words aloud. She shook her arm. "Can you let go? I've still got to go to my locker."

Aislinn released her, and Leslie left before she had to figure out how to answer the inevitable questions that

would follow her almost admission. *Talking won't change it.*
But sometimes it was what she wanted most, to tell someone; often, though, she just wanted to not feel those horrid
feelings, to escape herself, so there was no pain, no fear, no
ugliness.

CHAPTER 2

After school Leslie headed out before Aislinn or Rianne had a chance to catch up with her. She'd spent her free period in the library reading more on the history of tattooing, the centuries-old traditions of marking the body. The reasons—ranging from adopting a totem animal's nature to marking life events to offering visual cues to identify criminals—fascinated her. More important, they resonated with her.

When she walked in the door of Pins and Needles, the cowbell clanged.

Rabbit glanced over his shoulder.

"Be right with you," he called. As the man beside him talked, Rabbit absently ran a hand over his white-and-blue-dyed hair.

Leslie lifted a hand in greeting and walked past him. This week he had left a tiny goatee directing attention to his labret piercing. It was that piercing under his lower lip that had caught her attention the first time Ani and Tish had brought her to the shop. Within a week, she'd had her own piercing—hidden under her blouse—and found herself spending time in the studio.

She felt safe there—away from Bishop O.C., away from the unpleasantness of her father's drunkenness, away from whatever letches Ren brought home to share his drug of the week. At Pins and Needles she could be safe, quiet, relaxed—all the things she couldn't be most other places.

"Yes, always use new needles," Rabbit repeated to the prospective customer.

As Leslie walked around the shop, she listened to the snatches of Rabbit's comments that wound into the silence between songs: "Autoclave . . . sterile as a hospital."

The man's gaze drifted lazily over the flash on the walls, but he wasn't there to buy. He was tense, ready to bolt. His eyes were too wide. His posture was nervous—arms folded, body closed in on itself. Despite the number of people who came through the shop, only a few would actually lay down money for art. He wasn't one of them.

"I have a couple questions," she called out to Rabbit.

With a grateful smile at her, Rabbit excused himself from the man, telling him, "If you want to look around . . ."

Leslie walked over to the far wall, where she flipped through the flash—images that could be bought by and put on as many people as liked them. Flowers and crosses, tribal patterns and geometric designs—many were beautiful, but no matter how long she stared at them, none seemed right. The small rooms branching off the main room had other styles that were less appealing: old-school pinup girls, skeletal figures, cartoon characters, slogans, and animals.

Rabbit came up behind her, but she didn't tense, didn't feel that urge to turn so she couldn't be cornered. It was *Rabbit*. Rabbit was safe.

He said, "Nothing new there, Les."

"I know." She flipped the poster frame board that rested against the wall. One image was of a green vine entwined around a half-human woman; she looked like she was being strangled but smiled as if it felt good. *Idiotic.* Leslie flipped again. Obscure symbols with translations underneath covered the next screen. *Not my style.*

Rabbit laughed, a smoker's raspy laugh, although he didn't smoke and claimed he never had. "With as much time as you've spent looking the past months, you'd have found it by now."

Leslie turned and scowled up at Rabbit. "So design something for me. I'm ready *now,* Rabbit. I want to do this."

Off to the side, the would-be customer paused to look at a couple of the rings in the glass case.

With an uneasy shrug, Rabbit said, "Told you before. You want custom work, you bring me an idea. Something. I can't design without references."

The bell clanged as the man left.

"So help me find an idea. Please? You've had my parental

consent form for weeks." She wasn't backing down this time. Getting ink felt right, like it would help her put her life in order, to move forward. It was *her body*, despite the things that'd been done to it, and she wanted to claim it, to own it, to *prove* that to herself. She knew it wasn't magic, but the idea of writing her own identity felt like the closest she could get to reclaiming her life. Sometimes there's power in the act; sometimes there's strength in words. She wanted to find an image that represented those things she was feeling, to etch it on her skin as tangible proof of her decision to change.

"Rabbit? I need this. You told me to think. I've thought. I need . . ." She stared out at the people passing on the street, wondering if the men who'd . . . if they were out there. She wouldn't recognize them since Ren had drugged her before he gave her to them. She pulled her gaze back to Rabbit and was uncharacteristically blunt, telling him what she couldn't tell Aislinn earlier: "I need to change, Rabbit. I'm drowning here. I need *something*, or I'm not going to make it. Maybe a tattoo isn't the right answer, but right now it's something I can do. . . . I need this. Help me?"

He paused, an oddly hesitant look on his face. "Don't pursue this."

Ani and Tish peeked around the corner, waved, and wandered over to the stereo. The song changed to something darker, with heavy bass and growling lyrics. The volume grew loud enough that Leslie could feel the percussion.

"Ani!" Rabbit shot a frown toward his sister.

"Shop's empty now." Ani cocked her hip and stared at him, unrepentant. She never cowered, no matter how grumpy Rabbit sounded. It wasn't like he'd hurt her, though. He treated his sisters like they were the most precious things he'd ever seen. It was one of the things Leslie found comforting about him. Guys who treated their family well were safe and *good*—guys like her father and brother, not so much.

Rabbit stared at Leslie for several seconds before he said, "Quick fixes aren't what you need. You need to face what you're running from."

"Please? I want this." She felt tears sting her eyes. Rabbit suspected too much, and she didn't want pep talks. She wanted something she didn't have words for—peace, numbness, *something*. She stared at him, trying to figure out what to say to convince him, trying to figure out why he wouldn't help her. All she had was "Please, Rabbit?"

He looked away then and motioned for her to follow him. They stepped through the short hallway to his office. Rabbit unlocked it and led her into the tiny room.

She stopped just inside the doorway, less comfortable but still okay. The room was barely big enough for the things he had crammed into it. A massive dark wood desk and two file cabinets took up the back wall; a long counter cluttered with various artists' tools and media stretched the length of the right wall; the third wall had a matching counter with two printers, a scanner, a projector, and a series of unlabeled jars.

He pulled another key out of his pocket and unlocked a drawer on the desk. Saying nothing yet, he pulled out a thin brown book with words impressed into the cover. Then he sat down in his chair and stared at her until she felt like running, as if everything she knew about him had faded and he were somehow unsafe.

This is Rabbit.

She felt embarrassed by her brief fear. Rabbit was like the older brother she should've had, a true friend. He hadn't ever offered her anything other than respect.

She walked up to the desk and sat on it.

He held her gaze and asked, "What are you looking for?"

They'd talked enough that she knew he didn't mean what sort of picture, but what it represented. A tattoo wasn't about the thing itself, but what it meant.

"Being safe. No more fear or pain." She couldn't look at him when she said it, but she *had* said it. That counted for something.

Rabbit flipped open the book to a section midway through and sat it in her lap. "Here. These are mine. They're special. They're like . . . symbols of change. If the one you need is in here . . . just . . . do any of these feel like what you need?"

Images cluttered the page—intricate Celtic patterns, eyes peering from behind thorny vines, grotesque bodies with wicked smiles, animals too unreal to look at for long, symbols her eyes darted away from as soon as she glanced at them. They were stunning and tempting and repulsive, but for one image that set her nerves on edge: inky-black eyes gazed up from within black-and-gray knotwork surrounded by wings like coalescing shadows, and in the middle was a chaos star. Eight arrows pointed away from the center; four of these were thicker, like the lines of a spiked cross.

Mine. The thought, the need, the reaction were overpowering. Her stomach clenched. She pulled her gaze away, and then forced herself to keep looking. She looked at the other tattoos, but her attention returned to that image as if compelled by it. *That one's mine.* For a moment, some trick of light made it look as if one of the eyes in the image winked. She ran her finger over the page, feeling the slick-smooth plastic sheet covering it, imagining the feel of those wings wrapped around her—somehow jagged and velvety all at once. She looked up at Rabbit. "This one. I need this one."

A strange series of expressions came over Rabbit, as if he weren't sure if he should be surprised, pleased, or terrified. He took the book and closed it. "Why don't you think about it for a few days—"

"No." She put a hand on his wrist. "I *am* sure. I'm past ready, and this image . . . If it'd been on the wall, I'd already have it on me." She shivered, not liking the idea of anyone else having her tattoo—and it *was* hers. She knew it. "Please."

"It's a one-time-only tattoo. If you get it, no one else can, but"—he stared at the wall behind her—"it'll change you, change things."

"*All* tattoos change people." She tried to keep her voice even, but she felt frustrated by his hesitation. He'd been stalling for weeks. This was her tattoo, right there within reach.

Studiously avoiding her gaze, Rabbit slid the book into its drawer. "Those things you were looking for . . . those changes . . . you need to be absolutely positive those are the ones you want."

"I *am*." She tried to get him to look at her, bending down so her face was closer to his.

Ani poked her head in the doorway. "She pick one?"

Rabbit ignored her. "Tell me what you thought when you picked it. Were there any others that . . . called to you?"

Leslie shook her head. "No. Just that one. I want it. Soon. Now."

And she did. It felt like she was looking at a banquet and realizing she hadn't ever eaten, like a craving that she needed to fill immediately.

After another long look, he pulled her into his arms for a quick hug. "So be it."

Leslie turned to Ani. "It's perfect. It's a chaos star and knotwork with these amazing eyes and shadow wings."

Ani took one look at Rabbit—who nodded—and then she whistled. "You're stronger than I thought. Wait till Tish hears." She left, calling out, "Tish? Guess which one Leslie picked."

"No shit?" Tish's shriek made Rabbit close his eyes.

Shaking her head, Leslie told Rabbit, "You realize that you're all being über-weird, even for people who live at a tattoo shop."

Instead of acknowledging her remark, Rabbit brushed her hair back tenderly like he did with his own sisters'. "I'll need a couple days to get the right ink for this one. You can change your mind."

"I won't." She felt the unnatural urge to squeal like Tish had. Soon, she'd have it, the perfect ink. "Let's talk price."

Niall watched Leslie walk out of Pins and Needles. When she walked through the city, she moved with her shoulders squared, pace steady. It was at odds with the fears he knew hid inside her. Today, though, her confidence seemed almost real.

He stepped closer, pushing off the redbrick wall where he'd been leaning while she was in the tattoo shop. As she paused to survey the shadows in the street, Niall brushed his fingers over a lock of her hair that'd fallen forward over her cheek. Her hair—almost as wood brown as his own—wasn't long enough to tie back or short enough to stay back on its own, just right to be intriguing.

Like she is.

His fingers barely grazed her cheek, not enough for her to react. He leaned closer so he could smell her skin. Before work, she had a lavender scent, not perfume, but the shampoo she favored lately. "What are you doing out alone again? You know better."

She didn't answer him. She never did: mortals didn't see faeries, didn't hear them—especially mortals the Summer Queen had insisted be kept unaware of the Faery Courts.

Initially, at his king's request, Niall had taken a few of the shifts guarding Leslie. When she was unaware, he could walk beside her and talk to her as he couldn't when he was visible to her. The way the mortal girl looked at him—like he was better than he'd ever been, like he was attractive because of who he was, not because of his role in the Summer Court—was a heady thing, too much so, in truth.

If his queen hadn't asked it, Niall still would've wanted to keep Leslie safe. But Aislinn did order it. Unlike Leslie, when Aislinn had been mortal, she'd seen the ugliness of the faery world. Since becoming the Summer Queen she'd worked to find a balance with the equally new Winter Queen. It didn't leave a lot of time for keeping her mortal friends safe, but it did give her the power to order faeries to assure the mortals' safety. Such a task would not normally be handled by a court advisor, but Niall had been more family than mere advisor to the Summer King for centuries. Keenan suggested that Aislinn would feel better knowing that her closest friends' safety was under the direction of a faery she trusted.

Although it had been only a few shifts at first, more and more, Niall took extra duty watching over her. He hadn't done so with the others, but they didn't fascinate him as Leslie did. Leslie vacillated between vulnerable and bold, fierce and frightened. Once, when he had collected mortals for playthings, she would've been irresistible, but he was stronger now.

Better.

He forced away that line of thought and watched the sway of Leslie's hips as she walked through the streets of Huntsdale with a courage—*foolishness*—that ran counter to what he knew of her experiences. Maybe she'd go home if home were any safer. It wasn't. He'd seen that the first time he'd stood waiting on her front step, heard her drunken father, her vile brother. Her home might look charming from the outside, but that was a lie.

Like so much of her life.

He glanced down at the heelless shoes she had on, at her bare calves, at her long legs. The unexpectedly early start of summer this year—after ages of oppressive cold—was leading to mortals exposing more skin. Looking at Leslie, Niall wasn't complaining. "At least you have decent shoes tonight. I couldn't believe you went to work in those dainty little things the other night." He shook his head. "They were lovely, though. Well, really, I just liked the glimpse of your ankles."

She headed to the restaurant, where she would put on her fake smile and flirt with the customers. He'd see her to the door; then he'd wait outside, watching the bodies that came and went, making sure they didn't mean her harm. It was the routine.

Sometimes he let himself imagine how things would be

if she could *truly know* him—see him in a true light. Would her eyes widen in fear if she saw the extent of his scars? Would her face crumple in disgust if she knew the horrible things he'd done before he belonged to the Summer Court? Would she ask why he kept his hair shorn? And if she asked, could he answer any of those questions?

"Would you run from me?" he asked in a low voice, hating the fact that his heart sped at the thought of pursuing a mortal girl.

Leslie paused as a group of young men catcalled from their car. One of them hung halfway out the window, displaying his vulgarity as if it made him a man. Niall doubted that she could hear their words: the bass in their car was too loud for mere voices to compete with. Actual words weren't necessary to know threat. Leslie tensed.

The car sped away, the rumbling bass fading like thunder from a passing storm.

He whispered against her ear, "They're just children, Leslie. Come now. Where's that spring in your step?"

Her breathy sigh was soft enough that he would have missed it if he hadn't been standing very close. A little of the tension eased from her shoulders, but the drawn look stayed on her face. It never seemed to fade. Her makeup didn't hide the shadows under her eyes. Her long sleeves didn't hide the purpling bruises from her brother's angry strikes the other day.

If I could step in . . .

But he couldn't, not into her life, not into her home.

That was forbidden to him. All he could do was offer her his words—words she couldn't hear. He still said, "I'd stop anyone from taking that smile from you. I would, if I were allowed."

Absently, she put one hand on her back and glanced in the direction of Pins and Needles. She smiled to herself, the same smile she'd worn when she left the tattoo parlor.

"Aaah, you've finally decided to decorate that pretty skin. What will it be? Flowers? Sun?" He let his gaze drift up her spine.

She paused; they'd reached the restaurant. Her shoulders sagged again.

He wanted to comfort her, but instead he could only give her his nightly promise, "I'll wait right here."

He wished she'd answer, tell him she'd look for him after work, but she wouldn't.

And it's better this way. He knew it, but he didn't like it. He'd been a part of the Summer Court long enough that his original path was almost forgotten, but watching Leslie— seeing her spirit, her passion . . . Once, when he'd been a solitary fey, when he'd had another name, there'd have been no hesitating.

"I agree with Aislinn, though. I want you kept safe," he whispered in her ear. Her soft, soft hair brushed against his face. "I will keep you safe—from them *and* from me."

CHAPTER 3

Irial stood in the early morning light, silent, one of his faeries lying dead at his feet. The faery, Guin, had worn a mortal guise so often that bits of her glamour still clung to her after death—leaving part of her face painted with mortal makeup and part gloriously other. She had on tight blue denims—*jeans*, she and her sisters always reminded him when they spoke—and a top that barely covered her chest. That slip of cloth was soaked with blood, *her* blood, *fey* blood, spilling onto the dirty ground.

"Why? Why did this happen, *a ghrá*?" Irial bent down to brush her bloody hair from her face. Around her were bottles, cigarette butts, and used needles. None of these offended him the way they once had: this area was rough, grown more violent these past years as the mortals settled their territorial disputes. What offended him was the notion that a mortal bullet had taken one of his own. It might not have been intentional, but that changed nothing. She was still fallen.

Across from him waited the tall, thin beansidhe who'd summoned him. "What do we do?" She wrung her hands as she spoke, resisting her natural instinct to wail. She wouldn't resist for long, but Irial didn't—*couldn't*—answer yet.

He picked up an empty casing, turning it over in his fingers. The brass shouldn't hurt a fey, nor should the lead slug that he'd removed from the dead faery's body when he arrived. It had, though: a simple mortal bullet had killed her.

"Irial?" The beansidhe had bitten her tongue until blood seeped from her lips to drip down her pointed chin.

"Ordinary bullets," he murmured, turning the bits of metal over in his fingers. In all the years since mortals had begun fashioning the things, he'd never seen one of his own dead from them. Shot, yes, but they had healed. They'd *always* healed from most everything mortals inflicted—everything but severe wounds made by steel or iron.

"Go home and wail. When the others come to you, tell them this area is off limits for now." Then he lifted the bloodied faery into his arms and walked away, leaving the beansidhe to begin keening as she ran. Her cries would summon them, his now-vulnerable Dark Court faeries, bring them to hear the awful word that a mortal had killed a faery.

By the time the current Gabriel—Irial's left hand—approached mere moments later, Irial's winged shadow had spread like a pall over the street. His ink-black tears dripped onto Guin's body, wiping away the glamour that still clung to her. "I've waited long enough to address the threat of the Summer Court's growing strength," he said.

"Waited too long," Gabriel said. "Keep waiting and war comes on their terms, Iri."

Like his predecessors, this Gabriel—for the name was one of rank, not birth—had always been blunt. It was an invaluable trait.

"I'm not seeking war in the courts, just chaos." Irial paused at the stoop of a heavily shuttered house, one of the many such houses he kept for his faeries in whichever cities they called home. He stared at the house, the home where Guin would be laid out for the court's mourning. Soon, Bananach would hear the news of Guin's death; the war-hungry faery would begin her interminable machinations. Irial was not looking forward to trying to placate Bananach. She grew less patient by the year, pressing for more violence, more blood, more destruction.

"War is not what's best for our court," Irial said, as much to himself as to Gabriel. "That's Bananach's agenda, not mine."

"If it's not yours, it's not the Hounds', either." Gabriel reached out and brushed Guin's cheek. "Guin would agree. She wouldn't support Bananach, even now."

Three dark fey came out of the house; smoky haze clung

to them as if it seeped from their skin. Mute, they took Guin's body and carried her inside. From the open door, Irial could see that they'd already begun hanging black mirrors throughout his house, covering every available surface in the hopes that some lingering darkness would find its way home to the body, that some trace would be strong enough to come back to the empty shell, so Guin could be nurtured and heal. It wouldn't: she was truly gone.

Irial saw them in his street, filthy mortals with so much lovely violence he couldn't reach. *That will change.* "Find them, the ones who did this. Kill them."

The previously blank space around the oghams on Gabriel's forearm filled with scrolling script in recognition of the Dark King's command. Gabriel always carried out the king's orders with the intent plainly writ on his skin— to intimidate and to make clear that the king willed it.

"And send the others to bring some of Keenan's fey for the wake. Donia's too." Irial grinned at the thought of sullen Winter Court faeries. "Hell, bring some of Sorcha's reclusive faeries if you can find them. Her High Court's not good for anything else. I'll not sanction a war, but let's start a few fights."

At nightfall Irial sat on his dais looking out at his grieving faeries. They squirmed, paced, and wailed. The glaistigs were dripping dirty river water all over the floor; several beansidhes still keened. The Gabriel Hounds—in their human guise, skin decorated with moving ink and silver chains—joked amongst themselves, but there were under-currents of alarm. Jenny Greenteeth and her kin stared at everyone with accusing eyes. Only the thistle-fey seemed calm, taking advantage of the fear of the others, nourishing themselves on the panic that pervaded the room. They all knew that the rumblings of upheaval had already begun. With the reality of a faery death, the inducement to resort to extreme measures was inevitable. There were always factions, murmurs of mutiny: that was status quo. This was different: one of their own had died. That changed the stakes.

"Move away from the streets"—Irial let his gaze slide over them, assessing the signs of disagreement, determining who would sway toward Bananach when she began rallying them to her cause—"until we know how weakened we are."

"Kill the new queen. Both of 'em," one of the Hounds growled. "Summer King too if we need."

The other Hounds took up the cry. The Ly Ergs rubbed their bloodred hands together in glee. Several of Jenny's kin grinned and nodded. Bananach sat silently among them; her voice wasn't ever necessary to know her preference. Violence was her sole passion. She tilted her head in her avian way, not doing anything other than watching. Irial smiled at her. She opened and closed her mouth with an audible snap, as if she'd bite him. She made no other movement. They both knew she disapproved of his plans; they both knew she'd test him. *Again.* If she could, she'd kill him to set the court into discord, but Dark Court faeries could not kill their regents.

The snarls grew deafening until Gabriel held a hand up for silence. When the rest of the room quieted, Gabriel flashed a menacing smile. "Your king speaks. You *will* obey him."

No one objected when Gabriel snarled. After he'd slaughtered one of his own brethren for disrespecting Irial so many years ago, few ever challenged his will. If Gabriel had the political grace to go with the violence, Irial would try to cede the throne to him. In all the centuries Irial'd looked for his replacement, he'd only found one faery fit to lead them, but that faery had rejected the throne to serve another. Irial shoved that thought away. He was still responsible for the Dark Court, and considering what might have been didn't help.

He said, "We are not strong enough to fight one court, much less two or three working together. Can any of you truly tell me that the kingling and the new Winter Queen wouldn't work together? Can you tell me that Sorcha wouldn't side with anyone"—he paused and smiled at Bananach—"*most* anyone who opposed me? War is not the right path."

He didn't add that he had no desire for true war. It would look like weakness, and a weak king wouldn't hold his court very long. If there had been someone who could lead the court without destroying them all in unrestrained excess, Irial would step away, but the head of the Dark Court was chosen from among the solitary faeries for good reason. He enjoyed the pleasure of the shadows, but he understood that shadows needed light. Most of his court had trouble remembering that—or perhaps they never knew it. They certainly wouldn't appreciate hearing it now.

The Dark Court needed the nourishment of the finer emotions: fear, lust, rage, greed, gluttony, and the like. Under the last Winter Queen's cruel regime—before the newly empowered Summer King had come into his strength—the very air had been sustaining. Beira had been a malicious queen, inflicting as much agony on her own faeries as on those who dared to not kneel to her. It had been relaxing, if not always pleasant.

Irial said only, "Smaller conflicts can create the energy we need for sustenance. There are plenty of faeries you can use for nourishment."

In a voice that would disturb the calmest of the winter fey, one of Jenny's kin asked, "So we just feed on whatever random faeries we can find like nothing's happened? I say we—"

Gabriel growled at her. "We *will* obey our king."

Bananach snapped her mouth again; she tapped her talon-tipped fingers on the surface of the table. "So the Dark King is unwilling to fight? To allow us to defend ourselves? To strengthen ourselves? Just wait until we get weaker still? There's an . . . *interesting* plan."

She's going to be true trouble this time.

Another green-toothed fey added, "If we fight, maybe some of us might fade, but the rest . . . a war's apt to be good fun, my king."

"No," Irial said, glancing at Chela, Gabriel's sometimes mate. "No war right now. I'll not have any of you fade. That's not an option. I will find a way." He wished he could explain it to them in a way they'd understand. He couldn't.

"Chela, love? Would you?" Irial inclined his head toward a group of faeries who'd been smiling and agreeing with the green-toothed fey. Talk of disobeying him was intolerable, especially when mutiny was simmering in Bananach's eyes again.

Irial lit another cigarette and waited as Chela sauntered across the room. The knotwork hounds on her biceps snapped at each other as they ran around her arm at a blurring pace. A soft hum emanated from her, somewhere between a growl and a contented murmur. As she approached the table, she grabbed a chair from one of the thistle-fey, dumping him to the floor as she lifted it and settled amidst the grumbling faeries.

Several other Hounds dispersed throughout the crowd. Gabriel had spoken, said that they'd support the Dark King: they'd either need to obey Gabriel or kill him. Had he allied with Bananach, a faery war would be unavoidable, but Gabriel had stood with Irial for as long as he'd held leadership of the Hounds.

Irial resumed: "A mortal has chosen my symbol for her tattoo. She'll be bound to me within days. Through her, I will be able to feed on mortals and faeries both; I'll offset your own feeding until we have another option."

They didn't react for a moment. Then they lifted their

voices in a beautiful cacophony.

He'd never funneled his nourishment out to them, but he'd never needed to, either. He could. The head of a court was tied to each faery who swore fealty to him. His strength gave them strength; it was simply the way of things. It wasn't a permanent solution, but it would keep them alive until a better solution was in reach—one that wasn't full-out war.

He exhaled, watching the smoke writhe in the air, missing the dead queen, hating Keenan for defeating her, and wondering what it would take to entice Donia, the new Winter Queen, to become as ruthless as her predecessor. The alliance between Keenan and Donia had swung the balance too far toward a degree of peace that was detrimental to the Dark Court—but war wasn't the answer either. The Dark Court couldn't survive on violence alone, any more than terror or lust would be enough. Everything was about balance, and in a court where the darker emotions were sustenance, attending to that balance was essential.

Another squabble in the middle of the room caught his attention. Gabriel's growl shook the walls as he ground his boot into a Ly Erg's face, leaving the fallen faery bloody enough that there'd be another stain on the floor. Obviously, the Ly Ergs weren't being as cooperative as Gabriel would like. They enjoyed bloodshed too much, clustering to support Bananach every time she stirred mutiny.

With a gleeful grin, Gabriel watched the Ly Erg crawl

back to his table. Then Gabriel turned to Irial and bowed low enough that his face touched the floor, presumably to hide his grin as much as to show respect. He told Irial, "Once you collect your mortal, we'll ride with you to help evoke fear and confusion in the mortals. The Hounds support the will of the Dark King. *That* won't change." Gabriel's gaze didn't drift to Bananach or the glaring faeries who had gone to her side already, but his message was clear enough.

"Indeed." Irial ground out his cigarette and smiled at his most trusted companion. The Hounds had a lovely ability to induce terror in faery and mortal alike.

"We could get a bit of fear out of the disobedient in this lot . . ." Gabriel murmured, and his Hounds grabbed up some of the faeries who'd smiled in support of the earlier mutinous suggestions. "The Dark Court should show a little respect to our king."

Faeries clambered to their feet and talons and paws, bowing and curtsying. Bananach did not move.

Gabriel caught her gaze and grinned again. There would be no more overt objections or discussions tonight. Gabriel would organize the fey and threaten them if they refused to cooperate with Irial's precautions. They'd be almost perversely obedient. *For now.* Then Bananach would step up her attempts.

But not tonight—not yet.

"Tonight, we'll feast in our fallen sister's memory." Irial made a beckoning gesture, and several of Gabriel's Hounds brought in a score of terrified faeries they'd rounded up

from the other courts. None were from the High Court—
which wasn't surprising, as the High Court faeries so rarely
left their seclusion—but there were both Winter Court and
Summer Court faeries.

Irial folded a trembling Summer Girl into his arms. The
vines that clung to her skin wilted under his touch. She was
so filled with terror and loathing that he briefly considered
sharing her with the others, but he was still selfish enough
to want her to himself. Keenan's special girls were always
such a nice treat. If Irial was careful, he could draw enough
desire and fear out of them to stave off hunger for a couple
of days. A few times, he'd been able to leave them so
addicted that they returned willingly to his arms for regular
visits—and hated him for making them betray their king.
It was quite satisfying.

Irial held the girl's gaze as he told his court, "Their
regents did this, brought us to this when they killed Beira.
Remember that as you offer them your hospitality."

CHAPTER 4

The tattoo shop was empty when Leslie walked in. No voice broke the stillness of the room. Even the stereo was silenced.

"It's me," she called.

She went back to the room where Rabbit would do the work. The paper with the stencil of her tattoo waited on a tray on the counter beside a disposable razor and miscellaneous other items. "I'm a little early."

Rabbit stared at her for a moment but didn't say anything.

"You said we could start tonight. Do the outline." She came over to stare down at the stencil. She didn't touch it, though, strangely afraid that it would vanish if she did.

Finally Rabbit said, "Let me get the door."

While he was gone, she wandered around the tiny room—more to keep from touching the stencil than anything else. The walls were covered in various show and convention flyers—most faded and for events long past. A few framed photos, all black-and-white, and theater-size film posters were intermingled with the flyers. Like every other part of the shop, the room was impossibly clean and had a slight antiseptic scent.

She paused at several of the photos, not recognizing most of the people or places. Interspersed among them were framed pen-and-ink sketches. In one, Capone-era thugs were smiling at the artist. It was as realistic as any photograph, skillful to the degree that it seemed bizarre to see it hanging amidst the snapshots and posters. Rabbit returned as she was tracing the form of a stunningly beautiful man sitting in the middle of the group of gangsters. They were all striking, but it was him, the one leaning on an old twisted tree, who looked almost familiar. The others clustered around, beside, or behind him, but he was obviously the one with power. She asked, "Who's this?"

"Relatives," was all Rabbit said.

Leslie's attention lingered on the picture. The man in the image wore a dark suit like the other men, but his posture—arrogant and assessing—gave him the impression of being more menacing than the men around him. Here was someone to fear.

Rabbit cleared his throat and pointed in front of him. "Come on. Can't start with you over there."

Leslie forced herself to look away from the image. Fearing—*or lusting on*—someone who was either old or long dead was sort of weird anyhow. She went to where

Rabbit had pointed, put her back to him, and pulled her shirt off.

Rabbit tucked a cloth of some sort under her bra strap. "To keep it clean."

"If ink or whatever gets on it, it's not a big deal." She folded her arms across her chest and tried to stand still. Despite how much she wanted the ink, standing there in her bra felt uncomfortable.

"You're sure?"

"Definitely. No buyer's remorse. Really, it's starting to border on obsession. I actually dreamed about it. The eyes in it and those wings." She blushed, thankful Rabbit was behind her and couldn't see her face.

He wiped her skin with something cold. "Makes sense."

"Sure it does." Leslie smiled, though: Rabbit wasn't fazed by anything, acting as if the oddest things were okay. It made her relax a little.

"Stay still." He shaved the fine hairs on the skin where the tattoo would go and wiped her off again with more cold liquid.

She glanced back as he walked away. He tossed the razor into a bin, pausing to give her a serious look before coming behind her again. She watched him over her shoulder.

He picked up the stencil. "Face that way."

"Where's Ani?" Leslie'd rarely been at the shop when Ani didn't show up, usually with Tish in tow. It was like she had some radar, able to track people down without any obvious explanation how.

"Ani needed quiet." He put a hand on her hip and moved her. Then he spritzed something lightly on her back where the ink would go—at the top of her spine between her shoulders, spanning the width of her back, centered over the spot where Leslie thought the wings would attach if they were real. She closed her eyes as he pressed the stencil onto her back. Somehow even that felt exciting.

Then he peeled away the paper. "See if it's where you want it."

She went to the mirror as quickly as she could without running. Using the hand mirror to see her reflection in the wall mirror, she saw it—her ink, her perfect ink stenciled on her skin—and grinned so widely, her cheeks hurt. "Yes. Gods, yes."

"Sit." He pointed at the chair.

She sat on the edge and watched as Rabbit methodically put on gloves, opened a sterile stick, and used it to pull a glop of clear ointment out of a jar and put it on a cloth-covered tray. He pulled out several tiny ink caps and tacked them down to the drop cloth. Then he poured ink into them.

I've watched this plenty of times; it's not a big deal. She couldn't look away, though.

Rabbit did each step silently, as if she weren't there. He opened the needle package and pulled out a length of thin metal. It looked like it was just one needle, but she knew from her hours listening to Rabbit talk shop that there were several individual needles at the tip of a needle bar. *My needles, for* my *ink, in* my *skin.* Rabbit slid the needle bar into the machine. The soft sound of metal sliding across metal was followed by an almost inaudible *snick.* Leslie let out breath she hadn't realized she'd been holding. If she thought Rabbit would let her, she'd ask to hold the tattoo machine, ask to wrap her hand around the primitive-looking coils and angled bits of metal. Instead she watched Rabbit make adjustments to it. She shivered. It looked like a crude hand-held sewing machine, and with it he'd stitch beauty onto her body. There was something primal about the process that resonated for her, some sense that after this she'd be irrevocably different, and that was exactly what she needed.

"Turn that way." Rabbit motioned, and she moved so her back was to him. He smeared ointment over her skin with a latex-clad finger. "Ready?"

"Mm-hmm." She braced herself, wondering briefly if it would hurt but not caring. Some of the people she'd seen complained like the pain was unbearable. Others seemed not to notice it at all. *It'll be fine.* The first touch of needles was startling, a sharp sensation that felt more like irritation than pain. It was far from awful.

"You good?" He paused, taking away the touch of needles as he spoke.

"Mm-hmm," she said again: it was the most articulate answer she could offer in the moment. Then, after a pause that was almost long enough to make her beg him to get back to it, he lowered the tattoo machine to her skin again. Neither spoke as he outlined the tattoo. Leslie closed her eyes and concentrated on the machine as it hummed and paused, lifting from her skin only to touch back down. She couldn't see it, but she'd watched Rabbit work often enough to know that in some of those pauses Rabbit dipped the tip of the needle into the tiny ink caps like a scholar inking his quill.

And she sat there, her back stretched in front of him as if she were a breathing piece of canvas. It was wonderful. The only sound was the hum of the machine. It was more than a sound, though: it was a vibration that seemed to slip through her skin and sink into the marrow of her bones.

"I could stay like this forever," she whispered, eyes still closed.

A dark laugh rolled out of somewhere. Leslie's eyes snapped open. "Is someone here?"

"You're tired. School and extra shifts this month, right? Maybe you drifted off." He tilted his head in that peculiar way he and his sisters had, like a dog hearing a new sound.

"Are you saying I fell asleep *sitting up* while you were tattooing me?" She looked back at him and frowned.

"Maybe." He shrugged and turned away to open a brown glass bottle. It was unlike the other ink bottles: the label was handwritten in a language she didn't recognize.

When he uncapped it, it seemed as if tiny shadows slithered out of it. *Weird.* She blinked and stared at it. "I *must* be tired," she muttered.

He poured ink from the bottle into another ink cap—

holding it aloft so the outside of the bottle didn't touch the side of the ink cap—then sealed the bottle and changed gloves.

She repositioned herself and closed her eyes again. "I expected it to hurt, you know?"

"It *does* hurt." Then he lowered the tattoo machine to her skin again, and she stopped remembering how to speak.

The hum had always sounded comforting when Leslie had listened to Rabbit working, but feeling the vibration on her skin made it seem exciting and not at all comforting. It felt different from what she'd imagined, but it wasn't what she'd call pain. Still, she doubted it was something she could've slept through.

"You okay?" Rabbit wiped her skin again.

"I'm good." She felt languid, like her bones weren't all the way solid anymore. "More ink."

"Not tonight."

"We could just finish it tonight—"

"No. This one will take a couple sessions." Rabbit was quiet as he wiped her skin. He slid his chair back; the wheels sounded loud as they slid over the floor, like a boulder being pushed across a metal grate.

Weird.

She stretched—and almost blacked out.

Rabbit steadied her. "Give it a sec."

"Head rush or something." She blinked to clear her vision, resisting the urge to try to focus on the shadows that seemed to be walking through the room unattached to any-thing.

But Rabbit was there, showing her the tattoo—*my tattoo*—with a pair of hand mirrors. She tried to speak, and might have. She wasn't sure. Time felt like it was off, speed-ing and slowing, keeping pace with some faraway chaos clock, bending to rhythms that weren't predictable. Rabbit was covering her new tattoo with a sterile bandage. At the same time, it seemed, his arm was around her, helping her stand.

She stepped unsteadily forward. "Careful with my wings."

She stumbled. *Wings?*

Rabbit said nothing; perhaps he hadn't heard or under-stood. Perhaps she hadn't spoken—but she could picture them—dark, shadowy swoops, somewhere between feath-ers and slick-soft aged leather, that tickled the sensitive skin at the backs of her knees.

As soft as I remembered.

"Rabbit? I feel weird. Wrong. Something wrong."

"Endorphin rush, Leslie, making you feel high. It'll be okay. It's not unusual." He didn't look at her when he spoke, and she knew he was lying.

She felt like she should be afraid, but she wasn't. Rabbit had lied: something *was* very wrong. She knew with a certainty that seemed impossible—like tasting sugar and having it called salt—that the words he said didn't taste true.

But then it didn't matter. The missing hands of the chaos clock shifted again, and nothing else mattered in that moment, just the ink in her skin, the hum in her veins, the euphoric zinging that made her feel a confidence she'd not known in far too long.

CHAPTER 5

Although Rabbit had told him where to find her, Irial hadn't approached the mortal yet; he'd had no intention of doing so until he saw if she really was strong enough to be worth the effort. But when he felt their first tenuous link fall into place, felt her euphoria as Rabbit's tattoo machine danced across her skin, he knew he had to see her. It was like a compulsion tugging at him—and not just him: *all* the dark fey felt it, tied as they were to Irial. They'd protect her, fight to be near her now.

And that urge was a good one to encourage—their being near her would mean they'd taunt and torment the mortals, elicit fear and anguish, appetites and furies, delicious meals to sate his appetites once the ink exchange was complete. Where the girl walked, his fey would follow. Mortals would become a feast for king and court—he'd caught only slight drifts of it so far, but already it was an invigorating thing. *Shadows in her wake, for me, for us.* He drew a deep breath, pulling on that still-tenuous link Rabbit was forging with his tattoo machine.

Irial rationalized it: if he was going to be tied to her, it made sense to check in on her. She'd be his responsibility, his burden, and in many ways a weakness. But despite the reasons he could list, he knew it wasn't logic leading him: it was desire. Fortunately, the king of the Dark Court saw no reason to resist his appetites, so he'd co-opted Gabriel and was on the way to her city, seeking her presence the way he had sought so many other indulgences over the years. He leaned back, seat reclined all the way, enjoying the thrill of Gabriel's seemingly reckless driving.

Irial propped one boot on the door, and Gabriel growled. "She's fresh painted, Iri. Come on."

"Chill."

The Hound shook his shaggy head. "I don't put my boots on your bed or any of those little sofas you have everywhere. Get your boot off there before you scratch her."

Like the rest of the Hounds' steeds, Gabriel's wore the guise of a mortal vehicle, shifting so truly into that form that it was sometimes hard to remember when it had last looked like the terrifying beast it truly was. Maybe it was an extension of Gabriel's will; maybe it was the steed's own whim. All of the creatures mimicked mortal vehicles so well that it was easy to forget that they were living things—except when anyone other than the Hounds tried to ride them. Then it was easy to recall what they were: the speed at which they moved sent the offending faery—or mortal—

hurtling through the air into whatever target the beasts chose.

Gabriel steered his Mustang into the small lot beside Verlaine's, the restaurant where the mortal worked. Irial lowered his foot, scraping his boot on the window as he did so; the illusion of its being a machine didn't waver.

"Dress code, Gabe. Change." As Irial spoke, his own appearance shifted. Had any mortals been watching, they'd have seen his jeans and club-friendly shirt vanish in favor of a pressed pair of trousers and conservative oxford-cloth shirt. His scuffed boots, however, stayed. It wasn't the glamour he usually wore, but he didn't want the mortal to recognize him later. This meeting was for him, so he could watch her; it was not one he'd prefer her to remember.

"A face to meet the faces that we meet," but not my face— not even the mask I wear for the mortals. Layers of illusions . . . Irial scowled, unsure of the source of the strange melancholia that was riding him, and gestured to Gabriel to don a relatively unthreatening glamour as well. "Pretty yourself up."

Gabriel's appearance shift was more subtle than Irial's: he still wore black jeans and a collarless shirt, but the Hound's tattoos were now hidden under long sleeves. His unruly hair appeared to be neatly trimmed, as were his goatee and sideburns. Like Irial's, Gabriel's glamour was not his usual one. Gabriel's face was somehow gentler, without the dark shadows and hollows that he usually left visible for the mortals. Of course, the glamour did nothing for the

Hound's intimidating height, but for Gabriel, it was near conservative.

As they got out of the car, Gabriel bared his teeth at several of the Summer Court's guards in a taunting smile. They were, no doubt, minding the mortal since she was friends with the new Summer Queen. The guards saw him as he truly was and cringed. If Gabriel were to start trouble, they'd inevitably suffer serious injury.

Irial opened the door. "Not now, Gabriel."

After a longing look at the fey who lingered in the street, Gabriel went inside the restaurant. In a low voice, Irial told him, "After the meal, you can visit our watchers. A bit of terror so near the girl . . . It's what she's for, right? Let's see how the initial connection holds up."

Gabriel smiled then, happily anticipating a spot of trouble with the Summer Court guards. Their presence meant that neither Winter nor Summer Court would harm the girl, and no solitary fey would be foolish enough to try to engage in any sport with a mortal who was under such careful watch. Of course, it also meant that Irial would have the great fun of stealing her away without their noticing before it was too late.

"Just the two of you?" the hostess, a rather vapid mortal with a perky smile, asked.

A quick glance at the chart on the hostess station showed him which tables were in his mortal's section. Irial motioned to a table in the far corner, a darkened section fit for romantic dinners or stolen trysts. "We'll take that table in back. The one by the ficus."

After the hostess led them to the table in question, Irial waited until she—*Leslie*—walked up, her hips swaying slightly, her expression friendly and warm. Such a look would work well if he were the mortal he appeared to be. As it was, the shadows that danced around her and the smoke-thin tendrils that snaked from her skin to his— visible only to dark fey—were what made his breath catch.

"Hi, I'm Leslie. I'll be your server tonight," she said as she placed a basket of fresh bread on the table. Then she launched into specials and other nonsense he didn't quite hear. She had too-thin lips for his taste, darkened only slightly with something pink and girlish. *Not suitable for my mortal at all.* But the darkness that clung so poignantly to her skin was quite fit for his court. He studied her, reading her feelings now that they were linked even this slightly. When he'd met her she'd been tainted, but now she positively crawled with shadows. Someone had hurt her, and badly, since he'd first seen her.

Anger that someone had touched what was his vied with awareness. What they had done—and how ably she resisted the shadows—these were what made her ready to be his. Had they not wounded her, she'd be inaccessible to him. Had she not resisted the darkness so successfully, she'd not be strong enough to handle what he was about to do to her. She'd been damaged, but not irreparably. Fragmented and strong, the perfect mix for him.

But he'd still kill them for touching her.

Silent now, obviously done with her lists and recommendations, she stood and stared expectantly at him. Aside from a quick glance at Gabriel, her attention was riveted on Irial. It pleased him more than he'd expected, seeing the mortal look at him attentively. He liked her hunger. "Leslie, can you do me a favor?"

"Sir?" She smiled again but looked hesitant as she did so. Her fear spiked, showing in a slight shifting of shadows that made his heart race.

"I'm not feeling very decisive"—he shot a glare at Gabriel, whose muffled laugh turned into a loud cough— "in terms of the menu here. Could you order for me?"

She frowned and looked back at the hostess, who was now watching them carefully. "If you're a regular, I'm sorry, but I don't remember—"

"No. I'm not." He ran a finger down her wrist, violating mortal etiquette, but unable to resist. She was his. It wasn't official yet, but that didn't matter. He smiled at her, letting his glamour drop for a fraction of a moment, showing her his true face—testing her, seeking fear or longing—and added, "Just order whatever you think we'd like. Surprise me. I enjoy a good surprise."

Her waitress facade slipped a little; her heartbeat fluttered. And he *felt* it, the brief surge of panic. He couldn't taste it, not yet, not truly, but almost—like a pungent aroma wafting from a kitchen, teasing hints of flavors he couldn't swallow.

He opened the black-lacquered cigarette case he favored

of late and drew out a cigarette, watching her try to make sense of him. "Can you do that, Leslie? Take care of me?"

She nodded, slowly. "Do you have any allergies or—"

"Not to anything on your menu. Neither of us does." He tapped his cigarette on the table, packing it, watching her until she looked away.

She glanced at Gabriel. "Order for you too?"

Gabriel shrugged as Irial said, "Yes, for both of us."

"Are you sure?" She watched him intently, and Irial suspected that she was already feeling something of the changes that would soon roll over her. Her eyes had dilated ever so slightly when her fears rose and faded. Later tonight, when she thought of him, she'd think he was just an odd man, memorable for that alone. It would be a while until her mind would let her process the extent of her changing body. Mortals had so many mental defenses to make sense of the things that violated their preconceptions and rules. At times those defenses were quite useful to him.

He lit his cigarette, stalling just to watch her squirm a touch more. He lifted her hand and kissed her knuckles, once more being completely inappropriate for the guise he wore and for the setting. "I think you'll bring me exactly what I need."

Terror surged, tangling around an unmistakable blaze of desire and a bit of anger. Her smile didn't waver, though.

"I'll put your order in, then," she said as she took a step backward, pulling her hand free of his grip.

He took a drag on his cigarette as he watched her walk

away. The dark smoky line between them stretched and wound through the room like a path he could follow.

Soon.

At the doorway, she looked back at him, and he could almost taste her terror as it peaked.

He licked his lips.

Very soon.

CHAPTER 6

Leslie slipped into the kitchen, leaned on the wall, and tried not to fall to pieces. Her hands shook. Someone else needed to handle the odd guest; she felt frightened by his attention, his too-intense stare, his words.

"You okay, *ma belle*?" the pastry chef, Étienne, asked. He was a wiry man with a temper that flared to life over the oddest things, but he was just as irrationally kind. Tonight, kind appeared to be the mood of choice, or at least this hour it was.

"Sure." She pasted a smile back on her face, but it was less than convincing.

"Sick? Hungry? Faint?" Étienne prompted.

"I'm fine, just a demanding guest, too touchy, too everything. He wants . . . Maybe you could figure out what to order—" She stopped, feeling inexplicably angry at herself for thinking, even for that brief second, of having someone else order *his* food. *No.* That wouldn't work. Her anger and fear receded. She straightened her shoulders and rattled off a list of her favorite foods, complete with the marquise au chocolat.

"That's not on the dessert menu tonight," one of the prep cooks objected.

Étienne winked. "For Leslie it is. I have emergency dessert for special reasons."

Leslie felt relieved, irrationally so, that Étienne's rum-soaked chocolate decadence was available. It wasn't as if the customer had asked for it, but she wanted to give it to him, wanted to please him. "You're the best."

"*Oui*, I know." Étienne shrugged as if it were nothing, but his smile belied the expression. "You should tell Robert this. Often. He forgets how lucky he is that I stay here."

Leslie laughed, relaxing a bit under Étienne's irresistible charm. It was no secret that the owner, Robert, would do almost anything to please Étienne, a fact that Étienne pretended not to notice.

"The order for table six is up," another voice called out, and Leslie resumed her work, smile sliding back into place as she lifted the steaming dishes.

As the shift wore on, Leslie caught herself looking at the two odd guests often enough that she had a difficult time concentrating on her other tables.

Tips will be low if this keeps up.

It wasn't like touchy guests were unheard of. Guys seemed to think that because she waited tables she'd be easily swayed by a little charm and affluence. She smiled and flirted a bit with male diners; she smiled and listened a few minutes longer with older guests; and she smiled and paid attention to the families with children. It was simply how it went at Verlaine's. Robert liked the waitstaff to treat the guests personally. Of course, that ended at the threshold of the restaurant. She didn't date anyone she met on duty; she wouldn't even give her number.

I would with him, *though.*

He looked comfortable in his skin, but also like he'd be able to hold his own in the shadowy parts of the city. And he was beautiful—not his features, but the way he moved. It reminded her of Niall. *And he's probably just as unavailable.*

The guest watched her in much the same way Niall did, too—with attentive gazes and lingering smiles. If a guy at a club looked at her that way, she'd expect him to hit on her. Niall hadn't, despite her encouragement; maybe this one wouldn't go further either.

"Leslie?" The guest couldn't have spoken loudly enough for her to hear him, but she did. She turned, and he gestured for her to come closer.

She finished taking an order from one of the weekly regulars and just barely resisted the urge to run across the room. She navigated the space between the tables without taking her eyes off of him, stepping around the busboy and another waiter, pausing and moving between a couple leaving the restaurant.

"Did you need something?" Her voice came out too soft, too breathy. A brief flicker of embarrassment rolled over her and then faded as quickly as it had risen.

"Do you—" He broke off, smiling at someone behind her, looking as if he'd laugh in the next moment.

Leslie turned. A crowd of people she didn't know stood in a small circle around Aislinn, who was waving at her. Friends weren't welcome at work; Aislinn knew that, but she started walking across the room toward Leslie. Leslie looked back at the guest. "I'm so sorry. Just one second?"

"Absolutely fine, love." He pulled out another cigarette, going through the same ritual as before—snapping the case shut, tapping the cigarette on the tabletop, and flicking the lighter open. His gaze didn't waver from her. "I'm not going anywhere."

She turned to face Aislinn. "What are you doing? You can't just—"

"The hostess said I could ask you to wait on us." Aislinn motioned at the large group she'd come in with. "There's not a table in your section, but I wanted you."

"I can't," Leslie said. "I have a full section."

"One of the other waitresses could take your tables, and—"

"And my tips." Leslie shook her head. She didn't want to tell Aislinn how badly she needed that money or how her stomach clenched at the possibility of walking away from the eerily compelling guest behind her. "Sorry, Ash. I can't."

But the hostess came over and said, "Can you take the group and your tables, or do I need to have someone pick up your tables so you can take them?"

Anger surged in Leslie, fleeting but strong. Her smile was pained, but she kept it in place. "I can take both."

With a hostile look at the table behind Leslie, Aislinn went back to her party. The hostess left too, and Leslie was seething. She turned to face *him*.

He took a long drag off the cigarette and exhaled. "Well, then. She seems territorial. I suppose that little look was a don't-hit-on-my-friend message?"

"I'm sorry about that." She winced.

"Are you two together?"

"No." Leslie blushed. "I'm not . . . I mean—"

"Is there someone else? A friend of hers you see?" His voice was as delicious as the best of Étienne's desserts, rich and decadent, meant to be savored.

Unbidden she thought of Niall, her fantasy date. She shook her head. "No. There's no one."

"Perhaps I should return on a less-crowded night, then?" He traced a finger up the underside of her wrist, touching her for the third time.

"Maybe." She felt the odd urge to run—not that he was

any less tempting, but he was looking at her so intently that she was certain he wasn't anywhere near safe.

He pulled out a handful of bills. "For dinner."

Then he stood and stepped close enough to her that her instinct to flee flared to life; she felt suddenly sick in the stomach. He tucked the money into her hand. "I'll see you another night."

She stepped backward, away from him. "But your food isn't up yet."

He followed, invading her space, moving so close that it would seem normal only if they were about to dance or kiss. "I don't share well."

"But—"

"No worries, love. I'll be back when your friend isn't around to snarl at me."

"But your dinner . . ." She looked from him to the bills in her hand. *Oh my gods.* Leslie was startled out of her confusion by the realization of how much she was holding: they were all large bills. She immediately tried to hand some of them back. "Wait. You made a mistake."

"No mistake at all."

"But—"

He leaned in so he whispered in her ear, "You're worth emptying my coffers for."

For a moment she thought she felt something soft wrap around her. *Wings.*

Then he pulled back. "Go tend to your friend. I'll see

you again when she's not watching."

And he walked away, leaving her motionless in the middle of the room, clutching more money than she'd ever seen in her life.

CHAPTER 7

When Niall reached Verlaine's, Irial had gone. Two of the guards who'd been outside the restaurant were bleeding badly from teeth marks in their arms. Some embarrassing part of him wished he'd been sent for sooner, but he quashed that thought before it became one he had to consider. When Irial acted against the Summer Court faeries, Niall was always summoned. The Dark King often refused to strike Niall. Gabriel, on the other hand, had no compunction against wounding Niall and often seemed to be more violent toward Niall when Irial was near.

"The Gabriel"—one of the rowan shuddered—"he just walked up and ripped into us."

"Why?" Niall looked around, seeking some clue, some indication of a reason that Gabriel would do so. Niall might've chosen to avoid the Dark King's left hand as often as possible, but he hadn't forgotten the things he'd learned in the Dark Court: Gabriel didn't ever act without reason. It mightn't be a reason that the Summer Court understood, but there was always a reason. Niall knew that. It was part of why he was an asset to the Summer Court: he understood the less gentle tendencies of the other courts.

"Mortal girl talked to the Gabriel and Dark King," a rowan-woman said as she wrapped her bloody biceps. She clenched the end of a strip of spider silk between her teeth as she bound her arm. Niall would offer to help her, but he knew she'd trained with the glaistigs. It made her a great fighter, but it also meant anything that looked like mercy would be summarily rejected.

Niall looked away. He could see Leslie through the window: she smiled at the Summer Queen and refilled a glass of water. It wasn't an unusual task, or an exciting one, but as he watched her, his throat suddenly felt dry. He wanted to go to her, wanted to . . . do things he should not dream of doing with mortals. Without meaning to, he'd crossed the street, stepped close to that window, and rested his hand on it. The cold glass was a thin barrier; he could crack it with just a bit of pressure, feel the edges slice into his skin, go to her, and sink his body into hers. *I could let her see me. I could—*

"Niall?" The rowan-woman stood beside him, staring through the window. "Do we need to go in?"

"No." Niall pulled his gaze away from Leslie, forced his thoughts back to something less alluring. He'd been watching her for months; there was no reason for his sudden surge of irrational thoughts. Perhaps his guard was down from thinking of Irial. Niall shook his head in self-disgust.

"Go home. Aislinn has plenty of guards with her, and I'll watch the queen's mortal," he said.

Without any further comment, the rowan and her companions left, and Niall crossed back to the alcove where he'd waited out so many of Leslie's shifts at Verlaine's. He leaned against the brick wall, feeling the familiar edges press into his back, and watched the faces of the mortals and faeries in the street. He forced himself to think about what he was, what he'd done before he knew who Irial was, before he knew how twisted Irial was. *All things that mean I should not touch Leslie. Ever.*

When Niall had first walked among them, he'd found mortals enthralling. They were filled with passion and desperation, carving out what joy they could in their all-too-finite lives, and most were willing to lift their skirts for a few kind words from his lips. He shouldn't miss their dizzying willingness and mortal touch. He knew better. Sometimes, though, if he looked too closely at what he knew himself to be, he did miss it.

The girl was weeping, clutching Niall's arm, when the dark-haired faery approached. The girl had bared herself when she entered the wood and had innumerable scratches on her flesh.

"She's an affectionate thing," the faery said.

Niall shook her off again. "She's been drinking,
I suspect. She wasn't so"—he grabbed her hand as
she began unfastening his breeches—"aggressive last
week."

"Indeed." The dark-haired faery laughed. "Like
animals, aren't they?"

"Mortals?" Niall stepped closer to him, dodging
the girl's agile hands. "They seem to hide it well
enough at first. . . . They change, though."

The other faery laughed and caught the girl up
in his arms. "Maybe you're just irresistible."

Niall straightened his clothes now that the girl
was contained. She stayed motionless in the other
faery's grasp, looking from one to the other like she
was insensible.

The dark-haired faery watched Niall with a
curious grin. "I'm Irial. Perhaps we could take this
one somewhere less"—he looked up the path toward
the mortals' town—"public." The lascivious look
on Irial's face was the most enticing thing Niall
had ever seen. He had a brief flash of terror at his
tangled mix of feelings. Then Irial licked his lips
and laughed. "Come now, Niall. I think you could
use a bit of company, couldn't you?"

Later he wondered why he hadn't been suspicious at Irial's
knowing his name. At the time all Niall could think of was
that the nearer he got to Irial, the more it felt like stumbling

upon a feast and realizing he'd never tasted anything until that moment. It was an intensity he'd never felt before— and he loved it.

Over the next six years, Irial stayed with Niall for months at a time. When Irial was at his side, Niall indulged in debauched pleasures with more mortals than he'd known he could lie with at one time. But it wasn't ever enough. No matter how many days Niall lost in a blur of yielding flesh, he was never satisfied for long. There were equally dizzying days when it was just them, dining on exotic foods, drunk on foreign wines, touring new lands, listening to glorious songs, talking about everything. It was perfect—for a while. *If I hadn't gone to his* bruig *and seen the mortals there in Irial's domain* . . . Niall wasn't sure who he'd hated more when he realized what a fool he'd been.

"It's been too long, Gancanagh." Gabriel's voice was an almost-welcome interruption of the unpleasant memories. The Hound stood on the edge of the street, just close enough to traffic to be clipped by careless drivers but far enough to be mostly safe. Ignoring the flow of cars, he looked up and down the sidewalk. "The rowan gone?"

"Yes." Niall glanced at the dark faery's forearm, checking to see if there were words he should know, almost hoping Irial'd ordered Gabriel to do something that would allow Niall to strike out.

Gabriel noticed. With a wicked grin, he turned his arms so Niall could see the undersides. "No messages for you. One of these days, I'll get a chance to give you a matching scar on the other side of your pretty face, but not yet."

"So you keep saying, but he never gives you permission." Niall shrugged. He wasn't sure if it was because he was impervious to the terror of the Hounds' presence or because he'd walked away from Irial, but Gabriel brought up old pains every chance he could—and Niall usually let it go. Tonight, however, Niall didn't feel very tolerant, so he asked, "Do you suppose Iri just likes me more than you, Gabriel?"

For several of Niall's too-fast heartbeats, Gabriel simply stared at him. Then he said, "You're the only one who doesn't seem to know that answer."

Before Niall could reply, Gabriel slammed his fist into Niall's face, turned, and walked away.

Blinking his eyes against the sudden pain, Niall watched the Hound saunter down the street and calmly wrap his hands around the throats of two Dark Court fey who'd apparently been lurking nearby. Gabriel lifted the Ly Ergs and choked them until the faeries went limp. Then he slung them over his shoulders and took off in such a blur of speed that small dust devils swirled to life in his wake.

Gabriel's violence wasn't unusual, but the lack of obvious orders on the Hound's skin was enough to make Niall wary. It was inevitable that the semi-peace that resulted from Beira's death would cause ripples in the other courts. How Irial dealt with that should concern Niall only as far as protecting his true court—the Summer Court—but Niall had a residual moment of concern for the Dark King, a twinge that he had no intention of ever admitting aloud.

Leslie was pleasantly surprised that Aislinn was waiting on the curb outside the restaurant when her shift ended. They used to meet up after work sometimes, but everything had changed over the winter.

"Where's"—Leslie paused, not wanting to say the wrong thing—"everyone?"

"Seth's out at the Crow's Nest. Keenan's working on some stuff. I don't know where Carla or Ri are." Aislinn stood up and wiped her hands on her jeans, as if the brief contact with the ground had dirtied them. For all Aislinn's comfort in grungy places that made most people uncomfortable, she still had tidiness issues.

Aislinn glanced at a few unfamiliar guys across the street. When she looked away, one of them shot a grin at Leslie and licked his lips. Reflexively, Leslie flipped him off—and then tensed as she realized what she'd done. She knew better: caution kept a girl safer than provoking trouble did. She wasn't the sort to flip anyone off or speak up, not now, not anymore.

Beside her, Aislinn had finished her survey of the street. She was always cautious, enough so that Leslie had wondered more than a few times what Aislinn had seen or done that made her so careful.

Aislinn asked, "Walk over to the fountain?"

"Lead the way." Leslie waited until Aislinn started walking

before she glanced back to make sure that the guy she'd flipped off hadn't decided to cross the street. He waved at her but didn't follow.

"So did you know that guy tonight? The one you were talking to when I got there?" Aislinn tucked her hands in the oversize leather jacket she had on. She had a nice coat of her own, but she tended to wear Seth's beat-up jacket when he wasn't with her.

"I've never met him before." Leslie shivered at a sudden rush of longing that rolled over her at the mention of the strange guy—and decided not to tell Aislinn that he'd said he'd be back.

"He was kind of intense." Aislinn paused as they waited to cross the poorly lit intersection at Edgehill.

The headlights of a passing bus cut through the shadows, illuminating shapes that for a moment looked like a feather-haired woman and a group of red-tinted muscular men. Leslie's imagination was entirely too active lately. Earlier she'd had the disconcerting feeling that she was looking out of someone else's eyes, that she could see things that were somewhere else.

The bus passed, sending an exhaust-scented gust of air over them, and they crossed into the slightly better lit park. On a bench across from the fountain, four unfamiliar guys and two equally unknown girls nodded to Aislinn. She lifted her hand in a wave of sorts but didn't go toward them. "So did he ask you to meet him or something, or—"

"Ash? Why are you asking?" Leslie sat down on an empty

bench and kicked off her shoes. No matter how long she stretched or how much she walked, there was something about waiting tables that always resulted in sore feet and achy calves. As she rubbed her legs, she glanced over at Aislinn. "Do you know him?"

"You're my friend. I just worry and . . . He looked like trouble, you know? . . . The kind of guy that I wouldn't want near someone I care about." Aislinn moved so she was sitting cross-legged on the bench. "I want you to be happy, Les."

"Yeah?" Leslie grinned at her, suddenly calm despite the swirl of feelings that had been swarming through her tonight. "Me too. And I'm going to be."

"So that guy—"

"Was just passing through town. He talked pretty, wanted to be adored while he ordered his meal, and is probably already gone." Leslie stood and stretched, bouncing a little on the balls of her feet. "It's cool, Ash. No worries, okay?"

Aislinn smiled then. "Good. Are we walking or sitting? We just got here. . . ."

"Sorry." Leslie thought about sitting down for a half second. Then she looked up at the dark sky swallowing the moon. A wonderful rush of urgency filled her. "Dance? Walk? I don't care."

It was as if her months of fears and worries were slipping away. She reached back to touch her tattoo. It was just an outline still, but she already felt better. Believing in a thing—acting to symbolize that belief—really did make her feel stronger. *Symbols of the conviction.* She was becoming herself again.

"Come on." She grabbed Aislinn's hands and pulled her to her feet. She walked backward until they were several feet away from the bench and then spun away. She felt good, free. "You sat around all night while I was working. You have no excuse for sitting still. Let's go."

Aislinn laughed, sounding like her old friend for a change. "The club, I guess?"

"Until your feet ache." Leslie looped her arm with Aislinn's. "Call Ri and Carla."

It felt good to be herself again.

Better, even.

CHAPTER 8

Leslie walked down the hall of Bishop O.C., shoes held in her hand, careful not to swing her arm and smack one of the dingy metal lockers with her heels. It had been three days since she'd had the outline tattooed, but Leslie was unable to stop thinking about that dizzying energy. She had been having strange bursts of panic and joy, emotions that seemed misplaced, out of context somehow, but they weren't debilitating. It was like she'd borrowed someone else's moods. *Odd, but good.* And she felt stronger, quieter, more powerful. She was certain it was an illusion, a result of her new confidence, but she still liked it.

The part she didn't like was how many fights she seemed to notice—or that they didn't frighten her. Instead she caught herself daydreaming of the Verlaine's customer. His name was almost clear when she thought of him, but he'd never told it to her. *Why do I know . . . ?* She shook off that question and hurried to the open door of the supply room.

Rianne was motioning impatiently. "Come *on,* Les."

Once Leslie was in the room, Rianne shut the door with a quiet *click*.

Leslie looked around for a spot to sit. She settled on a pile of gym mats. "Where are Carla and Ash?"

Rianne shrugged. "Being responsible?"

Leslie suspected that she should be doing the same thing, but when Rianne had seen her in the hall that morning she'd mouthed, "Supply room." For all her flakiness, Rianne was a good friend, so Leslie ditched first period.

"What's up?"

"Mom found my stash." Rianne's heavily made-up eyes welled with tears. "I didn't think she was coming home, and—"

"How mad was she?"

"Livid. I have to go back to that counselor. And"— Rianne looked away—"I'm sorry."

Leslie felt like a weight was pressing on her chest as she asked, "For what?"

"She thinks it's from Ren. That I got it from him, so I can't . . . You shouldn't call or come over for a while. It's just . . . I didn't know what to say. I *blanked*." Rianne caught Leslie's hand. "I'll tell her. It's just . . . she's really—"

"Don't." Leslie knew her voice was harsh, but she wasn't surprised, not really. Rianne never did well with confrontation. "It wasn't from him, right? You know to stay away from Ren."

"I do." Rianne blushed.

Leslie shook her head. "He's a bastard."

"Leslie!"

"Shh. I mean it. I'm not mad at you for letting her think whatever. Just stay clear of Ren and his crowd." Leslie felt ill at the thought of her friend under Ren's influence.

"You're not mad at me?" Rianne's voice trembled.

"No." Leslie was surprised by it, but it was true. Logic said anger made sense, but she felt almost peaceful. There was an edge of anger, like she was about to be mad but wasn't quite able to get there. Every emotion the past three days floated away before it grew intense.

She had the irrational thought that her emotions would settle once she got the tattoo finished—or maybe it was just that she was yearning for it, that bone-melting sensation that she felt when the tattoo needles touched her skin. She forced the thought away and focused on Rianne. "It's not your fault, Ri."

"It is."

"Okay, it *is*, but I'm not mad." Leslie gave Rianne a quick hug then pulled back to glare at her. "I *will* be, though, if you go near Ren. He's hanging with some real losers lately."

"So how are you safe?"

Leslie ignored the question and stood up. She suddenly needed air, needed to be somewhere else. She gave Rianne what she hoped was a convincing smile and said, "I need to go."

"All right. See you in fourth period." Rianne pushed the stack of mats back into some semblance of a tidy pile.

"No. I'm out."

Rianne paused. "You *are* mad."

"No. Really, I'm just—" Leslie shook her head, not sure she could explain or *wanted* to explain the strange feelings compelling her. "I want to walk. Go. I just . . . I'm not sure."

"Want company? I could ditch with you." Rianne smiled, too brightly. "I can catch up with Ash and Carla and we'll meet you at—"

"Not today." Leslie had an increasingly pressing urge to run, roam, just take off.

Rianne's eyes teared up again.

Leslie sighed. "Sweetie, it's not you. I just need air. I guess I'm working too much or something."

"You want to talk? I can listen." Rianne wiped the mascara streaks from under her eyes, making them worse in the process.

"Hold still." With the edge of her sleeve, Leslie rubbed away the black marks and said, "I just need to run it off. Clear my head. Thinking about Ren . . . I worry."

"About him? I could talk to him. Maybe your dad—"

"No. I'm serious: Ren's changed. Stay away from him." Leslie forced a smile to take the sting out of her words. The conversation was becoming entirely too close to topics she didn't like. "I'll catch you later or tomorrow, okay?"

Not looking at all happy about it, Rianne nodded, and they slipped into the hall.

After Leslie left Bishop O.C., she wasn't entirely sure where she was headed until she found herself at the ticket window of the train station. "I need a ticket to Pittsburgh for right now."

The man behind the counter muttered something unintelligible when she slid the money across to him. *Emergency money. Bill money.* She was usually hesitant to spend her money on a few hours' trip to see a museum, but right then she needed to be somewhere beautiful, to see something that made the world feel right again.

Behind her, several guys started shoving each other. People around them began joining in, jostling one another.

"Miss, you need to move." The man glanced past her as he slid her ticket toward her.

She nodded and walked away from the fracas. For a brief moment, she felt like a wave of shadows surged over her, *through* her. She stumbled. *Just fear.* She tried to believe that, to tell herself that she'd been afraid, but she hadn't been.

The actual ride into Pittsburgh and the walk through the city were a blur. Odd things caught her eye. Several couples—or strangers to each other, by the looks of the very disparate clothing styles in one case—were embarrassingly intimate on the train. A beautiful boy with full sleeve tattoos dropped a handful of leaves or bits of paper as he walked by, but for a bizarre moment Leslie thought it was the tattoos flaking from his skin to swirl away in the breeze. It was surreal. Leslie wondered briefly at the oddity of it all, but her mind refused to stay focused on that. It felt *wrong* to question the odd things she'd been feeling and seeing. When she tried, some pressure inside her skin forced her to think of something, *anything*, else.

And then she walked inside the Carnegie Museum of Art, and everything felt right. The oddities and questions slid away. The very world slid away as Leslie wandered aimlessly, past columns, over the smooth floor, up and down the stairs. *Breathe it in.*

Finally her need to run eased completely and she slowed. She let her gaze drift over the paintings until she came to one that made her pause. She stood silent in front of it. *Van Gogh. Van Gogh is good.*

An older woman walked through the gallery. Her shoes clacked in a steady rhythm as she moved, purposeful but not hurried. Several art students sat with their sketchbooks open, oblivious to everything else around them, caught in the beauty of what they saw on the gallery walls. To Leslie, being in the museum had always felt like being in a church, as if there were something sacred in the very air. Today that feeling was exactly what she needed.

Leslie stood across from the painting, staring at the verdant green fields that stretched away, clean and beautiful and open. *Peace.* That's what the painting felt like, a bit of peace frozen in space.

"Soothing, isn't it?"

She turned, surprised that anyone could walk up to her so easily. Her usual hyperawareness was absent. Niall stood beside her, looking at the painting. His button-up was untucked and hanging over the waist of loose-fitting jeans; his sleeves were folded back, giving her a glimpse of tanned forearms.

"What are *you* doing here?" she asked.

"Seeing you, it seems." He glanced behind him, where a lithe girl with vines painted on her skin stood staring at them. "Not that I'm complaining, but shouldn't you be in classes with Aislinn?"

Leslie looked at the vine-girl, who continued to watch them openly, and wondered if she was a living art display. But then she realized that it must've been bad lighting or shadows: the girl had nothing painted on her. Leslie shook her head and told Niall, "I needed air. Art. Space."

"Am I in that space?" he said as he took a step back. "I thought I'd say hello since we never seem able to speak . . . not that we should. You could go. I could go if you have things—"

"Walk with me?" She didn't look away, despite the too-pleased look on his face. Instead of being nervous, she felt surprisingly bold.

He gestured for her to lead the way, acting more gentlemanly than she thought normal. It wasn't quite stiff, but he seemed tense as he glanced around the gallery.

Then Niall looked back at her. He didn't speak, but there was a strange tension in the way he held himself away from her. He lifted and lowered his right hand like he didn't know what to do with it. The fingers on his left hand were curled tightly together; his arm was held motionless against his body.

She rested a hand on his arm and told him, "I'm glad you're actually here instead of with Keenan for a change."

Niall didn't speak, didn't answer. Instead he looked away.

He's afraid.

Inexplicably, she thought of the strange guest at Verlaine's, could almost imagine him sighing as she breathed in Niall's fear.

Breathed in fear?

She shook her head and tried to think of something, anything, to say to Niall—and to avoid thinking about the fact that his fear was a little exciting. She just stood beside him and let the silence grow until it was uncomfortably obvious. It felt like the other museum patrons were staring at them, but every time she glanced at them, her vision would catch at the edges, as if a filter slid over her eyes and distorted what she saw. She stared at the painting, seeing only blurs of color and shape. "Do you ever wonder if what you look at is the same thing everyone else is seeing?"

He went even stiller at her side. "Sometimes I'm sure it isn't the same . . . but that's not so bad, is it? Seeing the world in a different way?"

"Maybe." She glanced over at him, at his nervous posture, and wanted to reach out to him—to frighten or calm him, she wasn't sure which.

"Creative vision creates art"—he motioned around the gallery—"that shows the rest of the world a new angle. That's a beautiful thing."

"Or some sort of madness," she said. She wanted to tell someone that she wasn't seeing things right, wasn't feeling them right. She wanted to ask someone to tell her she wasn't going crazy, but asking a stranger for reassurance was pretty far from comfortable—even with her feelings skewed.

She folded her arms over her chest and walked away, carefully not looking at the people watching her or Niall, who was following her with an expression of pain on his face. The past few days it seemed like people were behaving oddly—or perhaps she was just starting to pay attention to the world again. Perhaps it was a waking up from the depression she'd been fighting. She wanted to believe that, but she suspected she was lying to herself: the world around her had become off-kilter, and she wasn't entirely sure she wanted to know why.

CHAPTER 9

With a wariness that felt out of place in the museum, Niall watched the fey watch them. Vine-covered Summer Girls wore glamours to seem mortal. One of the Scrimshaw Sisters slid through the room invisibly, peering into mortals' mouths when they spoke. Another faery, whose body was nothing more than wafting smoke, drifted past. The faery plucked invisible traces from the air and brought them to his mouth, tasting mortals' breath, feeding himself with hints of coffee or sweets that they exhaled. None tested others' boundaries. Here was a place where the faeries all minded their manners, regardless of court affiliation or personal conflicts. It was neutral space, safe space.

And Niall was taking advantage of that safety to break his court's rules. He'd appeared to Leslie, spoken to her on his own. He had no explanation for it. It was an irresistible compulsion to be near her, worse than he'd felt at Verlaine's. He'd disobeyed his queen—not a direct order, but her obvious intent. Should Keenan not intercede with Aislinn, the consequences would be severe.

I can explain that . . . that . . . that what? There was nothing he could say that would be true. He'd simply seen Leslie, watched her blind wanderings, and revealed himself to her—stripped his glamour away right there in the gallery where any mortal could have seen, where plenty of faeries *did* see.

Why now?

The pull to go to her, to reveal himself, was like an order he simply could not refuse—nor, truth be told, did he want to. But he knew better. Until today he'd done fine with not approaching her, but that did not undo the embarrassing number of witnesses to his actions. He should excuse himself, turn back before he crossed lines that would result in his queen's anger. Instead he finally asked, "Did you see the temporary exhibition?"

"Not yet." She kept her distance now, after his too-long silence.

"There's a painting from the Pre-Raphaelites I wanted to see. Would you care to join me?" He had made a habit of viewing every Pre-Raphaelite painting he could. The reigning High Queen, Sorcha, had been inordinately fond of them and lent her likeness to a number of their canvases: Burne-Jones had almost done her justice in *The Golden Stairs.* He thought to tell Leslie—and stopped. He was visible to her. He shouldn't be talking to her at all, about anything.

He stepped away. "You're probably not interested, I can—"

"No. I am. I don't know what the Pre-Raphaelites are. I sort of walk around and look at the paintings. It's not . . . I don't know a lot about art history, just what"—she blushed lightly—"moves me."

"That's all you really need to know, isn't it? I remember the term, in part, because I know that their art moves me." He put a hand gently on the small of her back, allowing himself to reach out and touch her. "Shall we?"

"Sure." She walked forward, out of reach, away from his hand. "So who are these Pre-Raphaelites?"

That was something he could answer. "They were artists who decided to disregard the rules at their art academy, to create new art by their own standards."

"Rebels, huh?" She laughed then, suddenly relaxed and free for no obvious reason. And the beautiful paintings and fabulously carved pillars were less stunning with her for comparison.

"Rebels who changed the world by believing they could." He steered Leslie past a group of Summer Girls—invisible to her—whispering and pointing at him with pouts on their faces. "Belief is a powerful thing. If you believe you can . . ." He paused as faeries clustered nearer them.

Keenan will not be happy.

No mortals, Niall. You know better.

Unless Keenan agreed to that one . . .

She's Aislinn's *friend.*

Niall! Leave her alone. This last was delivered with an outrage that bordered on maternal.

"Niall?" Leslie was staring at him.

"What?"

"You stopped talking. . . . I like your voice. Tell me something else?" She wasn't bold like this, not during the months he'd been watching her, not a few moments ago. "The artists?"

"Right. They didn't follow the rules. They made their own." He refused to look at the faeries watching them and chattering their warnings. Their voices were angry and afraid, and although he knew better, he was excited by it. "Sometimes the rules need to be challenged."

"Or broken?" Leslie's breathing was uneven. Her smile was dangerous.

"Sometimes," he agreed.

There was no way she understood what breaking the rules would mean for him, for her, but he wasn't really breaking them. He was just bending them. He offered Leslie his arm as they walked toward the next gallery. Her hand trembled as she laid it on the curve of his arm. *My king sent me here to watch over her. He knows I can do this. I can be careful, stay within the rules.*

It will be fine. More often than not it was Niall who Keenan asked to guard Leslie. Despite the dangerous consequences of mortals being exposed to Niall's embraces, Keenan trusted him. They'd not spoken often of the way mortals lost themselves after they'd been too long with Niall; they'd not discussed how many mortals he'd destroyed under Irial's influence. All Keenan had said was, "I trust you to do what needs to be done."

Niall had intended to keep Leslie safe from the corruption of his affection. *And I will.* But today, all of Niall's good intentions had faded when he saw her looking so lovely and alone. After today, he would resume watching her invisibly.

I am able to do this: walk with her, talk, and be heard. Just this one conversation.

He'd keep himself distant; there was no harm in that. It wasn't like telling her what he was, or how often he walked with her unawares. He could walk next to her without kissing her.

"Do you want to grab a sandwich before we go to the exhibit?" she asked.

"A sandwich . . . I can do that. Yes."

It's still within the rules. Eating with her isn't dangerous. It would be if it were faery food he offered to her, but this was mortal fare prepared and delivered by mortal hands. *Safe.*

Her hand tightened on his arm, touching him, holding on to him. She murmured, "I really am glad I ran into you."

"Me too." He pulled his arm away, though. He could be a friend, perhaps, but anything more—that was forbidden him. *She* was forbidden.

And all the more tempting for it.

After a couple of too-brief hours, Niall excused himself and retreated, uncomfortably grateful when Leslie's evening guard arrived early. The time with her was painful—beautiful but painful in its emptiness—reminding him of what could not be his.

As he left the museum, he encountered several badly injured faeries, all but insensible from whatever drug they'd found in Irial's houses. It wasn't surprising to see such things so close to Irial's currently favored haunts, but it wasn't only the fey who shimmered with the taint of faery bruises. Mortals—far too many mortals—walked by with the ugly colors of healing bruises on their skin. The mortals might not recognize them as the handprints of something with talons where fingers should be, but Niall saw the bruises' true forms.

Why?

Winter fey passed him with uneasy glances. Solitary fey clustered in small groups at his approach. Even the usually implacable kelpies in the city fountains watched him warily. Once, he'd deserved such suspicions, but he'd shunned the Dark Court. He'd chosen to remake himself, to make amends for what he'd done.

But the sight of the wounded mortals and the anxious faeries made Niall's thoughts return to memories best left forgotten: *the glass-eyed awe as a tiny red-haired girl drooped in his arms, exhausted from too many hours in his hands; Irial's delicious laughter as a table crashed under the dancing girls; Gabriel's joy at terrorizing the people of another city while Irial poured more drinks; strange wine and new herbs in their dishes; dancing with hallucinations; objections from mortals taken out of his embrace* . . . And he'd reveled in all of it.

By the time Niall reached Huntsdale and went to the Summer Court's loft, his depression was far too pronounced for him to join the revelry. Instead he stood at the large window in the front room staring at the browning ring of grass in the park across the street. There they celebrated the Summer Court's rebirth, rejoicing at the court's new—albeit uneasy—accord with the Winter Court. Summer had come unseasonably early this year—a gift from the Winter Queen, a peace offering or token of affection perhaps. No matter. It was beautiful. It should soothe him but did not.

He sighed. He'd need to mention the state of the greenery to Keenan. *Think of duties. Think of responsibilities.* He'd spent a lifetime atoning for what he'd done. Whatever aberration was making him feel so off the past few days would pass.

He rested his forehead on one of the tall panes of glass in the main room. Across the street, faeries danced in the park. And as always the Summer Girls spun among them, darting in and out of the throng in that dervish way of theirs, trailing vines and skirts. Keenan's on-duty guards watched over them, keeping them safe, and off-duty guards danced with them, keeping them amused.

It looks like peace.

That's what Niall had fought for, what he'd pursued for centuries, but he stood alone in the loft—a silent watcher. He felt distant, disconnected from his court, his king, the Summer Girls, everyone but one mortal girl. If he could take Leslie to the dance, spin in the revelries with her in his hands, he'd be there.

But the last Summer King had made clear the terms of accepting Niall's fealty. *No mortals, Niall. That's the price of being in my court.* It wasn't so awful. Mortals were still enticing, but between his memories and his vow, Niall had learned to resist. He had not wanted for dancing—in revelries or in his bed—and it had been enough.

Until her. Until Leslie.

Chapter 10

By the end of the week, Leslie was more exhausted than usual. She'd taken extra shifts so she could afford to cover the groceries and still have money for the rest of her ink. She'd tucked that ridiculous tip away, not sure if she'd keep it. If it *was* a tip, she'd have a good deal toward getting a place later, enough to get started on her own, get some basic furniture. *Which is why it's not a tip. That much money doesn't come for free.* For now, she'd keep doing what she was doing before—earning her own money, paying her own way. *Which means being broke.* She knew Rabbit would let her do payments, but that would mean admitting she needed credit, and she wasn't keen on that plan either.

Better to be tired than sold, *though.*

But tired meant forgetting to control her words. Her cattiness slipped out after school while she and Aislinn were waiting for Rianne to finish meeting with a counselor. Apparently, a private counselor wasn't quite enough intervention; Rianne's mother had notified the school as well, and Sister Isabel had waylaid Rianne at the last bell.

Aislinn was watching up the street. She had folded her arms, one hand resting over the thick gold band on her upper arm. Leslie had seen it when they'd changed for PE. Now it was hidden under Aislinn's shirt. *What's she doing that she's getting all these baubles?* Leslie didn't think Aislinn was dumb enough to be trading herself for money, but lately it seemed that Keenan's wealth was in Aislinn's hands.

Without thinking it through, Leslie said, "So are you watching for the second-string boy-toy or the starting player?"

Aislinn stared at her. "What?"

"Is it Keenan's or Seth's turn to take you home?"

"It's not like that," Aislinn said. For a brief moment, it looked like the air around her shimmered, like heat rising off the ground.

Leslie rubbed her eyes and then stepped closer. "I'd rather believe it was like that than that you're letting Keenan use you because he's got money." She squeezed Aislinn's arm where the bracelet was. "People notice. People talk. I know Seth doesn't like me, but he's a good guy. Don't screw it up because of blondie and his money, okay?"

"God, Les, why does everything have to be about sex? Just because you gave it away so easily—" Aislinn stopped herself, looking embarrassed. She bit down on her lip. "I'm sorry. I didn't mean it like that."

"Like what?" Leslie had been friends with Aislinn since

almost the moment they'd met, but *friends* didn't mean she told Aislinn everything, not anymore. They were close *before*, but these days Leslie needed barriers. She didn't know how to start the conversation she'd needed to have for months now. *Hey, Ash, do you have the handout from Lit? By the way, I was raped, and I have these hella-awful nightmares.* She was holding it together, planning to move away, to start life all over again—and when she imagined trying to talk about it, about the rape, she felt like something was ripping her apart. Her chest hurt. Her stomach clenched. Her eyes burned. *No. I'm not ready to talk.*

"I'm sorry," Aislinn repeated, gripping Leslie's arm with an almost uncomfortably warm hand.

"We're cool." Leslie forced a smile to her lips and wished these emotions would fade away. Numbness was increasingly appealing. "All I'm saying is that you've got a good thing with Seth. Don't let Keenan ruin it."

"Seth understands why I spend time with Keenan." Aislinn bit down on her lip again and glanced back up the street. "It's not what you're saying, though. Keenan is a friend, an important friend. That's it."

Leslie nodded, hating that they couldn't really talk about their lives, hating that even her closest friendships were filled with half-truths. *Would she look at me with pity?* The idea of seeing that in Aislinn's eyes was awful. *I survived. I am surviving.* So she stood there, waiting with Aislinn, and switched the topic to one where they could both be honest. "Did I tell you? I'm finally getting my tattoo. I got the outline already. One more session—*tomorrow*—and it's done."

Aislinn looked somewhere between relieved and disappointed. "What did you pick?"

Leslie told her. It was easy to remember: she could see the eyes staring out at her, could picture them without trying. The more she thought of her art, the less tense she felt.

By the time Seth strolled up the street to meet Aislinn—looking like a walking advertisement for how hot facial piercings could be—Leslie and Aislinn were having a comfortable conversation about tattoos.

Seth draped an arm around Aislinn's shoulders and gave Leslie a questioning look. One pierced brow raised, he asked, "You got ink? Let's see."

"It's not finished." Leslie was barely able to contain the shiver of pleasure at the idea of getting the rest of it, but the thought of showing anyone felt surprisingly not-appealing. "Show you in a few days."

"Rabbit must have been pleased. Virgin skin, right?" Seth got a faraway smile on his lips and started walking, moving in that easy lope that was the only speed at which he seemed to do anything.

"It was. I got the outline last week." Leslie moved faster to keep up with Seth and Aislinn, who'd kept pace with Seth without pause, seeming as oblivious as he was. They had a synchronicity that came from truly fitting together. *That's how it's supposed to be: relaxed, good.* Leslie wanted to believe that someday life would be like that for her too.

Aislinn held Seth's hand and steered the two of them through the people passing on the street. As they walked, Seth talked a bit about friends' tattoos, about the shops up in Pittsburgh, where Rabbit did the guest-artist gig sometimes. It was one of the most enjoyable conversations Leslie had ever had with him. Until recently, he'd been terse with her. She hadn't asked why, but she suspected it had something to do with Ren. Seth wasn't very tolerant of dealers.

Guilty by association. She couldn't really blame Seth: Aislinn was too gentle to be exposed to Ren's crowd. If Seth thought being friends with Leslie would put Aislinn in danger, he'd have reason to disapprove. She shook off the thought, enjoying the banter with Aislinn and Seth.

They'd only gone two blocks when Keenan and Niall stepped out of a doorway. Leslie wondered how they'd known Aislinn was passing at that moment, but the awkward silence that came with Keenan's arrival made questions feel unwise.

Seth tensed as Keenan held out his hand to Aislinn and said, "We need to go. Now."

Niall stood to the side, watching the street. Aside from a curt hello to Seth, Keenan behaved as if he and Aislinn were the only two people there. He didn't look at anyone or anything other than Aislinn, and the way he looked at her was much the same as the way Seth did: like Aislinn was the most amazing person he'd ever seen.

"Aislinn?" Keenan made a weirdly elegant gesture with his hand, as if to direct Aislinn to walk in front of him.

Aislinn didn't respond or move. Then Seth kissed her briefly and said, "Go on. I'll see you tonight."

"But Niall . . ." Aislinn frowned as she glanced from Niall to Leslie.

"There's a guest in town. We need to find him. . . ." Keenan shoved his hair away from his face, elegance gone as quickly as it had arrived. "We should've gone hours ago, Aislinn, but you had your classes."

Aislinn bit her lip and looked at everyone. Then she started: "But Niall . . . and Leslie . . . and . . . I can't just *leave* them here, Keenan. It's not . . . fair."

Keenan turned to Seth. "You can stay with Niall and Leslie, right?"

"Planned on it. I got it, Ash. Just go with Sunshine"— Seth paused and gave Keenan a friendly grin that seemed at odds with the situation—"and I'll see you tonight. We're cool." He tucked a piece of her hair behind her ear and let his hand linger there, his palm resting around Aislinn's cheek, fingertips against her ear. "I'll be fine. Leslie will be fine. Go on."

When Seth stepped back, Keenan nodded to him and took Aislinn's hand. Whatever those three had going on was decidedly weirder than Leslie wanted to know about, and Niall's studious observation of the street was starting to make her feel angry. He hadn't even acknowledged her presence. The few moments of easy friendship with Aislinn and Seth didn't mean that she wanted to be caught up in whatever their drama was. "I'm out of here, Ash. I'll see you at sch—"

Aislinn put her hand on Leslie's wrist. "Could you hang with Seth? Please?"

"Why?" Leslie looked from Seth to Aislinn and back again. "Seth's a bit old to need a sitter."

But Niall turned toward her, the movement drawing her attention to his scar. Leslie froze, caught between wanting to stare and wanting to look away.

Niall said, "Surely you could join us for a while?"

Leslie turned to stare pointedly at Aislinn; there'd been enough "stay away" messages from Aislinn, but all Aislinn did was look to Keenan. And he smiled approvingly at them. *Maybe* he's *why Ash wanted Niall away from me.* Leslie shivered in a sudden rush of fear. Keenan might be Aislinn's friend, but something about him made her uncomfortable, more so today.

"Please, Les, could you? As a favor?" Aislinn asked.

She's terrified.

"Sure," Leslie said as a wave of dizziness rolled over her, like something in the core of her was being stretched and tugged. The force of it made her unable to move, unsteady to the point that she thought she was going to be sick if she tried. She started cataloguing everything she'd drunk or eaten or touched to her lips in any way. *Nothing unusual.* She stayed motionless, concentrating on breathing until she felt whatever it was recede.

No one else moved either. They didn't seem to even notice.

Seth said, "We're good. Go on, Ash."

Then Aislinn and Keenan got into a long silver Thunderbird parked at the curb and drove off, leaving Leslie standing there with Niall and Seth. Niall leaned back against the wall, not looking at her or Seth, just waiting on . . . *something.*

Leslie shifted from foot to foot, watching a group of skaters across the street. They were taking advantage of the traffic-less side street and doing tail slides on the curb—not that there weren't other places they could go, but they were content to be where they were. It was appealing, that sense of peace. Sometimes Leslie felt like she was chasing that—at Rabbit's, at her friends' parties. She just needed the right timing to catch it.

Seth started to walk away, and Niall pushed off from the wall, watching Leslie with a hungry expression. Something was different, unleashed. He stepped closer to her, slowly, and she felt sure his caution was to keep her from running.

"Niall?" Seth had stopped and called back, "Crow's Nest?"

"I'd rather go to the club." Niall didn't even glance at Seth. Instead he watched her with a pensive look, as if he were studying her. She liked it far too much.

"I need to bail," she said. She didn't wait for an answer but simply turned and left.

But Niall was standing in front of her before she'd gone more than a half dozen steps. "Please? I'd really like you to join us."

"Why?"

"I like being near you."

And she felt a surge of the confidence she'd been filled with in fleeting moments since she'd been tattooed.

"Come with me?" he prompted.

She didn't want to leave. She was tired of running every time she felt afraid. That fearful girl wasn't the person she'd been before; that wasn't who she wanted to be. She let go of the fear but couldn't answer.

He held her gaze as he lowered his head toward her. He didn't kiss her, though—just leaned kissably close and asked, "Will you let me take you in my arms . . . for a dance, Leslie?"

She shivered, confidence swirling with a surge of longing for the peace she could almost taste, peace she was suddenly sure she'd feel if she slipped into Niall's arms. She nodded. "Yes."

CHAPTER 11

Niall knew better. He knew not to allow himself so very close to temptation. He was to keep the queen's mortals safe while Keenan and Aislinn sought out the Dark King. Protecting Seth was easy: the mortal was the closest thing to a brother Niall had ever had. Leslie was more difficult: Niall knew he shouldn't even be considering seducing a mortal he was to protect.

This is work, just like any other day. Think about the court. Think about vows.

But it was hard to think about the Summer Court—or the Dark Court, for that matter. Niall had been a confidant to both kings, and now he was relegated to caretaker of the Summer Queen's mortals. Everything had changed when Keenan found Aislinn, the mortal who'd been meant to be his queen, and despite the fact that Niall was happy for his king, his friend, there was a sudden absence in his life. After centuries of advising Keenan, Niall was without purpose.

He needed direction. Without it he became . . . not of the sunlight. It frightened him, these too-frequent flashes of the memory of what he had been before he'd been taken into the Summer Court.

Being around Leslie had become a reward—and punishment. His unexpectedly intense longing to be near her the past week or so was complicating an already unstable situation. He was staring at her again, and Seth noticed.

"You think that's a good idea?" Seth glanced pointedly at Leslie.

Niall kept his expression carefully neutral; Seth knew him too well. "No, I don't suppose it would be."

Leslie seemed oblivious, lost in her own thoughts, and Niall wished she would share them with him. He had no one he could truly share such things with. Until he'd seen Aislinn and Seth, he hadn't realized—*admitted*—how he longed for that. Even Aislinn and Keenan had a beautiful bond, while Niall was increasingly disconnected from everyone. If Niall kissed Leslie, pulled her into his arms and let himself lower his guard, they'd be far from disconnected. She'd be his, willing to press her body against his, willing to follow him anywhere.

It was both the temptation and the trouble with mortals. The caresses of some faeries, Gancanaghs like him and like Irial once was, were addictive to mortals. Irial's nature had been altered long before Niall ever drew breath. Becoming the Dark King had changed him, made him able to control the impact of his touch. Niall had no such recourse: he was left with memories of mortals who'd withered and died for lack of his embrace. For centuries, those memories were reminder enough to restrain himself.

Until Leslie.

Niall could hardly look at her as they walked. If Seth weren't with them . . . Niall felt his pulse race at the images in his mind, at the thought of Leslie in his arms. Not for the first time, he was glad he had Seth's company. The mortal's calm seemed to help Niall remember himself. *Usually.*

Niall stepped a little farther away from Leslie, hoping— irrationally perhaps—that distance would bolster his self-control.

Keenan had been suggesting Niall pursue a relationship of his own now that the court was strong—*growing stronger by the day*—but Niall didn't imagine he'd be permitted to do so with a mortal, especially one Aislinn wanted sheltered. His king wouldn't ask him to disobey their queen.

Would he?

And Niall had no intention of betraying his king or queen's trust, not willingly. They'd asked him to keep the mortals safe, and so he would. He could resist the temptation.

But he still had to fold his hand into a fist at his side. The urge to lay his skin against hers was a compulsion he hadn't felt so strongly in centuries. He stared at her, looking for some clue as to why her, why now.

Leslie realized that Niall was staring at her again. "That's sort of creepy, you know?"

He looked amused, the corner of his scar wrinkling as he smiled ever so slightly. "Did I offend you?"

"No. But it's weird. If you have something to say, speak."

"I would if I could figure out what to say," Niall said. He put a hand on the small of her back and nudged her forward gently. "Come. The club is a safer place to relax than out here"—he gestured at the empty street—"where you are so vulnerable."

Seth cleared his throat and scowled at Niall. Then he told Leslie, "The club's right around the corner."

Leslie walked a little faster, trying to move away from Niall's hand on her back. Speeding up didn't help: he kept pace with her.

When they rounded the corner and she saw the dark building in front of them, she felt panic well up. There was no sign, no posters, no people hanging outside, nothing to indicate that the building in front of them was anything other than abandoned. *I should be freaking out.* She wasn't, though, and she couldn't understand why.

Niall said, "Head toward the doorman."

She looked back. Standing at the front of the building was a muscular guy with an ornate tattoo covering one half of his face. Spirals and lines disappeared under hair as black as the ink. The other side of his face was inkless. The only ornamentation was a small black tusklike piercing in his upper lip, the white match of which was in the corner of his mouth on the inked side of his face.

"Keenan cool with her being here?" The man pointed at her, and Leslie realized that she was still staring—in part because she couldn't fathom how she could've missed seeing someone like him standing outside the door.

"She is a friend of Aislinn's, and there are *unpleasant* guests in town. The"—Niall paused and crinkled his face into a wry smile—"Aislinn is with Keenan."

"So are Keenan and Ash good with it or not?" the inked man asked.

Niall clasped the man's forearm. "She is my guest, and the club should be near empty, yes?"

The doorman shook his head, but he opened the door and motioned to a short, muscular guy with the most incredible dreads Leslie had ever seen. They were thick and well formed, hanging like a mane around the guy's face. For a moment, Leslie thought it *was* an actual mane.

"We have a new *guest*," said the doorman as the dreadlocked guy came outside. The door thudded shut behind him.

Dreadlocks stepped closer and sniffed.

Niall quirked his mouth in what looked like a snarl. "*My* guest."

"Yours?" Dreadlocks' voice was low—harsh like he lived on cigarettes and liquor.

Leslie opened her mouth to object to the proprietary tone in Niall's voice, but Seth put a hand on her wrist. She glanced at him, and he shook his head.

Dreadlocks said, "My pride is in—"

Seth cleared his throat.

"Go tell them," the doorman said as he opened the door and motioned Dreadlocks back inside. "Two minutes."

They stood there awkwardly for a moment before the tension felt too unbearable for Leslie. "If this is a bad idea—"

But the door had already reopened, and Seth was stepping into the shadowy building.

"Come on." Niall went inside.

She went only a few steps before she stopped, unable to think what to say or do. The few people inside were all wearing strange and ornate costumes. A woman passed by with vines draped all over her arms; the vines seemed as if they flowered.

Like the living art at the museum.

Another couple wore feathered wigs; still others had blue faces and misshapen teeth, not like the vampire teeth the costume places sold at Halloween—but each tooth jagged, like sharks' teeth.

Niall stood beside her, his hand resting on her back again. In the odd blue lights of the club, his eyes looked reflective; his scar was a black slash on his skin.

"Is it okay that we don't have costumes, too?" she whispered.

He laughed. "Quite. These are their everyday wear."

"Everyday? Are they like one of those reenactment groups? A role-playing group?"

"Something like that." Seth pulled out a tall chair. Like the rest of the furniture, it was a polished wood. Nothing in the low-lit club seemed to be made of anything *other* than wood, stone, or glass.

Unlike the rough-looking exterior, the inside of the club was far from run-down. The floor gleamed like polished marble. Running the length of one side of the room was a long, black bar. It wasn't wood or metal, but it looked too thick for glass. As the rotating club lights hit the bar, Leslie saw streaks of color—purples and greens—shimmering in it. She gasped.

"Obsidian," said a raspy voice beside her ear. "Keeps the patrons calm."

A waitress in a skin-suit with shimmering silver scales all over her legs and arms stood there. She circled behind Leslie and sniffed her hair.

Leslie took a step away from her.

Although neither Niall nor Seth had ordered yet, the waitress handed them drinks—a golden-colored wine for Niall and a microbrew for Seth.

"No drinking age in here?" Leslie's gaze wandered over the room. The people in their odd costumes all had drinks, though some of them looked younger than she was. Dreadlocks was with a group of four other guys with pale brown dreads. They were sharing a pitcher that looked like it was filled with the same golden wine Niall was drinking.

A pitcher of wine?

"Now you see why I prefer to come here. Seth cannot

relax as well at the Crow's Nest, and they do not carry my preferred vintage"—Niall lifted his glass and sipped—"at any other club."

"Welcome to the Rath, Leslie." Seth leaned back in his chair and motioned to the dance floor, where several almost normal-looking people were dancing. "Weirder than anywhere else you'll ever see . . . if you're lucky."

The music grew immediately louder, and Niall tipped back his glass one more time. "You could relax more fully, Seth. Some of the girls—"

"Go dance, Niall. If we don't hear from Ash within the next couple hours, we'll need to get Leslie to work."

Beside her, Niall stood. He sat his half-full glass on the table and gestured to the dance floor. "Come join the dance."

At his words, Leslie felt a whispering need to refuse and a simultaneous tug of impatience to go toward the small group of costumed people who were dancing almost manically. The music, the movement, his voice—they all beckoned her, pulled her as if she were a marionette with too many strings. Out there in the throng of swaying, shifting bodies, she'd find pleasure. A sea of lust and laughter floated in the air around the dancers, and she wanted to swim in it.

To buy a moment to steady her nerves, she grabbed for Niall's glass. When she lifted it to her lips, it was empty. She stared at it, turning it in her hand by the fragile stem.

"We don't drink this in anger or fear." Niall put his hand over hers so that they were both holding on to his glass.

It wasn't anger or fear she felt; it was longing. But she wasn't telling him that. She couldn't.

The waitress stepped from somewhere behind them. Silently, she tilted a heavy bottle over the glass Niall and Leslie both held. From this close the wine looked thick as honey. Spirals of iridescent color shimmered as it filled the cup. It was tempting, smelling sweeter and richer than anything she'd ever known.

Her hand was still under his when Niall lifted the glass to his lips. "Would you like to share my glass, Leslie? In friendship? In celebration?"

He watched her as he sipped the golden drink.

"No, she wouldn't." Seth slid his beer across the table. "If she wants a drink, it'll be from my glass or my hand."

"If she wants to share my cup, Seth, it's her choice." Niall lowered the glass, still holding her hand over the stem.

The drink, the dance, Niall—too many temptations were in front of Leslie. She wanted them all. Despite how weirdly Niall was acting, she wanted that tumble into pleasure. The fears that had been binding her since the rape were loosening lately. *The decision to get tattooed did that. Freed me.* Leslie licked her lips. "Why not?"

Niall lifted the glass until the rim was touching her lips, close enough that her lipstick smudged the glass, but he didn't tilt it, didn't pour that strange-sweet wine into her mouth. "Indeed, why not?"

Seth sighed. "Think for a minute, Niall. Do you really want to deal with the consequences?"

"Right now, more than anything I can think of, but"—
Niall pulled the glass away from Leslie's lips and curled their
hands until her lipstick smudge was against his mouth—"you
deserve more respect than this, don't you, Leslie?"

He drained the glass and set it on the table but kept hold
of her hand.

Leslie wanted to run. His hand still held hers on the
glass, but his attention was no longer intense. Her confidence faltered. Maybe Aislinn had good reasons to keep
Keenan's family away from her: Niall alternated between
fascinating and bizarre. She licked her suddenly dry lips,
feeling denied, rejected, and angry. She shook off his hand.
"You know what? I'm not sure what game you're playing,
but I'm not interested in it."

"You're right." Niall lowered his gaze. "I don't mean to . . .
I don't want . . . I'm sorry. I'm not myself lately."

"Whatever." She backed up.

But Niall took both of her hands in his, gently so that
she could pull away if she wanted. "Dance with me. If
you're still unhappy, we'll see you home. Seth and I both."

Leslie looked back at Seth. He sat in a club that she
hadn't known existed, surrounded by people in extreme
costumes and bizarre behavior, yet he was calm. *Unlike me.*

Seth tugged at his lip ring, rolling it into his mouth as
he did when he was thinking. Then he motioned toward
the floor. "Dancing's fine. Just don't drink anything he
offers you—or that anyone else offers you, okay?"

"Why?" She forced the question out, despite her instant

aversion to asking, to knowing.

Neither Niall nor Seth answered. She thought to press the matter, but the music was beckoning her, inviting her to let go, to forget her doubts. The blue lights that came from every corner of the club spun across the floor, and she wanted to spin with them.

"Please dance with me." Niall's expression was one of need, of longing and unspoken offers.

Leslie couldn't think of any question—or answer—worth refusing that look. "Yes."

And with that Niall spun her into his arms and onto the floor.

Chapter 12

Several songs later, Leslie was thankful for the long hours of waitressing. Her legs ached, but not as much as they would have if she'd been out of shape. She'd never met anyone who could dance the way Niall did. He led her through moves that made her laugh and taught her strange steps that required more concentration that she thought casual dancing could ever need.

Through it all, he was curiously careful with her. His hands never strayed out of the safe zones. Like at the museum, he was almost distant as he held her. If not for a few flirtatious remarks, she'd suspect she'd imagined that delicious look when he'd invited her to dance.

Niall finally paused. "I need to check in with Seth before I"—he burrowed his face into the side of her neck, his breath almost painfully warm on her throat—"give in to my unconscionable desire to put my hands on you properly."

"I don't want to stop dancing. . . ." She was having fun, feeling free, and didn't want to risk that pleasure ending.

"So don't." Niall nodded to one of the dreadlocked guys who'd been dancing nearby. "They would dance with you until I return."

Leslie held out her hand and the dreadlocked guy pulled her into his arms and spun her across the room. She was laughing.

The first guy passed her to another dreadlocked guy, who spun her toward the next. Each of them looked identical to the last one. There were no pauses in their movements. It was as if the world had begun spinning at a different rate. It was fabulous. At least two songs passed, and Leslie wondered how many guys there were—or if she was dancing with the same two over and over. She wasn't sure if they really were identical or if the illusion was a result of being spun so impossibly fast. But then she stumbled to a halt. The music hadn't ended, but the dizzying movement had.

The dreadlocked guys stopped moving and she realized there were five of them.

A stranger walked across the floor toward her, moving with languid grace like he heard a different song than she did. His eyes were surrounded by dark shadows. *He* looked like he was surrounded by shadows, as if the blue lights glanced away without touching him. A silver chain glinted against his shirt. Dangling from the chain was a razor blade. He waved a hand dismissively at the dreadlocked guys and said, "Shoo."

She blinked when she realized she was staring. "I know you. You were at Rabbit's once. . . . We met."

Her hand drifted to the top of her spine, where her not-yet-complete tattoo was. It suddenly throbbed like a drum-beat caught under her skin.

He smiled at her as if he could hear that illusory beat.

Two of the dreadlocked quints had bared their teeth. The others were growling.

Growling?

She looked at them and then back at him. "Irial, right? That's your name. From Rabbit's . . ."

He stepped behind her, slid his hands around her waist, and pulled her back to his chest. She didn't know why she was dancing with him, why she was still dancing at all. She wanted to walk off the dance floor, find Niall, find Seth, leave, but she couldn't walk away from the music.

Or him.

Her mind flashed odd images—sharks swimming toward her, cars careening out of control in her path, fangs sinking into her skin, shadowy wings curling around her in a caress. Somewhere in her mind she knew she needed to step away from him, but she didn't, couldn't. She'd felt the same way when she'd first seen him: like she'd follow him wherever he wanted. It wasn't a feeling she liked.

Irial spun her against his chest, holding her firmly to him as he matched his movements to hers. She didn't want to like it, but she did. For the first time in months, the humming fear that was always just under the surface quieted completely, as if it had never been there. The stillness was enough to make her want to stay next to Irial. It felt good—natural, as if the rush of ugliness she was constantly fighting not to feel had drifted away when he took her into his arms. His hands were on her skin, under the edge of her shirt. She didn't know him, but she couldn't find any words to make him stop. *Or start.*

Laughing softly, he slid his hands over her hips, his fingers bruisingly tight on her skin. "My lovely Shadow Girl. Almost mine . . ."

"I'm not sure who you think I am, but I'm not her." She pulled back with a ridiculous amount of effort. She felt like a cornered animal. She shoved at him. "And I'm *not* yours."

"You are"—he put his hand over hers, capturing it as she pushed angrily at him—"and I'll look after you well."

The room felt like it was shifting, tilting, and she wanted to run. She shook her head with effort, and she said, "No. I'm not. Let go."

Then Niall was beside them, saying, "Stop."

Irial pressed his lips to Leslie's in a lingering open-mouth kiss.

She didn't like him, but she wouldn't have pulled away for anything. Her anger shifted into something territorial. The dual desire to resist being claimed as property and to claim him as hers surged through her. Irial stepped back, staring at her as if they were the only two people there. "Soon, Leslie."

She stared at him, not sure if she wanted to shove him again or pull him closer. *This isn't me. I'm not . . . what?* She didn't have words for it.

Niall was watching, and standing behind him were all of the dreadlocked guys and a larger group of people she'd not noticed earlier. *Where had they all come from?* The club had seemed mostly empty before; now it was filled. And no one looked friendly.

Niall tried to move her behind him, murmuring, "Come away from him."

But Irial slid his hands around Leslie's waist. His thumbs slipped under the edge of her shirt to stroke her skin. Her eyes blurred at the pleasure of that casual touch—not anger, not fear, just *want*.

Irial was asking Niall, "You didn't think she was yours, did you? Just like old times. You find them, and I take them."

Leslie blinked, trying to focus, trying to remember what she should be doing. She should be afraid. She should be angry . . . or something. She shouldn't be watching Irial's mouth. She stumbled as she tried to back away from him.

Niall bristled. Leslie could swear his eyes actually flashed. He stepped closer to Irial, hand clenched like he'd strike him. He didn't. He just ground out, "Stay away from her. You're—"

"Mind your place, boy. You have no authority over me or mine. You made your feelings on *that* quite clear." Irial pulled Leslie closer until she was right back where she'd been when they danced, in his arms and frighteningly unable—*unwilling*—to move.

Her face was flame red, but she couldn't move for several heartbeats.

"No," she said, forcing the word out. "Let go."

Then Niall stepped forward. "Leave her alone."

His eyes did *flash.*

"She's a friend of *our* court, of Aislinn's, of mine." Niall moved as close as he could to Irial without touching him.

Court?

"My girl claimed by your family?" Irial pulled her up so they were face-to-face and gazed at her as if there were secrets written on her skin. "She's not been claimed by yours."

Claimed? Leslie looked at him, at Niall, at the strangers around her. *This is not my world.*

"Let go of me," she said. Her voice wasn't strong, but it was there.

And he did. He let go of her and stepped away so suddenly, she had to grab his arm to keep from falling to the floor. She was mortified.

"Get her out of here," Niall said. From somewhere in

the crowd behind him, Seth stepped forward. He reached out for her hand, an uncharacteristically friendly move for him, and pulled her away from Irial.

"Soon, love," Irial said again as he bowed from the waist.

Leslie shivered. If her legs had been working, she would've run from the club. Instead the best she could do was stumble alongside Seth.

CHAPTER 13

Leslie and Seth had gone several blocks before she felt able to look at him. They weren't friends—by his choice—but she still trusted him more than she trusted most guys. She still valued his opinion.

They were almost at the Comix Connexion before she spoke. "I'm sorry."

She'd glanced at him as she said it but turned away at the sight of the anger on his face. His hands were held in loose fists. He wouldn't hurt her—Seth wasn't like that—but she still flinched when he reached out and caught her wrist.

"Sorry for what?" He quirked his eyebrow.

She stopped walking. "For making a scene, for acting like a big slut in front of you and Niall, for . . ."

"Stop." Seth shook his head. "That was not your fault. Irial's trouble. Just . . . just get away from him if you see him coming your way, okay? If you can, just go. Don't run, but get out."

Mutely, she nodded, and Seth pulled his hand away from her wrist. Like at the Rath, Leslie was sure he knew things he wasn't saying. *Is it a gang thing?* She hadn't heard of any real gangs in Huntsdale, but that didn't mean there weren't any. Whatever it was that Seth knew, he wasn't talking, and she didn't know how to ask. Instead she said, "Where are you going?"

"*We* are going to my house."

"We?"

"You have somewhere else safe to go before work?" His voice was gentle, but she felt certain that it wasn't a real question.

"No," she said, turning away from the too-knowing look on his face.

He didn't say anything else, but she'd seen the understanding in his eyes. And in that instant, she was sure that he—and therefore Aislinn—knew how ugly things were at home. They knew that she'd been lying to them, to everyone.

She took a deep breath and said, "Ren's probably there, so . . . you know, not exactly the safest place to be."

Seth nodded. "You're always welcome to crash at the house if you need."

She tried to laugh it off. "It's not . . ."

He raised an eyebrow.

And she sighed and stopped lying. "I'll remember that."

"You want to talk?"

"No. Not today. Maybe later." She blinked back the tears in her eyes. "Ash knows, then?"

"That Ren hits you or about what happened with his dealer?"

"Yeah." She felt like throwing up. "Both, I guess."

"She knows. She's been there, in a bad place, you know? Not the same, not as—" He stopped. He didn't offer her a hug or do any of those touchy-feely things that a lot of people would do, things that would make her fall apart.

"Right." Leslie folded her arms over her chest, feeling her world unraveling from somewhere inside, and knowing she couldn't fix it.

How long have they known?

Seth swallowed audibly before adding, "She'll hear about Irial too. You can talk to her."

"Like she talks to me?" Leslie held his gaze then.

"Not my business either way, but—" He bit his lip ring and rolled it into his mouth. He stared at her for several heartbeats before saying, "You'd both be better off if you started being straight with each other."

Panic welled up inside of her, a black bubble that made her throat feel tight. *Like it had when their hands . . . No.* She wasn't thinking about that, wouldn't think about it. Lately, the awful feelings had been so distant. She wished they would stay that way. She wished numbness would settle over her. She started walking faster, almost running, feet hitting the sidewalk with a steady *thunk*ing noise.

If I could outrun the memories . . . She couldn't, but it was better to think her heart raced from running than from the terror hidden in the memories. She ran.

And Seth ran steadily beside her, not behind or in front, keeping his pace measured to hers. He didn't try to stop her, try to make her talk. He just sprinted alongside her like running through the streets was perfectly normal.

They were at the edge of the railroad yard where he lived before she could bear to stop. Breathing deeply, she stared at one of the fire-blackened buildings across the street. Standing there in the patch of grass that shouldn't thrive in the dirty lot, she braced herself for the conversation she didn't want to have. She asked, "So how . . . what . . . how much do you know?"

"I heard about Ren setting you up to get out of trouble."

Hands, bruising, laughter, the sickly-sweet smell of crack, voices, Ren's voice, bleeding. She let the memories wash over her. *I didn't drown. I didn't break.*

Seth didn't look away, didn't flinch.

And neither did she. She might scream when the nightmares found her, but not by choice, not when she was awake.

She tilted her head back and forced her voice to stay steady. "I survived."

"You did." Seth's keys clinked together as he shook them

to find the door key. "But if everyone had known how bad things were before Ren let—" He stopped himself, looking pained. "We didn't know. We were so caught up with . . . things, and—"

Leslie turned away. She didn't—*couldn't*—say anything. She kept her back to him. The door creaked open but didn't slam closed, which meant he was standing there waiting.

She cleared her throat, but her voice sounded as tear-filled as it was. "I'll be in. I just need a sec."

She darted a glance his way, but he was staring into the empty air behind her.

"I'll be in," she repeated.

The only answer was the sound of the door closing gently.

She sat down on the ground outside Seth's train and let her gaze follow the murals that decorated it. They ranged from anime to abstract—dizzying, blurring as she tried to follow the lines, concentrate on the colors, the art, anything but the memories she didn't want to face.

I did survive. I still am. And it won't happen again.

It hurt, though, knowing that her friends, people she respected, knew about what *they* had done to her. Logic said not to be embarrassed, but she was.

It hurts. But she didn't want to let it. She stood up and ran a hand over one of the metalwork sculptures that sprouted like plants outside the train. She squeezed it until the sharp metal edges dug into her palm, until blood started to ooze between her fingers and drip onto the ground, until the pain in her hand made her think about *now*, not then, not other pains that left her curled into herself sobbing.

Think about this feeling, this place. She uncurled her hand, looking at the big cut in her palm, the smaller ones in her fingers. *Think about* now.

Right now she was safe. It was more than she could say some days.

She opened the door and went inside, fisting her hand again so the blood didn't drip on the floor. Seth was sitting in one of the weird curved chairs in the front of the train. His boa constrictor was coiled in his lap, one thick loop trailing toward the floor like the hem of a blanket.

"Be right out," she said as she walked past him to the second train car, where the tiny bathroom and his bedroom were. She almost believed he hadn't noticed the way she held her hand.

Then he called out, "There's bandages in the blue box on the floor if you need one. Should be some antibiotic junk too."

"Right." She rinsed her hand in the cold water and grabbed some toilet paper to hold. She didn't want to wipe her still-bleeding hand on Seth's towels. After she'd bandaged herself, she went back out.

"Feel better?" He was toying with his lip ring again.

Aislinn had said that the lip-ring bit was a stalling thing—not that Aislinn had been spilling secrets, but she seemed to find everything about Seth fascinating. Leslie smiled a little, thinking about them. Aislinn and Seth had something real, something special. It might not be easy to find, but it was possible.

"Some," Leslie said, sitting back on Seth's battered sofa. "I should probably rinse the, umm, sculpture off."

"Later." He motioned to the blanket he had put on the end of the sofa. "You should catch a nap. Here or back there"—he gestured toward the hallway that led to his room—"wherever you feel comfortable. There's a lock on the door."

"Why are you being so nice?" She stared at him, hating that she had to ask, but still needing to know.

"You're Ash's friend. *My* friend now." He looked like some freaky wise man, sitting in the weird chair with a boa in his lap and a stack of old books beside him. It was partly an illusion made by the surreality of the details, but not entirely. The way he watched her, watched the door. He knew about what sort of people waited out there.

She tried to make light of it all. "So we're friends, huh? When did that happen?"

Seth didn't laugh. He stared at her for a moment, stroking the boa's head as it slithered toward his shoulder. Then he said, "When I realized that you weren't a loser like Ren, but his victim. You're a good person, Leslie. Good people deserve help."

There wasn't any way to make light of that. She looked away.

Neither of them spoke for a few moments.

Finally, she picked up the blanket and stood. "You sure you don't mind if I crash back there?"

"Lock the door. It won't hurt my feelings, and you'll sleep better."

She nodded and walked away. In the hallway, she paused and said, "Thank you."

"Get some sleep. Later, you need to talk to Ash. There's other things. . . ." He paused and sighed. "She should be the one to tell you. Okay?"

"Okay." Leslie couldn't imagine what sorts of things Aislinn could say that would be any more awful or weird than what Leslie already knew, but she felt nervous at the tone in Seth's voice. She added, "Later. Not tonight."

"Soon," Seth insisted.

"Yeah, soon. I promise." And then she closed the door to Seth's room and turned the lock, hating that she felt compelled to do so but knowing that she'd feel safer with it in place.

She stretched out on top of Seth's bed, not pulling back the covers but wrapping up in the blanket he'd given her. She lay there in the darkened room and tried to focus on thoughts of Niall, of how carefully he'd held her when she was dancing with him, of his soft laugh against her throat.

But it wasn't Niall she dreamed of when she fell asleep: it was Irial. And it wasn't a dream. It was a nightmare to rival the worst ones she'd had: Irial's eyes staring back at her from the faces of the men who'd raped her, the men who'd held her down and done things that made the word *rape* seem somehow tame.

It was his voice that echoed in her head as she fought to wake and couldn't. *"Soon, a ghrá," he whispered from those other men's mouths. "Soon, we'll be together."*

CHAPTER 14

Since the Summer King was looking elsewhere for him, Irial had gone to the place where the court's darlings were most likely to be, the Rath and Ruins. *Better to let Keenan stew a bit longer before meeting.* The more the Summer regents panicked, the more emotional they'd be, and Irial could use a good meal. In the interim, he'd had the fun of watching Niall snarl over Leslie with a possessive streak that was quite unlike the Summer Court.

It made sense that the Gancanagh was already drawn to Leslie. Her growing bond with Irial was enough to make her tempting to everyone in the Dark Court. While Niall might have rejected the Dark Court so very many years ago, he was still connected to them. It was his rightful court, where he belonged whether or not he chose to accept it.

As does Leslie. She might not know it, might not realize it, but something in her had recognized Irial as a fitting match. She'd chosen him. Not even riding with Gabriel's Hounds was as satisfying as knowing that the little mortal was soon to be his, as knowing that he'd have her as a conduit to drink down emotions from mortals. The hints and teasing tastes he'd already been able to pull through her were a lovely start to how it would soon be. The Dark Court had fed only on fey for so long that finding nourishment from mortals had been lost to them—until Rabbit had started doing the ink exchanges. So much would be better once this exchange was finished. *And she might be strong enough to handle it.* Now he just had to wait, bide his time, fill in the hours until she was fully his.

Idly, Irial needled Niall, "Shouldn't you have a keeper or something, boy?"

"I could ask the same of you." Niall's expression and tone were disdainful, but his emotions were in flux. Over the years, the Gancanagh had continued to worry over Irial's well-being—though Niall would never say it aloud—and something had made that worry far more pronounced than usual. Irial made a note to ask Gabriel to look into it.

"A wise king has guards," Niall added. His concern had an edge of genuine fear now.

"A weak king, you mean. Dark Kings don't need to be cosseted." Irial turned his attention to finding a new distraction: Niall was too easily provoked just now, and Irial felt too much affection for him. At best, it was a bittersweet indulgence to taste Niall's emotions.

One of the waitresses, a wraith with crescent moons glowing in her eyes, paused. *One of Far Dorcha's kin.* Death-fey didn't usually linger in the too-cheerful Summer Court. Here was another lovely distraction. He beckoned her closer. "Darling?"

She glanced at the cubs, the rowan guards, and at Niall's glowering face—not in anxiety, but to track where they were. Wraiths could handle their own in almost any conflict: no one escapes death's embrace, not if death truly wants you.

"Irial?" The wraith's voice drifted over the air, as refreshing as a sip of the moon, as heavy as churchyard soil on his tongue.

"Would you fetch me some nice hot tea"—Irial made a pinching gesture with his first two fingers—"with just a kiss of honey in it?"

After a low curtsy, she floated around the assembled fey and headed behind the bar.

She'd be lovely at home. Perhaps she'd be willing to wander.

With a lazy smile at the scowling group, Irial followed her. None of them stepped in his way. They wouldn't. He might not be their king, but he was a king. They wouldn't—*couldn't*—assault or impede him, no matter how many of their delicate sensibilities he offended.

The little wraith set his tea on the slick slab of obsidian that made up the bar.

He pulled out a stool and angled it so he had his back to the Summer Court's guards. Then he turned his attention to the wraith. "Precious, what are you doing with this crowd?"

"It's home." She brushed his wrist with grave-damp fingers.

Unlike the rest of the faeries in the club or on the streets, the wraith was immune to him: he'd not provoke any fear in her. But she would pull it from others: hers was a sort of unpleasant beauty that they all feared—and sometimes longed for.

"By anchor or choice?" he prompted, unable to resist pursuing her—not when she'd be such an asset to his fey.

She laughed, and something quite close to the feel of maggots sliding into his veins assailed him.

"Careful," she said in that moon-sliver voice. "Not everyone is unaware of your court's *habits*."

He tensed briefly, watching her across the rainbow of color flaring in the obsidian bar. Between the purple streaks reflecting from the stone and the blue lights of the bar, she looked more terrifying than many of his own fey on their best days. And she brought fear to him with her intimation of knowledge. During the centuries of Beira's cruelty, the Dark Court's particular appetite wasn't hard to hide. Violence, debauchery, terror, lust, rage—all their favorite meals were amply available, floating in the very air. These new days of growing peace ruined that, required more careful hunting.

The wraith leaned forward and pressed her lips to his ear. Though he knew better, images of serpents coiled over his skin as she whispered, "Secrets of the grave, Irial. *We* aren't so forgetful or oblivious as the merry ones." Then she pulled back, taking the slithering sensation with her and offering a genuinely disturbing smile. "Or so chatty."

"Indeed. I shall remember that, my dear." He didn't look behind him, but he knew everyone there had watched, just as he knew that none would ask the wraith what she said. To learn a death-fey's secrets was to risk paying a price too high for any fey. He merely said, "The offer is there, should you ever want to wander."

"I'm content here. Do what you need before the king arrives. I've business to tend." She wandered away to wipe down the bar with a rag that looked like a remnant of a shroud.

She truly would be a lovely prize.

But the look she gave him made clear that she found the whole situation more amusing than persuasive. Far Dorcha's kin might not be organized within a court, but they didn't need to be. Death-fey walked freely in any house, separate from the squabbles and follies of the courts, seeming to laugh at all of them. If he amused her enough, she might deign to visit his house someday. That she chose to linger among Keenan's court spoke well of the young kingling.

However, it didn't change what Irial needed, what he'd

come to find—sustenance. He lingered, teasing the other waitresses, inciting the glares of the cubs and the rowanmen. Finally, the waitresses watched him through heavy-lidded gazes; the guards stood tense and angry, glaring at him. The combined dark temptations—to violence and lust—of the group still weren't enough to offer a proper meal, but it took the edge off his hunger.

He sighed, hating that he missed the last Winter Queen—not *her* but the sustenance she'd given him all those years. Her price had been painful, even by dark fey standards, but he'd rarely had a decent meal since her death. The ink exchange with Leslie would change that.

Maybe get a decent bit of chaos with the Summer Court too.

On that happy note, he stood and bowed his head to the wraith, who was now waiting attentively. "My dear."

Face as emotionless as when he'd arrived, she curtsied.

Irial turned to Niall and the scowling guards. "Tell the kingling I'll catch him on the morrow."

Niall nodded, bound by his fealty to his king to pass on the words, bound by law to tolerate the presence of another regent unless it threatened his own regents.

And hating it.

Irial pushed in his chair and stepped up to Niall. With a wink, he whispered, "I think I'll see if I can find the little morsel that was in here dancing. Pretty thing, isn't she?"

Niall's emotions flared, jealousy tangling with possessiveness and yearning. Although it didn't show on Niall's face, Irial could taste it. *Like cinnamon.* Niall had always been such fun.

Laughing, Irial sauntered out of the club, feeling almost satisfied with how unexpectedly well the day had turned out.

CHAPTER 15

By the time Irial left, Niall was sure that the Dark King would try to see Leslie again—if for no other reason than to provoke Keenan. *Or me.* Irial might not actively strike out at Niall for refusing the offer to succeed him, but they both knew it was an unforgiven insult. Leslie was doubly vulnerable for being Aislinn's friend and for being Niall's . . . *what?* Not his paramour, but perhaps his friend—that was something he could be. He could enjoy her company, be near her; he could have all of the things he wanted—save one. *If she's safe from harm . . .* The best Niall could hope for was that Leslie wouldn't ever cross paths with Irial again. *Hope isn't enough.*

A commotion at the door heralded Aislinn and Keenan's arrival.

"Where's Seth?" Keenan hadn't crossed the length of the room before he asked the question that was of utmost importance to the court. "Is he safe?"

Aislinn was not beside Keenan. She had been waylaid by the cubs to allow Keenan to speak to Niall first. It was a weak ruse, but it would buy the king a brief moment.

"I sent him away with Leslie. Well guarded, but—" Niall paused as the Summer Queen approached, her skin glowing with obvious pique. "My queen."

He bowed briefly to her.

She ignored him, her gaze only on Keenan. "That's getting old, Keenan."

"I . . ." The Summer King sighed. "If Seth was in peril, I wanted to protect—"

She turned to Niall. "Is he?"

Niall kept his face unreadable as he told them, "Fortunately, Seth did not attract the Dark King's attention, but Leslie did."

"Leslie?" Aislinn repeated. She blanched. "That's the third time he's met her, but I didn't think . . . he didn't pay any attention to her at Rabbit's, and he was dismissive at Verlaine's, and she said he wasn't . . . I'm a fool. I . . . never mind." She shook her head and refocused on the topic at hand. "What happened?"

"Seth took Leslie away. The guards followed, but—" He looked not at Aislinn but at Keenan, hoping that their centuries of companionship would weigh in his favor. "Let me stay nearer her until Irial leaves again. I can't touch him, but he has . . ."

Niall couldn't say it, even now with everything that had

passed; he wasn't sure how to finish that statement. Irial's random moments of kindness weren't something Niall liked to acknowledge.

A look of brief understanding passed over Keenan's face, but he did not ask the obvious questions. He did not point out that Niall was treading on unsafe ground. He merely nodded.

Aislinn spoke softly, "She is already interested in you, Niall. I don't want her to lose her mortal life because of a fleeting crush."

It was a warning. He knew it, but he'd been fey longer than his queen had drawn breath. Hoping Keenan wouldn't interfere, he asked, "What are your terms?"

"My terms?" She looked at Keenan.

"Terms under which he can go to her," Keenan clarified.

"Nothing's ever simple, is it?" Aislinn shoved at the gold-and-shadow streaks of her hair, looking like the sort of omnipotent deity mortals once believed the court fey to be.

"I will agree to whatever you ask of me if you let me keep her safe." Niall looked at Aislinn, but he spoke to Keenan as well. "I don't ask for many considerations."

Aislinn paced several steps away from them. For a newly fey monarch, the queen did exceptionally well, but Keenan and Niall had been together in the courts for centuries. There were habits, laws, traditions that Aislinn couldn't begin to understand so soon.

Niall looked at his king while Aislinn had her back turned.

Keenan didn't offer assurances. Instead he spoke softly to Aislinn. "You can set terms to Niall's presence in her life. He wants to protect the girl, to keep her safe. I would allow him to go to her."

"So I just need to figure how much he can get involved in her life?" Aislinn looked from Niall to Keenan, her observant gaze letting on that she knew there were nuances to the conversation that she was missing.

"Exactly," Keenan said. "None among us would willingly place a child in the Dark Court's hands, but if Irial's done no affront to our court, it's not our concern by law. I cannot act, not directly, unless he violates the laws."

Then his king walked away, having told Niall what he needed to know, what he'd already known: Keenan wasn't going to act. The Summer King didn't approve of Irial's predilections, his cruelties, or anything that happened in the shadows of the Dark King's court, but that didn't mean he was willing to enter a fight with the other court unless he could justify it by law. Those were *his* terms, whether he'd spoken them into the negotiations or not.

The Dark Court—like any of the courts—had volition. If Leslie belonged to the Summer Court, things would be different. But she was unattached, and thus fair game for any fey who wanted her. Years ago, Keenan had forbidden his fey from collecting mortals. Donia had made the same ruling when she took the Winter Queen's throne. The Dark Court, however, had no such compunction. Musicians who were particularly tempting "died young" to the mortal world. Artists retired to

unknown locales. The striking, the unusual, the enticing—
they were stolen away for the pleasures of the dark faeries. It
was an old tradition, one Irial had always permitted his court
fey. If he wanted her for himself, Leslie had no defense.

Niall dropped to his knees in front of his queen. "Let me
tell her about us. Please. I'll tell her, and she will swear fealty
to you. She'd be safe then, out of his reach."

The Summer Queen bit her lip. She almost flinched
away from him. "I don't want my *friends* under my rule. I
didn't want any of this. . . ."

"You don't know what the Dark Court is like. I do,"
Niall told his queen. And he didn't want Leslie to know.
Self-consciously he touched the scar on his face. Irial's fey
had done that to remind him of them every day.

"I want her to be free of all of this." Aislinn gestured at
the fey cavorting in the Rath. "To have a normal life. I don't
want this world to be her life. She's already been so hurt—"

"If he takes her with him, he'll hurt her worse than you
can begin to fathom." Niall had seen the mortals the Dark
Court had taken into their *bruig*, seen them after they left
the faery mound—comatose in mortal hospitals, muttering
and afraid in every city, shrieking in sanatoriums.

Aislinn looked across the room, unerringly finding the
Summer King where he stood waiting. She bit her lower lip
nervously, and he knew she was considering it.

Niall pressed her, "If Irial has decided to claim her, you
and Keenan are the only ones who can stop him. I can't
touch him. He's a king. If you invite her to our court first,

ask her to swear loyalty to you—"

"She's doing better lately," Aislinn interrupted. "She seems happier and more herself, stronger. I don't want to stop that and introduce all of this mess into her life. . . . Maybe he's just toying with us."

"Would you risk that?" Niall was aghast that his queen was being so foolhardy. "Please, my queen, let me go to her. If you won't bring her to you, let me try to keep her safe."

Keenan didn't approach—staying at a distance, making clear that it was the queen who was in charge—but he did speak. "Perhaps there is something to her we do not know, some reason for Irial to pursue her. And if not, Niall would still be there to try to keep her out of his reach, perhaps to distract her so she doesn't go willingly to Irial."

Keenan caught and held Niall's gaze. Although Aislinn could not see it, Keenan nodded at Niall; the king offered permission, consent to act. But Niall still needed Aislinn to assent. "She is *your* friend, but I am . . . grown fond of her as well. Let me keep her safe until he leaves. Remember how hard it was for you when Keenan pursued you. And she does not See him, not like you saw us."

"I want her safe from Irial"—Aislinn looked back at Keenan then, staring at the Summer King with some trace of the old fear in her eyes—"but I don't want her caught up in this world."

"Do you truly think there's a choice?" Keenan asked, his voice making clear that he did not. "You wanted to keep your ties to the mortal world. With that come risks."

"There are *always* choices." The Summer Queen straightened her shoulders. The wavering in her voice, the glint of fear in her eyes—they were gone now. "I won't make her choices for her."

Keenan did not disagree, although Niall knew him well enough to realize that he too thought Leslie's choices were growing limited. The difference was that Keenan didn't care; he simply couldn't involve himself in the life of every mortal who was plagued by a faery. This one didn't matter to Keenan, not really.

To Niall, however, she mattered more than any mortal ever had. He asked, "What terms, my queen?"

"You cannot tell her—about me or the fey or what you are. We need to learn more before we do that. . . . If there's a way to keep her safe from our world, to keep her unaware, we will." Aislinn watched his face, obviously looking for reactions, trying to gauge the wisdom of her terms.

Niall had centuries of experience, however. He stared unblinkingly at her. "Agreed."

"You may distract her, spend time with her, but no sex. You may *not* sleep with her. If Irial's interest is fleeting, you will be out of her life," Aislinn said.

Keenan did intervene then. "Don't start any wars without my accord. She might be important to you and to Aislinn, but I'll not go to war over one mortal."

She's more than just a mortal. Niall wasn't sure why that was or if it mattered. He nodded, though.

Then Keenan, half smiling, added, "Just be true to

yourself, Niall. Remember who and what you are."

Niall almost gaped at his king, but he'd spent too long practicing hiding his emotions. He merely let out his breath. Keenan's intimations were directly in conflict with Aislinn's expressed wishes.

He knows what I am. Addictive to mortals, leaving them willing to say or do anything to have another touch, another fix . . .

Oblivious to this, Aislinn peered down at Niall, shining so brightly that no mortal could've faced her without pain. Small oceans shimmered in her eyes; dolphins breached within them, breaking the blue surface. "Those are my terms. Our terms."

Niall took Aislinn's hand, turning it over to press a kiss into her palm. "You are a generous queen."

Aislinn let him hold her hand for a moment, and then she pulled him to his feet and asked, "Why do I feel like I've left out something important?"

"Because you are also a wise queen, m'lady." He bowed his head to her so she couldn't see his expression.

Then he left the Rath, not wanting to waste precious time to list all of the other terms she could have set upon him: time limits; alliances he could make with other courts and with solitary fey; vows he could make to Leslie that wouldn't reveal what they were yet would protect her more fully; renouncing the Summer Court to swear to another court for Leslie's safety; bartering his own person in her stead.

Keenan should've spoken some of those into the negoti-ation. He should've bound Niall more tightly. *Why hadn't he?* He should've supported Aislinn's intent; instead he'd suggested Niall seduce Leslie. Niall could pretend he hadn't understood the import of Keenan's words and gesture; Keenan could pretend he hadn't suggested such a thing. It all added up to a kind of lie, though, a deceit that made Niall uneasy.

CHAPTER 16

When Leslie woke with the nightmares still riding her, she had that awful first moment of not knowing where she was. Then she heard Seth talking, presumably on the phone since there were no answering voices.

Safe. At Seth's, and safe.

After stopping in the tiny bathroom, she went out into the front room.

Seth closed his phone and looked at her. "Sleep okay?"

She nodded. "Thanks."

"Niall's coming over."

"Here?" She raked a hand through her hair, attempting to unsnarl it. "Now?"

"Yes." Seth wore a bemused expression, not unlike the look he'd given her when she had sought his advice at the Rath. "He's a good . . . someone you can trust in the important things. He's close to a brother to me—a *good* brother, not like Ren."

"And?" She hated it, but she was embarrassed. Just thinking about the fiasco with Irial and Niall made her anxious.

"He likes you."

"Maybe he *did,* but after what happened—" She forced herself to meet Seth's gaze. "It doesn't matter. Ash has been pretty clear about the 'stay away' message."

"She has reasons." He motioned to a chair.

"Thought he was a good person?" she asked, ignoring the offer to sit.

"He is, but he's"—Seth toyed with one of the studs in the curve of his ear, a contemplative expression on his face—"in a complicated world."

Leslie didn't know what to say. She sat in silence with Seth for a few minutes, thinking over the day, the weirdness. Regardless of Seth's remarks, she wasn't keen on seeing Niall, not right now. It didn't matter, either: she needed her work clothes and they were at home. "I need to go home."

"Because Niall's coming here?"

"No. I'm not sure. Maybe."

"Wait for him. He'll walk you." Seth kept his tone casual, but the disapproval of her leaving was there all the same. "There doesn't have to be strings, Les; he can just be a person to get you safely to where you need to be."

"No." She scowled.

"Would you rather I walk with you?"

"I *live* there, Seth. I can't just not go home or take people with me all the time."

"Why?" He sounded far more naive than she knew him to be.

Leslie bit back her irritated reply and said only, "It's not realistic. Not everyone has the good luck to—" She stopped, not wanting to argue, not wanting to be unpleasant when he was only trying to be a friend. "It doesn't matter why. It's home for now. I need to change for work."

"Maybe Ash has clothes here that—"

"They wouldn't fit me, Seth." She stood up and grabbed her bag.

"Call me or Ash if you need anything? Put my number in your cell, too." He waited until she pulled out her cell, and he recited his number.

Leslie punched the digits in and slipped the phone back into her pocket. Forestalling any more objections, she said, "I need to go, or I'll be late for work."

Seth opened the door and stared out at the empty railyard. It looked as if he waved at someone, a sort of 'come here' gesture, but she saw no one.

"Are you all eating 'shrooms or something, Seth?" She tried to make her voice teasing, not wanting to fight, not after he'd shown her such kindness.

"No 'shrooms." Seth grinned. "Haven't licked any toads, either."

"So the staring off into space thing everyone's doing?"

He shrugged. "Communing with nature? Connecting with the unseen?"

"Uh-huh." Her tone was sarcastic, but she smiled.

In a brotherly gesture, he put a hand on her shoulder—not restraining her but holding on to her firmly. "Talk to Ash soon, okay? It'll make a lot more sense."

"You're freaking me out," she admitted.

"Good." He gestured toward the edge of the yard again and back at her. "Remember what I said about Irial. Get away from him if you see him."

Then he went back inside his train house before she could think of what to say.

When she walked into her house, Leslie wasn't really surprised to see the grungy crowd in the kitchen with Ren.

"Baby sister!" Ren called in a way that told her he was in the up part of his high.

"Ren." She acknowledged him with as friendly a smile as she could muster. She didn't look long at the people with him. Not for the first time she wished there were an easier way to determine whether they were just getting-high friends or if one was a dealer—not that it mattered. When people were high, they could be unpredictable. When they weren't high but jonesing for whatever they used, they were worse.

Her brother complicated things by dabbling with too many drugs and therefore too many circles of druggies. Today, though, there was no need to guess what they were using: the sickly-sweet smell of crack filled her kitchen the way the scents of home-cooked meals once had.

A skinny girl with lank hair grinned at Leslie. The girl

was sitting astride a guy who didn't seem to be high at all. He didn't share her pinched look, either. Without looking away from Leslie, he took the pipe out of the scrawny girl's hand and put the girl's hand on his crotch. She didn't hesitate—or look away from the pipe he held out of her reach.

He's the one to fear.

"Want a hit?" He held the pipe out to Leslie.

"No."

He patted his leg. "Want a seat?"

She glanced down, saw the skinny girl's hand moving there, and started to back away. "No."

He reached out as if to grab Leslie's wrist.

She turned, ran up the stairs to her room, and closed the door against the laughter and crude invitations that rang through her house.

Once she was ready for work, Leslie slid open the window and slung a leg out. It wasn't a huge drop, but when she landed wrong it hurt pretty badly. She sighed. She couldn't waitress with a sprained ankle.

I could go back in, just run down the stairs and out.

Carefully, she dropped her bag to the ground.

"Here goes."

She sat with both legs dangling from the window, then twisted so her stomach was on the wood and she was facing the house. Slowly she backed out, bracing herself with her feet on the siding and gripping the wooden window frame with her hands.

I hate this.

She pushed off, bracing herself for the impact. It didn't come. Instead she was caught in someone's arms before she touched the ground.

"Let go of me. Let *go*." She was facing away from the person who held on to her. She kicked backward and made contact.

"Relax." The guy holding her lowered her gently to the ground and stepped back. "You looked like you could use help. It's a big drop for a little thing like you."

She turned to face him and had to crane her neck to see his face. He was an utterly unfamiliar older man, not grandfather old, but older than most of the people who hung around Ren. He had a different look, too. Heavy silver chains dangled from both of his wrists. His jeans were faded and ripped in the calves to reveal the tops of scuffed combat boots. Tattoos of zoomorphic dogs covered his forearms. She should be afraid, but she wasn't: instead she felt still, calm, like whatever emotions churned inside had ceased to connect with the world around her.

She motioned to the tattoos on the man's arms. "Nice."

He smiled in what seemed to be a friendly way. "My son did that. Rabbit. He has a shop—"

"You're *Rabbit's dad*?" She stared. There was no family resemblance that she could see, especially when she realized that this meant he was also Ani and Tish's father.

The man smiled wider still. "You know him?"

"And his sisters."

"Look like their mothers. All of them. I'm Gabriel. Nice to meet . . ." He scowled then, causing her to step backward and stumble—not in fear, not even then, but in wariness.

But his scowl wasn't directed at her. The creepy dealer from the house had stepped around the corner. He said, "Come back inside."

"No." She collected her bag from the grass where it had fallen. Her hands shook as she clutched it and tried not to look at the dealer walking toward her or at Gabriel. Fear surged. Delayed and dulled as it was, it still made her feel like running.

Is Gabriel here to see Ren? Rabbit never talked about his dad; neither did Ani and Tish. *Is he a drug dealer too? Or just an addict?*

Gabriel stepped in front of the dealer. "Girl's leaving."

The dealer reached out toward Leslie. And without thinking, she grabbed his arm, wrapped her fingers around his wrist and held it immobile and away from her body.

I could crush him. She paused at her thoughts, at the weird calm settling back over her, at the weird confidence. *I could do it. Break him. Bloody him.*

She tightened her grip just a little, feeling bone under the skin, fragile, in the palm of her hand. *Mine to do with as I want.*

The dealer wasn't fazed by her grip, not yet. He was talking, telling Gabriel, "It's cool, man. She lives here. It's not a—"

"Girl's *leaving now*." Gabriel looked at Leslie and smiled. "Right?"

"Sure," she said, looking dispassionately at her hand curled around the dealer's wrist. She squeezed harder.

"Bitch. That hurts." The dealer's voice grew shriller.

"Don't cuss in front of the girl. It's rude." Gabriel made a disgusted noise. "No manners these days."

Something's wrong here.

Leslie tightened her grip again; the dealer's eyes rolled back in his head. She felt bones splintering and saw white through broken skin.

I'm not strong enough to do that.

But she stood there, holding the dealer's wrist in her hand, still squeezing. He'd passed out from the pain, dropped to the ground. She let go.

"Where you headed?" Gabriel handed her a dark rag.

She wiped her hand, watching the immobile man at her feet. It wasn't sadness or pity she felt. It wasn't . . . anything. *It should be, though.* She knew that, even if she didn't feel it.

"Why are you here?"

"To rescue you, of course." He grinned, baring teeth that looked like he'd filed some of them to points. "But you didn't need rescuing, did you?"

"No." She nudged the dealer with her foot. "I didn't. Not this time."

"So let me give you a lift, since my rescue services weren't needed." He didn't touch her, but put a hand behind her as if he'd rest it on the small of her back.

Not lying. His words felt true, not whole, not all there, but not lying.

She nodded and walked away from her house.

Some part of her thought she should be angry or frightened or ashamed, but she couldn't feel those things. She knew that somehow she had changed, as surely as she knew Gabriel hadn't truly lied.

He led her around the side of the house to a screaming-red Mustang, a classic convertible with black and red seats and vibrant detailing on the exterior.

"Get in." Gabriel opened the door, and she saw that what she'd initially thought were flames on the sides of the car were actually a throng of racing animals, stylized dogs and horses with odd musculature and what looked like smoke writhing around them. For a brief moment, the smoke seemed to move.

Gabriel followed her gaze and nodded. "Now *that* I did myself. Boy might look like his dam, but he's got my art."

"It's gorgeous," she said.

He slammed the door behind her and went around to the driver's side. After he slid the key into the ignition, he gave her a smile that was the exact same look she'd seen on Ani's face before she did something inevitably unwise. "Nah. Gorgeous is how fast she moves. Hook your belt, girl."

She did, and he took off with a scream of tires that could barely be heard over the roar of his obviously modified engine. She laughed at the thrill of it, and Gabriel gave her another Ani-ish grin.

She let the rush roll over her and whispered, "Faster."

That time it was Gabriel who laughed. "Just don't tell the girls you got to go for a ride before they did, okay?"

She nodded, and he accelerated until he topped out the speedometer and delivered her to work remarkably early—and laughing.

CHAPTER 17

"Leslie? Leslie!" Sylvie waved her hand in front of Leslie's face. "Damn. What are you smoking?"

"What?" Leslie tilted the glass of soda, pouring a little out so it wouldn't spill. Thoughts of Niall, of her nightmares of Irial, of her promise to talk to Aislinn, of the weirdly costumed crowd, of the surreal encounter with Rabbit's father, of her assault on the dealer at the house—they tangled and spun in her mind until she wasn't sure of what had really happened at all. *Did I break his arm?*

"Get some sleep or something tonight. You're a mess." Sylvie made a disgusted sound. Then she pointed to the main room. "The couple in section three need their check. Now."

"Right." Leslie set the drinks on her tray and headed back into the din of the restaurant.

The rest of the shift passed in a blur. Leslie smiled and kept herself on autopilot. *Bring the drink. Inane chitchat.*

Smile. Always remember to smile. Sound sincere. She was tired, exhausted really, but she got it done. Table by table, order by order, she got it done. That's how life worked: just keep moving, and it'll pass.

When her shift ended, she cashed out her tips and folded the money—*my ink fund*—into her pocket and made a mental note not to leave it out where her father or Ren could see it. She walked down Trestle Way, too tired to bother seeing who was out and about. *I just want to crash.* She'd gone a few blocks when she bumped into Ani and Tish.

"Leslie!" Ani squealed. She was terminally incapable of speaking at a reasonable volume. "Ohmygods, you look awful."

Tish shoved her sister. "Tired. She meant you look *tired.* Right, Ani?"

"No. She looks, you know, like she needs to go relax." Ani was unapologetic as always. "We're going to the Crow's Nest. You in?"

Leslie summoned up a smile. "I'm not sure I could walk that far tonight. . . . Hey, I met your father earlier. He's nice."

As they walked, Leslie filled them in on select details— omitting Gabriel's giving her a ride to work and her own impossible violence. Leslie felt her knees go wobbly when they turned on Harper. *Too tired for this.* She drew a few breaths, stopped moving. Near her were several people cowering in terror, backs to the wall as if something horrid were leering at them. One wept, begging for mercy. Leslie couldn't move.

"Just vagrants, Les. Bad drugs or something. Come on." The sisters kept walking, propelling her along with them.

"No." Leslie shook her head. It was something else. She tried to see it, sure something was there, like a shadow that lay atop the other shadows.

She started to walk toward the shadows, as if a string had found its way into the middle of her belly and she were being reeled in. A man was dancing manically on a stoop, which was weird enough, but he also seemed to be covered in thorns like shimmering green rose stems.

Ani looped an arm around Leslie's waist. "Come on, sleepy girl. Let's go play. You'll catch your second wind once you get moving again."

"Did you see him?" Leslie stumbled again.

Tish clapped her hands. "Oooh, wait until you see the new dartboards Keenan bought for the club. I heard that all his girlfriend said was that she wanted to try darts, and boom, there were three new boards the next day."

"She's not his girlfriend," Leslie murmured, glancing back behind them at the doorway. The thorn man waved at her.

"Whatever." Ani tugged Leslie forward. "There's new boards."

Leslie hadn't been at the club more than a half hour when Mitchell—her loudmouthed ex—showed up. Not surprisingly, he was ripped.

"Lezzie, girl!" He gave her a cruel smile. "Where's tonight's toy? Or"—he lowered his voice—"do you just take care of that with battery power these days?"

His dumbass friends laughed.

"Back off, Mitchell," she said. Dealing with him was never pleasant. After her mother had left, Leslie and Ren had both made some stupid choices, chasing a fix. Ren's fix had cost Leslie a lot, but even before that, she'd made a few choices that'd cost her. She'd tried to forget where she was, how wrong things were. It made her do stupid things. Mitchell had been one of those stupid things.

From out of nowhere, Niall was there. "Are you okay?"

"I will be." Leslie turned to walk away from Mitchell, but he grabbed her arm. Unbidden, the image of the dealer crumpling to the ground with her hand on his wrist rose up. *It would be wrong.* She stared at Mitch's hand on her skin. *So? He's wrong.*

"Don't touch Leslie," Niall said. He didn't move, but the tension in his body was obvious enough that people were backing away.

"Niall? It's cool. I've got it." She pulled her arm away from Mitchell, but when she turned around, Mitchell slapped her ass. His friends laughed again, but this time they sounded a little nervous.

Leslie swung back, hand curled into a fist, angry to a degree that felt obscenely good. For a moment, her vision was off. People all through the club were watching her, but they didn't look like people. Claws, thorns, wings, horns, fur, misshapen features, so many people looked *wrong*. It made her pause.

Niall stepped in front of her and asked, "Are you well?"

She was anything but well. Her pulse was racing like she had been chasing caffeine pills with espresso shots. Her vision was a mess; her emotions were a mess; and she wasn't about to say any of that aloud. Instead, she said, "I'm fine. It's fine. Everything's . . . fine. You don't need to—"

He cut her off. "He shouldn't disrespect you like that."

Leslie put her hand on Niall's shoulder. "He's no one. Come on."

Mitchell rolled his eyes. She hoped he'd leave it at that, but he was too drunk to have the sense to keep his mouth shut. He leaned in toward Niall. "You don't need to act all heroic to get in her pants, man. She'll spread those scrawny legs for anyone. Won'tcha, Lezzie?"

The sound that came out of Niall's mouth was more animal than human. He started forward, his body at an odd angle as if something were physically holding him back. Mitchell backed up. Leslie followed. She reached out then and gripped Mitchell's face with both hands. She pulled him toward her like she'd kiss him. When he was close enough to feel her words on his lips, she whispered, "Don't. Not tonight. Not ever again." She squeezed his face until tears came to his eyes. "I'll eat you alive. Got it?"

Then she let go, and he stumbled backward. The people who were watching her, those who'd looked just a moment ago feathered and oddly proportioned and otherwise not right, grinned. Some nodded at her. Others applauded. She pulled her gaze away from them. They didn't matter. What mattered was that her heartbeat was calm again.

A few steps away, Mitchell stood stuttering. "She . . . she . . . did you see . . . bitch threatened—"

Right then, Leslie felt invincible, like she could walk into a fight and not be touched, like there was some extra energy humming in her bones. It made her want to move, roam, see how far she could push it. She started to walk away, but Niall touched her arm gently.

"There's all sorts of dangers out there." He caught and held her gaze. "It would be safest if I walk with you."

Safe wasn't quite what appealed to her right then. *Safe* wasn't how she felt. Invincible, in control, *powerful*—those words felt closer to true. Whatever this fearlessness, this strength, this difference was, she was starting to like it. She laughed. "I don't need protecting, but I'd take the company."

Although Niall was mostly quiet as they walked through the dim streets, it didn't feel awkward or uncomfortable.

Her bad feelings, her usual worries and fears, seemed to be absent. It felt good; she felt good. The choice to change herself, to get her skin decorated, had been a turning point.

Niall caught her hand in his as they walked. "Will you stay at Seth's tonight? I have a key."

She wanted to ask why he cared where she slept, but the chance to stay somewhere safe was reason enough not to ask. She might feel invulnerable, but she wasn't entirely without logic. So she asked, "Where's Seth?"

"At the loft with Aislinn."

"And where are you planning to stay?" she asked.

"Outside."

"So you're going to sleep in the yard?" She looked away, and in doing so saw him out of the corner of her eye. Gone was the face she recognized. His eyes weren't just brown: they were shimmering with the patina of well-aged wood, the sheen of something caressed too often. His scar was red, like a still-tender wound, jagged as if an animal had slashed one long claw over his face. But it wasn't these things that made her draw her breath in so suddenly: he glowed faintly, as if he were being illuminated from some brazier inside.

As at the Crow's Nest, what she'd seen a moment ago and what she saw now weren't the same at all. She shivered, staring at him, reaching her hand out to touch the thick black shadows that lingered alongside his skin. Those dark shadows surged toward her hand, as if she were a magnet.

"Leslie?" He whispered her name, and it was the voice of wind racing down an alley, not a sound made by a person.

She blinked, hoping he wasn't one of those people who asked, "What are you thinking?" She wasn't sure what she'd say. The shadows pushed against her outstretched fingers, and she had a flash of the ink at Rabbit's shop: those shadows had wanted to crawl toward her from the uncapped ink bottle.

Niall spoke again. "I want to stay with you, but I can't."

Hesitantly she faced him, immeasurably relieved that he looked normal again. She looked at the street. Everything looked fine. *What just happened?* She was about to turn her head again, to see if he'd look different again, but he lifted her hand to his lips and pressed a kiss to the underside of her wrist.

She forgot about looking at him in her peripheral vision, forgot about the shadows that crept toward her. It was a choice. She could look at the ugliness, the oddities, the wrongness, or she could let herself enjoy life. She wanted that, pleasure instead of ugliness. Niall was offering it to her.

He leaned closer, his face hovering over the pulse of her throat now. It sounded like he said, "Do you know what I would trade to be with you?" But then he pulled away and distance returned to his voice. "Let me take you to Seth's tonight. I'll sit with you until you sleep if you want, if you'll let me."

"Okay." Leslie felt dizzy, swaying into him.

Niall put a hand on either side of her face. "Leslie?"

"Yes. Please." She felt high, blissed out. It was lovely—and she wanted more.

His lips were close enough that she felt his breath with each word. "I'm sorry. I shouldn't—"

"I said yes."

And he closed the slight distance between them and kissed her. She felt the same rush of fierce winds that she thought she'd heard in his voice. She felt it wrap around her like the air had grown solid and touched her everywhere at once, soft and unyielding at the same time. The ground felt different, like there would be thick moss under her feet if she looked. It was euphoric, but somewhere inside, panic was trying to force itself to the surface. She started to push him away, opened her eyes.

He tightened his hold and whispered, "It's okay. It'll be okay. I can stop. We can . . . stop."

But it felt like she was at the edge of a chasm, a swirling mass of tastes and colors she hadn't known could exist. The panic fled, and all she could think of was finding a way to reach that chasm, to slide down the slope into it. There was no pain there. There was nothing but ecstasy, mind-numbingly good and soul sating.

"Not stop," she murmured and pressed closer to him.

It isn't okay. She knew that, but she didn't care. Tiny slivers of shadows danced at the edges of her vision, gyrating like they'd stretch up to consume the moon. *Or me.* And in that moment, she hoped they would succeed.

CHAPTER 18

As Niall led Leslie through the street toward Seth's train, he wondered just how long he could handle being surrounded by that much steel. This part of the city was painful for any fey other than a regent to visit. It was why he wanted Leslie there, safe from the prying eyes of Irial's fey. It wouldn't stop Irial himself, but it would keep Leslie safe from the rest of the Dark Court—even as it would sicken Niall.

I deserve it, though, the sickness. He'd pushed her boundaries, crossed lines he knew not to broach. After all of this time, he'd come perilously close to giving in to what he was—and she'd die from it if he did.

"Are you still with me?" she asked.

"I am." He turned to look at her and saw them—Bananach and several of Irial's less-obedient faeries. They weren't near enough to see Leslie, but they would be if Niall didn't move her. He pulled her into a shadowed doorway and put his back to the street, keeping her out of their sight.

She didn't resist. Instead she tilted her head up so he could kiss her again. *Just one more kiss.*

When he pulled away he was more careful this time, enjoying the glazed look in her eyes, enjoying the knowledge that he made her feel so close to tumbled, but keeping his glamour firmly in place. He wanted to ask her what she had heard, what she had seen earlier, but that wasn't a conversation he could begin—not with Aislinn's rules still in place, and not with Bananach in the streets behind them.

That's what he should be concentrating on—the threat Bananach posed. Niall turned his head to better see the war-hungry faery, trying to think about safe retreat options. His mind was fuzzy, though. Bananach looked deadly beautiful as always, the raven-feathered head of her true image vying with her glamour of sleek black hair. She was one of the least-mannered faeries who lingered in Irial's court; she was the one who had once unseated Irial and continually sought to do so again—not to hold the court, but to create war within it. That she was prowling the streets with several Ly Ergs in tow did not bode well.

We should go. Now. We should—

Leslie pressed closer to him. He drew another deep breath of the curiously sweet scent that was uniquely her. Mortals always smelled so different. He'd almost forgotten how much he'd enjoyed that. He kissed her neck so she didn't find it odd that he was resting his face there. *Bananach hasn't seen us. We have a few more moments.*

Between kisses, he told Leslie, "I would stay with you always if I could."

And he meant it. Right then, he truly meant it. He'd been too long a part of the Summer Court to mean it for always, and before that he'd been even less capable of fidelity, but in that moment, as he stood pressed against her mortal body, he meant it as fervently as he was able.

Where's the harm in letting her linger with me for a while? If I am careful . . . She'd only sicken if he left her. He could stay with her for a few decades.

Behind him, he felt the street shiver as Gabriel and several of his Hounds came into it. Niall tensed. He wasn't able to stand against Bananach, Ly Ergs, and Gabriel.

And how do I explain to Leslie?

But when he glanced back, Gabriel and the others were all invisible. Leslie would not see or hear them.

Gabriel dispatched several Hounds whose names Niall did not recall—or care to—and they gleefully went after the Ly Ergs. Then he said, "Get going, boy, unless you want to help."

Niall held Gabriel's gaze, as answering was impossible.

"Take her out of here, Gancanagh." Gabriel leaned left as Bananach flew at him. She was glorious, moving with an elegance that few faeries could equal. Rather than step out of her path, though, Gabriel stayed between Bananach and Niall.

The raven-woman ripped a strip of flesh from Gabriel's forearm where Irial's orders were written.

Gabriel's snarl was wall shaking as he swung at Bananach. "Go."

Niall turned around as Leslie swayed into him, her eyes unfocused. She closed them and leaned forward like she'd topple over. Shame rose in him. Their kisses had injured her and distracted him beyond reason. If Gabriel hadn't been there, Bananach would've been on them in moments.

What's happening to me? He should be able to resist one mortal girl, especially in the presence of a fatal threat. He'd always been addictive to mortals, but they hadn't been addictive to him. They made him drunk, made him so intoxicated that he could barely stand, but they were never impossible to resist. He looked at Leslie. She was pretty, but he'd seen plenty of pretty girls over the years. Pretty wasn't reason enough to lose himself as he was doing. Nothing made sense. He needed to step away. He wasn't keeping her safe from Irial's faeries—or from himself.

He steadied her with his arm as they walked. Behind them, he could hear the horrific sounds of the tussle among the dark faeries. It had been a long time since Gabriel's snarls and growls were welcome sounds, but tonight the Hound had saved him and Leslie both.

Why?

A gleeful shriek from Bananach made him spin Leslie into a doorway. He felt the ominous rush of Bananach's movement toward them.

Leslie's back was pressed against a tall iron fence. She stared at him with the openness of so many mortals over the

years, her lips parted for a kiss he knew not to give her.
"Niall?"

"Just . . ." He had no words that he could say. He looked
away, counting each measured breath, concentrating on not
touching her. Behind them he heard Gabriel's Hounds
catch up. Bananach no longer crowed with pleasure.
Instead she hurled curses at the Hounds. Then there was
only silence in the street.

And he could hear Leslie's uneven breathing, matching
his own, proof that they were both more excited than either
of them should be. *She shouldn't be that drunk on just a
couple of kisses.* It wasn't as if he'd touched her in any intimate
way. *Yet.* He wanted to, more than he could remember ever
wanting a mortal. He put his hands against the iron fence
behind Leslie: the pain of it helped chase away his irrational
thoughts.

He looked behind him to assess the safety of moving.
Bananach was gone. The Hounds were gone. No other
faeries lingered in the street. It was only the two of them.
He let go of the fence and opened his mouth to find an
excuse to explain why he'd pushed her into the wall and
kissed her so—an excuse that would stop things before they
went further.

Is there such a statement?

But Leslie's hand slipped under his shirt, tentative but
there nonetheless. He could feel the edges of the cuts on her
palm and fingers as she slid her hand up his spine.

He pulled back.

Unable to keep her hand on his back as he stepped away, she slid it to his chest, lingering under his shirt. Her fingers traced upward to his heart.

Neither of them spoke or moved for several moments. Leslie's pulse had slowed back to normal. Her passion had abated. His guilt, on the other hand, wasn't leaving so quickly. There was nothing he could say to undo where they were, but he couldn't move forward either. His plan to be near her as a friend was failing horribly. He said, "We should go."

She nodded, but her fingers continued to trace lines on his skin.

"You have a lot of scars," she said, not asking but leaving the comment hanging there for him to answer or not.

Answering that implied question was something he didn't do, not when his king had been too young to realize that it was an awful question, not when he took any of the fey to his bed, not when his new queen had first seen him at guards' practice and looked at him with tears in her eyes. But Leslie had scars of her own, and he knew what had caused hers.

He kissed her eyelids carefully and told her, "It was a very long time ago."

Her hand stilled where it rested over his heart. If she thought anything of his erratic heartbeat, she didn't say.

Finally she asked, "Was it an accident?"

"No. It was very much on purpose." He brought her free hand up to the scar on his cheek. "None of these were accidental."

"I'm sorry." She leaned up and kissed his cheek. Her gentleness was even more dangerous than her passion had been.

If he thought on it, he could remember the pain as vividly as when it had happened. The memory of the pain cleared his head, helped him focus on where he was, and what he needed to be like for Leslie: strong, careful, a *friend*. He said, "I survived. Isn't that what matters? Surviving?"

She looked away. "I hope so."

"Do you think less of me?"

Her expression was aghast. "No. Gods no."

"Some would."

"They're wrong. Whoever hurt you . . ." She shook her head, her look murderous now. "I hope they suffered for it."

"They did not." He looked away then. If she knew how badly they'd broken him, would she pity him? Would she think him less a man for not being strong enough to escape them? He had, afterward. At the time he would've happily become a shade—faded rather than endure another moment of that pain, those memories. It would've been easier to give up, to end. Instead the last Summer King had found him, taken him into the Summer Court, and given him the space to recover his pride, to rebuild his mind.

"It's awful to think they're out there somewhere." She looked past him to the darkened streets, looking for faces in the shadows as he'd seen her do so many nights when he'd walked invisibly at her side. "I never know. I don't remember some of their faces . . . I was drugged when they . . . you know."

"Raped," he said gently. "And yes, I know exactly."

Her hand traced over one of his scars again, more hesitantly this time. The stunned look on her face confirmed that she understood. "You?"

He nodded. "It was forever ago."

Her eyes welled with tears. "Does it ever go away? The panic?"

And she looked at him with such hope he wished that fey could lie. He couldn't. He said, "It gets better. Some days, some years, it's almost gone."

"That's something, right?"

"It's almost everything some days." He kissed her gently, just a brush of lips, not seeking passion but offering comfort. "And sometimes you meet someone who doesn't see you any differently if you tell them. *That* is everything."

Silently she rested her face against his chest, and he held her and admitted the truth to himself: *For this mortal I would disobey my queen, abandon my king, the court that has protected me all these years. All of it.* If he took her into his arms, he would keep her. He wouldn't let her suffer the way the other mortals had when he'd left them. He would keep her, with his court's permission or without it. Irial wouldn't take her, and Keenan wouldn't stand between them.

CHAPTER 19

Leslie woke in the middle of the night to see Niall lying next to her, feverish, his skin damp with a sheen of sweat. He wasn't thrashing; he was perfectly still. His chest didn't appear to be moving at all.

She grabbed his shoulder and shook him. "Niall?"

He blinked at her, but it didn't take long for him to sit upright and look around. "Are you injured? Is someone here?"

"No." The skin under her hand was hot to the touch, far hotter than seemed possible. "You're sick, Niall. Stay here."

She went to the bathroom and grabbed a hand towel. After soaking it with cold water, she came back. Niall had closed his eyes and was lying back on Seth's enormous bed. If he hadn't looked like he was near passing out, it would have been a lovely sight to see. She knelt on the bed and wiped his face and chest with the icy cloth. He didn't react at all. His eyes stayed closed. His heartbeat thudded rapidly enough that she could see the pulse in his throat.

"Do you think you can walk to the front room? I can call a taxi," she murmured, glancing around the room to find her cell phone.

"Taxi to go where?"

"To the hospital." The wet cloth was already warm to the touch, and his body wasn't any cooler.

"No. We're not going there. Stay here or go to the loft." He opened his eyes and looked at her. There was no mistaking that look for anything remotely reasonable.

She sighed but kept her voice gentle as she said, "Sweetie, you're *sick*. Do you know what's wrong?"

"Allergic."

"To what? Do you have one of those pens for a shot?" She picked up his shirt from the floor and looked in the front pocket. There wasn't anything. She dropped it. *Where else?* There was nothing on the bedside tables. She reached down and felt inside the pockets of his jeans—which were still on him.

Niall grabbed her hand. "I did not bring you here to have sex, and I feel far from well enough to do so, but"— he pulled her forward until she was sprawled on his chest— "that doesn't mean I'm immune to your touch."

Using one hand on the wall to steady himself, he stood. "Help me get outside. I need air. Clear my head before I say something I can't."

"Something you *can't*?" She came to stand beside him,

though, offering him her support. He draped an arm over her shoulders; she put her arm around his waist.

Mostly talking to herself, Leslie said, "Seth. Ash. Everyone's keeping secrets." She looked up at Niall. "I ought to keep asking you questions until I get a few answers out of somebody."

She concentrated on getting him through the train and to the door. He hissed when he reached a hand out and brushed the door. They both stumbled when he recoiled.

"Are you okay?"

"No," he said. "Not so much. But I will be."

Not knowing what to say or do, Leslie looked around. She saw one of Seth's wooden chairs. "Come on," she said.

Niall leaned heavily on her as she dragged the chair far away from the train into the shadows of the yard. It was awkward, but she had plenty of practice maneuvering her drunken father into his room. Niall sat in the chair. She had just stepped away from him when Keenan appeared. He seemed to materialize out of the shadowed lot. He hadn't been anywhere in sight, and then suddenly he was in front of them—and angry.

"What were you thinking?" Keenan asked.

Niall didn't reply.

Leslie tensed, feeling an urge to run when he approached. She wasn't sure where he'd come from or why he was here. She *couldn't* wonder how he'd arrived so unexpectedly or why she felt so disquieted by his presence. All she knew was that he frightened her and she wanted him gone.

"I didn't know he had an allergy to"—Leslie glanced at Niall—"what are you allergic to?"

"Iron. Steel. He's allergic to iron and steel. We all are." Keenan scowled. "This serves no purpose, Niall."

Leslie stepped closer to Niall, decidedly uncomfortable with the hostility in Keenan's voice. *Salt for fury, like briny water in my mouth.* She touched Niall's shoulder and found his skin much cooler now.

"This is not the place," Niall muttered.

But Keenan continued, "If Irial wants her—"

Leslie lost her temper. "I'm standing right here, asshole. And where do you get off talking to him like that? You'd think—"

"Leslie." Niall laid his hand over hers.

"No. Why are you putting up with that?" She turned her glare briefly on Niall and then back to Keenan. "Don't talk about me like I'm not standing here. Don't act like some psycho friend of yours hitting on me means—"

"Just be silent for a change, would you?" Keenan stepped closer to her; his eyes seemed to glow with tiny flames. "You have no idea what you're talking about."

"Piss off." Leslie tried to raise her hand to slap the condescending look off his face, but Niall was now clutching both of her hands.

"I'm not sure why he wants this one, but"—Keenan shrugged—"if she's important to him, I want to know why. Your injuring yourself for her would upset Aislinn and serve no purpose for me."

Leslie's mouth gaped open as Keenan spoke: he sounded nothing like he did when he was with Aislinn, nothing like he had when he'd attended Bishop O.C. for those few weeks in the fall. He sounded old, far older than he could possibly be, and callous.

"Be more careful and enjoy your time, my *Gancanagh friend*." Then, after giving Leslie a brief once-over that made her feel so exposed that she wanted to hide her body, Keenan walked away.

Leslie stared at the shadowed yard. Despite the darkness, she could see the faint outline of Keenan's body as he strode off.

Beside her, Niall watched the shadows in silence.

Leslie stood next to him. She touched his forehead, his neck, his chest: the fever had broken. He seemed physically fine—tired, but fine.

"Keenan means well, but he has worries—"

"He's rude. He's demeaning. He's not the person he pretends to be when Ash is around. He—" She stopped herself and adjusted her tone. "If there's a reason to be nice to him, now might be a good time to tell me what it is."

"I can't. He's under a bit of stress. Aislinn helps, but there's so much I can't tell you. I would if I could. I'd tell you everything. You might not want to see me afterward, but . . ." He pulled her into his lap and stared at her.

"But what?" She wrapped her arms around him. And her anger at Keenan, her distrust, her unease—they all slid away.

Niall said, "I hope you do want to see me after our secrets are spilled. It'll be *your* choice, but I truly hope you still want to be near me."

She wasn't sure she wanted to know, but she *needed* to. She liked Niall, far more than she should after so short a time, but she wasn't interested in getting further involved if he was mixed up in something criminal. She'd had enough of that in her life already. "Are you involved in anything illegal?"

"No."

"No drug deals?" Her body tensed as she waited.

"Not me. No."

"Keenan?"

Niall snorted in laughter. "Aislinn would never tolerate that, even if he had inclinations that way—which he doesn't."

"Oh." She thought about it: the fact that Keenan rarely went anywhere alone, the weird club, the strange allergy, the secrecy Aislinn and Seth were somehow a part of. None of it fit together right; it didn't add up, no matter how she looked at it.

Which should terrify me. But her emotions weren't quite cooperating with that thought. *Which should also frighten me.*

She held Niall's gaze and asked, "What did he call you?"

"Gancanagh. It's a sort of family name. But I can't explain beyond that right now." Niall sighed and pulled her close. "Tonight I'll do my best to answer your every question, but Aislinn . . . She needs to speak with you before I can. No more questions until tonight. I'll explain to her, that we, that you . . . She'll understand. Meet me at the Crow's Nest? We'll talk to her."

She wanted to push him to tell her immediately, but she could tell by his tension and his worried tone that he wasn't going to. She turned so she was facing him. "Promise you'll tell me everything? Tonight."

"Promise." Niall smiled then.

Leslie kissed him cautiously. She knew he would tell her, felt certain of it, of him.

But he pulled back from their kiss almost immediately and asked, "So can I see what you have so far of the tattoo? Or is it somewhere improper?"

She laughed. "It's up by my shoulders. . . . Subtle topic shift."

It had worked, though—or maybe it was his kiss that made her feel so relaxed. Even though he was holding back, she felt her body responding in a way she hadn't thought she ever would again.

"So can I see the tattoo?" He started to tilt her forward, still holding her.

"Tonight. Rabbit is finishing it tonight after work. Then you can see it—when it's all done." She wasn't sure why, but from the moment she'd walked out of Rabbit's shop, she'd had a strong aversion to showing anyone her ink. *Not yet.*

"Another reason to look forward to our date, then. Talking, looking at your art, and"—he gave her a look that sent her pulse racing—"anything else that makes you happy."

He gently kissed her forehead, her cheeks, her eyes, her hair.

"I don't want you to go away," she whispered, finding it easier to admit in the darkness. "But Keenan's comments. The way he . . . I want you with me right now. I've wanted you with me for months."

He kissed her for real then, not gently as he had before, but fiercely.

Afterward he told her, "I'll leave Keenan and Aislinn's side if I need to. I'll walk away from everything, everyone, just for the chance to be with you. . . ."

While she didn't understand much of what was going on, she did understand that he was offering to give up his family for her. *Why? Why would being with me mean that?* She traced her fingertips over his face.

He said, "If you want me in your life, I'll be here. As long as you want. Remember that. It'll be okay. I'll stay with you, and we'll be fine. No matter what else happens or what you learn, remember that."

She nodded, though she felt like she'd wandered into a weird world where everything she thought she knew had faded away. But even with all the weirdness, being in Niall's arms made her feel safe, loved, like the world wasn't awful. She couldn't stay in Huntsdale, though, not living with Ren and her father, not where everything had gone so horribly wrong. "I can't ask you to give up everything when I'm not even sure where I'll be next year. College. And we don't know each other, not really. And—"

"Do you want to get to know each other?" he asked gently.

"Yes."

"Then we'll find a way." He stood then, with her in his arms, and walked toward the train. A yard or so away from it, he put her down. "Go in and sleep. I will be here when you wake. Tonight Aislinn will talk to you . . . or I will."

And when Leslie curled up in bed, she felt herself believing in Niall, believing in them, believing it really could be okay. Those dreams of finding someone who cared about her, who saw her as a person—maybe they weren't as impossible as they'd seemed.

CHAPTER 20

The morning was barely upon him when Irial walked into Pins and Needles, watching the mortals outside the shop with a new interest. Leslie would give him enough of her mortality that he'd be able to feed on them, to grow stronger. It had worked for a few of the thistle-fey, had worked for Jenny Greenteeth and her sisters. He couldn't grow weak. He couldn't allow his fey to grow weak and be ended by mortals. That wasn't an option. He'd have his mortal, nourish himself—through her—to feed his court. If they were strong enough, he and his mortal, they could survive it. If she was not as strong as he thought, she would die or slip into madness; he'd starve, fade, or worse—fail his court.

But she's a strong mortal. He hoped they would both survive. He'd never cared for one of them; there were a few halflings, like Rabbit, who'd mattered—but no true mortals.

"Iri." Rabbit's face lit with the inexplicable happiness he seemed to feel when Irial visited.

"Bunny-boy."

Rabbit scowled. "Man, you really need to stop calling me that. Ani and Tish are around somewhere. You know how they are."

"I know." Irial grinned. He couldn't see Rabbit as a grown man, despite the proof in front of him. "How are the pups?"

"Troublesome."

"Told you. It's all in the blood." Irial pulled out the book he'd brought with him. "Gabriel sends his best."

"He has a best? Been nice if they'd inherited it." Rabbit took the book, flipping it open as eagerly as he had the first time Irial had given him images of the more reclusive fey. The symbols and crude sketches were the start of what would be tattoos tying mortals to the Dark Court. Rabbit would re-create them in ways that faeries could not, capturing the flaws and beauties until they were pulsing on the page, seeking the mortal who could wear them. It was a disquieting skill—one neither of them spoke of.

Then Ani and Tish flew into the room, squealing in that eternally hyper way they had. "Iri!"

"How's Dad?"

"Did he send anything? He was here."

"He met Leslie."

"Rabbit won't let me go to the square anymore."

"Have you seen the new queens? We know the one, the Summer Queen."

"We don't *know* her. We *met* her. It's different."

"Isn't."

"Let Irial talk." Rabbit sighed. He might scowl a bit, but he watched the girls with a care their father wouldn't have. Halflings were typically too fragile to live in the Dark Court, too mortal, but the High Court would've broken their spirits—impeded their natural passions with unnatural restraints. Sorcha's court took the Sighted ones and all of the halflings—unbeknownst to the Winter and Summer Courts—but the Dark Court tried to keep their mortal offspring out of that rigid realm. Rabbit had repaid that secrecy by looking after the other halflings Irial'd found.

"There's trinkets from the Hounds." Irial held out the bag. "And one of Jenny's kin sent those garments you wanted."

The girls snatched the bag and scurried away.

"Exhausting beasts." Rabbit rubbed a hand over his face, then called out, "No clubs tonight, you hear me?"

"Promise," Tish yelled from somewhere in the back.

Ani ran back in. Grinning madly, she skidded to a stop a hairsbreadth away from Irial. "Did you like Leslie? I bet you did. Very hot." Her words all tumbled together. Then she stuck her tongue out at Rabbit. "We'll get to go tomorrow, then. Promise?"

As Rabbit put a hand over his eyes, Irial found himself offering, "I'll take them."

Rabbit made a shooing motion at Ani. Then he

flipped the sign on the door to CLOSED. "Now, let's give this a try."

The room was exactly as it had always been, immaculate and unchanging. Rabbit had aged some, not as fast as mortals, but he looked closer to early twenties than teens now.

Rabbit motioned to the black chair where his clients sat. "You okay?"

Irial squeezed Rabbit's forearm and admitted, "Tired."

After he handed Rabbit the cords Gabriel had sent, Irial sat down in the chair and stretched his legs out in front of him.

"I heard about Guin." Rabbit pulled out three needles and as many vials.

"Gabriel's got the Hounds patrolling; they think they're immune still. The leannan-sidhe are to stay out of sight." Irial leaned back in the tattoo chair and closed his eyes while Rabbit bound him with the cords. Irial always found himself talking freely with Rabbit. In a world of careful deceit, there were so few people Irial could trust without reservation. Rabbit had inherited all of his father's loyalty, but also the mortal sense to think things through, to talk rather than fight.

"I think the ink exchange will help." Rabbit rolled up Irial's sleeve. "It's going to hurt."

"Hurt *me* or the girl?" Irial opened his eyes briefly. "I saw her, the mortal."

"You. Leslie will just feel the tattoo. I think. She did well with the outline. The court's tears and blood are an easier adjustment for a mortal. Her emotions will be volatile, fleeting by now. She's coping, though. Your blood will be harder for her. . . ." His words drifted off. He picked up the brown glass bottle that held the strange ink he'd mixed for the exchanges. "I'm not sure how she'll do, since it's *you*. She's good people."

"I'll look after her," Irial promised. She'd be bound to him, but he'd make sure she was well cared for, satisfied. He could do that.

Rabbit tied another cord around Irial's arm to help raise a vein. Unlike the cords that bound him to the chair, this was a simple thing—a length of rubber like those in mortal hospitals.

"It'll be fine." Irial tested his bonds, then nodded to Rabbit. There were few creatures he'd trust to hold him immobile.

Silently, Rabbit located the vein on the inside of Irial's elbow.

"She's stronger than you know, or she wouldn't have picked me."

Rabbit jabbed a thick, hollow tube into Irial's arm. "Ready?"

"Yes." It was barely a sting, not anywhere near as painful as he'd feared.

Then Rabbit added the tiny filter only he could make to the tube.

Irial's spine bowed; his eyes rolled back. *It'll make me*

strong. Feed my court. Protect them. But the extraction of blood and essence was nightmarishly awful, as if tiny incisors were set to roam inside his body, ripping and tearing at places where sharp things should never enter.

"Keep the pups out of my reach," he gasped as his vision began to blur. "Need." Irial's stomach cramped. His lungs tightened, as if all the air he'd ever breathed were being sucked out all at once.

"Irial?" Ani's voice was in the doorway. Far enough away that he couldn't reach her; too close, though.

His hands clenched. "Rab . . ."

"Ani, go." Rabbit stepped in front of Irial then, blocking her from view.

"It'll pass, Iri. It always passes. Tell him, Rabbit, tell him he'll be okay." Ani's voice faded as she walked away.

"She's right."

"Starving." Irial dug his finger into the chair until the leather ripped. "You're destroying me. My court."

"No. It passes. Ani's right. It passes." Rabbit pulled out the tube with a *schluck*. "Rest now."

"Food. Need. Call Gabriel."

"No. Not until I finish the tattoo. Nothing until then. Else it won't work." Then Rabbit left, locking the door behind him, leaving Irial unable to move from the chair.

CHAPTER 21

Half afraid last night had been a dream, Leslie looked out the window. *He's still here.* Niall was doing some sort of stretching in the yard. Either he'd been awake for a while and was bored or he was just going about his routine. He'd shed his shirt, and in the light of day the spiderweb of scars that covered his torso was difficult to look at. Thin white lines crisscrossed thicker, uneven raised marks, as if something had clawed his skin. Seeing the full extent of it made her want to cry for him. *How is he even alive?* He was, though. He was a survivor, and it made him all the more beautiful.

With as little noise as she could, Leslie opened the door. "Hey."

He paused in midstretch, standing so still that he seemed frozen, as if he were carved of some rare dark stone. Only his voice proved that he was a living being. "Shall I take you to the school?"

"No." She shook her head as she walked toward him. Until then she hadn't decided, but looking at him—knowing that whatever happened next would mean they'd be changed from what they were in that moment—she knew that wasting the day was foolish. Spending the day at Bishop O.C. . . . it simply didn't make sense to her.

"What are you doing today?" she asked when she was standing beside him. Without conscious thought, she lifted her hand, letting her fingertips graze the scars on his chest, like following a map of chaos, lines bisecting lines, furrows branching into ridges and ripples.

He hadn't moved yet, staying as still as when he'd seen her walking toward him. "Taking a long swim in the cold river?"

She stepped slightly closer. "No."

He swallowed. "If I keep suggesting things, will you keep saying no?"

"Maybe." She smiled, feeling brave, confident with him in a way she hadn't felt with a guy in longer than she wanted to consider. "Do you want me to?"

"Yes. No. Maybe." He gave her a shaky smile. "I'd almost forgotten how much fun this dance was, the wanting without having."

"Is it okay if I lead?" She actually blushed when she said it. She was far from innocent, but he made her feel like this mattered, like *they* mattered.

"I'm rather liking it." He cleared his throat. "Not that pursuing you—"

"Shh."

"Okay." He watched her curiously. He still hadn't moved, feet and hands in precisely the same position as when she'd approached. It was odd.

"Did you go to military school or something?" she asked before she could stop herself. *What a dumb question!*

But he wasn't laughing at her or acting like she ruined the moment. He answered seriously, "Not like you're thinking, but I've had to learn a number of things because Keenan's father needed me to do so. Training . . . It's good to know how to protect yourself and those you care for."

"Oh."

"I can teach you how to defend yourself some. Not"— he held her gaze—"that it will always keep you safe. There are times when no amount of training will stop what others would do."

"So why . . ." She let the question drift away.

"Because it helps me sleep at night, because it helps me focus, because sometimes I like knowing that maybe if I were in danger again it would help." He kissed her forehead. "And sometimes because it gives me hope that it'll make me strong enough to be loved and protect the one I would try to love."

"Oh." She was at a loss once more.

He stepped back. "But you were going to lead this dance, so I'll work on following . . . after I ask if we could pause at the loft so I might bathe."

And just like that he eased her fears and brought the tension back to that comfortable zinging feeling they'd shared before he started talking about violence and love.

An hour later, Leslie walked through Huntsdale with Niall—sure that once she stepped away from him, the near illusory connection they had would end. It was so different from their walk the night before, when they'd stopped to kiss in alcoves and dark doorways.

Eventually he gestured at a tall old building in front of them. "We're here."

They stood at the edge of a small park that felt forbidden, as if the air before her had taken form and made a barricade around the greenery. Trees of all sorts bloomed in a riot of contrasting colors and scents; the grass, though, was trampled flat, browned as though by a fair or concert. The park was clean, too; there was no litter or debris at all. It was also empty of people: not even a vagrant lay on any of the odd wooden benches that were scattered throughout the park. Old stone sculptures glistened like they belonged in a museum, and the water in a fountain rose and fell as if a song controlled its flow. Leslie stared at it, the curiously enticing park, wondering how something so beautiful could be here and unused.

"Can we go there?"

"The park?" Niall looked from her face to the park, where she'd been staring. "I suppose."

"It's not private?" She watched as the flow of water shimmered like a girl undulating in some dance that she should remember, that her bones once knew.

There is *a girl.* The woman danced, hands lifted over her head, face tilted upward like she was speaking to the sun or moon. Leslie stepped closer, leaning into the weighty air that seemed to prevent her passing, to stop her from reaching the fountain. Without looking for traffic or for any conscious reason why, Leslie went toward the park. She paused, caught between longing and fear and not sure she truly felt either one.

"Leslie? Are you with me?" Niall took her hand, stopping her from entering the park.

She blinked. The image of the dancing girl vanished. The statues looked dim, and there weren't nearly as many as she'd thought. Nor were the trees all blooming: there weren't even as many trees as she'd thought. Instead, there were people she somehow hadn't seen: girls, many of whom seemed to be watching her and Niall, wandered around the park in small groups, giggling and talking to the guys who stood where she had thought there were only trees.

"Nothing makes sense, Niall." Leslie felt the edge of panic push against her, but it was less than real—more a murmur of an emotion that rose and faded before it found form. "I feel like . . . I don't know what I feel lately. I don't get scared, can't stay angry. And when I feel it, it's like it's not mine. I see things that aren't right—people with thorns on their faces, tattoos that move, horns. I keep seeing things that aren't real; I should be afraid. Instead I look away. Something's wrong with me."

He didn't offer her empty promises that it would be okay or that she was imagining it; instead he looked pained, leading her to believe that he knew something more than she did.

Which should make me angry.

She tried to summon it up, but her growing emotional instability had become so pronounced that it was like being a visitor in her own body. Calmly, as if the question didn't matter, she asked, "Do you know what's wrong with me?"

"No. Not really." He paused. "I know someone awful is interested in you."

"That should scare me." She nodded, still calm, still not frightened. *He* was, though.

"You taste afraid, jealous, and"—she closed her eyes for a moment, savoring some strange thread of emotion that she could almost roll on her tongue—"sad."

She opened her eyes. "Why do I know that, Niall?"

Confusion filled him then; she tasted that too. If his emotions were true, he didn't know any more than she did about her new ability.

"You can—"

"Taste your feelings." She watched him, *felt* him try to be still, like his emotions were being sorted into boxes she couldn't open. Glimmers of tastes—chicory and honey, salt and cinnamon, mint and thyme—drifted by like shadows.

"That's an odd choice of words." He waited, not quite a question, but close enough.

So she told him more of the things she'd been feeling. "There are bursts and absences. There are so many things I feel and see that I can't explain. It should frighten me. It should've made me talk to someone. But I haven't been able to . . . until now."

"Do you know when it started?" He was worried. Her tongue was heavy under a lingering lemony flavor, and she knew that *worry* was the feeling that went with that flavor.

"I'm not sure, not really. . . ." She tried to focus. There was a tumble of words—*the restaurant, the tattoo, the Rath, the museum, when, why*—but when she tried to speak, all the words were gone.

"Irial," Niall said.

His briny anger and cinnamon jealousy surged back until her throat burned with it. She gasped, nearly choking. But as she thought of Irial, everything felt better. She felt calm again. The tastes faded from her tongue.

Niall hurried her back across the street and into the old building. "We'll still spend the day together. He won't come here. Tonight we'll talk to Aislinn and Keenan. After that you'll be safe. Can we do that?"

His worry stretched inside her, filling her up, and then it slithered away as if it had found a tunnel to escape her. In its place she felt calmness. Her body felt as languid as when she was in Rabbit's chair. *Talking about this isn't necessary.* She shrugged. "We didn't have a plan yet anyhow, right? Hang out, work, see Rabbit, then more hanging out? Sure."

"Just a few hours, then, and it'll all be fine." He took her hand and started up a spiraling stone staircase.

"No elevators?" She looked around. The outside had been rather nondescript, worn down like most things in Huntsdale, but the inside of the building was beautiful. As at the Rath, obsidian, marble, and wood seemed to replace what would usually be metal.

"No steel allowed in here," he said distractedly.

She followed him until he stopped at a door that was too beautiful to be exposed to casual passersby. Stones—not cut jewels, but raw stones—were embedded in the wood to create a mosaic. She reached out, hand hovering in the air in front of the door. "It's gorgeous."

Niall opened the mosaic door. The inside was no less lovely. Tall, leafy plants dominated the room. Innumerable birds swooped through the air, nested in nooks in tall columns that supported vine-covered ceilings.

"Be welcome in our home, Leslie," he said.

The words felt strangely formal, setting off warnings that this was not the right place for her, that running would be wise. But Leslie could still feel Niall's emotions—he was happy, honored—and in the middle of it all was a thin cord of genuine love for her. So she stepped farther into the room, breathing the summer-sweet scent of flowers that bloomed somewhere in the loft.

"Make yourself at home while I bathe." Niall motioned

to an overstuffed chair. "Then I'll make us breakfast. We'll stay here. We'll figure it out."

She thought about answering, but he seemed to be talking to himself more than to her. She settled in the cozy chair, watching the birds dance through the air over their heads. *With Niall or with Irial, that's where I should be.* She wasn't sure why, but it was clear to her then. Every day her feelings had become further skewed from normal, and other people's emotions had been growing identifiable. She heard the excuses she'd been using to explain the changes away—and knew they were lies and self-deceits. She could see it all with a peculiar clarity. Something, the same source as the changes, was preventing her from thinking too much about the reasons why she was changing; it was somehow forbidden. *But why worry?* Whatever was changing made her feel good, better than she had in a very long time. So she closed her eyes and enjoyed the languor that had filled her during her conversation with Niall.

CHAPTER 22

They'd spent the day together playing video games, talking, and just being near each other. By the time Leslie had to go to work, she'd begun completely tuning out his worries and murmured warnings. She simply didn't *feel* those things. He was worried—she could taste that—but *she* felt good.

Niall left her at the door of Verlaine's with another reminder not to go anywhere with Irial or any strangers.

"Sure." She kissed his cheek. "See you later tonight?"

"I don't think you should be walking alone. I'll meet you and walk you to Rabbit's, and then I can walk you to the Crow's Nest after."

"No. I can call Ani or Tish or Rabbit to come meet me, or I'll take a cab." She gave him a reassuring smile before she went inside.

Work passed in a blur. They were busy enough that she had a nice amount to add to the money already in her bag. At the end of her shift, she cashed out and went over to Pins

and Needles. Between finally getting her ink and the promise of seeing Niall—*again*—later, she was almost giddy.
Everything was going better than it had in a very long time.

When she walked through the door of the tattoo shop,
all but one of the doors to the rooms adjoining the waiting
area were already shut. From the one open room came
Rabbit's voice, "Shop's closed."

"It's me." She went inside.

Rabbit sat on his stool. His expression was guarded.
"You could change your mind still. We could do something
else with—"

"Change the design midway?" She scowled. "That's
stupid. Honestly, Rabbit, your art is beautiful. I never took
you for insecure."

"It's not that. . . ."

"What then?"

"I just want you to be happy, Les." He tugged at his
goatee, seeming more nervous than she'd ever seen him.

"Then finish my tattoo," she said softly. She slipped off
her shirt. "Come on. We already had this conversation."

With an unreadable look on his face, he motioned to the
chair. "You chose this. You'll be all right. . . . I want you to
be all right."

Grinning, she sat down with her back to him again.
"And I will. I'll be wearing the prettiest, most perfect art on
my skin—my choice, my skin. How could I not be all
right?"

Rabbit didn't answer, but he was often silent as he

went about setting up his supplies. This routine was meticulous. It made her feel good, knowing that he was concerned about his clients' safety. Not all tattooists were so responsible.

She glanced back to watch Rabbit open a strange bottle. "What's that?"

"Your ink." He didn't look at her.

She stared at the brown glass: for a moment, she could swear black smoke danced like small flames above the lip of the bottle. "It's beautiful, like bottled shadows."

"It is." He glanced her way, briefly, face as expressionless as she'd ever seen it. "If I weren't so fond of the shadows, I wouldn't be doing this."

"Tattooing?"

He lifted the bottle and tipped it into a series of caps. Some of the caps already had a crystalline liquid in the bottom. In the dim light, it looked as if the ink separated into variations of darkness as Rabbit poured a little into each cap.

Tiny black tears, like a cup dipped into the abyss. She shook her head. *Too many weird events, making me think strange things.* She asked, "Is it the other liquid in there that changes the colors? Like two inks mixing?"

"They mix into what I need for your work. Turn." Rabbit motioned for her to look away.

She did, moving her body until her back was to him. He wiped her skin, and she closed her eyes—waiting.

Soon the machine hummed, and then the needles were on her skin. They barely pierced the surface, but that slight piercing changed everything. The world blurred and sharpened; colors bloomed behind her closed lids. The darkness grew and split into a thousand shades of light, and each of those shades was an emotion, a feeling she could swallow and cherish. Those emotions would make her live, make them all so much stronger.

Nourish us, save us, the body for the soul. Her thoughts were tangled with waves of feelings that fluttered through her and drifted away, like the strands of a lost dream after waking. She grasped at them, her mind struggling to hold the emotions in place, to identify them. These weren't just her emotions: she could feel the yearnings of strangers outside on the street—a montage of fears and worries, lusts and angers. Then cravings too bizarre to visualize washed over her.

But almost as soon as they touched her, each feeling skittered away, spiraling out onto some cord that led away from her into the shadows, into the abyss from which the ink in her skin had been collected.

Irial drifted in uneasy slumber. He felt her—his Leslie—being stitched closer to him with each brush of Rabbit's needles, tying her to him, making her *his,* far more truly than any of his fey were, than anyone had ever been.

And it felt like Rabbit's needles were puncturing Irial's

heart, his lungs, his eyes. She was in his blood as surely as his blood was in her skin. He felt her tenderness, her compassion, her strength, her yearning for love. He felt her vulnerabilities and hopes—and he wanted to cosset and love her. It was decidedly unfit for the king of the Dark Court to feel such tender emotion. *If I'd known, would I have done the exchange?*

He wanted to tell himself he wouldn't, but he'd allowed far worse to be done to him to ensure the safety of his fey.

In his nightmares, she was the girl he'd carried down the street, his Leslie, bleeding from wounds done to her by men whose faces came slowly into focus. He wasn't sure what was real and what was fear-distorted. She'd tell him, though. He'd walk through her memories as they drew closer. He'd comfort her—and kill the men who'd hurt her.

She'd make him stronger, nourish him by feeding him human emotions he couldn't touch without her. And he'd learn to hide how much she suddenly meant to him, how sickeningly mortal he felt. *What've you done to me, Leslie?* He laughed at the realization of his new weaknesses: by making himself strong enough to lead them, he'd simultaneously made himself far less of the Dark Court than he'd ever been.

What have I done?

As Leslie sat there—eyes closed and waiting—she heard the laughter again, but it didn't bother her this time. It felt good—welcome, even. She smiled. "It's a nice laugh."

"Stay still," Rabbit reminded her.

Then he went back to work, the hum of the machine sounding louder, as if her hearing had shifted. She sighed, and for a moment she could almost see the dark eyes that were now etched on her skin—except they seemed to be looking at her from beyond the room, just close enough that she wondered if she'd see them when she opened her own eyes.

She noticed the hum stop but couldn't quite open her eyes as Rabbit cleaned her back again.

Sleep now. It was just a whisper, but she felt certain that there was a real person talking to her—not Rabbit.

Who?

And he answered, her imaginary speaker. *You know who I am, Leslie. You might not like the answer just yet, but you know me, love.*

Beside her, she heard the bandage package rip, felt pressure as the pad was put over her tattoo.

"Just rest for a few minutes, Leslie," Rabbit murmured as he helped her stand, directed her onto the chair again, reclined now like a bed. "I'll be right back."

Listen to Bunny-boy. I need to wake up, and you don't want to be awake for it. Trust me, love. I want to keep you safe.

"Listen to who?"

"You're strong, Leslie. Just remember that. You're stronger

than you think," Rabbit said as he draped a blanket over her. "I'll be back in a few minutes. Just rest."

She didn't have much of a choice: she was suddenly more exhausted than she'd ever been. "Just a few minutes. Going out dancing, then."

CHAPTER 23

Irial woke with a scream half formed on his lips. He was unbound but still on Rabbit's chair. Red welts crossed his arms and legs. A bruise stretched across his arm where the tube had been. He tried to sit up, sending paroxysms of pain through his whole body.

Ani sealed her lips to his, swallowing his scream—and the ones that followed.

When she pulled back—lips blood red, pupils dilated, cheeks flushed—he gaped at her. Halflings didn't, couldn't, feed on faeries. Mortal blood overcame most of their fey traits. The traits that remained had never included this one.

More troubles.

"How?" he asked.

She shrugged.

"Ani, you can't stay here if you need to—"

"Feed?" she prompted with a smile that was all Gabriel, wicked and predatory.

"Yes, *feed,* like your father. No wonder Rabbit's had so much trouble with you." Irial concentrated on keeping his focus, on not trying to go check on Leslie, on dealing with Ani first. *Leslie's not ready to talk to me. Not here. Not when I'm so weak.*

"Your pain's like a big sundae. Didja know that?" Ani licked her lips. "Cherry. With extra sugar."

"What about Tish?" He pulled on the shirt Ani had given him. *Business first. Then Leslie.* Somehow she didn't seem like business anymore.

"Nope. Just me." Ani leaned closer. "Can I have another taste?"

She bit his chin, drawing blood with her sharp canines.

He sighed and pushed her away. *No violence in disciplining Gabriel's daughter.*

"I can feed off mortals without the ink exchange. No exchange. Just me." She sighed dreamily. "If they're rolling, it's like drinking rainbows. Rainbows. Big, sugary rainbows."

"Mortals?"

She swayed into him. "If I find a strong one, it's okay. It's only when I pick the wrong ones that they get all stupid. Not so different than what you're doing, is it?" She plopped down beside him. "She's fine, you know. Leslie. Resting and all that."

"Rabbit!" he yelled. Then he sent a mental message out to Gabriel. They'd need to take Ani with them for a while.

"What's she done?" Rabbit leaned in the doorway.

"Fed."

He nodded once. "I wondered if that's why—"

"You *wondered*? Why didn't you tell me? Warn me? She could've gotten hurt, could've gotten in trouble." Irial stared at him. "And she could have been what we needed to forestall . . ." He let his words drift away. The idea of finding Ani earlier, of not being with Leslie, made his stomach tighten in unfamiliar panic. Here was a solution that was too little, too late, and he was perversely glad of it.

Beside Irial, Rabbit was still, cautious, all the things Irial wasn't feeling. Rabbit said, "She's my sister, Iri. I wasn't going to turn her over for testing, not when you had a plan that might work."

Ani swayed and tried to step around Rabbit to leave. He scooped up his sister, holding her aloft and away from his body like she was feral, but looking at her with the same affection he'd had when Ani was just a newborn pup.

He pointedly changed the subject. "Leslie's leaving now."

To hide just how confused he was about the feelings he was having for Leslie, Irial focused on Ani, who was kicking her feet in the air and giggling. "Ani can't stay here," he said.

"I know." Rabbit kissed Ani's forehead. His eyes twinkled as he added, "Dad's going to have an awful time with her."

Irial felt the Hounds approach, a skin-prickling roll of terror that he let wash over him like soothing balm. Fey outside—not his, but summer fey—cringed as the Hounds passed. He let himself take nourishment from the horror they wrought by their presence.

"Daddy!" Ani squealed, kicking her feet again.

The Hounds stayed outside—all but Gabriel. He nodded at Rabbit. "Pup."

Rabbit rolled his eyes at his father and turned to Irial. "You ought to go after Leslie soon. *Daddy* can handle Ani." He grinned then, looking every bit like Ani's sibling. "In fact, I'll get Ani's bag together first so she'll be ready to leave with the pack."

Ignoring the look of panic that flashed over Gabriel's face, Irial answered, "Don't let Ani roam while you do."

After Rabbit carried the giggling Ani away, Irial brought Gabriel up to speed.

"What do I do with her?" Gabriel, the Hound who led some of the most terrifying creatures to walk the earth, sounded utterly intimidated. "How do I . . . She's female, Irial. Don't they have different *needs*?"

"She can't be worse than you were when you were younger. Ask one of your females for advice." Irial drew as much nourishment as he could from Gabriel's mingled panic and excitement and pride. Irial needed to be stable before he went to find Leslie, needed to be well fed so he didn't pull too many human emotions through Leslie just yet. *Let her get used to me first, talk to me.* He felt worry for his mortal. If the other dark fey had felt this weakness when they did the ink exchanges, they hadn't admitted it to him.

Gabriel was still talking; Irial forced himself to listen to the Hound.

". . . and they're just not good examples for my pup.

Have you seen them lately? Chela and her litter all but slaughtered the representatives of Sorcha's court the other moon."

"Month, Gabriel. The other *month*."

Gabriel waved a hand, utterly uncowed by his king. "They're too rough for Ani. She's so tiny." He started pacing as he rambled on about the female Hounds.

They were truly fierce, but Irial had trouble objecting to anything that kept Sorcha's court away from him.

"Can she *run*?" Gabriel stopped on the verge of a burst of pride that was almost chokingly sweet.

Irial closed his eyes and savored the orange-sugar rush of Gabriel's emotions. "Ask her."

"You need anything first?" Gabriel paused, as still as a wave before it breaks.

"No. Just take Ani home. Get Rabbit's telephone number so you can reach him if you need advice on her."

Gabriel snarled, but only once.

Irial glared, relieved to deal with the familiar challenge of Gabriel's pride. "He's raised her. You don't know her. Get his number."

The look on Gabriel's face would stop almost any fey or mortal. Accepting orders—even from his king—went against his instincts. Irial softened his tone. "If *you* don't need it, fine, but they should keep in touch. They're a pack of their own."

Gabriel bowed his head slightly. "Do you need someone else for your strength?"

Irial held out a hand to the once more visibly uncomfortable Hound. "After seeing you? Why?"

Gabriel straightened his shoulders. "Then I'll go fetch the pup. My daughter"—he had another burst of tangled emotions then—"it is just the one, right?"

Irial bit back his smile. "Just Ani."

"Right then. I'll get her."

"Be sure to say hello to Tish, though," Irial reminded him. "Then send her to me. We're going out."

I need to find Leslie. My Leslie, my mercy, my strength, my Shadow Girl . . . mine.

He drew a deep breath, pleased to realize that he knew exactly where she was, could see her if he tried. She had left the shop and now walked down the street, her step sure, her lips curved in the most enchanting smile he'd ever seen.

Soon. I'll be there soon. He pulled his hands through his hair, brushing it back, and checked that he hadn't any blood on his shirt. He didn't, but his pants were a total loss. He opened the door and called, "Tish! Five minutes."

Then he went to find his bag. *My mortal seeing me like this . . . no, not the best way to entice her, covered in blood.*

CHAPTER 24

Leslie felt a compulsion riding inside her, leaving her with an inexplicable need to move. Her skin felt tight and tingly. She reached back and tore away the bandage that Rabbit had put over her tattoo. The bandage was wet, not with blood but with plasma and traces of ink. Her shirt stuck to her damp skin, its fabric probably getting stained, but she couldn't stand having her beautiful tattoo trapped.

She tossed the bandage in the trash and headed down Crofter Avenue toward the Crow's Nest, grinning to herself when she saw the club's red neon sign. A few guys were hanging out in the shadowed alley alongside the building; it was a shortcut over to the railroad yard, but most people used it as a spot to smoke. As she approached, she saw one guy punch another. She smiled, feeling a pleasant jolt of adrenaline as the two men began hitting each other unreservedly.

At the door of the club, Glenn, the doorman, stopped her. His attention flicked to the fight in the alley, and the bars in his face glittered as the red light from the sign hit them. He shook his head at the fight. Then turned his attention back to her. "Five-dollar cover tonight."

"Least they're fighting outside." She pulled a crinkled bill out of her pocket and held her hand out for the stamp.

"They're staying out, too." He grinned at her. "You bringing trouble in your wake these days?"

She laughed, but privately she wondered if he was right. Inside the club the lead singer of the band all but screamed his lyrics; Leslie winced. "They don't sound like they're worth it."

"Could be worse." Glenn put the money in the box and leaned back on his stool. They listened to the guitar-heavy music for a minute; then he grinned again. "Or not."

"Anybody around?" She couldn't see far into the crowd.

"Seth and Ash are over by the wall." He inclined his chin toward the most shadowed part of the club.

"Is Keenan with them?"

"Yeah, he's there too." Glenn scowled, but he didn't say more.

The door opened behind Leslie. Glenn turned to the newcomer. "Ten-dollar cover."

Leslie leaned in and asked, "Inflation?"

"Nah. Doorman's prerogative." He quirked his mouth in a crooked smile.

She shook her head and started to walk off, but Glenn put a hand on her arm.

"Watch yourself. All sorts of freaks in town tonight."

Glenn shot a glance over the crowded room. The usual familiar faces were there, but a lot of strangers were in the crowd too. Maybe that's what all the fights were about: maybe gangs *were* moving in.

No. It felt weird to think it, but somehow she suspected that the fights were tied to her. It seemed solipsistic to consider it, but the idea felt true.

Or I'm losing it.

"You okay?" Glenn raised his voice to be heard over the increasing din, and she felt a wave of something—*protectiveness*—roll from him. "I could get Tim to watch the door and—"

"No, I'm cool." She didn't feel nervous, not tonight, not anymore. Her hand strayed to her tattoo, hidden under her shirt. "Thanks, though."

She squeezed her way through the crowd to Seth and Aislinn. They sat as close together as they could while still remaining on separate chairs.

Aislinn looked up. "Hey."

Beside her, Seth nodded and looked meaningfully at Aislinn and then back at Leslie. "You should talk."

"Sure." Leslie slid into the chair Seth pushed toward her. She leaned toward Aislinn. "Seth says you have something to tell me. Secret spilling and all that."

"I'm sorry about not telling you; I just wanted to keep you safe"—Aislinn bit her lip—"from things. When I heard about Ren's—"

"Don't," Leslie interrupted, waiting for the panic to hit,

but it was just a dull roar. "You know my secrets. Got it."

"You're right." Aislinn took a deep breath before looking at Seth for assurance.

Keenan approached the table with sodas for Aislinn and Seth and a glass of wine for himself. He handed Seth the drinks and turned to her. "Niall's not here yet. What shall I get you?"

"Nothing." She didn't have much cash on her, and accepting anything from Keenan made her uncomfortable, especially after the other night.

He scowled briefly at the crowd between him and the bar. "Soda? Tea? Water?"

"Nothing."

"Would—"

"Nothing," she interrupted in a firm voice. She stood back up. She *needed* to get away from Keenan. *Now.* She told Aislinn, "Come find me when you figure out what you're trying to say."

But Keenan came closer, beside Aislinn, putting himself between her and Leslie.

Get away from him. He's danger. Enemy. Not us. Leslie stared out at the throng of bodies. The band was awful but she wanted to move, burn some energy, ride out whatever rush she had going from the ink.

"We need to talk, Leslie." Aislinn sounded so serious, so worried.

Leslie forced herself to look at Aislinn. "Sure. I'll be on the dance floor when you're ready."

Leslie stepped away from the table, feeling the increasing pressure to get away from Keenan, to run. Her hands trembled from trying to stay still.

"Leslie, stop," Keenan said as he grabbed the bottom of her shirt.

Aislinn took hold of his wrist but couldn't push him away. "What are you doing?"

Keenan put his other hand on Leslie's hip and turned her. He lifted her shirt, baring Leslie's whole back to Aislinn and anyone who was near. "Look."

Aislinn gasped. "What have you done, Les?"

"Got a tattoo. You knew that." Leslie pulled out of Keenan's grasp. "Lots of people have them. Maybe you should be asking your idiot boyfriend here what *he's* doing. I don't appreciate being treated like—"

"She doesn't know, Aislinn." Keenan sounded weirdly gentle, soothing as if warm breezes were riding on his voice.

But Leslie felt her anger rising with each word that fell from his lips. This anger was not fleeting or fading.

Danger. He's dangerous to us. She paused. *Us?*

Keenan looked inhuman as he stepped closer to her. Some trick of the club lights made him glow like a golden effigy come to life. His voice burned her skin when he demanded, "Who did it?"

She crossed her arms, half-hugging herself, refusing to give in to the urge to run. Fear vied with anger, but she tilted her head to glare at him. "Why? You want one?"

"Tell me." Keenan gave her a look so predatory, she felt

her stomach twist in fear. It was a terrifying look—but no one else saw it. Aislinn and Seth were watching her, not Keenan.

She'd had enough. Her anger and fear fled again; she smiled with a cruelty she didn't remember owning. "Back off, Keenan. I'm not yours to command. Not now. Not ever. Don't cross me, kingling."

Kingling?

They weren't her words. They didn't make sense. But she felt better for saying them. She walked away and wiggled through the crowd until she reached the front of the stage. She felt like she was looking for someone, the one who would make it all better. *Where are you?* The thought repeated like a chant in her mind, so much so that she must have said it aloud.

He answered, "I'm right here."

And she knew who it was without looking. "Irial."

"How are you tonight, my love?"

"Furious. You?" She turned to face him, letting her gaze rake over him the way he'd looked at her at the Rath. He looked good, like sin in a suit. From the tips of his soft leather boots to the silk of his shirt, he was gorgeous, but a pretty package wasn't reason enough to forgive his near assault, to forgive anything. She summoned up her anger, her embarrassment, her fear. Then she looked him straight in the eye and said, "Not impressed *or* interested."

"Liar." He smiled then, and traced his finger down her wrist. He inhaled deeply, like he was trying to catch and hold an illusive scent, and she was suddenly calm. She wasn't afraid, wasn't anxious, none of the things she should feel. Instead she felt something uncoiling inside of her, a shadowy shape stretching and writhing under her skin.

Her eyes started to close; her heart fluttered. *No.* She stepped backward and told him, "You should go away."

"And leave you to fend for yourself?" He shook his head. "Now, why would I do that? I'll look after you when the kingling comes prowling this way in a moment. The boy's a nuisance."

"I have a date," she said, although she wasn't entirely sure how well that would go right now. *Focus on that.* Niall lived with Keenan, was his guardian, and right now the idea of crossing paths with Keenan made her want to strike someone. She froze then, as something pieced together. "Kingling?"

"The boy. But let's not talk about him." He took her hands. "Dance with me, Leslie. I'll be nice. Proper, even. Let's enjoy our moment before business interferes."

I should just go. But walking away from Irial didn't appeal to her. Everyone had warned her that he was trouble, but he didn't frighten her, not right now. It was *Keenan* who terrified her. Having Irial beside her felt right, natural. She didn't move—or answer him.

In the most enticing voice she'd ever heard, Irial said, "Come now, Leslie, would Niall really mind if we had one dance? More important, do *you* really mind?"

"I should." She didn't, though. Briefly she gave in to the

urge to close her eyes against the spiraling ecstasy that had begun to make her body hum.

"Call it an apology? I frightened you at the Rath, didn't I?" His voice seemed so inviting, easing her further into calm. "One song and then we'll sit and talk. I'll stay politely back if you but tell me to."

She swayed toward him like a cobra weaving to a snake charmer's songs. His arms slid around her.

The music was still fast, something suited to thrashing about manically, but Irial seemed oblivious to it. "See, love? Where's the harm, hmm?"

They danced, but she wasn't feeling trapped. She felt dizzy but confident, stepping away when the song ended.

Irial didn't touch her. He walked beside her. In the darkest corner of the room, he snagged two bottles of water from a waitress.

"So, how are you feeling after Bunny-boy's work?" He stood between her and the rest of the club.

She cracked the seal on the bottle of water and leaned against the wall, reveling in the feel of the bass thumping inside her skin. "What?"

Slowly, he reached out toward her. He slid his right hand up the back of her shirt along her spine to rest atop her still-tender skin. "The ink. Our tattoo."

"*Our* tattoo?"

He leaned in closer and whispered, "I know you heard me, saw me watching when Rabbit drew on that delicate skin."

He pressed his fingers over the tattoo until she winced. Her heart raced as if she'd been running for hours, as if the things in her nightmares had stepped into the room. *He's lying. Crazy . . . He's . . . not.* His words tasted true, felt right as they seeped into her mind.

"I felt each touch of the needle, drawing us closer and closer together. My eyes, Leslie, on your skin. My essence, love, buried inside you." Irial leaned back, giving her a scant bit of space, making it possible for her to look into his eyes. "You're my Mercy, my Shadow Girl, my banquet. Only mine."

She slid partway down the wall and would have hit the floor if he hadn't pulled her closer.

"That terror you feel right now"—he spoke softly, lips hovering over hers. "I can make it stop, just like that."

As he said *that*, he inhaled, and she felt perfectly calm, as if they'd been discussing nothing special.

Her mind couldn't process it—*refused* to attempt to make sense of what he'd said. Clarity filled her: all the weirdness of the past few days had brought her here. *He's what's changed. He's why I'm . . . wrong.*

"It's not possible," she said to him, to herself.

"You picked me. Rabbit told you it would change you."

"So Rabbit drew your eyes, my bad luck." She slid to the side, moving a little bit away from him. "That doesn't tie us together. It's just ink."

With sinuous grace, he turned to lean on the spot she'd

just vacated, putting them side by side. He didn't look at her but watched the dancers instead as he said, "You don't believe that. You know better. Somewhere inside, you *feel* different. I know that, as clearly as I know that you're watching for Niall, hoping he'll actually strike me this time."

She turned to look at him. "What?"

"He won't. Can't. There are only a few who can touch me, and he's not one of them. But"—he drew a deep breath and let it out in a long sigh, stirring tendrils of her hair— "I do like that you're wishing it. Healthy feelings, those ones—rage, dismay, fear, and a bit of guilty temptation. They taste good."

He laughed, a smoky sound curling around her like shadows taking form, like the shadows she'd imagined—*not imagined, but truly seen*—hovering over the bottle of ink at Rabbit's shop. She looked then, and saw shadows flowing through the room, crawling toward her from the bodies on the dance floor, stretching themselves out like they had hands that would stroke her skin—and she really didn't want them to. *Do I?* She licked her lips, tasting honey— *longing*—and pushed away from the wall.

Coming through those shadow-draped bodies were Keenan, Aislinn, and Seth. None of them looked happy, but it was Seth's worried expression that made her falter. She didn't want them to reach her any more than she wanted the shadows to. Rage at Keenan spiked, matching the cloud of salt-soaked anger that came through the air in front of him like fog coming in from the sea.

Irial twirled her into his arms and gave her a look that made her shiver with longing.

"Mmmm, I like that one, but"—he kissed her forehead tenderly—"I need to deal with business now. We'll have plenty of time for that soon enough."

She stepped away from him, stumbling into the crowd, where Keenan caught her without looking away from Irial. But being in Keenan's grip made anger flare purer than she'd thought she could feel, replaced the blood in her veins with salt. "Don't touch me," she hissed. "Don't you *ever* touch me, kingling."

"I'm sorry, Les. I'm so sorry," Aislinn whispered to her. For a moment it looked like golden tears slid down her cheeks, but then she turned away and said, "Seth?"

"I got her." Seth pulled her away from Keenan and tucked her under his arm protectively. "Come on, Les."

Keenan put a hand on Seth's shoulder. "Take her to Niall."

"I'm not going anywhere," she told the assembled group. "I don't know what's going on, but I'm—"

"Go home. You'll be safer away from this rabble." Irial inhaled again, and Leslie thought she could actually see shadows crawling across a twisting vine of ink—with feathers where leaves should be—that grew from her skin and vibrated in the air between them. When that shadow vine stilled, she suddenly felt calm again, at peace, quiet.

And she didn't want to be there any longer.

She didn't speak to any of them as she turned her back and left.

CHAPTER 25

Irial watched Leslie walk away with the Summer Queen's mortal. *What would he tell her?* It didn't truly matter, not now; she was his. Whatever they said or did wouldn't undo that.

"If anyone tries to take her from me, to come between us"—he pulled his gaze from Keenan to look at the Summer Queen—"*you* understand, don't you?"

She looked reluctant to answer.

"Aislinn?" Keenan took her hand in his.

She didn't react to either faery. "She's my friend. Leslie is not just some mortal; she's *my friend*. I should've acted when I saw you at the restaurant."

"It wouldn't have changed anything. She was already mine. That's why I was there." He reached out as if he'd touch her cheek, hand hovering by her sun-kissed face, and whispered, "What would you do to keep your mortal safe, Ash? Your Seth?"

"Anything."

"Exactly. You don't want to try to take Leslie from me. Your little kingling *did* tell you who it was that bound him, didn't he?" Irial waited for the flood of worry, of anger, of despair, and was surprised to find that the Summer Queen was in reasonable control of her emotions.

Looking rather like Gabriel's daughters, the Summer Queen cocked her head. "He did."

She stepped forward. Keenan didn't move to stop her. Instead he watched her with confidence, his emotions calmed. The Summer Queen let a trickle of sunlight seep into her voice, a tiny reminder of what she was, what she was capable of. She was close enough that the desert heat of her breath scorched Irial's face when she whispered, "Don't threaten me."

Irial held his hands up. "I'm not the one starting quarrels. I had business here: she's my business now." He felt ill at ease talking about her that way, his Leslie, his vulnerable mortal. So he changed the subject. "Thought I'd pay my respects to you while I was in the area . . . and check in on our Gancanagh. I find myself missing him lately."

Neither of the summer regents moved.

"To think of all the years he's wasted with you . . ." Irial shook his head. "What do you suppose it'd take to call him home to me?" Then he waited, looking forward to sating his hungers well enough to buy Leslie a few more hours to adjust before he started funneling the full weight of his appetite through her.

As the burst of Keenan's emotions seeped into Irial, the Dark King walked toward an open table. Keenan and Aislinn followed, as he knew they would, and sat down across from him. He traced a finger over the names—signs of mortals trying to leave a mark of their passing—that were carved into the surface. A waitress paused to offer them drinks, calling Aislinn and Keenan by name.

Irial accepted. "Whatever they usually have and coffee for me. Dark black."

The girl left, smiling a little longer than necessary at him.

If I could feed on them without an intermediary, like Gabriel's daughter had . . . He paused at that thought. *Had I known about Ani sooner* . . . But he hadn't. He was on this path, had found a solution. He'd look closer at Ani later.

First he'd get things with Leslie settled. If she was strong enough, she'd survive awhile, but in the end . . . in the end mortals always expired before faeries. They were such finite creatures. Their first heartbeat and memory were but a blink from death. To add the weight of nourishing his insatiable court in a time of peace was to hasten that unconscionably. Peace would kill his Leslie too soon, but war was never wise. It was a balance he needed. Being on the edge of violence but not down in it was what the Dark Court needed.

Irial returned his attention to the pair across from him. Aislinn was murmuring to Keenan, soothing him. "Calm down. Niall's not going anywhere . . . especially not to the Dark Court. He's safe—"

"Precious, you wound me." Irial laughed, immensely pleased by such naive belief, a true rarity in the courts. "Niall and I were *close,* if you will, before the young kingling was alive."

Keenan's anger flared. His fists were clenched so tightly, he was hurting himself. "And he's spent centuries suffering for it."

Irial leaned across the table. "Do you know how he struggles to deal with his yearning for Leslie? How very difficult . . ." He paused, pleased to see the tightening expression on Keenan's face. "But perhaps there's a reason he didn't tell you? Perhaps he's still more *my* court than yours. Perhaps he's been mine all along. . . ."

"Stay away from Niall," Keenan said. Waves of desert heat radiated from him, pulsing against them all.

Beside him, Aislinn absorbed that heat as quickly as Keenan released it. "Keenan. Damn it. We need to discuss Leslie's situation. Calm down or take a walk."

What a nice idea. Irial smiled at Aislinn. Then he turned back to Keenan, holding his gaze as he said, "He could reign in my court. What do you offer him? Servitude? Faeries? He's a *Gancanagh,* Keenan. He needs mortal touch or some focus to assuage the yearning. He has denied himself for centuries to protect you. What's he to do without a cause? Play nursemaid to the Summer Girls?"

Keenan struggled—and failed—to hide a flash of despair. A tiny rain shower began on the dance floor. The patrons squealed and laughed, no doubt explaining it away with a mundane answer—a faulty sprinkler head or leaky pipe.

"Niall is better off with me. His loyalty is to *my* court; that's cause enough," Keenan said.

"Did you know that he has seen Gabe of late?" Irial lowered his voice conspiratorially and added, "He's been under watch by Bananach. Do you think *she'd* bother with him if he weren't a part of my court?"

The heat radiating from Keenan's skin made the water in the room hiss into a steam. "He's not Dark Court. He belongs among faeries who don't torment him. He's happier—"

"No. He's not. The best we can hope for, kingling, is to find ways to be at peace with what we are. You understand that, don't you? He's teetering on the edge. You've given him the keys to his own destruction." Irial watched Keenan, saw the acknowledgment he knew he'd find if he pushed hard enough.

"Don't go there." Keenan was carefully not glancing at his queen, carefully not admitting that he'd manipulated Niall and put Leslie at risk.

"Walk away from this, kingling," Irial warned. "This isn't a conversation you really want to have. Is it?"

The Summer King lashed out, a sharp wind that burned across Irial's face, drawing blood to the surface. The intensity of the fury made it all the more nourishing for Irial.

Aislinn kissed Keenan's cheeks. "Go on. I can deal with him." She waved her hand at the crowd of mortals. Too many of them were watching, curious and eager. "They don't need to see this."

Keenan made an abrupt gesture toward several of the rowan-men, and the guards—who looked like nothing more than the ominous young men in the dark alleys of most cities—moved closer. They leaned against a nearby wall, shooting menacing looks at Irial. It was a charming little show, their posturing—as if any Summer Court fey could daunt the head of the Dark Court. Without another word, Keenan vanished into the half-drenched crowd on the dance floor.

Irial smiled at the young Summer Queen. "Now that he's gone, let's you and I get to know each other."

Aislinn gave him a smile that was caught between mortal innocence and faery cunning.

I could grow fond of this one. She was a more challenging adversary than Keenan right now.

"You shouldn't try Keenan like that. I'm not sure what secrets you two were exchanging, but this is *my* court now. Needling him isn't going to help." She didn't bother to keep the heat out of her voice, but unlike her king's, Aislinn's temper wasn't a concentrated slap. Instead the blistering summer heat pushed against Irial like a sudden gust, causing him to swallow hard against the taste of sand on his tongue.

Delicious. He drank down her acrid temper with relish. "Secrets? Keenan was brought up longing for power— power I took from him under the will of the Winter Court. We have a history . . . not quite as fulfilling as my bond with Niall, mind you, but the kingling has impotence issues with me."

"I know what your court is. I know what you do. You're responsible for the evil—"

"Evil?" He laughed then, letting every bit of his court's true nature into the sound.

The Summer Queen caught her breath. Her face flamed red, and the waves of anger radiating from her brought blisters to his skin.

"Not evil, child, and I'd rather you didn't insult me so"—Irial leaned closer, watching her face as she wrestled her emotions back into place—"because as much as I like your reaction, you've too many complications to interest me that way."

"If Keenan hears—"

"Tell him. Give him the extra reason to attack me." Irial licked his lips as if sand were truly a tangible thing, not simply a flavor in the air.

She switched topics. "Why are you trying to cause him troubles with Niall?"

"It behooves me." Irial saw no reason to be other than honest. "I understand addiction: it's one of my court's coins. Niall doesn't belong with Keenan, not now, not anymore. Keenan's mistreated him more than you know."

Aislinn's placid smile didn't waver, but tiny sparks of sunlight showed in her eyes. "What difference does it make to you?"

He leaned back and stretched his legs out in the aisle, as

comfortable as he could be in the crowd of frolicking mortals. "Would you believe I care for Niall?"

"No."

"Fey don't lie."

"Not overtly," she amended.

"Well, if you won't believe that"—he shrugged—"what can I say? I enjoy provoking the kingling." He reached out for her hand. Unlike most faeries, the Summer Queen had enough speed to avoid his touch—sunlight can move as quickly as shadows—but she didn't. Keenan would've.

Queens are so much more pleasing to deal with.

Irial was assailed by the seeping heat of summer's languor, steamy breezes, and a strange-sweet taste of humid air. It was lovely. He held on to her hand, knowing that she felt his court's essence as surely as he felt hers, watching her pulse flutter like a captured thing, caught and struggling.

She flushed and pulled her hand away. "Being tempted isn't the same as being interested. I'm tempted by *my* king every moment of every day . . . but I'm not interested in sex for empty pleasure, and if I were, it wouldn't be with you."

"I'm not sure who I should envy more—the kingling or your mortal toy," Irial said.

Sparks illuminated the club as her temper finally became less stable. But even as her mood vacillated, she wasn't as temperamental as Keenan. "Seth is not a toy"—she appraised him then with a clarity Keenan didn't have—"any more than Leslie is a toy to you. Is she?"

"Keenan won't understand that. When he took mortals, he took their mortality."

"And you?"

"I like Leslie's mortality the way it is." He shook out a cigarette, tapped it on the table. "This isn't a secret you'll get from me . . . any more than I'll tell you the kingling's secrets or Niall's."

"Why not just let her go?"

He stared at her, wondering idly if she'd light his cigarette. Miach, the last Summer King, used to derive curious amusement from lighting things afire. Somehow, Irial doubted Aislinn would, so he pulled out a lighter. "I'll not answer that, not now, not without a reason. She's mine. That's all that matters."

"What if I told you our court would take her back?"

He lit his cigarette, took a long drag, and exhaled. "You'd be wrong."

Irial didn't mention that the Summer King didn't care one whit about Leslie. The Summer Queen might care for his Leslie, but Keenan? He didn't truly care for anyone other than his own fey and his queen. *And not always to their best interests.*

Irritated but still in control of her emotions, Aislinn gave Irial a look that would send most fey to their knees. Before she could speak, he caught one of her hands again. She struggled in his grip, her skin growing hot as molten steel.

"Leslie belongs to me, as surely as your Seth belongs to you, as the Summer Girls belong to Keenan."

"She's my friend."

"Then you should've done something to protect her. Do you know what's been done to her? How lost she's been? How afraid? How very, very broken?"

As much as he found it touching that Aislinn cared for his girl, it wasn't reason enough to sacrifice Leslie. They hadn't protected her, hadn't kept her safe, hadn't made her happy. He would do those things. "When she adjusts to the changes—"

"What changes? You said she was still mortal. What did you do?"

Tiny storm clouds clustered around them until the club was hazy with them. The conversation wasn't going to improve, so Irial stood and bowed. "My court deals in darker things than yours. The rest is not mine to say. Later, if she wants to, she'll tell you."

Then he left the Summer Queen and her retinue of scowling guards. Despite his court's need for dissension among the denizens of Faerie, he had no patience for politics, not now. He had something—*someone*—more important to attend to.

CHAPTER 26

Leslie and Seth were several blocks away before she finally asked, "Do you know what's going on?"

Without missing a step, Seth said, "They're not human. None of them."

"Right." She scowled. "Thanks. Joking really helps."

"I'm not joking, Leslie." He glanced past her as if someone were there and smiled at the empty street. "Ask Irial for the Sight. Tell him you deserve it."

"The Sight?" She didn't smack him, but she wanted to. She felt utterly off-kilter, and he was mocking her.

"And guards," he added. Then he stopped and motioned to the open space in front of her. "Show her."

"Show me wha—"

A girl with black leathery wings appeared. She smiled in a predatory way. "Ooh, are we going to get to play?"

Niall's voice came from behind her, "Take a walk, Cerise. She belongs to Irial now."

"Irial took a mortal? Really? I heard rumors, but . . . hmm, she's a bit plain, isn't she?" The winged girl looked astounded, amused, and curious all at once.

Leslie stared at her: she couldn't turn to look at Niall, couldn't begin to get her head around what he had just said. *Belong? What about us? What about everything he whispered to me? Belong?* A burst of anger consumed her sadness but faded immediately. *Belong? Like a trinket? I* belong *to myself.* But she didn't say any of it, didn't turn to face him with confusion written plainly on her face. Instead she stepped up to the winged girl, Cerise.

Cerise flapped her wings. "They're real." And with her backless top, it was obvious that the wings were truly sprouting from her skin. "Oh, sweetie, you're in for a good time. That one has stamina you wouldn't believe—"

Then something—unseen—grabbed Cerise from behind; she started to move backward without any obvious effort on her part. Surges of loathing for Cerise rolled through the air from that unseen thing into Leslie's skin, filling her and fleeing before they settled.

"Fine. I'm going," Cerise snapped. Then she waved as she disappeared. Her disembodied voice called, "See you around, babe."

Leslie slid to the sidewalk. She was trembling, shaking from whatever was wrong with her. It wasn't just that she could tell what others were feeling: it was more now. The feelings around her were almost tactile, and they were slithering under her skin.

"She had wings," she said.

Seth nodded.

"And vanished? She really vanished?" Leslie tried to keep her focus. Somewhere in the apartments above her, a woman was weeping with a sorrow so heavy, it made Leslie think she was swallowing copper.

Niall reached down and helped Leslie to her feet. He bent so his lips were against her face. Gently he murmured, "I've failed you yet again. But I'm not giving up. Just remember that: I won't let him keep you."

Leslie looked from him to Seth. She wanted Seth to tell her this was a joke, wanted him to tell her things hadn't become hopelessly weird. Seth had been around as long as she'd lived in Huntsdale. If he told her it was okay . . .

But Seth shook his head. "Ask Irial for the Sight and guards of your own."

"Guards? They can't protect her from what she needs protection from, from *him*," Niall snarled before looking back at her. His expression softened then, and he whispered, "Don't forget: surviving is what matters. You can do this."

Tish stepped from the shadows in front of them. "You shouldn't touch Leslie."

Leslie tried to focus on the girl. The whole world had shifted, and Leslie was starting to believe that it wouldn't be getting stable again anytime soon. The symphony of flavors wafted from the walls around her, crept toward her from nearby rooms, and battered her skin. She closed her eyes and tried to catalogue the tastes as they ran through her. There were too many.

Niall slowly stepped back, assuring that she was steady on her feet before he let go.

"Are you sick?" Tish had her tiny hands on Leslie's forehead, her cheeks. "Is it from the ink? Let me see."

"I'm fine." Leslie slapped Tish's hand away from her shirt, anxious at the thought of sharing her tattoo—*our tattoo, mine and Irial's*—right now. "What do you want? Why are you—"

"I saw you at the club but couldn't expose myself there." Tish still stared only at Leslie.

Expose herself? With the deluge of emotions distracting her so, Leslie was having trouble figuring out what to say or do. All she could ask was, "Do you know Seth?"

Tish glanced briefly at Seth, sizing him up with a look that would've done Ani proud. "Ash's toy?"

Beside Seth, Niall stiffened, but Seth put a hand out.

"I don't get it, but"—Tish shrugged—"not my business."

Then she laced her fingers through Leslie's and started talking as if there were no one else around. "You seemed like you were having fun earlier. Rabbit would kick my ass if I didn't bring you to him, though. You're pale. The first day is rough for humans."

"Humans?" Leslie almost laughed at how very surreal the night had become. "What does that make *you*?"

But Tish was still talking, ignoring the question, "Let's

get you checked out. Make sure you're all good when he comes for you."

"I'm fine," Leslie insisted although she knew she wasn't. "But yeah, let's go see Rabbit. Just to . . . He?"

"Iri," Tish said gleefully. "You want to be ready for him, don't you?"

"For Irial?" Leslie repeated, looking back over her shoulder at Niall. He had a horrible expression of pain on his face. *Chicory tangled with copper sorrow.*

"Survive," he mouthed as he touched the scar on his face.

And she paused, remembering the way her vision had shifted when Niall had walked her to Seth's. She turned her head, looking at Niall and Seth from the corner of her eye: Seth looked the same as he always had. Niall didn't. His scar glared like a fresh jagged wound; his eyes reflected the streetlight like an animal's. His bones weren't quite right, like there were extra lengths or joints where she had none. His cheekbones were too severe for a human's face, too angular, and his skin glowed as if illuminated by a light inside him, as if his skin were too sheer, like parchment over a flame. She pulled her hand out of Tish's grasp and stepped toward him.

"He couldn't tell you," Seth said.

Leslie couldn't move closer, couldn't find words, staring at Niall as he glowed.

Niall held her gaze. "I negotiated with my queen to be allowed to protect you. I'm sorry I failed, Leslie. I . . . I'm so sorry."

"Your queen?" she asked, but she suspected the answer before she heard it. She looked at Seth.

"Ash," Seth confirmed. "She didn't want you involved in this world. She wanted to keep you safe from them."

He motioned behind her, where there were now almost two dozen people who didn't look anywhere near human. Like the crowd at the Rath, they all seemed to be wearing elaborate costumes. But they weren't costumes.

"What are they?" she asked.

"Faeries."

Leslie looked at them: no one was what they'd seemed a few minutes ago. Nothing made sense. *I am angry now. I am afraid.* Yet she couldn't feel those things. She felt curiosity, surprise, and a vague sense of euphoria that she knew—objectively—should be more terrifying than the rest.

"Ash rules one of the faery courts, the Summer Court. She shares the throne with Keenan," Seth said without any inflection, but Leslie felt—*tasted*—his worries, his fears, his anger, his jealousy. It was all there under the surface.

She looked back at Niall—not from the corner of her eye, but full on. He still looked like he was glowing. She gestured at him. "What? Why can I see you like this now?"

"You already know. I don't need to wear a glamour." Niall stepped forward, walking toward her.

"She's Irial's now. *Ours.*" Tish gestured toward the shadows, and at least six of the thorn-covered men stepped in front of Leslie, blocking Niall. As they did so, the dread-locked quints from the Rath appeared beside Niall. They were growling, as was he. He bared his teeth.

More people appeared as she watched. *No, not people, creatures of some sort, stepping out of empty air.* Some were armed with strange weapons—short curved knives that looked like they were made of rock and bone, long blades of bronze and silver. Others grinned cruelly as they lined up to face one another, except for a small group that encircled her and another that encircled Seth.

Tish—who looked no different, despite claiming affiliation with whatever weird creatures these were—stepped forward slowly, like a predator stalking prey. "I speak with Irial's blessing tonight, to look after Leslie, to keep her safe for him. You don't want to try us, Niall."

Niall's tense posture—his rage humming in his bones like an elixir Leslie could drown in—said what his words did not: he very much wanted to move toward violence.

And Leslie, for all the oddity of the moment, wanted him to. She wanted the lot of them to tear into one another. She wanted their violence, their excitement, their rivalry and hatred. It was a craving deep inside her, a hunger that was not her own. She swayed on her feet as their emotions tangled into her.

Then the circle around her parted. Tish bowed her head briefly and took Leslie's hand. She raised her voice enough to be heard over the growls and mutterings of the crowd. "Would you start a war over the girl, Niall?"

"I would love to," he answered.

"Are you *allowed* to?" Tish asked.

There was silence then. Finally Niall replied, "My court has forbidden me from doing so."

"Then go home," Tish said. She motioned toward the shadows. "Dad, can you carry her?"

Leslie turned and saw Gabriel. The tattoos on his arms shifted in the low light, as if they were poised to run. *That's not possible either. But it's real. And they want me . . . for what? Why?* She couldn't panic. She felt like it was there, though, a panic just out of reach, a thought of an emotion. *What did they do to me?*

"Hey, girl." Gabriel smiled gently as he approached her. "Let's get you out of here, okay?"

And she felt herself being lifted, held aloft as Gabriel ran through the streets faster than she'd ever moved in her life. There were no sounds, no sights, only darkness and Irial's voice from somewhere far away: *"Rest now, darling. I'll see you later."*

CHAPTER 27

Niall was only halfway into the front room of the loft when he said, "Leslie's gone. I don't ask much, haven't in all these years—"

Keenan raised a hand that glowed with pulsing sunlight. "Does Irial hold sway over you, Niall?"

"What?" Niall stood motionless as he reined in his own emotions.

The Summer King scowled but didn't answer. The plants in the loft bent under the force of the desert wind that was picking up speed as Keenan's emotions fluctuated; the birds had retreated to their safe nooks in the columns. *At least the Summer Girls are out.* Keenan sent the remaining guards away with a few terse words. Then he began pacing. Eddies of steamed air swirled through the room, twisting and spiraling as if ghostly figures were hidden in them, only to be slashed apart by the hot winds already shrieking around them—all of which were then washed away by bursts of rain. Made manifest by the king's warring emotions, the climates clashed in the small space and left disaster behind.

Then Keenan paused to say, "Do you think often of Irial? Feel sympathy for his court?"

"What are you talking about?" Niall asked.

Keenan gripped the sofa cushions, clearly trying to find a way to restrain his emotions. The storm whipped through the room, shredding the leaves of the trees, sending glass-work sculptures crashing to the ground.

"I've made the choices I needed to, Niall. I won't be bound again. I won't go back to that. I won't be weakened by Irial. . . ." Sunlight shone from Keenan's eyes, from his lips. The sofa cushions caught fire.

"You aren't making any sense, Keenan. If you have a point, make it." Niall's own temper wasn't as volatile, even after all these centuries with Keenan, but it was far crueler than Keenan could ever be. "Irial took Leslie. We don't have time for—"

"Irial's still fond of you." Keenan had a pensive look as he asked a question he'd not ever asked directly before: "How do you feel about him?"

Niall froze, staring at his friend, his cause, his reason for *everything* over so many centuries. That Keenan would ask such a question stung. "Don't do this. Don't ask me questions about *before*."

Keenan didn't answer, didn't apologize for salting old

wounds. He went to stare out the window as the sandstorm in the room stilled. The Summer King was calm again.

Niall, however, fought to control his own emotions. This wasn't a conversation he wanted to have, not now when he was worried about Leslie and furious with Irial. Once, Niall had placed his trust in another king, and that had been a mistake. Back then, Irial had revealed that he'd known all along that the mortals Niall had lain with were sickened and addicted. He'd told Niall that those mortals died—but not until after the dark faeries had brought the mortals to their *bruig* for entertainment. He'd explained that Niall's addictive nature was simply part of being a Gancanagh. Niall had run then, but Gabriel had come for him. He brought Niall back into the Dark Court's *bruig*, the faery mound where Irial was waiting.

> *"You could rule my court someday, Gancanagh," Irial had murmured as he brought forth the mortals who'd been addicted—and were mad with wanting.*
>
> *"Linger with us," he whispered. "This is where you belong. With me. Nothing has changed."*
>
> *Around them, the addicted mortals grappled at the willing fey like they were starving for touch, too sick with withdrawal to think of the consequences of contact with thorn-covered bodies and incompatible shapes.*

And Niall had been disgusted that he'd all but handed mortals over to the Dark Court, and when Irial offered him a trade—"*You entertain the court or they can, Gancanagh. Fear and pain is the coin for their ransom. It matters little to me who pays it*"—Niall had thought to do the right thing, giving his vow freely in exchange for the release of the addicts. In the end, it hadn't mattered: the addicts still withered away, pleading for the drug that was in Niall's skin.

Keenan was speaking again. "What you are has never been used as an asset to our court." He had a faraway look, both pensive and calculating. "If I'm to keep our court safe, I need to use all our assets."

Keenan uncorked a bottle that had been sitting on a warming tray, poured the honeyed drink into two glasses, and held one out.

Niall couldn't respond, couldn't speak. He just stared at his king.

"Even with Irial swaying her, Leslie will want you, and *he* still wants you. We can use this to learn the other secrets Irial's court hides from us." Keenan offered Niall the glass again. "Come now. He'll not strike out at you. Mayhap he'll share the girl, and—"

"You knew. That Leslie was marked by him, that—"

"No. I knew there were mortals being marked and taken in by Dark Court faeries. I hoped we'd have learned more by now, sorting out why or how they were bonding with mortals. Now we just need to reassess. This isn't over. She wants you. I saw her watching you before this all began. I

can't think Irial's claiming her will erase that. This could be
better than I'd hoped. If she survives, she'll be in a position
to learn much. She'll tell you. She'll do what you want just
to be near you." Keenan offered the glass a third time.
"Drink with me, Niall. Don't let this put us asunder."

Niall took the glass and, watching Keenan as he did it,
dropped it on the floor. "I've lived for you, Keenan. My life,
my every decision for nine gods-damned centuries. How
could you violate her like—"

"I'm not the one who violated the girl. It's not my blood
under her skin. Irial—"

"*Irial* wasn't the one playing me this time, was he?" Niall
bowed his head as rage vied with despair. "How could you
use me, Keenan? How could you keep secrets from me? You
manipulated me. . . ." He took a step closer to Keenan,
approaching his king with anger, with the temptation to
raise a hand to the faery he'd sworn to protect, to honor
with his last breath. "You *still* want to use me. You knew,
and—"

"I'd heard about their ink exchanges, suspected that
Leslie was one of them, but finding out the secrets of the
Dark Court is far from easy. She's just one mortal. I can't
save them all, and if one or two fall so we can keep them all
safe . . . This is no different than it's ever been." Keenan
didn't back up, didn't summon guards to his side. "We can
use this to have what we both want."

"You encouraged my interest in Leslie, set me up to disobey Aislinn, my queen, *your queen*."

"I did."

As Niall stood there, trembling in his anger, all of Keenan's statements of late came crashing in on him; the truth of what Niall hadn't seen, by trust or foolishness, was heart crushing. "And you don't feel any remorse, do you? What she's suffering—"

"Irial is a threat to our court." Keenan shrugged. "The Dark Court is too awful to be allowed to thrive. You know as well as I what they've done. You bear the scars. I won't have him strong enough to threaten our court, especially our queen. He needs to be kept in check."

"So why not tell me?" Niall watched his king, hoping for some answer that would ease the weight that threatened to break Niall's spirit as surely as the Dark Court once had.

But Keenan didn't offer such an answer. Instead he said, "And have you do what? Tell the girl? I saw you swaying to her as it was. Mine was a better plan. I needed you to have a focus, and she's as good a focus as any."

Niall heard the logic in the words, had heard his king speak thusly over the centuries when he seduced the mortals who were now Summer Girls. It didn't change anything: Niall's loyalty and partnership were rewarded by disregard and cavalier dismissal.

"I can't accept . . . won't accept this," Niall said. "I'm done."

"What do you mean?"

So Niall said the words that would undo his oath: "My fealty to the Summer Court is rescinded. You are my king no more." It was a simple thing to end what should matter so much. A few words, and he was alone in the world again.

"Niall, think about it. This isn't worth leaving." Keenan sounded nothing like the faery Niall had thought him to be. "What was I to do?"

"Not this." He stepped around Keenan. "I'd rather be solitary, courtless, without a home or king . . . than be used."

He didn't slam the door, didn't rage, didn't weep. He simply left.

Several hours later, Niall was still walking through the streets of Huntsdale. There was some sort of event, leaving the streets full and noisy, matching the din inside him. *I'm not any better than Irial. I'd have made her addicted like the junkies she fears.* And his king had known that, used that. *I failed her.*

It wasn't often that he lamented being the one who followed and never led, but as he walked through the dirty mortal streets, he wondered if he'd made the right choice so long ago when Irial'd offered to make Niall his successor. *At least then I'd have more choices.*

Niall waded through the mostly mortal crowd. The fey who mingled with them hurriedly stepped out of his path. As the crowd moved, Niall saw him: Irial lounged against a storefront.

"I heard you were out and about," the Dark King said, "but I was beginning to think my fey were wrong."

"I want to talk to you," Niall began.

"I'll always welcome you, Gancanagh. That hasn't changed." Irial gestured to the tiny park across the street. "Walk with me."

Vendors were selling sweets from their carts; drunken mortals laughed and shouted. A game of some sort or perhaps a concert must be letting out. People crowded the streets so much that traffic was unable to move. The Dark King wove through the stopped cars and angrily honking drivers, past a group of mortals singing quite poorly and doing what they seemed to think was dancing.

Once in the park, Irial motioned to a stone bench his fey had just finished clearing. "This is your sort of place, isn't it? Would you rather go—"

"It's fine." But Niall stood, leaning against a tree, not at ease with having his back to the fey roaming the street.

Irial shrugged as he folded himself gracefully onto the bench, looking perversely like an ingénue unaware of the effect he had on the gaping mortals around them. "So"—he lit a cigarette—"I expect you're here about my Leslie."

"She's not yours."

Irial took a long drag off the cigarette. "You think?"

"Yes. I do." Niall turned slightly, watching several faeries who were approaching from the left. He didn't trust Irial or the solitary faeries who were watching or—actually he didn't trust anyone right then.

Irial motioned several of his faeries closer and directed, "I want the immediate area empty." Then he turned his attention to Niall. "Sit. I'll not allow *any* harm to you while you sit with me—my vow on that."

Stunned by the generous vow Irial'd offered him—*no harm at all*, thus saying his own safety was secondary to Niall's—he sat and stared at the Dark King. It didn't change things, though: a moment of kindness didn't undo Leslie's situation or Irial's long-ago cruelty.

"Leslie's not yours," Niall said. "She's her own, bond or not. You just don't realize it yet."

"Aaah, you're still a fool, Gancanagh." Irial exhaled a cloud of smoke and leaned back. "A passionate one, but a fool nonetheless."

Niall said it then, the words he'd never thought to say to Irial, the start of a conversation that had once been his greatest nightmare. "Would you trade for her freedom?"

Something indecipherable flashed in Irial's eyes as he lowered his cigarette. "Perhaps. What are you offering?"

"What do you want?"

A weary look passed over Irial's face. "Sometimes, I'm not sure anymore. I've held this court through the wars between Beira and the last Summer King, through Beira's fits of temper, but this new order . . . I'm tired, Niall. What do I want?" Irial's usual facade—half amused and half callous—returned then. "What does any king want? I want to keep my fey safe."

"How does Leslie fit into that?"

"Are you asking for the kingling or for yourself?" Irial's tone was once more the needling one he so often used when they spoke: the Dark King had never quite forgiven Niall for running. They both knew that.

"What do you want from me in exchange? I'm here to bargain. What's your price, Irial?" Niall felt such a swirl of emotions at actually saying the words—self-disgust that he'd failed Leslie, anger that his king had failed him, dismay that he was touched by Irial's kindness. "I know how this works. Tell me what you're willing to give up and what it'll cost me."

"You never did figure it out, did you?" Irial asked incredulously. But before Niall could speak, Irial held up his hand. "Revel in the feelings you're fighting not to show me, and I'll answer you."

"Do *what*?" Niall had heard of odd bargains, but here he was exposing himself to Irial's whims, and the Dark King offered answers in exchange for "giving in to his feelings." Niall scowled. "What sort of—"

"Stop holding all those darker feelings in, and I'll give you the answers you need." Irial smiled like they were friends who'd been having a reasonable conversation. "Just let yourself feel your emotions, Niall. That's all I ask, and I'll share information commensurate in worth with what you feel and how fully you feel it."

"How will you—"

"Gancanagh . . . would you rather I ask for other favors? I'd rather not bargain with baser coins, not with you, not with anyone I have affection for." Irial leaned close enough and smiled such a wicked smile that Niall was reminded of more pleasant times with Irial long ago, before Niall knew who and what Irial was, before he knew what he himself was.

So Niall let his temper reign, released his hold on that pit of anger at Keenan's betrayal, let it bubble over. It wasn't an emotion he often let reign, but it was the one he'd been trying to quell for hours. It was almost a relief to feel the rage.

Irial's pupils dilated. His hands clenched. "That's one."

Niall thought about the mortals he'd wooed and left wasting away when he knew no better, thought of Leslie pliable and eager in his arms. He could picture her, kiss-drunk, and he wanted that—wanted *her* with a longing that was heavier for being denied.

"Two . . . Just one more emotion, Gancanagh," Irial murmured.

And Niall imagined wrapping his hands around Irial's throat, letting free the jealousy that he felt at the idea of Irial's hands on Leslie—or of her hands on Irial.

With a shaky hand Irial lit another cigarette. "You play the game well, Gancanagh. I wondered once what you'd do with the knowledge."

Niall watched, studying the Dark King with a distant calm now, feeling no true emotions at all. "What knowledge?"

"The dark fey starve without emotion, darker emotions. It's what"—Irial took a drag off his cigarette—"sustains us. Food, drink, air. Everything. There's a great secret, Niall.

There's the thing that the others would use against us if they knew."

Niall hesitated. Part of him wondered why Irial would take such a risk, why he would reveal his secrets, but another less easily embraced part knew exactly why Irial would do so: he trusted Niall. He looked away, lamenting the fact that Irial's trust wasn't misplaced. "So why doesn't Keenan notice? Or Sorcha? How did *I* not know?"

"His volatile nature? Her imperviousness to anything she doesn't like?" Irial tapped his ash onto the ground. "And you . . . I don't know. I thought you'd figured it out back then, and when I realized the kingling didn't know, I hoped that what we—"

"All of your court feeds like this?" Niall stopped him, not wanting to think about his time with Irial, the realization that Niall's blurry weeks of mad pleasures had nourished Irial—as, no doubt, had the horrific things that followed when Niall ran.

"They do, or they get weak." The Dark King's face revealed a raw pain that was almost embarrassing to see, like glimpsing someone's most private aches. "Guin died . . . from a mortal bullet. She was shot."

Irial stared at the crowd. A barefoot girl was dancing on the hood of a parked car. The driver was holding out her shoes and gesturing at the ground. Irial smiled at them before turning back and adding, "You care for Leslie. If you had known she was already mine, you would've tried even harder to keep her from me. You'd have fought for her."

I knew Irial wanted her and—Niall stopped himself, uneasy with the fact that Irial could read what he was feeling, and more important, that Niall could use this knowledge to destroy Irial. If the courts knew that they were so easily read and assessed, it would be hard to convince any of them to tolerate the Dark Court's continued existence.

"Beira knew all of this," Niall said.

"We needed her. She needed us. Else I wouldn't have helped her bind the kingling. She kept things in upheaval when my fey needed it."

"And Leslie fits in how?"

"I needed a backup plan." Irial smiled, but this time it was dark and deadly, tinged with more than a little challenge. "I need her."

"You can't have her," Niall started. But Irial gripped his arms: every lovely memory Niall had run from and every whispered horror of the Dark Court came rushing to his mind in a morass—then Niall felt like he was swallowing it, like he'd been drinking that too-sweet, forcibly forgotten wine. "Stop."

Irial let go of him. "I know Keenan has misled and deceived you. I know he was sending you to our girl, putting her in your path. Gabriel watched you struggle with your response to her. . . . I will not mislead you, not again. I would welcome you back into my home, where Leslie will be. I would still offer you my throne when you are ready."

Niall blanched. He'd been willing to endure whatever

he'd needed to in exchange for Leslie's freedom. *Kingship? Affection?* That was not at all what he'd expected. *It's a ruse, just like always. There was never anything real in what we once were.* Niall ignored all of it. "Would you let her go free in exchange for my fealty?"

"No. She stays, but if you want to be with her, you are ever welcome." Irial stood and bowed from the waist as if Niall were his equal. "I won't let my court suffer, even for you. You know what my secrets are, what I am, what I offer you still. I can promise you that she will be kept as happy as I can make her. Beyond that . . . come home with us or not. It is your choice to make. It has always been your choice."

And Niall stared at him, speechless, unsure of what answer he could offer that made any sense. He'd spent a long time not remembering the bond he'd shared with Irial, not longing for those years, and not admitting any of this each time he'd crossed paths with Irial. He realized now, though, that no matter how carefully he'd guarded his secrets, he'd been transparent to Irial. If the Dark King could read his emotions, could taste them, he'd known of Niall's weaknesses each time they'd met. *I've been exposed to him the whole time.* Irial didn't shame him for it. Instead he held out the same acceptance he'd offered centuries ago— and Niall didn't, couldn't, reply.

Irial said, "It's been a long time that you've been living for Keenan, paying back some perceived debt. We are what we are, Niall, neither as good or as evil as others paint us.

And what we are doesn't change how truly we feel, only how free we are to follow those feelings."

Then he slipped away into the crowd, dancing with mortals as he went and looking every bit like he belonged there among them.

CHAPTER 28

It was evening when Leslie woke in her own room, wearing the same clothes she'd worn the night before. She'd slept for more than twelve hours, as if her body were fighting off a flu or hangover. She still didn't feel right. The skin around her tattoo felt tight, stretched too thin. It didn't burn, or itch, or anything that would make her suspect infection. If anything, it felt too good, as if extra nerves were throbbing there.

Downstairs she could hear cartoons. Ren laughed. Someone else coughed. Others spoke in low voices and broken sentences she couldn't quite understand. She started to feel the familiar panic, terror that she was here, that she had no clue which of the others were down there.

Idly she wondered when her father had last been home. She hadn't seen him. *Someone would call if he died.* She didn't worry over him as she had done for so long. *I should.* Panic started to choke her. Then it just vanished. She knew that she had changed, and that Irial, who'd caused that change, wasn't human.

Am I?

Whatever Irial had done, whatever Rabbit had done, whatever her friends had hidden from her . . . She wanted to feel angry. Objectively, she knew she should feel betrayed, feel despair—rage, even. She tried to summon those feelings, but only the shadows of them rose. The emotions weren't hers for more than a moment before they fled.

Then Ren was calling up the stairs in a strangled voice, "Leslie?"

With a calm that should have been impossible, she rolled out of bed and went to her door. She was unafraid. It was a remembered feeling, one she liked. After turning the locks—which someone had thrown—she walked to the top of the stairs. As she looked down, she saw him, Irial, standing there beside her brother.

"What are *you* doing here?" she said. Her voice was even, but she shivered. This emotion, excitement, didn't flee. Unlike the others, this one stayed and grew.

"Seeing you." He held out a hand. "Assuring that you are well."

Ren stood beside Irial, trying to get his attention. "Umm, you need . . . anything? Anything at all?"

"Careful," Irial murmured, unmindful of everyone but her. His hands were on her hips then.

How did he get up the stairs so quickly?

"Don't. Please?" She wished she didn't feel so comforted

that he was here, wished she were sure what she was asking when she repeated, "Please?"

"I'm not here to hurt you, *a ghrá*." He stepped backward, not looking as he walked down the stairs, not removing his hands from her hips, either.

"You didn't lie, did you?"

"We don't."

Leslie stared at Irial. "Who are you? *What* are you?"

He held her gaze, and for an unreal moment she thought she saw shadows clinging to his skin like dark wings. Her body tingled all over, and she was sure that innumerable tiny mouths touched her skin all at once—soothing her, erasing everything but pleasure. She shivered against the sudden onset of cravings that made no sense. Her mouth was dry, her palms damp, her heart thundering in her head.

Without breaking her gaze, he said, "I'll take care of you, keep you from hurting or pain. You have my vow on this, Leslie. You'll never want anything again. Say the word, and it's yours. No more fear or pain. Just shadows of them, and I'll take them away. You won't have to feel them but for a moment. Look." He dropped his gaze to the air between them. A shadowy vine extended from his body to hers, coiling into her skin. She reached out as if she'd touch it; her hands brushed against the black feathers that curled from it like leaves. When she did, they both flinched.

"It's real. Whatever you did to me," she said.

"You wanted to be safe. You wanted to be without fear or pain. You have it." Irial didn't wait for her to move; he pulled her closer so she was leaning against him. He smelled like peat smoke, musty rooms full of sex and longing, sweet-strange and dizzying. She rubbed her cheek against his shirt, breathing in the scent of him.

"I'll never leave you," Irial whispered. Then he turned to the assembled crowd. "If anyone ever touches her again—"

The dealer started, "When I . . . I didn't know she was your—"

Irial made a gesture. Two very scarred guys appeared out of the empty air. They stepped forward and took hold of the dealer.

He was one of them. Leslie's knees buckled. *He . . .* Her stomach burned as she tried to let that thought finish itself. The terror of the other people in the room, of the dealer who was crying out as he was led away—she felt that too, all of it at once. The lust of the mortals—*mortals?*—in the room, the want, the desperate need. She felt a tangle of emotions assailing her. Flashes of need, of terror, of aching—they flooded her body until she swayed.

"Their feelings . . . I need . . ." She clenched Irial's hand.

"Shhh." He kissed her, and the feelings evaporated. "They just come through you. Those feeling aren't yours. Just a blink, and they're gone from you."

He had an arm around her, leading her to the sofa.

She stared at the door where the guys—*where did they come from?*—had led the dealer away.

Irial was kneeling in front of her. "It'll all be fine. No one will hurt you again. Ever. You will get used to the rest."

Mutely she nodded, watching him the way she'd never watched anyone in her life, transfixed. Irial could make everything good, right, happy. He was an answer to a question she'd forgotten to ask. Her body hummed in a pleasant blur. The feelings that had rolled through her were awful, ugly; she knew that objectively. After Irial took them, all she felt was bliss. Something heavy and floral was in her mouth, on her lips. *Lust. His. Mine.* Her veins sang with it, like fire coursing through her body, seeking her heart, flooding her nerves.

Then Niall's words echoed in her head, "Surviving is what matters. You can do this." *Do what? Survive what?* There was nothing bad here. Irial was making her safe. He was taking care of her.

"Come now. They'll pack your things." Irial motioned at three almost-androgynous guys who were headed up the stairs. "We need to get out of here. Away from so many mortals. Talk."

"Talk?" She almost laughed. Talking was pretty far from what was on her mind as he knelt there in front of her. Her eyes felt too wide. Every pore in her body was awake and zinging.

"Or whatever else would make you happy," he added with a wicked grin. "You've done me a great honor, Leslie. The world is yours."

"I don't need the world. I need—" She leaned forward until she was able to rest her face against his chest, hating the cloth that was in her way, suddenly furious at the damnable material. She snarled—then froze, realizing that her hand was already tearing at his shirt, that she'd made a sound that was so far from normal, so far from human that she should be terrified.

He pulled her to her feet, keeping her clutched tightly to his side. "It's fine. Just the initial changes. Shhh."

And as he breathed deeply, it *was* fine. He was still talking, though, asking, "What shall I do with them?"

Ren and the others were watching with looks of abject terror. But they didn't matter now; none of this mattered anymore. *Only Irial. Only this pleasure, this confidence.* That was all that mattered.

"Who cares?" she said.

Then he lifted her into his arms and carried her over the threshold into a world that was suddenly far more tempting than she'd realized it could be.

CHAPTER 29

Niall had walked out on his king; he'd failed Leslie; and he'd exposed his doubts and longings to Irial. He hadn't had such a complete feeling of loss in centuries. He'd spent part of the night and the whole of the day walking aimlessly but had come no closer to any answers or even the right questions.

He'd seen the faeries watching him: Keenan's and Irial's and those who were solitary. *Like I am again.* None of them, even those who'd tried to speak with him, had made him pause. Several times he'd had to move them bodily from his path, but he hadn't spoken a word or registered the words that they spoke.

But then Bananach was swaying toward him, moving like a shadow in the just-fallen night. The long feathers that spilled down her back fluttered and shifted in the breeze. She wore a glamour that made those feathers look like hair, playing mortal for him as she approached.

He stopped walking.

The smile she offered him was at odds with the malice in her eyes. She passed him, paused, looked back, and beckoned. She did not watch to see if he'd follow her as she walked into a narrow alley partway down the block. She did not glance back as she slipped under the metal fence or as she trailed her fingers over the razor wire that draped the top of that fence. It was only once Niall was standing behind her, like prey foolishly pursuing a predator, that she turned to face him.

Niall wondered if he was following her to his death: it was a fate he had considered and rejected after Irial allowed the Dark Court to torture him. *It wasn't the right choice then.* Bananach would gladly have taken Niall's life at the time had Irial not sent her away to indulge in her mayhem. *It's never the right choice.*

But he didn't retreat.

She leaned on the metal fence, her arm stretched over her head, her fingers curled around the loops in the fence. The barbed steel of the razor wire was just above her fingers, close enough that it looked like she was reaching for the poisonous metal. It was unhealthily attractive to him, her desire to touch pain.

He kept his distance and his silence.

She tilted her head to stare at him. The avian gesture contrasted with the mortal glamour she held on to as she waited. "Irial needs replacing," she said.

"And you're telling me this why?"

"Because *you* can give me change. He's not right for us. Not now." Her glamour shivered, flickering in and out. "Help me. Bring me my wars again."

"I don't want war. I want . . ." He glanced away, not knowing what he truly wanted. He'd followed her into a too-small space, pursuing the temptation of her violence. *And leaving Leslie to figure out the impossible on her own if I give in to the temptation of self-destruction.* He'd run away from Irial, from Keenan. He was still running. "I'm not going to help you."

"Smart answer, pretty boy." Gabriel appeared beside him. The Hound held an arm out, tattoos racing furiously over his skin, and motioned for Niall to step back. "You need to move along now."

Bananach snapped her mouth open and closed. Her glamour faded, revealing her sharp beak. "Your meddling is getting tiresome. If the Gancanagh wants to stay with me . . ."

Gabriel stepped in front of Niall just as Bananach launched herself forward. She shrieked, a sound that might have been laughter or anger or some combination of the two. Her hands were splayed open, her fingertips black talons.

"Court business, Niall. Go on now," Gabriel said without glancing back.

Gabriel lifted Bananach and hurled her into the metal fence. Her feathers snagged on the razor wire, but she yanked herself away. Shredded feathers drifted to the ground behind her and were lost on the shadowed pavement.

Niall wanted to leave, to stay, to tell Gabriel to get out of the way so Bananach could end the confusion and depression that had been weighing on him, to tell Gabriel to rip into her. Instead he stood still, watching, no more resolved than he'd been when Bananach had beckoned him to follow her.

It wasn't truly beautiful to watch Gabriel in action, but there was a brutal harmony in his movements. Like the Summer Girls' dancing, Gabriel's fighting had a rhythm to it, a song of its own. But the Hound's moves were well matched by Bananach's fury. The raven-woman was gleeful as she darted away and then returned to dive at Gabriel with abandon. From somewhere she drew a bone blade that glowed with preternatural light. Her black-taloned nails stood in relief against white bone and red blood as she slashed Gabriel from his left brow to his right cheek.

The fresh blood drew cries of pleasure from a group of Ly Ergs who filed into the enclosed lot from the street. Their red hands twitched in unison as they began circling Gabriel. They took some of their sustenance from freshly drawn blood, a habit that Niall had found disquieting when he'd learned of it. There weren't enough of them to over-come Gabriel, but with Bananach there too . . . *It's not really my business. It's Dark Court business. Which is not my court.*

Niall started to step out of their path, but leaving Gabriel to a half dozen Ly Ergs and a blood-mad Bananach wasn't something that set well with him. Gabriel's arrival had prevented Bananach from seriously wounding or killing him. He owed Gabriel for that. The Hound might not expect it, but Niall expected it of himself. That was one thing he hadn't lost, his honor.

He threw himself into the fracas—not for a court or a king, but because it was the right thing to do. Standing by while someone—even Gabriel—was outnumbered wasn't an option.

Niall didn't worry about consequences as he struck the Ly Ergs. He didn't worry about where his king was. He didn't worry about anything. He avoided some but not all of the Ly Ergs' blows. Although the red-palmed faeries were more concerned with drawing blood than with inflicting permanent injury, they had murdered their share of faeries and mortals over the years.

Bananach darted past Gabriel and caught Niall in the upper abs with the tips of her boots. Searing pain rocked him back as the boots' poisonous iron cut into his flesh. He stumbled, and she pressed her advantage with a swipe of her blood-soaked talons.

Then Gabriel grabbed her and steadfastly moved their fight away from Niall, back toward the fence, leaving Niall free to deal with the Ly Ergs. It was disturbingly good fun, salve for the gloom Niall had been trying to shake. It didn't change anything but was refreshing.

By the time Niall had most of the Ly Ergs retreating, Gabriel had bloodied Bananach severely enough that she was leaning against the one Ly Erg who'd held back from the melee. But even so, she fought until Gabriel punched her hard enough that she swayed backward and tumbled to the ground.

Gabriel told the single unwounded Ly Erg, "Take her out of here before Chela notices I've had another tussle with her." He snarled at the rest of the Ly Ergs, who'd eased closer. "I keep getting into fights with Bananach, Che's going to get all territorial. Don't none of us want that, do we?"

The Ly Erg didn't speak but merely stepped up beside the raven-woman. Bananach rested her head against his leg.

"You're inconveniencing me, puppy. If necessary, I'll see the ice queen or the kingling. Someone's"—she snapped her jaw at Niall in what was either an invitation or a warning—"going to help me get this court set right."

"Irial said how we'd handle things." Gabriel stretched out his arms to show the raven-woman the spiraling orders on his skin.

"*Iri* needs to go. He's in the way and not doing what needs done. War's what we want. Need some proper violence. It's too long." Bananach closed her eyes. "And you following me everywhere's getting old."

"So stay put and I'll stop following you." Gabriel lowered himself to the pavement with a graceless gesture and began inspecting his wounds. He grimaced, a decidedly unpleasant sight with the blood flowing down his face, as he poked at a gash on his forehead.

The Ly Erg reached an already red hand down to caress Bananach's bloody face and arms, nourishing himself on battle blood as his kind had once done on red-soaked fields. His skin shimmered as Bananach's fresh blood seeped into his palm. Another Ly Erg walked up and laid his hand on Gabriel's blood-covered face. Despite the fact that they'd all been trying diligently to skewer, maim, and otherwise incapacitate one another mere moments ago, they were almost cordial for a few bizarre moments. The Ly Ergs took the pain and blood into their skin, unmindful of past conflict in the moment of postfight pleasure and sustenance.

Then Gabriel swung at the Ly Erg who stood patting his still-bleeding wounds and said, "Enough. Get her out of here. Maybe you could try being obedient tomorrow?"

"Maybe you should try staying out of my way tomorrow." Bananach stood and flicked her long hairlike feathers over her shoulder with a look of disdain. She might be bruised and unsteady on her feet, but she wasn't cowed by anyone. Then, with a solemnity that was as eerie as her violence, she shifted her attention to Niall. "Think about what you want, Gancanagh—what's *right*. Forgiving the Dark King? Forgiving the Summer King? Or letting me bring you justice, pain, and war, and *everything* you desire. We'd both be happy."

Once she was out of sight, Gabriel asked, "You might have walked away from Irial, Gancanagh, but do you really want this lot influencing our court? Do you want to *help* her?"

"I'm not getting involved. It's not my court." Niall sat beside the Hound. He wasn't sure, but it felt like one of his ribs had been cracked.

Gabriel snorted. "It's yours as much as mine. You're just too much of an ass to admit it."

"I'm not like you. I'm not out looking for fights or—"

"You don't back down from them, though. 'Sides, Irial's not all about fighting either. That's why he keeps *me* around." The Hound grinned and gestured at the shattered windows and cracked bricks. "There's more to the Dark Court than violence. You bring out another sort of darkness. We both belong in the shadows."

Niall ignored the implications of Gabriel's words. "I left the Summer Court. That's why Bananach was here— because I am solitary, fair game, *prey.*"

Gabriel clasped Niall's shoulder approvingly. "I knew you'd get it figured out eventually: you don't belong with them. You get a few more things figured out, you'll be all right."

Then he lifted a broken brick and tossed it at a still-lit streetlight. As the glass shattered and clattered to the ground, Gabriel stood and started to walk away.

"Gabe?"

Gabriel's steps didn't slow or waver, but Niall knew the Hound was listening.

"I'm not letting him keep Leslie. She deserves a life. Irial can't take hers like this."

"You're still a slow learner, boy." Gabriel turned back.

"She's part of the court now. Just like you. Been part of it since that first touch of ink went in her mortal flesh. Why do you think we're all called to be nearer her? I watched you try to resist it. Like draws to like. You're both Irial's, and with her being a mortal . . ."

Niall froze.

Gabriel gave him a pitying smile. "Don't beat yourself up over things that are out of your control . . . or worry so much after the girl. You of all faeries ought to know Iri's not going to give up on the ones he claims as his own. He's just as stubborn as you."

Then the Hound was in his Mustang and vanishing into the darkened street, and for the third time in less than two days Niall was left with answers that did more to confuse him than ease his worries.

CHAPTER 30

Leslie rolled over, out of Irial's reach. Despite the vastness of the bed, she still felt too close to him. She'd meant to move several times already, to get up and leave. She didn't. She couldn't.

"It'll get easier," he said gently. "It's just new. You'll be fine. I'll—"

"I can't step away. I can't. I keep telling myself I'm going to go. But I don't." She wasn't angry even now, when her body ached. She should be, though. She knew that. "I feel like I'll throw up, like if I move too far from you . . ."

He rolled her back over so she was being held in his arms again. "It. Will. Fade."

She whispered, "I don't believe you."

"We were starved. It's—"

"Starved? We?" she asked.

He told her what he was, what Niall was, what Aislinn

and Keenan were. He told her they weren't human, not any of them.

Seth was telling the truth. She'd known somehow, somewhere, but hearing it said again, hearing it confirmed was horrible. *I am angry. I am afraid. I am . . .* She *wasn't,* though, not any of those things.

Irial kept talking. He told her that there were courts and that his—the Dark Court—lived on emotions. He told her that through her he would nourish them, that she was their salvation, that she was his salvation. He told her things that should terrify her, and every time she felt close to afraid or angry he drank it away.

"So you're what in this faery court?"

"In charge. Just as Aislinn and Keenan are for the Summer Court." There was no arrogance in his statement. In fact, he sounded weary.

"Am I"—she felt foolish, but she wanted to know, had to ask—"human still?"

He nodded.

"So, what does this mean? What am I then?"

"Mine." He kissed her to emphasize his point and then repeated, "Mine. You are mine."

"Which means what?"

He looked perplexed by that one. "That whatever you want is yours?"

"What if I want to leave? To see Niall?"

"I doubt that he'll be coming to see us, but you can go to him if you want." Irial rolled on top of her again as he said it. "As soon as you're able, you can walk out the door anytime you please. We'll look after you, keep you protected, but you can always leave when you want to and are able to."

But she didn't. She didn't want to, and she wasn't able. He wasn't lying: she believed that, tasted it, felt it in his words, but she also knew that whatever he'd done to her made her not want to be anywhere other than with him. For a brief moment, she felt terror at that realization, but it fled, replaced by a craving that made her sink her fingernails into Irial's skin and pull him closer—again and again, and still she was nearly shaking with need.

When Gabriel walked in, Leslie was dressed. She wasn't sure how the clothes had ended up on her, but it didn't matter. She was sitting up and covered. There was an apple in her hand.

"Remember to eat now." Irial stroked her hair back from her face, gentle like his voice.

She nodded. There were words she was to say, but they were gone before she could remember what they were.

"Troubles?" Irial asked Gabriel. Somehow Irial was at a desk far away from her.

She searched for the apple she'd been holding. It was gone. She looked down: her clothes were different. She had on a robe; red flowers and swirling blue lines covered it. She tried to follow them with her finger, tracing the pattern.

"The car's here." Gabriel had her hand and was helping her to her feet.

Her skirt became tangled around her ankles.

She stumbled forward and was folded into Irial's arms as they went into the club. The glare of lights made her hide her face against his shirt.

"You're doing fine," he told her as he combed out her hair, stroking his fingers through it, untangling it.

"It's been a long day," she murmured as she swayed under his caresses. She closed her eyes and asked, "The second day will be better, right?"

"It's been a week, love." He pulled the covers up over her. "You're doing much better already."

She listened to them laugh, the strange people—*faeries*— with Gabriel. They told her stories, amused her while Irial talked to a faery with raven feathers for hair. She was lovely, the raven-woman, Bananach. They all were. Leslie stopped staring at Bananach, trying to focus instead on the Vilas that danced with whichever of the Hounds beckoned, swaying through the shadows in the rooms like they felt the touch of shadows as Leslie did—like teasing hands, promising bliss that was too intense to allow for speech.

"Dance with me, Iri." Leslie stood and, ignoring the Hounds, went over to where Bananach was talking to Irial. It occurred to Leslie that this was a repetition of a tableau she could remember from other days: Bananach was around too often, taking Irial's time and attention. Leslie didn't like it.

"Move," she told the raven-woman.

Irial laughed as Bananach tried to raise a hand, only to

have it forced down by Gabriel and another Hound who both grabbed at her.

Irial said, "Bananach was just explaining why you aren't of any use to us."

Leslie felt the shivering in the tendrils that tied her to Irial, and she knew with perfect clarity in that moment that he had tamped down on their connection so she could have a few extra moments of lucidity. He did that.

"And what use am I, Irial? Did you tell her?" she asked.

"I did." Irial was standing now, hand outstretched, palm up.

Leslie put her hand in his and stepped closer.

Beside Irial, Bananach had gone still. She tilted her head at an angle that made her look far less human than the other faeries. Her eyes—which were similar enough to Irial's that Leslie paused—narrowed, but she did not speak. *She does not speak to me.* Leslie remembered that from other nights: Bananach refusing to address "the pet."

Leslie glanced at Gabriel, who stood waiting, and then around the club. They were all waiting. *For me. For food.* She thought she should feel frightened, maybe angry, but all she felt was bored. "Can you keep a leash on her while I relax?"

Gabriel didn't look to Irial for the Dark King's accord. He smiled. "It would be my pleasure."

Leslie knew that almost everyone in the club was watching her, but she suspected they'd seen her in far more mortifying circumstances. She slid her hands up Irial's chest, over his collarbone, and down his arms—feeling the tension in him that was utterly absent from his posture and expression. She tilted her head up and waited until he looked down. Then she whispered, "Am I just for using up, then?"

She knew it, knew that the ink under her skin was intended to let him—let *them*—do just that. She knew that the bone-melting bliss she felt each time he funneled the storms of emotion through her, forcing a tidal wave through a straw, was a trick to keep her insensible to the clarity that she had grasped *again* in that moment—and she realized that she'd had similar moments of clarity other nights and forgotten each time when the rush hit.

"Am I?" she repeated.

He leaned closer still, until she could feel his lips on her neck. There was no sound, only movement, when he said it. "No."

But she was willing to be: they both knew that as well. She thought about the life she'd had before—druggies in her home, drunken or missing father, bills to pay, hours waitressing, lying friends. *What's to miss?* She didn't want to return to pain, to worry, to fear, to any of that. She wanted euphoria. She wanted to feel her body go liquid in his arms. She wanted to feel the mad crescendo of pleasure that hit her with enough force to make her black out.

He pulled away to look at her.

She twined her arms around his neck and walked forward, forcing him to walk backward as she did so. "Later I'm going to be too blissed out to keep my hands off you. . . ." She shivered against him at the thought, at the admission here in public of what she was going to be like, not sure if admitting the desire was worse or better than telling herself some pretty lie to allay the blame. "This is fun, though. Being here. Being with you. I'd like to start remembering more of the fun stuff. Can we do that? Let me remember more of the good times with you? Let me have more of *this*?"

The tension fled then. He looked beyond her and gestured. Music filled the room; bass rumbled so heavily, it felt like it was inside her. And they danced and laughed, and for a few hours the world felt right. The disdainful and adoring looks on the faces of the mortals and faeries didn't matter. There was only Irial, only pleasure. But the longer she was clearheaded, the more she also remembered things that were awful. She didn't feel the emotions, but the memories came into sharper focus. There, in Irial's arms, she realized that she had the power to destroy every person who'd given her nightmares. Irial would do that: he'd find out who they were, and he'd bring them to her. It was a cold, clear understanding.

But she didn't want it, didn't want to truly destroy anyone. She just wanted to forget them again—even knowing she should feel pain was more than she wanted. "Irial? Feed them. Now."

She stopped moving and waited for it, the flash of emotions ripping through her body.

"Gabe," was all he said. And it was enough to start a melee. Bananach shrieked; Gabriel growled. Mortals screamed and moaned in pleasures and horrors. Cacophony rose around them like a familiar lullaby.

Irial didn't let her turn around. He didn't let her see anything or anyone.

Stars flashed to life in some too-close distance. They burned her up for a few brief heartbeats, but in their wake they pulled a wave of ecstasy that made her eyes close. Every particle of her body cried out, and she remembered nothing—knew nothing—but felt only the pleasure of Irial's skin against hers.

Chapter 31

Snatches of time were nothing but blurs and blank spaces, but the lucid periods were becoming more frequent. *How long has it been?* Her tattoo had been healed for a while. Her hair was longer. Often she could feel Irial close the connection, stopping the pull of emotions that slithered along the black vine that hovered between them. On those days almost everything was in order, sequential. So much of the time was a long blur, though. *Weeks?*

She hadn't left his side yet. *How long? How long have I . . .* Today she would. Today she would prove she could. She knew she'd tried—*and failed*—to do this more times than she could guess. There were bits of memories jumbled together. Life was like that now: just montages of images and sensations, and through it all there was Irial. He was constant. Even as she moved, she heard him in the other room. *Always at my reach.* That was dangerous too. The raven-woman wanted to change that, take Irial away.

Leslie slipped into one of the countless outfits he'd ordered for her, a long dress that clung and swirled when she moved. Like everything he bought, it was of material that felt almost too sensuous as she slipped into it. Without a word, she opened the door to the second room.

He didn't speak; he just watched her.

She opened the door to the hallway. Faeries followed her—invisible to any other human in the hotel, but she saw them. He'd given her the Sight with some strange oil he'd rubbed on her eyelids. Lanky creatures with tiny thorns all over their skin were silent, respectful even, as they followed her. Had she been able to, she'd have been terrified, but she was nothing but a conduit for emotions. The walls didn't keep her safe from them. Every fear, every longing, every dark thing those passing mortals and faeries felt flowed through her body until she couldn't focus. Only Irial's touch kept her from madness, calmed her.

The elevator door slid shut, closing the watching faeries out, taking her to the lobby of the hotel. Others would be there, waiting for her.

A glaistig nodded as she stepped out of the elevator. The glaistig's hooves clattered as she strode across the expanse of the room. Leslie's own footsteps weren't much quieter; Irial had bought her only ridiculously expensive shoes and boots with heels.

". . . the car brought around?" The doorman was speaking, but Leslie hadn't noticed. "Miss? Do you need your driver?"

She stared at him, feeling the flood of fear in him, feeling Irial several floors above her tasting that fear through her. It was like that, endless blurs of nothing but feeling emotions slither through her body to Irial. He said he was stronger. He said they were doing well. He said the court was healing.

The doorman stared at her; he spilled his fears and disdain onto her.

What does he see?

Irial had the appearance of someone far from responsible. He had the money and the constant flow of criminal-looking guests: the faeries' human masks did little to hide the aura of menace that clung to them. And she—when she left the suite—moved through the halls like a zombie, clinging to Irial, and on several occasions coming close to putting on a public show.

"Will you be going out today?" the doorman asked.

Her stomach cramped. Being away from Irial made her sick.

Gabriel swooped in behind her. "Do you need help?"

The doorman glanced away: he mightn't have heard the inhuman timbre of Gabriel's voice, but he'd felt the fear the Hound's presence elicited. All mortals did. It was what Gabriel was, and as he became agitated, he became more frightening.

The doorman's fear spiked.

"You made it to the door, Leslie. That's good." Irial's voice slipped into her mind. It was no longer surprising, but she still winced.

"Not his driver. Grab me a taxi?" she asked the doorman. She clenched her hands: she wasn't failing, not this time. She didn't faint or crumble. *Little victories.* She forced the words from her lips, "Taxi to take me to warehouse . . ."

She swayed.

The doorman asked, "Are you sure you're well enough to—"

"Yes." Her mouth was dry. Her hands were fisted tightly enough that it hurt. "Please, Gabriel, carry me to the taxi. Going by the river . . ." Then she toppled, hoping that he'd listen.

When Leslie woke in a patch of grass by the river, she was relieved. She could feel relief. Irial didn't drink her good feelings away. That should make her happy, knowing she wasn't numb. If not for the other thing—that maddening craving for Irial's touch, the awful sickening longing when darker emotions filled her to choking but didn't touch *her* emotions—she might be okay.

A bit away from her, several of Gabriel's Hounds waited and watched. They didn't frighten her. They seemed pleased that she liked them. A few times, she'd seen Ani and Tish— and in that shock-free way she lived now, she'd accepted their mixed heritage without pause. She'd come to terms with the realization that Ani—and Tish and Rabbit—had known that the ink exchange would change her.

"But you're strong enough, Les, really," Ani had insisted.

"And if I'm not?"

"You will be. It's for Iri. We need him to be strong." Ani had hugged her. *"You're his savior. The court's so much stronger. He's so much stronger."*

Ignoring the Hounds, Leslie walked along the river until she came to a warehouse where she and Rianne used to go to smoke. She slid open the window they'd climbed in together so often and made her way to the second floor—just high enough to see the river. Out here, away from everyone, she felt the closest to normal she had since the morning she'd left her house with Irial.

She sat watching the river race away. Her feet dangled out the window. There were no mortals, no faeries, no Irial. Away from all of them, she felt less consumed. The world was back in order, more stable somehow now that she was on her own. *Is it the distance?*

It didn't matter, though: she felt his approach. Then Irial was in the street, looking up at her. "Are you going to come down from there?"

"Maybe."

"Leslie—"

She stood up, balancing on the balls of her feet, hands above her head like she was preparing to dive into a pool. "I should be afraid, Irial. I'm not, though."

"I am." His voice sounded jagged, not tender this time, not reassuring. "I'm terrified."

She swayed back and forth as the wind batted against her.

In that implacable way he always seemed to have, Irial began, "We'll get better at this and—"

"Will it hurt you if I step forward?" Her voice was dispassionate, but she felt excitement at the idea. *Not fear, though.* There still wasn't any fear, and that's what she wanted—not to hurt, but to feel normal. She hadn't been sure before, but in that moment she knew that's what she needed: the whole of herself, all the parts, all the feelings. *And they're as far gone as normal is.*

"Would you feel it? Would *I* feel it if I fell? Would it hurt?" She looked down at him: he was beautiful, and despite the fact that he'd stolen her choices, she looked at him with a strange tenderness. He kept her safe. The mess she was in might be his fault, but he didn't abandon her to the madness it caused. He took her into his arms no matter how often she sought him, no matter that he'd had to move his court, that he looked positively exhausted. Tender feelings surged as she thought about it, about him.

When he spoke, it wasn't to say anything gentle. He pointed at the ground. "So jump."

Anger, fear, doubt, rolled over her—not pleasant, but real. For a brief moment, they were hers and *real* this time. "I could."

"You could," he repeated. "I won't stop you. I don't want to steal your will, Leslie."

"You have, though." She watched Gabriel walk up and whisper to Irial. "You did this. I'm not happy. I want to be."

"So jump." He didn't take his gaze away from her as he told Gabriel, "Keep everyone back. No mortals. No fey in this street."

Leslie sat down again. "You'd catch me."

"I would, but if the fall would please you"—he shrugged—"I'd rather you were happy."

"Me too." She rubbed her eyes, as if tears would come. *They won't.* Crying wasn't something she did anymore—neither was worrying, raging, or any other of the unpleasant emotions. Parts of her were gone, taken away as surely as the rest of her life. There were no classes, no melodramatic Rianne; there'd be no laughing in the kitchen at Verlaine's, no dancing at the Crow's Nest. And there was no way to undo any of the things that had changed. *Going backward is never an option.* But staying where she was wasn't true happiness either. She was living in a hazy dream—or nightmare. She didn't know if she could tell the difference just now.

"I'm *not* happy," she whispered. "I don't know what I am, but this isn't happiness."

Irial began climbing the building, grabbing hold of crumbling brick and broken metal, piercing his hands on the sharp edges, leaving a trail of bloody handprints as he made his way up the wall to her.

"Grab hold," he said as he paused in the window frame.

And she did. She clung to him, holding on to him like he was the only solid thing left in the world as he finished scaling the building. When he reached the barren rooftop, he stopped and lowered her feet to the ground.

"I don't want you to be unhappy."

"I am."

"You're not." He cupped her face in his hands. "I know everything you feel, love. You feel no sorrow, no anger, no worries. How is this a bad thing?"

"It's not real. . . . I can't live like this. I won't."

She must have sounded serious enough because he nodded. "Give me a few more days, and I'll have a solution."

"Will you tell—"

"No." He watched her face with something almost vulnerable in his eyes. "It's best for everyone if we don't talk of this. Just trust me."

CHAPTER 32

Irial had spent several days watching Leslie struggle with the urge to feel something of the emotions she'd lost now that he drank them through her. It was an unexpected dilemma. She'd stepped into traffic, provoked the increasingly aggressive Bananach, and interfered in an altercation with two armed mortals: the moment he relaxed his guard she was out endangering herself. She didn't make sense to him, but mortals rarely did.

Today she was exhausted—as was he.

He pulled the door to the bedroom closed, tearing his attention away from his sleeping girl. She required so much careful handling, so much hiding of his true feelings. He'd not expected a mortal to change him; that wasn't part of the plan.

Gabriel looked up as Irial sat at the other end of the sofa and resumed the conversation they'd been having every time Leslie napped. "We haven't had a good party with mortals in a while." He held out an already open long-neck bottle.

"That's because they break too easily." Irial took the bottle, sniffed it, and asked, "Is this actually *real* beer? Just beer?"

"Far as you know." Gabriel leaned back on the sofa, legs stretched out, boot-clad feet tapping in tune to some song that only he heard. "So, party with the mortals?"

"Can you get some that'll survive for a few nights?" Irial glanced at the closed door, behind which his own too-fragile mortal slept fitfully. "It'll be better if we don't need to replace them each week. Just gather the same ones up every few days until we see how it goes."

He didn't add that he wasn't sure how well Leslie would cope with channeling too many mortals' deaths, fear, and pain. If there were enough of them and they were terrified and angry and lustful enough, she'd be so intoxicated that he doubted that she'd notice a few deaths, but if too many of them died at once, it could upset her.

"A bit of war might be good too. Bananach is testing every boundary you set. Give her a small skirmish?" The fact that Gabriel had mentioned it at all was reason enough to worry.

"She doesn't have the support yet to get very far." Irial hated that she was always there at his heels, looking for weaknesses, stirring her small mutinies. In time, she would wear him down. If he didn't keep the court strong enough, she would rally them to true rebellion. It wouldn't be the first time. He needed to lull her back to moderate rumblings of war, not give her reason to get more bold. *First get Leslie situated.*

"Bananach tried for Niall again." Gabriel flashed his teeth in his glee. "Boy still holds his own in a fight."

Irial would've enjoyed seeing that. Niall tended to go for logic before violence, but when he did indulge in a fight, he did it like he did everything: with singular focus. "He's . . . well still?"

Gabriel shrugged, but his gleeful expression wasn't dimming. "He'll come back sooner or later, Iri. You need to think long term, that's all."

Irial didn't—*couldn't*—ponder what Niall would do just now. He had hopes, but hope wasn't a solution. Gabriel was right: Irial did need to think long term. He'd been too focused on his initial ideas. It had been too long since he'd needed to truly plan. During the nine centuries Beira ruled unopposed, Irial had allowed himself to grow weak, to assume that their nourishment would always be so easy. The past few months of having a true Summer King and a new Winter Queen had shown him how quickly change could come—and he hadn't been ready.

"Tell Bananach to gather whoever wants to go and start a little chaos with Sorcha. I can't nourish everyone long term. If the seasonal courts are determined to be uncooperative for now, let's see what we can do with her royal tediousness. If anyone can provoke Sorcha, Bananach is our best choice."

Gabriel's forearms grew dark with the details he'd carry

to Bananach—and hopefully satisfy her enough that she wouldn't be underfoot for a while.

"And Ani"—Irial paused to measure his words carefully—"bring Tish and Rabbit to stay with her. Have them move into the house where we took Guin. With Sorcha's penchant for stealing half-fey, they'll be too much at risk once Bananach starts her assault. Now that peace is here, Sorcha won't keep the High Court in seclusion."

For a moment, Gabriel hesitated. Then he said, "You'll be careful with my pups. Ani's being able to feed off mortals doesn't make her any less mine. Experimenting on—"

"We won't do anything she doesn't consent to." Irial lit a cigarette. He'd taken to smoking more frequently since Leslie had come to them. *Worry, for her.* He took a few drags before he spoke again. "Let Ani loose with the mortals, too. I want to see what she can drink off them. Maybe she's what we need to sort this all out."

"That'll mean two . . . parties . . . because I'm not going in there if my pup is." Gabriel's menace had vanished under his disgust at the idea of his pup loose in a crowd. "She's a good girl."

"She is, Gabe. Pick a few Hounds you'd trust to mind her. Two rooms, the ones across the hall. We'll see what it'll take to fulfill me—and the court, before Leslie slips into a coma. We'll watch her, keep track of her reactions, and stop when we get close to her limits." Irial cringed at the idea. A few of the mortals seemed to suffer neural damage if they were pushed too far.

"Gather up a few of Keenan's Summer Girls too. They work well as enticement for good behavior. Prizes for those with the most surviving mortals come dawn." Irial lowered his voice at the sound of movement in the bedroom. Leslie shouldn't wake just yet, but she was too stubborn to sleep as she should.

Irial held a hand out to Leslie as she walked into the room. She took his hand and curled into his arms.

"You'll take care of the party plans then?" Irial asked, absently petting Leslie's hair as she nestled closer.

Gabriel nodded. "Need at least two days, though."

"That works." Irial turned his attention back to his girl then, pleased to hear the soft click of the door closing behind Gabriel. "If you can be patient for two more days, we can work on your feeling a little less trapped by this." He motioned to the feathered vine that bound them together.

"What are—"

"No questions, Leslie. That's the condition." He kissed her forehead. "You want more freedom, room to roam?"

She nodded mutely.

"I just need you to stop putting yourself at risk. If you keep doing that, I won't be able to give you your space." He watched her face as he spoke, wondering yet again what she'd be like if she could keep some of her emotions, not all of them, but a few.

"Will what you're doing hurt?" She looked excited at the idea for a moment, interested in the idea of feeling the very thing from which she'd been seeking oblivion.

"Did the first couple weeks with me hurt?"

"I don't remember." She licked her lips as if she could taste his worries. She couldn't because of their tie, but sometimes he felt the tug as she tried to reverse the flow, as if she'd steal *his* emotions. "I don't have many clear memories of *that*."

"Exactly."

"You're cruel, Irial." She wasn't angry, accusing, none of those things. She couldn't be.

And for a moment, he realized that they both wished she could be. *My Shadow Girl.* He kissed her before he made the mistake of saying what he was thinking.

"I can be, Leslie. And if you keep trying to do damage to yourself, I will be." He had a brief hope that—even without feeling fear—her basic intellect would be enough to make her realize that this wasn't something either of them wanted. But she sighed, as if it weren't a threat but a reward, so he asked, "You remember Niall's scars?"

"I do." She watched him carefully, staying motionless.

"You won't like me if I'm cruel." He lifted her to her feet.

She stood motionless, hand outstretched. "I don't like you now."

"We don't lie," he reminded her as he took her hand and pulled her into his arms yet again.

"I'm mortal, Irial. I can lie all I want to," she whispered.

He let go of her, hating that it was hard to do. "Get changed, love."

They had a riot to attend. He hadn't walked her through

hospitals, sanitariums, or the like—*yet*—but tonight he'd take her to the feasts of anger. If he filled her up with all the darkness she could stand and channeled it out to his court, then he could let her breathe for a little while. It was either that or lose her, and right now, that didn't feel like an option. He'd been trying to build her tolerance slowly, but her stubborn streak—and his desire not to destroy her—had made his timeline no longer workable. Not for the first time since the damnable peace had begun, Irial wanted nothing more than to walk away from his court, from his responsibilities—except now he wanted to take Leslie with him.

CHAPTER 33

Over the next week, he pushed her until she was so shadow drunk that she retched, but they didn't discuss it.

They fell into a routine she thought she could accept. Irial didn't tell her what happened during the nights, and she didn't ask. It wasn't a solution—not really—but she felt better. She told herself it was progress of a sort. Sometimes, she felt brief tendrils of lost emotions when Irial kept the connection between them tightly closed, when the shadowed vine stretched like a sleeping serpent between them. In those moments she could lie to herself and say she was happy, that there were benefits to being cosseted so—then the weight of what she had become rolled over her until the cramps of need made her insensible.

No different than any other addict.

Her drug might have a pulse and a voice, but he was a drug all the same. And she'd sunk to depths that would make her dissolve in shame if such feelings were still in her reach. They weren't, though: Irial drank them down like some exotic elixir. And when the awfulness reached its pinnacle, Irial's touch was all that would assuage the maw that yawned open inside of her.

What is it doing to me? Will the darkness consume me?

Irial didn't have that answer; he couldn't tell her what it would do to her body, her health, her longevity—anything. All he could tell her was that he was there, that he'd protect her, that he'd keep her safe and well.

Now that she was able to go out walking regularly—away from Irial—she knew it was only a matter of time until she saw Niall. Of all the people from her life before the ink exchange, he was the one she was loath to encounter. He'd been beside Irial once: he knew what the Dark Court was like, what the world she lived in was like, and that lack of secrecy was something she didn't know how to deal with.

She'd looked for him, and today he was there. He stood across the street, outside the Music Exchange, the shop where Rianne was most often found. Beside him was a man—a human—playing music that was foreign and familiar on a bodhran. Her pulse picked up the rhythm, the pace of the music settling in her stomach as if each touch of the beater were on her skin, in her veins.

Then Niall turned and found her watching him.

"Leslie." His lips formed the word, but the sound was too slight to hear.

Traffic on the street moved faster than seemed safe to

enter, but Niall wasn't human, hadn't ever been human. He slid through gaps that weren't quite there, and then he was beside her, lifting her hands to his lips, crying tears she wasn't able to shed.

"He wouldn't let me see you," he said.

"I told him not to. I wasn't in a place where I'd have wanted anyone to see me." She looked away, watching the faeries watching them.

"I'd kill him if I could," he said, sounding crueler than Irial ever did.

"I don't want that. Not—"

"You *would* if he hadn't done this to you."

"He's not awful."

"Don't. Please." Niall held her, silent but for the sound of his tears. He acted like it was her he wanted, like all that she thought he'd felt was real, but she wondered. That urge she'd felt *before*, that compulsion to touch Niall, to press closer—it was gone. *Had it been an illusion? Was it there but swallowed down by Irial?* She looked at Niall's beautiful scarred face and felt a flash of tenderness, but there was no temptation.

Along the street, the faeries watched with expressions gleeful and heinous. Chattering and murmurs rose as they speculated on what Irial's fey would do, what Irial himself would do when he heard.

Kill the boy. He will.

Give him grounds to start a melee.

Nothing. She's not reason enough to—

Is. Irial never took a mortal till this one. She must be—

Irial hasn't allowed us to strike his lovely Gancanagh *in almost* always.

Torture him then? Make her *do it?*

They chortled and carried on until Leslie turned her eyes to the shadows and shot a pleading look at one of Gabriel's Hounds. In less time than it would've taken to speak, the Hound cleared the crowd, sent them scurrying by threat or force, hefting a few of them like misshapen balls and launching them down the street. Horrid splattering noises and shrieks resounded until even the man with the bodhran paused for a moment, looking about as if he heard some slight echo of the horrors he couldn't quite sense.

"They listen to you?" Niall asked.

"They do. They are good to me. No one has hurt me." She touched his chest where she knew his scars were hidden. Those scars told the answers to so many questions about him, about Irial, about the world she now called her home. She added, "No one has done anything but what I've asked of them. . . ."

"Including Irial?" Niall's face was as unreadable as his voice. His emotions, though, she felt those—hope and longing and fear and anger. He was a tangled mess.

Leslie wished she could lie, but she didn't want to, not to him, not knowing that he *couldn't* lie to her by word or emotion. "Mostly. He doesn't touch me without asking, if that's what you mean . . . but he made me this without asking, and I'm not sure anymore what's my choice and what's his. When I . . . I *need* him or I'm . . . it kills me, Niall. It's like starving, like something eating me alive from deep inside. It doesn't hurt. *I* don't hurt, but I know it should. The pain isn't there, but it doesn't stop me from screaming under it. Only Iri makes it . . . better. He makes everything better."

Niall leaned close to her ear and whispered, "I can stop it. I think I can undo it. I can get what I need to break his tie to you." And he told her that Aislinn would give him sunlight and the Winter Queen would give him frost, and he would burn and freeze the ink from her skin. "It should work. You'd be free of him. All of them."

Leslie didn't answer, didn't tell him yes or no. She couldn't.

"It's your choice." Niall cradled her face in his hands, looking at her the same way he had before, when she was not this. "You have a choice. I can give you that."

"What if it makes it worse?"

"Try to think what you'd choose if you weren't under his sway. Is this"—he paused—"what you would have chosen?"

"No. But I can't unchoose it either. I can't pretend I haven't become this. I won't be who I was before . . . and if the feelings come back, if I *can* leave, how do I live with what I've—"

"You just do. The things you do when you're desperate aren't who you are." Niall's expression had grown fierce, angry.

"Really?" She remembered the feeling, that moment when she looked at the ground and knew that even if Irial caught her the first time she jumped, there would be other times when she felt that desperation. The emotions she could just barely touch in that moment were a part of her as well. She was the person who chose this route. She thought back over the signs and warnings that something was amiss. She thought of the shadows she'd seen in Rabbit's office. She thought of the questions she hadn't asked Aislinn or Seth or Rabbit or herself. She thought of the shame she'd bottled up instead of seeking help. That was who she was; those were parts of her. They were all choices. To not act is a choice too.

"I don't think so, Niall," she heard herself say. Her voice wasn't soft or afraid. "Even under the addiction, it's me. I might not have had as many choices, but I'm still choosing."

She thought again of standing in the window of the warehouse. She could have chosen to jump. She hadn't. *It would be giving up, giving in if I actually jumped. Isn't it better to endure?* The person she was under the weight of her addiction was stronger than she'd realized she could be.

"I want a choice that doesn't hurt Irial or me," she said, and then she left him. Her choice would come—maybe not now, maybe not the choice Niall held out, and she wasn't going to let Irial or Niall or anyone else make it for her.

Not again.

CHAPTER 34

The moon was well overhead when Irial crept across the room. It wouldn't do for mortals to see doors opening and closing on their own, so he stepped into the hall wearing his mortal-friendly facade. Several of the Hounds were standing guard outside the room, invisible to any mortals that might pass. There weren't any in the hall, though, so Irial let go of his glamour and shut the suite door behind him.

"Keep her inside if she wakes," he told the Hounds. "No wandering tonight."

"She doesn't cooperate so well. We could just follow, keep her safe and—"

"No."

Another Hound objected, "We don't want to hurt her . . . and she's so unhappy if we stop her from going out."

"So block the doors." Irial grimaced. He wasn't the only one swayed too much by his bond with Leslie. His weak-

ness for her flowed into his whole court: they all had an
unreasonably hard time doing anything Leslie disliked.

I weaken them. My affection for her cripples them.

The only way to work around it seemed to be keeping
her from asking his faeries to do anything asinine. The
alternative, breaking her irreparably, wasn't a path he
wanted to consider.

Could I? He suppressed the answer before he let himself
go further in that thought. Handing Niall over to his court
had been horrific enough that he still dreamed of it. For
centuries, he'd dreamed of how Niall had rejected him
afterward. Weak kings didn't thrive. Irial knew that, but
knowing didn't undo the ache when Niall chose to go to
another court. That was a long-dead pain.

Being tied to Leslie, indulging in parties with the mortals as he and Niall once had, these things had brought
long-silenced memories back to the surface. It was yet
another proof that her mortal influence had tainted him,
changed him. It wasn't a change he liked. The vine that
stretched like a shadow between him and his mortal grew
suddenly visible in the air before him as his agitation
increased.

He told the Hounds, "Don't speak to her other than to
tell her that I forbade you to let her leave the room. Tell her
you'll bleed for it if she goes anywhere. If that doesn't work,
tell her *Ani* will."

They snarled at him, but they'd tell Leslie. Hopefully, it

would inspire her to obey his wishes for a few hours while he cleaned up the latest mess.

Inside the first room the floor was strewn with the weeping mortals who'd survived the most recent round of festivities. They'd endured longer than the last batch, but so many broke in mind or body too easily. They were wailing as the madness of what they'd seen and done settled on them. Give them a few drugs, a little glamour, and some simple entice-ments, and mortals willingly dived into the depths of hidden depravity. Afterward, in the light, when the bodies of those who'd died were entwined with the still living, there were those who didn't know how to hold on to their sanity.

"Chela's found a few sturdy ones to replace them. They're enjoying the amenities over in the other room." Gabriel tossed a girl's handbag into one of the bins and then motioned at a corpse.

"Dibs." Two of the Ly Ergs lifted her. A third opened the door. They'd take her somewhere else in the city to leave her for the mortals to find. "She's ours."

"No posing this one," Gabriel snarled as the Ly Ergs left. The faery who opened the door lifted his hand in a dismis-sive gesture, flashing his bright red palm.

Irial stepped over a couple who stared blindly past him.

"She kept encouraging them to fight over her. Whatever's spliced with that new X made her violent." Gabriel emptied pockets and stripped away some of the shredded clothes, directing grinning thistle-fey as he went about the grisly task. "They've been posing the ones they like. They set tea for several yesterday."

"Tea?"

One of the Ly Ergs grinned cheekily. "We got them proper things, too. They'd have been naked but for the hats and gloves we nicked."

A leannan-sidhe added, "We painted their faces, as well. They were lovely."

Irial wanted to chastise them, but it wasn't any worse than most of the things they'd done for sport over the centuries. *The Dark King doesn't require kindness for mortals.* He tamped down his unease and said, "Maybe we should set up a stage over in the park by the kingling's loft. . . . A scene from *Midsummer Night's Dream* . . . or—"

"No. The other mortal that was scrawling plays then. What's the one with the parade of sins?" A Ly Erg rubbed his blood-red hands over his face. "The fun one."

"I like sins," a leannan-sidhe murmured.

One of Jenny's kin picked up a corpse. "We've got our gluttony right here. This one serviced every willing faery in the room."

They were laughing.

"That's *lust*, sister. Gluttons have the extra meat on their middles. Like this one."

The surly Ly Erg repeated, "What's the play?"

"Faustus. The Tragical History of Doctor Faustus," Leslie said. Her voice was soft, but they all turned to the doorway where she stood. Her lacy pajamas were mostly covered by

the robe she'd slipped on. "Marlowe wrote it. Unless you believe the theory that Marlowe and Shakespeare were the same person."

None of the faeries answered. Had it been anyone else, they'd have snarled at her or invited her to join the fun. With Leslie, though, they did neither.

She pulled a pack of Irial's cigarettes out of her robe pocket and lit one, silently watching as they gathered the newly mad mortals. When they approached her, she opened the door for them.

They crossed the threshold and extended their own glamour to mask what they carried. She saw it, though. She got a close-up view of wide-eyed madmen, a fresh corpse, and bare flesh. Her horror and disgust peaked. She didn't feel it, of course, but the rush of emotions she should feel swarmed to Irial.

Once the faeries were all gone, she walked toward him, flicking ash on the red-stained floor. Her bare feet were stark white against those stains. "Why?"

"Don't ask me that." Irial saw the fine trembling in her hands, watched her resist the backlash from the feelings he'd sought out.

"Tell me why." She dropped the cigarette and ground it out under her bare foot. The trembling became worse as waves of mortal terror surged through her.

"You don't want this answer, love." He reached out for her, knowing that despite her best intentions, the backlash would soon pull her under.

She backed away. "Don't. I want to"—she stopped—"it's my fault, isn't it? That's why you're—"

"No."

"I thought faeries didn't lie." Her knees gave, and she dropped to the floor. She knelt on a wide red stain.

"I'm not lying. It's not your fault." His attempts to be the King of Nightmares, the Dark King, all faded because she looked lost. It was him who faltered, not her.

She gripped the carpet, bloodying her fingertips as she tried to hold on to the floor so as not to reach out to him. "Why were they here? Why are they . . ."

She obviously wasn't going to stop asking questions, so he stopped avoiding them. "If I'm sated, I feed the court enough that you can have some freedom. The court starves a little, but not enough to cripple them . . . and as long as you stayed in the suite you didn't need to know."

"So we tormented them so—"

"No. *You* didn't torment anyone." He watched her grasp at the horror she wanted to feel, felt it slither into his skin. He sighed. "Don't overreact."

She laughed, a sound as far from humorous as a scream would be.

He sank to the floor beside her.

"There are worse things." He didn't tell her that those worse things were inevitable if the peace between the seasonal courts grew much stronger, that this was just one step in their path. She stared at him for several heartbeats, and then she leaned forward and laid her head against his chest.

"Can you pick criminals or something?"

Somewhere inside he was saddened by her acceptance of these mortals' deaths, but that was her mortal essence tainting his judgment. He pushed the sorrow away. "I can try. . . . I can't change what I need you for, but I would spare you details of it."

She tensed in his arms. "And if I can't take it? What then? What if my mind . . ."

He said it then, admitted his weakness, "I hadn't planned this part, Leslie. I just needed your body to stay alive. Most of the mortals from the earlier exchanges . . . they didn't fare as well, but I'd like you not to be comatose. If that means a few other mortals die or slip into their own minds while you black out for a few hours or days—"

"Then that's what you'll do," she whispered.

CHAPTER 35

Niall had stopped by the loft to gather a few belongings when Aislinn walked in. "I don't want to discuss it again," he started, but then Aislinn stepped to the side. Leslie stood behind her. She was wan, with dark circles under her eyes. Bluish veins were so clear through her skin that, to his vision, she had a slight blue tint to her.

Aislinn said, "She wants to talk to you . . . not to me." Then his queen-no-more left, closing the door behind her, leaving Niall alone with Leslie.

"Has something happened?" he asked.

"Irial sends his regards." Her movements were as stilted as her words. She wandered away to stare out the window. Shadows danced in the air around her; he'd seen those same shadows dance in Irial's eyes, formless figures that leaped and spun on the edge of the abyss. Now they hovered around Leslie, a retinue of nightmare's handmaidens.

Niall didn't know what to do or say or think. So he waited.

"Can we leave?" She looked over her shoulder. "I can't do this here."

"Do what?"

She watched him, dispassionately it seemed. "What we talked about *before*."

And he knew that whatever she wasn't saying was horrific enough that she'd decided to leave Irial.

"Will you help me, Niall?" she asked. "I need to set things right."

For a moment, Niall wasn't sure if it was Leslie or Irial asking: her voice sounded wrong, her words not matching the intonations he'd heard from her before. But it didn't matter. The shadows danced around her, and he gave the only answer he could offer either of them: "Yes."

Leslie felt the strange whisper of Irial's nature rustling through her, even now. And it was a comfort, even though she was hoping to end it. What he gave her, what he cost her, it wasn't right for either of them. She would find it easier if she could call him evil, but none of this was about values or ethics. Those answers were too simple. Irial did what he deemed necessary to save his fey, what he thought best for his court—including her. It wasn't what was best for her or for the people who'd been brought to terror in the hands of the Dark Court. It wasn't best for the thousands of mortals who'd inevitably get drawn into Irial's plans once she grew less important to him or he grew more desperate.

She smiled at Niall. They stood in her old room. She hadn't been back there since she'd left with Irial. When she'd walked in, the house was empty, as if no one else had been there in weeks. If she could feel it, she might worry about her father, but as it was she merely noted that she wanted to worry.

Deal with that later. After.

Niall pulled her into his arms, holding her as securely as if she'd been falling only to be snatched back from the edge. His hand cradled the back of her head. "Will you look poorly on me if I admit that I wish I weren't the one to do this?"

"No." Later, though, when Irial's influence wore off, she suspected she might.

"Come on." She took his hand in hers and led him to the bed, her bed, inside her house. It was safe. *Because of Irial.*

Niall stood motionless as she sat down on the edge of the faded rose covers. She could feel rare brushes with her feelings—thanks to what Irial had done, thanks to the mortals who'd fallen into the arms of the Dark Court—not all of her feelings, but a few of the stronger ones. She felt disgust at the way the faeries treated the dead bodies, horror at the fact that people had suffered because of her. She cringed at the sin-sick weight of it . . . and at her yearning to return to numbness so she didn't have to feel it. That's what she'd pursued—numbness—and it wasn't worth the cost to her or anyone else.

She pulled Niall toward her; he looked at her with sad eyes.

Her stomach clenched at the fear that threatened to smother her—not in the way it once had, but in hunger.

Irial's hunger.

Then her fear fled, swallowed down by Irial as he sat in one of his clubs, surrounded by the fey who'd been slowly flocking to his side. Hopefully Irial's hungers would take the edge off the pain she knew was coming.

She rolled over, removing her shirt as she did, and tried not to think of what was about to happen. Eyes closed, she said, "Please?"

Niall lowered his hands onto her skin, onto her ink, onto that mark where Irial's presence was anchored into her skin. His touch burned from the small ball of sunlight that Aislinn had given him at the loft, that he'd carried inside him, that he'd brought.

At my request.

The frost that the other queen—the Winter Queen—had given him followed the sunlight: Leslie thought she felt icicles piercing her skin. And she screamed, though she tore at her lip to keep that sound inside. She screamed as she'd done only once before.

This isn't Niall's fault. MY choice. Mine.

"Forgive me," he begged as he forced the sunlight and

frost into her skin, freezing the tears in the ink, searing
away the tinge of Irial's blood that was blended into that
ink, killing the roots of the black vine that Irial's ink had
anchored in her body.

"*Leslie?*" *Irial whispered.*

She could see him clearly enough that he looked like a
hologram in the room. If her eyes hadn't been closed, she
would have believed he really was there. Startled, he stood,
unsettling the faery who'd been curled on his lap. "*What are
you doing?*"

"*Choosing.*" She bit the coverlet to keep from screaming
again. Her hands were fisted so tight that she felt the cover
rip. Her spine bowed. Niall's knee was on her back, holding
her down.

Tears were soaking the blanket under Leslie's face.

"*I'm* mine. *Not anyone else's.*"

"*I'm still yours, though. That won't ever change, Shadow
Girl.*" And then he was gone, and her emotions crashed
over her.

Niall pulled his hands away, and she turned her head to
look at him. He sat beside her, staring down at his hands.
"I'm sorry. Gods, I'm sorry."

"I'm not." She wasn't sure of much else, but she knew
that. Then the agony in her skin, the memories, the surge
of horror, it was too much: she rolled over and threw up in
the wastebasket. Her entire body clenched as pain coursed
through her. Tears joined the perspiration on her face as hot

and cold flashes switched in and out of control. Muscles she hadn't known she had were knotting up in response to the pain inside her.

She smiled despite it all; for just a moment, she smiled. She was free. It hurt like hell, but she was free.

CHAPTER 36

Leslie drifted in and out of consciousness for several days while the world moved around her. Niall stayed beside her. Aislinn and Seth visited. Ani and Tish and Rabbit visited. Gabriel visited, carrying more flowers than could be considered reasonable. He set the flowers down, clasped Niall's shoulder and nodded, kissed Leslie's brow, and left. The others all talked—words of support and apology from Aislinn, praise from Seth and Rabbit, forgiveness for leaving the court from Tish and Ani. Irial did not come to her.

She lay on her stomach wearing jeans and a bra. She hadn't spoken more than a few words yet. There had been too many things in her mind for her to try to formulate sentences. Neither her father nor her brother ever showed up at the house. She didn't know where they were, if they were coming back, or if they were being *prevented* from coming back. She was in her home—healing and safe. That was what mattered right then.

Niall was putting some sort of soothing cream on the sun- and frost-burned skin of her back. She turned her head to look at him. She saw them, stretched across the room: burned tendrils of the shadowy vine flowing from her skin—a connection still, but not a conduit. "It's never going to go away, is it?"

Niall stared at the blackened vine. "I don't know. I couldn't see it before. I can now."

"It's closed off. That's what matters. And it's not going to open again." She sat up and had to bite her lip to keep from crying out.

"Are you . . . how do you feel?" He was tentative, still not pushing her to words or actions. He was near enough that she could take his arm if she needed support, but he didn't get in her space.

"Awful, but real," she said.

"The aloe should help. It's the best I can do. The mortal things won't work since it was faery. . . . I called Aislinn and—"

"It's good, Niall. Really. I don't mind that it hurts." She watched him look at her with such sorrow that it broke her heart to see it, to realize how difficult the past days had been for him too.

"Help me up?" She held out a hand so he could steady her until she saw how she was going to handle moving. Sometimes standing was painful enough that she'd fallen back down. This time she wavered a bit as Niall helped her to the bathroom, but it wasn't as awful as it had been. She was recovering, physically and mentally. *It's time.* She leaned on the doorframe and motioned toward the cupboard under the sink. "There's a hand mirror under there."

Without comment he got it out, and she turned in front of the large mirror and held the hand mirror up so she could see her back. The ink in her skin had faded to white and gray. It was as beautiful as before, but it'd been bleached, lightened by the sunlight and frost Niall had pressed into her skin.

My *art now. My body.* She lowered the mirror and smiled. It wasn't the tattoo that had changed her, had given her repossession of her body. It was her actions, her choices. It was finding the path when it looked like there weren't any paths to be found.

"Leslie?" Niall stepped behind her and looked at her in the mirror, holding the reflection of her gaze. "Are you going to be all right?"

She turned so they were face-to-face and gave him back the words he'd offered her their first night together: "I survived. Isn't that what matters?"

"It is." He pulled her closer and held her carefully.

They stood there, quiet and together, until she started to sway. Blushing, she said, "I'm still weak, I guess."

"You're not weak at all. Wounded, but that's nothing to be ashamed of." He helped her to the bed. Hesitantly he said, "Aislinn would come care for you if you'd allow it. I've left them, left Keenan, but they'll look after you. We can sort it out, and then—"

"Niall?" She tried to keep her tone gentle as she said, "I . . . I can't deal with your faery courts right now. I just want my life. This"—she gestured around her room—"isn't good, but it's better than your world. I don't want to be a part of the faery world."

"I can't change what I am. I'm not a part of the court, but I can't *not* interact at all with my world. . . . I . . ." He let his words fade.

This wasn't a conversation she wanted to have, not now, but it was there. "I still feel . . . something, whatever it was, for you, but right now . . . I need to start over, somewhere else . . . on my own."

"I tried to keep you safe." He told her that he'd kept guard over her for months, that he—and other of Aislinn's faeries—had walked beside her in the streets of Huntsdale. He told her that he'd tried to not speak to her before because Aislinn had ordered him not to, that she didn't want Leslie drawn into their world—and that he'd thought his queen wise to decide thus.

"I want to be with you. I'm not with the court now. I'm . . . solitary. I could come with you . . . take care of—"

"I'm sorry," she said.

"Right. You need time, but when you're ready . . . or if you need anything *at all,* ever . . ."

"I know." She leaned back on the pillows. "Can you call Ash to come over? I need to talk to her before I see Irial."

"Irial? Why would you—"

"I'm not the only mortal. There's plenty of people he

could replace me with"—she kept the pain out of her voice, but she still had to pause—"if he hasn't already. I'm not going to walk away and leave someone else in my place." She thought about the weeping mortals on the floor, the bloody fights she'd seen the starts of before she blacked out, the knowledge that this was all Irial's being *careful*, gentle with her. What he'd be like without that caution was too much to consider. "I need to talk to Ash before I see him. I can't wait too long."

Niall sighed, but he went. She heard the front door open and close as he went to seek whoever waited outside. And she let herself drift to sleep, knowing that she was safe, free, and going to find a way to make sure that her freedom wasn't at the cost of another girl's life.

When Leslie walked into the suite that night, there was no one there but Irial. He didn't comment, didn't ask questions. He poured her a drink and held it out.

Silently she took it and walked over to the sofa. He followed but didn't sit near her. He pulled a desk chair over. It was uncomfortable to see him sit where she couldn't touch him.

"Are you okay?"

She laughed. "Niall thought it was unsafe to come here, and the first thing you ask is if I'm okay. Whatever you did to him must have been hellish."

"Our boy's not as quick to forgive as you are." Irial smiled, a sad smile that made her want to ask questions.

She didn't. She moved, trying to find a comfortable position that made the pain on her back less awful. She was glad it was there, but it still brought tears to her eyes when she moved. "I couldn't watch people die for me. Or whatever else you weren't telling me."

"It would've been worse in time," he admitted. It wasn't an apology, but she hadn't really expected one.

"Do I want to know?"

He lit one of his seemingly constant cigarettes, watching her in a way that was almost comforting in its familiarity. Then he made a dismissive gesture with his hand, the cherry of the cigarette waving in the air as he did so. "War, more effort on the drug front, an increase in the number of dark fey kept nearer to me. Maybe a bit of negotiation with Far Dorcha's fey in the sex and death markets."

"Would I have survived it?"

"It's possible." He shrugged. "You were doing pretty well. Most of the mortals don't stay conscious as long as you did. And since it was me that you were bound to . . . you really might have. I wanted you to survive."

"I've talked to Ash, and if you take another mortal—"

"Are you threatening me, love?" He grinned at her.

"No. I'm telling you that I don't want you to replace me."

His smile faded. "Well, then . . . and if I do?"

"Then Ash will work with the other one, the Winter Queen, and *they*'ll threaten you, hurt our—your—court." She watched him, not sure that her approach was the right one, but certain that she couldn't let someone else suffer like she had. "But here's the thing they *don't* get: I don't want you to be hurt. It would hurt me. If you let some other mortal channel that awfulness for you, that would hurt me. What they'll do to you when they find out, that will hurt me."

"And?"

"And you promised me that you wouldn't let anyone hurt me." She waited as he sat staring at her, smoking silently. Leslie's friendship with Aislinn might not be anywhere near repaired, but if the advice she'd given Leslie worked, it would go a long way toward setting things right. For now, that was Leslie's goal: getting things put to rights—her life, her future, and if she could, things with those who mattered to her. Irial was still on that list.

"The Dark Court is what it is. I won't tell them to change their natures to appease—"

"You're playing word games, Irial." She gestured for him to come closer.

His surprise was enough to offset her twinge of fear. He ground out his cigarette and moved over to sit on the sofa, near enough to touch—but not actually touching her.

She turned so they were facing each other. "You gave me your vow, Irial. I get that now. I'm telling you what will happen if you let them wound you: you will be hurting me, and if you know that and still take another mortal . . . What you are, what you do isn't my business, but doing another ink exchange, starting wars in my world, killing mortals, that *is* my business, and if my caring for you means that you can't do it . . . I'll admit that I still care."

He reached for her and she didn't flinch. She closed her eyes and gave herself over to his kisses. It was Irial who stopped.

"You aren't lying." He gave her the strangest look, a bit like awe and a bit like fear.

Having her autonomy back was a beautiful thing. And she realized that how she felt about Irial hadn't changed all that much.

"Tell me what you feel for me?" she asked.

He backed up just a little, no longer holding her. "Why?"

"Because I asked."

"I'm glad you won't end up comatose or dead," he said, his tone revealing nothing.

"And?" She watched him wrestle with his temptation to tell her. If he didn't want to, she couldn't make him.

"If you wanted to stay . . ."

"I can't." She squeezed his hand. "That's not an emotion, by the way; it's an offer. *You* of all people know the difference. What I'm asking—and you're avoiding—is whether you still care for me now that we're not connected. Was it just the ink exchange?"

"The only thing that's changed is that you're free of me and I'm left trying to figure out how to feed my court properly." He lit another cigarette and gave her his answer. "It was the exchange at first, but . . . that wasn't all. I do care for you. Enough to let you leave."

"So . . ." she prompted, needing the words.

"So, my vow's going to stay intact: no mortal ink exchange."

She stood awkwardly for a few moments. Leaving wasn't easy, no matter how right it was. There were so many things she wanted to say, to ask. They wouldn't change anything. They wouldn't make a difference, and really, they were all things that she suspected Irial already knew. So she said, "In the morning, I get the key for my apartment. Ash took care of it for me . . . not the money, but finding one and the paperwork and everything."

"You'll tell me if you need anything?" He sounded as tentative as she felt.

She shook her head. "No. I'm pretty sure seeing you—or Niall—is a bad idea. I told him, too . . . I don't want this world. Ash was right about that part. I want to go live my life, be normal, and sort out what happened—before you."

"You'll do well, better than if you stayed." He took another drag off his cigarette and exhaled.

She watched the smoke twist into strands in the air, not shadows, not anything mystical or ethereal, just the air that he'd exhaled—normalcy. And it made her smile. "I will."

EPILOGUE

As he often had over the past few weeks, Niall watched Leslie step out into the street. The mortal boy waiting there shrugged off whatever she said to him with a smile. He watched her with a protectiveness Niall approved of— putting his body streetside, keeping alert to the passing mortals. She needed friends like him. She needed the way the mortals made her laugh. *Not me. Not now.* The shadows under her eyes were fading; her stride was steadier, more confident.

"Looks good, doesn't she?" said an unwelcome voice behind him.

"Go away." Niall pulled his gaze away from Leslie, turning to face the king of the Dark Court.

Irial lounged against the newsstand, hat tipped low on his brow.

How did I not notice him?

"Healthier too, without that wretch of a brother causing her trouble," Irial added. With a friendliness that seemed at odds with the situation, he stepped forward and draped an arm over Niall's shoulder. They were of equal height, so it was an almost embracing gesture.

Niall shrugged off Irial's arm and asked, "What do you want?"

"To check on our girl—and you." Irial watched Leslie with a strange look that Niall would call protective if it were anyone else.

He's not capable of that, though. He's the heart of the Dark Court. But Niall knew he was trying to lie to himself, knew he'd been lying to himself for centuries: Irial wasn't what Niall had let himself believe. He was neither as awful as Niall believed nor as kind as he'd first seemed. *He still doesn't deserve to be near her.*

Leslie had been joined by several other mortals. One of them said something that made her laugh out loud.

Niall stepped in front of the Dark King. "She's free of you. If you—"

"Relax, boy." He laughed softly. "Do you really believe I'd hurt *her*?"

"You *did* hurt her."

"I took away her choices when I didn't warn her about the ink exchange. I used her. I did what we have both done with mortals forever."

Niall started, "It's—"

"*Exactly* what your last king did with his lovely queen and the rest of his formerly mortal playthings"—Irial paused, a strange solemn look on his face—"but you'll figure it out soon enough." Then, staring past Niall toward Leslie and her mortal friends, Irial said, "Once I gave you the choice between giving me the mortals you'd addicted or giving me yourself. You gave me yourself. That's what a good king does, Gancanagh—makes hard choices. You know what we are, yet you kept our secrets. You're setting aside your love for Leslie for her best interests. You're going to make an excellent king."

And before Niall could react, Irial pressed his mouth to the long scar that he'd once allowed Gabriel to carve on Niall's face. Niall felt his knees give out under him, felt a disquieting new energy flood his body, felt the awareness of countless dark fey like threads in a great tapestry weaving his life to theirs.

"Take good care of the Dark Court. They deserve that. They deserve *you*." Irial bowed his head. "My king."

"No," Niall stumbled back, tottering on the sidewalk, nearly falling into the traffic. "I don't want this. I've told you—"

"The court needs new energy, Gancanagh. I got us through Beira's reign, found ways to strengthen us. I'm tired—more changed by Leslie than I'll admit, even to you. You may have broken our tie, seared me from her skin, but that doesn't undo my changes. I am no longer fit to lead my court." Irial smiled sadly. "My court—*your court now*— needs a new king. You're the right choice. You have always been the next Dark King."

"Take it back." Niall felt the foolishness of his words, but he couldn't think of anything more articulate.

"If you don't want it—"

"I don't."

"Pick someone worthy to pass it on to, then." Irial's eyes were lightening ever so slightly. The eerily tempting energy that had always clung to him like a haze was less overwhelming now. "In the meantime, I offer you what I've never offered another—my fealty, Gancanagh, my king."

He knelt then, head bowed, there on the busy sidewalk. Mortals craned their necks to stare.

And Niall gaped at him, the last Dark King, as the reality settled on him. He'd just grab the first dark fey he saw and . . . *turn over this kind of power to some random faery? A dark faery?* He thought of Bananach and the Ly Ergs circling, seeking war and violence. Irial was moderate in comparison to Bananach's violence. Niall couldn't turn the court over to just anyone, not in good conscience, and Irial knew it.

"The head of the Dark Court has always been chosen from the solitary fey. I waited a long time to find another after you said no. But then I realized I was waiting for you to leave Keenan. You didn't choose me over him, but you chose the harder path." Irial stood then and took Niall's face in his hands, gently but firmly, and kissed his forehead. "You'll do well. And when you are ready to talk, I'll still be here."

Then he disappeared into the throng of mortals winding down the sidewalk, leaving Niall speechless and bewildered.

Irial didn't look back, didn't turn toward Leslie or Niall. He kept moving until he was lost in the crowd of mortals whose feelings he could read but not drink.

Not without her.

He could feel her out there, confident in her world, seeing the things that watched her from the shadows and not flinching. Sometimes he felt teasing tastes of her longing—for him and for Niall—but he'd not go to her, not now, not with her happy in her new world. She was making up the courses she'd missed during her time with him, proud of herself, rebuilding herself. She'd start college in the fall.

Not mine, not his, but Her Own. It pleased him, knowing that, and having those brief bursts of connection with her. He'd had a fear that relinquishing his throne would also end his tie with Leslie. He'd let that fear delay his stepping down. *Fear of losing my last link to my Shadow Girl.* Her actions had burned away the tendrils of vine where they'd burrowed into her flesh. He'd felt it, like losing feeling in a limb, setting him off-kilter so badly that he'd been despondent at the loss. But he could still taste the echo of her—not always, not even often, but there were moments when he felt her—like phantom pains in a missing limb. It was his craving for those moments that proved his inadequacy to lead his court. He might be out of her skin, but she'd left him as something other than what he'd been before—not mortal, but not strong enough to deserve the title of Dark King.

What does it mean when nightmares dream of peace? When shadows wish for light?

She might not be bound to him, but she was still his Shadow Girl. He'd given her his vow: to take care of her, to keep her from hurt or pain, from wanting for anything. Her leaving didn't negate his promises; they weren't conditional. And if Niall wasn't bound to a court, kept tied to some cause or purpose, he'd eventually go to Leslie. Their Gancanagh might mean well, but his nature—like Irial's—was to be addictive to mortals. He was still a thing of shadows despite how long he'd run from who he was. *Not now.* Now that Niall was bound to the Dark Court, his addictive nature was nullified. *And mine is returned.* Like Irial had once been, Niall was strengthened by his court, just as the court would be strengthened by Niall.

To look after the Dark Court, Irial had found them a better king. To care for Niall, Irial had given him the court. And to love Leslie, Irial would stay away from her. *Sometimes love means letting go when you want to hold on tighter.* It was the only way he knew to protect the court, the faery, and the only mortal who'd ever mattered to him.

Author's Note

I wanted the representation of all things tattoo-related to be as accurate and respectful as possible, so every tattoo reference in this book was handed to my tattoo artist, Paul Roe, to examine. Along the way, I've learned a great deal about the history of the art, the assembly of the machines, and minutia ranging from the metals one could use (what with faeries being sensitive to steel/iron) to why tattoo artists position the canvas in various ways. If there are errors, I hope you'll forgive me. If there aren't, the credit goes to Paul.

Leslie's tattoo is at the center of *Ink Exchange*. I knew that early on; I just didn't know exactly what the tattoo looked like. It needed to be a representation of Irial's nature, and while I had the words that made Iri come to life for me, I didn't have a visual that captured his essence. The universe gives us what we need, though; I believe that. What I needed was Paul's art and wisdom. To say that he was essential to the creation of this novel would be an understatement.

As with the tattoos I wear on my skin, I gave Paul my words; he answered with his images. The final result was the art that's hung in my direct line of sight for the past year. Thanks to Paul, Irial's eyes look back at me every day while I work.

It's an amazing thing when two people's muses can dance together.

The Superpower of Love

Also by Sophie Hannah

Fiction

Gripless
Cordial and Corrosive

Poetry

The Hero and the Girl Next Door
Hotels Like Houses
Leaving and Leaving You

Children's

The Box Room

The Superpower of Love

Sophie Hannah

First published in Great Britain by Century in 2001

First published in the United States in 2002
by Soho Press, Inc.
853 Broadway
New York, NY 10003

Library of Congress Cataloging-in-Publication Data

Hannah, Sophie, 1971–
The superpower of love / Sophie Hannah.
p. cm.
ISBN 1-56947-281-5 (alk. paper)
1. Friendship—Fiction. 2. England—Fiction. I. Title.

PR6058.A5928 S87 2002
823'.914—dc21

2002017563

10   9   8   7   6   5   4   3   2   1

The Superpower of Love

'Francis, phone Campbell!'

1

'Campbell has left Eve,' said Francis, without looking up, as Sim entered the flat. It was four thirty on Saturday afternoon; she always allowed a good half-hour between shopping and the *Potters Court* omnibus to unpack and pour herself a large, morale-boosting sherry, in case the scriptwriters had massacred her storylines. She thought she might have misheard Francis, whose voice was muffled by the sound of three large plastic bags and a ridged cardboard box brushing against the door frame.

Having squeezed her purchases into the hall, Sim let the box, which contained a silver bucket for chilling champagne, fall to the floor with a thud. 'What? What do you mean?' She thought Francis had said that Campbell had left Eve, but of course he couldn't have.

'Mm?' Francis had already lost interest. He sat on the hall floor beside the telephone with his glasses balanced on his knee, surrounded by newspapers. Beyond these was a trail of plates, coffee cups, strewn clothes and CD cases, which branched at strategic points and led to different rooms. It was as if Francis thought the carpets in their flat were perilous seas, requiring an emergency route mapped out in *Daily Telegraph* or pyjama-top stepping stones.

Sim sighed and struggled to keep hold of the good mood her shopping trip had instilled in her. Francis, she noticed, paid no attention to the champagne bucket beside him and certainly said nothing like, 'Oh, good, you've got

3

the wedding present.' He was wearing a red T-shirt and faded jeans, his blond hair falling over his eyes. Sim had recently incurred his wrath by telling him he looked like David Beckham.

'Francis, did you say Campbell had left Eve?'

'Mm. I think so. Somebody's left somebody, anyway.' Francis picked up a newspaper cutting and placed it on top of a pile of similar jagged grey strips. 'Dingleys,' he muttered, then turned his attention to the adjacent pile of cuttings, murmuring 'Kosovo'.

The flat's second bedroom made a light and spacious study, and Francis had a perfectly good office at the BBC in Leeds, yet his files and clippings invariably spilled out into the hall. Sim objected; deputy editors of news programmes belonged in leather-and-chrome swivel chairs, not on floors between rooms. She told herself the usual lie: if he was in the study, I wouldn't interrupt him.

'Francis, could you put your work down for a second, please?' This question was delivered with excessive polite-ness, the sort that hinted at its own abrupt end should the listener fail to comply. With her right foot, Sim pushed the champagne cooler towards one of Francis's newspapers, crumpling it at the corner, to herald the imminent invasion of what Sim called real life and what Francis called gossip. He abandoned his papers and looked up. Sim grinned at him and he grinned back. Each admired the other's stubbornness; it was one of the things that had brought them together.

'Right,' said Sim. 'Now, tell me everything I want to know, without my having to ask you a single other ques-tion.' Stories that came from Francis were always enhanced by prolonged suspense. It could take hours to squeeze the full low-down from him.

'Eve phoned while you were out. She said that Campbell had left her and gone off with some other woman. That's all.'

'That's all? What other woman?' Sim felt her mood darken. She'd assumed . . . well, certainly not *that*. God,

4

poor Eve, she thought, but the plunge of pain on her friend's behalf quickly gave way to puzzled irritation. Surely this couldn't be so. 'When? Why?' she barked at Francis, resisting the urge to stamp her foot. 'And why didn't you seem sure before?' Campbell couldn't leave Eve for another woman. Who did he think he was? Sim hadn't left Francis for Andrew Johnson. God, Campbell was a sly one. All these years he'd been so . . . still. Sim should have suspected his placid, immobile exterior was just a front. She felt unaccountably angry.

And why did she have to deal with this today, on the very day that she, Simone Purdy, had developed a world-view? Couldn't she rest on her laurels for a while, enjoy her new accessory without being required to put it to use? She'd left the flat this morning without a world-view and come back with one, thanks to a pair of stripy socks. She had neither expected nor prepared for the world-view's arrival, but she'd recognised it soon enough once it turned up. It manifested itself in the form of a sudden awareness that she knew everything, all the little secrets and techniques. Sim felt as if her brain had been fitted with an invisible but infallible guidebook to all aspects of life and immediately wondered how she'd got through twenty-eight years without such a useful device.

'I'm pretty sure it was Eve,' said Francis. 'But I was working. Why would I have got the idea it was Campbell and Eve if it wasn't?' He smiled mischievously.

Sim was often amused by his air of abstraction and had been known to kiss him when he confessed to having left his wallet or jacket on a train, but today she wasn't in the mood, not any more. 'Francis, it's about time you learned the difference between our friends.'

'I got the gist. Aren't most of your women friends essentially the same person?' he said in a hopeful final attempt to make Sim laugh. Francis knew she appreciated frivolous conversation, the effects that could be achieved by saying something one didn't entirely mean.

'No, Francis, they are not,' Sim replied, objecting to 'your women friends'. Weren't they his friends too, in spite of their sex? And it was only funny to act as if you didn't care when you either did or were right not to. Francis's remark had offended her world-view. Failure to notice the difference between things led to a lowering of standards. Sim knew this now that she'd found her ideal socks, a blend of soft cotton and lycra, not too woolly and not too shiny. They were supple without being excessively stretchy and their stripes were sharply distinct, a repeating sequence of blue, pink, green, white and yellow. Sim saw them in Next and instantly wondered what the hell she'd been doing all her life, sock-wise. She bought ten pairs and made a resolution: never again would she put up with greying, sagging toes and spider web heels. No more would she ignore the extent to which bad socks undermined the wearer.

Standing in the queue in Next, clutching the ten pairs to her chest in eager anticipation of the range of positive ramifications her purchase would have, Sim knew she was on to something. This wasn't only about socks; it went considerably deeper. It was connected to Matt and Lucy's wedding and to how much Sim loved Francis, to the absolute exclusion of all future Andrew Johnson-esque incidents. It covered Campbell leaving Eve, even though Sim hadn't known about that when she was in Next. But this was the beauty of the world-view. Once you knew it was there, securely in place, it could be applied to any situation. It could turn its hand to most things. Sim's world-view was one in which Campbell did not leave Eve. Certainty had descended upon Sim with great force. She felt she was unlikely to be unsure of anything ever again.

'How did Eve sound?' she asked Francis. Campbell was a sly bastard. All those years of being so kind, so tolerant of everyone else's character flaws – had he simply been laying the groundwork, calculating that his friends would feel they owed it to him to be not at all judgemental? And to pull a stunt like this with Matt and Lucy's wedding coming up; what was he thinking of?

'Dunno,' said Francis, sulky now that his attempts at humour had been rejected. 'No particular way.' He was still fiddling with his pile of papers. The faces of Dale and Wayne Dingley stared up at Sim, bumpy and doughy, with low, flat foreheads and slack mouths that made her think of adenoids. Beside that photograph was a grainier one of Bethan Wrigley, the murdered girl, with her mousy hair in a ponytail. How incongruous, thought Sim, not for the first time. Bethan didn't look like the sort of person who would be murdered. Sim, on the other hand, did, with her wild, bushy hair, floor-length cloaks, long lilac fingernails and now her stripy socks. It stood to reason that noticeable people were more likely to get killed. In Sim's view, it was a risk worth taking.

'Annette Wrigley's been bombarding us with complaints,' Francis grumbled, seeing Sim eyeing his papers. 'Doesn't want us to interview the Dingleys, but how else is the truth going to come out? Why's she giving us such a hard time?'

'She's a person with feelings,' said Sim impatiently. 'Her daughter was murdered and now it must seem to her as if the killers are getting their own radio show.' A huge potential for understanding had been unleashed in Sim with the arrival of her world-view. She was a newly minted motivation whizz-kid. 'Eve also has feelings. Did she sound upset?'

Francis struggled to remember. 'No. Don't think so.'

'She must be upset if Campbell's left her.' Sim's voice rose. 'Are you sure it was Eve who phoned?'

'Not absolutely, no.' Francis frowned at her bad temper, making it clear she had no right to smile at him one minute, then get cross the next. He began to skim-read an article that covered two full pages about whether ground troops should be sent into Kosovo. One page argued the case for yes, the other for no. This, Sim saw, was from today's

paper. Francis had written the date at the top in black
marker pen: 27 March 1999. No wonder he'd only half
heard the day's other big news if his mind was on ground
troops.

'Right!' She snatched the double-page spread from his
hand. 'Kitchen! Now!'

'Oh, no!'

Francis stood in the middle of the kitchen with his arms
folded and his eyes closed, while Sim took a large chopping
board out of a drawer, wondering how many more times
she was going to have to do this. She placed the chopping
board on top of the fridge and leaned it against the cork
noticeboard on the wall so that it covered the right-hand
side of a blue sheet of paper. Francis drummed his fingers
against his elbows and sighed.

'Right, you can open your eyes,' said Sim. The visible
part of the document read as follows:

OUR FRIE

Washington
Matt &

Cambridge
Vanessa &
Gillian

Manchester
Campbell &

Yorkshire
Us
Hazel

Sim was pleased with her list. She'd put a lot of effort into
drawing it up. Matt and Lucy were at the top, inevitably.
Sim felt it was appropriate for America to come first, and

8

even more appropriate that, of all their friends, Matt and Lucy should be the ones to live and work there.

Other than that, the order of the list was random, although the order in which each couple was presented had a logic to it. Sim had been friends with both Eve and Vanessa since secondary school, but whereas Vanessa was definitely, intrinsically, a 'Vanessa and . . .', Eve always signed Campbell's name first on cards; she was shrewd enough to see that precautions needed to be taken to prevent his fading into the background and confident enough to shine the spotlight elsewhere. Sim found this impressive, and referred to herself and Francis as 'Francis and Sim' whenever she remembered to.

Acquaintances had not been included, although one ex-friend remained on the list, with a line through her name. Sim could have made a new list, but she didn't want Gillian to disappear; she wanted her there, crossed out. In an oblique way it seemed to act as a deterrent, an example to their other friends, which was ridiculous because Sim made sure the list was hidden when anyone came round. Francis's inability to remember the names of some of his oldest and closest friends, let alone get the pairs right, was a secret Sim had kept successfully for years. This was what the list was in aid of. She had written it out a few months ago, dividing their friends into geographical locations for Francis's maximum convenience, and pinned it up on the notice board. The plan was that as Francis washed up he would commit the names to memory, including which ones were linked to which. Sim was sure he had it in him; he seemed to have no trouble remembering the names of the most obscure war criminals from the news, like the man Sim referred to as Grab-a-ditch Caravan. Sadly, the plan had a fatal flaw, which was that Francis never washed up, but Sim lived in hope.

'Oh, for God's sake!' he said, as Sim pointed to the first name on the list with a spatula. 'This is ridiculous.' Sim pursed her lips to indicate that she had no intention of backing down. The bond between herself and Francis relied, to a certain extent, on mutual infuriation. If either of them ever became noticeably less infuriating, the other would worry, particularly about the implications for their joint capacity to infuriate other people. 'I bloody know them, okay? Do we really have to go through this nonsense again?'

Sim thought of the recent illiteracy storyline in *Potters Court*, in which it was shown that this sort of denial was the first defence of someone who was ashamed of his ignorance. Not one of Sim's ideas, she was pleased to say. She wished the soap would stop recruiting social science graduates whose storylines necessitated the advertising of advice lines at the end of each episode and the constant dissemination of free helpful booklets. Nothing, in the infinite wisdom of Sim's world-view, was as helpful as pure entertainment. 'Go on,' she urged, holding the spatula aloft.

'Matt and Lucy . . .'

'Stop. Say the areas too.'

'Oh, for God's sake!'

'Francis, last week Matt phoned and you asked him how the weather was in Cambridge. I heard it with my own ears.'

'Okay, okay. Washington,' he underlined the word with mocking emphasis. 'Matt and Lucy. There, see? Told you I knew them.' Sim frowned, shook her head and pointed the spatula at the next section. She wasn't impressed. No one could forget the Alpha couple, as Vanessa rather snidely called them. Matt was Francis's oldest friend. They went to primary and secondary school together in Cambridge, then on to Trinity College.

'Cambridge. Vanessa . . . and Nicholas!' Francis sounded proud of himself. Big deal, thought Sim, who'd registered his brief hesitation. Their names were as inextricably linked as Punch and Judy's, and they got on about as well. But then, Vanessa had not once, to Sim's knowledge, gone so far as to like a boyfriend; she was never a soppy teenager, not even for an hour. While Sim, Eve, Gillian and every other self-respecting girl at their Manchester school had been busy scribbling hearts and arrows all over their exercise books, Vanessa was covering hers with doodles of herself dragging the boy of the moment behind her on the end of a chain.

After A levels, Sim and Vanessa went to Anglia Polytechnic in Cambridge to study English. Vanessa could barely contain her eagerness at the prospect of snarling at public school toffs from the university. Before long she'd moved in with one by the name of Nicholas Drogan, in order to be able to snarl at close range. In spite of his Marlborough College credentials, Nicholas was rapidly and substantially out-toffed by Vanessa, a state school girl from the north who felt that even without social and financial advantages she was innately superior to most people. Within months of arriving in Cambridge, her Manchester accent had disappeared and she had a voice you could drill holes with.

Sim had got together with Francis at around the same time, though not in any conventional manner befitting two students, not at Trinity College's May Ball, where Matt had met Lucy, or in the Jive Hive, where Vanessa had met Nicholas. Sim was in the Copper Kettle one lunchtime, having a coffee and a slice of cake, and cringing her way through the last chapters of *Lady Chatterley's Lover*, the subject of that afternoon's seminar, when she became dimly aware of a row taking place at the next table. She looked over and saw a gorgeous, sullen young man of about her own age sitting opposite a pouchy-faced woman in a floppy purple hat who was sobbing theatrically. 'You make me feel so worthless,' the woman ranted through her tears. 'You're so cold and hard. I'm trying to work through my stuff from childhood and . . .'

'You've had long enough,' the young man snapped. He radiated impatience and embarrassment, and looked not unlike a young Robert Redford (okay, so David Beckham

11

was a bit of a demotion; Sim could see why Francis had objected). Hundreds of tiny grey plaits erupted from beneath the woman's floppy hat and fell down her sloping shoulders. Her left nostril was pierced twice and a droplet of snot dangled from one of the rings. Sim couldn't believe Robert Redford, with his upright, no-nonsense posture, could have any connection with this soggy, sagging creature.

'You're so cynical,' the woman bawled. 'I gave up everything for you and your dad, and what do I get for it? He leaves me and you freeze me out. I was the one who made sacrifices for you, Francis . . .' On and on she went. Sim thoroughly enjoyed her peformance.

'Oh, stop whining!' The young man pushed back his chair and stormed off in the direction of the gents, slamming the door when he got there. The floppy-hatted woman turned and saw Sim staring. Her tears didn't quite go into reverse, heading back up her cheeks, but certainly her whole manner changed in an instant. 'My son, Francis.' She pointed after him and smiled at Sim, keen to ingratiate herself with her new audience. 'He's a shit,' she added, woman to woman.

'I don't mean to pry,' said Sim, though in fact she did, 'but any mother who says things like that about her son to a complete stranger ought to be spayed.'

When Francis returned, Sim had to explain why his mother was no longer present. He appeared utterly unmoved by the treacherous things his own flesh and blood had said about him, but when Sim told him what she'd said in response, he smiled as if he could hardly believe his luck in finding someone to whom the chore of insulting his mother could safely be delegated. He and Sim were inseparable after that.

'Manchester,' he now continued.

'Hang on,' Sim stopped him. 'You missed out Gillian, under Cambridge.'

'But she's crossed out.'

'She's still there. You should say "Gillian, crossed out".'

'Oh, don't be ridiculous. I'd have thought you'd want her off the list, now that you hate her.'

'I don't hate her. I have no strong feelings about her, other than that I don't want her as a friend.'

'Gillian's boyfriend isn't on the list. Andrew What's-his-name. Everyone else's is. It's not consistent,' said Francis, who sought to undermine, at every turn, the credibility of the object that regularly defeated him.

'I've explained that before, Francis.' Andrew Johnson wasn't a friend of theirs, nor had he ever been. He'd got together with Gillian after Sim had broken off all contact with her. Francis didn't know him and Sim, who had had an affair with him, pretended not to know him. Her stomach twisted at the sound of Francis saying Andrew's name, even half of it. 'Okay, Manchester,' she prompted.

'Campbell and Eve. Hm. You might have to make an amendment there. It's Campbell and someone else now. That's if it was Eve who phoned.' Francis beamed, proud of his poor recollection. Sim knew that this deliberate abstraction from friends' love lives was a luxury for him. He was the sort of man who stopped thinking about feelings the minute his own emotional needs were catered for. Sim was gratified that he trusted her to take care of the listening for both of them, but bloody hell, had Campbell left Eve or hadn't he?

Eve had stayed in Manchester when Sim and Vanessa departed for Cambridge, to do a Business and Management Studies degree. In her second year she'd met Campbell, a philosophy student with a motivation problem, then as now. Sim smiled. Eve had always had enough motivation for an army. Surely Campbell couldn't have left her. Without Eve's drive, Sim couldn't imagine he would get very far. It would all have blown over by the wedding, anyway, even if Sim had to blow it over herself. Lucy had insisted on inviting Gillian on the grounds that it would be mean not to and Sim wanted her ex-friend to see that

13

things were just the same without her, the gang every bit as solid. If Campbell and Eve were glaring at each other from opposite sides of the chapel, Gillian might think a general scattering had taken place and feel less personally excluded.

Gillian hated to be left out of anything, which was how she'd ended up in Cambridge. Determined to be where the majority was, she'd abandoned Eve in Manchester, sensing that the social power base had shifted, and followed Sim and Vanessa – somewhat stalkerishly, Sim always thought – in an attempt to form a cosy triangle. When this didn't work, when in fact a bigger group formed to include Nicholas, Francis, Matt, Lucy and Eve and Campbell at weekends and during holidays, Gillian was visibly put out. 'Serves her right for gatecrashing our lives,' said Vanessa, who felt that for Gillian to come to Cambridge with no particular activity in mind was a form of trespass. In those days, Sim was the one who encouraged the others to make allowances for Gillian. How ironic that she should now be the only one to have cut her out altogether. Lucy, Eve, even Vanessa – they still spoke to her when she phoned, felt obliged to invite her to weddings, excused her wrongdoings on the grounds that 'she's just a bit mad, isn't she?'.

How Gillian managed – after a couple of months of doing absolutely nothing apart from hang around lecture halls waiting for Sim and Vanessa – to get a place on a secretarial course and then a job in Cambridge University's Modern Languages department was a mystery to everyone. Her written English was atrocious. 'Computer spell-checks have got a lot to answer for,' Vanessa said bitterly every so often, when there were still no tidings of Gillian's sacking and transferral to her rightful place, the dole queue.

'Yorkshire,' said Francis, as the spatula hovered lower. 'Us.' He snorted. 'That's ridiculous, having us on the list.'

'Francis, we've been over this,' said Sim wearily.

'We are not our own friends.'

'Speak for yourself.' Sim wanted the list to be complete

14

and, since she was the group's central axis, she had to be on it. Sometimes she wondered whether the others would bother to keep in touch at all if it weren't for her active arrangement-making. Besides, her world-view seemed to feel she was her own friend in many ways. Francis also qualified in his less surly moments.

'I thought this list was an *aide-memoire*. I'm hardly about to forget us, am I?'

'I don't know. I'd say you're not unlikely to forget me,' Sim muttered.

'Nor am I likely to forget where I live. I wish I bloody could.' Francis had had it in for Yorkshire since the day they'd moved from Cambridge to their flat in Saltaire's New Mill two years ago. They'd had to drive their hired van the wrong way down a one-way exit road and had been yelled at by an irate neighbour-to-be. When Francis explained to her that the correct way into the car park involved going through a tunnel in the building with a maximum headroom restriction for which the van was several inches too high, she scowled and said, 'Is it 'eck!' Francis was shocked. He and Sim were no longer in touch with his mother and he'd grown unused to groundless attacks. He felt immediately unwelcome and ranted for two hours about how the carping neighbour's attitude was typical of mean-spirited Yorkshire folk. Was the old bat implying that if Francis were a good solid Yorkshireman instead of a namby-pamby southerner he would have been able to squeeze the van through, irrespective of the size of the tunnel? Francis had always had trouble with the idea that every person was an individual, distinct from all others (this was why politics appealed to him; one could abstract and generalise so easily – East versus West, Labour versus Tory). Sim had tried many times since that day to convince him that not everybody in Yorkshire shared their ungenerous neighbour's personality, but to no avail.

Sim loved Saltaire, could hardly wait to leave Cambridge. She hadn't foreseen that one little affair would tarnish her

15

whole view of the place, but afterwards she couldn't wait to get out. She and Francis needed a new start, far away from Andrew Johnson. Guiltily, she tried to cajole Francis into liking Yorkshire, but the north was Sim's territory; every time she begged him to admit that the hilly green, grey and purple landscape was beautiful, part of her was aware that she wanted Francis to be happy not so much for his own sake as to let her off the hook. Sim had persuaded him to apply for the job in Leeds and to take it when it was offered, having first secretly lined up a job for herself. Cambridge had been the one constant in Francis's childhood; it was what he'd relied upon in the absence of a stable adult and Sim had dragged him away. She hadn't even been able to tell him the truth about why it was so important to her. Still, self-criticism was not Sim's default setting. Optimism was, and she saw no reason why Francis shouldn't grow to love Yorkshire if properly trained.

'Right, and the last one?' She wielded the spatula threateningly. But not by any means least, she added silently, as if she could build up Hazel's confidence telepathically.

'Hazel and . . .' Francis seemed heartened now that the end of the list was in sight. 'Hazel and . . . oh, bugger!' Sim restrained a smug smile. She knew she'd get him. Hazel had always been one of his weak spots. She was a Saltaire addition rather than vintage Cambridge, and Francis, though he would never admit it, did not fully recognise single women, suspecting they were eschewed by men for a range of powerful reasons. He treated Hazel as a pet of limited appeal that Sim insisted on keeping and felt free to snap at her when she got under his feet. He was more politely baffled around Lucy, Vanessa and Eve, who were other men's to snap at.

'Calm down and think about it,' Sim counselled. 'Think laterally.'

'Laterally? I can't see laterally, there's a chopping board

in front of laterally. Hazel and . . . I give up.' His shoulders sank.

'Look carefully, Francis. Is there an ampersand next to Hazel's name?'

'What the fuck is . . . oh, right, an "and" symbol. No. Oh, Christ! Hazel and no one! Hazel and no one!' He punched the air in triumph, as if he hadn't only got the right answer thanks to Sim's clue. Despite resenting the chopping board test, Francis was chuffed when he acquitted himself well.

Sim rewarded him with a hug. 'Correct,' she said, kissing him as he tried to wriggle free. 'Hazel's single. Although try not to look so pleased about it. I promise you she's far from pleased. Now.' Sim put the chopping board and spatula back in their respective drawers. 'Look down that list and tell me who phoned, if it wasn't Eve.'

'I haven't got time to play games. I've got to go to the office.'

'Francis! It's Saturday.'

'The news doesn't stop at weekends.'

'Neither does real life. And if you'd paid attention in the first place, we wouldn't have to go through this rigmarole now. This is what you don't realise: you think you save time by not listening, but you actually increase the inconvenience to yourself.' Sim never tired of nagging Francis in an amiable sort of way, which she knew he appreciated. Her enthusiastic attempts to improve his behaviour were a sign that she regarded him as a worthwhile ongoing project; for so long Francis had feared he was a disappointing foregone conclusion. 'Now, come on,' she said. 'Who phoned?'

'Well, Hazel's got nobody to split up with. It obviously wasn't Matt and Lucy.' Sim nodded. Normally she would have questioned the assumption that a couple on the point of marrying were immune to break-up, but Matt and Lucy had spent a whole year planning their huge wedding in the minutest detail. Grand gestures, according

17

to Sim's world-view, were often the outward manifestation of grand feelings, and in the case of Matt and Lucy the content lived up to the form.

'Vanessa and Nicholas?' Sim suggested, not believing it possible for a minute. There was a palpable chemistry between those two; each represented for the other a sort of irresistible bogeyman. Sim could see how this might work; a cringe was not so far removed from a ripple of lust, after all. Vanessa had told her that both physical and verbal hostilities inflamed their sex life. They had nothing but contempt for one another's views but, as Vanessa once put it, Nicholas was as keen to fuck the right as Vanessa was to fuck the left. Sim had looked blank for a few seconds before saying, 'Oh, I see: wings.' Politics and football: both games bored her equally. Both – and on this point her world-view was unshakeable – were forms of escapism. One watched from a distance, supported either the red lot or the blue lot and fought, suffered and triumphed vicariously; it was entertainment for all those who had no instinct or appetite for the complexities of life and inferior to soap opera on every level.

Francis and Nicholas's interminable political debates, often umpired by a pensive and neutral Campbell, would have driven Sim mad with boredom, were it not for the fact that she enjoyed coaching Francis on the best way to argue. She'd taught him to eschew the sort of ideological bludgeoning Nicholas went in for, to keep calm, be charming, occasionally humorous, and every now and then add a dash of frivolity, the one thing Nicholas couldn't handle. Over the years she'd watched Francis's technique improve. These days he would turn to Sim eagerly the minute Nicholas was out of earshot and ask, 'How did I do? Did I win?'

Nicholas's reverent approach to politics fascinated Sim. In one respect he was like her: the most enthusiastic fan of everything he liked and a fearless critic of all he condemned. Sim admired him for this; too many people didn't distinguish sufficiently between the wonderful and the awful. If only Nicholas weren't such an enemy of the art of civilised conversation; if only he'd learn to season his convictions with wit and affability. The mildest opposition to his views made him bellow and he regularly described himself as 'a decent human being', which Sim regarded as an unpardonable triumph of substance over style.

Still, he unwittingly made her laugh, which was the next best thing to wittingly doing so. Sim had certainly never wished Vanessa would trade him in for a new boyfriend. Nicholas's reaction to Christopher Reeve's horse-riding accident was one of Sim's favourite comedy moments to this day. She had innocently remarked that it was a terrible thing to happen to anybody but for it to happen to Superman was all the more tragic, and Nicholas had had a fit. 'What about poor people who lose the use of their limbs?' he'd yelled, shaking his finger at Sim. 'Don't they matter?' She explained what she'd meant: it was worse in the case of Christopher Reeve purely because of the symbolism. If Superman was in a wheelchair, the world really was in trouble. 'I don't care!' Nicholas yelled. 'He's rich, famous and successful, okay? I refuse to feel sorry for him!' Sim and Francis had laughed about this for weeks; to approve of the almost total paralysis of all high achievers seemed a ridiculous extent to which to take one's left-wing sympathies.

'Well, was it Vanessa and Nicholas?' Sim asked, seeing that Francis's attention had wandered.

'No! For Christ's sake, it was Campbell and Eve.'

'Okay. Well, you'd better phone Campbell, then.'

'What?' Francis looked over his shoulder like a hunted animal checking out possible escape routes. 'Why had I better phone him?'

'To find out exactly what's happened,' said Sim.

'Bugger off. I've got to go to the office and pick up the Dingley trial notes.' There was scarcely a day when Francis didn't leave something crucial in the office.

19

'Can't it wait?'

'Let's see.' Francis rubbed his chin, pretending to think about it. 'We have two killers who walked scot-free from court on our programme in a few weeks, we have one opportunity to get them to incriminate themselves, we're being hounded by the victim's mother who can't see that we're on her side . . . no, it can't wait. Why don't you phone Campbell?'

'Because he might feel happier talking about it to you. You're a bloke.' Francis opened his mouth to deny this, then realised he couldn't. 'And I'm going to phone Eve, and I don't want to have spoken to Campbell already in case she asks me if I've spoken to him. If I say yes – and I'm not adding to her injuries by lying to her – she might feel less inclined to talk to me if I've heard Campbell's version first. I'll seem sort of . . . tarnished as a listener.'

'Sim, please. Fascinating though your stream of consciousness may be – and it isn't – I've got work to do. You phone Campbell, if you want him phoned.' Francis stomped out of the kitchen.

'I can't. I've explained why I can't.' Sim followed him into the lounge.

'If that garbled ejection of words is what passes for an explanation in your muddled mind . . .'

'. . . unless we do it the other way round. I ring Campbell, you ring Eve?' Sim called his bluff. She was always robust in the face of Francis's prickliness. He'd been astonished, when they first got together, to see that not all women flew into paroxysms of guilt-inducing grief when they spotted a criticism heading their way.

'God, no.' Francis shuddered at the thought of what phoning Eve might entail.

'Right, so therefore I can't ring Campbell. Which means you have to, because I want to get a bit of background before I speak to Eve. I don't want to force her to go through the whole thing in the kind of detail I want, namely a lot of detail, in case she's not up to it. If you've got the bare bones of the situation from Campbell, then I won't have to interrogate Eve. Also, you know, Campbell might be in a state. He might need someone to talk to.'

Francis looked trapped and confused. Sim guessed that the element of role reversal disturbed him. Since when did Campbell have needs that Francis was required to adapt to? Traditionally, Campbell was the one who adapted. He'd always admired Francis, tried to emulate him in many ways and with varying degrees of success. He certainly never put him out and that was the way Francis liked it. 'Sim, the last thing I need is to talk to someone who's in a state. Why would he be, anyway? He's the one who left. With another woman. What exactly do you want me to say to him?' Francis pretended to put a phone to his ear. '"Oh, hi, Campbell. It's Francis. By the way, why did you leave Eve?"'

'Yes, that would be a start, although the parodic tone could do with some adjustment. Oh, Francis, just ring him, will you? I'll write down the crucial questions you need to ask him.'

'It would be more helpful', said Francis icily, 'if you drafted a list of questions for Dale and Wayne Dingley. Or Tony Blair.' Sim looked puzzled. Francis sighed heavily. 'There's a war going on in Kosovo, in which our country is involved. Have you noticed that at all?'

'Francis, I know you're busy,' said Sim. 'I only want you to ring your friend.' The phone trilled loudly in the hall, as if suddenly reminded of its own importance. Francis stared doggedly at his feet. Seeing that he had no intention of moving, Sim went to answer it.

Campbell Golightly lay stranded on a strange bed, unaware that he was the subject of much vociferous debate on the other side of the Pennines. No one had come to rescue him, no one seemed likely to, therefore he assumed the world had forgotten him. Well, Eve had tried valiantly several times, to give her her due, but she was the one person

21

by whom Campbell didn't want to be rescued. None of his friends even knew where he was and to approach any of them would be to turn himself in to a higher authority. This solitary, adrift period was his window of opportunity, so why couldn't he enjoy it while it lasted?

Campbell could see his bewildered face in the skinny full-length mirror that made his cramped room seem smaller, not bigger as mirrors were supposed to, by reproducing its mean corners. He hadn't had time to be choosy. He'd walked out on Eve and it was either sleep rough or take the first place that came up. The house on Silderman Road, less than five minutes' walk from trendy, café-clogged Didsbury village, looked so perfect from the outside that Campbell filled in his mother's blank cheque on the doorstep, before he'd even seen the room that was free. He'd always wanted to live in a tall Victorian house with high corniced ceilings and a big garden. Too late, he discovered that he'd rented a tiny attic room with a bed directly beneath the sloping part of the roof. When he lay awake at night, unable to get comfortable on the lumpy mattress, he imagined he was in a coffin and the ceiling was its closing lid. It did not occur to Campbell to move the bed; it wasn't his, after all.

He would have preferred a room without a mirror, so far had his appearance deteriorated in the last fortnight. He hadn't been able to afford a haircut since leaving Eve, and as his hair grew up and out rather than down he was beginning to acquire a distinctly bouffant look. Also, his lips were disappearing. There used to be a line around them, a proper boundary that separated them from the rest of his face, but recently the chapped left side of his upper lip seemed to have merged with his cheek.

Campbell picked up the remote control and turned on the small, dusty television that Eve had brought round the day before. He had no idea where she'd got it from. She simply arrived with it, saying, 'I know you, Campbell, you can't live without a TV.' Had she gone out and bought it, as a kind of leaving present?

Apart from a brief bout of pettiness when Rory first appeared on the scene, Eve had been unbelievably reasonable. 'Why leave home and disrupt your life?' she'd said. 'Stay here and see Rory at weekends. See how it goes.' Campbell had pretended to consider her suggestion, though it disgusted him. He knew he wouldn't be able to live in the atmosphere of sanctioned sleaziness that it would undoubtedly entail. How could he spend weekends with Rory, then trot back to Eve and suffer her wise tolerance of his bad behaviour? He was determined not to let her rob his big new love of its nobility. Campbell wanted his passion for Rory to be a grand force that reduced obstacles to rubble, not a clock-watching, clerical creature that compromised and accommodated. And even if he had been amenable to Eve's suggestion, if he got Rory out of his system as Eve clearly expected him to, the whole business might be referred to in retrospect as a phase; Eve would use that very word. Oh, God, how undignified.

Funnily enough, he suspected that if Eve had reacted differently he might have stayed – if she'd either told him to fuck off and never come back or wept and begged him not to go – but she never entirely lost control. Her anger and misery took second place to a sort of strategic empathy. She persisted in looking at things from the angle of what was best for Campbell; that was why he had to get away from her. Her concern obliterated him, and the project-managerial nature of her kindness made him suspect she was plotting to keep him there against his will. It annoyed Campbell that Eve was so efficient, even in her bleakest moments.

For a few minutes the sound of Channel Four was muffled by a loud humming noise as the set warmed up. It could have been a hum of disapproval, as if the TV was reluctant to provide entertainment when there was an unfinished PhD in the vicinity. Campbell hopped through the channels, but found nothing more interesting than motor racing. Now would have been a good time to

23

do some work, if only he were in the right frame of mind. What was the big hurry about finishing his thesis, anyway? The incomplete dog-eared manuscript was within easy reach, under the bed in a Nike holdall; Campbell could pull it out and finish it any time, even if he couldn't quite bring himself to look at it right now. He was damned if he was going to put himself out to meet spurious deadlines, or feel guilty because Manchester University's philosophy department might cease to be recognised by some funding body. Campbell hated the way everything was about results these days. No one seemed to value thinking for thinking's sake, wrestling with life's big questions. You wouldn't catch Francis or Nicholas rushing their work, or Matt. And one day Campbell would have a proper job too, with a salary, and Eve would see that his long years of being a poor student had been worthwhile.

He hopped channels again. On BBC 2, Kosovan refugees stood in front of their wrecked homes. A woman in a headscarf shouted at the camera in a foreign language. A dead body lay at her feet, wrapped in a grey blanket. Serbian soldiers had shot her husband, said the subtitle. Campbell tried, as a fellow refugee from a life of safety and comfort, to feel something and failed, so he turned back to Channel Four. The Kosovan woman, in spite of her predicament, had looked healthier than Campbell. Her hair was in better condition, she had clearly defined lips and she was surrounded by people, other distressed refugees. I must speak to someone, thought Campbell, suddenly feeling the need to share his plight. But with whom?

Francis was out of the question. One simply did not say things like 'I've left my partner of seven and a half years and I feel lousy' to Francis. And Sim would whoosh Campbell towards insights and conclusions with terrifying speed, keen to pin everything down with words.

Campbell wasn't yet ready to make sense and wasn't convinced any of his friends would want to speak to this

24

version of him: the new, confused Campbell who created emotional disturbance. Sim, Francis, Vanessa, Nicholas, even Hazel – they all saw him as appreciative audience, not moody leading man. He was an extra in the drama of their lives, a peripheral comedy character, adaptable and unobtrusive. They'd be bound to resent him in his new incarnation, particularly with Matt and Lucy's wedding coming up, which they were all so bloody obsessed with.

There was nothing like a wedding for turning love into a competitive sport. When Matt and Lucy had announced their engagement last May, they'd set their other cohabiting friends a challenge whether they meant to or not. Eve started to badger Campbell as soon as she heard the news and no matter how many times he told her that real love didn't need to perform any bureaucratic rituals, she wasn't convinced. It was almost as if Matt and Lucy were experimenting with social control, forcing everyone close to them to inhabit a fake, magical land of bells and bouquets. Campbell lacked the stamina to invade that land and insist that his friends make room for his dislocation and uncertainty.

It occurred to him that he could phone Neil Temple, his squash partner. Neil wasn't one of Sim's lot and, never having met Matt and Lucy, would not be inclined to try to tidy away Campbell's messy feelings before the big day like an impatient parent stuffing his kid's toys into a cupboard before the guests arrived. On the other hand, Neil taught law at Eve's school. He'd been propelled towards Campbell at a tedious teachers' party a couple of years ago. 'This is Neil Temple. He plays squash, Campbell. Campbell used to play squash, didn't you?' was Eve's rather bizarre introduction. 'The two of you should fix up a date.' No, Neil was no good. Even though Campbell saw far more of him than Eve did, socially at any rate, Eve had discovered him first and spent five days a week in the same building as him. Campbell needed to talk to someone who only had access to one version of events: his version.

Of course: he could phone Rory. Wasn't she, after all, his new girlfriend? If only talking to her weren't so exhausting. Not that this was Rory's fault; it was bound to happen with a long-distance relationship. Campbell wondered how soon Rory would ask him to move in with her. Maybe her parents would donate their country house in Hampshire as a starting-out present. Wasn't that what those sorts of families did? Campbell tried not to think about what else Rory's family did; he'd denied it to Eve, would no doubt have to deny it again before long, and hoped that as time went on he'd fall for the story himself.

Several factors conspired to prevent him from phoning Rory. In this house he had to keep a record of his out-going calls and pay his share of the phone bill, unlike at home where Eve had paid all the bills without mentioning their arrival. And using either of the two phones would mean leaving his room. On the landing he would feel too exposed; all sorts of people in transit might pass him. The other phone was in the lounge and Campbell hadn't yet ventured that far. The kitchen, too, was unexplored territory. His five housemates (house-strangers would be more accurate) had lived together for years. Campbell felt very much the outsider and constantly expected to be asked to leave. He thought, though, that if he stayed out of the lounge, kitchen, bathroom and other communal areas as much as possible, the others would be less likely to object to his presence. He couldn't completely avoid the bathroom, but he spent as little time in there as possible. The landing, stairs and hall were equally difficult to bypass if he wanted to go out, but fortunately a PhD student didn't need to go out very often. All a PhD student really needed to do, in Campbell's experience, was watch *Neighbours* twice a day. This was something he and Eve had disagreed about.

He'd like to see Eve start something as complex as an investigation of the philosophical concept of vagueness, let alone finish one. She behaved as if Campbell's interest in the topic were a lovable eccentricity, laughing and ruffling his hair when he tried to engage her in a discussion of his work. 'Campbell, everyone knows what tall means,' she'd said scathingly when he first mooted his research plans. 'Can't you work on something a bit more . . . of general interest? What does it matter whether there's a fixed point where tall becomes not tall? Anything that's neither tall nor not tall is medium height.' Campbell was quietly livid. When Eve said 'of general interest' she meant financially viable.

'It matters to philosophers of language,' he replied gravely. 'And medium doesn't have fixed boundaries either; at its outer extremes, it's surely difficult to distinguish it from tall and short.'

'Jolly good.' Eve had switched off and was leafing through a copy of *New Woman*.

'It's interesting, Eve,' he'd tried to convince her. 'Look, we have to be able to assign a truth value to the statement "X is tall".'

'I don't,' Eve declared cheerfully.

'If X isn't tall, does that mean he must be not tall? Or is there a fuzzy area in between? Is it possible to say of someone "X is neither tall, nor not tall"? Eve?'

'Yes. Someone of medium height.' Eve sighed and shook her head.

'No, because if you're going to insist upon a category of medium in between short and tall, then someone medium would count as not tall. Okay, is it possible for someone to be neither medium nor not medium?'

'Who cares? God! Everyone knows what these things mean. Campbell, I really wouldn't apply to do a PhD on this tiny pedantic subject. You'll never get the funding.' That showed how much Eve knew; the Arts and Humanities Research Board thought Campbell's research was worth investing in, even if she didn't. It was only a pity they couldn't have extended their support for a couple more years. Campbell had been penniless for the past six months, and had relied on Eve and his mother to bail him out. 'You could always get a part-time job,' Eve had never tired of suggesting. 'It's not as if you spend every waking hour working on your thesis.' The irony was that if Eve had understood even the first thing about vagueness, she'd have realised that, as with short and tall, it wasn't so easy to fix the borderline between working and not working. Eve assumed that when Campbell had his feet up in front of the television he wasn't working, but sometimes his most profound thoughts came to him in front of *Through the Keyhole*.

A familiar melody made Campbell breathe in sharply. It was the *Potters Court* theme tune. Excellent. And it was Saturday, which meant that this was the omnibus edition, a whole hour and a half. Seeing Sim's name in the credits would be almost as good as talking to her, for now at least. Her personality was stamped all over the programme, which had a powerful but ever so slightly unhinged internal logic.

Television was one of the cornerstones of Campbell's relationship with Sim. They shared an all-time favourite episode of *Neighbours*, the one in which Bouncer the dog had a dream. Campbell cared about the details of things that most people thought were unimportant, which Sim took as evidence that he had a deeper appreciation of life. If Eve had a go at him in Sim's presence about lolling around in front of the telly, he only had to say, 'Eve, someone has to keep abreast of the issues in *Quincey*' and Sim would laugh so much that Eve found it impossible to pursue her complaint. Sim listened avidly to Campbell's explanation of why wrestling was the apotheosis of post-modernism, and he was grateful to her for making him feel more like an intellectual than a layabout.

He felt a cheerier mood creep up on him. *Potters Court*, with its sieges, bomb scares, second comings, coke-snorting eunuchs and alopecia-afflicted pornographers, suited his present mood. It struck him as ironic that Sim spent her working day (such as it was; she never seemed to be actually *at* work) dreaming up new ways to cause chaos for the residents of the Potters Court estate, and the rest of her time trying to prevent it from breaking out in her own home, easier said than done when one lived with Francis. Sim was forever patting his strewn papers into rectangular piles when she thought no one was looking. Campbell wondered whether, by writing about the disorder she feared, Sim felt she kept it at bay.

Campbell's new philosophy of soaps was that they were comfort viewing for those who felt themselves to be implausible, although an omnibus had always been cause for celebration, even in his more plausible days with Eve. Over the years Campbell and Sim had forced the others to sit through them all: *EastEnders*, *Coronation Street*, *Hollyoaks*. 'These people aren't real!' Francis regularly protested. 'Who gives a shit what happens to them?'

'Beware of anyone who says he isn't interested in fictional characters,' Sim warned their friends, eyeing Francis with mock disapproval. 'What that means is, he isn't interested in people full stop.' Francis didn't contradict her.

Campbell tried to ignore the current of anxiety that began, at that moment, to flow through him. How would Sim, who *was* interested in people full stop, react when Eve told her about Rory's family?

'Francis, turn the telly on, *Potters Court*'ll be starting,' Sim yelled as she picked up the phone.

It was Lucy. 'Sim? I've found my dream dress,' she said breathlessly.

'About time too.' *Potters Court* had indeed started. Sim stretched the phone wire as far as it would go, so that she could keep an eye on her programme from the lounge doorway. Anyone but Lucy would have been told to ring back in an hour and a half. 'You were cutting it a bit fine, weren't you?' she said, referring to Lucy's dress,

29

not the soap opera. The wedding was on Saturday the fifteenth of May, a mere seven weeks away. Matt and Lucy were getting married in the chapel of Summerton College in Cambridge, where Matt's dad was the Master. The reception, starting with a four-course wedding breakfast, was to be held in the dining hall, which the 250 guests would fill to capacity.

'Well, I'd bought another dress, just in case,' said Lucy. 'Quite an expensive one, too. I wish I hadn't wasted all that money now. It was lovely, but it wasn't the one. It wasn't special.'

'And this new one is?'

'Oh, yes. It's absolutely beautiful. I nearly faint every time I look at it.'

'What's it like?' It would certainly be either white or cream, thought Sim, very feminine, with a long train. She wondered what her own dream wedding dress might look like. Probably nothing like a wedding dress. There'd have to be some lilac, turquoise or fuchsia in it somewhere. Still, she couldn't see herself and Francis getting married. She had a feeling he'd be against it. His dad, with whom Francis was in touch intermittently, didn't bother to hide his view of marriage as something unsuspecting men were forced into by women they didn't love. He'd left home when Francis was eight. When Sim asked him how he'd felt, Francis muttered grumpily, 'I could see his point.'

'All my magazines say you shouldn't describe the dress to anyone,' said Lucy. 'Sorry – you'll have to wait and see. Now, what other news is there?' Sim didn't say anything. There was no point in telling Lucy about Campbell and Eve before the story had been confirmed. In any case, Lucy meant news for her to tell Sim. 'Oh, I've also bought some new shoes because the pair I bought originally went better with the other dress. The rings have gone off to be engraved.' Lucy speeded up. 'Matt's working on the seating plan . . .'

'Calm down,' said Sim. 'It'll all be fine. Are you panicking?'

'No, but . . . I really want it to be perfect, Sim.'

'It will be.' Most things that involved Matt and Lucy were. Summerton, Cambridge's richest college, had been stunning since 1583, so there was no reason to suppose it would be anything other than a blissful backdrop on the fifteenth of May, and Matt and Lucy looked as if they'd been designed with a wedding album in mind. Matt had a slim, athletic frame, dark hair and big brown eyes, and Lucy was petite with blonde, curly hair and smooth, pale skin on which Sim had never seen a spot. They'd certainly fulfilled their part of any bargain with the Almighty (in whom Sim only believed when it occurred to her that Matt and Lucy believed in Him) by keeping themselves in mint condition. Neither had ever smoked or taken drugs. They drank in a way that made drinking seem an uncomplicated, even a wholesome, pleasure. 'Get drunk with Matt and Lucy and you never have a hangover the next day,' Vanessa had once joked, but subsequent tests of the theory revealed it to be true.

Sim admired their quest for perfection, which didn't confine itself to their wedding plans. They would never have dreamed of using the same glasses for red and white wine, or allowing plastic or metal coat-hangers to dangle in their wardrobes when wooden ones were clearly superior. If Matt and Lucy had been shrilly or prescriptively fussy it might have annoyed Sim, but their gracious, happy pursuit of the best life had to offer impressed her, mainly because she felt they deserved it. Nothing even remotely unsavoury lurked in either of their pasts or in their present; Matt and Lucy had nothing to atone for. In return, it was almost as if heaven was meeting them halfway. For Sim they acted as a symbol, reviving her aspirations. She didn't want to be like them, or even want the same things – coat-hangers weren't important to her, nor was a big wedding for that matter – but there was something about

31

Matt and Lucy that made Sim strive to be her best self in their presence.

They'd moved three months ago, when Matt was head-hunted (though as the well-brought-up son of a Cambridge college Master he discreetly avoided using that word) by an American ice-cream manufacturer that was putting together a team of physicists to examine the particles that adhered to ice at different temperatures, investigating the effect these had on the texture of ice cream. Sim couldn't imagine an occupation, or a country, better suited to Matt's personality. He was startlingly clever at the same time as being unashamedly hedonistic, and was having the time of his life on Budweiser, baseball and an endless supply of free lollies from work. Lucy, an economist, now worked for the World Bank, much to Nicholas's horror. As a member of the Superman Paralysis Party (it wasn't called that, but it might as well have been), he objected to banks, be they World or piggy.

'Now, the stag-hen weekend . . .' Lucy's anxious voice interrupted Sim's musings. 'We've decided to go for Hollins Hall, on your recommendation. I booked it yesterday. Are you sure it's nice?'

'It's beautiful,' Sim assured her, feeling as if she'd sud-denly been made the hostess and silently awarding a few bonus points to Yorkshire. She'd expected Matt and Lucy to choose a Cambridge hotel. 'Like a castle, on top of a hill with huge gardens and a view across the Aire valley.'

'I had to book it quickly or we would have lost the rooms,' said Lucy, 'so I've booked four doubles and one single. That's right, isn't it? You and Francis, me and Matt, Vanessa and Nicholas, Campbell and Eve, Hazel.'

'Right,' said Sim after a pause. 'Listen, I can easily ring Hollins Hall if you're busy, but is there any chance of changing Hazel's single room to a double?'

'Sure, as long as they've got one available. Why, is there a prospective boyfriend on the scene?' Like everyone in love, Lucy wanted the same good fortune for all her friends.

'No, but you know how sensitive Hazel is. To be the only person with a single room would make her feel bad.' And if she had a double it could always accommodate Eve if she and Campbell weren't on bed-sharing terms by then, which they damn well would be if Sim had anything to do with it.

'I'll e-mail them and see if I can change the booking,' said Lucy. 'And you've got the dates written down, seventh to the ninth of May? Can you check everyone knows?'

'Already have and they do.' The purpose of stag and hen parties was not clear to Sim, but she was willing to be a farm animal for a while if it would make her friends happy; besides, it was a good opportunity for everyone to get together.

'Sim, I'm worried about Gillian,' Lucy said in between short, sharp breaths. 'What if she finds out there was a stag-hen weekend and she wasn't invited? What if someone lets it slip at the wedding?'

'I'll have a word with Francis,' said Sim. Francis tended to be the weak link in any chain of deception; he tried to save time by listening to only part of what he was told and invariably missed the '. . . but whatever you do, don't tell anyone' bit at the end.

'It's not just Francis. Any of us could give the game away and the last thing I need is Gillian having hysterics at my wedding. You know we actually thought twice about having round tables for the reception?'

Sim chuckled. Gillian was obsessed, in group meal situations, with sitting in the middle and hated restaurants where the tables were round because, short of sitting on top of the food, there was no way she could make herself more central than the other members of the party. 'Are you saying you want to invite her to Hollins Hall?' Sim asked. 'I can extend my wedding day truce to the weekend before, if you like. I won't be friendly to her, but I can try to be neutral and avoid an argument.'

'God, no. Thanks, but I don't think I could cope with Gillian for a whole weekend and we hardly know Andrew . . .'

'Andrew?' Sim felt her throat constrict. 'What's he got to do with anything?'

'Well, it'd be rude to invite Gillian without him, wouldn't it?'

'But . . . he's not coming to the wedding.' Sim was confused.

'Yes, he is,' said Lucy. 'Didn't you know? Oh – that was another thing I had to tell you – he wants you to ring him. Don't know why; I didn't think you knew him.' Sim was casting about for something convincing to say when Lucy went on, 'Maybe it's something to do with you and Gillian, if he knows you've fallen out. He said to ring him at work. Maybe he's scared there'll be a brawl at the wedding,' she concluded nervously.

'Did Gillian tell you Andrew wants me to ring him?' asked Sim, too unsettled by this news to reassure Lucy that her special day would be brawl-free.

'No, Andrew mentioned it when he RSVPed to the invitation. I kept meaning to tell you, but my mind's been all over the place.'

'Well . . . did he leave a number?' Or was he arrogant enough to assume Sim would remember it? Her composure was severely shaken. Nothing was more terrifying than past that thought it was present. She hadn't spoken to Andrew for over two years. What could he possibly have to say that was worth hearing? His conversation was by far his worst feature. It was bad enough that she'd have to see him at the wedding. Sim could picture it now: Andrew would corner her for a private chat, subject her to a string of crass innuendos to remind her of what she'd given up, then whisper 'toodle-pip' in her ear before scuttling back to Gillian.

Toodle-pip. Those two words (or that one word, depending on where one stood with regard to hyphens) had killed Sim's lust for Andrew Johnson with the speed and efficiency of a hired assassin. He'd introduced it into the vocabulary of their affair at a certain point, as a sign of greater intimacy. If only he'd started to say it before they slept together, Sim might have escaped unsullied, but in those more formal days he'd stuck to 'see you' and ''bye'. How was Sim to know that consummation would turn him into a toodle-pip man?

And how dare he attempt to communicate with her via Lucy; was he trying to scare her? Sim felt oddly vulnerable, as if it was bad luck to hear from Andrew less than half an hour after she'd found out Campbell and Eve had split up. She'd thought they were solid, as indestructible as herself and Francis, but maybe no couple was.

Sim tried to recall how she'd felt in the days when Andrew and Gillian were nothing to do with each other and quite separately distasteful to her. For over a year, Andrew was Sim's ex-lover and Gillian was first Sim's friend, then her ex-friend; if only Sim could have edited out, retrospectively, their meeting (at Cambridge Folk Festival of all places – neither of them even liked bloody folk music) and subsequent relationship. Their collective distastefulness added up to so much more than the sum of its parts. Andrew had linked Sim to Gillian, with whom she'd hoped to sever all ties, in the most shaming way possible, via a part of his body Sim had hoped to forget, and there was no undoing it, even if they split up tomorrow. Until the end of history, Sim and Gillian would always both have been toodle-pipped by Andrew Johnson. Sim felt not unlike a fashion designer on discovering significant wardrobe overlap with a tramp.

It was Lucy who'd first told her about Gillian's new boyfriend, scattering the seeds of countless worries. Had Andrew told Gillian he knew Sim? If so, had he told her the truth or pretended they were just acquaintances? Would

Gillian take the opportunity to get back at Sim by telling Francis? It was no longer merely the infidelity that needed to be concealed; Francis found Gillian repulsive, and would feel humiliated if he discovered that Gillian and Sim could be attracted, and attractive, to the same type of man.

Even if Andrew hadn't told Gillian already, there was always the chance he might, once they got really close, or if she succeeded in convincing him that Sim deserved no loyalty. As if he hadn't been disloyal enough by stealing a bit of her life. As soon as Andrew found out that his Gillian and Sim's were one and the same, he should have backed off. Was it ridiculous to be proprietorial over even the parts of one's life and past that one detested? If Sim caught Andrew rifling through her dustbin she'd be equally furious. Andrew had reneged on the severance deal. He and Sim were supposed to go their separate ways; he was surely not too stupid to realise that Gillian was not, and never would be, his separate way. Did he want Sim to live in dread? Was that why he hadn't told Gillian yet, to prolong his hold, keep back his trump card for as long as possible, or was it paranoid to imagine he would think in such a convoluted way? Not everyone, after all, was a soap opera storyliner.

Lucy recited Andrew's work telephone number and Sim pretended to write it down, though she had no intention of appeasing him with a call. If those two leeches wanted to tell tales, let them, and if anyone questioned the longevity of Sim's grudge against Gillian in the light of this new information, so be it. The truth was available to anyone who cared to look for it.

'Sim,' said Lucy tentatively, 'you're going to think I'm mad, but . . . well, the main reason I phoned is . . .' She stopped and sighed.

'What?' Sim forced herself to concentrate. What horror waited in the wings?

'I keep having these awful dreams. Do you think that's normal, before a wedding?'

'What sort of dreams?'

'Well, just one, really. But it's too disgusting . . .'

'Go on,' Sim urged. 'Say it out loud and it'll lose its power.'

'I haven't even told Matt.'

'Of course not.' The very idea, thought Sim.

'Okay. It's the morning of the wedding. I go to put on my dress and it doesn't fit. So I start moaning to my mum that I must have got fatter, expecting her to contradict me and say I look fine, but she doesn't say anything. So I turn round and look at her and . . .' Lucy took a deep breath. 'She screams. I ask her what's wrong . . .'

'And?' Sim demanded.

'She tells me to look in the mirror. Oh, God, Sim, this is so gross, really . . .'

'Tell me!'

'I look, and I've got this . . . this Siamese twin growing out of my side. That's why I can't get the dress on.'

'An identical twin?' Sim asked, trying to keep the shock and distaste out of her voice. A fat dream would have been clichéd but less disturbing.

'That's the weird bit. I can't see her face, but in the dream I know that she hasn't got any . . . you know, organs. She's sharing mine, and if I get rid of her, she'll die. Then I wake up. Told you it was weird.' Lucy tried to laugh it off.

'Hm,' said Sim. 'Are you and Matt getting on okay at the moment?'

'Fine. That's why I can't understand it. I keep wondering if something's wrong that I don't know about. I know I sound paranoid, but . . . there's nothing you're not telling me, is there?'

Sim assured her that there wasn't and that the nightmare probably wouldn't recur now they'd discussed it. 'Bugger,' she said as she put down the phone, feeling treacherous. If Lucy found out that Campbell had left Eve she'd connect it with her dream and imagine that her wedding was jinxed.

37

Campbell and Eve needed to be put back together, and fast. Who was the woman he'd left her for, anyway? It couldn't be a proper thing. Enough of this messing about. Sim dialled Hazel's number and left a message outlining the problem and inviting helpful suggestions, then left a similar message on Vanessa's mobile. The important thing was to make sure no one said anything to Lucy. Irrationally, Sim felt that if she succeeded in reuniting Campbell and Eve, she could also ward off Andrew.

She made a concerted effort to calm down, then returned to the lounge, where Francis was stuffing papers into his briefcase in front of *Potters Court*. The sight of her programme reminded Sim of the many characters' weddings she'd sabotaged. Each time, the challenge for the storylining team was to think of a new twist to ensure that the bride and groom left the church, mosque, temple, synagogue, hotel or register office without having tied the knot. Occasionally the ceremony was allowed to run smoothly, to lull the viewers into a false sense of security, and the trouble was saved for the reception. All the obvious devices had been used: bigamy, last-minute doubts and the like, but Sim had quickly got bored and started to suggest more outlandish things. One young woman turned out to have webbed feet, which her fiancé noticed for the first time when he saw her in her wedding sandals. One prospective groom admitted to his wife-to-be that he came from a family of cannibals and the buffet meat was human flesh.

Sim had proved she was resourceful when it came to disrupting weddings; what she had to do now was the exact opposite. She would imagine that Matt and Lucy's wedding was a *Potters Court* omnibus and anticipate everything that might conceivably go wrong, every tactless comment, feud or faux pas that might ruin the day. Then she'd channel all her creativity into defusing each potential threat. Starting with this silly business of Campbell and his new woman. She had six weeks before the stag-hen weekend; that was long enough. She settled down on the sofa, pleased with her resolution. 'Did you know', she said sadly, 'that in the last three years, the viewing figures have gone down from nine million to two?'

Francis looked up, adjusting his glasses. 'But . . . that must be us.' He looked bewildered. 'You and me.'

'Two million, you fool. Anyway, I'm not sure you'd count as a viewing figure. You aren't looking at the screen.'

'I don't need to. I get the gist.'

'It's our own fault,' said Sim gloomily. 'I keep telling the team that we need decent characterisation and genuine human drama, that's what gets people hooked. And proper conversations, not just short, sharp bursts that further the plot. Francis?'

'Mm. I'm not phoning him.'

'Who?'

'Campbell.'

'I was talking about *Potters Court*.'

'Oh well, Campbell, soap operas . . .'

'But since you brought it up . . . quick, it's the adverts!'

'Quick what?' Francis picked up the remote control and switched channels. On BBC 2, two men and a woman were discussing the ivory trade.

'Phone Campbell.'

'Sim, you're confusing me.' A copy of the *Spectator* lay open at Francis's feet with a tea bag on top, seeping russet liquid into its pages. He closed the magazine without removing the tea bag and it spurted brown juice on to his hand. He frowned, wiped his hand on his jeans and dropped the *Spectator*, complete with Earl Grey infusion, into his briefcase. 'Right, off I go,' he said, standing up.

'Francis, that's . . .'

'Ssh!' He put up a hand to stop her speaking, then pointed at the television. Sim looked at what had captured his attention. For once it was nothing to do with the news. There was no sign of the Dingleys or Annette Wrigley. Grab-a-ditch Caravan was nowhere in sight. This was an advert for Napper cigars, one Sim remembered from when she was a child. She concentrated on the screen. A young man with a floppy curtain of straight hair, dressed in a classic suit and leather brogues, sat in a maroon leather chair. Behind him was a large mahogany bookshelf which sported an array of leather-bound volumes with gold-lettered spines. Slowly, he reached into his jacket pocket and produced a fat cigar. Sim couldn't imagine why Francis particularly wanted to watch this advert now; he must have seen it before.

The young man turned on the table lamp beside his chair and examined his cigar in the light. It was wrapped in cellophane, with a white band round the middle. He smiled and pulled at the band, delicately uncoiling the cellophane before dropping it into a crystal ashtray on the table.

'I thought they weren't allowed to advertise cigars on telly any more,' said Sim.

'They aren't. They'll cut back to the studio in a minute. There.' The woman and two men reappeared and immediately started to shout at one another. 'Napper keep denying they're tangled up in the ivory trade, but new evidence keeps coming to light,' said Francis.

'The dapper unwrap a Napper,' Sim intoned in a deep voice, remembering how the advertisement had ended. 'I thought the white bands round the cigars were actually made of ivory. Or had some ivory in them, or something.'

'That's it,' Francis muttered. 'That's her.' He pulled the *Spectator* out of his briefcase. The pressed tea bag fell to the floor and Sim picked it up. 'Look.' Francis showed her the back cover, which sported a large picture of a cigar packet with the word 'Napper' written across it in white puffy writing, intended to represent smoke. 'The dapper unwrap a Napper', said the caption at the bottom of the page.

Sim couldn't see any sign of a 'her'. 'Francis, what are you on about?' she asked.

40

'Campbell's . . . oh, Christ, don't bloody moan at me. Campbell's new woman. She's a Napper.'

'What?' Sim sprang to her feet. 'She can't be a Napper as in Napper tobacco! How do you know? Why didn't you tell me?'

'I'm telling you now,' said Francis. 'Eve mentioned it when she phoned. I forgot until I saw the advert. I think so. I think that's what Eve said.'

Sim stood back with her hands on her hips and addressed an imaginary audience: 'Campbell, our close friend, has run off with the heiress to the Napper tobacco fortune and he forgets to mention it!'

'I didn't say that,' Francis protested. 'She may only be a distant relation. You made that last bit up.'

'Is it any wonder, when I'm starved of information? Right, that really is it. I insist that you phone Campbell this instant.'

2

Every Saturday it was the same: Hazel left work at four in order to catch the beginning of *Potters Court*, and every week without fail her train would be delayed and she'd miss the first half-hour. Today was no exception, but for once Hazel wasn't thinking about Sim's programme as she let herself into the flat. Her mind was elsewhere. 'It's a conspiracy,' she said loudly, slamming the front door behind her. 'And, um . . . it wouldn't surprise me if – Ian, are you here? – it wouldn't surprise me if it went all the way to the top!'

Ian smiled to himself and carried on washing up. Hazel liked to start conversations in the middle. In the old days this had confused him. Once he would have responded by saying, 'What's a conspiracy? All the way to the top of where?' but recently he'd started to enjoy guessing what Hazel was talking about. It seemed to Ian that she was challenging him to care enough about her to follow the peculiar machinations of her thought process, so he did his best. The more he understood her where others failed, the closer and more exclusive they would be.

'What have they done now?' he shouted towards the hall. This was a fairly safe response. Hazel was bound to be talking about her colleagues who, if her descriptions of her working life could be trusted, lurked in shadowy offices plotting to overthrow Hazel. Ian had the impression that being the literature development officer for Leeds was every inch as hazardous a career option as being a Catholic queen in a court full of Protestant arsonists. It was certainly time-consuming; Hazel rarely got back from the office before nine on weekdays and worked most weekends as well. If Ian hadn't changed his own timetable he'd never have seen her.

'Oh, they've only . . . See for yourself. Look.' Hazel appeared in the archway that separated the kitchen from the lounge. She was wearing the tall, fake-fur hat, woolly scarf, gloves and heavy floor-length coat that she always wore to go out, whatever the weather. She looked like a tiny Cossack. In her right glove she brandished a fat paperback book. 'What they forget is . . . um . . . um . . . that I know the world of publishing from the inside. They can't fool me.' Good, thought Ian, a clue. So this had something to do with the book Hazel was holding. Now he felt he had a fighting chance of understanding the conversation at some point in the near future. 'God, what an awful day. I've . . . um . . . um . . . got elephantitis in my ankles from running round the branch libraries, checking they'd put up my posters,' Hazel moaned. 'And guess what? They hadn't! I *hate* working with librarians. I'm going to become . . . um . . . um . . . an orthodontist!'

'What's that book?' Ian asked. Hazel held it up so he could see it. 'Oh. The new Cal Raynard. I didn't know . . .'

'Poor Cal Raynard. If I were him I'd slit my throat,' Hazel wailed.

Ian put the last pan on the draining rack, pulled the plug from the sink and dried his hands, taking a deep breath. 'Let's see it,' he said. 'I didn't know his new one was out yet.'

'Vanessa's his editor. I bet she and her cronies forced him to call it *Howdy*.' Hazel talked to Ian about her friends as if he knew them. Sometimes this made him feel less left out, other times more so. Bitterly, he thought of the many conversations he'd had about Vanessa since he'd known

Hazel; more than she'd ever had about him was a safe bet. A dark mood crept up on him. Why should he have to hear about the other people in Hazel's life, when they would never hear about him?

Ian took the book from Hazel, wincing as he stared at the brash cover picture of a handsome, square-jawed cowboy wearing a Stetson against a background of golden desert. 'The title's totally unsuitable,' said Hazel, who got steamed up about literary injustices above any other sort because books, unlike people, couldn't defend themselves. 'It should have been called *The Contrived Cowboy*. That would have had thematic relevance in all sorts of ways. It's the name of a bar the protagonist goes to and at the end when he dies . . . Oops. But you *must* still read it. It's worth it for the texture of the language alone,' Hazel solemnly pronounced. She often passed on books to Ian. She'd lent him her copy of Cal Raynard's first novel, *Cloudy*, which he hadn't read, although he'd pretended to read it so as not to upset her. He'd made sure to add new creases to the spine before giving it back.

'I think they made him call it *Howdy* to rhyme with *Cloudy*,' said Hazel. 'I refuse to believe Cal Raynard chose that title. I . . . um . . . um . . . spend my life being confided in by famous writers, so I know how their minds work.' Ian bit back a grin. A double 'um' from Hazel was a sure sign that she was about to exaggerate wildly. In truth she had one friend, Sim, who wrote for a mediocre soap opera and was not at all famous. And to say she knew the publishing world from the inside was a liberal interpretation of her having one friend, Vanessa, who was an editor at Gable Bazzard. Hazel didn't lie; Ian never suspected her of deliberately misleading him. It was simply that her mind distorted everything. All facts went through the Hazel filter and the result was that every story she told sounded disconcertingly like bullshit. Her double 'um's, in particular, made it sound as if she was playing for time while she invented the rest of her tale. Ian could imagine how this might annoy some people, but he found it hilarious. He was touched by her desire to improve upon the bare facts.

'Cal Raynard should have fought for his rights,' said Hazel in an injured tone, as if he'd let her down by failing to do so. 'It's his book, not the publisher's, and he'll never be taken seriously with rhyming titles and those dreadful garish covers . . . yuck. I intend to fight ceaselessly – ceaselessly! – until he gets the recognition he deserves.'

'So, is Vanessa part of this conspiracy?' Ian was amazed as well as impressed that Hazel cared so much. The unwelcome notion that he might be in love with her tried to present itself to his awareness, but he dismissed it.

'She must be.' Hazel shrugged. Ian waited for her to embark upon her ceaseless fight by condemning Vanessa's role in the atrocity, but wasn't particularly surprised when she said instead, 'I'm going to buy Matt and Lucy Cal Raynard's collected works for a wedding present. I'll have them leather-bound. They'll appreciate him.'

'Even if Vanessa doesn't, you mean?' Ian wanted to get off the subject of the wedding. He couldn't help resenting Hazel's enthusiasm for an event at which she would have to pretend he didn't exist. They'd become good friends over the past few months and it was in this capacity that Ian objected to being denied. All Hazel's other close friends would be there. Wouldn't she miss him and want at least to talk about him, make him part of this momentous occasion somehow? Wouldn't her inability to do so spoil her enjoyment at all? If only she hadn't gone on and on about the wedding, imbued it with such significance. Ian had long ago accepted that he must remain a secret, but on the morning of Saturday, May the fifteenth (he even knew the bloody date!) the point would be rammed home in a particularly sharp fashion.

'She slags him off to me,' said Hazel, 'but Sim says she's just goading me because she knows he's my favourite author, and that I shouldn't get upset. Sim says she wouldn't publish him if she didn't like his work.' Sim this, Sim that, thought Ian. The woman clearly had a blind spot the size of Baildon Moor and Ian wished Hazel would stop quoting her. Everything he knew about Vanessa, everything Hazel had ever told him, suggested she was a total bitch with no redeeming features. Hazel didn't mean to give this impression; on the contrary, she took pains to explain that Vanessa was only ever joking when she said hurtful, destructive things. Hazel provided the facts, but the interpretation was all Ian's own work. What frustrated him was her unquestioning acceptance of Sim's slant on Vanessa, one that flew in the face of all the evidence.

'She'd publish him if she were tied in to some sort of contract,' said Ian. 'Or if she inherited him from another editor.' He started to flick through *Howdy*. 'Could have been worse,' he muttered. 'It could have been *Howdy!* with an exclamation mark.'

'Don't look at the end, you'll spoil it,' Hazel shrieked, trying to wrestle the book away from him.

Ian, who was nearly a foot taller, held it open above her head. 'But you've told me what happens. Anyway, I'm not looking at the end, I'm looking at the . . .' Ian stopped abruptly. He was looking at something he didn't like the look of. 'At, er . . .' he muttered, distracted.

'Ian, what's wrong? What have you seen?'

'Nothing.' He smiled weakly. 'Here, take it.' He couldn't wait for Hazel to take the book out of his hands. In fact, if she didn't relieve him of it soon, he might not be able to stop himself from hurling it across the room.

'Ian, what's wrong? Is it something I've done?' Hazel began to cower and gesticulate.

'Nothing's wrong,' Ian said firmly. He couldn't allow himself to think about it now. 'I promise. Sim phoned while you were out.' A heavy-handed change of the subject, but it worked.

'Oh no! You didn't answer it, did you?' Hazel clapped a hand over her mouth.

'No, of course I didn't. Calm down. The message is on the machine.' Campbell had left Eve, apparently, but Ian thought he'd better let Sim's recorded voice break the news. He wished he hadn't needed to invoke her; in his present mood, he would have preferred to pretend Hazel's friends didn't exist. From what he remembered of her message, Sim wanted Hazel to help her get Campbell and Eve back together. A bit silly, really. What could Hazel do, or Sim for that matter? It wasn't their business. 'Why don't you ring her back?' Ian suggested, keen for Hazel to leave the room so that he could take a closer look at *Howdy*.

'Okay. I'll put her on speakerphone.' Hazel often did this, so Ian would feel included. 'Ian? You wouldn't ever answer the phone when I wasn't here, would you? You do know how important it is?' She shivered, still in her hat, coat, scarf and gloves.

'Yes, yes. Don't worry about that. Do you want a cup of tea, before you phone Sim?'

'Yes, please. It's just that ... I don't want anyone to disapprove of me. You do understand, don't you?' Ian did, but that wasn't to say he liked the situation. If Hazel's friends would disapprove, they didn't deserve to have Hazel as a friend. In any case, Ian refused to believe they would. 'My brothers would never speak to me again.' Hazel looked subdued, not elated as Ian would have looked at such a prospect. 'They'd tell my mum and dad, who'd ... um ... um ... cut me out of their will!' Double 'um' notwithstanding, Ian didn't doubt for a minute that Hazel's brothers were capable of doing this. They terrorised their timid parents just as they'd terrorised Hazel until she left home. Not that Mr and Mrs Ings had anything worth inheriting; if their mouldy back-to-back in Nuneaton was as grim as Hazel said it was, they were welcome to it.

Ings was a peculiar surname, though still preferable to Ian's, which was Boyle. Appended to Hazel it seemed cute

47

and cuddly; on her brothers it was more ominous, as if they'd concealed the first part of an appellation that might incriminate them. Privately, Ian thought of them as Badth and Wrongdo. He didn't share this joke with Hazel, unsure how she would take it. 'No one has any right to disapprove,' he shouted from the kitchen. 'What you do in the privacy of your own home is your business.'

'That's not true. I could be murdering people in the privacy of my own home.'

'Okay, but . . . this isn't a moral issue, that's my point.' Ian carried their cups of tea through to the lounge. 'It worries me that you think it might be.' He smiled warmly at Hazel. If he was going to use words like 'worries' he had to deflect them with reassuring facial expressions. Hazel's eyes widened in alarm until she saw his smile and understood that he wasn't angry with her. 'I mean, what if someone finds out? You might rather give me up, to stop them thinking badly of you.' There, he'd said it. Ian had craved reassurance on this point for some time, but because getting it involved mentioning a worst-case scenario to Hazel, never a wise course of action, he'd kept putting it off.

'Oh, Ian!' Hazel grabbed his hand. 'I'd never give you up. Never, never, never. I'd . . . um . . . um . . . collapse and die! You know that. God, I remember how I used to be, I was like an insane person. I couldn't have gone on for much longer. As you know, I've . . . um . . . um . . . spent most of my life in hospital.' Hazel hauled herself out of her chair and began to divest herself of coat, hat, scarf and gloves. A few moments later Ian heard her sling them into her wardrobe, shouting, 'Get in there, you infernal accessories!' He chuckled. She was starting to move back into theatrical mode, a sure sign that she felt better. Ian did too. He'd been afraid that Hazel was too weak to withstand peer pressure. If only she could defend herself as vociferously as she defended Cal Raynard. The problem, Ian guessed, was that Hazel wasn't convinced she deserved

48

a defence. Was it other people's disapproval she wanted to dodge, or her own? Did she regard Ian as the sin she could never confess? If so, Ian blamed Badth and Wrongdo for infecting her with their warped values.

Ian couldn't stand strong characters. All too often, like Badth and Wrongdo, they doubled as bullies, and even when they didn't they were profoundly irritating. As a child, reading his book of Bible stories, Ian had been convinced that Samson was a lot nicer after his haircut. Hazel was flamboyant, but she was also vulnerable. When they'd first met, before Ian realised what an exceptional person she was, Hazel had gone through a phase of leaving cliffhanger messages on his answerphone: 'Ring me quickly, something dreadful's happened' or 'Come round immediately – I've got something really exciting to tell you'. Gallantly, Ian rushed to the flat, only to find that the something dreadful was that Hazel couldn't get a stain out of a T-shirt and the something really exciting was a rerun of *Cagney and Lacey* on television. In those days Ian had been worried that she might turn out to be a strong character of the most annoying kind, but he'd soon cottoned on to what was really happening. Hazel was so insecure that she felt she needed special effects to make her interesting. Ian loved her surreal exaggerations but wished she didn't feel she had to bribe others to like her.

He was about to pick up *Howdy* again when he heard Hazel shriek, 'What? No!' as she replayed Sim's message. 'Campbell's left Eve! The sod! The absolute *bastard*!'

Ian was taken aback. Not that he knew the guy from a bar of soap, but Hazel had always liked him before. Wasn't Campbell the one who attended every single literary event she organised, including ones Ian wouldn't have been seen dead at, even if he could have appeared in public at Hazel's side? How had Hazel managed to ascertain that Campbell was a bastard on the basis of so little information? 'Give him a chance,' Ian suggested.

'I will not!' declared Hazel. 'And if he thinks he's getting an invitation to the launch of the Pudsey Poetry Postcards exhibition, he's got another think coming.'

Vanessa Willis gritted her teeth and murmured 'Come *on*' at the large iron gate in front of her that was taking an aeon to open. She could see Grange Road, but it would be some time before she'd be on it. Only in Cambridge, she thought, would one be expected to wait politely, maybe even smile and whistle along to Radio Three, while a gate yawned open as if it had all the time in the world. If this were London, someone would have ripped it out of the ground by now.

In London, though, no one would dream of sheltering university lecturers behind the high walls of a multimillion-pound model village with a chunky security gate. In London academics lived like normal people; some of them were even rumoured to be normal people. Nicholas's determination not to move there made a mockery of his left-wing posturing. He loved the cocooned, privileged life of a Cambridge don, which was fine, but why couldn't he admit it? Instead, he pretended that his chances of changing the world were significantly improved by staying where he was, in a centre of intellectual excellence where his ideas were treated with the respect they deserved. Change the world, indeed. He couldn't even change a tyre and, irritatingly, he never needed to because he refused to learn to drive.

Vanessa loathed Cambridge. However strenuously Nicholas tried to talk her into liking it, he would fail. Rather than bothering to find out what was at the root of her antipathy for the place, he bombarded her with a list of its attractions: 'It's clean, close to the countryside, there's no unemployment. Haven't you noticed how miserable and unhealthy everyone in London looks?' Of course Vanessa had; she wasn't visually impaired. And she'd noticed that in Cambridge people trotted around looking jolly and civilised, carrying straw baskets over their arms. 'Matt and Lucy are coming all the way back from Washington to get married here. And Francis would kill to live here again.' Nicholas always cited Francis when they had this argument, confirming Vanessa's suspicion that in a perverse way he respected Francis more than anyone, despite taking issue with him in public at every opportunity. 'You've heard him on the subject of Yorkshire.'

Yes, Vanessa had. One had no choice but to listen to Francis when he wanted to hold forth, pompous sod. And he saw no need for reciprocity either. Francis tuned in and out of what other people said as it suited him. Sometimes he even left the room, sticking his head round the door a few seconds later to see if the conversation had become any more interesting in his absence. You had to admire a person who was capable of being so effortlessly offensive.

If the Yorkshire yokels really were stupid and miserable, the county had to be doing something right. Stupid people deserved to be miserable. In Cambridge, people were stupid but happy because they believed they were clever, which was far worse. And nobody could accuse Yorkshire of being civilised, which was what Vanessa hated most about Cambridge. She'd heard on the radio the other day that, according to RSPCA statistics, Yorkshire was the cruelty capital of Britain. She could feel at home in a place like that. In Cambridge she was a pariah.

Unlike Nicholas, Vanessa was under no illusions about herself. She knew she was neither a normal person nor a good one; indeed, she suspected herself of being a latent sociopath. Why else would she get such a kick out of her warped home life with Nicholas, with its hair-pulling, bites and punch-ups, its ever present undertone of back-stabbing one-upmanship? Nicholas was equally addicted to it; no one loved a fight more than he did. Vanessa wasn't fooled by his so-called passionate political views; they were merely an accessory that maximised his opportunities for venting his aggression. If Nicholas had been born to poor white trash he might have become a wife-beating drunk instead of a politics lecturer. This idea appealed immensely to Vanessa, who gave as good as she got, both verbally and physically. There was no denying that, to use the language she reserved for that troop of whining ingrates, her authors, she was an unsympathetic character. Interesting, definitely; amusing occasionally, but nice? Perish the thought.

And her daily commute was making her worse. It was all right for bloody Nicholas. Last month his department had swapped buildings with Modern Languages, and his new office was five minutes' walk from home. Cambridge was his patch. The offices of Gable Bazzard, where Vanessa worked, were not so near. Every morning she got up at six, washed, dressed and took a taxi to the station where she caught the seven fifteen to King's Cross. She arrived at ten past eight and, along with a grisly coachload of swaying, greying, sweating automatons, took the tube to Hammersmith. This was the high point of her journey, seeing the misery of others at close range, smelling precisely how bad mankind's predicament was, summed up in the armpit of one businessman. It was the sort of genuine, gruesome life experience one didn't get in Cambridge. True, London was one giant toilet, but then so was human nature.

From Hammersmith tube station, Vanessa took a taxi if there was one or, if there wasn't, walked for fifteen minutes to Gable Bazzard's building, kicking used condoms out of her way and climbing over vagrants. By the time she arrived at work her face was covered with grey streaks (equal parts sweat and pollution) and she wanted nothing more than to crawl back to bed and sleep for a week. But the constant, ingrained tiredness wasn't the worst thing about commuting; Vanessa was plagued by the unsettling feeling that she was a mere visitor to her and Nicholas's life. He lived and worked in Cambridge, had a proper base there. He was the home team, with all the associated advantages, while Vanessa trudged back and forth like a fucking refugee.

He wouldn't have understood if she'd tried to explain. This, at least, was gratifying. Nobody understood Vanessa, a state of affairs that pleased her greatly. She couldn't fathom the keenness of some people to make their minds accessible to the troglodytes they encountered on a daily basis. Vanessa much preferred to be beyond everybody's grasp. 'Nobody understands me,' the imbecile Gillian Kench was always snivelling. On the contrary; how could anyone fail to understand a woman who wrote long lists each New Year's Eve entitled 'Gaols for Next Year', on which her every desire was painstakingly misspelt? The understanding of others was half voyeurism, half mental pillage, and left one's psyche feeling like the victim of a pogrom. Vanessa would never dream of debasing herself by descending to a comprehensible level.

Sim was big on understanding people, but Vanessa could forgive her because her primary motive was nosiness, not philanthropy. Her rampant curiosity was contagious, too; she managed to interest Vanessa in their other . . . well, friends would do for want of a better definition. Oh, they were okay, amusing enough – especially Gillian, who gave Vanessa a sense of what fun it must have been, in the old days, to sneer at the village idiot – but Sim was the only one she'd really miss, the only one who was real to her. About the others, Vanessa felt pretty much as she did about the characters in *Potters Court*: they were convenient chat fodder. Which reminded her: she must tell Sim about the strange man in Hazel's flat. Vanessa knew a juicy new source of gossip when she saw one and it'd make a change from talking about the wedding, which Vanessa was already thoroughly bored with.

The gate appeared to be having a rest, midway between closed and open. Fifty fucking years later! Vanessa turned on Radio Four and caught a snatch of yet another discussion about Kosovo, how terrible it all was. Yeah, yeah. The solution to stuff like that was obvious: anyone who wanted to avoid being raped, exiled, bombed or otherwise plundered should simply refrain from wearing a headscarf. Whenever victims were shown on the news, they had headscarves on; anybody who wore one, therefore, was asking for trouble and shouldn't come crying to Vanessa. She smiled, thinking of how she would bait Nicholas with this observation later.

She pulled a dark-brown Chanel lipstick out of her handbag and started to apply it, looking in the rear-view mirror. Vanessa hated bright colours; they reminded her of evangelical Christians. How Sim could bear to go round in those floor-length turquoise cloaks she would never understand. All Vanessa's clothes were black, but she was careful to buy only smart designer dresses and trouser suits with exquisitely tailored jackets, to distinguish herself from other people who wore black all the time, the lower orders who stank and had stained teeth.

It was quarter to six. She had exactly fifteen minutes to get to the Garden House Moat House Hotel (which idiot gave that place its name?) and find a parking space before her regular Saturday afternoon appointment at the beauty salon. This week she needed her aromatherapy neck, back and shoulders massage more than usual. Work had been hellish, with the controversy surrounding the title of Cal Raynard's next novel still raging. The author, in his infinite moronicness, wanted to call it *Considering Marmalade*. Sales had put their market-sensitive feet down and it was Vanessa's job to juggle the interests of the warring factions.

Ah, the gate was open, finally. About time too. With her lipstick-free hand, Vanessa reached into her bag for her cigarettes, steering with one elbow. Her mobile phone began to ring. Dropping the packet of Silk Cut, she grabbed it and pressed the green button. 'Hello?' she said, braking, but it was only her messaging service, then Sim's recorded voice: Campbell and Eve blah blah, something about Matt and Lucy's wedding . . . Vanessa switched off the phone. If she got drawn into Sim's gossip now she'd miss her appointment. She accelerated, moving her car out through the gate, which was starting to close. It could do that quickly enough, the bastard. A team of Cambridge scientists had probably been locked in a laboratory for years, charged with inventing an electronic gate that took eight times as long to open as it did to shut.

Vanessa headed down the private driveway that led from the university accommodation towards Grange Road. Just as she was about to move her right foot from the accelerator to the brake, at the point at which the gravel drive ended and the road began, she saw something out of the corner of her eye. It was a Chinese woman on a bicycle wearing a purple cycling helmet. Her bike was inches away, heading straight for Vanessa's car.

Vanessa grabbed the wheel with both hands and braked heavily. As she did so, the cyclist swerved to the right, trying to avoid Vanessa's Peugeot. Both were a little too slow and they collided with a loud thud. The Chinese woman parted company from her bike, flew into the air, then dropped to the ground. 'Fuck, fuck, fuck!' Vanessa murmured under her breath, resolving that, whatever else happened, she would not miss her salon appointment.

Seven and a half years. Four days. Seven and a half long, full, weighty years. Four paltry, measly days. There was no comparison, yet Eve couldn't help comparing them, knowing Campbell must have. What could have happened in those four days to cancel out the seven and a half years? Proportionally, in Campbell-units, each day he'd spent with Rory – before he left Eve, that is; he had no doubt spent more time with her since – must have been, according to his calculations, worth more than 1.875 years with Eve. She'd worked it out using a calculator.

Eve wondered if she would ever be so important to any man that one day spent in her company could wipe out more than a year and three-quarters of another woman's time and love. Those must have been some four days.

What did Rory do, dance naked with an elephant tusk between her buttocks while finishing Campbell's PhD for him? Unlikely, when she hadn't even completed her own, which was some rubbish about spin doctors being the only truly great artists of our time. Campbell, of course, had defended it. How romantic, thought Eve bitterly. Two unfinished doctorates beating as one.

Eve had been amazed at Campbell's strength of will. She'd counted on being able to keep him at home, in the house they'd bought together on Cromer Street. She was terrified of the new world she'd entered, in which there was no connection between what she wanted and what Campbell did. The idea that he was trying to turn himself into a stranger as quickly as possible made Eve sweat with dread. She wasn't stupid; she knew exactly how difficult it must have been for Campbell to alter his view of her, to make her, in his mind, someone whose words, actions and tears were not attached to any feelings of his. But he'd done it. Wishy-washy Campbell had finally displayed the sort of resolve she'd been trying to engender in him for most of the years they'd been together, except he'd used it to leave her.

Sim had always maintained Campbell wasn't as aimless and inert as Eve thought he was. 'He soaks up the texture of life,' she explained. Sits on his arse, more like, Eve translated. 'And he knows a hell of a lot, though he's modest about it. No man on this fair isle is a greater authority on Toadfish.'

'What the hell is Toadfish?'

'Who, not what. You know, from *Neighbours*.' No, Eve didn't know. Some people had jobs that required them to be away from their television sets occasionally. 'Campbell told me he's closer to the Toad than he is to most of his friends and relatives.' Sim laughed. She also defended Campbell's 'work', as she euphemistically called it, saying his attraction to such a small, specialised area was a sign of how deep a thinker he was, but Eve would take some persuading that a satisfactory resolution of the problem of vagueness would be of any practical use to anyone.

There was nothing vague about what Campbell had done to her, nothing reasonable either. His fancying another woman was neither here nor there; Eve had had brief flings, but she'd always made sure Campbell wasn't affected by them. She'd been through phases of finding him irritating, even of not particularly fancying him, but she'd never for a minute doubted they would pass because her commitment to Campbell was the governing force in her life. What had he been playing at for seven and a half years if he didn't feel the same way about her? Surely he'd known after a year or so that it wasn't the real thing, that Eve wasn't the one? He'd reacted huffily whenever she mentioned marriage or children, but he'd sworn he'd have felt the same whoever he was with. Weddings and kids simply weren't his thing.

And Eve had to admit she'd been going on about both a lot more since Matt and Lucy announced their engagement. Had she driven Campbell away? Oh, God, the thought of spending a whole day at a wedding in his company with things as they were made Eve ache with misery. Maybe she'd pretend to be ill, if she wasn't genuinely ill by then. Another week of feeling this bad would kill her, never mind seven weeks.

Eve wasn't sure whether she'd prefer Rory to be a symptom or the cause of her break-up with Campbell. She could hold her entirely responsible and hate her more if she were the cause, but then she'd also have to acknowledge Rory's superior power, her centrality. Eve had asked Campbell about this, but all he'd said in response was, 'I don't know. I can't talk.' He'd repeated this last phrase over and over and, while it was unhelpful, it appeared to be true.

Eve wiped her eyes, wondering when she'd last eaten. Saturdays and Sundays seemed disproportionately long without the distraction of work, as if they'd been stretched on a rack. Who'd have thought that mild, bumbling Campbell could alter time? And place. Eve's lovely terraced house that she'd decorated herself and was so proud of had become a den of horrors. Cromer Street, Rusholme, Manchester: all had become a menace, a taunting coagulation of misery.

The phone rang. Eve looked at her watch. Quarter to six. It was too early for Neil, who had taken to ringing between ten and twelve at night. Eve wondered whether he'd guessed that just before bedtime would be the worst time for her. The first few nights, Eve had practically devoured the phone in her eagerness to answer it, convinced it would be Campbell's 'terrible mistake' call. But she'd been expecting that for two weeks and it hadn't materialised. This was unlikely to be it, she thought as she got up to answer the phone. Was her lack of expectation in this regard a sign that she'd given up hope?

Neil, an affable Geordie with ginger hair and a stripe of freckles across his nose and cheeks, was the only one of her colleagues who knew what had happened. Eve didn't want her abandonment to become common knowledge just yet, but she'd had to confide in someone. She didn't know Neil very well – he taught law and she taught business studies, so they didn't have much to do with one another at school – but he was charming, cheerful and made Eve feel that the world wasn't an utterly wretched place. He'd also declared his intention, for the time being at least, to stop playing squash with Campbell, which Eve took as an indication that, insofar as sides could be taken, Neil was on hers. This comforted her. She needed to feel someone was firmly in her camp, and it had to be a person she and Campbell had shared, or it was no victory. And Campbell deserved to lose Neil, whom he'd always looked down on. Neil was a mere secondary schoolteacher with no PhD or fancy media job. Not that Campbell had either, yet. Eve's theory was that Campbell used Neil to balance out the inferiority he felt around the likes of Francis, Matt and Nicholas.

Eve had to admit she'd also used Neil when Campbell first left. She'd seen him as a shrink equivalent, someone to whom it was safe to show her weakest, most pathetic side, who could be discarded later when it suited her to pretend she'd never been in that much pain, and not be missed. She wasn't sure about that last part any more. Neil had been so kind and supportive. Still, it was odd and slightly depressing to think that for the last two weeks he'd been the main person in her life. It was such a big change. Perhaps that was better, though. Perhaps it was reassuring that things could be so different so quickly.

Eve stood in the hall beside the phone, her hand hovering over it. Was she ready to let the world in? This had to be Sim, back from town and keen to flesh out the scant details Francis had given her. How did Sim manage to keep her relationship in such good condition, Eve wondered, with messy, uncooperative Francis as a partner? She seemed happy, too, that was the weird thing, and assured Eve whenever the topic arose that Francis had a softer side. He would never leave Sim, Eve acknowledged with a pang of envy. Maybe that was all that mattered.

She'd been relieved when Francis picked up the phone, enabling her to deliver her news in a brisk, no-nonsense manner that got the point across but wasn't unduly painful. It was no substitute for discussing things properly with Sim, but it was useful to be able to practise on Francis, check she could get the words out of her mouth without crumbling. Since everything about Francis's demeanour seemed innately opposed to crumbling, unaware, even, that crumbling might ever creep on to the agenda of anyone he knew, Eve's task was made considerably easier.

She'd put off telling Sim and the others what had happened for so long because she wanted to keep the number of incoming calls to a minimum, dreading the abrupt swerve from soaring hope to crashing disappointment. Today, for the first time, she'd admitted to herself that this was real, that people should know about it. Eve wasn't a fool; she knew Sim would tell the others – Eve was counting on her to take care of publicity – and pretty soon Eve's telephone would be busier than that of the Liverpool passport office. She felt she could cope with this now. Sadly, she acknowledged what this meant: deep down, she no longer expected Campbell to call. She sighed and picked up the phone.

'Eve? Hi, it's me.'

'Thought it would be.' Eve was glad Sim's tone wasn't overly mawkish.

'Sorry you got Francis before. I imagine his reaction was everything you could have hoped for in your wildest dreams and surpassed even your most extravagant expectations?'

'It was, actually. He acted as though it hardly mattered, which is what I'm trying to convince myself of.'

'Is it true she's a Napper?'

'Yes. Rory Napper.' Eve remembered the days when that name hadn't been part of her life. Barely. 'Short for Aurora. Sim, Campbell wouldn't bring her to Matt and Lucy's wedding, would he?'

'You can't bring an extra person to that sort of wedding.' Sim laughed. 'Matt's been working on the seating plan since 204 BC.'

'Even if he's there on his own . . .' A loud ding-donging made Eve jump. What the hell . . . ?

'You've got a visitor,' Sim told her. To her embarrassment, Eve realised that she'd forgotten the sound her own doorbell made. No one had pressed it since Campbell left. Another punishment, thought Eve. She was always castigating him for forgetting his key and startling her with the loud chimes. Now she had a predominantly silent doorbell, which was infinitely worse. But it had just broken its silence. Could this be Campbell? It could, Eve thought. It was! Of course, a 'terrible mistake' visit was much more in character than a 'terrible mistake' phone call. It wouldn't surprise Eve if he simply walked back in, unzipped holdall over his shoulder, without even highlighting the terrible mistake component of his behaviour.

'Sim, can I ring you back?'

'Sure. Eve, it might not be him, so don't get your hopes up. But if it is, I want you to imagine that he's got his finger poised above the button of a nuclear bomb that could destroy the whole world. Don't do anything to alarm him. If he senses there's an easy opening for him to slide back in without any pressure, that'll bring out the best in him,' Sim gabbled. 'Campbell's not very confident. If he's confronted by what looks like devastation, he'll scarper and console himself by thinking the damage would have been irreparable anyway. He needs to see you, him and tranquillity and be aware that all he has to do is put the three together. Like a sort of remedial jigsaw,' she added.

The doorbell rang again. 'I'm coming!' Eve bellowed. 'Anything else?'

'Yes. If it's not him, if it's Rory Napper . . .'

'What?' This possibility hadn't occurred to Eve. 'If it's that bitch, I'll kill her,' she said and put down the phone before Sim had a chance to tell her that this course of action would only make Rory a martyr in Campbell's eyes.

Combing her hair with her fingers, Eve forced herself to walk slowly to the front door.

Nicholas Drogan pushed back his blue leather swivel chair and strode across his office to the window. The deadline for the amendments to his article on the Middle East peace process was creeping ever closer, so here he was, working on a Saturday, still in his office at quarter to six and resenting it. And enjoying resenting it. The stress, effort and long working hours involved in getting this article right and ready on time made Nicholas feel less like a member of a pampered intellectual class and more like a proper worker, a builder's labourer or something. He'd been up at seven every day this week. 'I believe you, thousands wouldn't,' Vanessa had scoffed when he told her. 'You're always fast asleep when I leave for work.' If he didn't make significant progress today, Nicholas would have to get up at six with Vanessa next week. That'd show her.

He stared out of the window at the Garden House Moat House Hotel across the road. Vanessa was probably in there at this very moment, having her over-indulged limbs tweaked and plucked. Nicholas was firmly opposed to that sort of nonsense. The amount of time people wasted beautifying themselves was a sign of the world's sickness. He wished he still had his old office in the Chesterton Road building. The sight of the Garden House made him think of Vanessa's body, a distraction he could do without when he had important work to do. The last thing he needed was images of her alabaster flesh swimming around his mind; her elegant feet with their long toes and absurdly high arches, the tattoo on her hip that was supposed to be a coiled snake but in fact looked more like an intra-uterine device. The physicality of Vanessa confused Nicholas; he was never quite sure what he wanted to do to her, or whether it was healthy.

The politics department's move had been pointless as far as he could see and he was unimpressed by the river view that his colleagues rhapsodised about. Still, he would endeavour to like his new office, with its original restored sash windows and marble fireplace. Vanessa had called him a natural conservative and accused him of hating anything new, which was rubbish.

He turned away from the window and forced himself to sit down at his leather-topped desk, where his article awaited him. The editor of *Global Issues* had strongly recommended that he make some substantial changes and one didn't mess about where *Global Issues* was concerned, not if one valued one's career. Nicholas began to read from where he'd left off: 'The history of the state of Israel is intimately tied in with . . .' Oh, blast. What was wrong with him? Why did his eyes keep sliding off the page? Fear, that was what it was. He was afraid that once he got properly stuck in, he'd discover that what the editor was asking for wasn't possible, not without destroying his precious article altogether.

He forced himself to concentrate. Factory workers didn't stop working when they hit a difficulty; nor would he. 'The history of the state of Israel,' he read aloud, 'is intimately linked to the dynamics of both European-style nationalism and colonialism abroad. The UN partition plans of the late 1940s grant a fundamental legitimacy to Israel which has since disregarded UN resolutions pertaining to Palestinian national self-determination. Indeed, the fight for the "security" of Israel and its dynamism as a modern economy and society has buried Palestinian national aspirations. Israelis should be prepared for greater compromise with the landless people given that their own sufferings in history have stemmed from their being a people without a land.'

Was that a good paragraph? Nicholas had thought so once, but he'd read it so many times that he could no longer tell. Should he take out the word 'buried'? If he started to tamper with the article in his present strained state of mind, he might do it irreparable harm. If only he could get it finished. Ideas for another essay he wanted to write, about the war in Kosovo, jostled in his mind; his attack on Blair and Clinton's obnoxious Western imperialism would be fluent enough, if only he could make a start. Instead, he was being forced to rake over old work, work he'd thought of as finished. It gave him a maddening sense of regress. As always when he felt powerless and frustrated, his head filled with anger towards Vanessa.

How disgustingly spoilt she was. It would serve her right to be a landless person for a while. She was lucky enough to live in Cambridge, the most beautiful city in England, in a college-owned flat for a ridiculously cheap rent, and the bitch wasn't satisfied. Porters brought her her mail, took her messages and ordered her taxis. As Nicholas's partner, she was entitled to free meals in Renshaw College and use of the tennis courts, private gardens, bowling green and wine cellars. They'd had a bedder, too, until Nicholas put his foot down and, ignoring Vanessa's furious protests, told the college that he had severe moral reservations about having a domestic servant. To punish him for depriving her of this amenity, Vanessa had boycotted all domestic chores, so Nicholas was the one who scrubbed the toilet bowl and scoured the bath to remove limescale. If this was the price he had to pay for sticking to his principles, Nicholas was happy to do it. 'How's your affinity with the world's peasants coming along?' Vanessa taunted him when he was on his knees wiping the lino with a cloth.

If she didn't want to feel that affinity herself, and clearly she didn't, why the hell was she so eager to move to London? Where did she imagine they could afford to live? They'd end up in a house with rotting window frames on a shabby, traffic-stunned road near a bridge covered in hardened pigeon droppings. Their closest tube station would have a sticky piss-stained floor and their local takeaway would pride itself on selling both pizzas and curries, as if such a mongrel of cuisine identity could ever be desirable. Litter leg warmers would adhere to their shins wherever they walked and they would dine in dingy pavement cafés run by balding, grease-splashed Cypriots. Vanessa mocked Nicholas's bourgeois sensibilities, but if he was vehement on the subject it was simply because he was angry that poor people were condemned to live in such squalor while he, Nicholas Drogan, had a choice.

He heard a metallic noise and looked up. Another sound followed, louder this time, a sudden click. A key in a door. He stood up. Nicholas hadn't given a spare key to anybody and the cleaners came in the morning so it couldn't be them. He watched the lock turn.

The door opened and Gillian Kench slipped into the office. The first thing that struck Nicholas was how drastically her looks had deteriorated. Her face, once oval-shaped, was round and puffy, her neck scrawny like an old woman's. Crinkly was the only word Nicholas could think of to describe her hair. It appeared to have the texture of cassette tape that had been mangled by a faulty car stereo and was streaked blonde at the front. In her right hand Gillian held a gold Yale key. She seemed to slide along the wall a few inches before stopping, as if she were on rails. 'Hello, Nicholas,' she said, with a look on her face that Nicholas was sure he'd be correct to describe as a leer. There was a thin black line around her artificially pink lips.

He opened his mouth, then hesitated. It was so long since he'd seen Gillian; he didn't know what to say to her. He'd found her weird and difficult to talk to at the best of times. What the hell was she doing with a key to his office? Come to think of it, why was she at work on a Saturday? Anyway, she was in the wrong place. Modern Languages had relocated to Nicholas's old building on Chesterton Road. It struck him that he hadn't once thought of Gillian in connection with his department swapping premises with hers, possibly because on one level he hadn't wanted to believe she really was a secretary in the Modern Languages department. According to Vanessa she was illiterate. How did she manage to hold down a job in the same university that employed Nicholas? He felt threatened, then embarrassed by his insecurity. It was no reflection on him; evidently different standards applied when it came to recruiting clerical staff.

'What are you doing with a key to my office?' he asked briskly.

'Charming. Aren't you even going to say hello?'

'Hello, Gillian. What are you doing with a . . .'

'. . . key to your office. I heard you the first time.' Gillian held up the key, examining it in the light. 'So, how *are* you?' Her languid voice drew out the question. 'How's Vanessa?' she drawled, emphasising every syllable.

'Gillian, what's going on?' Nicholas felt distinctly uncomfortable.

'Nothing.' She grinned, dropping the key into her blouse

pocket. Nicholas could see its outline, tilted upwards by her left breast. 'I bet you're both looking forward to Matt and Lucy's wedding, aren't you? I hope I'm on your table, Nicholas. It'll be nice to have a proper matey natter, won't it?'

Nicholas blinked and cast about for something to say. He'd tried to avoid thinking about the wedding, bourgeois charade that it was. Practically criminal, to spend that amount of money when half the world was starving. And to top it all, a stag weekend in a bloody Marriott hotel, with Nicholas's money ending up in some American fat cat's pocket. He'd only agreed to go along with the whole performance because Vanessa, fuelled by Sim, had worn him down. He should have protested more forcefully but there was no room in his head for anything but work, and certainly none for Gillian Kench. This needed to be made clear to her. 'Gillian, could you answer my question, please? What are you doing with a key to my office?' Nicholas was convinced there was some aspect of this scene that he was missing.

'It used to be my office,' said Gillian, wandering over to the window. Her heels click-clacked across the floor. 'I loved this view.'

'Really?' Nicholas struggled to keep the annoyance out of his voice. He didn't like to think of his office as having once belonged to a secretary. He'd imagined his new room was grander than that, full of the ghosts of brilliant minds. Administrative staff didn't normally have offices with marble fireplaces, even in Cambridge. She'd probably had to share it with several other secretaries, Nicholas thought.

'I pretended I'd lost the key when we moved, but I hadn't. I kept it.'

'Oh, right.' Why, for God's sake? 'Well . . . can I have it?'

'Do you want to come and see my new office?' Gillian asked in a sing-song voice. 'I think you'd like it. It's got a patch of mould on one wall in the shape of a fish.'

66

'No.' Could she be serious? 'I mean, I'm busy.'

'It's only on Chesterton Road. I've got the car, it wouldn't take long.' She must have seen Nicholas's expression because she scowled suddenly. 'Some friend you are!'

'Friend?' Nicholas stammered, unable to work out how such a misunderstanding could have arisen. He'd barely noticed Gillian; she'd simply been there, on the periphery of his and Vanessa's social circle, and then, later, not there. Nicholas had forgotten the details of her row with Sim that had effectively put an end to his connection with her. That was how little he cared about Gillian. This was crazy. 'Look, what exactly do you want?' Nicholas attempted to assert himself. His cheeks burned.

'Who says I want anything?' Gillian snapped, sucking her pink lips into her mouth before spitting them out again. There were pink and black smudges on her teeth. She folded her arms. 'God, you're a boring git. Sim's turned you against me, hasn't she?' Nicholas began to deny it, but Gillian talked over him. 'I'm not stupid, Nicholas. Well, don't worry, I won't bother you any more.'

She spun round and marched towards the door. 'I hope you like your new office, Dr Drogan,' she spat over her shoulder before slipping out of the room as swiftly as she'd slipped in.

Nicholas fell into his chair and wiped his forehead with the back of his hand. Nothing that made so little sense had ever happened to him before. It had to be a joke, one he didn't get. But why had Gillian bothered to go considerably out of her way to make such a joke? There must have been some other reason behind her visit that Nicholas had failed to discover.

He was furious with himself. He'd handled it all wrong, getting het up instead of keeping calm and finding out what was really bothering Gillian. And she still had a key to his office. Nicholas wondered how easy it would be to have the locks changed.

He sat with his eyes shut for a minute or two until his breathing returned to normal, ashamed of his irrational fear. She'd gone now, that was the main thing. Chances were it was an isolated incident with no logic to it. Maybe Gillian was just passing and popped in to see her old office and have, as she put it, a proper matey natter. Nicholas shuddered; she was a repugnant crinkly-haired bimbo. He decided not to mention the incident to Vanessa. There was no need. When he next saw Gillian, at Matt and Lucy's wedding, he'd be friendly and act as if nothing had happened. The more he thought about it, the more Nicholas was convinced nothing had.

'Damn!' Francis tunnelled through sheaves of paper on Steve McCargo's desk. The guy was a slobby fucker. Where was the Dingley trial transcript? How did Steve manage to get any work done, with this unstable paper mountain obscuring his computer's monitor? Francis picked up a mug that was encrusted with something orange, possibly cup-a-soup remains, in the hope that the transcript would be buried beneath it. It wasn't. The clock on Steve's desk trilled gratingly as it struck quarter to six, making Francis jump and knock a tower of folders on to the floor. 'Bastard,' he muttered.

Mess at work disturbed him; he saw it through Sim's eyes and had to fight the urge to clear away debris on other people's desks when they weren't looking. He'd grown up in a house where neglected vegetables turned to noxious liquids in cupboards and chicken carcasses were left to rot in the oven until flies colonised the kitchen. When he saw yet another empty crisp packet stuffed into yet another lipstick-stained styrofoam cup on a colleague's desk, his boyhood fear of being contaminated by the rubbish around him returned.

In the open-plan offices of *The North Today*, where chaos and order were constantly battling for *Lebensraum*, Francis was regarded as one of the tidy ones. His own desk normally had two or three separate piles of paper on it, but they were separate for a reason and each of them was more or less rectangular; Sim felt strongly that all piles of paper should be.

Francis had never told her that he was substantially tidier at work than in their flat. He didn't want her to be offended, to think he regarded *The North Today* as more deserving of his efforts. The truth was that he loved watching Sim tidy up. He grinned, thinking how livid she'd be if she knew. It was true, though; when Sim cleared up after him, he felt cared for. He liked to be able to relax his own vigil, safe in the knowledge that someone else was attending to things. It was the same with their social life, with Matt and Lucy's wedding. Francis never sought reassurance – outwardly, indeed, he positively discouraged it – but he noticed the way Sim tended to their life, home and friends, and it made him feel solid, established.

He wandered over to his desk to get Steve McCargo's home phone number and was about to ring him when he spotted two black folders labelled 'Dingley trial'. It hadn't occurred to him that Steve might try to be helpful and put the papers where Francis wouldn't need to rummage for them. Behind the folders was a large, framed photograph of Sim with her mouth open, next to the *Sun* headline 'Clobba Slobba' which Francis had cut out and pinned to the partition separating his desk from Justin Menasseh's. For once, the *Sun* had expressed Francis's sentiments precisely.

He was pleased with the optical effect he'd created; it looked as if Sim was shouting the headline. What had she been shouting, that windy day on a Cambridge punt, with her hair blowing out behind her and a bottle of Holsten Pils in her hand? Francis couldn't remember. Her mouth was open in every picture of her he'd ever seen. Sim tended to say a lot more than 'cheese' to cameras. He'd heard her promise Lucy she'd glue her mouth shut for the wedding photos.

Francis wasn't looking forward to the wedding. The

closer it got, the less comfortable he felt. Night after night, Sim gossiped about it, planned for it, immersed herself in its details, yet not once had she mentioned the possibility of herself and Francis getting married. When Matt and Lucy announced their engagement, Francis thought it would only be a matter of time before Sim instructed him to propose to her. When months passed and that didn't happen, he got a bit worried. She hadn't even raised the topic in a jokey fashion. Francis didn't like the idea that Sim might not want to marry him, and hated the prospect of spending a whole day and evening celebrating someone else's wedding while he was unsure if he'd ever have one of his own. He knew he ought to talk to Sim before the fifteenth of May, but couldn't bring himself to say the words. What if, on some fundamental level, he wasn't good enough for her and she knew it? What if he'd left it too late and Sim was already disappointed by his failure to propose? Francis didn't think this was likely; Sim rarely kept her thoughts to herself, but you never knew.

Even if he asked her and she said yes, Francis didn't see a way round the problem of his mother, to whom he hadn't spoken for years. He had no wish to re-establish contact, but how could he not invite her to his wedding? She was his mother. To exclude her would be too irreversible a gesture. Francis couldn't rely on other family members not to blab. The only solution he could think of was to get married in secret and invite no one, but that wouldn't be much fun for Sim. After witnessing Matt and Lucy's rigmarole, she'd be bound to want the same. Women liked all that stuff, didn't they? Francis sighed. He could have done without all this in his head with the Dingley interview coming up. Why couldn't Matt and Lucy have carried on living together? It would have made Francis's life much easier.

He picked up the files and left the office, momentarily forgetting where he'd parked his car. The centre of Leeds looked passable today. The pavements were a clean, light grey and the buildings commanded respect.

Francis would have preferred it if the pelican crossings didn't advise people on when to wait and when to cross in disembodied Yorkshire accents, but you couldn't have everything. And, of course, there was Harvey Nichols, which Francis invoked whenever he felt a pang of yearning for Cambridge. Leeds was on a different scale altogether. Francis often felt it had more in common with New York than with Cambridge. It was an exciting city to work in, with new bars, restaurants and apartment blocks springing up on an almost daily basis, but not as relaxing and friendly as Cambridge.

The sound of his own name wafted towards him, over the hum of traffic. He looked behind him, saw nothing, then looked across the road. A short, dark, middle-aged woman in a beige jacket and black trousers was staring at him. She waved at him to stop. Francis didn't recognise her. Her hair reminded him of the villain in *Blake's Seven*, one of his favourite programmes as a child. What was her name? Servilan, that was it. He was sure he didn't know this woman.

'Francis Weir!' she called again. This time Francis heard the voice more clearly. Unlike the pelican crossings, it had expression. Anger. Francis felt the hairs stand up on the back of his neck. Annette Wrigley. She'd cut her hair. He hadn't recognised her at first, so inappropriate was her presence here, on a road in broad daylight, in his life outside work. Aha, so she isn't too grief-stricken to go into town, Francis thought before he could stop himself.

Was this an ambush or a coincidence? Either way, Annette had no right to approach him when he was walking down the road on a Saturday, minding his own business. Francis quickened his pace and Annette did the same. She was almost running, her eyes darting to and fro, looking for a convenient gap in the traffic so that she could bolt across and catch Francis before he got to his car. She was playing tig with him, for Christ's sake. Francis wondered how sincere her bereaved-mother act was, how much of it was guilt.

He could see his car now and calculated that he'd reach it before Annette could get across the road. He speeded up, watching his feet to make sure he didn't trip. At last he reached the BMW. Once safely in the driver's seat with the doors locked, Francis cheered. He'd won. Sim agreed with him about the interview; it had to go ahead if there was the slightest chance of the truth being forced out of those thugs. Sim probably would not have run away from Annette Wrigley, or felt the urge to punish her for her persistence, but Francis was not Sim.

Dale and Wayne Dingley were savages; they were Francis's worst fears about the north of England personified. He had to confront them, or rather *The North Today* had to. The interview would be a journalistic triumph. Yorkshire, as the county where the programme was made, would be redeemed and Francis would feel happier about living here.

Annette was still in the middle of the road when he drove off. He felt her dark eyes pierce his back.

3

Eve opened the front door, her spirits plummeting when she saw that her visitor was not Campbell. A tall, skinny girl with centre-parted dark hair in two wonky plaits and glasses with tortoiseshell frames stood in front of her. She was wearing a Camborne Street High School T-shirt and and looked about fourteen. Her head jutted forward, one step ahead of her body. Eve didn't recognise her as one of her pupils. She didn't entirely rule out the possibility that this was Rory Napper's teenage emissary.

A neighbour across the road was washing his car. His fat, bleached-haired wife leaned on the bonnet, smoking. They fell silent when they saw Eve, eyeing her with suspicion. Did they know Campbell had gone? Did they blame her? Hers wasn't the first relationship on Cromer Street to break up, that was for sure. She and Campbell had often laughed at the loud slanging matches they heard through their bedroom walls, confident that such misery would never apply to them.

'Miss Hartigan?' the girl said. Her voice was mature and confident. 'I'm sorry to bother you at home. My name's Imogen Salt. I'd like to talk to you about something important. May I come in?' She had an odd way of talking, an accent Eve couldn't quite place. It didn't sound Mancunian. Eve nodded and stood back to let her pass, too stunned to speak. She was still getting over the shock of it not being Campbell. Still, might as well get used to it sooner rather than later, she thought. Everyone she encountered from now on would be not Campbell. She needed to get in training for the Campbelllessness ahead.

She followed Imogen Salt into the lounge and offered her a drink. As she prepared the requested glass of orange juice in the kitchen, washing and drying a tumbler and opening a new carton of Del Monte, she tried to pull herself together, to focus only on the present. She took a deep breath and returned to the lounge. 'What's this about, then?' she asked, handing Imogen her drink. Perhaps the school had burned down. In her current frame of mind, Eve doubted she'd have cared.

Imogen grasped the glass with both hands and took a sip, slurping loudly. On either side of her head, a wiry plait bobbed up and down. 'You were one of the judges of the school poetry competition, weren't you?' she said.

'Yes, I was.' Every year, the first three teachers to have their names pulled out of a hat were assigned the task of adjudicating Camborne Street School's annual poetry competition. Eve could have done without the extra work this year and thought the tradition was silly; what did she, a Business Studies teacher, know about poetry?

'I entered,' said Imogen. 'I've got a copy of my entry with me.' It wasn't so much the accent, Eve realised, as the inflection that was distinctive. Imogen spoke like a character from an old black-and-white film. She plunged into her sentences with great enthusiasm, like the kind of person who, in such films, would be described as a good sort or a brick. Imogen patted her pocket. 'I wondered if you could tell me why my poem didn't win.' Dimly, Eve became aware that questions needed to be asked, parameters established. 'I know you might think it's trivial,' Imogen continued quickly, 'but it won't take long. I've got a reason for asking, which I'll tell you, but first I want you to see if you remember the poem.'

'Look . . . how did you get my address?' Eve did think it sounded trivial. What was this pupil doing disturbing her on a Saturday? She forced herself to study the girl, to be fully aware of her presence. Imogen looked as if she might spring from her seat at any moment; barely contained energy seemed to radiate from her long, bony body. There was a kink in one of her plaits, as if the hair objected to being restrained. Eve was tempted to pull it straight but she imagined it would only spring back into its present position.

'My form tutor gave it to me. Mr Temple.'

'Neil Temple gave you my address?' If it was true, Eve resented it deeply. Neil had no right to inflict a pupil on her at the weekend. He could get into serious trouble if he went round handing out teachers' addresses to the kids.

'He wouldn't at first. But when I showed him the poem and told him what I'm about to tell you, well – he said you'd want to know about it.' Eve nodded, suspecting that this was Neil's idea of a good way to distract her from her misery. Hardly. A pupil with a poem was not exactly a free trip to the Bahamas.

'Go on, show me the poem, then,' Eve said wearily. She hardly remembered the school poetry competition. It was odd, she thought, the way the majority of her life – more than twenty-eight years – now felt shorter than the last fortnight, which seemed to stretch back into prehistory. 'But couldn't this have waited until Monday morning? It isn't on, you know, Imogen, turning up at a teacher's house.' Nor was it on for Neil to take advantage of her weakened state. What the hell was he thinking of? Eve would have to have words with him when he phoned later.

'I know. I've never done it before. I believe this is an exceptional case.'

Imogen's delivery of this line was so reminiscent of a black-and-white movie classic that Eve almost laughed. 'Why me?' she asked. 'I wasn't the only judge of the competition.'

'You're the only one who's normal,' said Imogen, sounding more like a regular schoolgirl. Eve couldn't argue with this. Phyllida Banborough and Walter Allnutt were regarded as stuffy, dull and unapproachable even by the staff.

'How old are you, Imogen?'

'Twelve.'

'Right. Year Seven, then.' Eve was surprised. Imogen had the manner and vocabulary of an older girl.

'Look here, Miss Hartigan, I would have waited until Monday but the prize-giving ceremony isn't too far off and I didn't want to lose any time.' Eve wondered where Imogen picked up her expressions. She'd never heard a pupil say 'Look here' in all her years as a teacher. Still, she sympathised with the sentiment, having recently lost seven and a half years. It was painfully ironic: Eve had prided herself on how long she and Campbell had stayed together, longer than many married couples. A good innings. But relationships were not like lives in this respect; if they were going to end at all, better that they should do so sooner rather than later.

Imogen reached into her trouser pocket and produced a folded piece of lined A4 paper. She handed it to Eve. The title of the poem was 'Memories' and underneath was written, 'by Imogen Salt, Form 7T'. Imogen leaned forward, nearly head-butting Eve, watching her intently as she began to read:

> Remember when the sea was blue
> The roaring waves swept to the shore
> The glistening sand so gold and bright
> These gorgeous gifts exist no more.
>
> The stony beach, the rolling sea
> Remember how we laughed and played
> The memories came back to me
> And in my mind for ever stayed.

Remember when the sun was bright
'Tis now a devil shade of red
The past was guided by the light
The trees are shrivelled now and dead.

Remember when the mountain peaks
Were covered by the crystal snow
The cold grey silence of today
Oh, where did all the beauty go?

Remember when the hills were green
The flowerless and depressing land
The stillness of the stony hills
They watch us coldly as they stand.

The dirtiness and poverty
The friendliness of olden days
The cruelty of modern times
It all has changed in many ways.

'Miss Hartigan, why are you crying?'

'I'm . . . nothing. I'm sorry, it's not you. It's not your poem.' Eve wiped her eyes. Neil was a bloody fool; hadn't it occurred to him that reading this sort of thing was unlikely to make her feel any better? 'It's great,' she said. 'Very . . . moving.' She held out the piece of paper for Imogen to take back. The poem contained some lines she didn't want to have to see twice.

'But you've seen it before,' said Imogen, puzzled. 'When you did the judging.'

'No. I definitely haven't. I'd remember,' said Eve. 'But that's easily explained. There were three judges, and each of us read a third of the entries. We shortlisted a few poems each and brought those ones to the final judges' meeting.' Eve realised as soon as this sentence was out of her mouth that she'd said the wrong thing.

'So whoever got my poem didn't even shortlist it,' said Imogen, nodding sadly. Eve felt terribly sorry for her all of a sudden. The poem was pretty impressive, considering it had been written by a twelve-year-old. *The trees are shrivelled now, and dead.* It would have been more straightforward to say 'The trees are now shrivelled and dead', or even 'The trees are shrivelled and dead now', but neither of these would have been as good, somehow, although Eve couldn't have explained why this was. She couldn't remember much about the poems that made it to the final meeting, but she had the vague impression that none of them had been particularly brilliant.

'If it's any consolation,' said Eve, 'I would definitely have shortlisted it if it had been in my pile of entries.'

'What did you think of the poem that won? Did you like it?' Imogen asked.

'I . . . well, I must have done. We all agreed it should win, out of the shortlisted ones, that is. I don't remember it very well. I've . . . been busy lately.'

Imogen produced another piece of paper from her pocket. 'Here it is,' she said. 'I copied it down when it was pinned on the noticeboard.' Eve wanted to ask why Imogen had done this; it seemed a bit extreme. Why did she care so much? It was only a poem. But then, she supposed you could apply the word 'only' to most things. Campbell had only left Eve; it wasn't as if anyone was dead. It was nothing compared with what was going on in Kosovo, for instance. Objectively, Eve knew this, but it wasn't how she felt. She took the winning poem from Imogen and read it:

'A Breezy Summer's Day'

by Katie Briscoe, Form 9G

A cold wind blowing
Whispering trees
Bending, twisting
Making patterns
In the breeze

78

Bowing flowers
Nodding gently
As the cold wind blows.

Eve stared at the poem for a few minutes. 'Yes, I remember it,' she said eventually. 'Well, it's not as good as yours,' she told Imogen, seeing no point in pretending. 'As I'm sure you know.'

'Miss Hartigan.' Imogen leaned forward. 'Now that you've read both poems I'll tell you why I'm here. I don't want you to think I'm big-headed, because I'm not. But when I saw that "A Breezy Summer's Day" had won the competition, I couldn't believe it. I wouldn't have minded not winning if I could see why the winner had won, but my poem is better.' Imogen blinked solemnly.

'I agree,' said Eve. 'And, as I said, if it had turned up at the meeting, I would have argued for it to win. I really would, Imogen. I'm not just saying that. But it didn't. I'm sure there are other competitions you could enter it in. Do you want me to find out for you?'

'No.'

'I bet it'd stand an excellent chance.'

'I'm not interested in that. That's not why I'm here,' said Imogen. Eve had never before met a twelve-year-old who was so composed, so sure of her own mind. 'I want to know why my poem didn't get shortlisted. Can you find out for me? I don't mind not winning. I just want to know. Until I hear a good reason it won't seem fair. Unfair things bother me,' she added, as if describing a quirk that was both inconvenient and particular to her.

Eve considered what she was being asked to do. It wouldn't change the outcome; the prize, even though it hadn't yet been officially awarded, couldn't at this stage be taken away from Katie Briscoe, but Eve believed Imogen when she said this wasn't her main concern. The prize was only a twenty-pound book token and Imogen didn't give the impression of being poor. Her clothes were clean and in good condition. Eve could well understand the need for an explanation. She too would be interested to discover why Phyllida or Walter had passed over 'Memories'.

'Okay, I'll try to find out for you,' she said.

Imogen's sharp eyes seemed to relax, looking immediately softer behind her tortoiseshell glasses. She smiled for the first time. Eve saw that she wore a brace on her top teeth only and thought, 'God, imagine being that young.'

'Thank you very much,' Imogen said. 'But promise me that if you find out the reason, you'll tell me the truth about it. Even if you think it'll upset me. I don't want to be protected.'

Eve couldn't help laughing. She'd said exactly the same thing to Campbell. And received a deeply unsatisfactory answer: 'I can't talk.' No explanation, nothing.

'I promise,' she said.

Vanessa felt her chest tighten with anger as two passers-by, both men, ran towards the Chinese cyclist and started to fuss over her. The woman was clearly all right; she'd stood up immediately and picked up her bike. There were smears of blood around her mouth, but her injuries had to be fairly minor. So minor, in fact, that Vanessa hadn't even got out of the car yet. Until these two men had appeared, she'd been considering simply driving off with a wave and a shrug to the cyclist as if to say, 'These things happen; oh well!'

One of the men wore a suit and carried a briefcase. The other must have been on his way to the university library, judging by his unkempt beard and battered rucksack. Both men stared at Vanessa through the windscreen, blinking their concern, supporting the purple-helmeted cyclist between them, even though she was quite capable of standing up on her own as far as Vanessa could see. It was her mouth that was affected, not her legs, for Christ's sake.

A swift exit was out of the question. Vanessa would

have to get out of the car and act concerned. Damn! If this were London, she could have counted on any witnesses being too busy and misanthropic to note down her car registration and take it along to the nearest police station like nauseatingly good citizens.

She opened her car door and got out, having adjusted her goals. The hit-and-run option was ruled out, but if she could appear caring and conscientious at high speed, she might be able to wrap up this tedious incident in less than five minutes and still get to the Garden House before she missed her appointment. The main problem here was the two men. They looked like the responsible sort who would want to follow correct procedures. If they sensed that Vanessa was in any way trying to get off the hook – not that she was on any particular hook, the crash having been equally the fault of both parties – they would insist on interfering in some tiresome way. If Vanessa could only shake them off, the cyclist alone would be a pushover.

'Are you all right?' Vanessa rushed over to her. 'Are you hurt?' She was careful to say nothing that could be construed as an admission of responsibility.

'Yes. I think I am okay, but my tooth is painful.' When the cyclist opened her mouth, Vanessa saw that one of her front teeth was bright red.

'Oh dear. But you're basically okay?'

'Someone should take her to casualty,' said the businessman sternly. Fuck. Vanessa knew she'd sounded too casual.

'Yes, I'll take her now. Come on,' she said gently to Redtooth. 'I've got some tissues in the car.' She nearly added 'to mop up all that blood' but stopped herself, thinking it would sound too macabre. There were disadvantages, Vanessa saw, to wearing dark make-up and black clothes. People might be quicker to think badly of you. If only she could have pulled on a pink woolly cardy – that'd mislead everyone nicely.

81

'The police should be notified,' the bearded academic said tentatively.

'Yes, quite,' agreed the businessman.

'Obviously,' Vanessa injected just the right amount of impatience into her voice, 'but the priority is getting her to hospital.' Who did these wankers think they were? Vanessa was the protagonist in this situation; it was nothing to do with them. 'Health comes first.' This last comment, with its overtones of matrons and lace-up shoes, was all the two men needed to hear. They shrugged and wandered off, shooting the odd foreboding glance back in Vanessa's direction. She knew they both thought the accident had been her fault.

Vanessa helped Red-tooth to padlock her bike to a nearby fence before opening the passenger door and ushering her into the car. She took a deep breath and went round to the driver's side. Things should be relatively easy from now on, she thought. The only thing she had to do was keep up her nicey-nicey act so that it didn't occur to Red-tooth to take down the car's registration.

'Okay,' she said, starting the engine. 'Where do you live? I'll drop you off.'

'Do you have a tissue?' Red-tooth asked, trying to smile politely. God, that was a point. Vanessa didn't want blood all over her upholstery. Well, maybe in a good cause – Cal Raynard's agent sprang to mind – but the thought of this woman dripping all over her car disgusted her. Vanessa found that she was beginning to dislike Red-tooth intensely, although she'd only known her a few minutes.

She rummaged under her seat until she found a tissue. It wasn't pristine, but it would do. She handed it to Red-tooth, who began to pat the area around her mouth. 'Right, where to?' Careful, careful. Don't act as if you want rid of the whining sissy.

'Hospital?' said Red-tooth hopefully.

'No, I'd better take you home first to . . . let your family

82

know what's happened.' And home had better bloody well be near.

'Oh. Yes. Do you know where Queens' College is?' Vanessa smiled. She did indeed. It was directly on the way to the Garden House Moat House Hotel. 'I am a student there. I have accommodation very near there.'

'Okay, off we go!' Vanessa said chirpily. God, I sound like Sim or Eve, she thought: as if it made sense to be happy, as if the world were not a dreadful place. They ought to try living in Cambridge and working in London, thought Vanessa. It was difficult to be cheerful when you were forced to waste a substantial proportion of your only life on this earth dealing with authors like Cal Raynard, who wanted to give their books titles that would ensure they never left the warehouse. Gray Jones, Gable Bazzard's head of sales, had made a suggestion last week and now considered the matter closed. Vanessa had passed on his idea to Raynard's agent and was waiting for the inevitable thumbs-down. Gray wanted to keep up the tradition of rhyming titles. 'Why must the hero drive a Saab?' he'd demanded, plonking himself down on the edge of Vanessa's desk and kicking his legs against it. 'Why can't he drive an Audi? It rhymes with *Cloudy* and *Howdy*. It's a car. It's perfect.'

Cal Raynard wouldn't think so, nor would his agent, and Vanessa could see their point. Somewhere between *Considering Marmalade* and *Audi*, Vanessa suspected there was a decent title to be had, one that bridged the gap between crass commercialism and pretentious artistry, but she for one couldn't be arsed thinking about it. She longed to leave publishing and do something else, but what? The *Bookseller* didn't advertise openings in germ warfare, which might have been better suited to her temperament.

Both Gray and Cal acted as if they had a God-given right to the final say. Neither of them had asked Vanessa what she thought. Why should she give a stuff about

Cal Raynard's books, when he refused to meet or speak to her? She didn't even know his real name, where he lived or what he looked like. His agent, Miff McGarvey, described him as a very private person. Not too private to be pally with Miff; not private enough to keep his turgid novels to himself, Vanessa thought bitterly. Clearly, he regarded her, his editor, as someone of no consequence. She'd spent three weeks working on *Howdy*, sent Cal twenty-six pages of editorial suggestions when most of her authors got no more than eight or nine. He'd ignored them all. His determination to exclude Vanessa from the creative process had ruined *Howdy*. She'd responded by disowning it as publicly as possible and planned to do the same with *Audi* or *Marmalade* or whatever the hell it was called, even though she was nominally its editor. This time she'd keep her ideas to herself. Let the novel be published in its present, sub-standard form. It'd serve the bastard right. Vanessa could imagine what sort of man he was: arrogant, devious, misogynist. Probably handsome.

'Was that your driveway you were coming out of?' Red-tooth asked. 'Is that where you live?' She smiled her polite red smile and Vanessa wondered if she was trying to gather information so that she could tell fuller tales to the police later on.

'Oh, no,' said Vanessa, as if by disavowing the site of the accident she could distance herself from any responsibility for it. 'I live in London, actually. I was just visiting a friend.'

'Oh. What do you do? What is your job?'

'I'm a bereavement counsellor,' said Vanessa. This was fun. Red-tooth looked impressed and didn't say anything else for a while. In retrospect, Vanessa saw that the profession she'd invented for herself on the spur of the moment had been a stroke of genius. Ha! She had more inventiveness in her little finger than Cal Raynard had in his whole body. Red-tooth now believed that Vanessa spent her days with the seriously distressed. If she had any sense, she would realise that a sore tooth was nothing in comparison.

'Here we are,' said Vanessa, pulling up outside Queens' College. 'Will there be anyone at home?'

'My husband, I think.'

'Right. Well, tell him what's happened, get him to make you a hot drink and ...' Vanessa paused, wondering what she could add. She hoped that a dazzling display of last-minute advice would distract Red-tooth sufficiently to prevent her from memorising the Peugeot's number plate. 'And then,' Vanessa continued, 'get him to take you to casualty. Do you know where Addenbrookes is?'

'Yes,' said Red-tooth. 'May I have your name and telephone number, please?'

'Yes. Of course.' Vanessa smiled, wishing Red-tooth had not survived the accident. She'd known from the minute she laid eyes on this woman, with her prissy purple cycling hat, that she would be nothing but trouble. Vanessa didn't mind trouble but she preferred the loud, cathartic sort. If Red-tooth had a problem, what was wrong with a slanging match on the pavement of Silver Street? Vanessa loathed the hypocrisy of this po-faced may-I-please crap.

She could hardly refuse to give her details, or ask why Red-tooth wanted them; if she came across as apprehensive it might imply guilt and put Red-tooth in a *Crimewatch* photofit frame of mind. No, Vanessa had to behave as if she was keen to monitor the progress of the damaged tooth.

She got out of the car a few seconds ahead of her bleeding passenger and, in a skilful manoeuvre, leaned against the bonnet, deliberately blocking Red-tooth's view of the licence plate. She guessed Red-tooth would probably have tried to memorise it if she could, but she was counting on her being too polite to insist on taking it down, especially after Vanessa had shown willing to give her name and number. To ask for any more would have been evidence of bad faith, too overtly discourteous for the hypocritical bitch.

Vanessa pulled a bit of paper and a pen out of her handbag, thinking quickly. She'd said she lived in London, so she couldn't give her home number. She wouldn't have, anyway. All she needed was for Nicholas to find out. She could imagine how he'd rush to side with Red-tooth and blame the accident on Vanessa's careless driving. As far as he was concerned, cars were a sign of consumerist individualism gone mad. Bikes, as vehicular underdogs, had his full support.

Vanessa considered making up a false name and phone number. Why not? Without her car registration, there was no way Red-tooth would be able to track her down. Unless she got the police involved. Vanessa could see her doing that. Once she realised the concerned act had been a sizeable con, Red-tooth would trot along to the police station and complain meekly about her ill-treatment. It was doubtful they would allocate much in the way of time and manpower to pursuing Vanessa when all that was at stake was a sore tooth, but was it worth taking the risk? Vanessa knew absolutely sod all about police habits. Maybe this was their month for cracking down on hit-and-run drivers.

Then there were the two witnesses, both of whom would beat a path to the cop shop door if they got the chance. Those two fuckers would be tripping over each other in their eagerness to do their civic duty. They might remember Vanessa's appearance, her car. They would certainly remember, as would Red-tooth, which driveway she'd been coming out of. Everyone in Cambridge knew Gentchev's Field. Vanessa didn't want to be caught by the cops in an undignified escape attempt.

She pulled off the pen's lid with her teeth and wrote 'Vanessa' on the bit of paper she'd torn from her notebook. She knew Red-tooth wouldn't ask for her surname, believing as she did in the intimacy of their post-collision bonding. Underneath her name, Vanessa wrote her mobile phone number. Let the stupid cow ring me, she thought. It would be easier to get rid of her over the phone. And if the worst came to the worst and Red-tooth went to the police, so be it. Vanessa had done nothing wrong; she'd not only given Red-tooth a lift home, she'd handed over her name and telephone number as any do-gooder would have done.

''Bye, then. Hope the tooth's okay!' she trilled, still shielding the Peugeot's registration plate with her body. Red-tooth hesitated, smiled tentatively, redly, then turned and walked away, disappearing into a driveway a few metres ahead. Once Vanessa was sure she'd gone, she climbed back into the car and started the ignition, feeling she'd handled the incident with reasonable success. She was a bit late for her appointment at the salon, but they wouldn't turn her away. They wouldn't dare.

'So, go on, then,' said Sim lightly when Eve phoned her back, after Imogen had left in sombre mood, clutching her neglected poem to her pre-pubescent chest. 'Let's hear the worst.' Sim managed to say 'the worst' in a way that implied it might not be all that bad. Maybe it isn't, thought Eve. Maybe everything would be okay. 'Tell me about it in a *PM*-ish sort of way.'

'What, in the manner of Tony Blair?'

'No, no. *PM* the radio programme. Give me a basic outline first, then go back and fill in more details. That drives Francis mad, you know. He hates details. He prefers gists, like most men.' Except Campbell, thought Eve, who'd never scaled the dizzy heights of a gist in his life.

The outline was so basic it was brutal. Two months ago a firm called Graduate Careers UK organised a four-day personal development and employment training course for graduate students in a hotel in Stratford. Campbell was on their mailing list and received a leaflet. He wasn't interested, but Eve persuaded him to go, hoping that the personal development part of the course would turn him into the sort of person who finished his thesis, got a good job and earned some decent money for a change.

On the first day he met Rory Napper, daughter of Guthrie Napper, the controversial tobacco impresario who many people claimed was also an illegal ivory trader. Rory was no longer a graduate student, but hadn't yet been deleted from the mailing list. She'd been expelled from the Communication Studies department of Warwick University after disappearing to Canada for a year without informing her supervisor.

Nothing happened between Campbell and Rory during these four days, if you didn't count the fact that each felt the other was special. Campbell was due back on the Friday evening and, while Eve waited for him to return, Rory phoned. Eve instantly disliked her voice, which sounded fluttery and clingy. She pronounced her 'r's as soft 'v's and made her own name sound like Vorvy, which at first Eve thought it was. Rory told Eve she'd met Campbell on the Stratford course and was ringing to invite him to stay with her in her family's country house in Hampshire. She did not invite Eve.

When Campbell returned, Eve told him about the call. Did Rory know Campbell had a girlfriend and if so, what was she playing at? Yes, she did know, said Campbell, and Rory wasn't playing at anything, as Eve so prejudicially put it. She was only being friendly.

From then on Rory phoned Campbell every day. A couple of weeks later she started to write to him every day too. Eve called her 'the stalker', which annoyed Campbell, who insisted that Rory was special and Eve would like her. He said he wanted the three of them to be friends. Eve wasn't interested. She was a principled vegetarian and had no desire to socialise with someone whose family caused needless suffering to elephants. Campbell both denied that the Nappers supported the ivory trade and, for added cover, put forward a hypothetical defence, one he claimed he didn't necessarily endorse, based on an unconvincing and unsavoury mélange of nature and Nietzsche.

Eve began to hate Rory Napper. She wished she could tell her to stop phoning Campbell and writing to him but, as Campbell pointed out, he'd never objected to Eve's male acquaintances. On the contrary, one of them, Neil, had become his good friend and squash partner. Eve didn't feel this was in any way analogous. However much Campbell insisted that his relationship with Rory was entirely platonic, Eve didn't believe him. His refusal to let her read any of Rory's letters made her suspicious.

One day Eve decided she'd had enough. Instead of taking Rory's stupid mauve envelope up to Campbell before she left for work, as she had done nearly every morning for a month, and placing it on his bedside table for him to find when he woke up, she opened the letter herself. Things appeared to be somewhat worse than she'd imagined. Rory's letter was full of declarations of love. She'd fallen for Campbell the moment she met him, apparently, and was terribly jealous of Eve. She wished she *was* Eve. She wanted to be with Campbell, she said, even though he belonged to a lower social class. Bloody cheek! According to Sim, soap opera shorthand for middle class was lots of books in the house, red wine, pens tucked behind ears and classical music, all of which applied to Campbell. Rory's family was simply a lot richer, from poisoning people's lungs and killing elephants. At the end of her letter Rory had written that she hoped Campbell didn't mind that they hadn't had sex in Stratford, because their relationship was about so much more than that.

Eve stared at the letter in horror for a few seconds, then marched upstairs to confront Campbell with the evident non-platonicness of his relationship with Rory. The human capacity for hope in desperate circumstances is astounding, Eve thought to herself, remembering that even then, even as she climbed the stairs with Rory's letter in her hand, she half expected Campbell to share her shock, to say 'What?

Why's she suddenly talking as if there's something going on between us?'

Campbell sat up in bed, rubbed his eyes and read the letter. Okay, he admitted, he was in love with Rory. And he intended to leave Eve. And now he had left.

'If only I hadn't opened that letter,' Eve said to Sim. 'That was what forced the issue. If I hadn't opened it, he might still be here.'

'Yeah, and he might still be the happy recipient of a daily mauve letter,' said Sim. 'Which would be completely unacceptable. Anyway, you wouldn't have opened the letter if you hadn't known something was wrong.'

'Yes, but he might not have gone. If I'd ignored the whole thing, maybe it would have petered out. I mean, until that morning he'd shown no sign of wanting to leave. All he seemed to want was for the three of us to be friends. Then suddenly, when he knows I've read the letter, he tells me he's in love with her and he's off, just like that. It was awful, Sim. I knew Rory was a problem, but I can't help feeling that ... I don't know, if I hadn't opened that envelope – which, let's face it, wasn't addressed to me – its contents might have been different. It's like I was punished for prying by having what I thought was a problem turn into a tragedy. That's what it feels like, a tragedy.'

'Look at it from another angle, Eve. Can't you see how brilliantly Campbell engineered this?' Eve couldn't. Campbell had many sterling qualities, but brilliant engineering was not one of them. 'He made it happen, not you. Whatever you'd done, the outcome would have been the same. Campbell created a situation which could only culminate in his leaving. First he met another woman, then he gave her his phone number and address, and allowed her to ring and write every day. Did he wake up extra early every morning to make sure he got to the post before you did? No.'

'But Campbell never wakes up early,' Eve protested.

'Eve, you're talking to the queen of lie-ins. And yet if I thought . . .' Sim paused. 'If I thought my other man was likely to be writing to me and knew that Francis was already suspicious, I'd make damn sure to get to the post before him. Campbell didn't do that, though. He allowed the daily phone calls and the mauve envelopes to flood in, forcing you to handle them and wonder about them. And why did he do that?'

'I don't know,' said Eve sadly. 'Why did he?'

'Because he suspected he wanted to leave. He wasn't sure; he was nowhere near certain enough to do it. So instead he sat back and allowed a situation to develop that forced you to take action. Which you did: you opened the letter and confronted him with it, which enabled him to leave, but feel the responsibility wasn't solely his. Clear?'

'Ish,' said Eve.

'Was he angry with you for opening a letter that was addressed to him?'

'Yes.'

'There you go, then. By focusing on your minor misdemeanour, he was able to give himself permission to leave without feeling too guilty.'

'Isn't that a contradiction?' Eve asked. 'How can he be the brilliant engineer of a subtle plan while at the same time being too spineless to leave if he wants to?'

'Easily.' Sim was warming up. It must have been a luxury for her, talking to someone who wasn't Francis. Eve wondered, briefly, if Sim had ever had an affair. If so, she probably wouldn't have told anyone. Eve knew from personal experience that the disloyalty felt so much less if it was never put into words and Sim more than anyone understood the power of words. 'Imagine you or me in his situation,' she was saying now. 'There'd be no need for a brilliantly engineered plan, or subtlety. We'd simply decide what we wanted to do, then do it. But Campbell – and this applies to most men – is illiterate when it comes to his own feelings. What would you say

91

if I asked you to talk about deep inelastic forward and non-forward lepton-hadron scattering?'

'What the hell is that?' asked Eve.

'That physics conference Matt went to in San Diego a few years ago.' Sim had a phenomenal memory for trivia. But then, Sim believed nothing was trivial. 'Would you rather live with a lepton or have an affair with a hadron?'

'I've no idea.' Eve laughed.

'Exactly, because you don't see the world in those terms. But Matt does. He's probably more comfortable talking about particles than people. Fortunately you and I can get by perfectly adequately without knowing about lepton-hadron scattering. But emotional illiteracy is more serious. It leads to a loss of control over your life. If you don't know what you want or how you feel, other people will be quick to mould you to their pattern. So men respond – not consciously, but out of some primeval survival instinct – by developing a weird mechanism whereby they can get what they want, before even realising what that is, without actually having to be seen to do anything definite themselves.'

'Hm,' said Eve. 'And you think Campbell's got a . . . mechanism like this?'

'I think he's got a spotless model, straight from the showroom and turtle-waxed,' said Sim.

'I still wish I hadn't opened that damn envelope,' said Eve.

'Eve, why didn't you throw Rory's letters away?'

'Is that what you would have done?'

'Definitely. Hi, Francis. Francis has just walked in,' Sim explained unnecessarily. 'Having first read them, of course.'

Eve didn't hear Francis say hello back. 'I would have felt bad tampering with his mail,' she said.

'Eve, if you succumb to that sort of conventional moral-ity, it makes it easier for Campbell's mechanism to have its way. Tampering with someone's mail isn't necessarily a bad thing,' said Sim. 'It depends whose mail it is and why you're doing it. It's not, for example, anywhere near as bad as making your partner bring your treacherous mauve envelopes upstairs every morning while you get an extra hour of beauty sleep. Still, I suppose he'd have found out if you'd thrown them away.'

'Exactly. Rory phoned him every night. What could I have done? I tried to talk to her on the phone once when Campbell was out. And I wrote to her.'

'You did? What did you say?'

'That she was putting a strain on our relationship and couldn't she lay off for a month or so. But it did no good. She phoned even more after that.'

'You astound me,' said Sim with heavy irony. 'Eve, why the hell didn't you tell me this was going on?'

'I know,' said Eve gloomily. 'I wish I had. But I thought it'd blow over.' This wasn't quite true. Every time she'd taken one of Rory's letters upstairs, Eve had thought of Sim and what she would have to say on the matter. But Sim was the obvious port of call for all love crises and if Eve told her nothing then she couldn't really have a crisis on her hands, could she? God, how stupid she'd been, like a woman who neglects the lump in her breast and dies rather than going to the doctor straight away. 'What would you have advised me to do?' she asked Sim, wanting to torture herself with the knowledge that the tragedy could have been averted.

'I'm not falling for that one.' Sim chuckled. 'The important thing is what happens now. Do you want him back?'

'I don't know,' said Eve. 'I did at first but . . . I keep thinking, if he can leave me after seven and a half years for someone he's known less than a week, is he really worth having? I mean, I've had flings in the past, but I would never have left Campbell. As far as I was concerned we were together for life.'

'You've had flings?' Sim sounded pleasantly surprised.

Eve waited for her to make a similar confession, then

remembered that Francis had returned and was probably stomping and rustling for attention in the background. 'Yeah,' she said. 'They didn't mean anything. I could have understood if he'd just fancied Rory. I even suggested he sleep with her a few times to get her out of his system. I tried everything, Sim. I was so reasonable.'

'Sounds like it.'

'All I wanted was to keep him here, whatever the conditions. That would at least have given us something to build on. I said he could stay in the house and we could sleep separately. I offered to move out of our bedroom on to the couch.'

'Did you also suggest that he disembowel you with a garden rake?'

'No.' Eve laughed.

'Eve! How remiss of you. So, this alleged specialness of Rory's – what does it consist of? Is she stunningly beautiful?'

'No! Thank God for that, at least. Campbell took his camera to Stratford, so I've seen photos. She's got long, stringy, piss-yellow hair which she tucks back with a hair-slide at the front, a huge, slabby chin, sunken eyes the colour of babies' diarrhoea – you know, sort of yellowy-brown – and her skin's all pimply. She's a massive snob too, really right-wing. How can Campbell think someone like that's special? I just keep thinking . . .' Eve coughed, to avoid crying. 'I keep thinking, what if he hasn't come back before the wedding? I don't know if I can face going . . .'

'Everything will be sorted by then,' said Sim. 'I'm so confident, I'm not even planning to tell Matt and Lucy.'

'Really?' Eve found this comforting. 'Maybe Francis could talk to him. He'd listen to Francis. I kept asking him if he was sure he was doing the right thing and he kept saying no, he wasn't sure, but there was no alternative, as if he was a robot or something.'

'Of course,' said Sim. 'Because it's much easier for a robot with no alternative to leave than for the autonomous and many-optioned Campbell Golightly who, of course, is far too out of touch with his feelings to make a decision like that.'

'I'm worried he's having some sort of breakdown. I mean, why Rory?' Eve picked at the sore. 'It's so insulting that he'd choose someone like that over me. If she's special, what does that make me? She sounds awful, Sim. She got kicked off her PhD course. She's never managed to hold down a job. She doesn't believe in penetrative sex . . .'

'Can I stop you right there,' Sim cut in sharply. 'Run that last one by me again.'

'She doesn't believe in penetrative sex.'

'Eve! How can you toss that nugget of good fortune into my lap so casually? If Rory doesn't believe in penetrative sex, Campbell will be back next week! There's no two ways about it. I may, in fact, send Francis out for some champagne.'

Hazel opened her study window and leaned out, hoping the fresh air would calm her down. Sim had phoned on the dot of half past six, when the *Potters Court* omnibus finished, and announced she was coming round at seven for what she described as a Campbell and Eve symposium. Hazel had bundled Ian into the hall in a panic. This had happened before a couple of times and she always feared Sim would detect Ian's recent presence in the flat.

She focused on Baildon Moor and listened to the roar and foam of the River Aire until her heart stopped pounding. Hazel loved the view from her study. At first she hadn't been able to bring herself to call it a study, didn't feel she was the sort of person who needed or deserved one, but these days the word almost came naturally to her. The only people in whose hearing she would still say 'the little room', or even 'the junk room' for added security, were her family, who she knew would greet the word 'study' with peels of mocking laughter. It was bad enough that Hazel lived in a converted mill next to the

David Hockney gallery in Saltaire. Her two brothers were constantly on the lookout for signs that she was getting ideas above her station and was about to start hanging around with celebrities such as Jerry Springer and Noel Edmonds. Hazel had assured them that those particular celebrities didn't live in West Yorkshire, but her brothers wouldn't have put it past her to commute in order to hang around with Noel and Jerry.

Hazel looked at Sim's green Volvo in the car park below the window and Francis's white BMW beside it. If only they didn't live in the same building. It was comforting to have friends within easy reach, but this was too close. Hazel had told Ian to make sure Sim and Francis weren't getting in or out of their cars before letting himself into the flat, the front door of which was visible from the car park, and to keep away from front-facing windows as much as possible. He'd assured her this wasn't a problem.

Hazel touched the wooden window frame superstitiously, in case she'd tempted fate by wishing Sim and Francis further away. If they hadn't been neighbours, Hazel would never have met them, would still be friendless. Sim had taken an instant liking to Hazel – something no one had ever done before – and had wasted no time in sweeping her up into a wider social circle that seemed willing to accept her on Sim's say-so alone, providing her with a programme of activities that stretched several months into the future. For the first time in her life she'd been invited to a wedding.

The doorbell rang. Hazel jumped, pricking her arm on the large cactus on the windowsill, half concealed behind the curtain. 'Ow! Gatting!' She tutted and rubbed her arm. Ian was always telling Hazel to move him (although Ian had called Gatting 'it' at first, before he knew better) so that she didn't spike herself every time she drew the curtains, but she couldn't do that. Gatting liked it where he was and might react badly to a change of scene.

'That'll be Sim,' Hazel told the cactus as she went

to open the door. 'Isn't that nice? She's come to see us.' Gatting looked forward to Sim's visits. She was the only one of Hazel's friends who fully understood his significance.

When Hazel was little the Ings family's favourite cricketer was Mike Gatting. As a general rule, Ingses were not encouraged to have their own opinions; there was always a party line. Hazel, keen to fit in, became a fanatical Gatting supporter and cried whenever he was bowled out. She took Gatting fever several steps further than the other Ingses, to the point where it began to annoy her brothers, who held a meeting behind her back to discuss how to deal with it. One day, Hazel found to her horror that the entire family, nuclear and extended, had switched its allegiance from Gatting to David Gower. Such was the power of her brothers.

No one offered Hazel an explanation, least of all her shadowy, oppressed parents; they simply ostracised her on cricket-watching days and mocked her for her adherence to the old regime. This put Hazel off her food and within a few weeks she'd lost half a stone. Her mother bought her a cactus to cheer her up but her brothers, to reinforce the point still further, insisted on calling the cactus David Gower. Her parents, scared to defy them, simply cowered and nodded. Hazel didn't say anything, but privately she changed the cactus's name from Gower to Gatting. She vowed that as soon as she left home, it would be called Gatting publicly.

It was with this story that Hazel introduced herself to Sim when they first met two summers ago. Hazel was sitting in the car park with Gatting so that he could soak up some rays of sunlight before the long Yorkshire winter descended. Sim pulled up beside them in her car and asked Hazel if she was all right. A person sitting in a car park next to a cactus was not necessarily okay, Sim explained. Hazel told her all about Gatting, his history and importance in her life, and Sim, rather than nodding politely and sloping off as Hazel had expected her to, invited her and Gatting in for a coffee. At first Hazel thought there had to be a catch; was Sim trying to trick her? Was she planning to hide Gatting to make Hazel panic? Hazel lived in fear of practical jokes; she felt she was practically a joke herself.

But no, unbelievable though it was, Sim genuinely liked Hazel. As soon as she heard the story of Gatting – Hazel knew this now because Sim had told her – she knew she wanted Hazel as a friend. The aspect of the story that had really impressed Sim was Hazel's resolve and loyalty. It would have been easy, Sim said, to go over to David Gower when the rest of the family did, or to let the cactus gradually assume the identity of a Gower cactus rather than a Gatting cactus, given that that was how the rest of the family thought of it. But Hazel had stood firm and given Gatting his proper name as soon as she left home. A lesser person, Sim said, might have thought it didn't matter after all those years. Sim was of the view that everything mattered. Her only criticism of Hazel's behaviour, Gatting-wise, was that she still hadn't told her family about the renaming of the cactus. 'They need to know about it,' said Sim, 'or else they'll think they've won.' But standing up to her family was not Hazel's strong point.

She peered through the peephole in her door. A distorted Sim stared back at her. The glass was convex and made people look as they did in the backs of spoons. Hazel thanked God every day for her peephole. She hadn't even thought about it when she rented the flat, but it enabled Ian to screen visitors. Sim was the only one of Hazel's friends likely to get so close. Francis never came round and anyone who didn't live in the building had to press the intercom outside even to get as far as the entrance hall. If he saw Sim through the peephole, Ian knew to hold his breath and keep still until she went away. He was under strict instructions only to admit meter readers from utility boards and Hazel, when she'd forgotten her key.

'Sim!' She swung open the door. 'Those bastards have . . . um . . . um . . . ruined Lucy and Matt's wedding present! I'll never forgive them.'

'How come, and which bastards?' Sim frowned. Her long, lilac thingie (Hazel was never sure if it was a cloak, cardigan or shirt) followed her into the flat.

'Jacket designers! I was going to get them Cal Raynard's complete works, but you should see the cover of the new one – it's revolting.'

'So get them something else,' said Sim. 'Matt only reads science journals and the sports pages, anyway, and maybe the odd Andy McNab.' Her mind was elsewhere. She walked through the lounge into the kitchen. Hazel ran after her, trying to think of something compelling to say, to give Sim an incentive to carry on talking to her.

Hazel always tried to hook Sim right at the beginning of a conversation. This was a legacy of the introductory Gatting incident. Hazel's vivid depiction of a family so dysfunctional that it waged psychological war using cricketers and cacti as weapons had captured Sim's imagination. Unfortunately, most of Hazel's life was much duller than that. How far could one sick slice of autobiography take you? Not very far, Hazel was afraid. She felt urgently in need of reinforcements. Sim must never suspect that the Gatting incident was the only one in Hazel's childhood that rose to such a peak of traumatic eccentricity.

'The wedding present can wait,' said Sim, filling the kettle. 'Tea?' Hazel nodded. 'What can't wait is Rory Napper. We have to get rid of her well before Matt and Lucy's wedding. Have you got Lapsang?'

'Who's Rory Napper?' Hazel pointed to a cupboard above Sim's head. Of course she had Lapsang. Everyone Sim visited or was likely to visit had it; it was mandatory. She listened as Sim summarised what Eve had told her, but found herself unable to wait until the end of the story before interrupting, so outraged was she. 'The bastard!

He left Eve for someone else? That's even worse. The callous shit!'

'I'm sure he didn't do it callously,' said Sim, giving Hazel an odd look. 'He must have had his reasons, and if Francis would only bloody ring him, we'd have his reasons too.'

'I'm surprised Francis is willing to ring him. I wouldn't.'

'Willing is perhaps an overstatement.' Sim grinned.

Hazel couldn't see that there was anything remotely amusing about the situation. Eve was lovely; how dare Campbell hurt her? Hazel wanted to punch him. 'Seven years and he deserts her for a woman who kills elephants!'

'I don't think she personally . . .'

'I don't care! Poor, lovely elephants.' Indignant tears pricked the backs of Hazel's eyelids. 'Well, that's it, as far as I'm concerned. I won't be taking him to the Horsforth Poems and Pints night, that's for sure. I'll find someone else to take.'

'Come on, Hazel.' Sim was looking worried. 'People leave people all the time. You have to be able to change your partner if you want to. It happens. I don't mean we should reduce it to a generalisation. Obviously this is a specific leaving with its own character, but . . . we have to consider Campbell, don't we, as well as Eve and the elephants. Maybe he felt he'd hurt Eve more by staying. It'd be no fun for her to live with someone who'd rather be somewhere else.'

'Well . . .' Hazel wasn't convinced. 'He won't be getting an invitation to the launch of the Limericks in Libraries project. Over my dead body.'

'That'll be a crushing blow for him,' Sim muttered, opening the fridge. Hazel stiffened. Was she being mocked? Sim straightened up, looking very serious all of a sudden, holding the milk bottle like a microphone. 'The problem with disapproval is that it impedes understanding. If you dismiss Campbell as a bastard, you miss out on the . . . potential for investigation. Besides, it's not really a moral issue.' Hazel blushed. Ian had used those exact words earlier. 'We can't just turn against our friends when they behave badly,' said Sim. 'Where are the cups?'

'Top cupboard on the right,' said Hazel distractedly. If the truth came out, would she be seen by the world as more or less guilty than Campbell? Less, surely. She and Ian weren't hurting anyone, that was the difference.

'They're not,' said Sim, holding open the door to the top right-hand cupboard.

Hazel looked up and saw plates of all sizes and a few bowls, but no cups. 'Um . . . um . . .' she stammered, frantically trying to think. Ian had been washing up when she got back from work this afternoon. He must have put the cups in a different cupboard, but Hazel could hardly explain this to Sim, who didn't know Ian existed. 'I can't remember where they are.' She shivered. 'I'm sorry. This . . . news about Campbell and Eve is . . . um . . . um . . . well, it's a catastrophe!' Sim smiled sympathetically, and opened a few more doors until she found the one that contained cups and mugs. Hazel felt terrible; it was unforgivable to use Eve's misfortune to get out of a sticky situation.

'I know what you're thinking,' said Sim, making Hazel shiver with guilt and fear. 'That I turned against Gillian.' Oh, thank God. 'That was different, though. Gillian committed a friendship-invalidating offence, then failed to apologise properly.' Hazel didn't need reminding. Gillian's inadequate apology had become a staple joke, mentioned at least once during every social occasion. She'd written to Sim after the night of the big row, not to say sorry but to suggest that they 'berry the hat shed'. Sim had shown the letter to the rest of the gang, to demonstrate Gillian's evasion of her responsibility for what had happened, but most of them were more interested in laughing at the spelling. 'This proves I'm right,' Vanessa had declared triumphantly. 'Without spell-check, she'd be finished.'

'Also, there's no incentive to forgive Gillian,' Sim went on, handing Hazel her tea. 'I don't feel as if I'd benefit from a reconciliation. She's not kind. She's not clever, interesting or funny. In fact, she possesses no good qualities. I should have got rid of her ages ago. It's important to have standards. It's a deliberate policy of mine.'

'What?'

'To be as horrible to the people I dislike as I am nice to the people I like and love. It's the only way of conducting yourself that makes any sense and it's much fairer than the blanket approach, adopted by the unenlightened, of treating everyone the same.'

Hazel nodded, then realised there was a discrepancy in what Sim had said about Campbell. 'But . . . if people are allowed to change their partners, as you say . . .'

Sim laughed. 'There's no if about it, Hazel.'

'. . . then why do you want to get rid of Rory Napper?'

'Hey?'

'You said we had to get rid of her well before Matt and Lucy's wedding. And on the phone you said we needed to get Campbell and Eve back together. But why, if you think he'd hurt her more by staying with her?'

Sim looked momentarily puzzled. 'I didn't say that. I only said . . . well, I was talking hypothetically. Anyway, that's not the point.' She bit her lip, emitting a loud huff. Hazel had never seen Sim flustered before. 'Rory Napper sounds awful. I'm sure Campbell's capable of seeing that, given a few pointers in the right direction.'

'I don't think Eve should take him back,' Hazel ventured. 'Not after what he's done. She'd be better off with someone new, someone loyal.'

Sim nearly choked on her tea. Recovering quickly, she laughed uneasily and said, 'Hazel! I can't believe you're being so anarchic. Campbell and Eve are an institution.' Despite the comic tone, Hazel believed Sim meant every word. 'Lucy's frantic as it is. It'll ruin her day if Eve's a wreck. She and Matt have been planning this wedding for a year. Given the amount of money they've forked out and the effort they've put in, I think we owe it to them to make sure things are perfect. Lucy'll freak if she finds out Campbell and Eve have split up, which means they've got to be back together by the the stag-hen weekend.'

Hazel frowned. Sim had always shielded Matt and Lucy from anything problematic, believing they weren't kitted out for it. She seemed to feel any disharmony might puncture the aura of perfection that surrounded them. To put even a minor quibble before them would be as gross an affront as spraying Special Brew around the Sistine Chapel. Hazel had absorbed this attitude to a certain extent, but to take it this far struck her as ridiculous. Sometimes one's friends split up before one's wedding and that was that. Hazel doubted Matt and Lucy would disintegrate, or even postpone the ceremony. They might be sad for Eve but . . . well, so they should be. There was something that didn't quite add up about Sim's slant on the situation.

'I'd better go home and ring Vanessa.' Sim swallowed the rest of her tea in one gulp. 'Make sure she knows not to mention it to Lucy.'

Hazel was immediately beset by anxieties. Was Sim leaving so soon because she, Hazel, had said the wrong things, and too many of them? For a second, she considered shouting, 'I've got a big secret!' to make Sim stay a bit longer.

She'd been tempted to tell Sim before, but always decided against it. She wasn't absolutely sure Sim would think it was okay, and as for the others . . . Hazel shuddered to think how Nicholas would react. She remembered how ungraciously he'd greeted Gatting the first time he came to Hazel's flat. 'I can't believe you called your plant after that wanker who went to South Africa,' he said, shaking his head in disbelief. Plant, indeed. Gatting was a cactus. Hazel had never quite forgiven Nicholas for that remark. Didn't it occur to him that Gatting might have been christened years before his cricketer namesake did anything wrong? By the time Mike Gatting went to South Africa, the name was an essential part of her Gatting's character. Would Nicholas expect Hazel to change her own name if somebody else called Hazel Ings made a bad decision?

The rest of her friends might be okay about Ian, though. No, she couldn't risk it. It wasn't that she feared censure; what she thought of others mattered far more to her than what others thought of her. It was her own mind she had to live with, after all, her own beliefs from which she couldn't escape. Hazel desperately wanted to believe in her friends, but if any of them made an issue of Ian in any way – even if all they did was laugh dismissively – she would think less of them, permanently. Ian wasn't negotiable; he was crucial to her well-being. If anyone condemned, mocked or denied this, it would seem to Hazel as if they were making their disregard for her happiness apparent. To use Sim's expression, that would be a friendship-invalidating offence.

As she closed the door in Sim's wake, it occurred to Hazel that the one person she could have counted on not to judge her was Campbell. He was good like that. The bastard.

Vanessa was driving back from the Garden House Moat House when her mobile phone started to ring. Oh, goodie: Red-tooth's first call. Vanessa was fully prepared. She pulled her phone out of her bag with one hand, steering with the other, glad, now, that Red-tooth had asked for her name and number. This way the game would last longer. 'Hello?' she said.

'Vanessa, it's Sim.'

'Oh. Hi.'

'You sound disappointed. Were you expecting someone more interesting?' There was no resentment in the question; Sim would genuinely have been fascinated to learn of the existence of someone more interesting than herself. Vanessa considered telling her about the accident and Red-tooth, her new toy, but decided to err on the side of caution. Despite Sim's reluctance to disapprove in case she was excluded from future gossip, she'd surely have something to say about Vanessa's plan to torment an injured cyclist. 'I'm only disappointed by life,' said Vanessa. 'Not by your phone call in particular.'

'Did you get my message?'

'The one that made no sense? Why mustn't I tell Lucy? Why must Eve and Campbell be got back together?'

'You sound like Hazel,' said Sim glumly. 'I don't get it. Where's everyone's enthusiasm?'

'If I display enthusiasm, will you take back that I sound like the runt?'

'Vanessa, Hazel's . . .'

'Nice. I know. So, go on, tell me the goss.' Vanessa turned into Grange Road. As she approached the entrance to Gentchev's Field, she noticed that Red-tooth's bike was still chained to the fence beside the gate.

Swiftly, but without missing out any crucial details, Sim summarised what Eve had told her. She barely paused for breath. 'What I don't get is this,' she said, once the facts were out of the way. 'Campbell could have gone off with any number of people . . .'

'Only ones who didn't mind his inertia.'

'Campbell isn't inert,' Sim protested. 'Not mentally.' Vanessa smiled. She'd only once seen Campbell animated and that was when he was holding forth about *Bergerac*; it didn't inspire confidence. What Sim meant was that he was good at chatting. Sim loved anyone who could chat well, prizing this skill even more highly in a man because it was rarer. 'Why would he choose this Rory person?' she demanded. 'According to Eve, she's a slab-chinned, snobby, spotty, unemployable, elephant-killing stalker who won't have penetrative sex. Whereas Eve is attractive . . .'

'. . . and penetrable. I know. But Eve's appearance is

irrelevant; Campbell's fed up of looking at her after seven years. She's pretty in a tidy, well-proportioned way, but you can imagine that would get boring after a while. Maybe Rory Napper's more striking.'

'Well, if Eve's description is at all accurate . . .' Sim began.

Vanessa sighed heavily. 'Think back over what you've just said and look for the clue.'

'What?'

'Of course Eve's description isn't accurate.'

'Oh, come on,' said Sim. 'I know Eve won't be keen to present Rory in the best possible light, but there are some details she couldn't have made up. Like the penetrative sex. And the elephant killing.'

'Sim, I hate to embarrass you by bringing this up, but you were enamoured of a certain Andrew Johnson for a while. Rory can't possibly be worse than him.' Vanessa crossed her fingers and waited. Sim, who traditionally had always been keen to talk about the Toodle-pipster and her own foolish involvement with him, had been monosyllabic on the subject since he got together with Gillian. Vanessa had taken the hint and stopped mentioning Andrew, assuming Sim felt significantly tarnished by having her sexual history snarled up with Gillian's. Vanessa understood this completely and hoped Sim would permit her this one small lapse if she could prove relevance.

She'd been flattered at the time of the affair to be the sole recipient of Sim's confidences, although she was realistic about why she, of all Sim's friends, had been chosen. Sim could talk openly about her bad behaviour to Vanessa, who had no interest in promoting goodness in herself or others and could be relied upon to bring her ruthless intellectual rigour to the matter. What disgusted other people delighted Vanessa, which she could see might be refreshing for the would-be wrongdoer. Sim couldn't have hoped for the same exhaustive dissection from any of her other friends, not without the added weight of disapproval.

She seemed to be struggling to reply, so Vanessa helped her out by changing the subject. 'What's all this got to do with Matt and Lucy's wedding, anyway?' she asked.

'It won't be perfect if Campbell's still with this creature,' Sim explained. 'It'll be marred.'

'So? What can you do about it?' Sim's reverential attitude to the colossal waste of money scheduled for the fifteenth of May irritated Vanessa. Sim treated Lucy and Matt like some kind of National Trust preservation area, one in which you wouldn't be prepared to live yourself but liked to pay homage to every now and then, to justify spending the rest of your time having much more fun pumping petrol fumes into the air like every other normal person.

'I can interfere, until things are as I think they should be,' said Sim.

'Have you ever considered applying for a job as president of the United States?'

'Why?'

'You've just defined American foreign policy,' said Vanessa. 'Interfering in the domestic affairs of others, using your position as a superpower to make weaker countries submit to your will. But if you tell Nicholas I put it like that I'll kill you. Why bother getting involved, anyway? Personally, I couldn't care less whether Campbell and Eve are together or not.' Vanessa knew Sim would assume she was joking. People were so reluctant to take unpleasantness seriously; Vanessa was convinced that was how the idea of comedy came into being.

'You know I can't adopt that sort of laissez-faire attitude,' said Sim. 'If you neglect a situation it gets worse. Like Eve ignoring Rory's letters. What would you do if someone started writing to Nicholas every day on mauve notepaper?'

'Pack up his possessions in large crates and have them

107

and him sent on to the other woman's address,' said Vanessa. 'Erase his voice from the answerphone and begin my life anew. What about you?'

'If someone started sending Francis mauve letters?'

'Yes. Although Francis wouldn't notice, unless the sender was Kofi Annan.'

'I'd throw the real letters away and substitute fake ones I'd written myself.'

'Why would you want to engage in such a pointless activity?' asked Vanessa. She believed Sim really would go to those lengths to keep Francis and wondered if she loved Nicholas as much. She loved screwing him, but was that the same thing?

'If Eve had thrown them away, Campbell would have found out the minute Rory said "Did you get my letter?" and Eve would have looked like the bad guy. But let's say she'd transcribed the letters, word for word except that in each case she added one sinister phrase that would be guaranteed to scare Campbell off . . .'

'"Darling Campbell,"' said Vanessa. '"Can't wait to see you. Just found out I'm a carrier of the herpes virus . . ."'

'Exactly. Although it'd have to be something Campbell wouldn't mention to Rory over the phone, otherwise she'd deny having written it.'

'Go on, then, do better,' Vanessa challenged her.

'Well,' Sim began enthusiastically. She'd clearly given a lot of thought to the perfect method of sabotaging Campbell's mauve envelopes. Where did she get the energy, Vanessa wondered. 'How about, "Please don't mention this when we speak because it's too painful for me to talk about . . ."'

'Good. Nice silencing order, convincingly passed off as trauma.'

'Erm . . . "but I spent some time in a young offenders institute after I set fire to my boyfriend when I was seventeen . . ."'

'Appalling.' Vanessa laughed. 'You were doing well

and then you blew it. My idea was much better. Herpes is gross, whereas serving time for murder has a certain mysterious allure. Talking of which . . .' Vanessa's tone changed suddenly.

'Yes?' There was an almost audible pricking up of ears at Sim's end.

'The runt . . .'

'Vanessa, stop. If you didn't insist on terrifying Hazel into silence, you'd discover that she's a really interesting and unusual . . .'

'Not the cactus anecdote again, please. I've got a more recent story starring Runtelstiltskin.'

'Vanessa! What story?'

'Last week we did a Gable Bazzard roadshow in Leeds.' Vanessa knew Sim would interrupt at this point and ask for more details. Sim did. Her mind had already gone off at a tangent, wondering how Hazel might be connected to the roadshow. 'Sim, it's impossible ever to get to the point of a story with you. The roadshows are irrelevant, as you'll see in a minute if you let me carry on. Please trust me to tell you everything you need to know. I'm not Francis.'

'Sorry, sorry.'

'We did a roadshow in Leeds and I thought I'd pop round and see you, as I was in the area. Anyway, you weren't in, so I buggered off, but while I was in your car park I saw a man in Hazel's flat.'

'What? Really?' Sim's tone was hushed and ceremonial. Vanessa imagined her with bowed head, entering into solemn communion with the gossip god. 'Well, I suppose it could have been her dad or one of her ghastly brothers,' Sim said eventually. 'But they never come round.'

'It wasn't them. I've been bored rigid by photos of the runt's family on more than one occasion.'

'Are you sure it was the right flat?'

'Positive. The window immediately to the left of that bit where the bins are.'

'Yeah, that's Hazel's. What did this man look like?'

109

'Hideous,' said Vanessa. 'He had a shaven head and a thick neck. And a tattoo, I think. Even Hazel could do better. Sim? You're not saying anything. Has your tongue been cut out by the Saltaire noise pollution police?'

'I was round at Hazel's a minute ago. She did seem a bit . . . well, I just thought she was being her usual self . . .'

'Which, let's face it, is hardly very usual.'

'Why wouldn't she tell me if she had a boyfriend?' Sim wondered aloud. 'Maybe he's married.'

'I'll leave the matter in your capable, meddlesome hands,' said Vanessa. 'Do let me know if you find out. I yearn to be entertained with tales of Runtelstiltskin's secret life.' She pressed the 'end-call' button on her phone before Sim could scold her.

4

It was seven thirty. Outside, the River Aire sped along the valley, making a swishing, burbling sound that floated in through the open kitchen window. Sim chopped fresh spinach and coriander to put into a curry for herself and Francis. The two chicken breasts she'd bought in town were still in the fridge, unopened. She didn't fancy eating meat tonight; it would feel as if she were taking Rory Napper's side against Eve. She hoped Francis, a dedicated carnivore, wouldn't be too disappointed.

She'd been doing a lot of thinking since her conversations with Hazel and Vanessa, interrogating her own motives. Hazel's puzzled look lingered in her mind. It was the sort of look you gave someone when you thought their inner logic didn't quite tally. To be such a person bothered Sim, even temporarily. Her world-view had stepped in and given her an ultimatum: either she was honest with herself now or all future investigations might be doomed.

Could she be jealous of Campbell? Before today Sim had believed she was the only one of their circle to dabble in infidelity. This was as it should be: herself at the cutting edge of social and sexual configurations. And then along came Campbell with an illicit romance that at once disinterred the shameful spectre of Andrew Johnson and made Sim's affair with him look positively amateurish. Campbell had taken the concept of infidelity one step further, first by being passionately pursued, then by eloping, and Sim envied him the high drama of the experience. That drama should rightfully have been hers. She'd put in the hours, after all, working for *Potters Court*, immersing herself in upheaval.

Andrew had never said anything about wanting Sim full-time, and the feeling – a sort of erotic indifference – was mutual. Sim didn't know why she'd bothered, really. If only she could rewrite history, erase her betrayal of Francis. There'd be no competition then; Campbell would not have outdone her.

Had her unfaithfulness been merely an overspill of her avid interest in people? She remembered one thing: a substantial part of Andrew's appeal had been his willingness to listen to Sim endlessly, especially before they'd first slept together. Sim liked nothing more than to give a stunning verbal performance to an appreciative audience; it was her idea of great foreplay, in fact. She had a strong belief in her power to improve other people's lives and often felt it was a shame that Francis, whose mind was elsewhere so much of the time, should be the only beneficiary.

Sim put the chopped spinach in a colander and rinsed it under the tap. No, she must resist the temptation to blame her lapse on Francis. True, he could be impatient and abrasive, but Sim had known that all along. Without a hard shell, Francis would never have survived eighteen years in his mother's house. Francis loved Sim in a fierce, demanding way that kept her on her toes. He wasn't always easy to live with, but Sim had risen to the challenge of loving him and succeeded in making both of them happy. There was distinction in that; only someone with Sim's talent for love, her immense power to transform, would have been able to thaw out Francis to the extent that she had.

Sim smiled, recalling that as a child she'd had two pet bumps in the road – Humphrey and Len – which she fed with privet leaves every day on her way to and from nursery. Even then the affection of a concrete mound

112

seemed worth more than the love of, say, a dog, which any fool could get. Sim had never regretted choosing Francis's ill-mannered devotion over the soft-centred splutterings of a chocolates-and-flowers man.

She put the water on for the rice and leaned out of the window, hoping the mild breeze would blow her thoughts into order. How could she be jealous of Campbell? He'd lost Eve, while Sim was lucky enough still to have Francis. Poor Campbell. Rory sounded dreadful and as for Eve . . . Sim hadn't realised how admirable a person she was until today. Eve had acted with the dignity of a Gandhi or a Martin Luther King. Instead of turning against Campbell and baying for revenge, instead of letting bitterness set in, she'd taken the noble view, that hers and Campbell's was a relationship worth saving, and given him permission to try Rory out if that was what he needed to do. Even now she'd let him resit the love examination if he wanted to.

It's up to us, his close friends, to make sure he seizes the opportunity, thought Sim. Eve's essential excellence could withstand the bleakest conditions but Sim feared Campbell's soul was at stake. He'd always been alarmingly malleable. In the wrong hands, he could become a force for darkness.

She felt arms round her waist. 'Love you,' Francis muttered grumpily into her ear. She turned round, smiling. What had brought this on? 'Have you finished on the phone?' he asked.

'Yeah.'

'Good.'

'Feeling neglected, are you?' He shrugged and Sim kissed him. Despite Francis's disapproval of unrestrained chatting, he got worried when Sim took her gossip elsewhere.

'It's distracting when I'm trying to work,' he complained mildly. 'I keep hearing myself referred to in all sorts of worrying contexts. First there's some plan afoot to send me fake mauve letters, whatever that means . . .'

'No, that was . . .'

'. . . and before I heard you saying you "may send Francis out for some champagne", like some sort of irritating Sloane.' He grew angrier as he remembered this. 'I'm fed up of it! I'm not having you changing my character to amuse your friends. When, I'd like to know, did I become the butler? There I was, under the illusion that I'm the deputy editor of a serious news programme, but no, it turns out I'm someone who receives mauve letters and is sent out for champagne!'

Sim laughed nervously, hoping that was all Francis had heard. She'd always assumed he was too wrapped up in his own private world to listen to her calls. What had she said to Vanessa about Andrew? Had she mentioned his name? She'd have to be more careful in future. 'Francis, I had no intention of sending you out anywhere. I only said that because I wanted to end my conversation with Eve on an upbeat note.'

'Why bring me into it?' he demanded. 'Why didn't you say you'd go out and get the champagne yourself?'

'I don't know. It appealed to me as something to say.'

'You obviously see me as some sort of bloody cartoon character that comes in handy for fleshing out your imaginings,' Francis grumbled. 'Not as a person in my own right.'

Sim felt bad. She realised, even if Francis didn't, that he was accusing her of behaving like his mother, constructing a false image of him and then using it against him. Why *had* she said what she'd said to Eve? When you were as experienced a chatterer as Sim, talking became like touch-typing – you skipped the process and got it right instinctively. She tried to go back and rationalise it.

'It wouldn't have been as good from Eve's point of view if I'd said I'd go out for champagne. That would imply a normal celebration – I'm the bubbly type, a natural optimist. For you to go out and buy champagne sounds almost parodic at the same time as suggesting a bigger cause for celebration. It's a more comic image.'

'I see. So what am I, a flat pessimist? I've bought champagne in the past.' Francis looked hurt.

'Yes, but you'd never celebrate the frigidity of one of our friends' romantic rivals. Whereas I might. Do you see what I mean?' Francis shook his head in distaste. He didn't ask how frigidity came into the equation, Sim noticed. 'If you'd heard my whole conversation with Eve . . .'

'I'd rather have my head stamped on by sumo wrestlers,' said Francis.

'. . . you'd have seen what I was trying to do, why my comment was exactly right. God, I didn't realise how good I was!' Sim giggled. 'I was maintaining a safe comic distance from reality. I wanted to sound upbeat, but in an unlikely way. For me to buy champagne would sound too plausible; it would have raised Eve's expectations. She might have taken it as a promise that everything would be okay in the end, which it might not be.'

'Forget it.' Francis grimaced, acknowledging defeat with a wave of his hand. 'I don't care.'

'The image of me sending *you* out for champagne for this particular reason is so surreal, it sort of implies hope can be fun, even without expectation.'

'Sim, I'm losing the will to live,' Francis warned. He wandered back into the lounge and sat down in front of the television. Contrary bugger, thought Sim. How come he cared so much about Grab-a-ditch bloody Caravan when he didn't want to talk about his own friends? She followed him, unwilling to let it lie.

'Did you know Rory Napper won't have penetrative sex with Campbell?' she said.

'I don't care. What? Really?' He scowled, annoyed to have fallen into the trap of slight interest.

'Really.'

'That's absurd. It's . . . downright unreasonable.'

Sim watched him ponder the bottomless pit of suffering she'd just evoked. 'You must ring him, Francis, quickly, before dinner.'

115

'Absolutely not.'

'Oh, come on. Eve thinks he's having some sort of breakdown.'

'In that case I'm certainly not ringing him.'

'Francis, for God's sake, he's your friend. Don't you care about him?'

'Simone, you know I don't discuss things in those terms. Campbell is a friend of mine, yes, which is why I have no intention of pestering him to satisfy your nosiness.'

Sim sighed. 'Annoying type,' she said, smiling at the thought of him as a cartoon character. Maybe he was right. Maybe she had been trying to create a cartoon world for Eve. In cartoons, awful things happened but the goodies always bounced back, while the baddies ended up getting squashed by steamrollers.

'You know, Francis,' she said, 'you could be pretty perceptive if you tried. Sometimes you say things which . . .'

'Ssh!' Francis pressed the volume button on the remote control. A row of little green squares appeared on the screen and a green arrow moved along them until the noise made Sim wince. 'Look, the Dingleys!'

Dale and Wayne Dingley were twenty and seventeen respectively. In March 1998 they stood trial for the rape and murder of Bethan Wrigley, an eighteen-year-old student from Roundhay in Leeds. The Dingley boys lived with their grandparents on an estate in Pudsey, a rougher part of town.

Bethan Wrigley had lived with her mother, Annette. It was Annette who waited up for Bethan on Friday, 30 August 1997, the night of Bethan's best friend's eighteenth birthday party. It was Annette who phoned the police at 5 a.m. when Bethan failed to return. Bethan's body was found at eight the next morning, in a field of overgrown weeds beside some waste ground, metres from where the Dingleys lived.

Dale Dingley had a criminal record for burglary and it

hadn't taken the police long to match up his fingerprints with those found on Bethan Wrigley's torn clothing. Different fingerprints were found on the victim's handbag, which later turned out to be Wayne's.

The police arrested the Dingley boys and searched the house. Under Dale Dingley's bed, rolled into a ball, they found a bloodstained T-shirt. The blood was examined and found to be Bethan Wrigley's. Subsequent tests identified semen taken from the dead body as belonging to Dale Dingley.

The case was very newsworthy, partly because the killers were brothers, which seemed to capture the country's imagination, but also because of the apparent motivelessness of the crime. Despite the Dingleys' protests that 'We never done it' and their grandparents' spirited defence ('They never done it'), the nation believed the Dingleys were guilty. Since their trial in March 1998, countless documentaries had been broadcast about the case. Some of the more controversial ones put forward the view that the Dingleys were only the final link in the causal chain, that Dale and Wayne were no more guilty of this awful crime than society as a whole. Bill Clinton was guilty. Tony Blair was guilty. The Royal Family were guilty. The official line of the Superman Paralysis Party, endorsed by Nicholas, was that the Dingleys were victims of social exclusion and anyone who wasn't doing his or her bit to redistribute global wealth might as well have put the knives into their hands.

But in spite of the televised disagreements about whether Dale and Wayne Dingley were the sole culprits or whether the government's failure to introduce proportional representation was equally responsible, there was one thing about which everyone agreed: Dale and Wayne Dingley did the deed.

They were acquitted. There was an unfortunate accident at the police laboratory which compromised the physical evidence taken both from the scene of the crime and from the Dingleys' home, rendering it all inadmissable. This was an enormous stroke of luck for Dale and Wayne, so fortuitous that some people speculated about whether the accident could really have been an accident. But why would anyone want to protect the Dingleys? They had no friends in high places; the public and the press were dead against them. The only people championing their cause were the Superman Paralysis Party – all fourteen of them – and they were not subtle enough to infiltrate a police laboratory. They wouldn't have been able to resist the urge to yell 'Kill the pigs!' which might have alerted astute observers to their illegitimate presence.

Dale and Wayne Dingley were acquitted and went into hiding immediately after their trial. They'd received numerous death threats and were placed under police protection. Ever since, Annette Wrigley's lawyers had been trying to get to the bottom of the matter of the compromised evidence. If they could find out whose fault it was, that person could be charged with negligence. Annette Wrigley wanted somebody to be punished for allowing the murderers of her daughter to walk free. Ideally, she wanted the murderers to be punished, but there didn't seem to be much chance of that happening.

The Dingleys disappeared from the public eye until about a month ago, when a PR firm claiming to represent Dale and Wayne phoned *The North Today* and said that the boys would like to be interviewed, tell their side of the story. Their lives had been ruined, apparently, by the fact that everyone thought they were killers. *The North Today* (in the form of Francis) agreed to the interviews, in spite of Annette Wrigley's protests.

The documentary that had just started, the one for which Francis had entreated Sim to shut up, was called *Siblings Who Kill* and featured the Dingleys as well as a pair of ten-year-old twin sisters from Chippenham who had beaten their baby brother to death for no real reason,

118

and two brothers from Salisbury in their late twenties who had shot their mother and stepfather while on holiday in Italy, claiming their victims had locked them in the apartment and deliberately tried to starve them. Are they evil, the programme asked, or victims themselves? Should we demonise them or berry the hat shed?

'Do you know when I first knew Gillian was evil?' Sim said to Francis. 'Or had the potential to be?' The Dingley component of the programme was over so it was safe to speak.

'No, but I sense enlightenment is close.' Francis picked up a folder from beneath his chair and started to rummage through it.

'It was when we first moved here and she refused to call Saltaire Saltaire. She called it Bradford. Even though Saltaire is a world heritage site, a well-known place in its own right, famous for Sir Titus Salt *and* David Hockney. Have we ever referred to where we live as Bradford? Have any of our other friends? No. Saltaire, Yorkshire, up north, but never Bradford. And Saltaire and Bradford have both got two syllables, so it's not as if it works as an abbreviation. But Gillian's so petty, she wanted to make where we live sound worse than it is.'

'If that's your idea of evil, you need to get out more,' said Francis, with a pen lid in his mouth. He scribbled illegible notes on a piece of paper.

'On the contrary,' said Sim. 'You need to get *in* more, into people's minds. Evil starts small. I bet massacring Albanians wasn't the first sign that Slobodan Milosevic was a bad person. You're not telling me that he spent most of his life having tea with old ladies, then suddenly turned. No. As a young man he probably . . . refused to eat at restaurants with round tables. But people missed the warning signs and now he's committing genocide. If his friends had dealt with his flawed character early on, when he kicked a dog or refused to give some children back their football . . .'

119

'Give some children . . . !' Francis spluttered.

'What? What's wrong?'

'I've got better things to do than listen to made-up incidents in the lives of war criminals and I don't give a shit about Gillian bloody Kench. I'm going to phone Campbell.'

Sim opened her mouth as he marched out of the room, then closed it again. It wouldn't do any harm to let Francis think of this as a successful mutiny.

(ii)

'Oh, Francis, no!'

1

The *Potters Court* omnibus had finished over an hour ago, since when Campbell had been lying on the bed with his eyes closed. He needed to go to the toilet, but his feet were bare and he wanted to avoid direct contact with the sticky blue carpet. There was a long, thin worn patch in the middle of it, as if a previous occupant of the room had lain on the floor sobbing once too often and eventually sunk through it. The rust-coloured walls were beginning to make him feel as if he were living inside a blood clot. Eve believed all walls should be white; Campbell couldn't get that thought out of his mind and it bothered him. Eve's influence extended too far for comfort. If she and Campbell were two stones thrown into a river, she would have many ripples – stretching all the way to the sea, perhaps – and Campbell would have none.

He missed his and Eve's house on Cromer Street. Terror gripped him suddenly, as if a black hood had been slipped over his heart. This was happening more and more often when he thought about his decision to leave Eve. Not so much the actual leaving as the decision-making. Campbell was about to give this matter further consideration when the phone rang.

He reached for the television remote control and turned up the volume, unsure what his housemates would expect from him. There was a phone on the landing outside his bedroom, which he'd gladly answer every time it rang if he could be certain the others wouldn't think he was a paranoid control freak trying to monitor their calls. It wouldn't help that they saw him so rarely because he confined himself to his bedroom day and night (he had yet to set foot in either the lounge or the kitchen); that would surely add to their suspicions. Campbell didn't want them to think he was using his attic room as a starting point for some sort of coup.

He decided to leave it. He'd answered a call earlier. In any case it was unlikely to be for him. Everyone but Rory seemed to have forgotten him and she didn't have his number. He'd lied and said there was no phone in his new house. Campbell doubted Rory's telephonic habits had changed in the last fortnight, and thought he ought to spare his housemates the multiple midnight calls and, from a selfish point of view, guard against eviction.

Since his move to Didsbury, Campbell had had a grand total of one visitor: Eve. Where were Francis and Sim? Why hadn't Neil phoned? Campbell could have done with a cathartic game of squash. He clutched his duvet in horror. It didn't for a minute occur to him that everyone he and Eve knew had taken her side and dropped him; what froze his blood was the idea that they might not really exist, they might have been no more than an illusion created for him by Eve. He wouldn't have put it past her to hire a posse of actors to make Campbell think he had a big group of friends when in fact he had none.

There was a loud banging on his bedroom door, which made Campbell jump and also, fortunately, caused a flood of sanity to wash over him. Of course his friends weren't actors. 'Campbell? It's for you,' said a male voice. Campbell hadn't yet matched up the house's voices with its faces.

He hauled himself off the bed and, as he ran to the door, had the mad thought that he would beg whoever was on the other end of the line to rescue him. The man Campbell thought of as Housemate 2 perched precariously on the

124

bannister, holding the phone. He frowned when he saw Campbell, shocked, no doubt, by his gravity-defying, tufty hair and ill-defined lips. Housemate 2 had a proper mouth with a line round it, which now said, 'If it rings again, can you get it? I just had to run all the way upstairs.'

'Sure,' said Campbell. As soon as Housemate 2 was out of sight he slapped his forehead and hissed under his breath. How was it possible, after so much deliberation, to end up doing the wrong thing? It could only be a matter of time, surely, before the house's other residents asked him to leave.

'Hello?' he said tentatively, in case the call wasn't really for him.

'Campbell? Francis.'

'Francis, hi.' Campbell tried to sound casual. Instantly, he abandoned the idea of pleading to be rescued.

'So. How's it going?' There was a note of suspicion in Francis's voice.

'Oh, you know . . .'

'Haven't seen you for a bit.'

'No, no.'

'Have to go out for a few beers soon.'

'Yeah. How's . . . er . . . how's Sim?' Campbell thought it might be an idea to bring up the topic of girlfriends.

'Fine. Cooking, which is why I have the rare privilege of being able to choose all my own words.' Campbell smiled. Usually Sim could be heard in the background, reminding Francis of crucial information that he was failing to impart at every stage of the conversation. 'How's the PhD going?' Francis asked.

'It's not, really. I haven't been able to do much recently. I'm . . . I'm living in Didsbury now. I haven't really settled back into work, you know?'

'Oh. Hmph.'

Talking to Francis was hard at any time and Campbell didn't feel well enough to tackle it in his present condition. To fill the silence he said, 'How's your work?'

'Kosovo's keeping us busy. And the Bethan Wrigley case.'

'Yeah? What about it?' Campbell felt a sudden urge to immerse himself in the details of wars and sex murders. It comforted him that these things, at least, had not happened in his life.

'We're having Dale and Wayne Dingley on the programme. Telling their side of the story. Annette Wrigley's furious.'

'Shit.'

'Yeah. She thinks it'll win them public sympathy. I'm hoping it'll have the opposite effect.'

'Have you told her that?'

'No, don't want to get her hopes up. We need to keep her at a distance. Won't do her any good to get too involved.'

'Totally.' Campbell suspected any mother would be too involved in the murder of her daughter, but he kept this insight to himself. He wondered whether he should raise the matter of Eve and Rory if Francis didn't.

'So. I hear you've had . . . er . . . a spot of bother,' Francis said finally.

'Yeah.' Campbell's body slumped with relief. At last!

'So. You're living in Didsbury now?'

'That's right.' It didn't sound too bad put like that: living in Didsbury. There had to be some cool places to live in Didsbury, even if Campbell wasn't in one of them.

'Some excellent restaurants there,' said Francis. 'Pacos is very good. Although their Irish coffee's a disgrace.'

He tutted and Campbell wondered whether he was annoyed with himself for changing the subject. Still, why should he leave it to Francis to lead the conversation? He, Campbell, could also have a hand in directing it. 'I feel a bit weird, you know?' he said, and was sure he heard a stifled groan. No, it couldn't have been. Francis didn't say anything so he went on, 'I was thinking about it before you rang. It's as if . . . oh, I don't know.'

126

'Oh well. There's no point . . .'

'No, that's it.' Campbell wasn't prepared to let this chance slip away. 'There's a sinister feeling that creeps up on me sometimes, as if all the decisions I made – you know, to leave, to give it a go with Rory – were actually made by someone else. I know it's ridiculous, but I feel as if I'm in a trance, carrying out the orders of a higher power.'

'Well, Eve and Sim think you're probably having a breakdown,' said Francis. Campbell heard Sim shouting from far away that Francis was bloody stupid to have said that. 'For God's sake,' Francis huffed. 'Why doesn't she talk to you herself if she doesn't like the way I do it?'

'Mm,' Campbell agreed. It comforted him to know that the possibility that he was having something as mundane as a breakdown was being bandied about. If it was a breakdown, it could be put right by experts: doctors, psychologists, chemists. Sim didn't sound worried, from what little of her tone Campbell had managed to pick up. People had breakdowns all the time. Campbell's greatest fear was that something was happening to him that had never happened to anyone before. 'It's like they're laughing at me,' he told Francis.

'Who?'

'I don't know. Well, no one, obviously. I'm being daft.'

'Right. So you're not having a breakdown?'

'No,' Campbell said confidently, hoping to impress Francis.

'Good. And this new woman of yours . . . ?'

'Rory.'

'Yes.'

'She's not having a breakdown either,' said Campbell.

'Should hope not.' Francis sounded surprised and Campbell realised that wasn't what he'd meant. 'Is she . . . well, what's she like?'

'She's great. You'd like her. You'll have to meet her.'

'Excellent. Good. So, things are shaping up okay, then.'

'I suppose so.' Campbell was beginning to feel uncomfortable with the level of all rightness he was claiming for himself, but he didn't want to frustrate Francis, who clearly thought they'd dealt with the bad patch and it was now behind them. Francis used the telephone to clear up practical matters; a call that didn't end in firm clarification or a resolution was a wasted call as far as he was concerned. But in his desire to satisfy Francis's need for progress, Campbell was being slightly dishonest. He felt like a sick schoolboy, about to embark upon a cross-country run and risk collapsing rather than be accused of malingering by a robust PE teacher.

'Why don't you and Sim come over one night?' Campbell suggested. As he said it, he felt that this might be exactly what was needed to make him feel more at home in the Didsbury house. One slap from the sole of Sim's shoe and the worn patch in his bedroom carpet would be bound to beat a hasty retreat.

'Good plan. We could go to Pacos.'

'Yeah, that's a good idea.' Campbell felt unsettled by Francis's failure to consult with Sim, as if this meant that the meal at Pacos was doomed never to take place. Why, in fact, was Francis the one who'd phoned him? 'Francis?'

'Mm?'

'Tell Sim I'm not a bastard, will you?'

Francis tutted. 'There's no need. At no stage has that been her opinion and, believe me, I'm well-versed in what her opinion is.'

'But tell her, will you? Not to think of me as a bastard who jilts women?'

'No, I won't,' said Francis. 'That's not the sort of thing I say, I'm afraid.'

'Oh.' Campbell could see his point. It wasn't the sort of thing Francis said.

'I doubt I'll need to tell her anything. There's probably a wire attached to my clothing somewhere. Sim is listening to all this on earphones in the kitchen.' Campbell heard something rude being shouted in the distance. 'Anyway, we'll be in touch soon to arrange this meal, yes?'

'Yeah, sound.' Campbell prepared to put the phone down.

'Erm . . .' Francis cleared his throat awkwardly. 'So where will you be?'

'When?'

'For us to ring you. Next week, say.'

'Well . . . here.' Campbell was puzzled. Where else would he be?

'Fine. That's where we'll ring you, then.'

Only after he'd hung up did it occur to Campbell that this last question had been Francis's way of asking whether he intended to go back to Eve.

'I hate this lounge. Triangular rooms have bad Chi,' said Vanessa, yawning. She looked out of the window. 'What kind of architect built this dump, anyway? You know what it looks like? Twelve Toblerone tubes in a field.' It was Thursday evening. Vanessa lay stretched out on the window seat, with a glass of wine in one hand and a red pen in the other. A fat manuscript rested on her stomach.

Nicholas ignored her. He stared at the pages spread out in front of him on the coffee table. 'Dance and bloody gastronomy,' he muttered.

'When can we move out of this unsightly barracks and live somewhere decent, like London?'

'Oh, shut up. You don't know how fucking lucky you are.' The rent on Nicholas and Vanessa's flat in Gentchev's Field was subsidised both by the university and by Renshaw College, where Nicholas was a fellow. They paid £200 a month for a three-bedroom flat set in landscaped gardens that were studded with ornamental ponds, bridges, fountains and gazebos, and still Vanessa, contrary bitch that she was, wanted to move to that emporium of scabby-legged prostitutes that had the nerve to call itself England's capital city. Nicholas could have done without her carping tonight.

His deadline from *Global Issues* was flying towards him and he hadn't even started his rewrites.

'What's wrong with you?' Vanessa demanded.

'Work.' He didn't want to go into it. What was stopping him getting stuck in? This had never happened before. For weeks he'd been staring at his article until the words swam before his eyes, unable to do anything. Nicholas had an inkling of how awful it would be to suffer from impotence and shuddered. Vanessa would leave him like a shot.

'At least you don't have to read this shite.' Vanessa pointed to the manuscript on her stomach, *Audi* or *Considering Marmalade*, depending on whose side you were on. Vanessa was on neither. 'The new Cal Raynard. Every time that man writes another book I feel like wading into the sea with a pocket full of heavy bricks. If someone were to drag him into the middle of Trafalgar Square and beat him to death with clubs, they would have my entire admiration.'

'Lives in London, does he?' said Nicholas bitterly. 'Why don't you fuck off and join him, then?'

'I don't know where he lives, or even who he is. He's one of these privacy-obsessed arseholes . . .'

'Oh, *God*!' Nicholas swept all twenty-three pages of his article on to the floor and slammed his fist down on the table.

'What's wrong?' Vanessa looked up.

'This . . . *stupid* editor wants me to consider the effect dance and gastronomy might have on the mediation of the Israel–Palestine conflict! Can you imagine? Come on, Palestinians, do the can-can. How about a nice waltz while we drive you out of your homes and shoot your children! What bullshit. I'm not doing that. I'm going to have to withdraw the article.' Nicholas wandered over to the window and flung it open.

'Don't you dare. For God's sake, Nicholas. Considering it doesn't preclude the possibility of arriving at the verdict that it's nonsense, does it?'

'You don't understand. Anyway, that's a minor detail. The main thing they want is more balance, in other words, more pro-Israeli propaganda. Idiots!'

'Hang on. Balance might only mean . . .'

'Forget it. You wouldn't understand.'

'I would, actually,' said Vanessa indignantly. 'Editing is what I do for a living and I happen to be rather good at it.' *Howdy*, Cal Raynard's second novel, published this week, could have been a brilliant book if only its author had taken Vanessa's advice. To think she'd actually been excited, when her colleague Camilla Pearson was discreetly fired, at the prospect of inheriting the mysterious Cal, whose first novel *Cloudy* had shown real promise. But Raynard, who had taken advice from the brainless Camilla, wouldn't let Vanessa anywhere near his precious prose, so fuck him. 'Three words of advice,' she said to Nicholas. 'Roman Polanski's foreskin.'

'*What?*'

'I don't know whether the story's true, but it's a good metaphor. To avoid persecution by the Nazis, Roman Polanski made himself a fake foreskin out of wax so that he'd look like a non-Jew. It saved his life.'

'That sounds like crap,' said Nicholas.

'Doesn't matter if it is. The point is, he couldn't change what he was, but he also didn't want to be killed. It wasn't as if he was selling out by making himself a fake foreskin. He was still Jewish and, more importantly, he was alive.'

Nicholas frowned. 'Isn't Roman Polanski a rapist?'

'God, you're boring.' Vanessa put Cal Raynard's manuscript on the floor and rested her bare feet on it. 'It was only statutory rape, and it was after his wife had been carved up by Charles Manson. I'm sure you'd behave impeccably in those circumstances,' she said sarcastically.

'His films are sick as well.' Nicholas turned away.

'Why do I bother?' said Vanessa under her breath. 'Look, you don't want to change your article, but if you tell *Global Issues* that, they'll reject it. So you need to give it a fake foreskin. Make it look like what they want it to be, but at the same time protect what it is, what you want it to be. Instead of thinking about how to change it, think about how to disguise it. Balanced doesn't have to mean pro-Israeli, or even sitting on the fence. Balanced could simply mean allocating equal space in the text to the cases for both sides.'

'Why should I allocate . . .'

'Because then, when you demolish the Israeli case in your conclusion, it'll be all the more devastating. Whereas if the whole article's one-sided it's as if you're arguing against nothing.'

Nicholas felt the lump of tension in the pit of his stomach begin to dissolve. Disguise instead of change; he hadn't looked at it that way. Could she be right? He sat down again, retrieved the scattered pages and reassembled them. Roman Polanski's foreskin. Hm. Nicholas hid a smile beneath his hand. So Vanessa cared about his work; she hadn't calcified completely into a nasty bitch. It was reassuring to know that she could still offer the occasional life-enhancing moment of the sort that had first attracted Nicholas to her. He'd been worried that physical compulsion was the only thing keeping them together, but what Vanessa could do with her body was nothing compared with what she could do with her brain when she tried. Nicholas remembered the brilliant arguments they used to have – which invariably ended in great sex – when their sparring had been sharp and witty. These days they picked at each other with a listless, dispiriting pettiness. The sex was still good, though, and Vanessa was right about his article. Of course he couldn't abandon it.

'Thank you, Vanessa. What an excellent suggestion, Vanessa,' said Vanessa. 'Once you've applied the wax foreskin, you send the article back to them with a letter telling them that you've done exactly what they asked and they feel immensely flattered.' She kicked Cal Raynard's manuscript. 'This isn't even high enough to make a good footstool.'

'Sh!' Nicholas hissed, engrossed once more in his endangered article. He'd got as far as paragraph six:

> In his book *A Place Among the Nations*, Netanyahu argues that there is already a Palestinian state, namely Jordan, and therefore there is no need for another. But Netanyahu's plan would involve the wholesale transfer of millions of people, against their will, from one place to another. This is as unreasonable as it would be to suggest that the Northern Ireland issue might be resolved by the entire Catholic population decamping to Italy; after all, Irish Catholics and Italians are all Europeans. Leaving aside the question of how Jordan would react to such an idea, there is the more fundamental question that needs to be asked: why should the Palestinians leave what they regard as their home?

Yes, Nicholas could see a way forward already. He'd reduced Netanyahu's views to one line, hadn't even quoted from his book. What he had to do was present the Israeli angle in greater detail, more sympathetically even, so that the final demolition would be a more meaningful victory.

'Oh, Campbell's left Eve for another woman,' said Vanessa. She had a habit of speaking when Nicholas least wanted her to. 'So I don't know what's going to happen this weekend.'

'Oh, Jesus.' Nicholas scowled. He'd forgotten the hoards were descending. Another one of Sim and Vanessa's bloody arrangements. 'Can't we put it off? I can't work with guests all over the place. And I'm not having Hazel sleeping in my study, you can forget that. Last time . . .'

'Hazel's not coming. She's busy inflicting another festival on the unsuspecting populus. Did you hear what I said about Campbell leaving Eve?'

133

'Yeah.' Nicholas didn't take his eyes off his article. What was the point in helping him with his work if Vanessa was only going to distract him from it immediately afterwards? Not wanting to seem uncaring, he added, 'Well, it might do him good to be on his own for a while.'

'He isn't on his own, dufus. He's got a new girlfriend. A Napper, no less. Hello? Am I talking to myself?' There was a knock at the door. Nicholas didn't move. Sighing, Vanessa got up to answer it, kicking *Audi* on the way.

A porter in a suit and bowler hat looked past her and bowed in Nicholas's direction. 'A letter for you, sir,' he said, handing a small white envelope to Vanessa without moving his eyes, which were fixed on the only Renshaw College fellow in the room, as if the rest of the world were invisible. Vanessa threw the envelope down on the table in front of Nicholas.

'Thanks,' he said distractedly.

'Mention it,' Vanessa replied bitterly. Her mobile phone started to ring on the windowsill. 'Maybe this'll be a human being,' she said, picking it up.

Nicholas ripped open the envelope, his mind still on his work, and pulled out a small sheet of yellow lined paper that looked as if it had been torn from a toddler's ring-bound notebook. There was a picture of a fluffy white rabbit in the bottom right-hand corner. The fat, cursive handwriting was unfamiliar. A child or a very stupid person might write like this, but Nicholas had no correspondents in either category. Puzzled, he turned the letter over, searching for a signature. A sour taste filled his mouth when he saw Gillian's name. What did that fool want with him now? He looked over his shoulder to check Vanessa wasn't trying to read the letter. Mercifully, she was looking out of the window, busy with her call. 'Yes. Of course. Yes, that's right,' she said. If Nicholas hadn't been so preoccupied, he might have noticed her uncharacteristic politeness.

He took a deep breath and began to read. 'Dear "Doctor" Nicholas,' Gillian had written. 'Hi! How have U been since i last saw U? i did enjoy our little chat. We must do it again sometime.' What the fuck was going on with her 'I's and 'You's, Nicholas wondered. Was it an attempt to be trendy? Chillingly, there was more: 'But U and VANESSA probably want nothing to do with me and Andrew. Hes only clark of works and Im only a secretray. U are a fellow, letters after you're name and VANESSA is a big publisher in London.'

Nicholas swallowed. An icy ripple travelled from his throat down to his stomach, as if he'd swallowed cold marbles. Why was Vanessa's name in capitals? Irrational though it undoubtedly was, Nicholas felt that anyone whose spelling was this bad was capable of unimaginable horrors. And she was lying about her boyfriend, Andrew Johnson. He had a job in the works department of Renshaw College, but only as an underling. He certainly wasn't Clerk of Works. That was a much more senior position, held by a man named Gilbert Rawlins whom Nicholas knew well.

'We should get together sometime, if were good enough for U,' the letter went on. 'Our phone number at home is 319937. Anyway, the reason im writing is because U didn't answer my question. i asked U what U liked best about Ur new office. U didn't answer. Did U know that it was once the office of Kenneth Scantlebury who won a Nobbel Prize? No. U never bothered to find out.' The letter was signed simply 'Gillian', no regards or best wishes.

Nicholas's heart thudded. Suddenly, Benjamin Netanyahu was the least of his worries. Gillian hadn't asked him any questions, apart from whether he wanted to go with her to look at her new office. What was she talking about? Nicholas would have assumed that her visit and this letter were part of some sort of campaign of persecution, but there was absolutely no reason for Gillian to take against him; he'd never crossed her in any way. The cold marbles nestled in his gut. Nicholas would have been a lot happier if the mad bitch's boyfriend didn't work at Renshaw.

He tried to remember what he'd overheard Vanessa and Sim say about Gillian. He was sure he'd been present during numerous discussions that, if he'd only listened, might have helped him now. Why had Sim turned against Gillian? He'd known once, but he'd forgotten the details; they seemed so unimportant. Still, Sim and Francis were coming to stay this weekend and Sim wasn't shy when it came to gossip. Nicholas was sure he'd only have to mention Gillian's name and she'd tell him all he needed to know.

'Oh yes, I quite see that,' said Vanessa in her new, strange tone. 'I tell you what – why don't you pop the receipts in an envelope and send them to me? I'll send you a cheque by return of post. I certainly can. Flat two. Sorry, the reception on my phone isn't great. That's Flat two, Staircase M, Gentchev's Field, London.' If Nicholas hadn't been too busy regretting his failure to listen to old conversations, he might have attended to this one and been justifiably suspicious. Vanessa would never offer to 'pop' something in an envelope. Gentchev's Field was in Cambridge, not London, Nicholas and Vanessa's staircase was N, not M, and their flat was number twenty-two, not number two. But Nicholas, distracted by Gillian's lunatic missive, remained oblivious to the lies that were being told only metres from where he sat.

'This isn't too bad,' said Sim cheerfully, following Campbell up the long, narrow stairs. Francis trudged after them carrying two bottles of wine in a Harvey Nichols bag. Campbell had been ridiculously excited all week at the prospect of Sim and Francis's visit, then childishly disappointed when he opened the front door to them and there was no instantaneous revelation, only Sim's wild hair filling the doorway, the odd ray of light and Francis creeping in around it. Campbell had expected to know his own mind as soon as he saw them, for everything to become clear and perhaps even for a veil of mist to part. None of this had happened. A gust of outside world had blown in, scattering things a bit, but nothing was resolved.

He knew exactly what Sim meant when she said the house 'wasn't too bad'; there was an unspoken 'for the time being' appended to her comment. Meaning he could still go back to Eve? 'I'm afraid it's a bit basic,' said Campbell as he ushered Sim and Francis into the confined space of his room. 'You two can have the bed and I'll sit on the floor.'

'Why don't you buy some chairs?' said Francis, who had been known to reject the comfiest and deepest of sofas in favour of the floor, contrary sod that he was.

'Campbell doesn't want to have to worry about buying chairs.' Sim rolled her eyes. Worry's got nothing to do with it, thought Campbell, whose funds wouldn't even stretch to an Ikea floor cushion.

'No, but he seems to be worried about where we're all going to sit,' said Francis with deliberate patience.

'We'll be fine,' said Sim in a sing-song voice. 'Honestly, what a fuss!'

'I didn't say we wouldn't,' said Francis wearily. 'I was simply suggesting a way to relieve anxiety on the seating front. It's very easy. It's called buying a chair. I'm sure Campbell won't be too squeamish about my mentioning it.' Campbell laughed weakly, but neither Sim nor Francis seemed to notice.

'Francis, the last thing Campbell needs at the moment is a head full of chairs,' Sim insisted, shooting a quick sideways glance at Campbell as if to check that he had the air of a furniture-oblivious man. He flushed slightly, wondering how neutral he looked. He felt as if he ought to stand up straight, as if Sim were grooming him for something. Yes, there was definitely an implication along those lines; the air in his room was thick with it. That must be why Sim doesn't want me to have chair worries in my head, he thought. It was as if she were saving him for some unspecified future event, keeping his mind pristine so that it would be ready when the time came. But for what?

'We wanted to pop round and see Eve as well, but she's out with a colleague tonight,' said Sim, perching on the edge of Campbell's lumpy bed. 'Do you know if she's still coming to Cambridge this weekend?'

'She isn't,' said Campbell. 'She's got too much marking.' Eve had rung to tell him this yesterday. 'So you can go, if you want to,' she'd added, as if they couldn't both have gone. Campbell thought it beneath her to be so immature. Frostily, he'd told her he wasn't going either.

'Oh, well. I'll see if she wants to go for a curry next week,' said Sim, who evidently felt Eve should be mentioned as soon as possible. It would have been disrespectful not to refer to her, Campbell could see that. Sim's jolly, 'in-passing' tone forced him to think of Eve as someone who still existed in the arena of carefree social encounters, who might enjoy a pint of lager with a balti sag paneer and a peshwari nan. Her life could not be entirely reduced to the repository of misery Campbell had come to think of it as. He had vainly imagined that he'd ruined her. Sim was here to tell him Eve's life went on and – although there was no element of gloating – that she was still involved in its most rewarding components. Francis noticed none of this.

'I'm not going this weekend either,' said Campbell. He waited for Sim to ask why not so that he could tell her he was seeing Rory, but she said nothing. Campbell suspected her of deliberately withholding the question. 'Which colleague?' he asked.

'Hm?' Sim was looking at the ceiling. 'Nice skylight,' she said.

'Which colleague is Eve out with tonight?'

'Um . . . Neil somebody?'

'Neil?' Campbell was surprised.

'Yeah. Why, do you know him?'

'Better than Eve does,' said Campbell, puzzled. 'I play squash with him. Or did, until recently. I haven't been in the mood for a while.' And Neil hadn't phoned.

'I think she went out with him on Tuesday as well,' said Sim.

Francis turned on the television, murmuring, '. . . catch the news'. Slobodan Milosevic was defending himself in an interview with an accusatory reporter.

'That makes no sense,' said Campbell. 'Eve doesn't even like Neil. She used to moan when I invited him back for a drink after playing squash. She said he was a nerd and she saw enough of him at school.'

'Maybe she's changed her mind,' said Sim.

'She must have. How odd.' And not entirely comfortable, either. Campbell wondered whether he ought to phone Neil. He didn't want to leave it too long. Come to think of it, a game of squash might do him good.

'Campbell, it's not odd at all.' Sim laughed gently. Clearly she felt his error was so huge that it had to be handled with care, coaxed down from its great height before it did any serious damage. 'Things have changed for Eve. The people we like when we're feeling fine often aren't the same ones we're drawn to when we're down on our luck,' said Sim.

'I'm down on my luck when it comes to being able to hear the news,' Francis murmured, edging closer to the television.

'Exactly,' said Campbell. 'Neil's a fucking ambulance chaser.' He had no idea where this came from, hadn't planned to say it at all.

'Not necessarily,' said Sim. 'He might just be a kind, caring bloke who doesn't hold it against Eve that she's not in tip-top condition at the moment. Admittedly there are people – usually competitive, insecure women – who deliberately seek out weak or unfortunate friends, ones who've had their insides replaced by tubing or who compulsively eat dog food, so that they can feel superior and disguise their crowing as sympathy . . .'

'That's true,' Francis chipped in glumly. Campbell wondered who he was thinking of.

'. . . and there's the opposite syndrome too,' Sim went on. 'People who are scared that their friends' unfortunateness will be contagious, or bring down their value by proximity, as if they were houses.'

Campbell thought about Rory's parents' house in Knightsbridge. He'd never been in the home of a truly rich family before, but as soon as he arrived he felt underdressed in his T-shirt, baggy combat trousers and trainers. Everything inside the house seemed to radiate wealth and Campbell felt as if the only way he could credibly remain on the premises was if he offered to do a spot of chimney-sweeping before dinner.

Campbell and Rory had not shared a bedroom. This, Rory said, was partly because her parents were old-fashioned about such things but also because having her own space was important to Rory. Mr and Mrs Napper had had the top floor of the house converted into a self-contained flat for her when she was a teenager. She had a large bedroom with a balcony and steps leading down to her own private roof terrace, a fully fitted kitchen, a lounge-cum-study area and a bathroom with a large, oval-shaped sunken bath that doubled as a jacuzzi. Rather alarmingly, she also had a vibrator that she coyly showed Campbell, a bright pink transparent rubber penis, with multicoloured floating beads at its base. There was a smaller pink thing sticking out of the side of it in the shape of a rabbit. Rory laughed at Campbell when he asked what it was. 'It's for clitoral stimulation, silly,' she said, giggling and nudging him. He backed off, hoping Rory wouldn't suggest they involve this peculiar object in their love life at any stage. Not that they really had one yet.

Campbell had been allocated a strange underground room that must once have been the cellar, with high, narrow slits for windows, level with the bottom of the garden. He felt a bit like a prisoner in a dungeon, albeit a luxurious one, and slept only fitfully. Every hour or so he woke up with a racing heart and a reservoir of sweat in the middle of his back. Eventually he resigned himself to sleeplessness and decided to have a cigarette. He got out of bed and pulled a chair over to one of the windows. The Nappers (bizarrely, given that they'd made their fortune from tobacco) did not allow smoking in their house, unless one was prepared to hang out of an open window. Campbell climbed on to the chair and drew the curtains. What he saw in the Nappers' garden nearly made him lose his balance.

Right in front of him were two thick grey legs that looked as if they belonged to an elephant. Campbell jumped down from the chair and ran to the en suite bathroom where there was a bigger window. He could see the garden clearly now, although nothing else was clear. Quite the opposite, in fact. There appeared to be two people dressed up as elephants standing on the Nappers' lawn. They had big ears and floppy trunks, and their bodies looked puny compared with their immense heads. Whoever had made the costumes needed to learn a thing or two about proportion.

One of the elephants spotted Campbell in the window and pointed him out to the other. Together they bent down and lifted a white rectangle of card so that Campbell could see it. On it was written 'BUSINESS THRIVES MEANS ELEPHANT LIVES'. Campbell stood rooted to the spot and held his breath, waiting for something to happen. Nothing did. The two elephants stood still, holding their sign and watching. It was as if they were trying to out-stare him.

He grabbed the yellow and blue checked curtains and yanked them closed, breathing heavily. For a few seconds he did nothing. Then he moved away from the window and started to run a bath, adding some kind of scented oil from a little bottle by the side of the basin. This did not have the relaxing effect that Campbell had hoped for. After only a few seconds his skin began to tingle, then to burn, and he had to leap out of the water to avoid real pain.

Had the elephants spiked the bath oil? He didn't dare to look out of the window again in case they were still there. The words on the sign kept repeating themselves in his mind: business thrives means elephant lives. It wasn't grammatical, yet somehow its peculiar, back-to-front incorrectness made it catchy in a threatening sort of way.

At breakfast the next day Mrs Napper breezily announced, 'Our elephants made an appearance last night.' She looked not unlike an elephant herself, with her bulk and many wrinkles. Campbell nearly fell off a chair for the second time in one visit. He'd decided not to mention his trunkly encounter to anybody, not wanting to alarm his hosts. But Mrs Napper didn't sound at all fazed.

'I . . . I saw them,' Campbell mumbled.

'Did you?' Mrs Napper smiled indulgently. 'You didn't say.'

'I . . . er . . . I wasn't sure whether you knew . . . I didn't want to . . . er . . .'

'How sweet. Campbell didn't want to worry us.' Mrs Napper smiled at Mr Napper, who shrugged. He clearly didn't think it was sweet but wasn't going to object if his wife chose to see it in those terms. He was thin with a strange, trapezium-shaped chin, much worse than Rory's. 'No, they're perfectly harmless. They turn up once a fortnight or so and just stand quietly in the garden, holding up their silly sign. They would never dream of damaging the property.'

'We've had worse,' Mr Napper said stoically.

'Oh, yes, we've had bricks through the window, dog dirt through the letter box, everything,' Mrs Napper told Campbell. 'That's why Rory's on the top floor; she didn't feel safe lower down.' This sounded oddly sexual to Campbell, although he was disgusted with himself for reading this meaning into Mrs Napper's innocent remark.

Campbell didn't quite know what Rory meant when she said she didn't believe in penetrative sex. Did she mean she disapproved of it, denied its existence altogether or merely preferred to abstain from it herself? And what about the pink rabbit vibrator? Surely she put that inside her, or else what was the point of having it? Perhaps that didn't count, not being a person. Campbell had always thought vibrators were the sexual equivalent of tinned meat: artificial and gross. Sim would no doubt have views on this and all related matters, but Campbell had to draw the line somewhere. It was bad enough Sim getting inside his head without involving her in his sex life as well. He also had no intention of telling anyone what he'd found out from Rory the morning after his ordeal in the bath – that the scented oil he'd used was intended to relieve the symptoms of gum disease, from which Mr Napper suffered, by burning the sore areas into a state of numbness.

Campbell realised suddenly that Sim and Francis had been in his room for ten minutes or so and neither of them had mentioned Rory yet. He could understand this from Francis, who had made an awkward enquiry over the phone last weekend about 'the new woman' and probably thought Campbell's answer ('She's great') had furnished him with all the information he needed. But Sim's silence on the matter was more worrying. When someone as nosy as Sim didn't bombard you with questions, something was usually wrong.

'Rory was sorry she couldn't be here tonight,' Campbell blurted out. Sim couldn't ignore this, direct as it was. She would have to respond in some way. For a second, Campbell was terrified she would say, 'Who?'

'Was she?' Sim smiled. 'Campbell, are you sure you've done the right thing?'

Campbell beamed with relief. So Sim was in no doubt that Rory existed (of course she bloody existed!) and that

Campbell's new life was real. The least he could do in return was be honest. There was no need to be defensive now. 'No,' he said.

'You're not,' Sim repeated matter-of-factly. Campbell could see the effort that went into her act; she hid her shock very well. Sim was a person who was much given to sureness, but she was realistic about it. She knew she was outnumbered in the world. More people were uncertain than were certain, so Sim made the effort to assimilate.

'No,' said Campbell. But it didn't matter, couldn't Sim see that? At some point in the future he would be sure and when he was, there would be genuine possibilities awaiting him. Either Rory or Eve: one right for him, one wrong, but both valid. 'It's hard to be sure, you know?' he clarified. 'I mean, Eve and I were together for nearly eight years. I've known Rory only a couple of months.'

'I hear Eve gave you the option of having an affair with Rory but staying at home?' Sim said.

'Here we go,' Francis muttered.

'Yeah, yeah, she did,' said Campbell, his good mood ruined. God, the thought of Eve and Sim talking, unrestrained by his or Francis's interjections, was profoundly disturbing. What if Eve had told Sim about the penetrative sex embargo? He should never have mentioned that to Eve; it had felt like a mistake at the time, but he'd wanted to give her a small consolation, a reassuring titbit to cling to. Sex was the one area in which Eve was undoubtedly superior to Rory. They were at opposite ends of the spectrum when it came to enthusiasm. About innate aptitude for the act itself Campbell wasn't in a position to comment. It could be worse, he told himself. He could have told Eve about the vibrator. His account would have been incomplete even if he had. With the best will in the world, Campbell doubted he could make the words 'clitoral stimulation' emerge from his mouth.

'You didn't fancy that?' Sim asked.

144

'No. It wouldn't have been right to stay with Eve once I'd had those feelings for Rory.'

'That wasn't what Eve thought,' Sim pointed out.

'Leave Campbell alone,' said Francis. 'Sorry about this, Campbell.'

'It's okay.'

'Do you still love Eve?' Sim asked.

'I don't know, Sim.' Campbell was really in for it now, he could tell. He didn't feel ready. The warm-up had not been adequate. 'It's difficult, you know? I do and I don't. That's normal, isn't it?'

'Never mind normal; is it possible?' said Sim. 'You should know, you're the expert on vagueness. Ah, Eve'll have to admit defeat now. I told her philosophy was useful for everyday life. Can it ever be true to say that X both loves and doesn't love Y?'

'Yes,' said Campbell quickly, annoyed at falling into the trap.

'Oh, right.' Sim looked surprised. 'I didn't realise you'd got that far with your research. I thought you were still undecided.'

'Well . . .' Campbell blushed, trying to hide his crossness. He hadn't thought about his thesis for weeks. Sim was more interested in his work than he was. 'If there isn't a fixed point at which love becomes not love . . .' he began.

'There is,' said Francis abruptly. 'The point at which you dump Eve for someone else.' Sim gave him a stern look.

Campbell felt winded by the directness of Francis's comment. 'No,' he insisted. 'There's an intermediate category in between love and not love.' Sim and Francis were forcing him towards a conclusion he wasn't yet ready to draw. He had grave doubts about the intermediate category argument and felt uncomfortable defending it. He saw another way round the problem. 'Look, it's not that simple, okay?' he said. 'There could be a fixed point where love becomes not love and I just don't know on which side of the border my feelings for Eve fall.'

145

'Whatever.' Francis stood up and turned off the television. 'Life's too short,' he said. 'Shall we go for a nice, long, cool pint before our meal? Did you book the table, Sim?'

'In a minute, Francis. Short is also a vague predicate. I happen to think life is long. You make it short by reducing it in your mind,' she ticked him off, 'boiling things down all the time.'

'What am I, a sauce chef?'

'It feels long to me, because I take time to notice the small things, the particulars. Whereas you hurtle through life and probably lose years in the process.'

'I hurtle through life?' Francis laughed. 'Rubbish. I'm one of the most sedentary people I know. I've got an unusually slow metabolism.' Francis pushed out his stomach and patted it, to prove his point.

'Physically you're stationary but mentally you hurtle,' said Sim.

'Do you want to see a photo of Rory?' Campbell asked suddenly.

There was no response for a few seconds. Then Sim said 'Sure' and Francis said 'Not especially'.

'Francis! Don't be so rude.'

'It's okay,' said Campbell quickly.

'I'm not being rude,' said Francis. 'It doesn't matter to me what she looks like. Campbell obviously thinks she looks nice and that's good enough for me.' He sat down on the floor and turned on the television again. He did not look like a man who was inwardly hurtling, it had to be said. Campbell produced a small packet of photographs from under his bed. 'These were taken the other week, at her parents' house,' he said.

'So . . . her family's pretty rich, then. "The dapper unwrap a Napper."' Sim mimicked the voice from the advertisement.

'Yeah. She doesn't make a big deal about it, though.'

'If you're not sure you've done the right thing, you can always think of it as provisional and see how it goes,' Sim counselled, flicking through the photographs. 'Wow, look at the front porch. This house could be the setting for a Merchant ... Ivory film.' It was less than a second long, but Campbell heard the pause. If Sim had stopped abruptly after 'Merchant' it would have looked even more suspicious. So she'd said 'Ivory' too, although she regretted saying either word, Campbell could tell. Particularly since 'Merchant' meant someone who made money, making the whole phrase sound like a damning indictment of the Napper family rather than an innocuously genteel film partnership.

So it was an issue for Sim. Campbell wasn't sure who to be furious with, her or the Nappers. 'There are some things about Eve that I don't like,' he blurted out, as an obscure form of punishment.

'Jolly good,' Francis declared, looking at his watch. 'Come on, let's go and eat. I'm bloody starving.'

'Like what?' Sim asked.

'I don't know. She's into all that conventional stuff. Marriage and kids. I mean, what difference does it make if you're married or not?'

'It seems to make a difference to you,' said Sim. 'In the opposite direction.'

'She's also a bit manipulative.'

'Are you sure? Manipulation is when pressure is covertly applied. Isn't Eve, on the contrary, quite open about what she wants?'

'Well, strategic, then. That's what I meant.' Campbell wished he'd never got into this.

'But strategic means no more and no less than making a plan,' said Sim gently. 'The three of us arranging to go for a meal tonight, that could be seen as strategic.'

'So far the strategy has proved ineffective,' Francis grumbled.

'She was really horrible about Rory as well. She called her a slag.'

'Campbell!' Sim laughed. 'Anyone in her position would

have been horrible about Rory. From Eve's point of view, Rory's the person who stole her boyfriend and ruined her life.'

'No, but . . . even before, when Rory and I were just friends. Whenever I said to Eve that the three of us should get together or Rory should come and stay, she said no. She refused to meet her. She called her "the stalker". It seems a bit hypocritical, that's all. Eve's always had male friends. And now she's started seeing Neil Temple every night . . .'

'Can we go and eat?' asked Francis. 'Before Lenny Henry appears at my side with a camera crew, having mistaken me for a famine victim.'

Sim stood up and stretched, laughing. She handed the packet of photographs back to Campbell without commenting on Rory, who featured in nearly all of them. Campbell was furious. Suddenly, because Sim said so, the conversation was over and they were going out. He looked back on the evening so far and saw that Sim had basically ignored Rory, as if she could disregard her out of existence. Well, fine. If Sim wouldn't pay attention of her own accord, Campbell would have to take more active steps to ensure that his new relationship got the recognition it deserved.

Ian had a problem. In a fit of temper the previous day, he'd ripped a page out of Hazel's copy of *Howdy* by Cal Raynard. If he could have gone round every bookshop in the country and torn the same page out of every copy, he would have. That wasn't feasible, so he'd had to make do with the one he had to hand. It was a pointless act but it made him feel better, as if he'd protested in a small but crucial way.

Later he calmed down and was on the point of going out to buy Hazel a new *Howdy* to replace the one he'd defaced when he noticed that she'd already written 'This book belongs to Hazel Ings, and has the wrong title!!!!' on the inside cover. He grinned and began to panic at the same time, pulling another book off the shelf. It had the same inscription, only without the comment about the title. Shit, why hadn't Ian noticed before that Hazel did this? He'd borrowed enough of her books, for God's sake. He selected another one at random, with his eyes closed. It turned out to be *The Observer Book of Cacti*. Ian smiled as he read the inscription: 'This book belongs to Gatting Ings'. Mad though Hazel undoubtedly was, Ian couldn't help – he resisted the word 'loving' – being immensely fond of her.

He ran through his options: he could buy another copy of *Howdy* and attempt to forge Hazel's writing. Would she be able to tell, if he did it carefully enough? Probably not. At most she might think her writing looked a bit funny, but the explanation for this was so unlikely that Ian could safely assume it would never occur to her.

On the other hand, maybe there was no need to go to such lengths. Ian looked at his watch: nine thirty. If he set off to Waterstone's now it would be at least an hour and a half before he could start work. That would throw him off course for the whole day. Besides, Hazel had read *Howdy* already. If he slotted it neatly into the bookshelf, perhaps she wouldn't look at it again for a few months, or indeed ever. He was overreacting, he told himself. Even if Hazel noticed the missing page, Ian could feign complete ignorance; why, after all, should a book with a page ripped out of it implicate him in any way?

He opened the window in Hazel's study, closed his eyes and listened to the river as it churned along the valley. The air in Saltaire seemed to smell and taste fresher than in other places. Was it only because Hazel lived here that he thought this? He couldn't risk telling her the truth. If only she had a different group of friends . . . no, that wasn't fair. Ian wouldn't have wanted to deprive her of Sim, Eve or Lucy. And Hazel might resent the fact that he'd deceived her until now, even if she understood his reasons. The last thing Ian wanted to do was hurt her. Apart from anything else, she'd come to be his best friend; he couldn't risk losing her. 'What do you reckon, Gatting?' he nudged the brown pot beside him with his elbow. 'What would you do?' At first he'd only spoken to Gatting ironically, to please Hazel, but these days he did so without thinking. The cactus had proved to be a good sounding board, cheaper than a therapist and equally reliant upon sexual symbolism, shaped as it was like a thick, green, spiky phallus. Ian nodded. 'I know. It's tricky,' he replied to what he imagined Gatting would have said if he could speak.

Ian retreated several paces so that he couldn't be seen from the car park, wishing he didn't have to take such precautions. He loved the moor with its green and purple patches, could have leaned out of the window and stared at it all day. It was a sight that nourished the soul. Ian could get on with his work here; at home he wouldn't have stood a chance. His mam had the television on full blast from the minute she got up until she went to bed and his dad chain-smoked, turning everything in the house yellow. Ian couldn't wait to move out.

It had taken him years to pay off all his debts from his reckless early twenties, but he'd done it eventually and had now saved almost enough money for a deposit on a house of his own, a big, detached stone mansion with grounds, somewhere in the Yorkshire countryside. He would marry Hazel – or someone, he corrected himself, embarrassed by his out-of-control thoughts – and have three children. Probably it could never be Hazel, he realised sadly. She'd find it too complicated to reconcile their present relationship with any sort of romance, even if Ian wouldn't. That was his dream, though. For the time being, he saved as much money as he could and spent the bulk of his time at Hazel's, working and avoiding his parents.

A green Volvo swerved into the mill's car park. Sim. Ian looked at his watch: nine thirty-five. Where was she coming back from at this time? Did the woman never go to work? Hazel wouldn't be back for at least another twelve hours. Ian stepped back into the hall so that Sim wouldn't spot him as she approached the door, wondering which of the two deceptions in his life would come to light sooner and which would have the more awkward repercussions.

Neil Temple stood beside his pigeon-hole in the staff room, waiting for Phyllida Banborough to walk over and pick up the two letters he could see were waiting for her, so that he could have a word with her without attracting too much attention. In his hand was a folded copy of Imogen's poem, 'Memories'. The original plan had been for Eve to talk to Phyllida and Walter, the other judges, but she'd been too upset to stay at work today, so Neil had offered to do it instead.

He'd never seen her so miserable, not even the day after Campbell left. Neil had reserved judgement then. From an aesthetic point of view he'd thought Campbell was mad, but madness was pardonable. What was totally, utterly unforgivable was to ring Matt and Lucy, mutual friends whose wedding both Campbell and Eve were due to attend in the very near future, and ask if he could bring his new girlfriend, Eve's supplanter, to flaunt in front of her. Neil had been with Eve this morning when she'd opened Lucy's e-mail. He'd seen her run out of the room, then return a few minutes later looking pale and red-eyed. Ignoring Neil's advice, Eve had e-mailed Lucy back to say yes, it was fine. 'It bloody well isn't fine,' he'd insisted. 'Tell her to get straight back to Campbell and say, sorry, she's changed her mind. She needn't blame it on you. She shouldn't have said it was okay in the first place.'

Eve had simply shaken her head. 'If Campbell wants to bring Rory, let him,' she said. 'It might make me feel better in the long run.'

'How so?' Neil had asked. Eve certainly didn't look as

if she felt better. Her face looked like a strained dam struggling to hold back a tidal wave.

'If he's capable of doing this, I'm better off without him.' Neil couldn't disagree with that. All the guilt he'd felt about having taken Eve's side and put his and Campbell's ongoing squash tournament on hold vanished, as if someone had pressed a delete button in his brain. He could admit it now: he wanted to be more than a friend to Eve and, what was more, he would be, or at least he'd try as hard as he could. A residue of loyalty to Campbell had held him back until today, but stuff that. The man didn't know the meaning of the word. Neil knew Campbell thought of him as a mate and would expect his mates not to censure him too severely, if at all. How convenient. The way Neil saw it, he'd be doing Campbell a disservice if he allowed him to delude himself. The sooner Campbell found out Neil was after Eve the better. Maybe that'd teach him not to throw away a good thing so thoughtlessly in future.

And not just any good thing: Eve Hartigan. She was pretty, clever, kind, capable – a prize picnic hamper of a person, thought Neil, containing everything you needed and a few little surprises too. Eve was the sort of woman who carried a warm glow around with her and Neil badly needed some warmth in his life. He'd lived on his own for too long, with only Radio Four to welcome him home when he got in from work. He wondered how Eve felt about men with ginger hair. Many women Neil had met were funny about it.

The bell rang and Phyllida Banborough wandered over to her pigeon-hole. A cigarette dangled from the corner of her mouth, the ash just about to fall. Neil found her repulsive. Her skin was as beige as the staffroom wallpaper; both were irretrievably nicotine-stained. 'Have you got a minute, Phyllida?' Neil asked.

'I've never got a minute.' Phyllida's lips formed a snarl around her cigarette. 'I'm a teacher, remember? I haven't had a minute since nineteen seventy-two.'

'I wanted to show you this.' Neil handed her Imogen's poem.

'Seen it before,' said Phyllida, trying to give it back.

'You have? When?'

'It was one of the entries in the poetry competition. I've never read anything so morbid in my life. Where did you get hold of it?'

'Oh, I . . . er, found it on the floor in a classroom. In north block,' Neil added, hoping this concrete detail would make the story credible.

'Best place for it.' Phyllida sniggered. Her tower of ash toppled and landed on the slope of her sagging bosom. 'Bugger,' she said, brushing the greyness into her brown blouse.

'I think the poem's very moving,' said Neil. 'And sophisticated for a twelve-year-old.' Eve thought it was brilliant; it had made her cry. It wasn't only Imogen that Neil was defending.

'Bit too sophisticated if you ask me,' said Phyllida, slinging her handbag over her shoulder. 'Look how long it is, for a start.'

'Six verses isn't long.'

'It's too long for a twelve-year-old,' said Phyllida.

'What are you talking about?' Neil swallowed a laugh. Surely the woman had to be joking. The human hand was fully formed by the age of twelve and easily capable of penning twenty-four lines.

'This wasn't written by a twelve-year-old!' Phyllida thrust the poem back into Neil's hands, giving him a paper cut in the process. 'One of her parents must have done it for her.' She picked up her letters and hurried out of the staffroom before Neil had a chance to reply.

Poor Imogen. Her poem had been unfairly dismissed from the competition, bathed in fag smoke and now bled upon. Neil was surprised by the depth of his anger and the surge of confidence that came with it. It was as if

Campbell's sudden descent into moral lowliness empowered Neil, enabled him to get a leg-up to some higher level of existence. This was his chance to make an impact. He'd show Phyllida Banborough what was what, and Campbell. He'd show everyone.

2

It was Friday night, late. Sim lay beside Francis in Vanessa and Nicholas's superior spare bed (for once there had been no competition for it) wiping tiny beads of sweat from her brow and upper lip as they appeared. Her throat was dry and felt drier with every sip she took from the glass of water on her bedside table. She wondered whether this was what was known as a panic attack. It seemed likely. She'd received a letter from Andrew Johnson today. It was sheer luck that Francis didn't see it. He was in the kitchen getting himself a bowl of cereal when Sim opened it and she'd had time to stuff it into her pocket before he emerged.

Later, locked in a service station toilet cubicle somewhere along the M1, on neutral territory, she'd taken it out and read it. Andrew wanted to meet her for lunch when she was next in Cambridge. He needed to talk to her. That was all the letter said, apart from 'Toodle-pip' at the end. How sickeningly predictable. Sim pulled her mobile phone out of her handbag, still in her cubicle, and phoned the Works department of Renshaw College. As soon as she heard Andrew's voice she demanded to know what was going on, but he insisted he'd only talk face to face. He sounded serious, not flirtatious as Sim had expected. She'd agreed to meet him on Sunday for lunch at the Galleria and had no idea, yet, how she'd get away from the others. Before that, though, there were two sleepless nights to get through.

Had Andrew told Gillian? The possibility that Francis might find out, that Sim might lose him, loomed very large all of a sudden. Why had Sim imagined she could get away with it? Was it being a soap opera writer that gave her the illusion that other people were no more than characters in her drama who could be manipulated indefinitely?

Sim tried to divert the flow of anxiety to her other preoccupation: Campbell, the sneaky little shit, had got permission from Matt to bring Rory to the wedding. Sim didn't blame Matt, who existed outside the realm of complications, being totally uncomplicated himself, but Campbell should have known better. He understood about motivation, and implications; Sim had watched and discussed enough soaps with him over the years to be sure of this. This was no casual move on his part. It was as if he wanted to punish Eve.

Sim sat up jerkily, hoping to wake Francis, and took another sip of water. She loathed mess, and had tried so hard to prevent the Campbell, Eve and Rory clutter from contaminating Matt and Lucy's wedding. That she'd failed was bad enough, but what irked her most was that the bride and groom didn't seem to care. Lucy hadn't even phoned to discuss it. Sim had got the story from a distraught Eve. Vanessa and Nicholas, when Sim told them, took the news in their stride and Francis barely looked up from his paper. Sim was beginning to fear she and Eve were the only ones who mourned the old world order. 'Francis? Are you asleep?' She prodded him in the ribs. 'Francis?'

'Mm.' Francis stroked Sim's thigh. 'I was.'

'I can't work out what Campbell's playing at. Why's he trying to squeeze Eve out of the wedding?'

'Sim, it's the middle of the night.'

'I think she should still go,' said Sim. Focusing on this distracted her from portentous thoughts about the Toodle-pipster, as Vanessa called him. God, that made him sound alluringly harmless. 'For her own sake, so that

Campbell hasn't won, and for his sake too,' she said. 'He needs to be subjected to Eve's positive influence. Look how far Rory's already pulled him in the direction of scumminess. The old Campbell would never have done something like this.'

Francis sat up and fumbled in the dark for his glasses and watch. 'It's half-two, for fuck's sake!' He blinked at Sim, outraged.

'I know. I can't sleep. Francis?'

'Don't ask me anything. Think of me as asleep.'

'Did you think Campbell said anything odd last night, anything that . . . struck a peculiar chord?'

'I'm not listening.' Francis took off his glasses and dropped them on the floor.

'Did you hear him say "Rory was sorry she couldn't be here"? He'd obviously invited her. If she'd been able to come, we would have turned up and there she would have been. I'm surprised Campbell'd take the chance of that happening. Francis?'

'What, for Christ's sake?'

'Aren't you surprised?'

'No, I'm not. This . . . oh, God, what's her name?'

'Rory.'

'. . . is his girlfriend. Why shouldn't he invite her to his house?' Francis buried his face in a pillow. 'Would it do me any good to close my eyes and pretend?' he asked. 'Or are you monitoring the wave functions in my brain?'

'By the same token, you could say why shouldn't he invite her to his friends' wedding.'

'Well . . . yeah.'

'Because he can't expect to rush people. Not Eve and not us. I'm not saying he should hide Rory away for ever, but it's undignified to try to engineer a foursome situation too soon, which last night would have been. Didn't he think it might make us feel a bit uncomfortable?'

'It wouldn't have made me feel uncomfortable,' said Francis.

'It would me,' said Sim. 'To expect us to switch suddenly from evenings with Campbell and Eve to evenings with Campbell and Rory, without asking us how we feel about it . . .'

'I don't feel anything about it.' Francis sounded puzzled. 'It's Campbell who's switched, not us. What's it got to do with us? If we arrange to go out with Campbell, it's fair enough for him to bring whoever he wants.'

'Even to the wedding?'

'It's Matt and Lucy's fault for saying . . . What's-her-name could come. Maybe Campbell just thought, "Fuck it, I'll bring my new girlfriend." I can understand that. Etiquette can be oppressive. Big weddings like Matt and Lucy's . . . impose expectations on people. Like not bringing your new bird if your old one's going to be there. Also . . .' Francis sat up and put on his glasses again. 'The wedding's at Summerton. Very plush, very establishment, which calls for even more etiquette. Sim . . .'

'I see what you mean.' Sim nodded. 'By rebelling against establishment norms, Campbell can link this in with his unfinished PhD and make a sort of ethical stance out of fucking things up.'

'Sim!'

'What?'

'Do you think a wedding has to be like Matt and Lucy's in order to be . . . proper?' Francis looked nervous. 'Or could a cheaper, more private sort of wedding be just as good? One to which, say, no relatives were invited?'

Sim frowned. 'Don't change the subject. I've just had another idea. Of course! Francis, you keep referring to Campbell as "bringing" Rory.'

'So?' Francis demanded sulkily.

'I think he's trying to rush through the transition from Eve to Rory, to create the impression that he's the bringer and Eve was only ever the brought. If there's no awkward

158

in-between phase, with Rory being tentatively mentioned to gauge our feelings on the matter, it somehow denies Eve's importance.'

'That's because she hasn't got any any more.'

'Francis, that's an awful thing to say!'

'I don't mean to me, you fool. I mean she's no longer important to Campbell. He's ditched her.'

'Well, if she isn't, she should be after nearly a decade. Anyway, you're wrong. Eve still matters deeply to Campbell. That's why he's foisting Rory upon us all without a proper introductory period, trying to pull off this absurd image of himself as the "bringer", as you said, and relegate both Eve and Rory to "brought" status. But that isn't the real Campbell, he isn't a bringer, everyone knows that. He's playing a role that doesn't suit him to make us focus on him, not on them. Look, there's clearly something wrong with Rory; that's what Campbell doesn't want us to notice. Similarly, he knows Eve still matters. Not only to us, but to him. He thinks that his acting as if she doesn't matter will make her stop mattering. And to think his plan nearly worked! Remember what I said when I first brought this up, about how out of order Campbell was to invite Rory to the wedding and our meal last night? Don't you see? The focus was on Campbell's callousness, just as he intended it to be. Not on the crucial difference between Eve and Rory.'

'Sim, please, please, shut up.' Francis pulled the duvet over his head.

'Francis, this conversation has been very useful. It's lucky I didn't cut it short to please you. If you skimp on the process, you get skimpy results. I've made an important discovery tonight. Why would Campbell feel the need to whizz his changing love life before our eyes like some sort of psychedelic kaleidoscope if he was happy with his decision? He wouldn't. He'd have done everything more gradually, with proper attention to procedure. The corners he's trying to cut can only mean one thing: he's regretting what he's done already. He doesn't know it yet, but he wants Eve back.'

Sim was having difficulty keeping her eyes open – unusual for her, thought Vanessa, especially this early on a Saturday evening. She'd nodded off several times in front of the *Potters Court* omnibus and only fully awoke, bleary-eyed, when Nicholas started to shout at Francis: 'But we've helped create this situation, that's what's so hypocritical! Just war, my arse! All we're doing is making the Serbs feel protective towards Milosevic. If we'd mind our own fucking business, they'd get rid of him of their own accord sooner or later. But no, we steam in there and end up killing more people than the alleged bad guys!' Francis sneered amiably in response.

Vanessa didn't care if the others were crotchety or comatose; she was in a good mood. Things were going swimmingly on the Red-tooth front. The first call had come, as expected, but from Red-tooth's husband. 'Hello, Miss Vanessa?' he'd said. 'You have an accident with my wife?' It was typical of that little wet to get her husband to ring. Red-tooth was basically okay, he said, but she'd been hurt and upset by what happened.

Vanessa hated people who fished for sympathy. Anyone with any dignity would have stuck to the facts, which were that Red-tooth would survive, although the hospital had advised her to get checked out by her dentist. The husband wanted Vanessa to pay for the taxis that had taken Red-tooth to casualty and home again, and the taxis that would take her, on Monday, to the dentist and back. Vanessa had agreed and told him to send her all relevant receipts. 'Oh, yes. Thank you very much,' he'd said. 'Your address, please?'

She'd enjoyed lulling him into a false sense of security, letting him think he was sorting things out in an efficient, husbandly way, protecting his little woman. In fact, Vanessa had no intention of paying for any of Red-tooth's taxi journeys. The address she'd given was so close to her own that if it ever came to it she could claim he'd misheard the details: flat two instead of twenty-two, staircase M instead of N. So contemptuous was she of Mr Red-tooth, she didn't even bother to amend Gentchev's Field, pretending it was in London when everyone who wasn't a complete mong knew it was in Cambridge. Mr Red-tooth, who lived in Cambridge, hadn't spotted this discrepancy, which was reassuring. It would be easy to outmanoeuvre someone so dense.

Vanessa guessed he would be meticulous about sending the receipts, accompanied by a neat, handwritten breakdown of costs. None of which would reach her. The communication would get lost in a wormhole of the postal system; the chances of it being returned to sender were bound to be slim. And without receipts, the Red-teeth could hardly expect Vanessa to reimburse them, could they?

Vanessa was very clear about her strategy henceforth. What surprised her, though, was that when she trawled her mind for details of the accident she couldn't remember whether Red-tooth had been cycling on the road or on the pavement. If the latter, Vanessa was off the hook, and she thought it was only fair to accord herself the same rights as any defendant in a British court and place the burden of proof upon the prosecution. Unless she could swear that Red-tooth had been cycling along the road, she had no alternative but to acquit herself. And if her memory was fuzzy on this point, how – given the inaccuracy of human recall in emotionally charged situations – could Red-tooth's be otherwise? How could she and her husband be so sure that Vanessa was the guilty party and Red-tooth the helpless victim? It was some victim, thought Vanessa, who so easily made the transition from the distraught to the bureaucratic, from pain to processing receipts.

Vanessa looked forward to seeing what the Red-teeth's next move would be. Whatever it was, she was covered.

Even if the police were brought into it (and Vanessa seriously doubted they'd squander their already stretched resources following up a sore tooth) she could plead good intentions. She'd given Red-tooth a lift home after the accident, handed over first her phone number then her address; it wasn't her fault if Mr Red-tooth had misheard and sent the receipts to the wrong place. All in all, Vanessa felt she'd handled the situation rather well.

'Loss of life isn't the only issue,' Francis replied to a further tirade from Nicholas. 'Some people might feel death is a reasonable price to pay to put an end to tyranny.'

'Huh! As if Blair and Clinton aren't tyrannical! As if America isn't the most fucking murderous country in the world! Have you forgotten Vietnam, Kuwait? It's not about morality, it's about American self-interest, as always. Why else would Bill Knob-head Clinton risk turning a small Balkan war into world war fucking three? Jesus, Francis, you're so moderate!' he spat, red-faced.

Vanessa loved the way he pronounced the 'h' in 'knob-head', just like a public schoolboy. 'Nicholas and moderation don't get on,' she said. 'You prefer rudeness, don't you, darling? Where rudeness is absent, he fears freedom of speech is being stifled.'

'Oh, fuck off!'

'Don't you think it's good that America tries to sort things out in other countries?' Sim chipped in. 'Someone has to be in charge, don't they?' Nicholas's face froze. Vanessa willed Sim to continue, hoping for a good fight to get her teeth into, and Sim obliged: 'I mean, I don't know anything about politics, really, but I think it's good that America's got an idea of how things should be that doesn't just stop at its own borders. It tries to save the world from bad things like ... well, communism, fascism and stuff. Isn't that comforting?' Vanessa clapped her hands together in glee.

'I can't believe I'm hearing this!' Nicholas yelled. The

162

window behind him rattled in its frame. 'Sim, you know sod all!'

'Well . . . possibly that's true, but I *think* I know that Slobodan Milosevic is much more of a tyrant than Bill Clinton,' said Sim. 'Isn't he?' she asked Francis, who nodded.

'I can't believe you're nodding! I can't believe it!' Nicholas roared.

'I agree with Francis about loss of life not being the be all and end all,' said Sim, yawning. 'Sometimes you have to stand up for what's right.' Vanessa tutted. Not much chance of a scrap when Sim kept diluting the tension with her placidity. She never raised her voice, even at her most passionate. She spoke quickly when something mattered to her, but never aggressively.

'America doesn't give a damn about *right*!' The same could not be said for Nicholas. Lucky, really; Vanessa found calm men like Campbell too effeminate. 'How the fuck can you say Clinton's motives in Kosovo are ethical?'

'I don't know Bill Clinton,' said Sim. 'I've no idea what his motives are.'

'They're instrumental! The guy's a complete twat!'

'You can't avoid instrumentalism when you're personally involved in a situation,' Sim countered, looking amused. 'As for what Clinton's thinking, none of us can know. We've never met him. All I know is, I'd rather die accidentally in a bomb that was intended to wipe out Gillian Kench, even if it missed her by a mile, than be killed by Gillian Kench. Either way I'd be dead, obviously, but it would still make a difference. There's more to it than life and death, that's all I'm saying. There's an important symbolism involved in declaring war on baddies, even if one's motives aren't totally pure. Of course America isn't perfect, but, I mean, is anyone? Are you?'

Vanessa closed her eyes and waited for a voluble eruption from Nicholas. When it didn't arrive, she opened them again to find him chewing his fingernails. A mottled flush suffused his face. 'Just remind me why you fell out with Gillian,' he said to Sim.

'Oh, for God's sake,' Vanessa snapped, disappointed by the anticlimactic end to the discussion. 'Do we have to go into all that again?'

'Keep the fuck out of it! I was talking to Sim.'

The phone rang. 'This is probably our curry delivery guy, lost,' said Vanessa. 'Or scared to come up because of Conan the Barbarian over here.'

Nicholas picked up the phone, giving Vanessa a one-fingered retort with his other hand. 'Hello? Oh, hi, Eve. Do you want Sim?'

'Ask her how she is,' Sim hissed.

'How are you?' said Nicholas quickly, then blushed as he realised he'd obeyed an order from an apologist for American foreign policy. Vanessa made a gloating face at him. 'Yeah. Yeah. I know. Guthrie Napper's daughter, as well. I can't believe Campbell would sell out like that, join the fat cats,' he said pointedly, scowling at Vanessa to make it clear that she was the nadir of feline obesity as far as he was concerned. 'What? Yeah, she's here.' Nicholas passed the phone to Sim.

'Hi, Eve. What are you up to? Oh, right. Great. Did you have a good time?'

'I'm starving,' said Francis. 'Where's our food? Sim, get off the phone so I can phone the curry place again.' Sim waved him away. She took the phone through to the hall and closed the door behind her.

'How's work?' Nicholas asked Francis, turning his back on Vanessa.

'Okay. The Dingley interview's coming up, we're busy preparing for that. I can't say I'm looking forward to seeing those thugs again.'

'They were acquitted,' Nicholas reminded him tetchily.

'Yeah, because our legal system's better at protecting criminals than victims.'

'Poor people don't stand a chance in British courts,' Nicholas huffed.

'What do you know about courts, darling?' Vanessa teased. 'You've never been near one in your life. Or poor people, for that matter.'

'Fuck you!'

'The Dingleys did it, all right,' Francis said quietly. 'It's a joke. All the evidence is there but it's inadmissible.' Vanessa was heartened to hear this. If the police couldn't nail the Dingleys, who were clearly guilty as hell of a vicious crime, there was no way they'd be able to build a case against Vanessa for last week's accident when there was no evidence, only her word against Red-tooth's. She beamed at Francis, who had unintentionally boosted her confidence. He looked away, surprised and embarrassed.

Sim came back into the lounge. Francis seized the phone and began to dial the number of the Indian restaurant on Huntingdon Road that should by now have delivered their food.

'How's Eve?' asked Vanessa.

'Fine. She's at home with Neil and Imogen,' Sim answered slowly, her mind elsewhere.

'Who? Oh, the swotty poet. Eve's spending a lot of time with Neil, isn't she? Does she actually like him or would anyone do?'

'How weird,' said Sim, who hadn't heard the question. 'Eve and Neil took Imogen to Saltaire today and they called for Hazel. Eve reckons she saw a man in Hazel's flat – sounds like the same one you saw, Vanessa. Shaved hair, big blue tattoo on his arm.'

The doorbell rang. 'At last!' said Francis, tossing the phone on to the sofa.

'Nosh!' Nicholas perked up. He and Francis rushed downstairs to collect the curry, their political differences forgotten.

'Well, have you found out who he is yet?' Vanessa asked Sim.

'No. Haven't had a chance. I wanted to wait and broach the subject face to face, and you know Hazel – she works longer hours than the speaking clock. He must be a boyfriend, a married one.' Sim tutted and shook her head. 'But that doesn't fit. Hazel wouldn't have an affair with a married man.'

'He's got a neck that's so thick, it's almost a deformity,' said Vanessa. 'She's probably ashamed of him. If she isn't, she should be.'

'If Hazel had a boyfriend, there's no way she'd be ashamed of his looks, however bad they were,' said Sim. 'She's a very loyal person.' Francis and Nicholas reappeared with two satisfyingly large plastic bags full of curry cartons wrapped in orange oil-stained newspaper.

'Yum,' said Vanessa. 'Who says he's a boyfriend? He could be a gigolo, a drug dealer, a pimp, any number of things.'

'What's going on?' demanded Francis, who lived in fear of peculiar conversations interfering with his dinner.

'No. Not Hazel.' Sim ignored him.

'You'd make a crap detective, Sim. You ignore the evidence and speculate about what people would or wouldn't do.'

'Character is a fact, Vanessa. It counts as much as anything else.'

'Come on, you two,' said Francis. He and Nicholas were unpacking the goodies in the kitchen. 'Sim, chuck these away, will you?' He thrust some stained sheets of newspaper at her as she approached, dropping half of them on the floor in his impatience.

Sim sighed and picked them up. In the presence of curry, Francis forgot everything else. It amazed Sim that the scent of a Lamb Rogan Josh could erase from his mind, for instance, the way Nicholas had just yelled at him. Look, the two of them were beaming at each other across the foil-wrapped chappatis like a pair of newly-weds. It would be a while before Sim would feel inclined to beam at Nicholas. Passionate beliefs were one thing; trying to annihilate any opinion that differed from your own was quite another. What was the point of discussing anything ever, if one wasn't prepared to take anyone else's thoughts into account? For Sim, hearing an alternative viewpoint was alluringly exotic, like looking at pictures of sun-baked pools in holiday brochures and thinking, 'I could go there, if I wanted to.'

If irretrievably spoiling the mood of an evening hadn't been almost at the top of Sim's list of terrible things to do (on account of the innocent having to suffer along with the guilty) she might have put it to Nicholas – tentatively, politely and in a tone that made it clear it was okay to disagree – that he tended towards tyranny. Shouting, Sim's world-view butted in and told her, was the conversational equivalent of fascism. Nicholas used words as weapons, to wipe out the opposition, and in doing so he reduced other people to the status of objects, obstacles in his righteous path. He might as well change his name to God, thought Sim, with all the claims he makes to being in possession of the absolute truth.

She was about to crush the oily sheets of newspaper into a little ball and throw them in the bin when the words 'Stand By Your Man', in large, bold type, caught her eye, on a page that came from the *Sun*. Underneath the headline was a photo of Dale Dingley, with his arm round a woman. Sim took a closer look. Normally she didn't so much as glance at a newspaper from week to week, apart from to look at the TV listings, but she was interested to see Dale Dingley's other half. Francis had never mentioned a girlfriend. But then, he wouldn't.

Tricia, she was called. She wasn't a pleasant sight. Her teeth were pointy, like a dog's, and she had a bad footballer hairstyle: page-boy around the head and long at the back. Dale was standing next to her, bare-chested, with his arm slung over her shoulder. The *Sun*'s photographer had obviously told him to go for a roguish grin.

Sim was about to draw Francis's attention to the piece when she noticed something on Dale Dingley's left arm: a navy-blue tattoo of a mermaid with large bare breasts. A blue tattoo. Like the man in Hazel's flat. Also like that man's, Dale's head was newly shaven, with a visible red scab in between the ridges of his scalp, where he must have nicked himself with a razor. Oh God. Sim's heart began to race.

'Sim, it's going cold,' Francis complained.

'I'm coming.' She tore the *Sun* article into little pieces so that no one could reassemble it later, and threw it in the bin.

Eve, Neil and Imogen Salt sat at Eve's kitchen table drinking Lapsang Souchong from matching china cups. Neil said it tasted of ashtrays, but Eve had been determined to use her pink Wedgwood teapot, which meant they all had to drink the same thing. Her own first choice had been Earl Grey, but Imogen had asked if she had any Lapsang Souchong and it occurred to Eve that she did – Sim had brought round a packet ages ago, raving about it. Eve had stuffed it in a cupboard and forgotten all about it, but now was as good a time as any to sample it. She thought it was hilarious that this should be Imogen's favourite tea; how many twelve-year-olds had even heard of it? Eve liked the name, which conjured up sophistication and ceremony, but the taste took a bit of getting used to.

As did the blow Campbell had delivered the day before, via Lucy, from which Eve was only just beginning to recover. She was still in pain, still crying a lot, but the despair that threatened her with extinction at any moment had passed. Neil and Imogen helped, warming up the house with their combined presence. They made Eve's home feel colourful again. She appreciated the pinkness of the teapot, the ring of yellow roses around the rim of each cup, the golden beech of the kitchen table. It was as if the house had sprung back to life after a long coma.

Campbell's mum had given them the teacups as a seventh anniversary present. How could he have left them behind, Eve wondered? He'd hardly taken anything with him, only a few clothes and his toothbrush. Eve could never have done that. Even if she'd fallen madly in love with another man (this she could imagine) and decided to leave Campbell for him (this she could not), she wouldn't have been able to float out of her environment so easily, being the sort of person who quickly grew attached to the little accessories of life.

Anyone who could leave behind a beautiful china teaset that was a present from his mother was capable of leaving behind a girlfriend of seven and a half years. It was easy to conclude this now, of course, since Campbell had done both already, but what interested Eve was the connection between the two leavings. To Campbell, a cup was a cup. He made no distinction between Royal Doulton and the chipped mugs that turned up at car boot sales. There was a danger, Eve thought, that if you treated objects like objects, you would eventually begin to treat people in the same uncaring way. But why should that be? Objects were only objects, after all. But the whole point was that they weren't; not if you allowed them to mean more to you.

'What did Sim say about the man in Hazel's flat?' Imogen asked.

'That Vanessa's seen him too. No one knows who he is. Still, I doubt it'll take Sim long to find out.' Imogen had quickly familiarised herself with Eve's friends and now referred to them as if she'd known them all for years. Eve wondered whether Imogen was popular at school. Her odd maturity might put off the other kids. Eve hoped not; Imogen deserved to have friends of her own. And she deserved better treatment than she'd had from Camborne Street School recently.

Eve and Neil had taken Imogen to Saltaire for the day. It was irregular for teachers to spend time with a pupil out of school hours, but they both felt they owed her some compensation for Phyllida Banborough's mean-mindedness. Imogen had always wanted to go to Saltaire because, as she put it, it was named after her. She'd taken a book out of the school library about Sir Titus Salt, the mill owner who built the model village so that his workers could live in sanitary conditions, and she insisted he was her ancestor. Neil bought her a postcard with a photograph of Sir Titus on it and Imogen claimed she could detect a family resemblance, his long bushy beard notwithstanding.

After lunch in Salt's Diner and a quick look round the David Hockney exhibition and the shop, they went to the New Mill to call for Hazel. Eve rang the bell and waited. A few seconds passed before a male voice said 'Hazel, is that you?' over the intercom. Funny, thought Eve.

'No, it's some friends of hers. Is she due back soon?' There was no reply. Eve rang the bell twice more but the man didn't speak again. She moved over to Hazel's study window and peered in. There he was, in the hall. He disappeared after a second, but Eve could still picture him clearly, hours later: a skinhead with a blue tattoo on his shoulder. It was very strange indeed and a bit worrying. Eve had thought he might be an intruder but, as Imogen pointed out, the man was not hiding from Hazel as a burglar would have been. He'd been expecting Hazel, had responded to the bell on the assumption that it was Hazel at the door. Might he be a Gatting-sitter, Eve wondered. Her gran used to hire someone to mind her cats when she went out for any longer than half an hour. Was Hazel mad enough to do the same for her treasured cactus? Eve hoped not, for the sake of her friend's sanity. She'd phoned Sim at Vanessa's as soon as she, Neil and Imogen had got back to Rusholme, thinking that if anything juicy was going on in Hazel's life, Sim was bound to know what it was. Sim didn't know, but there had been an on-the-case seriousness about her tone.

'So, what are we going to do about your poem, then?'
Neil asked Imogen.

'There's nothing we can do, is there?' Eve tried to hide
her surprise. Why was Neil raising Imogen's hopes when
the matter was over and done with? The competition
already had its winner.

'I don't mind,' said Imogen. 'I only wanted to know the
reason.' She sounded like the weary heroine of a David
Lean film. Where had she picked up this way of speaking,
Eve wondered. From her parents?

'There might be something we can do,' said Neil enig-
matically.

'Neil . . .' Eve cautioned.

'What do you mean?' Imogen's eyes glowed.

'Leave it to me.' Neil winked mischievously. Eve nearly
laughed. She wasn't used to men who said 'Leave it to me',
nor to ones who winked. Campbell never winked. None of
their male friends did. Eve considered how much they must
all have rubbed off on each other over the years, and the
possibility that Campbell's defection, his sin (she couldn't
help thinking of it in this way), might belong somehow
to the whole group, or at least to the males within it.
Matt was the best of them. At least he'd bought Lucy a
solitaire diamond engagement ring and proposed to her
on one knee. But Eve only knew this because Lucy had
told her. Whenever she saw Matt he was guzzling beer and
leaping up and down in front of televised sport. Francis
was practically a robot and Nicholas's remarks on the
phone a minute ago had left much to be desired. How
dare he make out that Campbell's defection had a political
element? Campbell had betrayed Eve, not some abstract
cause. How was it possible to be so wide of the mark? The
idea of Campbell aspiring to be a fat cat was ludicrous.
If only he were that ambitious. Eve couldn't imagine him
setting his sights much higher than a slender squirrel.

Eve thought of herself as a generally public-spirited
person, but she was determined not to share Campbell's

desertion with anyone. It wasn't a universal tragedy; it was *her* tragedy and she was proud to own it. Nicholas had no right to claim it for some campaign of his own.

There was, Eve felt, a sort of ingrained shoddiness about Campbell's male friends (she didn't include Neil, who had never been more than a squash partner). None of them had phoned him since he'd moved to Didsbury apart from Francis, and he'd had his arm twisted by Sim. Certainly none of them had advised him against chucking away a seven-and-a-half-year relationship on the basis of having spent four days with a stranger.

Why do I care how they've treated Campbell, Eve wondered. She was furious with herself for putting his needs before her own; was that what people meant when they talked about unconditional love? None of them has phoned me either, she thought. Of course they hadn't; they left that sort of thing to their girlfriends. Eve hadn't even minded until now, taking it for granted that this sort of benevolent neglect was the most one could expect from men. How dare Neil come along and highlight her other male friends' inadequacies by being so damn caring and noble? He made Eve feel a fool for having underrated him for years. She'd seen him as someone who got Campbell out from under her feet once a week and never recognised his potential to be a real friend, opting instead for weekends of shallow fun with his inferiors. Why had she overlooked Neil? His hair was orange and he had a bit of a beer belly; he wore white socks sometimes, but so what?

Eve poured more Lapsang Souchong, filling Neil's cup first. He didn't like its flavour, but he thanked her and drank it as if he did. Neil was a gentleman. Even his taste buds were honourable. Eve wished she'd gone to Cambridge this weekend and taken him with her. Sim would adore him and . . .

Slowly, Eve's smile widened. Of course. Why hadn't she thought of it before? What better opportunity for Neil to meet the gang than at the wedding? Eve wasn't prepared to go alone, not if Rory the stalker was going to be there, but to go with Neil would be a different matter altogether. There was no way Matt and Lucy could complain either, not after they'd said Campbell could bring Rory. Lucy felt guilty enough already; she'd leap at the chance to salve her conscience. 'What are you doing on May the fifteenth?' Eve asked Neil.

3

Cambridge was always hectic, even on Sundays. Sim pushed through the crowds on Bridge Street, pretending she felt brave, trying to blend in with tourists and men in straw boaters selling chauffeured punt trips. She hovered on the Galleria's threshold. No sign of Andrew. Sim was annoyed with him for being late until she looked down and spotted him waving at her through a gap in the stairs. He'd chosen a table on the basement floor, the darkest part of the restaurant, instead of on the balcony overlooking the river; perhaps he too was concerned about secrecy.

His hair was longer, layered and almost shoulder-length. He'd lost about a stone, and looked at the same time more handsome (not that Sim could ever find him sexy again) and less healthy The whites of his eyes were flecked with red, she noticed. 'You're looking well,' he said, standing up to kiss her, squeezing her hand. He was wearing ribbed black trousers and a blue-and-white pin-striped shirt. He smiled warmly and appeared almost breathless, which made no sense to Sim, unless he could barely contain his glee at the prospect of blackmailing her.

'What's all this about, Andrew?' The question came out more sternly than she'd intended.

He frowned. 'Aren't you going to sit down?'

Telling herself she'd find out soon enough – a few minutes didn't matter – Sim sat down and began to flick through the menu, wanting to fix her eyes on something

174

neutral. 'I might just have a drink,' she said. 'I'm not very hungry.' Andrew wasn't solely responsible for driving away her appetite. Dale Dingley's resemblance to the man seen twice in Hazel's flat had put Sim off her curry last night and she'd ended up giving most of it to Francis. She forced her Hazel worries out of her mind. One thing at a time.

'Oh, come on! Surely there's something you fancy?' said Andrew suggestively. Then, fearing he'd been too subtle, he added almost mournfully, 'I know what I fancy.'

'Cut the crap, Andrew,' Sim snapped, hating the feeling of not being in control. 'I'm not pissing about with small talk until you tell me what you want. Why are we here?'

'All right, keep your knickers on. On the other hand . . .' He tried to grin, but it was clear that his lascivious remarks were having no effect on Sim's mood or his own. Sim gave him the most withering look she could manage. 'Christ, what's wrong with you?' he asked. 'You're not being very friendly.'

'Andrew . . .'

'Okay, okay.' He held up his hands. 'God!' He cleared his throat. 'You're not making this any easier. I'm just trying to . . . relax the atmosphere a bit. You seem so tense.'

'I'm not tense,' Sim lied. 'Just busy. So can you say what you've got to say, please?'

'It's Gillian.' Andrew swallowed hard, his Adam's apple leaping up and down.

'Thought as much. Have you told her, then? Is she going to tell Francis?'

'About us? Of course I haven't told her. Jesus, what do you think I've got, a death wish?' Sim was puzzled, then relieved. It hadn't occurred to her that Andrew might keep the affair from Gillian out of self-interest; she'd been so caught up in her own agenda that she'd never got as far as wondering whether Andrew had one. It stood to reason, though. Anyone so obsessed with sitting in the middle that she'd go as far as to boycott round tables in restaurants

175

would react badly to the news that her boyfriend had slept with her friend-turned-enemy. Andrew sighed and closed his eyes, and Sim noticed dark shadows under them. 'Look, I have to ask you a question,' he said. 'What's going on with you and Gillian?'

'Nothing. We haven't spoken for months.'

'I know that, but . . . is it temporary? Is it a best mates' tiff? I mean, you used to be quite close from what I can gather. Do you have any surviving loyalty to her?' Andrew watched Sim carefully. 'She says you hate her, even though there's no reason why you should . . .'

'Hang on just one fucking second,' Sim interrupted. 'Are you quoting her, or is that your opinion?'

'What?' Andrew looked confused. 'Why are you *fucking* swearing at me, Sim?' he mimicked her. 'Is what my opinion?'

'That I've taken against Gillian for no reason. I don't hate her, incidentally.' Sim wondered whether there was any point in speaking to anyone, ever. Andrew wasn't the first person to get it wrong. All Sim's friends continually misrepresented her position, reducing it to hatred; there seemed to be nothing she could do to stop them. Nicholas, who'd never seemed interested before, yesterday asked to be told the full Gillian story and, having heard it, said, 'But she must have done something else. You wouldn't hate her just for that.' Sim objected to being so severely misunderstood when she was painstakingly vocal with her every opinion. Why did she bother?

Hate was the wrong word, too emotional. Sim had made an informed judgement about Gillian, based on standards rather than an excess of sentiment. It was no wonder her harsh stance was the part of the incident that stuck in people's minds. Gillian's original attack on Sim had been equally harsh, but it was generally taken for granted that anything Gillian said was a hormonal outburst that could be overlooked; she was seen as being beyond reason and therefore, perversely, less responsible

176

for the rift than Sim, who operated within the arena of rationality.

No stupidity or hysteria could be offset against Sim's verdict, which was why Lucy, Eve and Hazel regularly tried to talk her out of her . . . *not* hatred, but irreversible disdain for Gillian. They were scared to acknowledge that the worth of a human being could be objectively assessed and found wanting. To do so would strike them as cruel, and might require difficult action; it was far easier to make these things relative, a matter of clashing personalities, mood swings or breakdowns of communication. But Sim believed it was cruel to the world to be soft on the unpleasant things inside it.

Why had Nicholas insisted that Gillian must have done something else? Wasn't it enough that she was vile, or would Nicholas find the idea that some people were innately more loathsome than others offensively inegalitarian? Equal rights for total fuckers, was that his motto? Perhaps Sim was doing him a disservice. He hadn't defended Gillian, which at least was something. Maybe he'd been dissatisfied with the story from a narrative point of view. Sim could understand that. It was a bit thin, really. Such a flimsy plot would never turn up in *Potters Court*; Sim wouldn't stand for it. In a soap, if a major fallout between two characters was required, one would have to kidnap the other's child at the very least.

Gillian had done nothing so dramatic. At a party at Sim and Francis's house last year, she'd made a bizarre and unsubstantiated accusation, that was all. She'd arrived in a bad mood, tight-lipped. Nicholas and Vanessa, with whom she'd travelled up from Cambridge, had no idea what was wrong with her; she'd been in a strop all day and wouldn't say why. Eventually alcohol loosened her tongue and when Sim asked her for the fourth time what the matter was, Gillian said, 'It's you.'

'Me? Why, what have I done?'

'You've ruined everything!'

177

'What?' Sim had done nothing but give Gillian cocktails and try to thaw her out with chat since she arrived. 'Are you kidding?'

'Just like you always have! You ruined my childhood, and my teenage . . . hood. You've always had it in for me.' Her face was monsterish, puffy and contorted.

'Gillian, what are you talking about? Can you be more specific?'

'You've been talking to Vanessa *all* night and leaving me out! That's not *all* you've done, either.'

'What do you mean?' Sim asked, confused. 'I've hardly said a word to Vanessa. And what else am I supposed to have done?'

'If you don't know, I'm certainly not going to tell you!'

No matter how hard Sim tried to persuade her to part with a few details, Gillian refused to elaborate. After an hour or so she announced that she was leaving and stormed out of the flat. Sim followed her, saying, 'Gillian, there's no point going now, how will you get home? Can't we talk about this, see if we can sort it out? What have I done, for God's sake?'

'I'll stay in a hotel,' Gillian hissed, pressing the down button on the lift so hard that her fingertip turned white. 'And another thing . . .'

'What?' Sim had no idea what to expect. Gillian seemed capable of anything. Perhaps green juice would spurt from her eye sockets.

'I was on a bus in Cambridge the other day and I heard two women talking about you. They were both saying you were a right cow. Neither of them liked you at all and they said they had good reason!' she spat at Sim.

'Really? What were their reasons?' Sim was genuinely curious.

Gillian clearly hadn't anticipated the question. Blushing, she stammered, 'Well, I didn't hear them actually because . . . the bus went under a . . . loud bridge at that point. But . . . from what I *did* manage to hear,

178

it was something to do with you being a really bossy cow!'

That was it, end of story. The lift arrived. Gillian got into it. Two weeks later she'd written to Sim asking if they could 'berry the hat shed', but she neither apologised nor withdrew her accusations. Sim didn't reply and hadn't spoken to Gillian since. She'd never known whether to believe the story about the two women on the bus. Either way, Gillian evidently meant Sim harm, as people who passed on bad gossip in a supposedly neutral manner always did.

The Galleria's head waiter approached, with a bottle of red wine and two glasses. 'Would you like to taste it, sir?' he asked Andrew.

'No, thanks, I'm sure it'll be fine.'

'You ordered wine?'

'Yes. Would you have preferred white?' Andrew looked worried.

'I'd . . .' Sim was speechless, a condition she rarely suffered from. 'I'd have preferred to choose my own drink. What the fuck is this, some sort of romantic reunion?'

'Well . . .' Andrew blushed.

'I don't have to sit here and listen to you defend Gillian . . .' Sim stood up. Andrew grabbed her arm. She felt sick. The thought of those hairy hands all over her . . . ugh.

'Sim, wait, please. You've misunderstood me, I wasn't . . .'

'I don't care.' Now she was confident that Andrew wouldn't tell Gillian about the affair, there was no reason to stay. 'Andrew, do me a favour. Don't ring me again, okay?' She didn't even have to be nice to him. She'd seen the look on his face when she asked if he'd told Gillian; the very idea filled him with horror. If only Sim had thought of that before; she could have saved herself months of anxiety. 'Don't try to speak to me at Matt and Lucy's wedding. In fact, I'd prefer it if you didn't go.'

Andrew shook his head sadly, as if Sim had let him

down. 'It isn't as simple as that,' he said. 'Gillian'll make me go. Look, will you sit down and hear me out? There are things you need to know. I'm desperate, Sim . . .'

'No, I won't. Goodbye, Andrew.'

Sim couldn't get to the door quickly enough; she jumped up the steps two at a time. A gust of fresh air hit her as she tumbled out on to Bridge Street. She could feel the part of her mind that contained Andrew awareness flushing itself out. He didn't matter any more. 'Toodle-pip.' His voice trailed weakly after her, so faint that Sim wondered if she'd imagined it.

From: lucyfairclough@worldbank.org
To: n.drogan@cam.ac.uk
Subject: Campbell and Eve
Date: Sun, 5 April 1999

Hi Nicholas and Vanessa
I'm sending this on the off-chance Sim and Francis are still there. If they are, can you ask Sim to e-mail or phone and tell me the gossip? What's going on with Campbell and Eve? Why did no one tell me they'd split up? The first I heard was when C phoned and asked if he could bring his new girlfriend to the wedding. Matt and I don't mind if Eve doesn't, but who is this Rory? C was v. cagey on the phone, couldn't get anything out of him. I e-mailed Eve and she swore she didn't mind. Isn't she upset, though? Why did he leave – was there more to it than new girlfriend? I've been meaning to phone Sim, but haven't had time for last few days. Then Eve phoned this morning and asked if she could bring someone called Neil Temple to wedding – who he? New boyf? E couldn't tell me anything cos he was there in the background, so urgent updating required!
Lucy

PS Also, ask Sim what she reckons to some sort of fancy dress thing as part of stag-hen w/end (Matt's idea – I

180

It was Sunday evening and Sim and Francis were driving
home, zooming past petrol station after petrol station on
the A14. Sim longed for the day to end so that she could lie
in bed in the dark and devote herself entirely to considering
the matter of Hazel and her mystery man. If she thought
about it now she'd stop speaking and Francis would be
suspicious. Pleased, perhaps, but suspicious. She decided
to open another subject altogether. 'Francis, remember last
Thursday, when Campbell said there were some things
about Eve that he didn't like?'

'No,' Francis affirmed, as if he'd got mixed up and
thought he was saying yes. He fiddled with the radio
buttons to find a news programme. The car swerved.

'One of them was that she was horrible about Rory
before anything had happened. Eve was against Rory from
the very first time she phoned, before Campbell had even
got back from Stratford.'

'Stratford?' Francis shook his head crossly, as if to say
'Oh, I give up!'. He had no idea how Stratford was
connected to anything, but rather than enquire so that
the discussion could proceed, he saw this as a possible
loophole to get himself off gossip duty.

'Yeah, the course he went on, where he met Rory.' Sim
ignored his attempt to shirk conversational responsibility.
'Don't you think that's significant?'

'What, that he met her in Stratford?'

'No.' Sim sighed heavily. 'That Eve hated Rory from
the start and referred to her as "the stalker".' She turned
down the volume on the radio. It was only another boring
Kosovo debate, for heaven's sake.

'I don't know.' Francis shrugged, turning it up again in
time to hear someone mention the possibility of Russia
using nuclear weapons if NATO didn't backtrack.

'Campbell wants to pass it off as nastiness on Eve's part

because he can't admit the truth. Francis? He can't admit the truth.'

'Which is?' said Francis with a sigh, resigned to sharing an enclosed space with Sim and her stream of consciousness.

'Rory's a bad egg. Eve sensed it straight away. Some people have a sixth sense that enables them to detect evil. Rory activated Eve's in the way that Gillian activated mine. It's like . . . I don't know, tuning in a television. Once you've found Channel Six, it's always there. But Campbell can't get it, just like we can't get Channel Five in Saltaire,' Sim concluded sorrowfully, wondering when this deprivation would end. She hated to think how many episodes of *Sunset Beach* she'd missed. 'Most people haven't got Channel Six,' she went on, 'and they try to undermine the power of those who do by making out that it's somehow mean to notice badness in others.'

'Are you saying Campbell never notices anything bad?' Francis asked impatiently.

'Oh, yeah, he notices bad *things*, but that doesn't tell you anything. Without Channel Six, it's impossible to distinguish between a good person who does lots of things wrong and an evil person who behaves well most of the time to mislead you.' Francis shook his head and smiled tolerantly in Sim's direction. 'Like Rory. Except it sounds as if she doesn't really bother with the behaving well bit.'

'You don't know she's so terrible,' Francis objected.

'I believe Eve.' Even though she still doesn't believe me about Gillian, thought Sim sadly. There was a difference, though: Eve had known Gillian since their schooldays, whereas Rory was a stranger; Sim faced neither an adjustment nor a loss if she accepted Eve's version of her rival. 'You should believe her too,' she told Francis. 'Think how satisfactory she is in lots of little ways. You only have to tell her a date once and she writes it on her calendar. When she borrows a novel, she posts it back as soon as she's read it with a little note saying what she thought of it.'

'Big deal!'

'It is! If the little things are right, chances are the big things will be too. Look at Matt and Lucy's wedding. Think how much time and effort they put into the invitations alone, finding the right sort of card . . .'

Francis grimaced. 'Sim, about weddings,' he began with a deep breath. 'Imagine if we were getting married. Would it matter to you if . . .'

'Francis, why are you indicating left?'

'I was in the middle of . . . oh, forget it!' Francis sighed. 'You see, this is where I start to have doubts about your heightened powers of perception. You appear to be lacking Channel Seven: basic deduction.' He frowned. Had Sim deliberately changed the subject because she hated the thought of marrying him? He ought to try to be a bit more charming, just in case. Funnier, too. What if he was a diseased organism, though, and all his efforts were doomed to failure? Francis had always suspected as much.

'Don't be sarcastic,' Sim ticked him off. 'You're planning to stop at these services.'

'Correct.'

'What were you saying?'

'Forget it. It doesn't matter.' Francis was annoyed with himself. He knew he'd never have given marriage a second thought if it weren't for Matt and Lucy, and was annoyed to be a follower rather than a leader. But if Sim would agree to a quick, secret wedding, maybe they could squeeze it in before . . .

'Francis?'

'Mm?'

'I think something's going on with Nicholas. He's withholding something.'

'I wish he bloody would.' Francis chuckled. 'His thoughts, opinions and beliefs would be a good start.' Nicholas had only mentioned Matt and Lucy's wedding in order to condemn it as bourgeois and call them Lord and Lady

Muck. He applied those titles loosely: to anyone who arranged to do anything even remotely pleasant, anyone who displayed the slightest reluctance to do something unpleasant, anyone, indeed, who wasn't up for sticking his or her head into a toilet bowl whenever the chance arose.

Francis guessed that neither Nicholas nor Vanessa would ever dream of getting married; they weren't temperamentally suited to happy occasions. And there's no way they love each other as much as Sim and I do, Francis thought smugly. It was crucial, he realised, to have someone to whom one felt superior: another problem with Nicholas's naïve egalitarianism. Francis suspected Nicholas didn't believe in the concept of superior character, since it was a commodity one was arguably born with, like inherited wealth.

'No, really.' Sim's voice broke into his thoughts. 'He's hiding something, I know it.'

'Don't be stupid. People don't hide things. That only happens in films. You just want our friends to be more interesting than they are.'

Sim wondered if this was true, if she was being overly vigilant. Better to err on the side of caution, though. She was furious with herself for not having detected that something was wrong with Campbell and Eve long before Campbell walked out, during the mauve letter epoch. The signs must have been there, but Sim had been concentrating on Matt and Lucy's wedding. She had no doubt she could have talked Campbell out of leaving. Persuading someone with his temperament to stay put was a doddle; persuading him to move again after having moved so recently was more tricky. I can do it, though, thought Sim, I *will* do it.

Maybe Nicholas's oddness this weekend was all in her imagination and the tattooed man in Hazel's flat wasn't Dale Dingley. What a relief that would be. Sim wanted to ask Francis whether he thought there was any chance the Dingleys were innocent, but he'd parked the car and was already climbing out. 'Won't be a minute,' he said.

Sim opened the passenger door and stretched her legs, thinking. Surely everyone in the country was familiar with the Dingleys' faces; the case had had endless news coverage. Wouldn't Eve and Vanessa have recognised Dale Dingley, if he it was? Sim would have, but only because he was a central character in Francis's life at the moment, with the interview coming up. She wouldn't have recognised John Venables or Robert Thompson, Neil or Jamie Acourt, although she knew the names well enough. She knew whom they'd murdered and allegedly murdered, but if she'd spotted any one of them in the window of a friend's flat, she wouldn't have known him from a Dove Cream Bar.

It had to be Dingley. He was in hiding, wasn't he? It would explain such a lot: Hazel's nervous temperament, her tendency to mislay teacups. Anyone'd be jumpy if they were harbouring a murderer. Except that if Hazel was hiding Dale Dingley in her flat then he couldn't be a murderer. Of that Sim was certain. Hazel had a Channel Six, albeit an erratic, oversensitive model. Long before Sim banished Gillian, Hazel took against her for laughing at Gatting's shape and saying he could double as a spiky dildo. Hazel was petrified of Vanessa's sharp tongue, recoiled from Francis's occasional put-downs as if she'd been struck. And then there was her reaction to Campbell's recent behaviour, her hurt on Eve's behalf. She'd die of horror if a rapist or murderer went anywhere near her.

Sim wondered how Hazel knew Dale Dingley wasn't guilty. Perhaps she'd been with him on the night in question. No, she would have come forward if that were the case. Maybe she just knew. Maybe she trusted him in the way that Sim trusted her. But were they only friends or was there a romantic involvement? If so, how did Tricia, the pointy-toothed girlfriend from the *Sun*, fit into the equation?

Thank God Vanessa hadn't spotted the photograph of

Dale when Francis and Nicholas unpacked the curry. She might have made the connection then if she hadn't before. Sim knew this was something she could mention to no one. Who apart from Sim had a high enough opinion of Hazel to trust her instincts over the instincts of the nation's judiciary and media? Nobody. Without Sim's help, Hazel would get none. This depressed Sim hugely. Why couldn't Hazel rely equally on Vanessa, Eve or Lucy? Or any of the men. Weren't they supposed to be a group of close friends?

Sim was determined to be of assistance. Her years of writing for soaps had stood her in good stead. How often, on *Potters Court*, did it happen that a goodie who told the truth was doubted and disbelieved by everybody, with disastrous consequences? Almost every week. Hazel was that goodie now. Next time Sim saw her, she'd make a point of voicing her doubts about the Dingleys' guilt. A few well-crafted comments should be enough to open the floodgates.

Sim heard Francis's footsteps. 'Campbell just rang,' he said, snapping his mobile phone shut as he got back into the car. 'It's okay if he comes to stay next weekend, isn't it?'

'Sure,' said Sim. What better opportunity to persuade him not to bring Rory to Matt and Lucy's wedding? Sim thought she could probably accomplish this in an hour, but to stretch it out over a whole weekend would be more fun. There could be various stages to the procedure, layer upon layer of wit, lovely dinners and subliminal suggestions until, before Campbell knew it, he'd be agreeing to whatever Sim said.

'He says he's fed up of sitting in that little room,' said Francis.

'Has he still not been into the lounge?'

'Nope.'

'The more he builds it up, the harder it'll be for him ever to do it. Still, he might not be there much longer.'

'Oh?'

'This coming to stay – he's teetering on the brink of regret. He isn't quite ready to admit that he wants Eve back, so he's coming round to ours where he can soak up an Eve-friendly atmosphere and be talked into a reconciliation by me.'

'That's rubbish.'

'No it's not. Why is it?'

'Because he's bringing Rory.'

'He's what?'

'He's bringing Rory.'

'Oh, Francis, no!'

(iii)

'No way, Francis.'

1

Sim opened a bottle of lavender aromatherapy gel and poured a large globule into the bath she was running. Lavender was supposed to relax you. The water turned cloudy and foam began to swirl. She closed her eyes and breathed in and out a few times, deeply and slowly. She'd been feeling panicky all week. A slippery sort of chaos had broken out in her social circle, one she could see no way of grasping and knocking back into shape.

Eve had struck back at Campbell by asking Lucy if Neil Temple could come to the wedding and Lucy had agreed without pressing Eve for details of who Neil was or why she wanted to bring him. Communication seemed to be breaking down all over. In other circumstances, Sim would have been vehemently in favour of any plan to make Campbell jealous, but she was alarmed by Eve's sinister failure to consult her, not to mention Lucy's. All her friends had started to behave with frightening autonomy. Sim blamed Campbell, who'd been the first, asking Matt if Rory could come to the wedding without so much as notifying Sim. Campbell's attempt at independent action irritated her more than Eve's. He was so far from being self-sufficient that it was embarrassing to watch him try. Sim felt that Campbell, who'd never been a man of action, should stick to what he was good at: philosophy, chatting, compliance, watching TV. Who did he think he was, Andy McNab?

Lucy's attitude was also disturbing. Her paranoid phase had passed, her sinister Siamese twin dream had not recurred and she'd risen to a higher plane of pre-marital elation. She no longer felt anything was capable of ruining the best day of her life and was sending breezy, frivolous e-mails as if she hadn't a care in the world. It didn't seem to matter to her one jot whether Campbell and Eve were back together in time for the wedding. She'd laughed when Sim told her she'd been trying to protect her and Matt from the messy truth in the hope that order would be restored before the fifteenth of May. Sim tried not to feel discouraged. She had a vision of how things should be, namely how they were until recently, and she would strive to bring it about, with or without allies.

She could have done with Francis's support, but even he was being idiotic, granting permission for Rory Napper to be brought to Saltaire when he could easily have made an excuse. All the way back to Yorkshire last Sunday Sim had tried to persuade him to phone Campbell back and pretend he'd remembered a prior engagement. 'It's disloyal to Eve,' she'd pleaded with him. 'Can't you see that?'

'No, I can't.' Francis looked mystified, then grumpy. 'We can't tell Campbell he can't bring his new girlfriend to stay and that's that. Haven't you got any manners?'

Sim thought he was a fine one to talk. 'But you wouldn't have to say that. You could make up another reason. It's too soon, Francis. Maybe after some time has passed, when Eve's feeling better about things, but not now.'

'What difference does it make when it happens? If it's disloyal now, won't it still be disloyal in a few weeks or months?'

'I don't know. I'll worry about that when I have to. In the meantime we can easily arrange to see Campbell on his own. Look, we'll meet Rory soon enough, at the wedding, on neutral territory. We can't have her in our flat, at our invitation. It's not fair on Eve.'

'Neutral territory! This isn't a war.'

192

'Of course it is, Francis. All right, if you won't ring him, I will.'

'And say what?'

'That my aunt and uncle are coming to stay.'

'No! I'm not letting you lie to Campbell.' Francis flexed his shoulders to show that he was serious. Every now and then he took it upon himself to intervene in Sim's handling of Campbell, challenging the advice she gave him about how to write his thesis or make his grant cheques last longer, and they argued like parents over the best way to bring up a child. Sometimes, bizarrely, they even quarrelled about which of them Campbell took after more. When talking to Francis, he found nothing more fascinating than the Channel Four News, while in Sim's company soaps were his favourite viewing. Campbell was like an abstract painting; he meant whatever you wanted him to mean. 'If you don't want him to bring Rory, fine, but tell him the truth,' said Francis.

'Leave it to me.' Sim planned to deal with it in her own sweet way. Truth and sweetness were frequently incompatible.

'No, I won't,' said Francis. 'I'll tell Campbell what you're up to if you feed him some bullshit.' Sim knew what this was about. Francis, too, wanted to believe he was autonomous. He needed to reassure himself every so often that he was stronger than Sim's manipulations.

'Francis, that's totally out of order,' she said. 'Your main loyalty should be to me.'

'My main loyalty's to what's right!'

'So is mine, but . . . what about what you said to Nicholas on Saturday night? About lives sometimes having to be sacrificed to defeat tyranny. Doesn't the same apply to truth?'

'Oh, come on! The only tyranny here is you and Eve taking it upon yourselves to conspire against this poor woman who's probably very nice. You're acting like a pair of hairdressers. How can you dislike someone you haven't met?'

'You're happy enough to dislike Grab-a-ditch Caravan and his pals.'

'Don't be stupid, that's not the same.'

'Yes it is. You can dislike someone because of what you know they've done. I know Rory's upset Eve – that's good enough for me.' Sometimes it was positively disloyal to be objective.

'Don't even think about lying to Campbell, all right?' For once Francis had the last word. Since Sim was unwilling to tell Campbell the truth – that she didn't want Rory Napper in her flat – she had no choice but to let Francis's arrangement stand. She couldn't risk doing anything that might make Campbell think of himself as a man in possession of a forbidden love. No fusses of any kind should be made about Rory, in case Campbell panicked and did something extreme in the name of heroism or romance. He might marry her, God forbid.

Sim wished that Francis understood. Her angle on Rory was not at all hairdresser-ish (not that Francis knew the first thing about hairdressers; every two months a drunken pensioner of Latvian extraction hacked at his neck and ears for five minutes in a city centre basement). Sim's attitude was far more complex than Francis gave her credit for. Of course she knew that in situations like this the Rory figure was not the thieving harlot any more than the Eve figure was the wronged saint. Nobody had stolen Campbell from anybody else; Campbell had chosen and the responsibility was all his. Rory owed Eve nothing. Sim firmly believed that it was impossible to care about someone you didn't know, and if you didn't care personally, no amount of abstract theorising about the rights and wrongs would sway you.

Sim didn't believe there was a woman on the planet who could honestly say she'd never go off with another woman's man. If you wanted something enough, it was understandable, forgivable even, to try to get it. Unfortunately Sim's open-mindedness on this matter was the cause of the problem, not its solution. If only she'd been more intolerant, a happily blinkered member of the moral majority, she could have spent a pleasant weekend directing vibes of strait-laced condemnation at Rory, muttering 'Slag!' and 'Homewrecker!' across the dinner table, and disloyalty to Eve would not have been an issue.

Sim only hated Rory because she was Eve's friend and Eve needed an ally, someone who would actively participate in vilifying the beast that had savaged her life. When Campbell described Rory as 'great', Sim did not contradict him, although she was inclined to think that Eve's interpretation was closer to the mark. Campbell's was too vague. He did not make Rory come alive as a character, whereas Eve conjured up a hideous frigid demon in whom it was difficult not to believe.

As long as Sim didn't meet Rory, it was possible for her to glide in and out of both perceptions of her, Campbell's and Eve's, as and when the occasion demanded. Rory herself didn't matter; all Sim cared about was her two friends and how they felt. All this was doomed to change as soon as she met Rory and had her own independent reaction to her. What if Vanessa was right and Eve's depiction of her rival was not a fair one? What if Sim liked Rory or, even worse, found that she had a magnetic, wondrous quality that vindicated Campbell's choice? Sim would not then be able to continue to give Rory a verbal shredding in conversations with Eve.

Quite aside from the matter of Rory herself, there was the added hazard of the impact that Campbell and Rory might make as a couple. What if they radiated a shining oneness, like Matt and Lucy? Sim had always thought Eve and Campbell made a good couple, but not so good that she couldn't imagine it being improved upon. She'd heard Eve make disparaging comments about Campbell's continuing studenthood and failure to bring in any money which had worried her at the time, and sometimes Campbell looked embarrassed by things Eve said, as if he thought her his intellectual inferior (although his idea of intellectual prowess seemed to consist of little more than the ability to deconstruct *Columbo*). And then there was the marriage-and-children power struggle.

It occurred to Sim that when a man anxious to avoid fatherhood runs off with a woman who won't have penetrative sex some might say it was more than a coincidence. She perked up a bit; at least if the frigidity thing turned out to be true it would firmly establish Rory as a laughing stock. Still, there was something distasteful about the whole dynamic, however gruesome Rory might be. Meeting her would make comparisons inevitable. It was revolting to subject Eve to that indignity, and more revolting still to come out in her favour in an aren't-you-the-lucky-one sort of way. Couldn't Campbell see this?

He was so wrong about wrongness, that was his trouble. Much as he probably regretted hurting Eve, Sim knew he'd kidded himself that he had no alternative, not once he'd started to have feelings for Rory. He would have told himself that leaving was fairer to Eve, kinder even, than lying to her, when in fact to leave someone was the ultimate insult, the final washing of hands. Campbell could have kept his infatuation to himself until it passed, or exorcised it with an affair the way Sim had with Andrew Johnson. Surely one owed that much to one's long-standing relationship; disloyalty of the groin was a minor offence compared with disloyalty of the heart and mind.

Not so minor, though, that Sim could forget it, put it from her mind for ever. She wished she hadn't been at Vanessa's that evening three years ago, when the smoke alarm started to wail for no apparent reason. Vanessa had phoned Renshaw College's Works department, who were on call twenty-four hours a day for just such emergencies, and the Toodle-pipster was dispatched to Gentchev's Field to sort out the problem.

He and Sim chatted flirtatiously while Vanessa hissed profanities. 'Are the smoke alarms in Cambridge so bored

196

that they go off every time someone misquotes Ovid?' she snapped. 'Fix it, will you.' Andrew fixed it. Two days later he and Sim were in bed together. The bed they were in was Sim and Francis's, which was Sim's biggest regret of all. Their flat felt contaminated after that, as if it wasn't quite theirs any more. Strangely, the same didn't apply to Sim; she was still entirely Francis's because she defined herself as such. The bed, having no consciousness, could not reject Andrew Johnson after the event, so his imprint and aura lingered, nestling in its springs and fibres. Sim had insisted on throwing it away when she and Francis moved to Saltaire.

The sex was disappointing. Sim phoned Vanessa the morning after the first time, anxious for a thorough analysis. 'I'm not sure it was normal,' she said.

'Well, don't ask me about that,' Vanessa replied caustically, stroking her bruised neck. 'I've only slept with Nicholas recently, and we know nothing of sexual normality. Why, what obscene, base practices did your paramour engage in?'

'No, nothing like that, but . . . I think he might have been a bit . . . small.'

'Small?'

'Yeah.'

'Oh, I see. What do you mean, you think he might have been?'

'Well, I didn't look too closely . . .'

'Sim, you fucked him. You must know if his knob's small.'

'No, I didn't get to touch it much,' Sim explained. 'He was too busy doing things. It sort of . . . stayed out of reach. I grabbed it a few times, but it slipped away before I could be sure about its dimensions.'

'I resent having to think about the man who balances my radiators in this context,' said Vanessa.

'It felt small when I touched it, though, even though it was . . . you know.'

'I do, more's the pity.'

'And when we did it, it was really weird. I could hardly feel it was there.'

'What? Don't be ridiculous. You must have felt it.'

'Yes, I felt it,' said Sim impatiently, 'but it hardly seemed to go in at all, if you see what I mean. I kept having to push myself closer to him to make it go in a bit more.'

'In that case he's very, very small. Unless Francis is immense and you're just used to a different scale of fuck.'

'No, I'd say Francis is about normal, the same as most people I've slept with.' And he'd probably object to this conversation more than he would to my affair, thought Sim.

'Well, Andrew must be tiny, then. Although . . .'

'What?' Sim had asked eagerly.

'Well, the size of a dick can feel different, depending on . . . you know, certain factors.'

'Like what?'

'Sim, don't push your luck. You must know what I mean.'

'I don't, I swear.'

'Well, tough. I've said all I'm going to say.'

'Oh, please, Vanessa. It might be crucial.'

'Oh, bloody hell! If you're not in the mood, you're likely to be less accommodating, aren't you? So it'll feel bigger because it has to push its way in. Whereas if you're lubricated . . .'

'Oh, I see. No. I know what you're saying, but while that might make someone seem narrower, it wouldn't make them seem shorter, would it? Think about it. If you're pressed up against the person, however lubricated you are, they'd still go in a certain number of centimetres. You'd feel how far they'd got, wouldn't you?'

'Thank you so much for giving me the unmissable opportunity to participate in this conversation. Yes, I suppose so.'

'And Andrew felt as if he was only just in.'

'Then he's small.'

'I'm not convinced. I keep thinking it must have been the angle, or some external factor. If he really was as small as he felt, surely he would have said something.'

'Like what?' Vanessa laughed.

'Like . . . I don't know, something to warn me.'

'What, like, "Beware, I have a very small penis"?'

'No, obviously not that. I don't know, it just doesn't add up. Blokes are notoriously self-conscious about cock size, aren't they? I can't believe that any man who was as small as Andrew is, if my impression was correct, would cheerfully enter into a fling and allow his inadequacy to be revealed. I mean, wouldn't he have some sort of complex?'

'Maybe he's exceptionally confident. Look, Sim, much as I'd love to discuss Andrew's knob for a few more hours, I have to go. I'm in the middle of a meeting with an author.'

Sim smiled, cheered by this memory, especially the idea of the poor writer who'd had to hear Vanessa's side of the dialogue. She imagined Saul Bellow or Anita Brookner waiting patiently while Andrew's dimensions were debated, and laughed out loud. That conversation with Vanessa had been the highlight of her fling with Andrew, come to think of it.

Sim undressed and got into her lavender bath. Francis would be back soon, having picked up Campbell and Rory from the station. Very shortly, Rory Napper would be in her home and there was nothing Sim could do, which topped her list of least favourite situations.

Still, she couldn't deny that she was curious. Much as she feared the weekend's ramifications, it would be fascinating to observe Campbell in a new context, one in which he felt he was more effectively offset. And at least Eve had approved the whole thing, which made Sim feel slightly better. She'd even expressed a certain degree of enthusiasm, keen to hear Sim's impression of Rory and to be reassured that Campbell's mental condition was stable.

The phone rang. 'Great,' Sim muttered, clambering out of the bath. She ran to the hall, dripping water and lavender-scented foam over Francis's files, notebooks, chewed pen lids and other assorted carpet sculptures. Serves him right for being so messy, she thought.

'Hello?'

'Sim? It's Eve. Guess who I've just had on the phone?'

'Rory Napper?'

'No. Campbell's mum, Sheila. She and Mark have met Rory. And guess what? It's official. She's awful!' Eve announced with glee.

Leeds station was cold, grey and noisy. Campbell stood in a pool of slush, shifting from foot to foot, waiting for Francis's car to zoom into view. He was nervous about explaining why Rory wasn't with him, and debated whether to tell Sim and Francis the truth or invent a more palatable lie.

His encounter with Neil Temple in the alleyway yesterday preyed on his mind. Eve had phoned him on Wednesday to say that as they'd split up it would make sense to sell the house. Campbell couldn't bear the thought of doing this. He'd told her gruffly that he wasn't sure and wanted at least to talk about it first. Eve had a free period the following morning so she told Campbell to come round and they could have a chat about it. It was on his way to this chat that he bumped into Neil, the treacherous bastard, sneaking out of the back gate and into the alleyway, buckling his belt as he hurried away, pretending he hadn't seen Campbell. So he'd spent the night and, knowing Campbell was due to arrive any minute, Eve had sent him out the back way: how sordid. It was pure chance that their paths crossed. Normally Campbell would have walked down the road, but he'd been daydreaming and missed his bus stop and the alleyway was the quickest way of getting to the house from the other end of Rusholme.

Neil was quite astonishingly out of order. Campbell

wouldn't have thought him capable of such trespass. Didn't Eve see what sort of a person Neil was, the sort that would nick a mate's girlfriend the minute his back was turned? The Toad, Campbell's friend from *Neighbours*, would never do that. Campbell was furious with himself for being a deluded, trusting dupe. No wonder Neil hadn't returned any of his recent calls. Campbell had assumed he was busy. Instead, all along, Neil had been plotting to steal Eve, distancing himself from Campbell to put an innocuous gloss on what he was trying to do so that by the time his betrayal was complete, it would no longer be a good friend he'd betrayed. That Campbell had left Eve rather than the other way round was no excuse. Neil should have realised that it took far more than the act of ending a relationship to end a relationship; there was a sense in which Eve was still Campbell's and always would be.

Still, if Rory turned up tomorrow, everything could still be okay. What bothered Campbell more than their separate arrival was the knowledge that he would spend between now and tomorrow afternoon worrying that Rory would fail to arrive altogether.

He assured himself this was unlikely. He'd spent what felt like hours on the phone to National Rail Enquiries, planning her travel schedule in detail. He'd spent what really was hours – an hour and twenty minutes, to be exact – on the phone to Rory this morning, explaining to her about the necessity of changing trains ('No, there isn't a direct service from Knightsbridge to Saltaire. You'll have to change twice. Yes, fifteen means three').

Campbell couldn't believe that Rory, with her background and advantages, was flummoxed by the twenty-four-hour clock. He'd suggested that, if getting the train presented too much of a problem, Rory could drive to Saltaire, but this provoked shrieks of dismay. She'd accused him of being unsupportive: didn't he know that her back seized up if she spent too long in a seated position?

'Could a Mr Campbell please come to the information

desk?' an amplified female voice boomed, filling the station concourse with its echo. 'Mr Campbell to the information desk. Thank you.' Campbell jumped, assuming immediately that he was the one being summoned. People often mistook his first name for a surname. He looked quickly to his left and right, feeling as if everyone was watching him, wondering why he alone had been chosen. What had he done? As unobtrusively as possible, he approached the information kiosk.

'I'm Campbell,' he said to the girl behind the desk, hoping she couldn't smell his T-shirt, which had acquired an unpleasant odour after he'd left it for too long in the washing machine, scared to return to the utility room until he was sure all the house's other residents were out.

'Pardon?' The girl looked at him with distaste. Campbell didn't blame her. He'd passed the mirror this morning and yelped with shock; the transmutation of his upper lip into a borderless expanse of chafed flesh was complete. He hoped this wouldn't put Rory off him, or that Sim had a magic cream that would cure him tonight, before Rory arrived. (She'd have to volunteer it, though; Campbell didn't like to ask.) God, he couldn't stand to lose Rory, especially if Eve was with Neil now. What would he be without her? Rory was a Napper. Yes, *the* Nappers, Campbell had told his own less famous relatives. He'd liked the idea of being linked to such a prestigious family, possibly even marrying into it. It'd show Eve, for doubting his ability to achieve anything. But now that he was officially Rory's man, he still didn't feel like a success, like a person who'd made it. Rory never seemed to have any money when Campbell was with her, although she bought jumpers for £400 and boasted about not having to do a day's work in her life if she didn't want to. Campbell thought it was a bit mean of her to keep her wealth and privilege to herself when he had nothing. Wasn't love supposed to be about sharing?

'I'm Campbell,' he said, sticking out his lower lip, which

202

was still presentable. 'You asked for me.' The girl looked blank. 'Well, someone did. That voice . . .' He pointed upwards.

'Oh, right.' She yawned and picked up a piece of paper from the desk in front of her. 'Message for you. Francis is supposed to be picking you up?'

'Yes.' Campbell blushed, hoping the girl didn't think he was gay.

'He'll be half an hour late, but you should wait in Starbucks, have a cappuccino, and he'll collect you from there when he's ready.'

'He said all that?' Campbell asked, confused. Why would Francis want to tell him what to drink? Campbell found himself suddenly in the grip of his recurring panic. Leeds station was peopled with Eve's spies. Did she know Campbell had seen Neil? Was this her revenge?

'No, it was a woman who phoned.' The girl in the kiosk consulted her notepad. 'Sympathy?' Campbell felt beads of sweat break out where his upper lip used to be. Was this railtrack employee offering him her pity? Did he look that badly in need of a shoulder to cry on? Maybe Sim would give him twenty quid for a haircut and a new T-shirt . . .

An alternative occurred to him. 'Sim Purdy?' he asked.

'Must have been that, yeah.' Campell beamed with relief. So nothing sinister was afoot. He didn't need to worry; he could relax and have a coffee while he waited for Francis. Everything would be all right: Rory would come tomorrow and as for Eve and Neil, well, it was probably just a one-night stand. Doubtless Eve was blushing about it already. Neil wore shirts with elbow-length sleeves, for Christ's sake.

Campbell eyed Starbucks dubiously, then decided to flick through magazines in John Menzies instead. There was no room for complacency. In all probability there was no one out to get him, no one who had been assured that a man fitting his description could be found at a Starbucks table in the coming half-hour, but it wouldn't do any harm, Campbell thought, to take a few elementary precautions.

Neil looked good in a suit. His orange hair worked well as the one splash of colour against the black jacket and white shirt. He should wear that outfit to the wedding, thought Eve, making a mental note to tell him. She listened as he delivered his speech about Imogen's poem to a tired headmistress who, at this hour on a Friday afternoon, would much rather have been on her way home than stuck in her small, airless office listening to the concerns of two members of staff.

Neil had offered to do the talking and Eve had agreed eagerly. As a law teacher, she'd joked, he ought to know how to build a convincing case. She needn't have worried. Neil's tone was so reasonable and engaging that it was bound to make anyone who failed to be won over by it question their own soundness of mind.

Claire Morgan, Camborne Street's headmistress, was a thin, middle-aged woman with hennaed red hair that was always grey at the roots. She frowned as she listened to Neil. Imogen's poem was in front of her; she glanced at it from time to time and sighed. When Neil had finished speaking, she shook her head sadly. 'It's a very good poem, but I don't see that there's a lot I can do. Phyl Banborough, as a legitimate judge, decided the poem didn't deserve a prize. I can't overrule her and award a second prize to a poem she disqualified.'

'Of course you can't.' Neil nodded understandingly. 'But what if we approach this from another angle? You appointed three judges: Phyllida, Walter and Eve. I've read the competition rules . . .'

'You have?' Claire Morgan smiled tightly and a mesh of lines appeared round her mouth. 'I'm afraid I can't say the same. They were drafted by my predecessor years ago.'

'Well, the rules say that in a situation where the judges'

verdict is not unanimous, a majority of two to one is acceptable.'

'I see. I assume Walter knows nothing of this?' She looked at Eve, who started to shake her head.

'He does, actually.' Neil's tone was a subtle blend of apology and smugness. 'I showed him the poem yesterday . . .'

'You did?' said Eve, cross that he hadn't told her. What if Neil turned out to be like those men in the sort of crappy TV movies Campbell and Sim liked, charming strangers who seemed too good to be true at first but quickly became control freaks who bugged their girlfriends' telephones and shot all their friends on the back porch? Neil grinned at Eve and winked, and her irritation dissolved. He'd wanted to impress her with his revelation, that was why he didn't tell her beforehand. And Imogen's poem wasn't Eve's property or business any more than it was Neil's; Eve told herself to stop being paranoid. Just because she'd slept with Neil a few times didn't mean he was going to mutate into a psychopath. If anything, he was becoming gentler, more considerate.

She was impressed by how unselfish he was in bed, how much time he was willing to devote to . . . Eve banished this thought, feeling her face heat up. The head's office was no place for sexual reminiscences. But what if Neil's considerateness in this department, his concern for Imogen – everything, in fact – what if it was just an act, designed to make Eve fall for him?

'Walter said he was happy to see "Memories" awarded a joint first prize,' Neil told Claire.

'You've clearly done your research,' she said. 'I'll have to dig up the rules and have a look at them when I've got a minute.' Eve guessed that it took considerable self-control on the head's part not to add 'whenever *that* might be'.

'I've got them here.' Neil opened his briefcase. 'I've highlighted the relevant sections.' He had? Was this what people meant by 'masterful', Eve wondered. Her life had been distinctly lacking in male masterfulness so far, so it was hard to tell.

Neil passed the papers to Claire, who was shaking her head within seconds. 'No, it's no good, Neil. No can do.'

'Why not?' Neil asked, without a trace of anger or disappointment, as if he'd expected this reaction. Eve wondered if he ever got upset. Would he take it equally calmly if she told him she wanted to go back to being friends? Eve didn't think that was what she wanted but it was hard to be sure. For the past week, emotions had been rioting in her head and she couldn't seem to bring them to order.

'The majority of two rule only applies at the final stage,' said Claire, 'after each of the three adjudicators has got his or her initial allocation of entries down to a shortlist. But Phyllida didn't put Imogen Salt's poem on her shortlist, so officially it shouldn't even have reached the other two judges.'

'I've anticipated this objection,' said Neil, to Eve's amazement. Again, she wondered if he was simply showing off, before telling herself that wasn't fair; he'd seemed genuinely concerned about Imogen and her poem from the start. 'And I think I can answer it. If you look carefully you'll see that nowhere in these rules is it explicitly stated that the majority of two clause applies only to the shortlisted poems.'

'Yes, it is.' Claire Morgan looked at her watch and eyed her office door, as if planning an escape. 'Listen: "A third of the total number of entries will be given to each adjudicator, who will select a shortlist of between five and ten to show to the other judges. The winner will be chosen from a maximum of thirty poems which must have been read by all three adjudicators" . . . dur-de-lur-de-lur . . .' Eve smiled to herself. Claire used the expression 'dur-de-lur-de-lur' in the way that Campbell used 'blah blah blah', to signify the presence of something irrelevant that could be skipped over – usually, in Campbell's case, a letter from his credit card company threatening to take him to court or a warning from his supervisor that if he didn't get his act together he'd miss his PhD submission deadline. Neil said 'yar-dee-yar-dee-yar-dee'. Eve quite liked this expression and considered switching to it. There was no reason to stick to 'blah blah blah' now that Campbell had left her and she needed some form of abbreviation. Sim was the only person Eve knew who never skim-spoke and got annoyed if other people did, demanding to know what all the blahs stood for.

'"If there is any disagreement between the judges,"' Claire read on, '"the winner or winners may be decided by a vote, in which a majority of two in favour of any poem will make it permissible to award a prize to that poem."' She looked at Neil. 'How much more explicit could it be?'

'Okay, let's take this point by point,' said Neil. Eve tried to imagine Campbell taking anything point by point and failed. 'First, let me be candid. I agree with you, basically, that to award a second prize to Imogen on the basis of a majority of Eve and Walter would be against the spirit of these rules. Being intelligent people, we can all see what's intended. But if we take what's written here literally it's a different story. Listen: "A third of the total number of entries will be given to each adjudicator, who will select a shortlist of between five and ten, to show to the other judges." That happened, didn't it?' Eve and Claire nodded. 'So no rules broken so far. Right, next bit: "The winner will be chosen from a maximum of thirty poems which must have been read by all three adjudicators." Now, we know that whoever wrote these rules intended the maximum of thirty poems to mean the amalgamation of the three shortlists, but it doesn't explicitly state that.'

'Oh, Neil, this is absurd,' Claire snapped. Neil smiled at her with a slight frown around his eyes and forehead, as if he couldn't understand this sudden eruption of rudeness just when things seemed to be falling into place. 'Sorry,'

Claire muttered under her breath after a few seconds. Neil's silence had made her feel guilty. Quite right too, thought Eve, who by now had guessed what Neil intended to argue and was trying not to be too impressed.

'As long as there's nothing written down that says the maximum of thirty poems necessarily has to mean the combined three shortlists, Imogen's poem can get a prize. I don't know how many poems Phyllida shortlisted, but I know Eve had six on her list and Walter had seven on his. Even if Phyllida had her full quota of ten, that would still be a total of only twenty-three. All three of them have read Imogen's poem, therefore it falls within the category of "a maximum of thirty poems that have been read by all three judges". Now, there's obviously strong disagreement between said judges, which is where the last bit comes in: "The winner or winners may be decided by a vote, in which a majority of two in favour of any poem will make it permissible to award a prize to that poem." And we've got our majority – Eve and Walter.' Neil smiled almost apologetically and waited for Claire's reaction.

Eve couldn't help wishing she'd come up with this angle. She was the poetry prize judge, not Neil. She'd never have thought of this, though, not in a million years. Neil had no responsibilities as far as the competition was concerned and yet here he was, trying to save the day, making Eve feel negligent. She knew it was petty, but she felt competitive with Neil in a way that she never had with Campbell. She wasn't used to being the less dynamic and inspired one in a relationship. If that was what she and Neil were having.

After a few seconds and a raising of the eyebrows, Claire Morgan said, 'Let me think about it.' Neil stood up to leave and Eve did the same automatically, although she hadn't expected the meeting to end so soon. She couldn't help feeling deflated; she'd hoped for an immediate resolution. Neil gathered together the documents he'd brought with him and put them back into a blue file, on which Eve noticed he'd written 'Imogen Salt/Poetry Competition'.

'Forgive me for saying this,' said Claire as they were about to leave the room, 'but isn't it a big fuss about nothing? It's only a piffling school competition. What does it matter, really?' Neil, whose hand had been on the doorknob, turned and walked slowly back to Claire's desk, even though he could have answered her from where he was. The deliberate symbolism of his gesture implied that Claire's question had been unhelpfully retrogressive, undoing all the progress the three of them had made.

'I think it matters,' said Neil, 'in the sense that everything does. If we don't fight little injustices, how are we ever going to work our way up to challenging big ones? One of our pupils has done something excellent. We're always going on about excellence in this school. I'll feel like a fraud if we don't ensure this piece of work gets the reward it deserves. I agree, the stakes are relatively low, which is all the more reason for us to act. There's a clear benefit and no cost. Whereas if we ignore this, what do we do when a bigger problem comes along, something more difficult to resolve? We've got to start as we mean to go on, or else we'll always give in to the temptation to do nothing.'

'Okay, I get your point.' Claire looked peeved. 'Leave it with me.'

Once they were out in the corridor, Eve turned to Neil and stared at him, open-mouthed. 'Wow!' she said. 'I feel as if I should salute you.'

'Don't be silly.' He grinned, pleased with himself. 'Just address me as "Oh, Captain, my Captain" in future, that'll be sufficient.'

'But, Neil, I didn't have six poems on my shortlist. I had ten.'

'Yeah,' Neil whispered, looking over his shoulder. 'And I've no idea how many Walter had. But if Claire agrees to our proposal, you had six, okay? That still leaves room for Imogen's.'

'Neil!' Eve laughed. 'Isn't that a bit corrupt?'

'That depends whether you believe in natural justice or

institutional justice. Look, I've got to go and get my bag from the staffroom. Meet you in the car park in a few minutes?'

Eve nodded, thinking that she could definitely fall in love with Neil, given time. Something had slotted into place in her mind when she heard him tell Claire Morgan that everything mattered. That was what Sim was always saying. Could it be true? Perhaps life was like a sea with two shores: one good, one bad. Every little event, each tiny action, pushed the tide ever so slightly in one or other direction. The more small victories good won over evil, the more the sea pushed towards the good shore. Eve blushed, embarrassed to be having such a hippy-ish idea. Anyway, it was more complicated than that. If Imogen got her prize on the strength of Neil's lie, wouldn't it be a contaminated triumph at best, a bit like winning Campbell back after he'd sullied himself by associating with Rory Napper?

Eve decided she disagreed with Sim and Neil. Everything couldn't matter; it would make life impossible, far too complicated. Some things had to be discounted, overridden, in order for people to move forward. Eve couldn't at the same time want Campbell back and want a new life with Neil. She felt as if there were no answers, only questions. I'm turning into Campbell, she thought.

Opposite Hazel on the train, a purple-nosed man and a cackling woman were drinking Special Brew and exchanging slurred insults. Hazel tried not to look at them. Unpredictable drunks were among her least favourite people. She was used to seeing them on the last trains, the 11.06 or the 11.36 from Leeds to Saltaire, but the afternoon trains normally contained no one more frightening than Francis, who growled at Hazel about the primitive wagons that serviced the Leeds to Skipton line before burying his face in the *Daily Telegraph*.

This was the first time in two weeks that Hazel had left work at a reasonable hour. The 'Voices in the Aire' festival was in progress, which meant evening events almost every night. Hazel was so tired that she felt she might suffer a stroke. She wished she could be more like Ian. His job was far more demanding, yet he never seemed stressed or allowed himself to be ground down by it, and was efficient enough to get everything done between Monday and Friday, leaving weekends free for hikes and fishing trips. He always invited Hazel, but she was scattier than Ian and spent most weekends getting right the things she'd got wrong during the week.

Hazel would have liked to have a photograph of Ian to keep in her wallet and show people, pretend he was her husband. A horrible thought struck her: what if Ian got married one day? How would she cope? She'd be tempted to say she never wanted to see him again, that it would hurt her too much, but how could she? Given the nature of their relationship, it would make no sense to Ian. Hazel wouldn't be able to break off all contact with him without confessing to how she felt. Which, of course, she could never do.

The man opposite her belched loudly and Hazel peered into her handbag to avert her nose from the fumes. Damn, she still had *Howdy* by Cal Raynard. She'd promised to send it to Eve first class today, but had forgotten to post it. She'd decided not to buy Lucy and Matt Cal Raynard's collected works as a wedding present. They weren't big readers, either of them, and she couldn't bear to think of her favourite novels being neglected. She'd have to think of something else.

Hazel took the book out of her bag and held it in front of her face as protection from her unsavoury travelling companions. It fell open at the back. She ran her finger over a jagged ridge of paper. How odd. A page had been torn out. It wasn't part of the novel but one of the end pages that were normally used to promote the publisher's other titles. Hazel took a closer look at the stump that ran all the way down the length of the book, puzzled that

211

she hadn't noticed it before. It nestled between a page of reviews of *Cloudy* and its blurb, and an advertisement for a novel called *The Gazebo* by Javier Galan. Hazel always read the adverts in books, especially books she'd enjoyed, in case they led her to other good things. She recognised the blurb of *The Gazebo* so she must have seen it before, when she'd got to the end of *Howdy*. She would have noticed the missing page then if it had been ripped out already.

But how odd. No one had touched *Howdy* apart from her. Unless Ian had looked at it while she was out. Hazel's heart jolted as she remembered how strangely he'd acted when she first brought the novel home. He'd started to flick through it, then stopped abruptly. His face had turned white but he'd denied anything was wrong. Could the page that was now missing be what had offended him? Had he ripped it out when Hazel wasn't looking?

She shivered, wondering why Ian would hide something from her. He obviously doesn't like me as much as I like him, she thought sadly. She would never have defaced a treasured possession of Ian's. Wasn't it bad enough that the publishers had defaced it with the wrong title and cover?

There had to be an explanation. Perhaps Ian had seen something on the missing page that he desperately needed, although Hazel couldn't imagine what. And why couldn't he have bought his own copy instead of attacking hers? At least he hadn't torn a page out of the body of the novel; that would have been unforgivable.

Hazel felt as torn as her book. She adored Ian, and didn't want to think badly of him, but she couldn't dismiss an attack on her treasured Cal Raynard, to whom she also wanted to be loyal. She wished she'd made this discovery while she was still at work. She could have nipped out to Waterstone's and examined a pristine copy of *Howdy* to establish what was missing from hers. Now she would have to wait until tomorrow. It didn't occur to her to ask

Ian straight out; he would have every right to be furious with her for accusing him, invading his privacy.

Why can't I trust him, thought Hazel, and leave the matter alone? Her natural inclination was to run away from anything mysterious in case the explanation turned out to be too scary, but because this involved Ian she had to know. Please let it be something minor, she prayed.

'Francis? Where are you?' Sim was still in the hall, naked (though she never felt more dressed than with a phone at her ear), surrounded by a pool of lavender-scented water.

'In the car, on my way to pick Campbell up.' She heard road noise in the background so she believed him. Francis had been known to pretend to have left work when he hadn't and not realise he'd been rumbled even when someone stood beside him and said loudly, 'See you in the editing suite in five.' 'What do you want?' he asked.

'To check you weren't still in the office. I know you find it hard to drag yourself away and it's a bit much to keep them waiting for over half an hour. Even if one of them is Rory Napper.'

'I left as soon as I could and it wasn't soon enough,' said Francis angrily. 'The Dingleys were smuggled in by police escort a couple of hours ago. I resent having to share a building with those murdering thugs.' Sim didn't respond. What Francis was saying couldn't be true, not if Dale was a friend or lover of Hazel's. A small doubt lodged itself in Sim's brain. Francis sometimes had good instincts about people, when he went so far as to notice them. But if Hazel believed Dale Dingley was innocent, he had to be. Oh, it was too confusing! Sim had been trying to get hold of Hazel all week, but according to her colleagues at Leeds city council she'd been spending an inordinate amount of time escorting a performance poet called the Throat Parrot around North and West Yorkshire. It was all most unsatisfactory.

'Anyway, one of them isn't Rory Napper,' Francis went on. 'She's not coming . . .'

'Well, that's probably just as well, because . . .'

'. . . until tomorrow. What was that?' Francis shouted as a lorry passed in the background.

'I said it's probably just as well. But you say she's coming tomorrow?'

'Yeah.'

'How come?'

'I've no idea, Sim. Ask Campbell. What were you about to say?' his voice crackled as his phone's signal grew weaker. 'Why would it be better if she wasn't coming?'

'I've just had Eve on the phone with confirmation of Rory's horrendousness.'

'Eve is hardly an impartial witness.'

'No, but it isn't only her opinion any more. Sheila and Mark have both met Rory now and they both hated her. They think Campbell's made a big mistake.'

'That's interesting,' said Francis sarcastically. 'Who the fuck are Sheila and Mark?'

'Francis! Campbell's mum and his brother.'

'How the hell do you know their names?'

'Because I listen to people when they speak, Francis. Apparently Rory shouted at Mark for nearly an hour because he made a flippant remark about the Dalai Lama. And she does yoga and chants in the middle of the night. When Campbell took her to Sheila's, she demanded a room and a bed to herself, said she'd never sleep otherwise. In the end Sheila gave Rory her double bed and slept on the sofa-bed with Campbell. Sheila's got a nickname for Rory: she calls her Grimbelina.'

'Oh, God!' Francis wailed.

'What?' Sim was alarmed and pictured a truck heading for the side of his car.

'I don't want someone like that in my flat!'

'Francis, you were the one who made the arrangement.'

'That was before I knew this. Right, that's it.'

'What's what?' Sim didn't like the sound of this.

'You'll have to tell Campbell she can't come.'

'*What*? No way, Francis. If you don't want her here, you tell him. You were the one who said she could come.'

'All right, then, I'll tell him.' There was grim determination in Francis's voice.

'No, you won't. Francis, don't dare to say anything.' It was all very well for him to show a sudden interest in interfering in their friends' lives, but he had to learn the ropes. He wasn't yet qualified to butt in, any more than a keen Biology A level student was qualified to authorise a hysterectomy.

'I bloody will say something.'

'Oh, God. I wish I hadn't told you now.'

'I don't see why I should have to have a lunatic in my home. She made him sleep with his *mother*. Is she sick or what?'

'Francis, calm down. She won't turf us out of our bed.'

'Damn right she won't. If she doesn't want to share the spare bed with Campbell she can sleep in the bath. And if I find her doing yoga at four in the morning, I'll evict her on the spot. Any chanting, she's out.'

'Francis, calm down and be reasonable. We can't kick her out. She's Campbell's girlfriend.'

'That's his lookout.'

Sim took a deep breath. 'Now, listen,' she said. 'You're not to say a word against Rory to Campbell. You're not to criticise her in any way. Understand?'

'I'll say what I want,' Francis protested.

'But . . . oh, for God's sake!' Sim clenched her fist in frustration. 'Francis, you never want to say anything to anyone, so don't pretend that you're suddenly desperate to . . .'

'Sim, my battery's going. Look, I'll . . .' There was a loud beep and the line went dead.

*   *   *

Vanessa had spent another tedious day in her tiny office (she thought of it more as a hutch) at Gable Bazzard, surrounded by bright, glossy posters of books she wished had never been written. The phone rang and she picked it up with low expectations. 'Is that the Loch Vaness monster?' a well-bred voice drawled. Vanessa scratched her black nails across the surface of her desk and stuck out her tongue in disgust. 'It's Miff McGarvey here.' Great. Cal Raynard's bloody agent. Miff always addressed Vanessa as if she were a cute but infuriating dog. 'You can guess what I'm ringing about, can't you?' said Miff in her habitually languid tone. Vanessa wondered if she was phoning from a Turkish bathhouse. 'Callypoos is terribly upset.' The nickname was Miff's feeble attempt to win Vanessa's sympathy for her author. Vanessa had seen through this ruse months ago and had no trouble resisting it. Callypoos made her think of callipers, an image as abhorrent to her as all images of weakness. 'Absolute no to *Audi*,' said Miff. 'On no account. Over Callypoos's dead body. And mine.'

Vanessa hoped the dead body remark wasn't an idle threat. She couldn't stand Miff, who regularly boasted that she was the only person Cal would allow to edit his books. She wasn't even an editor. She'd been a landscape gardener before becoming an agent. Vanessa wished she'd fuck off back to her wheelbarrow full of manure. 'It's a good title, Miff,' she lied. 'Especially coming after *Cloudy* and *Howdy*. If he changes the pattern now it'll be bad for sales.'

'He insists his main character would never drive an Audi.' Miff's voice sharpened. 'He's abso*lute*ly a Saab man. And Callypoos is worried about future books. He's afraid it'll constrain his choice of subject if he knows when he starts writing that the titles have to rhyme. He might get writer's block.'

'Why don't we worry about that when it happens?' said Vanessa brightly.

'Novel number four, the one he's just started, is set in China,' Miff began enthusiastically and Vanessa immediately thought of Red-tooth. Since the accident, she'd developed an antipathy towards people of oriental extraction in case they turned out to be Red-tooth, whose features had become a blur in her mind. The passing of time certainly fuzzed things up; Vanessa had never realised quite how much until now. In the matter of who was in the road and who on the pavement, her memory grew more distorted with each day that passed.

Red-tooth, on the other hand, was experiencing no such doubts. Her husband had left several messages on Vanessa's mobile, saying 'I am trying to speak to Miss Vanessa. She run over my wife.' Aha, thought Vanessa, so now we're getting nasty. The Red-teeth's unshakeable belief in her guilt was beginning to piss her off. It was so easy to blame the driver of the heavier vehicle, so ethically lazy not to question one's own part in what had happened. Vanessa thought it highly unlikely that she would have driven out into the road without first checking for traffic on both sides. How many bloody times had she driven out of Gentchev's Field? Too many for her liking, and she always stopped at the point that divided the pavement and driveway from the road. Then she checked for traffic. The fact that she and Red-tooth collided before Vanessa had looked left and right had to mean, didn't it, that Red-tooth, stupid twat that she was, had been cycling on the pavement. 'You run over my wife' indeed!

Yesterday Vanessa had decided the matter had dragged on long enough. When her phone rang and the Red-teeth's number flashed up on the screen, she answered it in an estuary accent and announced that Vanessa was out of the country on business for at least the next three months. 'Oh. Thank you very much,' Mr Red-tooth had replied gravely. Surely now they'd give up.

Vanessa would consider herself cursed indeed if the

Red-teeth turned out to have the staying power of Miff McGarvey, who'd begun to coo about Callypoos's artistic needs. 'Why don't you tell him to ring me?' Vanessa interrupted the flow.

'We've been through this. He's a very private . . .'

'Person. I know. In that case, let him suffer privately.' What about Vanessa's privacy, her right not to be harangued by Cal Raynard's minions? It was all right for him, sneaking off to lead his reclusive life, pretending to be JD fucking Salinger while Vanessa was obliged to sit at the end of a phone all day, taking flak from Miff. Did Raynard think Vanessa was some unimportant flunky whom he could order around by remote control?

She loathed people who couldn't stand up for themselves. Red-tooth was as bad. If she wanted her taxi fares refunded, she should have been prepared to ask for them herself. If she didn't have the guts to do that, she deserved everything she got. The modern world was wet, that was its problem. Everyone wanted to be tucked in with a teddy bear at night and told that everything would be all right in the end. Well, tough: it wouldn't. At best we're all going to die, thought Vanessa. She wanted to ask Miff if she didn't think the three of them – Miff, Cal and Vanessa – should just forget about the business of writing and publishing novels, and proceed immediately to the glue factory. Instead, she said, 'Tell Cal either the book's called *Audi* or there'll be no book' and hung up, knowing she didn't have the authority to make a decision like that without consulting senior colleagues. But fuck it, quite frankly.

Nicholas sat opposite Gillian Kench in the Baron of Beef on Bridge Street, a dark cave of a pub where no one he knew ever drank. He was furious with himself for having agreed to meet her, but he'd been unable to ignore her second demented letter. Like the first, it was full of lower case 'i's and upper case 'U's, and exuded an atmosphere

218

of non-specific threat. Nicholas's anxiety had started to interfere with his work on his article, just when the Roman Polanski's foreskin approach was starting to pay off. He had to get this sorted out.

Talking to Sim last weekend had been anything but reassuring. She'd made it clear she believed there was no depravity of which Gillian wasn't capable. Comfortingly, she had little evidence to back this up, no more than Gillian's bad behaviour at that silly party last year unless there was something she wasn't telling Nicholas, and she'd sworn there wasn't. Still, he couldn't ignore her opinion. Women understood each other, which made her an expert witness. Vanessa had chipped in and said that Gillian always had a self-serving agenda that was pitifully transparent. Sim had agreed with the first part of this, but questioned the transparency. 'I still have no idea what prompted her to accuse me of ruining her life,' she said.

'She's far too thick to do any real harm,' said Vanessa.

'On the contrary,' said Sim. 'The only thing worse than evil with a brain is mindless evil.'

Nicholas had put her opinion and Vanessa's together, added his own experience of Gillian and figured out that she must want something from him. His plan was to see her once, find out what it was and tell her she couldn't have it, not on any account.

He'd arrived to find Gillian already in the pub, sitting at a corner table with a long red drink that looked like fizzy blood. He'd bought himself a pint of bitter, though he preferred white wine, wanting to look more macho than he was.

Gillian's mouth was outlined in purple this evening, and filled in orange. She was wearing a low-cut V-necked dress without a bra and looking even more like a crinkly-haired philistine than she had the last time Nicholas had seen her. Her hands kept straying to her cleavage, as if she was searching for a necklace that ought to be there.

Seeing no point in wasting time on small talk, Nicholas

blurted out the questions that had been keeping him awake at night, one after another. 'What do you want from me? Why do you keep writing to me? Why don't you write your "I"s and "You"s properly?'

'Ah, so you noticed that.' Gillian grinned.

'Of course I noticed it.' Nicholas searched her face for signs of sarcasm. Could she honestly have thought he wouldn't?

'So you know why, then.' Gillian folded her arms beneath her breasts, making them stick out across the table like a balcony. Nicholas leaned back. He could smell her skin, a faint tang that reminded him of urine and made him retch. 'Little i, big U,' she said. 'It's clear enough, Dr Nicholas Drogan.'

'It isn't clear to me,' said Nicholas.

'Think about the way things stand. In our relationship. That's a clue.'

'We haven't got a relationship! And I don't want one, not with you.' Nicholas realised he was shouting.

'Don't lie!' Gillian shook her head vigorously and her hair swayed. Today it reminded Nicholas not of mangled cassette tape but of crispy seaweed from a Chinese restaurant. 'How can you say that?' she sounded hurt. 'We've been friends for years, haven't we? In a few weeks we'll be at Matt and Lucy's wedding together, with all our other mates.'

'No . . . we won't. Not really. I mean, we may both be there . . .' Nicholas found himself in a frustrating predicament. He wanted to deny what Gillian had said about the two of them being friends, but technically he supposed she was right. Before Sim changed the rules, Nicholas had spent nearly every weekend in Gillian's company. Why had he allowed that to happen, when he'd never cared an iota about this woman? He'd accepted her as one of Vanessa's friends, but even Vanessa had mocked Gillian for as long as Nicholas could remember, calling her the village idiot. Was it Sim's fault? She was the one who made all the arrangements, the one who'd forced Hazel upon them, another 'friend' Nicholas couldn't care less about who called her house plants after foul right-wing cricketers who accepted bribes from the apartheid regime.

Nicholas wondered which of his friends he truly liked. His political comrades were no more than that; they'd never made any social advances. Francis was tremendously knowledgeable about current affairs and Nicholas found him stimulating company, but was he a nice person? Or Matt, another supposedly close friend? Nicholas didn't think he'd ever spoken to Matt about anything but sport. Of the whole bunch, Nicholas felt the most warmth for Campbell, who was genuinely kind-hearted and ideologically sound most of the time, apart from when he pretended to see Francis's point of view for the sake of fairness. Shit, Nicholas kept meaning to ring Campbell to check he was okay, but work and Gillian had pushed everything else out of his mind.

He sighed, deciding not to insist that he'd never regarded Gillian as a friend. There was no point in hurting her feelings unnecessarily. 'Look, Gillian, if this is a crush or something . . .'

'A crush!' She guffawed, her unrestrained breasts wobbling.

'Well, what's this about, then? You barge into my office . . .'

'My office.' Gillian gulped down a mouthful of her fizzy blood drink.

'What . . . what do you mean?'

'It was my office, until you stole it.'

'What?' Nicholas stared at her in amazement. 'Is that what all this is about?'

'Of course,' said Gillian. 'Don't pretend you didn't know.'

Nicholas exhaled slowly to calm himself. Now that he knew the crux of the problem and saw how patently absurd it was, he felt stronger. And a lot angrier. 'I did not steal your office, as you well know,' he said firmly. 'Your department moved out of the building and mine moved in.'

'That's a convenient way of putting it,' said Gillian quietly.

'It's the only way of putting it.'

'Frankly, your cavalier attitude makes a mockery of everything we've been through together, Nicholas. I *loved* that office. It was like a second home to me. It had sentimental value.'

Everything they'd been through? What, a few weekends of drinking and fucking pointless banter? Nicholas wondered whether Gillian really cared about the office, or if it was some sort of ploy. Perhaps she simply wanted to attack Nicholas and this was as good an excuse as any. 'Don't be ridiculous,' he said. 'Look, what do you want me to say?'

'You *knew* it was my office and you *deliberately* made sure you got it so you could lord it over me!' Her voice had become a wobbly squeal.

'Gillian, that's rubbish. I never even gave you a thought. My head of department assigned me your . . . that office.' Damn, that was a mistake. Gillian noticed it and her eyes glinted in triumph. 'I had no idea it was yours,' Nicholas went on. 'As far as I was concerned it was just any old office.'

'Liar! You knew I'd been booted out and you've been gloating ever since.'

'Gillian, that's completely untrue. It would never have occurred to me that you'd give a damn. University rooms are much of a muchness.'

'So you don't love it, then?'

'What?'

'You don't love the office?'

'Of course I don't . . . *love* it.' Nicholas winced. 'It's just a room. Look, this is insane. What about your letter? What does all that I-and-you shit mean? Why did you write Vanessa's name in capitals?'

'Because she's *so* important.' Gillian giggled nastily. 'Little i, big U.' She mouthed the words with mock laboriousness. 'As in I'm little, I've got nothing. You, the big man, you've got everything.'

'What? You're deranged. Leave me alone!'

'Don't be aggressive.' Gillian's face crumpled into a mask of hurt. Her expressions changed with alarming frequency; Nicholas could hardly keep up. Her purple and orange mouth drooped. 'I only wanted to ask you what you thought we should do. I wanted to resolve things before Matt and Lucy's wedding, so there wouldn't be an atmosphere.'

'Do?' Nicholas was confused.

'I see.' The hurt expression vanished and hard resentment took its place. 'You think this is enough? We've had a chat and that's it?'

Nicholas wished he'd brought Vanessa with him. She'd have known how to handle this. I'll tell her as soon as I get home, he thought. Vanessa would deal with this mess in two seconds flat. Having decided to delegate responsibility for the problem, Nicholas was keen to get away. 'Gillian, our departments have swapped buildings,' he said. 'There's nothing we can do about it.' He downed the rest of his drink in one.

'I see.' She sighed. 'Well, I had hoped we could resolve this amicably.' Her eyes flashed. The bitch was threatening him. Who the fuck did she think she was?

Nicholas's hurt pride took over and without thinking he said, 'Listen, I could get you sacked, you know. You're only a secretary, an illiterate one at that. If I tell my head of department . . .' He tailed off, unable to believe he'd just pulled rank like that, like some obnoxious Tory.

'Try it,' Gillian dared him. 'I'll say you tried to rape me.' She got up to leave, sticking out her red-stained tongue at Nicholas. 'I will, Dr Drogan. I never say anything I don't mean.' She marched out on her spiky stilt shoes. Nicholas wanted to run after her and shake her into taking it back, but felt dizzy, as if he might faint if he moved an inch. He sat alone at the table for a few seconds, then hobbled to the gents where he threw up his pint of bitter.

2

The best part of sleep, Sim had always thought, was the moment when you were on the verge of drifting off, conscious of how close you were to unconsciousness. It was at this moment precisely, at half past one in the morning on Friday night, the first night of Campbell's visit, that the phone started to ring.

Normally Sim would have tumbled out of bed and dashed into the hall to answer it, assuming someone had died. No one she and Francis knew was in the habit of phoning later than eleven o'clock. Tonight, though, she lay still. The machine'll get it on the next ring, she thought, knowing exactly who it would be.

Francis, who had been fully asleep, sprang into a seated position. His hair stuck out in triangular tufts all over his head and he squinted as he reached for his small rectangular glasses. He looked like a late, arty addition to the Sex Pistols. 'Shit . . . what . . .' he said, throwing back the duvet on his side.

'Don't bother, it's only Rory Napper from the planet Headcase,' said Sim drily. They listened to Francis's voice on the answerphone, followed by the beep. The machine was clearly audible from their bedroom even with the door closed.

'Um, hi, this is Vorvy, Campbell's friend again. Well, his girlfriend, actually.' There was a pause and a giggle. 'Can you answer the phone, Campbell? Camp-bell!' she trilled in a sing-song voice. 'Um, okay, I know some answerphones cut off if you stop talking, so I'm just going to talk and talk and talk until you pick up the phone. Tra la la la la! Boop de doop de doop. Oops, I hope I don't use up all the tape. Anyway, Campbell, answer the phone, I know you're there, so I'll just prattle on about nothing until you come and speak to me . . .'

As Sim's eyes adjusted to the darkness, she noticed that Francis's face was twisted with rage. She chuckled quietly. This was most satisfactory. Rory was doing a perfectly good demolition job on her and Campbell's relationship all by herself. At this rate, Sim wouldn't need to lift a finger. Even someone as sedate as Campbell couldn't put up with this level of unhinged self-obsession for another five weeks. Things would be back in order by the wedding: Eve and Campbell together, Rory and Neil abandoned like weapons that were no longer necessary.

Sim tried not to think about Hazel, whom she still hadn't succeeded in contacting. Whoever this Throat Parrot chap was, he seemed to require Hazel to carry his poems all over the county for the foreseeable future. Sim supposed that if Hazel was working even harder than usual, it had to mean she was coping, but the matter of Dale Dingley would have to be confronted sooner or later. God, if that crisis erupted just before Matt and Lucy's wedding . . . Sim forced her thoughts back to Grimbelina, who was infinitely more entertaining.

Francis had arrived back at the flat with Campbell in tow at about seven o'clock. They'd barely taken off their coats before Rory rang for the first time. Sim had asked Campbell why she wasn't with him and Campbell muttered something to the effect that Rory hated to rush. 'She said she needed this evening to deal with herself,' he explained with a puzzled frown, as if unsure what this might consist of. That was all the conversation they'd managed to squeeze in before the phone interrupted them. Sim had known who it was even then, and she'd suspected that this initial communication from the Napper would be the first of many. Calmly, feeling like someone in a rather good film, she picked up the receiver, excited at the prospect of hearing Grimbelina's voice for the first time. Now that the eyewitness accounts were in from Sheila and Mark Golightly, and Sim was confident she would loathe Rory, she couldn't wait to experience her first-hand.

She said hello neutrally, anxious not to prejudice her experiment by sounding either friendly or unfriendly. It didn't for a moment occur to her that it might be someone else, and she felt rewarded when the call turned out to be in keeping with the great Sim tradition, that of not being wrong.

'Is Campbell there?' a light, tinkly voice enquired.

'Yes,' said Sim.

'Could I speak to him?' Rory talked to Sim as she would have to the operator. Her words and tone in no way acknowledged that she was about to spend most of the weekend as a guest in Sim's flat.

Sim passed the phone to Campbell and dragged Francis into the living room in order to create the illusion that they were giving Campbell some privacy. As soon as she'd pulled the door closed behind her, Sim pressed her ear against it. She had no intention of leaving the Campbell-Rory dialogue unattended. She was a relationship scientist, involved in ground-breaking research, and it delighted her to think that her hall was shortly to be filled with primary evidence.

'Simone, remove your ear from that door right now,' said Francis wearily. Sim waved him away. 'No, I won't shut up,' he protested. 'There's something I want to talk to you about. You know, er, weddings?'

'Sh!' Sim waved him quiet and pointed towards the hall, in which Campbell was mumbling.

'Can I suggest that you leave other people's relationships alone and pay some attention to your own?' said Francis sharply, making for the kitchen.

Sim often wondered how Francis had managed to rise through the ranks of BBC researchers to his present position. It seemed to her that whenever he was presented with an opportunity to delve investigatively into the crevices of a situation, he wasn't interested; he would simply amble into the kitchen in search of a snack rather than put himself out to chase a new morsel of information. It wouldn't have surprised Sim to learn that the news she heard on the television and radio was a mere fraction of the whole picture, of what might come to light if ever someone who was genuinely curious were to be put in charge. It's no wonder, thought Sim, that Francis assumes the Dingleys are murderers. Then it occurred to her that Wayne Dingley, as far as she knew, was not absolved by any connection to Hazel and might well be guilty even if Dale wasn't, so perhaps Francis wasn't entirely wrong. That would explain why the police had found so much incriminating evidence in their house. Yes, the more she thought about it, the more likely that seemed.

While Francis assembled his favourite between-meals meal, a chopped-up green apple and a few small cubes of cheese, Sim stood still and listened. 'Yeah . . . yeah . . . no . . . okay . . . o*kay*,' Campbell whispered, as if he were talking to an invalid. 'No, it won't . . . Yes, they will . . . It'll be fine . . . No . . . *Yes*.' He seemed to be reassuring Rory and pleading with her at the same time. Sim couldn't hear Rory's end of the conversation, but it was hard not to draw the conclusion that she was in some respect being an immense pain in the arse.

Sim listened as Campbell tried, without much success, to bring the conversation to a close. Finally he managed it, and Sim made no comment when he strolled casually into the lounge, trying his hardest to look like somebody who had just taken part in an ordinary, common-or-garden phone call. Sim smelled denial all over him. He was trying to make the best of the situation because he assumed his choice was carved in stone. Sim guessed that Campbell felt he'd used up his one allotted change of mind when he left Eve and couldn't possibly allow himself another. Men, she believed, were far more defeatist than women when it came to solving problems. Francis would often step outside and say bitterly 'Oh, great, I'm going to get soaked' rather than go back upstairs to fetch an umbrella.

After that first call, Rory telephoned three times, not including this verbal midnight feast, her fifth communication of the evening. The second followed hot on the heels of the first – there couldn't have been more than ten minutes between them – and the third came at ten o'clock, just as Sim, Francis and Campbell were walking through the front door after having been out for a meal. Rory phoned again at half past eleven when they were in the middle of watching a video. Each time, it had taken more of Campbell's nos, yeses and okays to get rid of her. He was evidently embarrassed by her behaviour, but he determinedly made no apology for it, nor did he acknowledge that it was in any way unusual.

Sim took Campbell's lead and also pretended that a normal time was being had by all. Francis grew more irate with each call and Sim had to employ her best emergency calming techniques to prevent him from stomping off to bed in a huff. 'For God's sake, Francis, don't let Campbell see you're angry,' she hissed. 'The disapproval of one's friends is the most powerful aphrodisiac known to man. Don't push him closer to Grimbelina than he already is.'

'But these conversations don't seem to be achieving anything,' declared an aghast Francis, who could imagine nothing worse than an under-achieving conversation.

All in all, it had been a more than usually exhausting evening, and now the night looked set to follow suit. A thin strip of light appeared under Sim and Francis's bedroom door. They heard Campbell grab the phone and whisper, 'Rory, it's half past one, you know?'

'I've had enough of this,' said Francis. 'I'm going to have words in the morning.'

'No, you aren't, Francis,' whispered Sim, sitting up. 'Shush. I want to listen.'

'Why should I shush? It's Rory Napper who should be shushing. Who does she think she is, plaguing us with phone calls day and night? I'm going to tell her exactly what I think of her when she arrives. She's a complete succubus and a phoney. I can hear it in her voice. You know who she reminds me of, don't you?'

'Of course I do, but, Francis, this is brilliant, can't you see?'

'No, I can't. I was asleep and now I'm not. How is that brilliant?'

'Ask yourself this: why do you think Campbell hasn't apologised for Rory's constant telephonic harassment this evening?'

'He obviously doesn't give a shit whether I get any sleep or not.'

'You're wrong, Francis. He cares desperately. He's terrified that we're forming a bad impression of Rory.'

'We are!'

'I know. So to arm himself against our negative perception, Campbell's refusing to let himself acknowledge that Rory's done anything wrong tonight.'

'Of course she bloody has!'

'I know. But Campbell's got a romantic narrative in his head. It goes like this: things weren't working out with Eve. Campbell met Rory, who was special, and went off with her into the sunset. Happily ever after. Every time she inconveniences us, it's like another rock of reality hurled against his version of events and he's petrified it'll shatter. Campbell yearns for romance, Francis.'

'Well, for God's sake, don't say it in that way.' Francis looked alarmed. 'What do you want me to do about it?'

'Nothing. But he does, he yearns for it. That's why he wasn't happy with Eve: he found her too practical. She paid too much attention to the organisation of their day-to-day lives. She wanted to get married and have children and be an ordinary person who gets on with things. Campbell isn't ready to get on with things. Look how indecisive he is, how reluctant to settle down to finishing his thesis. He's looking for a way out, maybe some kind of lost youth. He wants to suspend time, escape to a kind of wonderland . . .'

'Sim, you don't know any of this.'

'. . . and he thinks Rory's his ticket to this lost world.'

'What lost world? What ticket?' Francis asked impatiently. 'You talk about these things as if every educated person ought to be familiar with them. I have no idea what you mean.'

'I mean, Francis, that Campbell's seeking the intangible. What Eve was offering him was a partnership that involved all levels of existence. Yes, they shared an emotional bond, obviously, but they also shared the bills and the housework . . . well, actually, they didn't, Eve always did more and paid more . . .'

'I'm bored of this.' Francis took off his glasses. 'I'm off to sleep.'

'. . . but the point is, Campbell couldn't handle that. Francis, I'm not saying all this to exercise my vocal cords, you know. I happen to believe it's important.'

'You think every fucking thing's important!'

'Precisely!' Sim hissed.

'Whereas earlier, when I wanted to talk to you about something I think is important . . .'

'Francis, tell me later, whatever it is. I need to follow this train of thought or I'll lose it. Where was I? Oh, yes. Campbell couldn't handle it. It made him feel too mundane, and inadequate as well because Eve was so much better at day-to-day life than he was. He wanted a purer love, a mystical partnership of souls. That's what he thinks he can achieve with Rory, but he's got it all wrong. She's obviously a complete disaster in every practical sense, so Campbell assumes she's on a higher plane. When in fact she's just on a crap plane.'

'Mm.'

'Deep down, of course, he senses the truth: that he's made a terrible mistake. That's why he can't risk apologising for her phone calls. On one level he knows his illusions about Rory are so frail that they couldn't withstand any sort of proper examination.'

Francis didn't respond. Sim could hear Campbell in the hall: 'No . . . yes, it will . . . no, it's fine . . . okay . . . okay . . . no . . . yesss . . . Rory, I've got to go. I don't want to wake up Sim and Francis . . . What? . . . Don't be silly . . . Don't be . . . Of course I don't prefer them to you.' Sim cheered silently; she could hardly believe her luck.

'For fuck's sake!' Francis sat up again. 'This is blatantly antisocial behaviour!' He tried to climb out of bed. Sim laughed and grabbed his arm so that he couldn't escape. 'Let go of me. I've had enough. I'm going to unplug the phone if that's what I have to do to get a decent night's sleep.'

'Francis, stop it.' Sim giggled. 'Did you hear what Campbell said before, about not preferring us to Rory? The woman must be demented.'

'I don't understand you.' Francis shook his arm free. 'What are you so pleased about?'

'The more conspicuously out of order Rory is, the happier I am. It puts pressure on Campbell to amend his view of her, to bring it into line with what he knows our view will be. Eventually the dream will deflate and then he'll go back to Eve.'

'But he's not even saying anything.' Francis was astounded. 'Why doesn't he tell her to pull herself together?'

'Obviously she has the power,' said Sim. 'The more irritating person in any relationship usually does, because the other poor sod will do anything to avoid being irritated any more than he or she has to be. Stiff competition, in our case.' Francis smiled reluctantly. 'Another difference, you see?' said Sim.

'No, I don't. Between what and what?'

'Between Campbell and Eve and Campbell and Rory.

Campbell was the more irritating out of him and Eve, on paper at any rate. Eve had ticks in all the right boxes: job, money, willingness to commit. But I bet Campbell told himself those boxes were meaningless social norms or something. He probably knew Eve would be perceived by many people as a better catch than him and resented it. He feels, innately, that he's the better one – you know, more cerebral, less conventional – and he couldn't live with the dichotomy.' Francis scratched his head. Sim could see he was impressed by her theory, but reluctant to admit it. 'With Rory, things are clearer,' she went on, encouraged. 'Campbell's got a less objectionable personality, and his lack of worldly success is less noticeable than hers because she's had all the advantages money can buy and still got kicked off her PhD course. She's drippy, needy and destined for failure – in every way the opposite of Eve, which is why Campbell chose her.'

'He can't think very much of Eve, then.'

'Of course he does. It's life he's afraid of, not Eve. Eve knows what she wants and that frightens him. He wants to be able to look down on it. It's essential to his well-being to believe that an aimless, self-indulgent amble through life is somehow the more sensitive, soulful option. It's a fear that he'll never achieve anything that's behind it, I'm convinced. That's why he picked Rory, who could never reasonably expect him to amount to anything because she plainly never will herself. Campbell thinks she's deep, with an inner life that elevates her above normality. And he's right to think she lives entirely within her own head, but that isn't because she has a heightened intellect or imagination, it's because she's pathologically self-absorbed and useless. Again, this suits his purposes. Eve is a person who notices other people, whereas Rory's aware of no one but herself. And Campbell doesn't want to be noticed.'

'What? What was all that?'

'Nothing, dear. Actually, it was something, but if you aren't paying attention . . .'

233

'The thing is, I generally lie on my side with my eyes closed for a few hours every night. I don't know whether you'd noticed that at all?' Sim laughed and hugged him. He smiled reluctantly, shaking her off.

'Francis? Sorry.'

'Oh, what now?'

'Do you remember when Eve adapted the lyrics of that "Do You Have a Girlfriend" song by Billie?'

'Who's Billie? Campbell's brother?'

'No, Billie the pop star.'

'Sim, please!'

'"Do you have a girlfriend?"' Sim began to sing in a whisper. '"You're looking real cool. Can I have your number? You don't have a pen, do you?" That was the bit Eve made up. The real lyric is "You don't have a thing to lose", but Eve thought "You don't have a pen, do you?" was better.'

'Oh, God,' Francis yelped through clenched teeth.

'That's what I call a heightened imagination,' said Sim. 'It's the little things, Francis . . .'

'Yeah, right. Whatever.'

It was Saturday morning and Hazel was the only customer in Waterstone's. She felt like a criminal as she gingerly approached the 'R' alcove in the fiction section. Fortunately, none of her literary event contacts seemed to be working today. She didn't have the emotional energy to make polite conversation. She hadn't slept well and had been standing outside the shop for half an hour this morning in the hope that someone would let her in before the official opening time of nine o'clock.

Hazel looked left and right, feeling like a double agent. What if Ian chose this Saturday to come into town? If he saw her pick up *Howdy* and turn straight to the back, he'd know she was checking up on him. I'm a doubting, niggardly woman, Hazel castigated herself. I'm the sort of person who would ask Chitty Chitty Bang

Bang if he had RAC cover before going for a magic ride.

Both Cal Raynard's novels were on the shelf. Hazel trembled, realising that she'd been hoping they wouldn't be – anything to defer the revelation. Assuming there was to be one. With shaking fingers, she picked up *Howdy* and opened it near the back. She found the advertisement for *The Gazebo* by Javier Galan. Bracing herself, she closed her eyes, flicked back a page, took a deep breath and looked, prepared for the worst, uncertain of what the worst might be.

Her cheeks puffed out with relief when she saw nothing more sinister than further praise for *Cloudy*, spilling over from the previous page of panegyrics. Nothing out of the ordinary; only the *Mail*, *The Times Metro* and *GQ* having their say. Puzzlement was beginning to set in when it struck Hazel that pages had two sides. She steeled herself and flicked.

Oh, thank God. Only an advertisement for another book: *His and Hers* by Debbi Naismith and Greg Pendry. Original paperback, £5.99. Hazel frowned and chewed her bottom lip. Ian had to have torn out this page for a reason. She turned back to the reviews of *Cloudy* and read each one carefully. Most were good but unremarkable. The only one that attracted Hazel's attention was the *Guardian*'s: 'A promising debut'. Some patronising oaf's idea of praise, she thought huffily. One only had to apply such a comment to *Wuthering Heights* to see how uncomplimentary it was. She wished reviewers would think in terms of individual books rather than writers' career trajectories, but this was her own personal *bête noire*. Ian wouldn't care what the critics had said about *Cloudy*. Hazel had lent him her copy and he'd delivered a harsher verdict than any of these papers and magazines. The style was sloppy, he said, quickly adding that he basically loved it when he saw Hazel's wounded expression. Could it be that Ian resented having to listen to her witter on about how wonderful Cal

Raynard was? Was he jealous? Hazel was embarrassed, knowing that buried somewhere in the recesses of her imagination was a fantasy about Ian and Cal Raynard fighting over her, each desperate to win her undying love and hand in marriage. But that was all it was, a fantasy. Ian had ripped out the page after seeing something specific that had frightened or shocked him; Hazel remembered the look on his face. Romantic rivalry had nothing to do with it.

She turned back to the *His and Hers* side of the page. Under the title and the authors' names, in jazzy lettering, hovered the quote 'the novel that grabs you by the short and curlies'. How revolting. Hazel read the blurb and a dark flush of indignation suffused her face.

When Annie and Rob meet at a party, they rub each other up the wrong way. But their private parts know better and have their own ideas about exactly what sort of rubbing up should take place. Join Annie the Fanny and Rob the Knob in their quest to bring their stubborn owners together, as they travel round the world, from Soho to Islington to Notting Hill. *His and Hers* is their story, a hilarious, heart-warming tale of secrets and secretions, of sobbing and throbbing, of groping and hoping. This novel will have you clitorally on the edge of your seat!

Hazel slammed *Howdy* shut. She was no literary snob, but the idea of this book offended her. Was nothing sacred? Vanessa would say not. Had Ian known how Hazel would feel about this thinly disguised pornography and torn out the page to protect her from its crassness?

This appealed, but did not quite convince her. Perhaps Ian knew one of the authors, Debbi Naismith or Greg Pendry. What if he was afraid he was in the book, unflatteringly portrayed? Poor Ian; that would be awful. The more she thought about it, the more strongly Hazel felt that *His and Hers* was the key, somehow. She'd have to buy it. Not here, though; what if it got back to one of her contacts that she'd bought such a lowbrow publication? No, she'd ask Sim to buy it for her. Sim often bought lurid, trashy books that were an insult to the great English literary tradition, claiming they were 'fun'. What naïve, short-sighted philistinism! *Potters Court* had dragged Sim down aesthetically. Hazel couldn't believe, sometimes, that she had a friend who had never read *Tristram Shandy*, or anything by Stendhal. That was a polytechnic education for you. Still, now wasn't the time to be snobby, when she needed Sim's help. Sim could breeze into a shop and buy *His and Hers* without feeling culturally abused, not being the . . . um . . . um . . . guardian of good taste for the whole north of England. What a grave burden to carry! What a weight upon mortal shoulders!

'I suppose you know about Eve's new boyfriend,' Campbell said to Sim after breakfast. He sat at the table, watching her back shake as she washed up. Francis had gone to work. The imminent Dingley interview entailed working seven days a week, apparently. Campbell, never having had a full-time job, couldn't imagine how a person could end up having to work every single day and not consider committing suicide, or resigning at the very least. He was appalled by what the world expected of its grown-up population.

He was having a bad weekend. In his dreams last night a creature with Eve's body and the head of an elephant had whispered, 'Business thrives means elephant lives' in his ear over and over again. It was Rory's fault for disturbing his sleep with her manic phone calls.

Campbell had been determined not to mention Eve and Neil, not to reveal how much he cared, but Sim hadn't brought it up and he was beginning to suspect that she didn't know. If Eve hadn't told Sim, it couldn't be that significant. Campbell prayed it was only a one-night stand, never to be repeated.

'What?' Sim's eyes widened. Then she grinned and said, 'Oh, you mean because she's bringing Neil to the wedding?'

'She's *what*?'

'Oh. You didn't know.' Sim looked apologetic, then amused.

'The . . . I can't believe . . .' Campbell didn't complete the sentence. Sim was watching him avidly, waiting to pounce. Okay, so he'd got Rory an invitation to Matt and Lucy's wedding, but that wasn't the same. He'd fallen in love with Rory. Eve was only doing this to get at him. Still, he bit back what he knew Sim would regard as a hypocritical remark. As if to reward him, she said, 'He's not her boyfriend. She's invited him as a friend.'

'So how come I caught him sneaking out of the back door the other day, when Eve knew I was coming round, doing up his fucking trousers?' Campbell embellished Neil's state of undress to highlight the injustice of which he, Campbell, was a victim. He wanted to incriminate Eve. Sim was less likely to feel sorry for her and demonise Rory if she knew that there was another man on the scene, especially one who snuck.

'But . . . Eve hasn't said anything to me.' Sim looked puzzled. For a moment Campbell feared she'd be angry. She liked to be kept informed. Campbell hated the thought of Sim being angry with Eve, even though he was livid with her himself, and was relieved when she said, 'Oh, well, I can understand why she hasn't. She's probably worried I'd think she was only seeing Neil on the rebound.'

'She obviously is on the rebound.' Campbell sneered, irritated by Sim's easy acceptance of the new man in Eve's life, by her lack of doubt. Perhaps Neil had only looked guilty because of how he knew it would appear to Campbell. I'll break the fucker's legs at the wedding, he thought, wishing he were the sort of person who could carry through such a resolution.

'Not necessarily,' said Sim. 'It's not as simple as that.'

'Yes, it is.' Campbell knew how dogmatic he sounded, but he was damned if he would let Sim rob him of all his comforts: first the idea that nothing might be going on, then his rebound certainty. 'Eve never showed any interest in Neil before we split up. He was my squash partner. He meant nothing to her, just some colleague. It's pathetic! She's so desperate not to be single that she grabs the first person who comes along.'

'Don't you think there might be more to it?' Sim suggested. 'When the things you value most highly turn out to be worth nothing, what choice do you have? You either write off your whole life as a disaster or you create a new value system. Eve's a strong character, so she's done the latter.'

'She's not a strong character,' Campell protested. Why did no one ever challenge Sim? Not in a minor way, as he was now, but properly, fundamentally. No one ever demanded that Sim account for the vast amount of knowledge she claimed to have. Where did she get it all from? Campbell wanted to see the paperwork. He wanted to prove that Sim's wisdom was laundered or counterfeit. 'She can't bear to be on her own so she takes up with a random teacher. What's strong about that? And even before I left, she wasn't strong then either. All the time we were together she made life too easy for me, you know? She didn't have any desires of her own. All she cared about was keeping me happy. She never expressed an opinion until she knew my opinion. We always did what I wanted.'

'Darling, it must have been hell.' Sim smiled.

'I'm serious. That's one of the things I like about Rory. If she thinks I'm talking crap she'll say so. She doesn't pander to me.'

'But do you pander to her?'

'Well . . .'

'Because I agree that the ideal situation is no pandering from either party.' Sim allowed an ominous silence to

239

reign for a few seconds. 'Did you ever say this to Eve?' she asked.

'No.'

'Why not?'

'Probably because I wanted to have my way,' said Campbell. 'For a while. But it wasn't healthy. Eve should have resisted my will, you know?'

'I can think of occasions when she did,' said Sim.

'Such as?'

'When you announced your intention to leave. She did everything she could to persuade you to stay, on almost any terms. And she didn't give in about marriage and kids.'

'But she should have backed down on that. That's the sort of thing that she was ridiculously stubborn and unreasonable about. But other times, when I'd pester her to express a slight preference – Indian or Chinese, a pint or the pictures – she'd have no opinion, she'd . . .'

'Campbell.' Sim eyed him sternly. 'Eve's easygoing. That's not the same as being weak.'

Campbell shook his head. 'If she really liked Neil, she'd have the courage of her convictions. She wouldn't care what anyone thought. She'd have told you by now, definitely. The idea that those two have got together – it makes no sense!'

'It makes perfect sense,' said Sim lazily, stroking her coffee cup. It infuriated Campbell that she evidently felt so little effort was necessary in order to be more right than him. 'You know what you sound like? The endless letters of complaint we get at work about *Potters Court*, people saying it's not realistic that such and such a character who used to be straight is suddenly gay, or that someone who used to be a mugger is now a magistrate. But of course it's realistic. However much we like to think of our personalities as fixed, stable things, the evidence suggests otherwise. And the more dramatic a life crisis is, the more it can change us. That's what's happened to Eve. You rejected her. If Neil appreciates her and makes her feel wanted again, what's wrong with that?'

Campbell tutted. 'She's making do. She never gave him a second thought before.'

'The key word is "before". Look, let's take an analogy. If one day you went into Marks & Spencer to buy a shirt and they told you that a new law had been passed and money was no longer a valid form of payment, what would you do?'

Campbell sensed that a lot depended on his answer. What would he do? He couldn't think. 'Nothing, I suppose,' he said. 'Not buy the shirt.'

'Not buy the shirt?' Sim repeated seriously.

'Well, I couldn't, could I? If my money was worth nothing.'

'Right, but . . . more generally, what might you do?'

'I don't know, Sim. Try to forget about the shirt. Maybe I never liked it that much in the first place.'

'No, no.' Sim waved an impatient hand at him. 'Don't get too fixated on the shirt. The point is that if money's suddenly worthless, pretty soon you're going to have to come up with an alternative way of getting what you need. Maybe you can pay with something else. Let's say you've got a goat at home. You might be able to swap that for your shirt. The woman on M & S's shirt counter will need to find another way of getting milk, if she can't use money. See what I'm saying?'

'No.' Only someone on LSD would, surely.

'You're the money. Neil is the goat. It may not have occurred to Eve to pay by goat before because she always had money. But now she hasn't. You know, to a certain extent, Rory's also a goat.'

'What?' Campbell didn't like the sound of this.

'I think it's interesting', said Sim, 'that you see Eve turning to Neil as desperation when you and she have done exactly the same thing. Each of you, in some way, was made unhappy by the other and you both found new people who you hoped would make you happier.'

'It's totally different! It's not the same at all,' said Campbell frantically. He knew he was less adept than Sim at articulating his thoughts but it seemed imperative to make the effort now. 'I met someone who I . . . who I thought might be . . . well, was – is! – better. Eve's deliberately chosen someone she knows is worse because she couldn't have the person she really wanted, you know?'

Sim stared at him. Campbell blinked a couple of times, trying to convince himself that he hadn't just said something incredibly mean. 'So one's a grand passion, the other's desperation?' Sim summarised.

'Something like that,' said Campbell defensively.

'And are you sure it wasn't partly desperation that led you to Rory?'

'I had Eve.'

'But you might have been desperate to avoid facing some seemingly insoluble problem in your and Eve's relationship. Or desperate to blame a more general sense of unease on one specific area of your life: Eve.'

'No,' said Campbell flatly. 'That isn't it. That wasn't it at all.' Ah, yes, now he saw. This was the way to deal with Sim. Give her too many words and she'd twist them to suit her own interpretation. The best policy was simply to tell her she was wrong without specifying how or why. It was possible to do that and reveal very little of oneself. Campbell intended to deprive Sim of the raw materials for analysis.

'So Rory's better, is she? Than Eve?'

If Campbell could have said yes to this, the matter would have been dealt with once and for all. But he couldn't bring himself to say it. Sim saw that she had the upper hand and built on it by adding, 'I mean, you've been listing all Eve's faults, but what about Rory's? Another coffee?'

'Yes, please. Rory's nice, okay?'

'Is she perfect?' Sim rinsed out the cafetière. Water

242

glugged down the sink. Campbell felt a pang of longing for his own kitchen, for the sight of Eve washing up. Like Sim, she rinsed everything in hot water after washing it. Campbell favoured the dunk and drain approach. The soap suds slid off eventually; what was the problem? He and Eve had argued about so many trivial things for so many years. In a way Campbell was glad that real pain and anger had replaced the niggling; it made him feel more stately, as if he'd moved up a level. He was unhappier than he'd ever been, but at least he no longer felt like the household pet of the group, patted on the head by Eve and her friends when he did something cute or amusing, as if they thought that was the best or the most he could do.

'Nobody's perfect,' Campbell concluded sagely.

'So Rory must have flaws.'

'Not really.'

Sim glanced at him sceptically. 'Campbell, in a few hours I'm going to meet her.' Shit, she was right. If Campbell made out Rory was brilliant in every way, Sim would like her even less than she otherwise would because of the raised-hopes-followed-by-let-down factor. Yesterday, he'd prayed Sim and Francis wouldn't make a fuss about Rory's telephonic stalking and they hadn't, thank God. Maybe they understood that it was an adjunct of her free-spiritedness. One of Rory's best features was her ability to flout convention. Sim also didn't care a damn about anyone else's rules, so perhaps it was a quality she would admire in Rory. Although Eve was conventional and Sim seemed to think Eve was fantastic. Campbell didn't get it.

'She can say some odd things,' he conceded.

'Such as?'

'Well . . . when she met my mum, she kept going on at her to buy me a flat in London, so that we could live near each other. It didn't occur to her that Mum might not be able to afford it. And the other day she said she wished I was rich like her.'

'What?' Sim's eyes widened. Campbell couldn't tell whether she was horrified or thrilled.

'I think she meant it for my sake,' he said.

'Yeah. Uh-huh.' Sim's whole face gleamed.

'She's happy with me as I am,' Campbell clarified, 'but she doesn't want me to feel inadequate when I go to her family's house.'

'Anything else?'

'Well . . .' There was something else, actually. Probably nothing, though. Campbell had almost forgotten about it. Oh, what the hell? If he told Sim, that'd prove he wasn't worried about it. 'Rory's having a big party for her thirtieth birthday and she hasn't . . .' A ringing interrupted him.

'Do you want to get that?' Sim asked, a smile hovering around her mouth.

'No.' Campbell pretended not to understand what she meant. She got up to answer the phone and he let out a long breath. It was just as well he hadn't had time to finish his sentence. Sim would only have mocked him, the smug cow. Besides, he was being silly. Rory would invite him to her party eventually. It must just have slipped her mind.

Vanessa's mobile phone could be relied upon to ring every time she negotiated the Newnham roundabout. Today, it saw no reason to break with habit. The Peugeot swerved as she grabbed it with her free hand, ignoring outraged beeps from goody-goody Cambridge drivers who kept both hands on the wheel at all times. She pressed the green button, confident that it wouldn't be either of the Red-teeth. Vanessa hadn't heard from them in a while and had therefore had no occasion to tell them – as if she would ever have admitted it – that her slant on the accident had changed.

She was beginning to come round to the view that the collision had in fact been her fault, not Red-tooth's. She had a distinct recollection, one that had surprised her by surfacing unexpectedly, of reversing several feet before getting out of the car to see what state Red-tooth was in. Why would she have done that unless her car was jutting out into the road, a potential obstacle to the flow of traffic?

Vanessa had become fascinated, for the first time in her life, by the workings of the human mind, amazed that it was possible for a blurred picture to come belatedly into focus. Her new angle on the accident made her despise Red-tooth even more. If Red-tooth had given it half as much thought as Vanessa had, her impression of what happened would surely have fluctuated. She would have gone through phases of thinking that she was the one to blame and, unsettled by her imprecise memory, told her husband to stop pursuing Vanessa for taxi fares, to let it lie. This wasn't what was behind the Red-teeth's recent silence, Vanessa was convinced. They had given up for practical reasons, not because of any element of self-doubt, arrogant wankers that they were.

'Hello?' she said, swan-necking on to the Fen Causeway.

'Hello, is that Vanessa?' a male voice asked in an accent that sounded Cockney and was definitely not Chinese.

'Speaking.'

'This is PC Phil Stickles at Parkside police station in Cambridge.' Vanessa's mouth dropped open. She braked and swung over to the kerb, to a cacophony of horn beeps. 'I'm phoning about a road accident you were involved in, with a cyclist.'

'Yes.' Vanessa saw no point in denying it.

'It's nothing, really,' PC Stickles was eager to reassure her. 'The cyclist doesn't want to take things any further. She just hasn't been able to get in touch with you and she said you'd agreed to pay her taxi fare to casualty and back. Apparently she had no luck getting through on your mobile.'

'Oh, dear,' said Vanessa irritably. What sort of person would go to the police rather than write off a couple of measly taxi fares? Even Vanessa wouldn't be that evil; laziness would prevent it. 'She was probably ringing the wrong number. I've done everything I can to be reasonable and helpful, but she's been so difficult to deal with. I gave her my address so that she could send me her taxi receipts . . .'

'Ah, yes. Let me check that with you now. Flat two, Staircase M . . .'

'No, no, no, that's all wrong,' said Vanessa impatiently. 'It's flat twenty-two, staircase N, Gentchev's Field, Cambridge.'

'In that case she certainly has got it wrong. She's got London written down here.'

'London?' Vanessa did her best to sound aghast. 'I did tell her I worked in London . . .' She let the unfinished sentence hang in the air.

'Oh, well, that'll be it, then. She's obviously not among the brightest and best of the suns of the morning, your cyclist.' Vanessa felt a small glow of pleasure to hear Red-tooth thus described; my cyclist, she thought, to do with as I wish. 'Anyway, it shouldn't be a problem. I'll have to pop round and take a statement from you at some point . . .'

'Why?' Vanessa didn't like the sound of this. Her life was difficult enough without a criminal record. Still, didn't they say you might as well be hung for a sheep as a lamb? Maybe now was the time to commit all the other crimes she'd dreamed about, like setting fire to the Gable Bazzard offices.

'Oh, yes, we have to for all road accidents, however minor,' said PC Stickles. 'Don't worry, it won't go any further. It's only so our paperwork's in order. Now, is it okay if I pass on your correct address to the cyclist?'

'Of course. Tell her to send her taxi receipts to the right address and I'll send her a cheque by return of post.'

'Oh, that's very kind of you.'

'Well, it is rather, even if I do say so myself.' Now that

she knew an official statement would have to be made, Vanessa was taking no risks. Red-tooth was such a bitch. It was a shame she hadn't been more severely injured in the accident. And, what was more, the silly cow probably agreed. Vanessa wouldn't have put it past Red-tooth to wish she were crippled so that she could squeeze more compensatory cash out of Vanessa. Sick fuck. 'The thing is,' Vanessa told PC Stickles, 'I only offered to pay her taxi fares as a gesture of goodwill. She was cycling on the pavement as I was edging out of my driveway and she slammed into the side of my car.'

'Is that so? That's terrible. Cyclists, eh?' said Stickles. 'Well, in the circumstances it's very good of you to offer to pay her taxi fares.'

'And I gave her a lift home after the accident. But she's acted all along as if the accident was my fault, when it was plainly hers.'

'Yes, she did seem to be approaching it from that angle, I'll grant you that,' said Stickles.

'I can't believe she's doing it,' Vanessa inserted a tremor into her voice. 'It makes me feel like withdrawing my offer to pay her taxi fares.'

'I don't blame you,' said Stickles. 'Some people have got no common decency. As I say, though, you needn't worry. The matter won't go any further, whether you pay for her taxis or not. I do need to take this statement, though, love. When could I pop round?'

'I'll come to the station,' said Vanessa, imagining Nicholas's earnest intervention if he found out about this. He'd probably be glad if Vanessa went to prison. He was always complaining that British jails were concentration camps for the underclass. To see his bourgeois girlfriend banged up would restore his faith in social equality.

Vanessa wasn't at all happy with Nicholas at the moment. Last night she'd made several blatantly offensive comments and he'd ignored her. He turned his back on her in bed and either fell asleep straight away or pretended to. This morning he'd scuttled from between the sheets like a frightened cockroach before Vanessa could grab him. This was most unusual. Whatever faults Nicholas had, he'd always been a diligent and inspired sexual associate. Vanessa refused to believe he'd gone off her, or was having an affair. Who else could offer what she offered?

Besides, there was no need to mention this episode. Nicholas was right, Vanessa's type didn't go to prison. Didn't the police realise that their function was to protect people like herself from the rabble, the riff-raff? The Red-teeth? The sooner she satisfied PC Stickles's bureaucratic needs, the sooner Vanessa could revert to a life that did not involve unpleasant skirmishes with the law. 'Why don't I come in right now?' she said sweetly.

It was Saturday afternoon and Eve, Neil and Imogen were watching a musical called *The Slipper and the Rose* on television, killing time before the *Potters Court* omnibus. Campbell never used to let Eve watch musicals, but she found she was getting her own way a lot more these days. Neil was keen to please her, and Imogen seemed to regard Neil as a minor deity, following his lead on most things.

Imogen was spending more and more time at Eve's. So was Neil, for that matter. The other night he'd mentioned the possibility of moving in. Eve had wanted to say yes straight away but thought it wouldn't do him any harm to be forced to try a bit harder. Neil's obvious devotion to her made Eve feel for the first time in her life that she had some power. She wanted to use it, even though she knew this was a petty impulse. There were also other advantages to delaying Neil's moving in. If and when that happened, Campbell would find out, and Eve didn't want to give him a convenient justification for drawing a line under his old life. She was reluctant to draw that line herself, even though she could see now that Campbell wasn't half as wonderful as she'd thought he was. She'd been so busy admiring the funny, kind, wise Campbell she'd wanted to believe in that she'd overlooked his alter ego, the lazy, selfish, immature leech. It was as if Campbell's body was disputed territory for which these two characters were vying. Eve was no longer convinced she'd want him back, especially not now she had a boyfriend who was clearly passionate about her in a way that Campbell never had been, but she certainly wanted him to want to come back. The words 'terrible mistake' had still not been uttered and Eve needed to hear them.

If she let Neil move in so soon, all her friends would think she was on the rebound, except possibly Sim who was very much in favour of the immediate snapping up of anything that might improve one's quality of life. She'd already made a few impressed noises when Eve told her how solicitous Neil had been since Campbell left, but there was more to tell, all of it impressive. Neil had said he loved Eve already; he'd called her the love of his life. Yesterday when she was feeling suspicious and insecure, and had accused him of using Imogen and her poem to prove to her, Eve, what a hero he was, Neil had calmly reassured her: 'Perhaps initially there was an element of that,' he admitted, 'but you try asking me now to give up on getting a prize for Imogen's poem. I wouldn't do it. Not even for you, Hartigan.' Eve could see he meant it. She loved the way Neil called her by her surname when he wanted to subdue her irrationality.

It might not be a bad idea to tell Sim about Neil and let her pass on the information to the rest of the group. Sim never relayed merely the facts; she always took care to package them in an appropriate interpretation. It wouldn't convince some of the gang – Hazel would still furrow her brow and say how brave Eve was to trust another man so soon, meaning how insane, and Vanessa would think Eve was sad and desperate – but it would certainly help. And people needed to know before the wedding so that they weren't shocked to see Neil's arm round Eve's shoulder or his hand reaching for hers. He was far more tactile than Campbell, who reacted like an embarrassed schoolboy to public displays of affection.

Come to think of it, Matt and Lucy's wedding would be a good opportunity to consolidate things with Neil. If Campbell had shown no sign by then of wanting to come home, Eve would ask Neil to move in with her. That way they could claim a slice of the day's high romance for themselves. The fifteenth of May was still over a month away, and would be two months from the day Campbell left; that was a decent enough interval, wasn't it? Eve smiled, cheered by the prospect.

The phone rang and Imogen ran to answer it before Eve could tell her not to. Presumptuous little madam, she thought. Imogen had never been given permission to answer the telephone, nor to turn up of an evening and assume she could eat with Eve and Neil, and watch television with them. It didn't seem to occur to her that she might not be entirely welcome. Yesterday she'd asked Eve if she could go to Matt and Lucy's wedding. 'It's not fair for you and Neil to go without me,' she'd said, as if they were a family. This caught Eve so off guard that she was unable to answer.

'You don't want to spend a whole day at some boring wedding, watching a load of old biddies getting chicken flesh trapped in their false teeth,' said Neil.

'Ugh! Horrid!' Imogen had giggled, succumbing to Neil's charm as she always did. Eve found she was able to appreciate Neil even more when she viewed him through Imogen's eyes, although she couldn't work out why she trusted the judgement of this strange twelve-year-old more than her own.

Eve wondered about Imogen's parents, why they didn't seem to mind her developing a second home. Thinking this might be a delicate issue, particularly since she and Neil were teachers at Imogen's school, Eve had left a couple of messages on the Salts' answerphone to the effect that she hoped they didn't mind the amount of time Imogen was spending at her house, but she'd had no response. Mr and Mrs Salt seemed to have no desire to meet Eve or Neil, and never came to pick Imogen up, giving her money for taxis instead. Eve thought this was deeply irresponsible, but Imogen behaved as if it were normal and changed the subject whenever Eve mentioned her parents.

The situation was highly irregular, but deep down Eve was profoundly grateful for the girl's intrusion. The transition from Campbell to Neil was awkward and the presence of another person was a welcome distraction. Eve wasn't sure she would have been able to handle the intensity of immediate, private coupledom with Neil. Having another person around to dilute the essence of what was taking place made the change seem more organic somehow. The combination of Neil and Imogen created the impression of a whole new life. Without Imogen, it would have seemed more as if Neil had been plucked from his natural habitat and squeezed anomalously into Eve's old life, where he didn't belong.

'It's Sim,' Imogen yelled.

'Ow! I'm here, there's no need to shout.' Eve, who'd followed her into the hall, took the phone with a stern glare. Why wasn't Mrs Salt teaching her daughter proper manners? 'I'll answer it next time, if you don't mind.'

'Was that your poet prodigy?' Sim asked eagerly. 'Has she become a fixture?'

'Sort of. It's okay, though.'

'She sounds nice,' said Sim. 'So ... any other new fixtures I should know about?'

'What? Like what?'

'Oh, I don't know. Neil, perhaps?' said Sim wryly. 'Campbell saw him sneaking off down the alleyway.'

'Neil never mentioned it,' said Eve. Come to think of it, Neil didn't mention Campbell at all any more. Eve thought there was a superstitious element to this, as if he believed that to utter Campbell's name would be to acknowledge that he still had power over their lives. So Campbell knew. Damn!

'Well?' Sim demanded. 'Are you an item?'

'Sort of.'

'Congratulations. I think it's brilliant.'

'You do?'

'Yes. It'll be a new experience for you, having a relationship with someone who isn't likely to run off with an elephant killer.'

Eve closed the door between the hall and the lounge, making sure not to meet Neil's eye as she did so. 'What does Campbell think?' she asked.

'He's incensed. With you for appropriating his squash partner and with Neil for pinching his bird. He thought you were both his, and then you go and become each other's without his permission.'

'God!' Eve felt rage brewing in her stomach. 'I certainly don't owe him anything and Neil was more of an acquaintance than a friend. I mean . . . don't you think?' She was momentarily confused. Neil wasn't a treacherous person; that was Campbell's forte.

'Relax,' said Sim. 'I know Campbell. He'll have assumed you were still marked as his territory, even after he left you for Rory, but Neil rushed in to plant his flag . . .'

'I like your feminist analysis.' Eve laughed.

'Thank you. The point is, Campbell needs to grow up and learn that actions have consequences. Neil's presence at the wedding will symbolise that very fact. Campbell will see the two of you together and realise that if you trade something good for something awful, you might never get the good thing back, nor do you deserve to! I'm not saying Campbell doesn't deserve a second chance, but he only does if he learns this valuable lesson, and if anyone's going to make that happen it's Neil. So your new man's an agent of justice in my book.'

'I think you're making Neil sound more noble than he

is,' said Eve. 'It's more likely he just fancies me and hasn't given a thought to Campbell.'

'I'm glad you pointed that out,' said Sim. 'It shows that you're going into this with your eyes open. And you'll need twenty-twenty vision when it comes to the crunch.'

'What crunch?' Eve saw no such thing on the horizon, open eyes or not.

'You're going to have to choose between them. Any day now, any *minute* now, Campbell will commence his descent from the summit of Mount Imbecility. I can say that with great confidence now I've met Rory.'

'Oh, my God! I thought she wasn't coming till tonight.'

'No, she got here a couple of hours ago.'

'So she's there now?'

'No,' said Sim. 'She left one of her suitcases at Leeds station. Francis is driving her and Campbell back there now. He was thrilled, as you can imagine. She thinks she might have left it in WH Smith's.'

'Ha!' said Eve. 'I hope she doesn't find it.'

'Well, if she doesn't, she's got enough in the two cases that made it safely to our flat to last her a fortnight, never mind a weekend. I've just had a thorough rummage.'

'Sim!' Eve laughed. 'Did you find any blood-soaked tusks?'

'No, but I'll tell you what I did find. A bright pink vibrator!' Sim's voice rang out in triumph at her discovery. It had clearly been an effort for her to restrain herself from blurting out this choice morsel of gossip earlier in the conversation. 'With a prong sticking out of the side, in the shape of a rabbit!'

'What?' Eve squealed with delight. 'What sort of prong?'

'You know, for ... added ...'

'Oh, I get it,' said Eve, who wasn't sure she did but didn't like to ask whether the rabbit-shaped protruberence was north- or south-facing. 'Jesus!'

'I know. Isn't that just the best bit of dirt to have on one's worst enemy?'

'Yes, but . . .' Eve felt deflated all of a sudden. 'What can I do with it?'

'Enjoy it, of course! Savour the knowledge,' Sim instructed. 'I've taken a photo of it for you.'

'Do you think Campbell knows about it?' asked Eve. 'Has he seen it or . . . used it?' The latter seemed most unlikely. The Campbell Eve knew would have turned up his nose at all sex toys, being very firmly a missionary position man.

'Who knows? Eve, what's Campbell playing at?' Sim's voice became suddenly serious.

'Don't ask me. Is she really awful, then?'

'Grimbelina is an apt nickname, put it that way.'

'Oh, God. This is terrible, Sim. I wouldn't mind Campbell leaving me for someone else if I thought he'd be happier, but she's not going to make him happy, is she?'

'Surely his obvious wrongness is a consolation. Eloping with Grimbelina isn't a choice any sane person would make, it's an aberration. It's no more a reflection on you than if he'd left you for a Pot Noodle. Campbell's judgement has clearly undergone an inversion of some kind. Look at it that way and you could almost take his leaving as a compliment. Bugger, there's someone at the door. Hang on, let me shift over to the peephole.'

'I wonder if he deliberately picked someone putrid because secretly he wants it not to work out so that he can come back to me,' Eve thought aloud. A silence followed, which was long by the standards of any conversation that involved Sim. 'Sim?' said Eve. 'Are you still there?'

'Aha! A cry for help, you mean. Like someone who swallows some pills but not enough to kill them,' said Sim. 'Brilliant. That didn't occur to me, but I think it's got legs. Oh . . . look, I've got to go, it's Hazel. I'll keep you abreast of developments and ring you soon. 'Bye!'

Eve put down the phone. It rang again while her hand was still on it. She picked it up. 'There can't have been a development already,' she said.

'Eve? It's Claire Morgan here. Sorry to phone at the weekend, but I thought you'd want to know.'

'Oh, I do! Sorry, I thought . . . never mind. How are you?'

'Fine,' Claire said briskly. Evidently she hadn't phoned to be sociable. 'I've just tried to ring Neil but he's not in, so I thought . . .'

'He's here,' said Eve. There was no point in pretending. Claire would find out eventually. Many of the other teachers already knew; Eve had spent half of last week accepting the congratulations of her colleagues and the other half overhearing them whispering behind her back, saying she must be desperate. Sod them. Who wasn't on the rebound on some level? How many people, if they could be with anyone they wanted, would choose to be with their current partners? Very few, Eve suspected. Would she have stayed with Campbell if she'd had an offer from Tom Cruise? She sighed. Yes, she probably would. 'Do you want to speak to Neil?' she asked.

'No, I can speak to you. It's about Imogen Salt and the poem.'

'Neil's just in the lounge,' said Eve. 'I can easily . . .'

'Eve, I'm sure you'll be able to cope,' Claire snapped. When, Eve wondered, had she become the sort of woman who passed anything difficult over to her man to deal with? As soon as she could, was that it? Until Neil came along it hadn't been an option.

The idea of asking Campbell to shoulder any sort of burden was laughable; Eve had gone to extreme lengths in the opposite direction, sheltering him from things as mundane and inoffensive as the washing up and the shopping. Campbell had once remarked that such chores (as well as others: ironing, hoovering, cleaning the bath) made him feel as if he was plunging head first into an abyss of non-achievement. 'No, that's your PhD,' Eve had teased him, but he hadn't found it funny.

'As soon as you wash things they start to get dirty again,'

Campbell complained, as if he were the first person ever to think of this. 'It's ridiculous.' Asked to take the bin out, he'd adopt a mystified expression and say, 'But I only took it out yesterday.' Eve had assumed all men were like Campbell in this respect – only prepared to do things that had the good manners to stay done – but Neil had no problem with chores. He accepted them as a necessary and not even particularly unpleasant part of life.

Eve saw in retrospect that she'd been wrong to create huge expanses of free time for Campbell. It wasn't as if he'd used them to finish his thesis. She should have forced him to share the housework, but her love for him had made her weak, which had the knock-on effect of weakening Campbell. Oh well, there was no point worrying about it now. Let's face it, he hadn't left her because she'd let him off the hoovering.

'I've taken advice and it seems to be okay,' said Claire Morgan.

'You mean . . . ?' Eve drifted back to reality.

'What Neil suggested. The two-one majority. If Walter agrees with you that Imogen's poem should be given a second prize or joint first prize, that'll be in accordance with the rules.'

'That's brilliant,' said Eve. 'That's . . . great.'

'It isn't great for me,' Claire said in a martyred voice. 'Phyllida won't be at all happy.'

'But she won't be able to complain if no rules are being broken.'

'Oh, she'll complain. Still, it won't be your problem. But tell Neil he'd better not find any more loopholes in school policy. I can do without headaches like this.'

'Miserable old boot,' Eve muttered after the loud click. She'd have to speak to Walter first thing on Monday, check they had his vote. She stood in the hall, grinning like a clown. It was Imogen and Neil's victory really; Eve's role in it had been minor, but she was thrilled nonetheless. If she'd been superstitious she'd have taken this as a sign of something – that Campbell hadn't arranged for all good news to be redirected on the day he left, for instance. Eve didn't know whether she was imagining it, but she felt as if her fortunes were about to turn round, like a boomerang, and start whizzing back in the right direction.

3

Sim was tempted to laugh when she saw the tiny cloaked figure in the doorway. 'Hazel,' she said gently, glimpsing a slice of face beneath the tall Russian hat. 'Are you okay? I'm glad to see you've finally taken some time off from launching storytelling grottos and encouraging senior citizens to carve their memoirs on to stones in the Aire valley.' With Francis, Campbell and Rory on their way back from Leeds station, this was hardly the ideal moment for the Dale Dingley symposium, but Hazel seemed ominously subdued and Sim couldn't bear to miss an opportunity.

'Something . . . um . . . um . . . terrible's happened,' said Hazel, hovering in the hall.

'What?' Sim pushed her friend towards the kitchen. 'You can tell me, whatever it is.' Make it quick, she added silently.

'Why might you tear a page out of a novel that belonged to someone else?'

'I wouldn't,' said Sim. This wasn't the question she'd been expecting. 'Why? Has someone torn a page out of one of your books?'

'Yes . . . um . . . I can't tell you who.'

'That's okay. Drink?' It had to be Dingley. 'Let's call the person X.' Sim prepared to be wise and open-minded. Maybe no one else would believe Hazel that Dale was innocent, but Sim would. Everyone needed a sole believer, no one knew that better than Sim, who, in the matter of Gillian, still didn't have one.

'Okay.' Hazel smiled weakly, relieved to have got away with keeping something to herself. 'No, thanks, I just had a coffee. X is . . . a friend of mine and he . . . he or she tore a page out of my copy of *Howdy* by Cal Raynard.' She opened her handbag and pulled out a black Waterstone's carrier bag. 'Here, I bought a new copy so I could show you.' She flicked through *Howdy* until she came to the advertisement for *His and Hers* by Debbi Naismith and Greg Pendry. 'This page here,' she said, handing the book to Sim.

'Ooh!' Sim read the blurb. 'That's my holiday reading for this year sorted out. But . . . you're wondering why your friend tore out this page.' Hazel wasn't the only one.

'He's not the sort of person who would do that to a book,' said Hazel. 'I can't understand it. He loves books, and he . . . appreciates the value of things.' Sim was acutely aware that this did not coincide with the impression of Dale Dingley projected by the media, but she let Hazel go on. 'I knew something was wrong when I first showed him *Howdy* and he went all funny, although he denied it. Then I found a page missing.'

'Are there no other suspects?' Sim asked, meaning for Bethan Wrigley's murder as well as this silly book business. She was keen for everything to be out in the open and was trying to steer things in the right direction with her choice of words.

'None. He was the only person who had access to the book between my reading it and discovering the torn-out page. I know I should ask him but I'm scared in case it's something bad. I'm afraid it must be, for him to do that. He normally looks after things, especially things that are mine. He looks after them better than I do. He notices when Gatting needs to be repotted and . . .' Talking about Gatting always made Hazel emotional and for a moment she was unable to continue.

Sim murmured appropriately soothing phrases and thought hard. Something didn't add up here. For God knew how long Hazel had been harbouring a man whom the entire country believed to be a murderer in her flat without buckling under the pressure and now here she was, being pushed over the edge by something as unspectacular as a missing page. Or perhaps Sim was thinking too literally. Perhaps Hazel had never doubted Dingley's innocence until this small, weird incident alerted her to the fact that he didn't necessarily tell her the truth at all times.

'You must be wondering why I've never mentioned this friend before.'

'Hazel . . .'

'Oh! I've decided what I'm getting Lucy and Matt for a wedding present,' Hazel declared out of the blue. 'I don't know why I didn't think of it straight away, it's . . . um . . . um . . . the best gift anyone could possibly give a friend!'

'What?' Sim asked patiently. Hazel underestimated her persistence if she thought this detour would put her off the scent for more than a few seconds.

'A cactus! It can be Gatting's friend. It'll have to be named after a cricketer. I thought perhaps Embury.'

'Is he a cricketer?'

'Sim!'

'Well, I don't know. Yeah, that's a great idea.' Sim reread the blurb of *His and Hers*, not seeing how it could be significant to Dale Dingley. It was overtly sexual. If Dingley were a rapist . . . but he *wasn't*, he couldn't be. Sim decided to take the plunge; she'd been patient enough. Francis, Campbell and Rory wouldn't be back for at least another fifteen minutes. 'Hazel, I've got a confession to make,' she said. Good, inspired, clever to say to Hazel exactly what she wanted to hear from her and set the tone. 'I know about . . . your friend.' Hazel froze. 'Don't worry. I want to help you in any way I can.'

'You do? There is something . . .'

'What? Anything.'

'I need to read *His and Hers*. But I refuse to buy it.' Pompousness overtook Hazel. 'I'm a literature development officer and I have standards to uphold.'

'What?' Sim tried not to sound too outrageously disappointed. She'd had visions of herself escorting Dale Dingley's cloaked form over Baildon Moor at midnight, with snarling policemen in hot pursuit. 'Hazel, leaving the book aside for a minute . . .'

'But it's important!'

'I know. I'll buy it for you, I promise, but . . .'

'Oh, thank you, thank you!'

'Hazel, I'm trying to tell you something,' said Sim slowly. 'I *know*.'

'How?' Hazel retreated into her large coat, pulling in her head like a turtle.

'I saw him in your flat.' Sim decided to keep Eve and Vanessa out of it, keep it simple. 'And then, you know, on TV and in the papers. I recognised him.'

'What?' Hazel looked mystified. 'I didn't know he'd been on TV.'

'Come on, Hazel, of course he has. But the point is, if you believe he's innocent then so do I.'

'Oh no! No!' Hazel wailed, taking Sim entirely by surprise. 'Has he committed a crime? Oh, God, tell me it's not true!' She started to sob, rocking to and fro.

Sim scratched her head, utterly bewildered. Could there have been a major misunderstanding? Sim didn't see how, but she thought it best to clarify. 'Hazel, let's get this into the open once and for all,' she said. 'I know you're hiding Dale Dingley in your flat. Right?'

Hazel's tear-streaked face emerged from behind her collar, resembling that of a bleached turtle. She looked around the room as if she'd never seen it before, then looked at Sim in the same way. For a few seconds she seemed to be suspended in time and space. Sim was afraid she was about to suffer an irreparable nervous breakdown. Then she started to mutter. 'Dale Dingley in my flat, Dale Dingley . . .'

'Well?' said Sim gently, smiling to assure Hazel that everything was fine. Hazel nodded. 'Okay.' Sim sighed with relief. Progress at last. 'I also know you wouldn't do that unless you were sure he didn't rape and murder Bethan Wrigley. Am I right?' Another nod, jerkier this time. 'Hazel, are you and Dale Dingley in love?' Hazel blinked and blushed, which Sim took as an affirmation. 'What about Tricia?' she asked.

'Who?'

Oh dear. This was getting complicated. Was Tricia a front, to divert suspicion from Dingley's real whereabouts? It would be awful if Hazel's first serious boyfriend turned out to be a two-timer. Sim decided to skip over this issue for the time being. 'It must have been a nightmare for you,' she went on, 'loving a man that half the country wants to lynch, being the only one to believe in him. He must love you so much, Hazel. I'm sure he did even before all this happened but especially now that you've been so loyal and stood by him.' Hazel nodded tensely. Sim wondered why she still looked so wary. She'd expected a stream of relieved babble and a handing over of all future responsibility for the situation to herself. But for the first time since Sim had known her, Hazel appeared to have nothing to say.

It wouldn't be so bad to move to London, would it? Nicholas stood by the window, staring out at the neat rows of small blue flowers in the flowerbeds of Gentchev's Field, thinking for the first time that he could bear to leave this place. In fact, since his drink with Gillian the previous night he'd been desperate to get out. Cambridge was not safe and comforting as he'd thought. It was too small; it contained too many people one knew. The anonymity of London would offer more protection, Nicholas would feel less visible in it, but how long would it take him to find a job there? And what would he tell Vanessa? She wouldn't believe he'd simply changed his mind any more than she'd believe that he'd never laid a finger on Gillian if she accused him of rape. Given the nature of Nicholas and Vanessa's physical relationship, it might ring all too true.

Nicholas had felt sick all day and been unable to work. He couldn't bring himself to do anything about his problem, having no idea what to do, but neither could he push it from his mind and get on with his life. He hadn't even bothered to get his article out of its envelope this morning, and had spent nearly a whole day staring out of the window, dashing back and forth to the bathroom. Gillian had upset his stomach. He felt guilty, like a monster, although he knew this was mad, he hadn't done a single bloody thing wrong. All he'd ever done was try to be a decent human being and improve the world with his writing, but work seemed laughably trivial in the light of recent events, like a game Nicholas had played when he was happy. At this moment in time he didn't give a stuff if the Israelis stole all the Palestinians' land. He had other more pressing concerns, ones that had kept him awake all night.

Gillian was evil, there were no two ways about it. Sim was right. Nicholas had always liked to think of himself as a fighter back – against the system, against Vanessa – but while both could be distinctly unpleasant, vicious even, they at least made sense and were capable of engaging in rational discourse. One could see how they worked, predict with a reasonable degree of accuracy how they might behave in the future. Gillian, in contrast, felt like a random force of darkness that destroyed lives for no reason at all. Like cancer.

Nicholas jumped as a loud ringing filled the room, sounding to his anxious ears like a siren. It was probably Vanessa. He prayed it was. Nicholas rushed to answer the phone, thinking that if this were a horror film, the call would turn out to be perfectly innocent, a red herring. But it wasn't a film and the caller was Gillian.

'Nicholas?' She giggled, turning his insides cold. 'God, I was pissed last night. Were you?'

'I . . . I . . .' Nicholas stammered. Gillian was speaking

as if they'd shared a jolly, boozy evening rather than the nightmarish scenario that was engraved upon his memory.

'I was steaming!' she went on. 'Anyway, look, Nicholas, I phoned to try and patch things up.'

'Right.' He held his breath, still too wary to sigh with relief. But this had to be a good sign.

'There's no need for any of this unpleasantness, you know.' Oh, thank God. So she wasn't going to accuse him of molesting her after all. 'I only want you to do the decent thing,' said Gillian dolefully. 'If I had any sense that you cared, that you genuinely gave a shit about what's happened to me, that'd be enough. I'd leave you alone.'

'I care,' said Nicholas desperately. 'Of course I care.'

'No, you don't.'

'I do!'

'Prove it.' Her tone had hardened into sullenness.

'But . . . I thought all I had to do was care. You didn't say anything about proving it.'

Gillian sighed loudly. 'Nicholas, you are so incredulously selfish! The real joke is that if you'd only offered to give me back the office, I would have said you could keep it.'

'Give you back the . . . Gillian our departments have swapped premises.' Nicholas found her stupidity repulsive. Anyone who confused incredible with incredulous deserved to be . . . Nicholas shied away from the unpleasant half-formed thought. He was a feminist, he reminded himself. How could he have been so naïve as to think that her conciliatory tone at the beginning of the conversation was a good sign? Again, he'd made the mistake of assuming logic could be applied to the problem of Gillian. 'You can't be a Modern Languages secretary based in the International Relations building,' he snapped. 'Your head of department wouldn't allow it.'

'You should still have offered,' said Gillian. 'You've failed to make or mend in any way.' Nicholas shook his head in disgust. Had the woman been lobotomised?

Fearlessness flowed through him suddenly. There was no way he was going to be intimidated by such a spaz. Nicholas swallowed and shook his head, ashamed of his instinctive reactions. He hadn't used the word 'spaz' since his Marlborough College days. It was Gillian's fault; she was corrupting him. People like her needed to be culled. 'I'm going to give you the benefit of the doubt,' she went on. 'I don't think you're intentionally cruel, just a bit stupid.' Gillian said this softly, as if to cushion the blow to Nicholas's ego. 'If you can't think of a way out of this mess, I can.'

'What?' Nicholas latched on to the words 'a way out'. Please, please, he thought. He'd pay her, if that was what it took.

'We share the office,' Gillian suggested happily.

'Share it? But it's mine.'

'It's big enough for two people.'

'But . . . no, Gillian. Your head of department . . .'

'Leave him to me,' said Gillian with terrifying certainty.

'Gillian,' Nicholas tried to sound authoritative, feeling desperation wash over him. 'I need an office of my own. I've *got* an office of my own. My work is the most important thing in my life . . .'

'Saddo,' Gillian interjected merrily.

'Fuck you! Do you know what? I hope you die.'

'Nicholas, don't overreact. We've got a huge office to share between us. There's easily enough room for both of us. We can even rig up some sort of barrier . . .'

'Leave me alone,' Nicholas spluttered, his whole body shaking. 'Or I'll kill you, understand?' Was this what madness was? When Vanessa calmly applied the word to Gillian, did she have this sort of malignancy in mind? If so, how could she laugh as she said it?

'I'll tell the police you said that,' Gillian replied coolly before hanging up.

It was eight thirty on Saturday evening by the time Rory

got round to asking her first question of her hosts: 'Am I like you expected me to be?' Sim noticed because she'd been waiting for it. Although Rory's question was staggeringly self-centred, it did at least contain an awareness of Sim and Francis as people who might have expectations. We exist, thought Sim, only insofar as we react to Rory, reflect her back to herself. Until now, Rory had shown no interest whatsoever in either Sim or Francis. Or Campbell, come to think of it. All she'd done was implore everybody to be supportive and help her recover – those were the words she used. She'd found her case, but the effort of being driven around Yorkshire by Francis had been altogether too much for her. After two cups of some hideous tea she'd brought with her that stank of weeds and a long rest on the sofa beneath Sim and Francis's spare duvet, Rory had finally felt 'well enough' to be chauffeured to Bingley for her evening meal.

The four of them sat at an upstairs window table in Valentino's, Sim and Francis's favourite Italian restaurant. The starters had not yet arrived and Francis was becoming grumpier by the second. His body language – folded arms, averted eyes – made it plain that he had no intention of fielding Rory's question. Sim would have to deal with it.

She took a while to answer, unprepared for an enquiry of this nature, which seemed on the face of it to be an alarming call to honesty. It was either brave or arrogant of Rory to invite opinions in this way. Sim was fascinated by the whole Rory package, with its prominent shovel-shaped chin, pink pimply skin like uncooked quail flesh and lank blonde hair, held back at the front by a child's hairslide, a smiling yellow sun stuck on to a metal grip. Here was a woman who plainly didn't care what impression she made on other people, adding to the bad impression she'd already made by asking people for their impressions of her.

Sim saw that a response of some kind was required; Campbell's complexion was turning grey. Since Rory's arrival, Sim had noticed a tangible force field of tension around Campbell that she hadn't felt before in all the years she'd known him.

Rory's question had unsettled Sim. Suddenly she was expected to be a participant, not merely a spectator. Normally she wouldn't be caught without a reaction, a handy phrase that could be whipped out if the need arose, but her mind was full of Hazel worries. Something was definitely amiss, but Sim couldn't put her finger on what it might be. Hazel had been so odd earlier and hadn't answered the door when Sim went round to see if she was okay, though Sim knew she was in. This retreat into silence, together with Rory's self-absorption, made Sim feel oddly invisible. She didn't mind this at all; visibility could become tiring and she'd welcomed the prospect of a weekend off. Being Sim Purdy full-time was quite some performance; she'd looked forward to being an observer for a couple of days. The Hideous Grimbelina should have known she was this weekend's spectacle and Sim had never been keen on shows that leaned too heavily upon the crutch of audience participation. 'Yes, you're pretty much what I expected,' she replied. Another long silence followed, during which Campbell looked at Sim imploringly in the hope that she might add 'You're every bit as wonderful as Campbell said you were' and Francis stared at her with a frozen half-smile, as if daring her to add, 'You're every inch as revolting as we'd been led to believe.'

'Because I know you were friends with Eve, you see,' said Rory, impatient for Sim's answer so that she could move on to her next comment. So she wasn't curious about whether Sim's 'Yeah, pretty much' implied a double positive or a double negative, in terms of expectation and actuality.

'Are, not were,' said Sim cheerily. Campbell's face twitched.

A waiter arrived with four starters on a tray. 'Who is having the veal sweetbreads?' he asked.

'Meee!' Rory twittered.

'And who is having the . . .'

'Excuse me, waiter.' Rory put up her hand as she said this.

'Yes, signora?'

'What's that?' She pointed at an extractor fan on the far wall.

'Pardon, signora?'

Sim pursed her lips, keen to get back to more important matters. She wanted to make it clear that as far as she was concerned Eve existed in the present tense. 'What's that thingie on the wall?' Rory asked, trance-like. Why the fuss about the fan when she'd shown no curiosity about anything else, Sim wondered.

'It is to remove food smells. To keep air fresh,' said the waiter.

'Could we have our starters, please?' Francis said gruffly. They were still on the tray.

'Of course, signor. Who is having the soup?'

'It's lovely,' said Rory, still staring at the fan, tilting her head to one side as if to view it from another angle. 'How long have you had it?' Sim noticed that Francis was glaring at her in a threatening manner, as if she were somehow responsible for Rory's behaviour.

'Rory, don't be silly.' Campbell blushed. 'He doesn't want to talk about that, he's busy.'

'I'm having the soup,' said Francis.

The waiter ignored him. 'No, no. Is all right,' he said to Campbell. 'I don't know how long we have it. I only am here a year.'

'Who is it made by?' asked Rory in a dreamy, aerated tone. 'I'd like to get one.'

'Rory, don't be absurd,' said Campbell.

'Could you have a look and see if there's a brand name on it?' Rory smiled sweetly at the waiter.

'Rory, let him serve the food,' said Campbell.

'Campbell, for God's sake, I only want him to look . . .'

'Mine's the soup,' Francis growled. The waiter looked

at him anxiously, then at Rory, then at Francis again. He shrugged helplessly, balanced his tray on the edge of the table and thumped Francis's arm as they both reached for the soup at the same time. Sim and Campbell had each ordered a bowl of fresh mussels, but neither minded the delay. There were more important things to be considered.

'It's an ordinary bloody fan,' Francis muttered, vigorously stirring the creamy green contents of his bowl.

'Francis, that's a terrible thing to say,' Rory squeaked. 'You shouldn't shut yourself off from new experiences. There are so many marvellous things . . .' Her voice trailed off.

'Indeed there are,' said Sim raucously, 'although perhaps not in our immediate vicinity.' Good old Campbell, she thought, for laying on this entertainment. Rory was monstrously mad. It was such fun to see her in action. If only Eve were an extractor fan on the wall; she would have loved every minute of this.

The waiter, who had obediently gone off in search of a brand name, returned. 'It is made by Ventilair,' he said.

'Thank you,' said Rory. 'I must write that down. Has anyone got a bit of paper and a pen?' Nobody had. 'Could you possibly bring me a pen and paper, if it isn't too much trouble?' she asked the waiter. Sim couldn't bear her mooning drawl. She sounded like someone under hypnosis and looked the part as well, her face solemn and looming.

'Rory, don't be so demanding,' Campbell whispered.

'Campbell, leave me alone!' All the other tables fell silent. 'I only want a pen and paper. He doesn't mind.'

'No, I don't mind,' the waiter agreed. 'Is fine. I get pen and paper.' He scurried away.

'Don't boss me around, Campbell,' said Rory. 'It's a control thing, okay? When you try to stop me from talking, it makes me feel I haven't got control over my own body, which is a scary feeling. It feels like a violation. Do you understand?' Sim and Francis looked at Campbell, willing him to stand up for himself. Two couples at an adjacent table began to giggle and nudge one another. Such conversations were not a common occurrence in Bingley.

'Sorry,' said Campbell, biting his hopelessly chapped lips.

'It's not good for either of our souls, Campbell,' Rory said loudly, shaking her head as if inestimable damage might already have been done.

'Look, Sim and I eat here a lot . . .' Francis began. Sim shot him a stern glance. It was best to avoid a full-blown row. Sim didn't want this weekend to be a categorical disaster; that would imbue Rory with too much importance. Disasters could be formidable and magnificent in their way. If Campbell perceived Rory in that light there would be no hope of saving him. Rory had to be kept at the level of a farce. 'And . . . uh . . .' Francis stopped reluctantly in response to Sim's silent pressure.

'Try to get some words out,' Rory mocked him.

'Rory!' Campbell gasped. 'Don't be so rude.'

'Anyway, where were we?' Sim said quickly, tapping Francis's leg with her foot under the table. The waiter emerged from the kitchen with a scrap of paper, on which he had written the word 'Ventilair', and handed it to Rory.

'What's this?' she asked.

'Rory,' Campbell hissed from the side of his mouth. 'It's the name of the extractor fan.'

'Oh,' said Rory sadly. 'Thank you.' She didn't look up. After the waiter had gone she said, 'I don't want it any more. You three have spoiled it.'

'. . . demented,' Francis mumbled.

'What?'

'He said we never meant it.' Sim smiled.

'This is very difficult for me, you know, meeting Campbell's friends.'

'It's no picnic for us,' said Francis. Sim adored the way

270

he was spontaneously unpleasant to the loathsome and hypocritical.

'Is he being horrible?' Rory asked Sim.

'Of course he isn't,' said Campbell.

'I don't know how you all feel about me . . . replacing Eve. I mean, you were a foursome with Eve and now . . . I've come along. I was a bit nervous about whether I'd be accepted.'

So this is what's going on, Sim thought. Rory wanted nothing less than a cast-iron guarantee that Eve was history. 'That's entirely understandable,' said Sim. 'I doubt Paul McCartney and the Frog Chorus would be keen to play to a football stadium full of Beatles fans.' Francis chuckled, beaming appreciatively at Sim.

'I don't understand.' Rory looked at Campbell, who looked angry. Tough luck, Sim told him in her head. If he wanted her to stop making comments like that, he'd have to do something about it. She could see her respect for Campbell taking a dive if he kept up this pathetic behaviour. Why was he being such a jelly? It occurred to Sim that gelatin was used to make both bombs and bouncy red desserts for children's parties. What if Campbell was similarly versatile?

He didn't seem prepared to stand up to anyone, not Sim and not Rory. Telling facial contortions were the closest he got to action. Did he imagine that was enough, or did he genuinely have no desire to shape his own destiny? Sim guessed he was kidding himself that a sharp twitch of his chafed lip represented him manfully springing into action. 'I hope it's okay for me to come to Matt and Lucy's wedding,' Rory said to Sim. 'I know Eve's going to be there and I don't want Campbell's friends to feel uncomfortable, you know, divided loyalties, that sort of thing.'

Sim laughed. 'If and when my loyalties divide, I'll let you know,' she said. Rory emitted a small, poignant sigh, which Sim translated as meaning, 'You're only damaging yourself by being sarcastic.' Sim had never felt better in her life.

When Rory got up to go to the bathroom a few seconds later, Campbell buried his face in his hands and groaned. 'Sorry she's so mad,' he said.

When Vanessa got back to the flat, two communications awaited her. The first was a note from Nicholas, saying he'd gone to the pub. She scowled. Nicholas never went to the pub on his own. Why start now? Had some-one told him that was what the lower orders did of an evening? He'd better get his arse back here sharpish, thought Vanessa. Weren't men supposed to need sex more than women?

Underneath Nicholas's note was a brown envelope. Vanessa's name and address were handwritten and there was no postmark. She only knew one person who was likely to deliver a letter to her by hand. Fucking hell, talk about keen; Vanessa had only spoken to PC Stickles this morning. She turned the envelope over and found the sender's details, all present and correct: G C Li, Flat 4, Heron House, Newton Site, Silver Street, Cambridge. Above it Red-tooth had written, 'If undelivered, please return to'. Of course, Red-tooth would never be in too much of a hurry to take sensible postal precautions. Vanessa prised open the envelope, unfolded the sheet of lined A4 paper and began to read:

Dear Vanessa

I am the girl you had an accident with some weeks ago. After you took me home, I took a taxi to the local hospital and had a medical check-up. I was lucky enough to just have my teeth hurt as well as a few bruises in my knee. Doctors there helped me to adjust one of the front teeth which was knocked in by the pavement and found one third of my other front tooth missing. I went back to the hospital for

272

an X-ray exam two days later and was told that my teeth was strong enough to survive the accident but they might die early in future. The doctor then sent me to the University Dental Service where I had another examination by a dentist and had my missing teeth filled two weeks later.

I have suffered a lot from the accident. My face looked strange for the first week after the accident. I can still only eat liquid food.

My husband and I tried to contact your mobile phone for several times. We were told you were on a business trip abroad for three months. Then we phoned again and were told you were away for six months 'at the very least'. Not knowing how to contact you, we have to seek help from the police. I hope the call from the police has not brought you an unpleasant surprise.

I am enclosing receipts of taxi fee and dental charge for you. As a full-time student I am covered by NHS treatment, so it's actually not a large sum of money, totally about £60.

I look forward to hearing from you.

Best regards

Gang Chuen Li

A little bundle of receipts, secured with an elastic band, was enclosed. Four of them were for taxis and three had NHS logos on them. Vanessa added up the amounts and found that they came to £56.92. Totally £60 indeed. Red-tooth was attempting to defraud her of nearly £4. Well, she could bugger off. PC Phil Stickles was ardently on Vanessa's side after their intimate little chat at Parkside police station this afternoon. Now that she had official backing, reimbursing Red-tooth was the last thing on Vanessa's mind.

Red-tooth's claim that she hoped the call from the police hadn't been an unpleasant surprise made Vanessa want to puke. Why did she hope that? If she believed Vanessa's reckless driving had caused her all the suffering she so painstakingly detailed in her letter, why did she care how many unpleasant surprises came Vanessa's way? She didn't, of course. She was lying in order to appear nice and reasonable.

Vanessa opened her stationery drawer and looked through her selection of postcards. Most of them were Gable Bazzard book covers. There was nothing with a car on it, which would have been Vanessa's first choice, but she perked up again when she realised she had something even better: a postcard of the Dustin Hoffman film *Marathon Man*. Vanessa grinned. Red-tooth probably hadn't seen the film, probably didn't know about the gruesome dentistry scene it contained, but that didn't matter. It was still brilliant; Vanessa would appreciate the artistry of the act even if its target didn't.

On the back of the card she wrote,

Dear Ms Li,
Thank you for your letter. I agreed to pay your taxi fares as a gesture of goodwill. As I was not responsible for the accident, and as you were driving on the pavement where you shouldn't have been, I don't see why I should have to pay for your dental treatment. I've spoken to the police at length and they agree with me. Please, therefore, send me an invoice to cover the taxi fare only.
Yours sincerely
Vanessa Willis

Vanessa stuffed Red-tooth's letter, the receipts and the *Marathon Man* card into a white A5 envelope, addressed it and summoned a porter by telephone to take it to the post office as a matter of urgency.

'Sim, I want you to know that I would never have gone

274

near Campbell if I'd known he had a girlfriend,' Rory drawled. It was Sunday evening. Francis and Campbell had gone out to collect a Chinese takeaway, leaving Sim alone in the flat with the Grimble (the name Grimbelina seemed overly formal now they'd met). Rory lay on the lounge floor and stroked the sofa with one arm. She'd changed into her nightie, although it was only eight o'clock, and covered herself with a pink woollen blanket that she'd brought with her in one of her many cases. Not once during the entire weeked had she sat upright in a chair.

'Really?' Sim replied coolly. 'Well, that's funny.' Her abiding memory of this weekend would feature the Grimble as she was now: horizontal and nestling in soft material, talking utter drivel.

'What?' Rory demanded, sensing a challenge.

'Well, I don't know whether I've got things mixed up, but that's not what I heard.'

'Oh.' The Grimble lifted her arm and made a slow arc with it in mid-air.

'No,' Sim went on chattily, ignoring the modern ballet that was in progress on her living-room floor. 'What I heard – I mean, maybe wires have got crossed somehow – was that you knew about Eve and even spoke to her several times on the phone.'

'I've never phoned Eve in my life,' said Rory smugly. Her voice really was atrocious, a gloopy secretion that slid out of her mouth.

Sim wanted to hit her, but a physical assault would have ended the conversation, which looked set to be rather fun. 'No, but you phoned Campbell every day and Eve often answered the phone,' she said. Rory shrugged. 'Thereby alerting you to the fact that she lived in the same house as Campbell and was his girlfriend.' Sim smiled sweetly, in the manner of someone helping to clear up a misunderstanding. Rory's gooey fakeness disgusted her. A more upfront approach would have been preferable: 'Sim, look, I know Eve's a friend of yours but quite frankly I had to have

Campbell so I went for it and didn't give a damn who got hurt.'

'You probably don't know this,' said Rory, poking a bare leg out of her blanket and extending it towards Sim, 'but Campbell only told me he had a girlfriend on the fourth day of our Stratford course.' She put on a martyred face. 'I don't think I'll ever be able to forgive him for that.'

Sim considered this for a few moments. Was Rory trying to deflect blame from herself by any means possible, or changing the subject in order to confuse Sim, to make her think that carrying on the conversation was a waste of energy? Either way, Sim had no intention of being beaten. 'Maybe so,' she said. 'But what you originally said was that you wouldn't have gone anywhere near Campbell if you'd known he had a girlfriend. If he told you on the Stratford course . . .'

'But only on the fourth day!' Rory insisted. Sim noticed that her leg was particularly quail-like: skinny, pinkish-white and covered in tiny raised bumps, as if she were cold, which she couldn't be with that blanket round her. An image of Eve's well-proportioned tanned legs appeared in Sim's mind and she thought of the scene from the film *The Shining* where the beautiful woman Jack Nicholson is kissing turns into a hideous, scabby corpse. Nicholson must still be sane at that stage in the film because he starts screaming. Sim concluded that Campbell, who had put himself through a transition of comparable grotesqueness by choice, had to be nuts.

'Yes, but then, after the fourth day, you knew,' she persisted. 'And you still chased him. I might do the same myself, except I'd have the guts to admit what I was doing instead of coming over all morally pious.'

Rory retracted her leg and curled her body into a tight ball. 'I would never chase any man, let alone one with a girlfriend,' she said haughtily.

'Rory, you phoned and wrote to Campbell every day.

276

Eve wrote and asked you to lay off but you didn't. Why don't admit it? You went all out to get him.'

'Oh! If you'd seen her letter!' Rory shook her head.

'What do you mean?'

'Sim, I swear to you, if I'd read that letter and thought Eve and Campbell had a future together, I would have kept well away, but it was clear from Eve's letter that she was totally wrong for Campbell.'

'Really,' Sim said coldly, unimpressed by Rory's ever shifting position on the matter. 'Why was that, then?' Rory winced as if she couldn't bear to elaborate. Something would have to be done about the Grimble. Normally in a situation like this Sim would nip round to Hazel's to share the gossip, but there was still no response from that quarter and Sim had decided that she couldn't tackle the Hazel issue until she and hers were rid of the Napper. 'Rory? What was it about Eve's letter that led you to this conclusion?'

'Oh, I can't explain.' Evidently she regarded specifics as crude and beneath her.

'Forgive me if I'm being slow,' said Sim, 'but I'm not sure I see what you mean. Are you trying to say that you were only happy to purloin Campbell because you could see his relationship with Eve wasn't working? Would you never break up a relationship that was going well?'

'I would never break up any relationship, Sim. What do you think I am?' Therein, thought Sim, lies a tale. 'If that's what all Campbell's friends think of me, there's going to be a lot of unconstructive energy floating around at Matt and Lucy's wedding. It seems a shame to spoil their day. I've been thinking . . .'

Chicken, thought Sim scornfully. Rory was scared of meeting Eve; anything to avoid facing up to what she'd done. Not long ago Sim would have been thrilled if Rory had ducked out of the wedding but now she was torn; if Neil went and the Grimble didn't, it wouldn't be symmetrical. Sim had adjusted to the new shape of the wedding and didn't want it to become lopsided. If Campbell was there alone, Eve might take pity on him and neglect to flaunt her relationship with Neil. Sim passionately believed that such flaunting was the short, sharp shock Campbell needed; nothing less would be strong enough to blast him out of the abyss. 'Yes?' she said to Rory, who hadn't completed her threat, or promise, depending on how you looked at it.

'I don't want Campbell to be in a difficult position, or anyone else,' said Rory. Just as Sim was beginning to wonder whether there was a glimmer of hope for her as a human being, Rory added, 'I think it'd be better for everybody if Eve didn't go.'

Ian pushed the hoover across Hazel's living-room carpet, slamming it into the skirting board. He turned round, aimed it in the other direction and was about to pursue dust even more aggressively on his return journey when Hazel turned off the power at the socket. 'Did you hear what I just said?' she asked timidly.

'Yes, I did and I can't believe it,' Ian said tightly. 'What the hell . . . ?' He stopped, afraid of letting loose his true feelings on the matter. He and Hazel had never rowed before. He took a deep breath and forced his voice to come out normally. 'Why did you tell Sim that I'm Dale Dingley?'

'Oh, I'm sorry, I'm sorry! Don't be angry, please. Oh, I've ruined everything! You'll never forgive me.' Hazel ran in little semicircles around him, popping up first on one side of Ian, then the other. She was frantic.

Ian took pity on her. 'All right, all right, I'm not angry, but . . . Jesus, Hazel.' He shook his head.

'I wish I hadn't now, but it's too late. She believed me. What are we going to do?' Hazel's teeth chattered. 'Oh, God, I've let you down!'

'Why didn't you tell the truth?' Ian asked. 'I mean, wouldn't it have been preferable? It's a bit insulting to think that you'd rather let your friends think you're living

278

with a murderer than tell them about me. I must really be a guilty secret.'

'You're not, you're not . . .'

'No one's ever made me feel ashamed before, Hazel, but I have to tell you, you're coming close.'

'It's not you who should be ashamed, Ian, it's me.' Hazel's face was blotchy with fear.

'But that's the whole point. You *shouldn't* be!'

'I know, I know. I just meant . . . it would be me, if anyone.'

'Hazel, don't just agree with me because you're scared of an argument,' said Ian gently. 'I'm not going to storm out and never come back. I'm yours as long as you want me, okay? You know that.'

'But I don't deserve . . .'

'Shut up a minute and listen. We need to get to the bottom of this. If you think we, or you, are doing something wrong, you should put a stop to it. We can just be friends. I'd be happy with that. I wouldn't hold it against you.'

'But I don't think it's wrong,' Hazel protested.

'Neither do I. Then why did you just tell your friend I was Dale Dingley, when you could have told her the simple truth?'

'I didn't tell her! She guessed . . . oh, you know what I mean. And she didn't disapprove.'

'Well, she bloody well should have done,' said Ian, thinking that Sim had to have a screw loose. First Vanessa Willis, then Dale Dingley; did Sim befriend the obnoxious out of sheer perversity?

'Sim thinks he's innocent,' Hazel explained. 'She trusts my judgement. Oh, Ian, she sounded so impressed when she was telling me we were in love – me and Dale Dingley – as if she so admired me. I could tell I'd gone up in her estimation. I know I should have told her the truth, but I suppose I was flattered. Not that Sim wasn't perfectly nice to me while I was single – while she thought I was single, I mean – but no one properly respects a woman who isn't loved by anyone and she was making it sound so romantic, I . . . I didn't want to give that up. I didn't want to tell her I haven't got a man who loves me. I wanted to pretend it was true.'

'It *is* bloody true,' Ian shouted.

Hazel frowned. 'What? What do you mean? You mean . . . Ian, I know you aren't Dale Dingley.' She seemed reluctant to remind them both of this.

'For Christ's sake. I'm in love with you, Hazel. No, I'm not Dale Dingley, but you can't have everything. Do you think you could make do with me instead?'

Monday, 12 April 1999, 10 a.m. Studio Four, Broadcasting House, Montgomery Lane, Leeds. **Steve McCargo** *sits behind a table, wearing headphones.* **Dale** *and* **Wayne Dingley** *sit opposite him, also wearing headphones. In front of each man is a styrofoam cup full of lukewarm coffee. It is ten minutes into the interview.*

S McC   So let me get this right: you're claiming you have no idea how a blood-soaked T-shirt found its way under your bed?

D D   Yeah.

S McC   But you don't deny that the T-shirt was yours?

D D   Nuh.

S McC   So what do you think might have happened? (*Long pause.*) When had you last seen that particular T-shirt, before the police found it under your bed?

D D   Dunno.

W D   How the *bleep*'s he s'posed to remember that? S'a *bleep*ing T-shirt. He's got loads of *bleep*ing T-shirts. (**Wayne** *is saying* 'fuck', *not* 'bleep', *but this is being altered in transmission because of the time of day.*)

S McC   Dale?

D D   Uh?

S McC   This is your chance to put your side of the story . . .

W D   Yeah, s'about *bleep*ing time we 'ad our say. We're the *bleep*ing victims here.

S McC   Wayne, you'll get your chance to speak in a minute. But if I could go back to Dale . . .

W D   He told yer. He don't know nothing about how that T-shirt got there.

S McC   The T-shirt was covered in blood. Do you know whose blood?

D D   Bethan Wrigley's.

W D   Stop *bleep*ing around wi'im! We read the papers. We i'n't thick.

S McC   How did Bethan Wrigley's blood get on to your T-shirt, Dale? DNA tests proved it was hers.

D D   Dunno.

W D   The pigs *bleep*ed up all them tests.

S McC   Dale? Do you think someone borrowed your T-shirt, or stole it, murdered Bethan Wrigley and then put the T-shirt back under your bed? And what about the fact that your semen was taken . . .

W D   Leave him the *bleep* alone. Them tests was rigged, right?

S McC   Do you at least concede that somebody raped and murdered Bethan Wrigley?

W D   Must have done, 'ey?

S McC   What's your opinion of the men who raped and murdered Bethan?

W D   You don't know it was men. Could have been girls. Anyway, how do you know it was more than one person? Might have been one woman what done it.

S McC   Whoever it was, then. What do you think about them?

W D   I don't think nothin' about 'em.

S McC   Dale, do you agree with Wayne that a woman might have killed Bethan Wrigley?

D D   Yeah. Dunno.

S McC   There must have been a man involved as well,

281

mustn't there? (*Long pause.*) Because semen was found.

W D   (*cockily*) She might have slept with her boyfriend before she died.

S McC   The physical evidence made it clear that a violent attack had taken place. And tests showed that the semen belonged to Dale.

W D   Look, it's like all these miscarriages of justice you keep hearing about.

S McC   Your fingerprints were found all over the body, Wayne. What do you say to that?

W D   I say it's a *bleep*ing lie. I never touched her.

S McC   What's your explanation, then?

W D   It's obvious, innit? We was framed.

S McC   Where were you on the evening of Friday, 30 August 1997?

W D   Where we told the pigs we was: in All Bar One in Leeds.

S McC   So you weren't in your local, the Bell Tower?

W D   No. *Bleep*, how many times . . . ! We was in All Bar One.

S McC   No one saw you there.

W D   We kept ussen to ussen.

S McC   You were, on the other hand, seen coming out of the Bell Tower in Pudsey. The witness who reported seeing you testified that you appeared to be extremely drunk.

W D   Can't have been us she saw. We wasn't in the Bell Tower that night.

S McC   Don't you usually go to the Bell Tower every Friday?

W D   What if we do? Don't want to get in a rut, know wha' I'm sayin'?

S McC   What if I were to suggest that you did go to the Bell Tower on Friday, 30 August 1997, that you did fall out shortly before midnight, roaring drunk, and that you bumped into Bethan Wrigley who was on her way home from the nightclub down the road, Lazy Lou's? What if

282

I were to put it to you that you dragged her on to the area of waste ground where the playground used to be and proceeded to rape and murder her?

W D   I'd say, prove it.

(iv)

'Francis? Francis!'

1

The first thing Sim saw when she pulled over by the kerb was Campbell's face, framed in the pub doorway. His expression was slack and dejected. Sim hadn't seen him for just under a fortnight and was shocked to observe the rapid decline in his appearance. He still hadn't had a haircut and his mouth resembled a large scab. Bloody hell; Campbell was supposed to be cheering Francis up.

The Rusholme night air smelled of curry and exhaust fumes as Sim opened the car door and stepped out. Francis didn't move. 'We've arrived,' Sim told him in a more neutral tone than she would normally have used. Francis hadn't been himself since the Dingley interview and even more sinister was his refusal to talk about it. Silence was the one thing Sim couldn't deal with.

The Dingleys' appearance on *The North Today* had won them more public support than they'd had previously. Letters had flooded in after the interview from people who purported to understand what they were going through, many of them teenage girls and middle-aged women. Sim couldn't fathom this. Anyone who'd listened to the interview could be in no doubt that Wayne Dingley was scum through and through. Dale hadn't said much. Did he know his brother had done it? It must have been tough to live with if he did. Did he and Hazel talk about this, or did they both believe Wayne hadn't done it? Hazel was still avoiding Sim, using the Throat Parrot as an excuse.

Something would have to be done. Worried though Sim was about Francis, she couldn't allow that to blot out everything else.

The tabloids had run numerous stories about the 'Dingley Fan Club' and published interviews with pretty young blondes who claimed to be the soulmates of either Dale or Wayne, depending on which brother they fancied more. Annette Wrigley had attempted suicide two days after the interview and Francis had barely spoken since.

Sim's suggestion that he should see his doctor and ask to be signed off work with depression was rejected with a level of verbal violence that was rare even for Francis. She shouldn't have been surprised; Francis saw it as disgraceful to be in the grip of any emotional state other than contented apathy. Emotions were things that happened to other people; Francis merely watched them on the news.

Sim had given up trying to talk to him about Annette Wrigley; there was no point. The barriers came up immediately. Discussing how one felt, in Francis's book, was akin to picking one's nose in public. He preferred to emulate a robot who proceeded methodically through life without falling prey to such girlish disabilities as guilt and remorse.

Sim couldn't recall having been so worried about anything before, though she'd forbidden herself to give in to tormented guesses as to what was going on in Francis's mind. Her worst fear was that he was single-handedly battling against spasms of dread, too proud to seek help. She told herself that most people, at some point in their lives, went through brief periods of morbid depression – mini nervous breakdowns, if you like – and survived them. The difference was that Francis was particularly ill-equipped to deal with anything of that nature. He'd always been scathing to the point of arrogance about psychological conditions, refusing to believe in the pull of the subconscious, or indeed in anything that couldn't be filmed with Kate Adie standing in front of it.

This evening was supposed to be the latest in a series of distractions: meeting up with Campbell in Manchester for a drink at the Whitworth pub and a curry at Francis's favourite Indian restaurant, the Sangam, which served, Francis insisted, the best mushroom pakora in the country. Normally Sim would have been opposed to any plan for recovery that did not involve direct confrontation with the problem, but Francis's case was different. In its honour, she'd formulated a brilliant new therapy; one in which the cure was entirely unrelated to the disease. Sim didn't want Francis to wrestle with his conscience. He'd done enough of that already. Forcing him to do something as uncharacteristic as talking at length about how he felt would only freak him out even more; he'd feel as if his whole identity were being snatched away from him and would recoil from what he'd perceive as his new, weakened self.

So day after day Sim kept up a cheery façade, hoping Francis would eventually relax and let himself off the hook. She'd stopped mentioning Annette Wrigley and the Dingleys altogether, and arranged a programme of ceaseless fun in the hope of demonstrating to Francis that he could slip back into his old, comfortable life without even having to pay a toll of relevant words.

Ceaseless fun was evidently not on the agenda tonight, however. One look at Campbell's face reminded Sim that this was the pub in which Hindley and Brady had hatched their plans. Damn, bad choice; she should have suggested the Clarence down the road. But didn't Karl Marx and Matthew Engel also drink here? Sim had heard something to that effect but she wasn't sure. Besides, that fact might have cheered Nicholas up but it would do nothing for Francis.

The jukebox was on full blast. 'Come on, come on, come on,' an ardent male voice sang, 'love's the greatest thing.' Campbell was hunched, unshaven, thinner than Sim was used to seeing him, over a small round table. He stared into his pint with watery eyes. There were no two ways about it: he was decaying. Sim felt guilty. She'd been so worried about Francis that all thoughts of Campbell had been driven from her mind. Seeing him now, she remembered the last thing she'd said to him, before he and Rory left Saltaire: 'By the way, I wouldn't use that vibrator again if I were Rory. I dunked it in the River Aire this morning.' Campbell had stormed out without saying goodbye. It had seemed funny at the time. Sim was enraged by Rory's suggestion that Eve stay away from Matt and Lucy's wedding. Her comment was intended to punish Campbell for his execrable taste. Let him worry about whether or not it's true, she thought. Sim predicted he wouldn't tell Rory; being the jelly that he was, he was more likely to say nothing, hope Sim was joking and worry at the same time in case Rory contracted a hideous venereal disease that he could have prevented.

Was that why he was in such a state tonight? Had he spent the past fortnight fretting about Rory's quail-like innards? God, Sim hoped not. She wanted Campbell to pull himself together, not waste away. If he could, she added humbly, feeling for the first time in her life that there might be forces at work that were greater than all of them – even her, the fearless Simone Purdy.

'Eve's over there,' Campbell told Sim, pointing grimly at the bar. He and Francis had not yet acknowledged one another's presence. Sim couldn't think of a single word to say in response to this. Well, in the absence of ceaseless fun, surprise would do nicely. Her heart was beating fast as she turned to look. Yes, indeed, there Eve was. This went way beyond surprise and into shock. What a brilliant shock, though. Sim felt overpowered by sentiment; here she was, meeting Campbell and Eve in the pub, like old times. It was so unquestionably right. Unbidden, a scene from *The Railway Children* sprang to mind: a platform, mist clearing, a longed-for face emerging and Jenny Agutter shouting, 'Daddy, my daddy!' Sim choked back a tear. I must be going soft, she thought. To ground herself, she focused on the fact that Campbell was looking as bleak as Saddleworth Moor in the rain, so this couldn't be the loving reconciliation she hoped it was.

Eve, hearing her name mentioned, turned and waved. She too had lost weight since Sim had last seen her, but not unhealthily. On the contrary, Eve seemed to radiate happiness and power. Her hair was shorter with blonde highlights. Those black trousers and boots were new too. Sim had difficulty imagining what could have happened between Eve and Campbell before she and Francis arrived that would have resulted in Eve looking so triumphant and Campbell so dishevelled and ethereal, as if he were barely clinging on to the tangible world.

'Hi, you two!' Eve pushed through a crowd of students with her gin and tonic and another pint for Campbell. 'You've just missed my round, you'll have to buy your own drinks. Only kidding. What do you want?' Eve sounded hyper-upbeat, as if someone had wound up a key in her back.

'Francis?' Sim nudged him.

'Hm?'

'Eve's offering to buy you a drink. What do you want?'

'Oh . . . um . . .'

'Kronenbourg,' said Sim, raising an apologetic eyebrow at Eve. 'And I'll have a Southern Comfort and lemonade. Ta.' The second Eve was safely out of earshot she said, 'What's wrong with Eve?'

'Nothing,' said Campbell, making a visible attempt to rally round. 'She and Neil have got engaged.'

'*What?*'

'They're engaged. Neil proposed. Eve said yes. She's got a ring.' He stared at Sim accusingly.

Sim took off her jacket and sat down, thinking quickly. She needed to get with the programme, to use an American expression. Francis might have opted to retreat from life, but Sim couldn't afford to. In fact, she needed a project now more than ever, to keep her busy, since all she could do on the Francis front was wait and hope. She looked at him and saw that he hadn't heard a word Campbell had said. If only he were more interested in the love lives of his friends, this news might have been sufficient to jolt him out of his depression. But there was only one sort of news Francis recognised, the Radio Four sort. Had he learned nothing from his recent experiences? He'd thought Annette Wrigley was just a news item and been badly shocked when she did something messy and personal like try to kill herself.

A new thought struck Sim: was there an element of narcissism, even of selfishness, in Francis's behaviour? Did his interest in himself so outweigh his interest in others that he could allow himself to be swallowed up by his own mind without feeling he was missing much? Sim wished she could feel properly irritated with him for being spoilt and thoughtless enough to put her through this ordeal, but one look at him told her he was too weak to be an object of crossness. She hated having to adjust to an idea of Francis as an invalid.

Back to Eve, though, before she got too upset. Sim was not willing to accept Eve's engagement on any level. The joyous, revelatory feeling she'd had when she first saw Campbell and Eve together in the pub had left her in no doubt as to what should happen. Everything could still be – *had* to be – as it was before. Eve needed to rescue Campbell; without her he would become an amorphous mass, and Sim wanted the old Campbell back, the laid-back armchair philosopher and connoisseur of soap operas that he'd once been.

Neil was a good stop-gap and, in some ways, sounded superior to Campbell, but there was only one measurement that counted and that was love. For all Francis's flaws, Sim would never dream of leaving him for someone more attentive and polite. Andrew Johnson, for instance. Ugh. The Toodle-pipster had left two messages on Sim's mobile phone this week, asking her to call him. She'd ignored both, hating Andrew for reminding her of a time when she hadn't appreciated Francis quite as much as she did now. Even if Francis never spoke again, Sim wouldn't abandon him in favour of somebody who did. For better or for worse. Sim had never said it, but that didn't mean it wasn't true.

Eve came back from the bar and bounced on to a stool. 'Well?' she demanded. 'Has Campbell told you my news?'

'Yes,' said Sim. It occurred to her that Eve's engagement might be a ploy, designed to bring Campbell to his senses, but that alternative was no better. Sim knew what Neil had done to get Imogen's poem a prize in the school competition. She was impressed. Not many people would have bothered. She hoped Eve wasn't using Neil; he deserved better. 'Congratulations!' she said, attempting the sort of smile that would keep Eve guessing. 'Francis? Francis!'

'Hm?'

'Eve and Neil are engaged.'

'Who's Neil?' Francis murmured. No one told him and he didn't ask again.

'So when's the wedding?' Sim thought she might as well know the worst.

Eve laughed. 'May the fifteenth,' she said.

'But that's . . .'

'Matt and Lucy's wedding day. I know.' Eve beamed. Sim felt peculiarly leaden. This was not good. She'd counted on Eve saying she and Neil hadn't yet set a date. Sim did not respond well to deadlines. She had trouble with anything that didn't get out of the way sharpish when it saw her coming. 'It'll save everyone turning out twice,' said Eve. 'We thought we'd get married in the morning, at Cambridge Register Office, then go to Matt and Lucy's wedding in Summerton chapel and have a joint party afterwards, to celebrate both marriages.'

'But Matt and Lucy have already arranged their reception . . .'

'Don't worry.' Eve smiled. She seemed frighteningly calm. 'I'm sorting it all out with Lucy. I e-mailed her yesterday. They'll have their sit-down dinner as planned, and then mine and Neil's guests will arrive in time for the next bit, the dancing and stuff. We've offered to pay for half the booze.' Sim pretended to be reassured. She couldn't believe Lucy had agreed to this. It was a terrible idea, disastrous. Why did Eve and Neil have to cram their wedding into a day that was quite full enough already? For nearly a year, Sim had looked forward to having an excellent time on May the fifteenth, and now Eve proposed to bugger it up by marrying the wrong man on the same day. The grandness and symbolism of the occasion would be entirely undermined. 'I was saying to Campbell that it'd be him and Rory getting engaged next.' Eve giggled.

'Really? Ha, ha!' Sim guffawed, hoping to indicate to all present that this could only be a joke. What was Eve playing at? Was she drunk? Poor Campbell; Sim had been way too hard on him. She'd thought of him as the stupid one and Eve as the more sussed, but at least Campbell wasn't going so far as to marry a virtual stranger just to make a point. Sim had never even met Neil.

'Don't you want to see the ring?' Eve asked.

'Oh. Yes.'

'Neil insisted on buying an expensive one,' she said, stretching out her arm towards Sim. On cue, the large pear-shaped diamond caught the light and flashed.

'Wow,' said Sim. 'It's beautiful. So where is Neil tonight?'

'In bed with a stomach upset,' said Eve briskly. 'The ring cost two and a half grand. I was a bit shocked when Neil told me that, but as he pointed out, that's because I'm used to economising. And I don't need to as much now that I haven't got a useless waste of space to

294

support.' She elbowed Campbell in the ribs and laughed. Campbell winced and pushed away his pint as if it had turned sour under his nose. Sim looked at Francis, who was staring morosely at the silent TV screen above his head. He hadn't once tried to hurry them all to the restaurant. Neil wasn't the only unknown force Sim had to deal with. I'm sitting here with three strangers, she thought. What had become of the pompous, irritable Francis she adored, the happy Campbell and Eve combination she relied upon?

Change: never was a commodity more overrated. She, Simone Purdy, had not changed in any significant sense since she was four years old. It was a wildly inconsiderate thing to do to one's social circle. Sim intended to put a stop to it, all of it. She straightened her back and reached for her handbag. Pulling out her diary and a pen she said, 'When are you free for lunch, Eve?'

Gang Chuen Li
Flat 4 Heron House
Newton Site
Silver Street
Cambridge
CB2 0PR

Monday, 26 April 1999

Dear Vanessa

Sorry for a late reply. I have just come back from my dissertation research in Geneva. I was surprised to read your postcard. I didn't realise that my kind silence has led to a misunderstanding on your side. In order not to embarrass you, I have never blamed your careless driving which has caused me great suffering in recent times.

The pavement where you thought 'I shouldn't be' is actually specified by Cambridge City Council for bicycle riders' use. There are several clear signs along the road. One especially at the gate where you drove out suddenly without looking around. As a matter of fact this is a popular path for student cyclists as it leads to the university library.

Under such circumstances I would insist that you pay the total amount of the cost of the terrible accident, which is £59. The police judgement you quoted is based on the wrong information you provided. I don't mind contacting them again to clarify the whole story should you wish to do so.

I am invited by the British government to study in your best university. And according to what I have learned here, I have enough confidence on the honesty of the British people as well as your sound legal system.

Best regards
Gang Chuen

Nicholas pressed his lips tightly shut to stop the bile that was rising in his throat from spewing out of his mouth. He put a hand against the door frame to steady himself. Then, because he didn't want anyone who happened to be passing to see or smell what was in his office, he forced himself to walk in and shut the door behind him. Once he was in an enclosed space with the mess, the urge to vomit was even stronger. Nicholas wanted to run to the windows and throw them open, but in order to do that he would have to pass the thing.

Why hadn't he had the lock changed? All he'd have had to do was tell a porter and it would have been attended to, but he'd felt paralysed by Gillian's threats as thoroughly as he was now paralysed by what he saw in front of him. In the middle of his office floor was a large, roundish pool of urine. Funnily enough, it was exactly the same shape, though smaller, as the pond where his dad had taken him to feed the ducks as a boy, in the park, next to the rusty climbing frame. Floating on its surface was an empty packet of the breakfast cereal Shreddies, surrounded by what looked like its contents: lots of tiny, square, brown parcels. Nicholas had to exercise considerable self-control to stop himself from howling in anguish. This was the sort of thing that happened to people in nightmares, in horror films. It couldn't be happening to him in Cambridge, in his real life. He tried to think beyond his disgust and panic. It didn't take a genius to work out that Gillian had to be responsible.

Tiptoeing around the horror with his nostrils clamped shut, Nicholas grabbed the phone from his desk. He dialled the number of the Modern Languages office, wondering about the sheer volume of liquid. She must have saved it up . . . no, he couldn't bear to think about it. He heard the words 'Modern Languages', followed by a loud sniffle.

'Why? Just tell me why,' he demanded. He tried to sound furious to conceal his terror. Nicholas couldn't believe that his life, that he himself, had come to this. Once he'd have vigorously denied he had a violent streak; now he prayed for its return. He felt shrivelled by fear and worried that he'd never again feel the red-blooded urge to hit someone very hard, not even Vanessa.

'Don't shout at me,' Gillian reprimanded him tearfully. 'How can you be so insensitive, today of all days?'

'What?' Once again, she'd succeeded in putting him off his stroke.

'Don't you care that Jill Dando's been shot?'

'*What?*' The name was familiar but it took Nicholas a few seconds to work out who Gillian was talking about. When he realised it was a TV presenter he said, 'No, I fucking don't care!' How dare Gillian prattle on about some pampered, rich celebrity after what she'd done to his room?

'That's typical of you, Nicholas Drogan. Well, I care. I *loved* Jill Dando. She was my namesake.'

'Gillian, I'm phoning about what you've done to . . . in my office.'

'What did you expect?' she said nastily. 'You stole that office and then refused to share it with me. You ignore my feelings completely. You've *shredded* me, Nicholas. That's what the Shreddies mean, in case you're too thick to guess.'

'Gillian . . .' Nicholas fought the urge to bash his head against his office wall until he knocked himself out. 'Look, please come and clean up this mess. And then we'll talk, okay?'

'You clean it up.'

'For fuck's sake, you were the one who did it!' Nicholas couldn't understand why he bothered to argue with her, as if she were capable of seeing and responding to reason.

'I don't want to talk to you, Nicholas. Put the phone down, right now. I want to ring the police.'

'Gillian, please . . .'

'No, you've had all your chances. Get off the phone.'

'Wait!' Nicholas pleaded. 'I'm sorry. Look, you win, okay?'

'How do I win?' Gillian asked suspiciously.

'I'll . . . clean up the office.' Nicholas felt faint with humiliation, as if he'd ceased to be a person.

'And?'

'I'll share the office with you,' he heard himself say.

From: lucyfairclough@worldbank.org
To: francis.weir@bbc.co.uk/thenorthtoday
Subject: FAO Sim
Date: Tue, 27 April 1999

Hi Francis
Please could you print this out and give it to
Sim? I assume she's working from home, since I
e-mailed her at work and she hasn't answered. Ta.
Matt says hi.

Hi Sim

I suppose Eve's told you about her plan to get married to Neil on the same day as me and Matt. I can't believe you think this is a good idea and I'm hoping you can talk her out of it. She'd listen to you. She can't possibly be over Campbell yet and even if she is, it's too soon for her to be sure she wants to marry Neil. I love Eve dearly and don't want to hurt her, but Matt and I both think she's making a big mistake. Why can't she and Neil give their relationship a year or so, see how it goes and then get married later if they still want to? I don't want to say anything to her in case she thinks it's because Matt and I are reluctant to share our party. We aren't at all – we just think it's silly for her to rush into such a big step. Please talk to her. I'll ring you tonight.

Luce

PS Ta for info on costume shops. Still not sure about fancy dress idea – may be too much hassle. Where is Eldwick, anyway? Isn't the hotel nearer to Bradford?

'Ladies and gentlemen,' a crackly voice filled the carriage. 'I'm sorry to announce that this train will be subject to a delay of approximately fifteen – one five – minutes when we reach Saltaire. This is due to one of the carriages catching fire.'

Never mind catching; it had been on fire since Keighley, where Hazel had got on. A flame had licked at the window nearest to her as the train rolled into the station. She'd moved diplomatically along the platform and chosen another door further down, hoping to arrive at work uncharred. She really ought to learn to drive, the Leeds to Skipton line being what it was. Still, who cared if she was late back to the office? Hazel had Ian now; little else seemed to matter. She was someone's other half. For the first time ever, she was loved! Gatting loved her, of course, but not in the romantic sense. This was something so new and exciting that Hazel could hardly contain herself. She would have given herself up entirely to contented daydreams, were it not for a few worries that gnawed at her mind.

Why had Ian torn the *His and Hers* page out of her copy of *Howdy*? Hazel was scared to ask, in case Ian's secret turned out to be something with the power to ruin their new-found happiness. They hadn't slept together yet. Hazel couldn't risk taking things forward a stage until she trusted Ian completely. She hoped he'd tell her whatever it was soon; maybe he was just waiting for the right moment.

The barbecued train slid into Saltaire where it seized up with a violent clinking sound. The door nearest to Hazel was flung open and Francis jumped into her carriage, depositing his briefcase on her lap without comment while he took off his jacket. He looked as if he'd just been roughed up by the ghosts of Christmas past, present and future, getting in some early training. 'Fucking thing's on fire,' Francis snapped. 'Whole country's grinding to a halt. That's what comes of most people being *stupid* enough to vote for Tony Blair!'

Hazel cowered beneath his angry gaze. What must Sim think of her now that she'd heard Dale Dingley on the radio? He'd come across as a monster, couldn't have sounded guiltier if he'd tried. Hazel couldn't face Sim at all; she'd studiously avoided all her advances ever since what Hazel had dubbed Dingley Day. She prayed Francis wouldn't mention it and that, if Sim had told him about Hazel's ridiculous confession, he'd missed it because he wasn't listening, as with most things. 'You're late in,' she commented feebly.

'Didn't sleep,' said Francis. He eyed her with suspicion, reclaiming his briefcase with a sharp jerk, as if Hazel had snatched it from him. 'How come you're already on? Don't you live in Saltaire?'

'I live in the same building as you, Francis.' Hazel tried

not to feel offended. 'I've just been in Keighley with the Throat Parrot.' Sim probably hated her for consorting with a murderer. She must have told Francis to act cool if he saw her.

'What the hell is that?' Francis scowled.

Hazel wished she'd sat amid the flames and ashes of the burning coach. Anything was preferable to Francis in this sort of mood. 'Who, not what,' she corrected him. 'He's a performance poet.'

'Jesus!' Francis shook his head in disgust. Hazel was feeling more depressed by the second. Francis sometimes had that effect on her. What if Sim had never believed the Dingley story? What if she hired a detective who found out the truth about Ian? For the first time, Hazel realised how stressful being happy was in comparison with being miserable; one had so much more to lose.

'Are you looking forward to Matt and Lucy's wedding?' she changed the subject.

'No.'

'Oh. Right.'

'It's an illusion.'

'What do you mean?'

'Why do people bother getting married?' Francis opened his briefcase and pulled out the *Daily Telegraph*. He unfolded it, but continued to rant from behind its pages. 'I mean, life's fairly shit, isn't it? It's sheer lunacy to be happy. Vanity, that's what it is. We're all living on borrowed time. Any minute now a giant foot could come along and squash us.'

Hazel didn't know what to say. She gulped uncomfortably. This sort of thing happened all the time in *Potters Court*. In all soaps, actually. One character unwittingly strolled up to another and, quite by chance, made a comment that was highly relevant to the second character's preoccupations, without realising its relevance. The first character then breezed away innocently, leaving the second wearing an 'Oh no! That applies to me!' face for

301

the remaining few seconds of the scene. In soaps, Hazel realised miserably, it was almost always a bad omen when this happened.

'Sim probably wouldn't marry me anyway, would she?' Francis asked irritably. 'Well?'

'I've never asked her,' said Hazel truthfully.

'You haven't? Well, why not? I thought you were supposed to be her friend.'

'I thought you were supposed to be her boyfriend,' Hazel retorted sharply. Francis muttered something inaudible and retreated behind his paper. I can't believe I said that, in that tone, to Francis, thought Hazel. What had possessed her? She didn't regret it, though. Ian was always telling her she should stick up for herself.

'Ladies and gentlemen,' a more cheerful voice boomed from the speakers. 'I'm pleased to announce that we shall shortly be recommencing our journey to Leeds. I would just point out, however, that we're having a slight problem at the moment with water seeping into carriages B and C, so if you'd be so good as to make sure no bags or coats are on the floor. Thank you.'

'Water in one carriage, fire in another,' Francis snapped. 'What next, fucking locusts? Sod this!' In one swift movement, he'd grabbed his jacket from the luggage rack and was out on the platform again, glaring at Hazel as he marched away, as if the failure of the train were all her fault. How would he get to work, she wondered. Would he come back and catch the next train? He didn't look in any fit state to drive. Hazel wanted to phone Sim to tell her that Francis appeared to be more than usually unbalanced this morning, but she was terrified of what else the conversation might involve. How was it possible to get oneself into such a predicament?

'I told Campbell quite seriously', said Eve, facing Sim across the sort of round table Gillian Kench would have hated, 'that if Rory comes to the wedding, I'll punch her.

302

I've never hit anyone in my life, but I'd hit Grimbelina. It's not just Matt and Lucy's day any more, it's mine too and I don't want Rory there.' Eve and Sim had met for lunch at the Tai Pan in Victoria Park, the nearest restaurant to Eve's school.

'Did you tell Campbell this?' asked Sim, picturing an aghast Campbell receiving the unwelcome tidings that his ex-girlfriend would feel duty-bound to punch his present one.

'Oh, yes.'

'How did he respond?'

'Stunned silence at first. Then he said I was being nasty and unreasonable, and told me to control myself.'

'Like he has, you mean?' Sim laughed.

'That's what I said. He didn't control himself when he was tempted to leave me for Rory. But he said that was different.'

'Let me guess,' said Sim wryly. 'It's okay to exchange one girlfriend for another, but never okay to hit someone, whatever they've done.'

'That was about the size of it, yes,' said Eve.

'Ah, you see. It's Campbell's wrongness wrongness again.'

'He tries to have it all ways. He says he didn't choose to leave me, he *had* to do it. So I said, how's that any different from me having to hit Rory if I see her? I told him I'd rather be punched in the face any day than go through what he's put me through.'

'Campbell needs to believe that things can be civilised,' said Sim. 'Unfortunately, they can't always, especially when a creature like the Grimble's involved. She's so warped, it's impossible to be constructive in her presence. I tried, but it was like trying to make a flower arrangement out of a heap of shit. I mean, I told you what she said about your letter and how she wouldn't have gone anywhere near Campbell if she'd known he had a girlfriend . . .'

'That's a complete, outrageous lie! I told Campbell she

303

told you that, but he dismissed it completely. He said she's just a bit mad.'

'Mad, hey? Well, whatever you want to call her, it was like trying to reason with an abscess. Anyway, if she does come to the wedding and you do hit her, I'll hit her too.' Sim realised this was true. Things had certainly changed. Only a few weeks ago her prime concern had been to preserve the perfection of Matt and Lucy's special day; now here she was committing herself to assaulting one of their guests.

'Why? You didn't hit her when she stayed with you.' Eve tried hard not to make this sound like a criticism.

'That was a different context. Hitting wasn't right for that weekend. What I did was better: I made it clear that I wasn't buying into the Rory Napper myth. It would have been absurd for me to hit her when you weren't there. Whereas if you hit her' – Sim bit into a small triangle of prawn toast – 'and I was there and I didn't, that would be as bad as failing to stand up and say "I'm Spartacus" immediately after Kirk Douglas had said it.'

'Anyway, Campbell says he probably won't bring her.'

'Oh.' Sim was sorry to lose her righteous punching fantasy so soon after being given it to play with. 'Eve?' she began reluctantly. This could be a nightmare, but she'd promised Lucy; she couldn't let her down.

'Mm?' Eve popped a vegetarian dumpling into her mouth.

'Don't you think it'd be better if you and Neil got married on one of the other three hundred and sixty-four days of the year?'

Eve smiled understandingly. 'I know what you're thinking, Sim. I'm not stupid. Normally I wouldn't tag along on someone else's special occasion, but . . .' She looked sad.

'What?' Sim asked.

'It'll sound silly. I'm not usually superstitious, am I?'

'Not at all.'

'I just . . . want to be happy with Neil. I want everything to be right and I suppose I kind of think that . . . well, Lucy and Matt are so happy and their wedding'll be so idyllic . . .'

'You're hoping it'll rub off on you and Neil. Like a good luck charm.' Sim finished Eve's sentence for her.

Eve nodded. 'Neil and I couldn't afford to have a wedding party at Summerton College on our own, and I can't think of anywhere better to get married. I feel I deserve some good things after what I've been through.'

Sim couldn't disagree. How could she blame Eve for wanting to soak up a bit of the golden aura? Didn't they all do that, to a certain extent? Wasn't that why Sim herself was so looking forward to the wedding? Let's face it, she was unlikely ever to have one of her own; Francis would find the whole process too upsetting. He thought too much of his father to make him spend a whole day in the company of 'the Great Satan', as Philip Weir liked to call his ex-wife. 'How does Lucy feel about it, though?' Sim asked gently.

'I don't think she's that thrilled, but I'm hoping she'll come round. Can't you talk to her, try to persuade her? It really means a lot to me, Sim. Lucy can't see that it's a tribute to her and Matt more than anything else. They should be flattered. The day could be doubly romantic if we all approach it in the right way. Will you have a word with Lucy?'

'Of course,' said Sim, stifling a sigh. Great. At this rate she'd forever be going back and forth between Lucy and Eve, relaying the opinion of one to the other. As for her own world-view, it had never been so torn. Lucy and Matt led such a blessed life; they couldn't be in a stronger position. And Eve's world had been turned upside down. On the other hand . . .

'Is Francis any better?' Eve asked, interrupting Sim's deliberations.

'Slightly.' She sighed. 'He's speaking occasionally, which

305

is an improvement. Do you know, I never realised how jolly his grumpiness was until now.'

'If you say so.' Eve looked doubtful.

'It's true. He was grouchy, but always in an upbeat way. I know it sounds mad, but I'd sacrifice a hell of a lot to have him be normally irritating again.' She smiled sadly. 'Do you think I should invite Annette Wrigley round for a confrontation?'

'Sim, you can't do that!' Eve was shocked. 'She might have a real go at him. She begged him to cancel the interview and then tried to top herself after it was broadcast.'

'I know. A direct attack might do him good, though. Don't look at me like that, Eve, I've tried everything else. At the moment Francis doesn't need to defend himself because we're all so busy defending him.' Eve wondered who that 'we' was intended to include. She certainly hadn't defended Francis; she'd thought the Dingley interview was a crazy idea from the start. But she knew Sim was keen to see them all as a group, united in every respect, so she said nothing. Nor did she point out that if Lucy had a problem with sharing her wedding day, she could bloody well lump it. Eve had her own happiness to consider.

Sim was still thinking aloud about Francis. 'There's a danger that if we all cosset him too much, he'll continue to wallow. If Annette Wrigley came round and laid into him, it might sharpen his defensive instincts, that's all. He's a stubborn, awkward bugger, let's not forget that.'

'Well, I wouldn't risk it if I were you.' Eve speared a vegetable spring roll with her fork. 'Campbell was really upset, wasn't he?' she said. 'About me and Neil getting engaged.'

'He looked a wreck,' said Sim. 'But was he like that at the beginning of the evening?'

'No, he was fine before I told him. Well, not fine, but . . . well, how he's been since we split up.'

'Like a man in a health club changing room who can't understand why the key pinned to his trunks won't open his locker,' Sim summed up. 'And then you told him and he disintegrated.'

'He was obviously shaken,' Eve agreed. 'But he didn't try to talk me out of it.'

'Yes, but Campbell's clutch is very high, isn't it?'

'Hey?'

'When a car's clutch is high, it takes longer to accelerate. You put your foot on the gas and nothing happens for a while. Then gradually it creeps forward.'

'Yeah, but that's no good,' said Eve impatiently, as a waiter placed Sim's duck in plum sauce and Eve's mushrooms in black bean sauce on the table in front of them. 'What sort of idiot is he if he'll stand back and let me get engaged to someone else?'

'Eve, are you sure you want to marry Neil?' Sim asked. Eve was prepared for the question. She'd made a few notes in her head, knowing Sim would get round to asking at some point. Any friend would, but one as nosy as Sim would require a particularly thorough answer.

Neil had grown on Eve, there was no doubt about that, and before too long she'd be thirty. She wanted to get married, have children. That had always been a central part of her life plan, and she didn't care a damn about taking things slowly and sensibly. Sim wouldn't either, if someone had just seized seven and a half years of her life and ripped them up right under her nose. Neil would make a wonderful husband and father, and he adored Eve. What more could she want?

'I know it seems rushed,' she said, 'but, yes, I'm beginning to love him, Sim. Really. And in many ways we're so much better suited than Campbell and I were. Neil's got a job, he helps around the house, he can drive . . .'

'Eve, these things are neither here nor there,' said Sim. Very occasionally Eve came out with this sort of nonsense. Sim didn't hold with the idea of people as useful. Anyone could be useful, even donkeys and Gillian Kench. It took a rare talent to be successfully ornamental. Was Neil as good at chatting as Campbell was, that was what Sim wanted to know.

'I know Neil would never leave me and run off with someone else,' said Eve. 'That's the main thing.'

'What would you have said if Campbell had asked you to marry him the other night in the Whitworth?'

'I don't know. He never would, anyway.'

'Still, you say you don't know,' Sim repeated hopefully.

'Well, I still love him.' Eve shrugged, seeing no harm in admitting it. 'It'd be a bit odd if I didn't, wouldn't it? And I think he still loves me. He said he did in the Whitworth, before you and Francis arrived.' Her voice went flat. 'But he said he loves the Grimble too.'

'Eve, you're not bringing Neil to Matt and Lucy's stag-hen weekend, are you?' said Sim.

'No. Don't worry, we're leaving them something to call their own. Campbell wouldn't dare bring Rory, would he?'

'Even Campbell's not that stupid,' said Sim. 'So you'll both be there without your other halves. Good.'

'Why?'

'Because I've got a plan,' said Sim.

Vanessa stood on Grange Road and stared down at the pavement, clenching her fists until her knuckles whitened. There, a few yards from the driveway that led to Gentchev's Field, was a wobbly white bicycle symbol that, despite having been pounded by feet and tyres for years, was still clearly visible. Vanessa had never noticed it before. Across the driveway, where the pavement started again, there was another identical symbol. Since the only way of getting from one stretch of pavement to the other was by crossing the Gentchev's Field driveway, it appeared Red-tooth was right: this was intended as a cycle path.

There was no feeling Vanessa hated more than that of being caught out. There had to be a way round this. She was damned if she was going to be the one responsible for the accident in her own fabrication as well as in the true version of events.

Something was very wrong here. Red-tooth, in her latest martyred, self-satisfied letter, had not denied cycling on the pavement. On the contrary, she'd defended her right to do so. Whereas Vanessa's memory of the event, which became more vivid as time elapsed, now placed Red-tooth firmly in the road at the time of the collision. Besides, what did it matter, road or Gentchev's Field driveway, if both Vanessa and Red-tooth had the right to be on both? Whose fault the accident was depended not on where it took place, but on who was driving without appropriate care and attention.

As long as there was no consensus, no stable, shared reality, Vanessa was damned if she was going to accept even a sliver of blame. If the situation's two protagonists couldn't agree on the simple fact of where the crash took place, what were the chances of getting to the truth about which of them was going too fast? Pretty bloody small, thought Vanessa. Red-tooth could have been hurtling along carelessly as Vanessa edged gently out, or perhaps it was Vanessa who did the hurtling. Everything was in doubt. I have no alternative but to let myself off the hook, thought Vanessa.

It occurred to her that perhaps Red-tooth was lying too. Perhaps she knew full well that she'd been in the road, but knew also that the pavement doubled as a cycle path and had decided it would be easier to defeat Vanessa within the terms of Vanessa's own story, the one Red-tooth had in writing on the back of the *Marathon Man* postcard.

Vanessa still had one clear advantage over Red-tooth, as far as she could see: she was Vanessa Willis. And the game was far from over. She could put forward a defence based on several points. Gentchev's Field's driveway was unmarked, uninterrupted gravel; there was no white line, no bicycle symbol painted on it at any point to alert emerging drivers to the possibility of cyclists crossing their path. Surely that meant the onus was on cyclists to stop at the edge of the drive and check there was no car on its way out.

The crux of the matter was who had priority over that shared patch, the few square feet that were both driveway and cycle path. What did Cambridge City Council intend? Did they imagine cars would hang back until they were sure no bikes wanted to pass, or that cyclists should give priority to drivers?

A brilliant idea struck Vanessa as she stood on the white bicycle symbol. What if she were to produce a witness or two, people who could say they'd seen Red-tooth cycling recklessly. Talentless first-time novelists who were desperate to get into print might be good for a corrupt project of this sort, and there was no shortage of them in the Gable Bazzard files.

Vanessa walked back to the flat, forcing herself to smile at the two porters she passed. She ignored Nicholas, who was hunched over the coffee table, staring morosely at his article. Vanessa guessed that the Roman Polanski's foreskin technique hadn't worked for him, but she had no intention of asking and giving him the opportunity to tell her her expert advice was useless. Besides, Nicholas had avoided sex with her now for four days, so Vanessa didn't see why she should bother to speak to him at all.

She went upstairs and pulled a small paper bag out of the top drawer of her bedside cabinet. Inside, there was a postcard of the film *Bicycle Thieves* that Vanessa had bought in London last week with Red-tooth in mind. 'Dear Ms Li,' she wrote.

I do not accept responsibility for the accident. I do not intend, therefore, to reimburse you for the taxi fares or your dental treatment.
    Yours sincerely
    Vanessa Willis.

*   *   *

When the doorbell rang insistently for three or four seconds, Ian knew who it was. He could picture the determined finger pressing it down. That finger meant business. Ian could have sat tight until Sim went away, but what would have been the point? He had to enter and leave Hazel's flat at least once a day; Sim would catch up with him eventually. Ian was fed up of dodging her. Curiosity about what she would say to him if she got the chance was distracting him from his work.

'Hello?' He spoke into the entryphone.

'It's Sim, Hazel's friend. Is that Dale Dingley?'

Ian sighed. Cheers, Hazel. 'No,' he said.

'I know it's you, Dale. It's okay, Hazel told me. Now, let me in.' She sounded grave, like a Victorian matriarch. Ian couldn't believe this was the same fun-loving woman Hazel described so rapturously. She did think he was a rapist and murderer, though, which might explain it.

'Come up,' he said. At last he was to meet someone from Hazel's other life. He felt nervous, then wondered how Sim felt about confronting the person she believed him to be. She couldn't possibly still think Dale Dingley was innocent after the interview on *The North Today*.

A couple of minutes later there was a loud rapping on the door of the flat. 'Come in,' Ian called. Nothing happened, so he walked over and opened it. A large woman with curly brown hair and tinted glasses stood before him, wearing a long black dress and a floor-length lilac cardigan. She looked elegant and terrifying, and was armed with a copy of *His and Hers* by Debbi Naismith and Greg Pendry. 'Come in,' said Ian, staring at the book. A couple of weeks ago he'd have been furious, but his anger had dissipated and he felt no more than mild distaste.

'You're . . . er, you're not Dale Dingley,' was the first thing Sim said.

'No.' Ian smiled.

'Phew. Well, that's a relief, I suppose.' Sim looked

disappointed. 'I was going to ask you . . . you know, if you'd done it.'

'I doubt he'd have confessed,' said Ian. 'Why don't you come in? My name's Ian Boyle. It's good to meet you. Would you like a coffee?'

Sim nodded. She followed him through to the kitchen and put *His and Hers* down on the worktop. 'I brought this for Hazel,' she said. Ian put the kettle on and waited for an explanation, but when he turned round Sim had left the room. It had to be a coincidence, surely, nothing to do with him. Ian told himself firmly not to be paranoid. Everyone was reading it; he'd seen it on buses and trains. It was this spring's most popular rubbish. He made the coffees and took them through to the lounge. Sim had taken up residence on Hazel's sofa and resembled a technicolour Buddha in her long robes.

'Well,' she said, 'I've made a complete idiot of myself, haven't I? The thing is, you've got the same hairstyle . . .' She stopped abruptly. 'Hazel *told* me you were Dale Dingley. Why?'

'You'd assumed they had a glamorous doomed romance going.' Ian smiled. 'She thought you respected her more because you thought she had a bloke and I suppose . . . well, you seemed happy and she didn't want to upset you.'

'Oh, God, poor Hazel. So you aren't her boyfriend?'

'Well, yes, I am now.' Ian explained how Hazel's distress at getting entangled in the Dingley fabrication had led to his rather unromantic declaration of love. Once she'd got over the shock, Hazel had said that she loved Ian too, and since that day there had been a lot of kissing and hand-holding. Nothing more, though. Hazel was still a virgin – something Sim didn't know and Ian had no intention of telling her – and wanted to wait until she knew Ian well enough to trust him completely. Or thought she did. Ian felt a twinge of guilt.

'But that's great!' Sim perked up. 'So some good's come

of my, er, misunderstanding. In fact, you could say that I got you together! But . . .' Here comes the question I've been dreading, Ian thought. 'If you and Hazel weren't an item before I waded in with my Dale Dingley theories, why were you living in her flat?'

'I wasn't. I live in Baildon at my mam and dad's. I spend a lot of time here, though. Hazel and I were . . . friends.'

Sim's eyes narrowed. 'She would have told me about you.'

'We *were* friends . . .'

'But there's more to it,' Sim finished his sentence.

'Yes,' Ian admitted, finding it odd that he and Sim were gabbing away as if they'd known each other for years. It was quite nice, actually. 'This is where it gets tricky, Sim. I can't tell you. I'm sorry. I've tried to persuade Hazel, but she insists on keeping it a secret. She thinks her friends would disapprove. I don't agree with her. I think there's nothing to disapprove of, but she won't be persuaded.'

'Disapprove?' Ian could see from Sim's face that she was concentrating hard, as if trying to solve a cryptic crossword clue. He found her amusing and had to remind himself that he didn't usually like strong characters. Sim was different; she added colour to her surroundings, consolidated them. And if she was strong, she didn't appear to want to bash everyone else over the head with her strength. She was easy to talk to. Ian felt he could have said anything to her, if only he hadn't had to make sure he said nothing. How ironic. 'You aren't members of the same family, are you?' Sim asked eventually.

'No!'

'Okay, sorry. Had to ask. Are you colleagues, embezzling Leeds council funds?'

'No. And please don't keep guessing or I'll have to stop answering your questions. I'd happily tell you but Hazel won't let me. What can I do?'

'Hm.' Sim chewed her bottom lip. 'Has it got anything to do with *His and Hers* by Debbi Naismith and Greg

Pendry?' Ian tried not to look stunned. Evidently he failed, because Sim started to laugh. 'Hazel told me you ripped an advert for it out of another of her books. She's convinced there's some sinister reason and asked me to buy it for her so she could study it for clues.' Ian groaned and shook his head. No wonder Hazel didn't trust him enough to sleep with him. What was he going to do? 'She wouldn't buy it herself because she thinks it's too lowbrow,' Sim explained.

Ian would have hugged Hazel if she'd been there. Of course it was lowbrow; how could anyone think otherwise? It belonged in a literary underclass all of its own. 'No, it's nothing to do with that,' he said. 'Oh, God, this is mad. The thing is, there are two secrets.'

'Two! Marvellous.' Sim settled in for the double bill.

'One Hazel knows, the other she doesn't. The *His and Hers* thing, well, that's the one she doesn't know about. I'm really sorry, Sim, but I can't tell you either secret. I'd love to, believe me. I'd love to tell you both, but I can't. And I know I've got no right to ask you this, but please don't mention the second secret to Hazel. It's nothing that'll harm her. I do have my reasons, honestly.'

'Okay.' Sim nodded thoughtfully and Ian congratulated himself. He'd approached it perfectly. If he'd clammed up, Sim would have fought him with all her best underhand tactics. By laying out in detail what he couldn't tell her so that she had a precise map of exactly what information was missing, Ian had created the impression of confiding in Sim without giving anything away. 'But you'll have to tell her I came round, that I know you're not Dale Dingley,' she said. 'Tell her you told me she pretended you were because she didn't want to tell anyone she had a boyfriend until she was sure it was going to last.'

'Okay.' This struck Ian as a sensible suggestion.

'In return for not mentioning the second secret to Hazel . . .' Sim began with a sly smile.

314

'Go on.'

'What are you doing on the weekend of the seventh to the ninth of May?'

'Hazel's going to Matt and Lucy's stag weekend. I've got no plans.'

'Why don't you come with her? Now that you're her boyfriend, you should meet her friends. No one needs to find out you were ever anything else, if you see what I mean.'

'Well . . .' Ian wasn't sure he should agree without consulting Hazel.

'Oh, come on. Look, you'd be helping me out. I can't tell you how pleased I am about you and Hazel.' Sim beamed at Ian. 'You know our friends Campbell and Eve split up recently?' Ian nodded. 'Well, I could have prevented it if I'd been more on the ball. But I wasn't and it happened. So hearing that I've inadvertently got you and Hazel together is a real sort of . . . what do you call it? Like in films where couples who tragically lose a child at the beginning have a cute baby at the end and that makes everything okay. Redeemed! That's how I feel.'

Ian thought Sim had a colossally exaggerated sense of her own importance, but he kept that thought to himself. 'The stag weekend?' he prompted. 'How would I be helping you out if I came?'

'Oh, right. Well, my mission is to get Campbell and Eve back together. When Lucy was booking rooms at Hollins Hall, she booked them a double, not knowing they'd split up, and she booked a single for Hazel. I told her to change Hazel's single to a double, thinking that Eve could go in with Hazel if she and Campbell weren't back together by then. Anyway, there were no doubles left, but we got the last room available, a twin. If you're in there with Hazel, Eve and Campbell will have to share their double room and bed, won't they? It's brilliant!'

315

'But . . . isn't Eve marrying someone else?' Ian asked, confused.

'We'll see about that,' said Sim.

2

Eve pulled a small white envelope out of her pigeon-hole, too distracted to recognise Walter Allnutt's right-sloping handwriting. All she'd thought about since her lunch with Sim at the Tai Pan was the plan and whether it would work. She'd tried to express her doubts, but Sim had an answer for everything. 'He can't refuse to share a bed with you,' she'd said. 'I'll tell him there are no spare beds or rooms in the hotel. Campbell couldn't afford one, anyway.'

'He'll just sleep on the floor in someone else's room,' said Eve.

'He'll be too embarrassed. We're all couples, aren't we? He won't want to spoil the amorous atmosphere in our boudoirs.'

'He'll sleep on Hazel's floor, then.'

'Hazel's a woman, Eve. He'd be too embarrassed to suggest it, in case she thought he was coming on to her. Anyway, Hazel's very anti-Campbell at the moment. She didn't send him that leaflet she sent the rest of us about that Verses on Hearses thing. He's been struck off her mailing list. There's no way she'd share a room with him.'

'Sim, he'll think of a way round it.'

'Excuse me, this is Campbell Golightly we're talking about. When has he ever thought of a way round, through, or past anything? You know what a map drawn by Campbell would look like, if he were a cartographer?

It would be a big, blank sheet of paper with nothing on it apart from a red dot and the words "You are here". I'll tell him it'll be a purely platonic bed-sharing and he won't suspect a thing. Not consciously, anyway. His mechanism – remember I told you about that? – will know what's going on, though, and make sure he leaps at the chance. Subconsciously, he wants to get back together with you, but he won't admit it in case he loses face.'

'And if he agrees?'

'You don't have to leap on him. Just lie there looking like a tempting prospect and be nice to him. Hopefully he'll get nostalgic for the old days, when he got laid without any trouble and everyone he knew didn't loathe his girfriend. Once he remembers what that feels like, he'll want you back. Deffo.'

'But will I want him back?' Eve felt the need to remind Sim, occasionally, that she had free will. 'Would I ever be able to trust him again, after what he's done?'

'Yes,' said Sim. 'Campbell's no serial deserter. In fact, he's not even a one-time deserter. His attempt to desert you is about to be revealed as a total flop. And luckily the Grimble is *so* awful that she'll make a great cautionary tale. Campbell's not stupid. I predict that if you and he do get back together, he'll appreciate you more and treat you better than ever.'

'But, Sim, I'm engaged to Neil. I love him. We're good together. I'd have to lie to him.'

'It's hardly a lie. He knows Campbell's going to be there. Just . . . don't go into detail about sleeping arrangments. I'm not for a minute suggesting you leave Neil,' said Sim. 'If you decide you prefer him and want to marry him, fine. All I want is to put you in a position where you're able to make a proper decision. At the moment you aren't because you've got Neil at his best and Campbell at his most bonkers, in the grip of his obsession with old Cruelty-without-Beauty. Campbell needs to be cured, Eve, whether you get back with him or not. Then, once he's better, you can make an informed choice about who you want to be with. But listen, do me one favour, okay?'

'What's that?'

'If, during the night, Campbell makes a move . . . well, would you mind . . . you know?'

'Accommodating him?'

'Yeah. I think it'd help to get him back on track.' Eve couldn't think how to respond to this request and had changed the subject at that point. She wasn't sure she wanted to have sex with Campbell, either physically or . . . politically, for want of a better word. She liked the idea of his wanting to have sex with her, though. If Sim's plan worked, Campbell might say he regretted what he'd done in an attempt to get her to screw him and then she wouldn't need to.

The school bell rang and Eve quickly ripped open the envelope in her hand, smiling and tutting at the memory of Sim's lunacy. 'Dear Eve,' Walter Allnutt had written. 'I am writing to inform you that I am unable to support the idea of a prize of any sort being awarded to Imogen Salt for the poem "Memories". I'm sorry if this is disappointing news. Bests, in haste, Walter.'

Oh, no. Eve blinked several times and reread the note but the words didn't change. But, wait, how could this be? She'd spoken to Walter at length and he'd been all in favour of giving Imogen a prize. Why the sudden derailment? After all the effort poor Neil had put in.

Eve couldn't help feeling this was a bad omen. She'd agreed to Sim's plan and now this had happened. If she rang Sim and said she'd changed her mind, would Walter change his? I can't do that, she thought, however much she wished she could for Neil's sake and Imogen's. Eve was a goer-through with things. She didn't back out or run away, not like Walter Allnutt. It was lucky he wasn't in the staffroom now, or Eve might have pulled his gold-rimmed bifocals off his nose and stamped on them. Wasn't it bad enough that she was treating Neil unfairly, without one of their colleagues joining in?

From: mattc@hopkinsandgreen.org
To: francis.weir@bbc.co.uk/thenorthtoday
Subject: Mainly girl stuff
Date: Thur, 29 April 1999

Hiya Frankie boy
Looking forward to getting v. trolleyed with you at stag weekend (girls can bugger off and be hens somewhere else!) Could you pass this next bit on to Sim? Cheers. Hope your liver's ready for the onslaught.

Matt

Dear Sim
Hi, it's Matt here. Listen, sorry to land all this shit on you, but Luce is a bit upset and I think she's pussyfooting around the issue so I thought I'd try and sort it out. I know she e-mailed you and said she didn't think Eve and Neil should rush into getting married for their own sake, not because we mind them muscling in on our wedding day and party. Well, that's crap. I told her to be honest, but Luce is too nice and polite. Apart from the fact that it's obviously an arsehole of an idea to marry some bloke you've just plucked off the staffroom sofa because you're desperate, Lucy does mind them getting married on the same day as us. Things like that mean a lot to girls, and she feels Eve's copying her and trespassing on her big day. She doesn't want to share her wedding day with anyone (except me, obviously!) and she especially doesn't want to share it with the most farcical marriage of the century! I don't mean to be tight on Eve or anything, but come on, you must agree. Sort it out, mate – I know I can rely on you. Everyone listens to you.

Matt

From: alj@renshaw.cam.ac.uk
To: simone.purdy@potterscourt.co.uk
Subject: DON'T IGNORE!
Date: Thur, 29 April 1999

Sim

This is ridiculous. I've left three messages on your mobile and you're not responding. I've phoned you at work but you never seem to be there, unless your colleagues are lying for you. Please get in touch. I really need to see you before the wedding on May the fifteenth. There's a lot I need to tell you, things you'd want to know. You misunderstood me when we met at the Galleria. I wasn't criticising you for falling out with Gillian. I was asking because I need your help, Sim. I can't go into it here, but please ring me. I still have feelings for you, you know. Always have had.

Toodle-pip

Andrew

xxxxxxxxxxxx

Sim lay with her eyes closed, breathing evenly as Francis writhed and wriggled beside her. She thought he'd find it easier to fall asleep if he didn't know she was awake, aware of his insomnia. It was difficult to appear asleep when you weren't, though; you had to make sure your eyelids didn't look clenched.

No wonder Francis wasn't making a speedy recovery if he was having such restless nights. Sim didn't know if he was always like this because she was usually asleep herself. Tonight, however, she was an edgy insomniac in her own right. She had no idea how to handle the conflict that was brewing between Eve and Matt and Lucy. Both parties expected her to act on their behalf and Sim couldn't think of any compromise solution. Nor was she sure whose side she was on. Matt and Lucy had early bird rights, having claimed the fifteenth of May almost a year ago, but Sim couldn't help thinking they were being a bit mean. The last thing Eve needed was to be made to feel unwanted again after the rejection she'd already suffered.

If she and Campbell fell into one another's arms in the foyer of Hollins Hall, that would solve a lot of problems. Eve might think Neil was better for her than Campbell, but he certainly wasn't better for her friendship with Matt and Lucy, in that Campbell almost definitely would not want to marry Eve on the fifteenth of May.

Sim refused to think about Andrew. Feelings for her, indeed. Could there be a more meaningless phrase? Everyone had feelings of one sort or another – positive, negative or indifferent – for everyone else. Sim was working hard on cultivating the last variety with regard to Andrew.

This is ridiculous, she thought, after another half-hour of lying as still as a statue, listening to the material of Francis's pyjamas scratch softly against the sheet as he rolled back and forth. 'Francis,' she said loudly, startling him. 'If you can't sleep, you should see Dr Vine and get some sleeping pills.'

'No.'

'But you aren't sleeping. You need sleep to be able to work. Francis? Well?'

'Leave it.'

'Oh, well, suit yourself. Francis? You know at the stag-hen weekend?' If he wasn't prepared to talk about his own preoccupations, he could damn well talk about hers.

'Sim, for fuck's sake . . .'

'What? You're not asleep, so we might as well chat.'

'That doesn't follow, logically.'

'I think we should be vegetarians, just for that weekend. No fish, either; anything Eve doesn't eat, we don't eat.' Sim sat up in bed. This idea had been feeling its way around the back of her mind for some time, but it had only bloomed just now. 'I think it's important, symbolically,' she said. 'The huge potential for elephant indignation is an as yet untapped resource in the war against Grimbelina. Animal rights issues play a large part in the imagery of it all. We have to take the right side, Francis, and be seen by Campbell to be taking the right side. Francis?'

'I thought you wanted me to get some sleep,' said Francis, who had a pillow over his head. 'Leave me alone.'

'But do you agree?'

'Whatever!' The word came out as a groan.

'Good. I'll try to get the others in on it too. Now, the way we present this to Campbell is crucial. He needs to know we've gone vegetarian so that the imagery can do its work upon him, so that he's aware of a gradual landslide in Eve's direction. That means we have to tell him directly. He's bound to be in an emotional fug and unlikely to notice that we're eating carrot roulade instead of roast beef. So I'll slip it into the conversation at some point, but I won't explain why. Don't you explain why either, Francis. If he asks, which he probably will, make a wistful face as if you've given the matter deep thought and change the subject. The only way we can make it plausible is by saying nothing. The one thing you absolutely mustn't do is tell him the truth. If he knows we're trying to create an effect, the gesture will instantly be sapped of all its power. Now, what we . . .'

'For fuck's sake!' Francis bellowed, jumping out of bed as if he'd been electrocuted and banging his head on the wall in his haste. The free-standing wardrobes shook. Sim gasped and clutched the duvet. She'd never seen Francis move so quickly. He yanked open the curtains and stood in the middle of the room, panting. 'Leave me alone! Leave me alone! I tell you to shut up and you don't shut up! You're the most annoying person I know, has anyone ever told you that? You witter on and on, and I'm fucking sick of it. Sick of it! Do you have any idea how banal all this sounds to me now?'

'Now?' Sim prompted. 'What, you mean I didn't sound banal to you before? That wasn't what you said at the time,

I'm sure of it.' Yelling was considerably more than she'd had from Francis for a good long while.

'Yes, now, now!' Francis opened a cupboard door, then slammed it shut again. 'Now that I'm responsible for the near death of Annette Wrigley! She tried to kill herself! Dale and Wayne Dingley are still free! Nothing is any better than it was before.'

Sim was amazed and relieved. This was the first time since the interview that Francis had mentioned the names Dingley and Wrigley. Now here he was, shouting about them, being his old lovable crotchety self again, only a bit louder.

Sim lay down and threw the duvet over her head, smiling to herself. ''Night-night, Francis.' If she wanted him to keep talking, the very worst thing she could do was appear interested.

'Sim! Didn't you hear what I just said?' Francis pulled the duvet off Sim's curled body and threw it on the floor.

She ignored him and yawned. Her strategy was working like a dream. There could be no obvious flagging up of the cathartic moment; Francis loathed that sort of thing. 'I'm not listening to you unless you listen to me,' she said. 'Did you take in any of what I said about Campbell and Eve and the meat?' Sim continued to let Francis believe her mind was elsewhere. If he thought she'd noticed him 'being psychological', he would get embarrassed and withdraw.

'No!' Francis sounded more bewildered than angry. 'Sim, what I'm trying to say is important.'

'As is what I'm trying to say,' she retorted.

'Campbell and Eve? How *dare* you compare that gossip crap to what I'm talking about? Lives have been ruined . . .'

'Francis, you could easily be describing the Campbell and Eve situation, can't you see that?' Sim sat up, taking pity on him. 'The bad way in which you now find yourself is entirely a result of this spurious distinction you make between ordinary people's real lives – gossip, as you call it

– and the politicsy, newsy things you take so seriously, the things that are safely far away. Annette Wrigley crossed the line, didn't she? She tried to kill herself, which made you realise she isn't just a headline, she's a person. You couldn't handle it when she did something that went beyond the professional you and impinged upon the personal you. If you want to avoid shocks like that in future, you've got to start noticing people, taking their feelings into consideration.'

'I do all that,' said Francis defensively.

'No, you don't. Whenever I try to talk to you about what's going on with anyone we know, you're not interested. You think there's no difference between *Potters Court* and our friends' lives. You put them all in the same category. And then you're shocked when Annette Wrigley downs a bottle of sleeping pills.'

'So what are you saying?' Francis yelled. 'I'm the worst person in the world, ever – is that it? I'm an evil bastard because I didn't give in to Annette Wrigley's blackmail and cancel the interview? I deserve to be punished, just because I don't find it fascinating to spend hours discussing who Campbell happens to be rogering at the moment?'

'Or not, as the case may be,' Sim muttered. 'Look, I'm not saying that . . .'

'Go on, tell me! You think I'm a shit. I knew it!'

'I don't think that and I never will,' said Sim calmly. 'Look, I spend most of my time thinking about what's going on in other people's minds and I thought – I still think – you were right to do the interview. In its way, the truth came out. Anyone with a brain who heard it will be in no doubt that the Dingleys did it.' Sim decided not to mention her own doubts at the time. Now that she knew Dale Dingley was nothing to do with Hazel, she could see that he was probably a rapist and murderer. There was nothing like loyalty for clouding the issue; only the friendless could afford to be moral purists. 'It's not your fault Annette Wrigley took it so badly,' she told Francis, wondering if this was also loyalty talking.

'So why do I feel it is?' asked Francis.

'Because there are a few things you don't understand, but I'm too tired to explain them now. I'm going to sleep.' Sim faked a yawn. Her world-view was playing hard to get. Never in her life had she felt more awake.

'No fucking way,' Francis shouted. 'We're going to settle this now, tonight. I want to know exactly what you mean.'

'Okay, Francis.' Sim turned on her bedside lamp. The radio alarm clock's digital display told her that it was quarter to three in the morning. 'Bring me a cup of Lapsang Souchong and I'll tell you about my world-view.'

'Hello, you Loch Vaness monster, you!' First thing on Friday morning Miff McGarvey's well-bred tones seeped into Vanessa's office-hutch via that treacherous double agent, her telephone.

'Miff. Hi.' The agent's jokes were as repetitive as Cal Raynard's titles. Vanessa sighed and took a large gulp of coffee from her *His and Hers* mug. The novel had been a huge hit and its accessories were all over Gable Bazzard's offices. Everywhere Vanessa looked she saw the cover image replicated, a clothed male groin and a clothed female groin pressed together indecently on posters, postcards, mouse mats and crockery. It wasn't what one wanted to see when one's boyfriend had inexplicably withdrawn his sexual favours. Nicholas had better get his act together pretty soon or he'd be history.

'Presumably Gray's told you.' Miff's tone suggested that Gray had told everyone who was anyone.

'Our Gray?'

'The very same. I met him at a party the other night and we drank rather a lot of tequila – oh dear! – and we sorted out our teensy-weensy wrangle. And *everybody*'s happy with the new title, so that's wonderful.'

326

'Excuse me?' Fury billowed through Vanessa. 'What is the new title?'

'*Rowdy*. It's *so* wonderful, so relevant. It makes a real statement about the tone and the main character.'

Vanessa was too stunned to speak. How dare Gray forget to tell her that a new title had been agreed upon? Never mind tell her; she should have been consulted. She was the book's editor. 'I'm surprised you're happy with it,' she said stonily. 'I thought Cal didn't want a title that rhymed with his others.'

'Yes, but *Rowdy* is a vast improvement. The problem with *Audi*, you see, is that Callypoos was absolutely convinced that his salesman would drive a Saab and we all know that you can't argue with an author's intuition about one of his precious characters. But I had a little wordarooney in his ear and he came round. Sometimes one has to compromise, doesn't one?'

No, one fucking does not, thought Vanessa. She was glad this had happened, actually. It made her realise that she'd let Red-tooth off far too lightly. She should have done much more than refuse to pay taxi fares and dental costs. 'Come on, darling,' said Miff. 'If Himself can live with it, surely you can?'

'Can he live with having written his novels?'

'What do you mean?'

'I rest my case,' Vanessa muttered, before slamming down the phone. She pulled her wallet out of her bag and started to flick through a fat wad of receipts. The one she was looking for was headed 'G P Motors'. Ah, there it was: a bill for a service Vanessa's car had had three days after the crash with Red-tooth. It listed four items that had been replaced: a headlight bulb, the fan belt, the stepper motor and the vacuum pipe. How was Red-tooth to know these parts were faulty long before she came along?

Vanessa took a sheet of white A4 paper from the printer on her desk and began to write:

Dear Ms Li

After taking extensive legal advice, I find I have no alternative but to insist you reimburse me for the damage you caused. I enclose a receipt for the work I needed to have done on my terribly ruined car after you so carelessly rode into me. I know you will want to do the right thing. [Vanessa grinned. It was fun to parody Red-tooth's style.] The sum comes to a total of £278.68. I would appreciate it if you could send me a cheque by return of post.

    Yours sincerely
    Vanessa Willis

From: simone.purdy@potterscourt.co.uk
To: mattc@hopkinsandgreen.org
Subject: Campbell and Eve/Costume shops
Date: Fri, 30 April 1999

Hi Matt!

Got your message loud and clear. Okay, listen. I've got a plan to get Campbell and Eve back together at stag-hen weekend. They'll be sharing a room. They've both agreed to this, which I take as a sign that they're amenable. If they get it back on at Hollins, there'll be no wedding with Neil – problem solved. It's the only solution that'll make everyone happy (except Neil, but if Eve loves Campbell more, as her going back to Campbell will prove she does, it's better for Neil in long run too). Can we all be vegetarians for the weekend? It's v. important. Haven't got time to explain why – got soap mayhem to create. See you soon.

Sim xx

PS Tell Lucy Eldwick is much nearer to hotel than Brad or Leeds and the costume shop there, Dutton's, is the best in West Yorkshire. It's run by a little bearded man (whose pipe is bigger than he is!) who used to fish off *the Suffolk coast – he's a real character. Warn Lucy, though, that fancy dress might have to be optional – Francis might insist on going as the belligerent deputy editor of The North Today. Soz!*

Neil leaned against the school railings beside Walter Allnutt's battered Nissan Bluebird, feeling like a gangster. This, at least, was one problem he was determined to tackle head-on. In the case of Eve, his strategy was to say nothing. She'd been doing a lot of whispering on the phone to Sim recently. Neil knew something was up and guessed that it involved Campbell.

The life Neil had lived – not happily but with a sort of grudging acceptance – before he and Eve got together was unthinkable now; he'd die rather than be that lonely again. Whole weekends had passed during which he hadn't spoken to a soul. Embarrassingly, he'd even thought this was relatively normal.

In those days Neil used to believe he wasn't fussy; any woman would do, he'd thought, within reason, of course. But after only a few weeks with Eve, the idea of climbing into a bed beside anyone else was grotesque to him. Neil felt as if he'd found the one place in the world where he belonged. No, not found; that was wrong. He'd *created* that place. Until very recently he'd thought Eve was as happy there as he was.

Neil told himself that Eve was still engaged to him and that he had to trust her, to cling to the hope that she'd never do to him what Campbell had done to her. Eve, like Neil, was a person who stuck to the commitments she made. She was fair and wise, and Neil deserved her more than Campbell did, surely she could see that. Perhaps Neil was naïve, but he believed in the power of justice to win through.

Here came Walter Allnutt, the creep. Neil tried to look relaxed and friendly. 'Are you waiting for me?' Walter asked.

'Yes. I wanted a quick word about the poetry competition.' It hadn't taken Neil long to cobble together a plan. The prospect of Imogen's poem not getting the prize it deserved, when things had been looking so hopeful, brought him close to raw despair, though he couldn't quite understand why he cared so much.

'Oh?' Walter raised a bushy eyebrow.

The guarded tone of a turncoat, Neil thought bitterly. 'Just a bureaucratic endnote to the whole process, really. I'm tying up the paperwork and as there's been some disagreement about this one girl's poem, I wondered if you'd mind putting it in writing. Just so I can stick it in a file, you understand. You know what this place is like about keeping records.'

'What do you want me to put in writing?' Walter's eyes narrowed.

'Oh – only a couple of lines about why you didn't think a prize should be awarded to Imogen Salt's poem. Nothing too detailed.' Neil knew he was handling it well; his tone was just right.

'Well, I . . . I . . .' Walter's mouth twisted. Bastard, thought Neil. He didn't have a reason, unless you counted fear of Phyllida Banborough. One minute Walter had been telling Eve how marvellous he thought 'Memories' was, the next he was writing a curt note to say that he'd decided to form a two-to-one majority with Phyllida. Walter's trouble was that he had no backbone; he was morally incontinent. Rather like a certain Mr Golightly of Didsbury, formerly of Cromer Street, Rusholme. Emphasis on formerly.

Neil's chest swelled with confidence. All he had to do was adhere firmly to the path of righteousness, a sort of ethical yellow brick road, and all opposition would fall away. He'd buy Eve something expensive on his way home, too, something Campbell would never be able to afford.

'I think I . . . er . . . Phyllida and I both thought the poem couldn't possibly have been the girl's own work,'

330

said Walter. 'It was too mature. She must have copied it, was our feeling.'

'Sure, sure, whatever,' said Neil breezily. 'Just dash off a few lines to that effect when you've got a minute and wham it in my pigeon-hole.' Dash? Wham? He was going overboard in his attempt to sound casual but it seemed to be working.

'Of course,' said Walter.

'Cheers. Oh – are you likely to be seeing Phyllida tomorrow?'

'We're going to the cinema tonight.'

Oh, you are, are you? 'Great. Could you ask her to do the same?'

'If I remember,' said Walter, pulling his car keys out of his jacket pocket.

'Cheers.' Neil smiled, looking forward to telling Eve about the satisfactory progress of Plan B and how he'd fooled Walter. It seemed crucial to remind her whenever the opportunity arose that this time she'd backed a winner.

Francis got out of the taxi and paid the driver, aware of Roundhay Park behind him, opposite Annette Wrigley's house. He wondered how Annette felt about living so close to its dark expanse, whether she ever looked out of her bedroom window at night and imagined she saw Dale and Wayne Dingley's shadowy forms emerging from the blackness.

He rang the bell and waited, observing that he was not afraid of what was about to happen. It was inevitable. He could no longer indulge his misery in the abstract manner to which he'd become accustomed, thanks to Sim. His grim mood now had a cast of characters, at least one of whom was within his grasp. Sim seriously believed – and she'd put the case quite convincingly during their recent nocturnal seminar – that what one did and said to the piddling everyday people one encountered in one's piddling

331

everyday life could have a profound effect upon . . . well, all sorts of things.

Annette Wrigley would not be keen to see him, Francis knew. What she would say to him was likely to make him feel worse, not better, but he didn't care. One thing he'd learned since becoming what Sim called depressed (Francis hated the word) was that change, not improvement, was what one craved, change in any direction.

The house was a tall Victorian semi with a stained-glass panel above the front door and a bay window to the left of the porch. Francis focused on the spots of rust on the letter box. If he thought about anything else he might lose his nerve and run away.

He heard feet slowly descend the staircase. Seconds later the door opened. Annette Wrigley was still in her dressing gown. Her face was lined and pale. Her hair was even shorter now, and clung to her head like a tight swimming cap. 'Francis Weir,' she said quietly, as if to a third party. She stepped aside and gestured for Francis to come in. He tried to gauge from her face whether she was preparing to attack him, taking a few quiet moments first to assemble her curses in an appropriate order.

He followed her through to the dining room at the back of the house. Francis guessed that Annette avoided the front room as far as possible – the legacy of too many journalists leaping over the hedge with their microphones and cameras. On one wall there was a large framed photograph of Bethan wearing a red school uniform with a shield logo on the blazer. Something was written on the shield, probably the name of the school or a motto in Latin, but the writing was too small for Francis to read. Annette, he remembered, had paid to send Bethan to Rivington, the best private school in the county.

Francis approved. His own mother hadn't bothered to do the same for him. Actually, Francis suspected she felt threatened by the prospect of his doing well at school, in case he ended up in a stronger position than her. She impressed upon him, all through his teens, that for boys his age to play truant, drink, smoke, take drugs and generally go off the rails was a standard part of growing up. She'd been quick to mock kids like Matt, who worked hard, had aspirations and were firmly on the rails, implying that they were somehow abnormal, arrogant even, as if screwing up your life made you a better person. Francis had even fallen for this for a while. If he hadn't had Matt as a best friend, whose parents had encouraged both boys to apply for Cambridge University because it was the best, Francis might never have come to his senses in time.

No child of mine and Sim's will go to a state school, Francis vowed. You didn't have to be married to have kids any more, did you? Francis rejected the idea as soon as it occurred to him. It was important to do things in the right order.

Annette was staring at him, saying nothing. There was no offer of a drink, no banter to help ease Francis into what he had to say. This did not flummox him; he hadn't expected Annette to help him and saw no reason why she should. They faced each other across a large mahogany table that was covered with pieces of the orange glass Francis had heard Sim call 'carnival'. He cleared his throat. 'I'll get to the point,' he said. 'I want to apologise to you. For failing to be . . . properly aware of you as a person.'

No response.

'I'm concerned about you,' Francis went on.

'Oh, really?' said Annette dully.

'I wanted to say sorry. I'm sorry. I know it can't make up for . . . but I wanted to say it anyway.'

'You got your scoop. What do you care?'

'That wasn't why . . .'

'Boosted the ratings, did it?'

'That's not fair,' Francis began crossly, then remembered the context and adjusted his voice accordingly. He wasn't used to speaking gently but he gave it a whirl. 'You know that had nothing to do with it,' he said. 'I was hoping to expose the Dingleys for the evil scum that they are. I think we did that, to a certain extent.'

'Get out!' Annette hissed through clenched teeth. Francis didn't move. Sim had warned him he might have to push Annette through the hostility barrier. Would he have got a more favourable response if he hadn't mentioned the Dingleys by name? He could have sworn he'd felt the temperature in the room drop by a few degrees when the word exited his mouth. If only Sim were here to help him; it would have been a different story with her around, Francis was convinced. Kettles would be on by now, biscuits would be out, life-affirming chatter would be rampaging around the house. But Francis knew he had to get through this on his own. I am a grown man, he told himself, and Sim might not always be there to look after me. It was a sobering thought.

'Why are you still here?' asked Annette. 'I'm not willing to talk about this with you. I'm Bethan's mother and you're a stranger.' She turned away.

'But . . .' How best to express this, Francis wondered. 'We're both involved in this *mess*!' he blurted out. 'Well, this . . . this tragedy, I mean.'

'It's my tragedy.' Annette's voice shook with controlled fury. 'The Dingleys were acquitted long ago. All I want you to do – all I've *ever* wanted you to do – is let me grieve in peace and stop poking around in my business.'

'Bethan's your daughter,' Francis began clumsily, 'but that doesn't mean you have sole ownership of the situation. What happened to her isn't only your business. You shouldn't want people to think it is. Don't you want the world to care? That was all I wanted. That's why I arranged the interview.'

'You're unbelievable,' Annette murmured, still facing the window.

'I want to help if I can,' said Francis.

'You can . . .' she turned to face him – '. . . by leaving. You're the person who turned the Dingleys into celebrities. How dare you come to my house?'

334

Francis frowned. He had one more thing to say and he needed to say it quickly, as it looked as if he was about to be ejected from the premises. 'I've always thought you were a very nice . . . a very *good* mother,' he said. 'Bethan was lucky. I mean . . . I don't mean . . .'

'Please go,' said Annette.

> Phyllida Banborough & Walter Allnutt
> Camborne Street High School
> Camborne Street
> Rusholme
> Manchester

> 2 May 1999

Neil Temple
(address as above)

Dear Neil Temple

As requested, we are writing to inform you of the reason why we both feel that the poem 'Memories' by the pupil Imogen Salt of form 7B should not be awarded a prize in this year's school poetry competition.

Evidently the poem is not Imogen Salt's own work. Several of the phrases and ideas are undoubtedly too sophisticated for a twelve-year-old. It is a very accomplished piece of work, but Imogen Salt has copied either all or part of it from somewhere, either a book or else it was written by one of her parents or older siblings. We do not feel that cheating should be rewarded.

Yours sincerely
Walter Allnutt and Phyllida Banborough

(cc Claire Morgan, Eve Hartigan)

(v)

'Oh, Francis, it's so romantic!'

1

Joseph Hawkins
Hawkins, Whitmore, Nedderman Solicitors
Forward House, 34 Prince Street,
Manchester M21 6HU
DX 14331
Tel: 0161 718 2399/0777-876546 (mobile)

Mrs Phyllida Banborough and Mr Walter Allnutt
Camborne Street High School
Camborne Street
Rusholme
Manchester
M14 7QN

6 May 1999

Dear Mrs Banborough and Mr Allnutt

Ms Imogen Salt vs Mrs Phyllida Banborough
Ms Imogen Salt vs Mr Walter Allnutt
Without Prejudice

I am the legal representative of Ms Imogen Salt and I am writing to inform you that we intend to take legal action against both the above-named parties for their slander to her in their letter of 2 May 1999, a copy of which is enclosed.

My client will proceed with the case against the above-named parties unless she receives a written apology, including a categorical withdrawal of the allegation that Ms Salt copied the poem, cheated, or contravened the rules of the contest in any capacity, within ten working days of the date of this letter, and unless her poem 'Memories' is reconsidered as an entry in Camborne Street High School's 1999 poetry competition.

If we have not heard from you within ten working days of the date of this letter, we will commence proceedings. You should be aware that, should this case reach court, the onus will be on the above-named parties and their legal representatives to provide proof that the poem 'Memories' is not the original and exclusive work of Ms Imogen Salt.

    Yours sincerely

      Joseph Hawkins

      Solicitor

Enc

(cc Mrs Claire Morgan, Ms Eve Hartigan)

Imogen handed the letter back to Neil. 'Ace,' she said. 'Dead convincing. I still think my solicitor's the best.' Imogen had invented the name 'Nedderman'. 'He'd be a cute, doddery old lawyer,' she'd said firmly. 'With a Zimmer frame.' Neil had been responsible for Hawkins and Whitmore, or rather for the fabrication of Whitmore and the adaptation of Hawkins. Joe Hawkins was Neil's brother-in-law who lived in Chorlton at the address on the letterhead. Joe had been briefed and had promised to ring Neil the minute Phyllida and Walter responded.

'What does "without prejudice" mean?' Imogen asked. 'Why does it say "DX 14331" under the address?'

'It's all legal jargon. Most solicitors' offices have DX addresses as well as normal ones. Walter and Phyllida are more likely to fall for it if it looks like other correspondence they've had from lawyers.'

Imogen's eyes widened behind her tortoiseshell glasses. 'Why, do you reckon they've been sued for slander before?'

'No!' Neil sighed, knowing that under normal circumstances he'd have found Imogen's suggestion highly amusing. 'But they'll have bought houses, made wills and stuff.'

'What if they ring up?'

'Joe'll have to pretend he's a lawyer, won't he?'

There was determination in Neil's voice that bordered on anger. Eve was, at this moment, giving Campbell a lift to Hollins Hall. 'Come on, Neil, it makes sense,' she'd placated him. 'We both live in Manchester and he hasn't got a car, or any money to get the train.' If it weren't for Imogen, Neil would have had to spend the whole weekend on his own, like in the bad old days. Eve had told him not to worry, but Neil had a strong hunch she was keeping something from him. As her fiancé, he should have been invited to this stag weekend. It was bloody rude of Matt and Lucy not to think of it. Were all Eve's friends conspiring to get her and Campbell back together? Was Eve going along with it on any level, even subliminally? Neil cursed himself for allowing her to leave the house this morning. He should have put his foot down; he was a fool for trusting fate to provide the outcome he wanted. What sort of coward was he? Hartigan, you'd better not let me down, he thought.

'Are you all right?' Imogen asked.

'What? Yeah, fine. Fine.' Neil forced himself to smile.

'So you sent this letter today?'

'Yesterday. They'll have got it today, hopefully.'

'What if they ring and your sister answers?'

'She'll be his secretary. Don't worry, Imogen. I've gone through it with them. They'll know if it's Walter or Phyllida – no one else would call Joe Joseph. It isn't his name.'

'How come?' Imogen's speech, Neil noticed, had become slangier over the past few weeks as she'd picked up his and Eve's most frequently used phrases. She no longer sounded like an elegantly scripted movie.

'He was christened Joe. His parents knew it'd get short-
ened so they thought they'd do it themselves. Don't your
family ever shorten your name?'

'No.' Imogen's eyes clouded over.

'They always call you Imogen?'

'Yes. What's wrong with that?'

'Nothing. I'd have thought they might have abbreviated
it to Imo.'

'That sounds stupid,' she said huffily. 'Anyway, I thought
it was better to have a name that you couldn't shorten.
You can't shorten Neil. Why's it okay for you and not
for me?'

'Imogen, calm down. I'm not criticising your name.'

She turned away. 'Do you think if you give someone
a nickname it means you love them more?' she asked
eventually.

'No,' said Neil, thinking of the Hideous Grimbelina. He
prayed she wasn't quite as grim as everyone made out; all
Neil needed was for Campbell to go off her.

'I might start calling you Eel.' Imogen giggled.

'If you do, I'll call you Moge.'

'Ace! I like that name. Eel? Eel!'

'Oh, sorry. Mm?'

'I'm missing Eve. Are you?'

'Yes,' he admitted. This was intolerable. It couldn't go
on for a second longer.

'Eel?'

'Mm?'

'I've got something to show you too.' Imogen pulled a
small yellow envelope out of her pocket. 'But you've got
to promise not to get emotional or anything. You're a man,
remember, and a teacher.'

Neil stared at the envelope, which he felt sure contained
some awful message from Eve, and wished he could simply
flick an 'off' switch in his brain and opt out of the part of
his life that was coming next.

*   *   *

342

Sim heard the door slam. 'Is that you, Francis?' she called, throwing her nightie into the open holdall on the bed. 'You need to pack. Francis? Is that you?' Normally Sim would have packed for him, but she'd been impressed to note some significant changes in his attitude and behaviour since his visit to Annette Wrigley. In less than a week, Francis had matured considerably and mature people did not fly into impatient rages when asked to think about what they might want to wear in one or two days' time.

'No.' Francis appeared in the bedroom doorway. 'It's Ferdinand Marcos.'

'Who?' Sim looked puzzled, then irritated. 'From *Eldorado*? That hasn't been on for ages, Francis. No, I'm thinking of Marcus Tandy,' she corrected herself.

'And I'm thinking of a Filipino dictator,' said Francis.

'We haven't got time for Filipino dictators,' Sim told him. 'You need to pack. I want to get to Hollins Hall as soon as possible. When do you think you'll be finished packing?'

'About two seconds after I start. Why are you flapping?'

'I want to get there before Campbell and Eve, see how the land lies, so to speak. I don't want them to arrive and find a vacuum.'

'Won't they find a hotel? Hollins Hall exists even when you're not in it, you know.'

'I was going to send Hazel on ahead,' Sim explained, ignoring Francis's sly dig, 'but Ian's working late and so devoted is she that she doesn't want to arrive without him. I wonder what Ian does for a living; I forgot to ask. Anyway, Hazel adores him. I think they'll be the next to get married, you know.'

'Maybe not,' said Francis pointedly.

'Why?' Sim glanced at him, surprised. 'Oh, you mean Campbell and Eve? No, even if my plan works, they'll need a while for things to settle down. Whereas Hazel and Ian . . .'

'I didn't mean Campbell and Eve,' said Francis. 'Sim,

343

you know you told me I need to talk about my feelings more? Well, I've been wondering . . .'

'Francis, first pack.' Sim dashed over to give him a quick, encouraging kiss. 'Then wonder.' She grabbed her toiletries bag from the glass shelf in the en suite.

'I thought it wasn't good for me to repress things,' said Francis. 'Women! Bloody inconsistent.' He shook his head crossly. And while he was on the subject of women . . . 'Sim? You know Annette Wrigley?' He hovered in the doorway.

'Mm?'

'I'm a bit worried I might have said something really bad to her,' Francis confessed.

'Aha!' Sim looked up from her packing. 'Finally! I've been asking you to tell me what you said to her for *days*. I knew you hadn't forgotten.'

'I told her I thought Bethan was lucky.'

'What? But she was raped and murdered.'

'I know.' Francis looked despondent. 'I meant before that, though. Annette must have known I meant that, don't you think?'

'I don't know, Francis, I wasn't there.' Sim sighed. 'But what should you have done, if you weren't sure?'

'Erm . . . said it again? More clearly the second time?'

'Exactly. Well done, Francis! If someone doesn't get your drift immediately, don't just slope off and regret the misunderstanding. Explain. Which reminds me . . .' Sim looked at him sharply. 'I want to check your best man's speech, if you ever get round to writing it. Matt'll never forgive me if it contains some horrendous faux pas.'

'It won't,' said Francis indignantly. 'I think I'm getting the hang of saying the right thing at the right time.'

'Well . . . good.' Sim eyed him doubtfully.

'I wonder who'd be my best man. I mean, it was easy for Matt – I'm obviously his best mate, but it'd be harder for me. Thanks to you, we appear to be equally best friends with everyone.'

'Well, luckily we don't have to worry about it,' said Sim cheerfully. 'Now, come on. Pack!'

Eve wound down her window saying, 'Phew! Hot!' and hoping Campbell would fall for it. The truth was, he was making her newly cleaned car pong. His clothes smelled of washing that had taken too long to dry and the hedge of hair crowning his head was greasy. He still had that sore on his mouth too; shouldn't it have healed by now, Eve wondered. She was gratified to see how badly he was managing without her, but she'd have to make him wash before getting into bed. Eve was excited, almost hysterical, at the prospect of sharing a bed with Campbell, something she thought she'd never do again, and tried not to think about Neil, who would spend the next two nights alone. *You should be with Neil*, said a voice inside her head, *that's where you belong*. Another voice said, *Rubbish! You belong with Campbell*. Eve couldn't tell which voice was her heart and which her conscience.

'Put your belt on,' she said, doing her best impression of a calm person. 'You don't want to turn into an elephant.' This was an old joke, one Campbell had invented. A few years ago there was a television advertisement that showed a back-seat passenger who'd neglected to fasten his seat belt being hurled through the windscreen. At the moment of impact, the passenger rather mysteriously turned into an elephant. The point, presumably, was that one's body weight increases substantially in a crash. 'Still,' Eve went on, 'Rory might like that. She could slaughter you for your tusks.' She laughed at her own witticism as they drove along Wilmslow Road through Didsbury village, past pavement cafés in which idle arty types like Sim sipped mochas when they should have been working.

'Don't,' said Campbell, fastening his seat belt with a sigh.

'Oh, lighten up! What's wrong?' What if Campbell couldn't stand to be near her any more? Sim had assured

Eve he was keen, but he didn't exactly look delirious with anticipation.

'Rory slept with someone else.' At first Eve thought she'd heard wrong. She took her eyes off the road and looked at Campbell, whose face struggled to keep itself in order.

'What? How do you know?' The bitch. Eve would kill her.

'She told me. She said she didn't want there to be any lies between us.'

'Oh, Campbell! I'm really sorry. I hope you finished with her straight away. Campbell? You didn't, did you?'

'She says . . . she got lonely because I was far away and she felt that shagging this guy . . .' He broke off. 'She says sex is the only way she knows of communicating with the world.'

Eve frowned. 'I thought she didn't do penetrative sex.'

'So did I,' said Campbell bitterly. 'When I got upset, she starting having a go at me for being petty. She said I should channel my energies into something more constructive.' Campbell gritted his teeth. 'And she gave the example of baking bread.'

'I hope you told her to fuck off, Campbell. You should have known she was lying about not going in for penetrative sex. She's got a vibrator, for God's sake.'

'How do you . . . ? Oh, let me guess. Sim told you.' Eve didn't see any point in denying it. She kept her eyes diplomatically on the road. Campbell grimaced. 'And she's having a fucking thirtieth birthday party tomorrow night, which I'm not invited to,' he said. 'She told me I'm not the sort of person her friends would get on with. Meaning I'm not posh enough.'

'Campbell, I can't believe you're being so pathetic,' Eve snapped. 'It's your own fault for letting her treat you like shit. God, and I thought you were clever! Why are you such a useless blob?'

'Cheers.' Campbell tried to sound ironic but there was a tremor in his voice.

346

'I mean, even if you don't want me, you could get someone miles better than Grimbelina.'

'Than who?'

'That's what we all call her,' Eve explained. 'Your mum made it up. Or the Grimble, or Cruelty-without-Beauty. Sim thought of those.'

'Don't be horrible.' Campbell's voice turned cold. 'She's still my girlfriend.'

'Like I was, you mean, before you dumped me?'

'I didn't ... anyway, it's not necessarily true, what you said.'

'What? What did I say?'

'That I don't want you.'

'Well, do you?' said Eve in a brittle voice, thinking she shouldn't have to ask, that Campbell should volunteer the information. Just as she'd told Neil, voluntarily, innocently, that she was giving Campbell a lift to Yorkshire but there was nothing to worry about, it was all over between them? The most ridiculous thing of all was that Eve was already missing Neil quite a lot, at the same time as tingling all over because Campbell – unfragrant and unreasonable as he was – was sitting beside her. She never thought she'd be a woman who loved two men. It was so impractical.

Silence filled the car. Why hadn't Eve noticed while they still lived together that Campbell was a conversational terrorist? He held words hostage, releasing them a few at a time, only when his interlocutor complied with his unreasonable demands. He had an infuriating way of looking as if he was about to say something of lasting significance while in fact saying nothing, his closed mouth bulging with the words he'd decided to detain further.

'Gillian Kench phoned me yesterday.' He changed the subject.

'What?' Eve was so surprised that for a second she forgot she was driving and narrowly missed a cyclist on Wilbraham Road. 'Why?'

347

'She didn't know we'd split up. She accused me of telling everyone except her and leaving her out deliberately. I could have done without that, on top of everything else. Why the fuck did you give her my number?'

'I didn't,' said Eve angrily. 'I haven't spoken to Gillian for ages.'

'Then who did?'

'I've no idea.'

'She's pissed off that Matt and Lucy haven't invited her this weekend.'

'What? Oh, Campbell, you idiot! She wasn't supposed to know about it.'

'Well, I didn't fucking tell her! And before you ask, I haven't a clue who did. Is there any point in us speaking at all, if we're just going to blame each other for stupid things?'

'You're the one who left me,' said Eve before she could stop herself.

'Why are you marrying that wanker Neil?' Campbell demanded. 'It's crazy. You're not going to do it, are you?'

'Yes, I am. Next Saturday. And if Rory's there, I'll cut her tongue out.'

'Neither of us'll be there,' said Campbell with grim satisfaction. 'I'm not coming along to celebrate you making the worst mistake of your life.'

'Oh, so you're going to miss Matt and Lucy's wedding, are you?'

'Yes, if it means I won't have to see you with that arsehole.'

'Neil's not an arsehole,' said Eve. 'He's lovely. Anyway, why shouldn't I marry him? I don't want to be a spinster all my life and you refused to marry me. For years you gave me all that crap about how we didn't need to be married because our relationship was stronger than that . . .'

'All right, all right.'

'And look where it got me . . .'

'I still think our relationship's strong,' said Campbell quietly.

'Oh, right.' Eve laughed bitterly. 'And I suppose that was why you left.' Before she knew it she'd have talked herself out of loving Campbell by reciting a list of his offences. Sim wouldn't be happy.

'Give me a chance, for God's sake,' said the serial offender.

'A chance to do what?' This was daft. Neil was better for her. She'd have a happier life with Neil. But this had nothing to do with happiness; it was about necessity. Or habit or tradition, Eve wasn't sure.

If Campbell had a response, he was holding it to ransom. Eve looked at him out of the corner of her eye. I don't even fancy him as much as I fancy Neil, she thought. Especially not with that blister on his lip. It made no difference, though. Her feelings for Campbell had gone beyond the stage where that mattered, beyond Campbell himself and his good and bad points. He was simply part of her life and she was part of his. 'Okay, then, I'll give you a chance,' said Eve, prompting him.

'Good. Thanks,' he said.

'Well?'

'Well what?'

'Is that it?' Eve shook her head in disbelief.

'Is what what?'

'Can't you remember the history of this conversation? You said you thought our relationship was strong and asked me to give you a chance. I agreed and then you didn't . . . say or do anything.'

'It's not that simple, you know?' Campbell sighed.

'Do you still want to be with Rory? Do you want me back? What do you want, Campbell?' Eve slammed down her foot on the accelerator, imagining it was Grimbelina's head, and the car zoomed on to the M602.

'You always . . .' Campbell began.

'What? What do I always do?'

'Not now. Before. All that marriage and babies stuff. It's just not reasonable, you know? You knew I wasn't ready. You could have waited instead of trying to rush me. I haven't even finished my PhD, let alone got a job.'

'Exactly!' said Eve, thinking Campbell must really have lost the plot if he was citing his lack of professional achievements in his defence. 'I was scared that if I didn't rush you, you'd be happy to vegetate for ever.'

'Thanks a lot. That's how you've always seen me, isn't it? A vegetable.'

'Don't be stupid. I've always been really proud of you. Look, you've got nothing to complain about – you won. If it'd been up to me we would have got married years ago. We'd have three kids by now.'

'All I wanted was for you to put me first,' said Campbell. 'And you wouldn't.'

'What?' Eve was confused. He'd never said any of this before. Come to think of it, shouldn't this discussion have taken place a good deal sooner? Or would that have been impossible? Perhaps Campbell felt he could only say these things to Eve from the safe distance of his new life. 'What are you on about?' she asked. 'I put you first all the bloody time. My whole *life* was about putting you first!'

'There's no reason why we can't be happy, if you'd just stop pressuring me. I'm not saying I'll never want to have kids, but . . . can't you put those plans on hold?'

'I can't believe I'm hearing this,' Eve muttered, incensed. Finally, Campbell was articulating his emotions, revealing precisely how selfish and immature he was, just in case Eve had been in any doubt. 'You were the one who left me for someone else. You're asking me to give up all the things I want and you haven't even said you want me back yet.'

'Well, that's kind of implied, isn't it?' said Campbell.

'Implied isn't bloody good enough! Let's get things the right way round. Do you want me back? Have you realised that running off with that frigid animal-torturing cow was a terrible mistake and that you love me more?'

Eve heard herself shout. She was in no fit state to be driving a car.

'It's impossible to assess things like more and less when it comes to love,' said Campbell condescendingly, as if Eve were a simpleton. 'Love is a vague predicate . . .'

Eve wanted to shove him on to the motorway. 'Forget it!' she said, wishing Neil were beside her instead. Had she come to her senses at last? She'd make Campbell sleep on the floor tonight and tomorrow night; she didn't care what Sim said.

'What about my question?' asked Campbell innocently, as if he weren't the bastard who'd ruined everything. 'What about your side of the bargain?'

'There's no bargain,' Eve told him. 'I'm marrying Neil next week and nothing you can say will stop me.'

The Marriott Hollins Hall Hotel was an imposing stone mansion at the top of Hollins Hill in Baildon, on to which the newer, more angular country club had been built in similar light stone. Vanessa drove up the wide concrete path that spiralled up the hill to the car park at the top. She was looking forward to a weekend of saunas, massages, beauty treatments and excessive drinking, and with all the others cooing like mad about the wedding, she expected to get away with making only a minimal contribution. What was the big deal, for Christ's sake? Lucy and Matt had been living together for years like everyone else. Vanessa hoped the marriage bug didn't start to go round, like flu. 'We're here,' she yelled at Nicholas to wake him up. He didn't jump, which confirmed Vanessa's suspicion that he hadn't really been asleep.

She parked, climbed out of the car and took in the panoramic view of the sprawling Aire valley, invigorating after the flat neatness of Cambridge. The weather was cool but bright, and patches of sun made the hills in the distance glow. You wouldn't see light like that in London.

Now that Nicholas wanted to move and had even gone

so far as to apply for a job at Thames Valley University (which was bound to be some sort of hideous ex-poly-cum-disused-warehouse) Vanessa wanted to slow things down. The new Nicholas scared her; he wouldn't talk about why he'd changed his mind and Vanessa was still hoping it was a phase that would pass. Humiliating though it was, she'd been forced to admit to Nicholas that she didn't really want to move to London. She'd been having fun in Cambridge recently, clashing with Red-tooth, sweet-talking PC Stickles. She wanted to stay put and have Nicholas be his old vituperative self again. Vanessa hadn't realised in time to appreciate it, but until a few weeks ago she was actually very happy; she'd had a fulfilling sex life, fights, a routine – what more could a girl wish for?

'Get the cases,' she ordered. 'Nicholas! Chop chop.' If he wasn't a lover, he could be a servant, she'd decided. Nicholas roused himself and climbed out of the car, proceeding obediently to the boot to retrieve the luggage. He'd been virtually silent for over a week. 'You realise, don't you, that if you move to London, you'll become the sort of person you've always claimed to hate,' said Vanessa. 'Every time you come somewhere like this for a weekend, you'll say "Oh, it's so good to get out of London", as if you'd forgotten the rest of the country existed.' Nicholas shrugged. 'That's what you want, is it? Traffic fumes? Black snot?' Nastiness was the only way Vanessa knew of displaying concern. Still, it didn't seem to matter how vile she was to Nicholas; he was like a man in a trance. He'd stopped going to his office altogether and Vanessa saw no evidence that he was working on his article. She refused to entertain the possibility that he was having an affair.

Nicholas walked towards reception like a robot, carrying their cases. 'Do me a favour,' said Vanessa, and he paused. 'Try to act normal when we're with people. I'd rather our friends didn't know what a farce our life has become.' For the first time in several days Nicholas's eyes met hers. He nodded, conceding that this was a valid point.

Vanessa wanted to scream. If he could look at her and nod, why couldn't he go a little further and tell her what was wrong?

At least she'd finally had satisfaction on the Red-tooth front. She was confident that by the time she got back to Cambridge, a cheque for £278.68, the full cost of her car's beauty treatment, would be waiting for her. Red-tooth had ignored Vanessa's last letter, in which she'd been instructed to pay for the Peugeot's service by return of post, and no further demands for taxi or tooth money had made their way to Gentchev's Field. Red-tooth was clearly hoping for a truce. She didn't know whom she was dealing with if she thought such a feeble petering-out of hostilities would be satisfactory to Vanessa. It was all right for Red-tooth. As things stood, she came out on top financially; the sum she claimed Vanessa owed her was less than a quarter of what she owed Vanessa.

When more than a week passed and still no cheque was forthcoming, Vanessa decided to teach the arrogant bitch a lesson. Every night after she'd got back from work, had a shower and changed, Vanessa drove to the spot near Queens' College on Silver Street where she'd dropped Red-tooth off and waited, hoping her quarry would emerge. The first night was a waste of time; she didn't even get a glimpse. On the second night, after waiting for two hours, Vanessa saw both Red-teeth, which was deeply frustrating. She needed Red-tooth on her own. The happy couple cycled along Silver Street from the direction of King's Parade and into their driveway. Red-tooth's face looked unfamiliar – Vanessa had completely forgotten it since the accident – but she recognised the bike and purple cycling helmet. She forced herself to concentrate on her target's facial features, unappealing though they were; she had to be able to spot Red-tooth on foot or she might miss a good opportunity.

She had no joy again the following night, which made her insides fizz with frustration. Giving up wasn't an option. Winning became more important to Vanessa every day and it wasn't as if she had anything better to do with her evenings lately. Nicholas didn't notice whether she was there or not. Yesterday, finally, her opportunity had presented itself and Vanessa took full advantage of it.

At twenty past nine, just as she was about to give up hope for another evening, Red-tooth and her bike appeared on Silver Street and set off in the direction of the university library. Red-tooth didn't notice Vanessa's car by the side of the road, if indeed she remembered it at all. Vanessa followed at a gentle pace, not wanting to alert Red-tooth to her presence. At the traffic lights, Red-tooth turned left and headed towards the Newnham roundabout, which was a surprise. Where could the swotty specimen be going, if not to the university library? Vanessa pursued her over the roundabout and on to Barton Road. When Red-tooth stuck out her arm, Vanessa indicated left and they both turned on to the road that led to Grantchester, home of the Rupert Brooke pub, one of Sim's favourite haunts.

Vanessa felt adrenalin surge through her. Perfect. She knew this road well; a hundred yards or so from Newnham it narrowed and went into countryside. There was never anyone around, only fields on both sides. There were no more houses until Grantchester.

Vanessa waited until the Barton Road had been safely left behind, then steadily accelerated. Within a few seconds her bumper was only inches behind Red-tooth's back wheel. Vanessa depressed the accelerator ever so slightly and her car nudged Red-tooth's bike, making it wobble, though not enough to unseat its rider. Surprisingly, Red-tooth didn't turn round to see who'd bumped her. Perhaps the knock was so mild that she hadn't even felt it, or had attributed it to the wind. What a lenient soul I am, Vanessa thought to herself. Still, she wanted to make a bit of an impact. She accelerated again and this time bumped Red-tooth a bit harder, forcing her into a hedge at the side of the road. Perfect. A bit of comic indignity was exactly what Red-tooth needed; she might learn to laugh at herself and stop being so pompous.

Vanessa didn't want to hang around too long. While Red-tooth pulled herself and her bike out of the greenery, Vanessa drew level with her in the car. 'I want my cheque by Monday,' she said, before driving off. The 'or else' was implied. It wasn't necessary to spell everything out, as Vanessa kept telling her more heavy-handed authors. She thought she might frame Red-tooth's cheque when it arrived and put it on the wall instead of paying it into her bank account. She needed to remember her triumph more than she needed the money.

The hotel's automatic doors slid open. Vanessa followed Nicholas into the domed foyer, which was dominated by polished dark woods. Clusters of red velvet chairs were arranged mock-casually around small glass-topped coffee tables. A row of squat trees with fat trunks and spiky, rubbery foliage lined one wall. The shiny brass reception area gleamed. 'Let's go straight to the bar,' said Vanessa. 'The others'll be there already and I'm desperate for a drink. Can you have our cases taken up to our room?' she barked across the desk.

'Yes, after you've checked in.' The receptionist produced the relevant form and Vanessa filled it in. Nicholas asked for directions to the Long Weekend Café Bar. There was an urgency in his voice which suggested he too was dying for a drink. Vanessa had noticed the speed at which the bottle of vodka in their cupboard had emptied last week. Damn Nicholas. If he proceeded with his selfish decline, she'd have to start an affair, but with whom? Vanessa quite fancied her mental image of Cal Raynard, but she was unlikely ever to meet him and even if she did, the reality would undoubtedly prove disappointing. Besides, she didn't have the energy to pretend to be nice for long enough to attract a new man. Charming PC Stickles had been exhausting enough.

The Long Weekend Café Bar was cavernous. Insipid

watercolours of famous sports personalities, obviously copies of photographs, covered the walls. Sim and the others, with the exception of Campbell and Eve and the unwelcome addition of Hazel's unsightly new boyfriend, were sitting at two corner tables. Vanessa hadn't seen Matt and Lucy for over three months and was struck by how American they looked. Their teeth were whiter, as were Matt's trainers. He was also wearing a baseball cap with a bloody American flag on it. Vanessa wondered if he had napalm in his pockets, then realised this was Nicholas speaking from inside her head. She waited for him to comment on Matt's attire and felt inexplicably bereft when he didn't. 'Gin and tonic,' she barked at him. Nicholas nodded and went off to the bar.

'She can't play house with Campbell this weekend and marry Neil next Saturday. It's just not on,' Matt was saying in a heated tone. Brows around the table were furrowed.

Goodie, thought Vanessa, a controversy. 'Quite,' she chipped in by way of greeting. 'Doesn't this particular pantomime break all records?' She caught sight of an Yves St Laurent label on the cuff of Hazel's boyfriend's jacket pocket and wondered whom he was trying to kid when his face and the shape of his head clearly identified him as white trash. 'I don't believe we've met,' said Vanessa. The runt sat beside him looking tense in a clingy grey dress that made her look like Moby Dick's dwarf sister.

'Sorry,' said Sim. 'This is Ian, Hazel's boyfriend. Vanessa . . . and Nicholas over there at the bar.' Ian gave Vanessa a peculiar look. Had she been the paranoid type, she'd have wondered if he knew something she didn't, though she conceded it was unlikely he knew anything at all. He looked as if he spent his spare time at car boot sales hunting for second-hand packets of pork scratchings.

'Look, hopefully after this weekend Eve and Campbell'll be back together, so there'll be no problem,' Sim said to Matt, as Nicholas returned from the bar with two double gins and tonic.

'Apart from the embarrassingly undignified behaviour of all involved, you mean.' Vanessa chuckled. 'None of them can have been first in the queue when God handed out pride, that's all I can say. You can't tell me Neil's anything other than a contingency plan for Eve. He must know it, too, unless he's totally thick, yet they're desperate enough to marry each other rather than be single. And if Campbell crawls back to Eve because things don't work out with Rory that'll be just as farcical.'

'Vanessa's bang on,' said Matt, adjusting the stars and stripes on his head.

'Matt, come on.' Lucy looked uncomfortable. 'Don't be so . . .'

'What kind of way is that to talk about your friends?' Ian addressed Vanessa. 'They'll walk in in a minute. Would you say all that to their faces?'

'Oh, God!' Vanessa rolled her eyes. 'Not the old behind-my-back-or-to-my-face distinction! Do you think it's better to say things to people's faces that are going to make them feel like shit?'

'It's better not to say those things at all, if they're your friends,' said Ian coldly.

'Hazel, your boyfriend is suffering from terminal adolescence.'

'Look, I don't think . . .' Ian began angrily.

'Guys, guys,' Sim talked over him. 'Come on, now. Vanessa, look at it another way. You mentioned pride before. I think Eve's being positively saintly, putting her pride aside and sharing a bed with Campbell, basically offering herself to him in the full knowledge that he might still trot back to Rory after this weekend. Imagine how hard it'll be for her, knowing that we're all aware she's being tried out, when she used to be Campbell's proper partner. That's quite some loss of status, yet she's willing to do it in order to save her and Campbell's relationship.'

'Campbell's awful to put her through that,' said Hazel.

'He can't ever have loved her if he's willing to make her suffer so . . . publicly.'

'Is it really any of our business?' Ian ventured.

'The good samaritan pipes up again,' Vanessa muttered under her breath.

'Hang on,' said Sim, darting a placatory look at Ian. She hadn't finished sticking up for Eve. 'If Campbell rejects Eve, she'll marry Neil. Again, she'll have to put her pride aside. She knows we'll all be there . . .'

'Yeah, because it's *our* wedding,' said Matt.

'. . . congratulating her and Neil, with the memory of this weekend fresh in our minds. Eve's not stupid; she knows people'll look at her and whisper about how she's marrying Neil on the rebound, but she's willing to put herself through that in order to have a chance of happiness with Neil.'

'So what are you saying?' asked Lucy. 'She wants to be happy with one of them and either will do?'

'Sim's point is that Eve's being optimistic and realistic at the same time, which Sim thinks is admirable,' said Francis. 'She's not bothered about her image, or any of the trivial things most people get hung up about. She wants to be happy, yes, and she clearly has feelings for both Campbell and Neil. She doesn't want to admit defeat too soon with Campbell, but she also doesn't want to rule out the possibility of being happy with Neil just because in some ideal world she might have preferred to be with Campbell.'

'Sim, Francis is gossiping,' said Vanessa. 'Is he ill?'

'Exactly!' Sim ignored her. 'And it could be even more sophisticated than that. Perhaps as things stand Campbell's her first choice, but if he fails to appreciate the grand gesture of this weekend, his last chance, maybe that'll be the final straw and Neil will become her genuine first choice.'

'He'd be my first choice,' said Hazel, who was making a colossal effort to appear relaxed. She'd been badly shaken by Ian's unpleasant exchange with Vanessa. How had they got off to such a bad start? She was cross with both of them for not biting their tongues for her sake. 'Neil really loves Eve,' she said. 'He'll look after her properly. Campbell'll just leave her again and . . . um . . . um . . . run off with a Scandinavian air hostess!'

'I don't buy your theory, Sim,' said Matt, yawning. 'Let's get some more beers in, anyway, get shit-faced and do mad, zany things.'

'Fancy dress has been vetoed, hasn't it?' said Francis.

'Yeah, by you, you boring old fart! And I veto just sitting around talking about boring Campbell and Eve. This is supposed to be mine and Lucy's weekend, in case you've all forgotten. Waiter!'

'Matt!' Lucy blushed. 'He's just jet-lagged,' she told the others.

'No, I'm not,' said Matt. 'I object to their poxy love life interfering in our plans and upsetting you, babe.'

'I'm fine,' said Lucy in a tone that suggested otherwise.

'What do you reckon to it all, Nicholas?' asked Francis. Vanessa cursed him silently. It would surely become obvious as soon as Nicholas opened his mouth that he wasn't himself. Had he even been following the conversation?

She sighed with relief when he started to speak. 'If Campbell loved Eve, he wouldn't have gone off with Rory,' he said flatly, 'and if he loved Rory, he wouldn't share a bed with Eve.'

'Quite right, darling,' Vanessa took over. 'Likewise, if Eve gave a damn about Neil or Campbell, she wouldn't be able to adapt in the way you're saying, Sim. Loved ones aren't so easily interchangeable, to anyone with a modicum of taste.'

'Cor-rect,' said Matt, looking around to see what was keeping the waiter he'd summoned.

'I take all your points.' Sim nodded. 'But on the other hand . . .'

'Who gives a shit?' Matt cut her off. 'They're idiots,

359

that's all there is to it. Could someone please tell me, I mean, I've always wanted to know: why do so many people deliberately set out to fuck up their lives?'

'Dark forces are at work within their souls,' Vanessa explained.

'Hey?'

'You wouldn't know a dark force if it hit you in the face, Matt.'

Sim wasn't so sure about this. There was something frightening about the mood Matt was in tonight. He was so vehemently anti-Campbell and Eve. Was it only because their break-up had affected his wedding? Sim realised she'd never seen anyone cross Matt before.

'It's Neil I feel sorry for,' said Lucy. 'He proposed to Eve in good faith, thinking Campbell was out of the picture. And look how she's treating him.'

'He couldn't possibly have thought Campbell was out of the picture,' Francis argued. 'We're talking, what, a couple of weeks before he started buzzing around Eve? Neil was Campbell's mate. It's a bit off to steal your friend's ex-girlfriend the minute his back's turned.'

'Oh, come on! Campbell left her. She was fair game,' said Vanessa.

'Poor Neil,' said Hazel. 'I feel as if we're participating in Eve's deception of him by joining in with this trial weekend for her and Campbell.'

'Excuse me!' Matt snapped. 'I don't even fucking know the guy and this is our weekend, mine and Luce's. I've had enough of this!'

'I know, Matt, I'm sorry,' said Sim. 'Look, let's stop talking about Campbell and Eve and start enjoying ourselves. We need some champagne, to toast Matt and Lucy.' What's this: offerings to the gods, thought Vanessa irritably. Hadn't anyone noticed the change in Nicholas? Was it only glaringly obvious to her? Sim leaned over and put her hand on Matt's arm. 'Don't worry,' she said. 'I'll be very surprised if Eve marries Neil next weekend.'

'Sim, don't you think you should keep out of it?' said Ian.

'Right, sorry about that, ladies and gents!' A gangly young man in a Hollins Hall T-shirt sprang forward with a pad and a pen. 'What can I get you?'

'Two bottles of your best champagne,' said Matt, pleased to be getting appropriate attention at last.

'Special occasion, is it?' asked the waiter.

'Sure is, Craig,' said Matt, reading his badge. Craig grinned. Vanessa could see both men were itching to tell each other to have a nice day. Any minute now they'd start saluting. 'Lucy and I flew in from Washington yesterday,' said Matt. 'We're getting married next . . .'

'Ian?' Craig's smile widened. 'Sorry.' He looked at Matt and blushed. 'Ian Boyle?' What an ugly surname, thought Vanessa. Fitting though; Ian's head, which he'd turned away as if he didn't want to be recognised, was shaped just like a boil. 'All right, mate! How are you doing? I used to work for Ian,' Craig explained to the rest of them. Matt, still angry at being interrupted, pulled down his baseball cap so that the American flag covered his eyes.

'Oh yes?' said Vanessa. 'Assistant good samaritan, were you?'

'No. Cleaner.' Craig was confused. 'Ian's got a business, cleaning. You know, people's houses and stuff. I used to help him when I was a student. How's it going, mate?'

'Oh, no,' Hazel whispered.

'Hazel, it's fine,' said Sim quickly, sitting forward in her chair. She and Ian exchanged a peculiarly knowing look that Vanessa couldn't interpret. 'What about that champagne, then?' Sim asked Craig in a high-pitched voice.

'We need it now,' Ian insisted. What the hell was going on? Craig skulked off towards the bar, looking as mystified as Vanessa felt.

'So now you all know!' Hazel blurted out, making Lucy jump.

'What the hell's going on?' Matt pulled off his cap and slammed it down on the table.

'Nothing,' said Sim briskly. 'Nothing's going on, and no one knows anything, Hazel. Let's all carry on enjoying . . .'

'What don't we know?'

'Francis!'

'Here are Eve and Campbell,' said Lucy, in a tone that might have sounded neutral if she'd limbered up a bit more.

'It's all right, Sim,' said Hazel, who appeared to be steeling herself like a person facing the scaffold. 'If you've guessed, it won't be long before everyone else does.' She stood up. Vanessa half expected her to produce an over-head projector and some transparencies from her pocket, so formal was her manner. 'Ian's a cleaner,' she announced to the group. 'Okay? He's my cleaner. Does anyone have a problem with that?'

Campbell slid into the bar behind Eve, who'd stomped angrily ahead all the way from the car park. She ran towards the others, waving and mouthing silent greet-ings as if to show Campbell that it was only him to whom she wasn't speaking. They'd stewed in silence for most of the journey. Eve had started it. She was the one who'd clammed up after their row. Pathetic, thought Campbell, who hadn't been sent to Coventry since he was about nine.

This situation was freaky: he and Eve driving to Yorkshire together in Eve's car to meet up with their friends, as they had so many times before. It felt so natural in some respects and so unnatural in others. 'I'll get us a drink,' he called after Eve, wanting to postpone the moment of facing the crowd. Campbell prayed Sim had told the others what was going on; he certainly wasn't up to explaining anything to anyone, even assuming he could.

Sim was hoping he and Eve would sort out all their problems this weekend, that much had been obvious from her last call. Campbell wanted to oblige – it was the only way to make sure Eve didn't marry Neil – but wasn't sure it was as simple as that. He'd said as much to Sim on the phone. 'What about Rory? I can't just tell her I've changed my mind.'

'I'll finish with her for you,' Sim offered. 'It would be a pleasure. Just give me the word and I'll make sure she never bothers you again.' Campbell was sorely tempted, but only at the level of fantasy. Besides, he wasn't sure he wanted to end it with Rory, despite her infidelity. At least she'd been honest about it, and he valued absolute honesty even if Eve and Sim didn't. There *was* something special about Rory; he'd felt it when they first met. And Eve had really pissed him off on the way over with her refusal to see things from his point of view, her stubborn insistence on marrying Neil just to prove a point.

'How can I tell which one I prefer?' he'd asked Sim on the phone. She told him that on the news the previous day, a panel of knowledgeables had been discussing the possibility of Russia starting a nuclear war unless NATO's forces stopped bombing Kosovo.

'Imagine they're going to nuke us in two weeks,' she said enthusiastically. 'Who would you rather spend your last days on earth with, Eve or Rory?'

'If it was only two weeks, it wouldn't really matter, you know?'

'That's ridiculous.' Sim laughed. 'Why do you think so many people with terminal illnesses get married?'

'Do they? How do you know?' Campbell trusted Sim least when she veered towards the statistical.

'In *Potters Court* they do,' said Sim. 'And everyone knows life imitates soap opera. You can't judge something symbolic by how long it lasts. You could even argue that symbols last for ever.'

'No, that's rubbish. If the whole world's been destroyed by nuclear bombs, there's nowhere for the symbols to exist, is there?' said Campbell, thinking how superior he was to

Neil, who'd be incapable of such advanced philosophical debate. Sim must be aware of this too. Why wasn't she telling Eve, before it was too late? Campbell had no doubt Sim could stop the wedding if she wanted to, so why didn't she? He couldn't ask; it felt wrong, somehow, to demand that Sim explain her behaviour. She was so busy interpreting the actions of others that it would seem ridiculously cheeky, like asking an undertaker to bury himself.

'A symbol doesn't have to continue to exist,' she said. 'Maybe it's enough that it once existed, if what it symbolises is a wrong being righted. Anyway, who would you choose?'

'I don't know,' said Campbell. 'There are things about both of them that I like, you know? And things I don't like. I keep waiting for . . . something to happen that'll make it clear. Some definite sign.'

'And you a vagueness expert!' Sim scoffed. Campbell was comforted to hear that someone still thought him an expert on something. 'You of all people should know better than to wait until you feel you've crossed a clear line. Look, it's the same as short and tall.' Sim reverted to the standard example. 'It's hard to point to an exact boundary between them, but what's our response? We don't just give up and say "Oh, well, I don't know whether anything's short or tall", do we?'

'No,' Campbell had to concede.

'So what do we do? That's not a rhetorical question, by the way.'

'Well . . .' Campbell remembered a brilliant paper he'd heard at a conference a couple of years ago. He really ought to get to more conferences. They were good for meeting new women, ones he could impress, with whom he had no history. 'There's the supervaluation theory,' he said. 'If according to all reasonable definitions of the term something is tall, then we can say it's tall.'

'What counts as a reasonable definition?' asked Sim. 'There's bound to be disagreement about that.'

'Yeah, but that's a normative question and we have to avoid them.'

'Oh, absolutely. Like the plague,' said Sim, who didn't understand what he meant. 'So what do we do, if we don't get into wondering what reasonable means?'

'Okay, look,' Campbell began. 'We ask a load of people to say where they think tall begins, from what height upwards. If they give a range of answers, from five foot five to six foot, say, then we conclude that anyone who's six foot or over is tall, because according to none of our definitions would they be not tall.'

'Ah, I see!' Sim sounded thrilled, as if new light had dawned. Campbell realised he was an intelligent, knowledgeable person. If only he could remember that about himself and take it with him into the rest of his life. 'Okay, so if according to all reasonable definitions of you preferring Eve to Rory . . .'

'But that's much harder,' said Campbell. 'It's comparative.'

'It's still possible,' said Sim. 'One reasonable definition might be your willingness to share a bed with Eve. Another might be your blatant unhappiness and physical decline – soz, but you are a bit of a wreck, you've got to admit – since you left Eve.'

'Yeah, and a reasonable definition of me preferring Rory is that I left Eve for her,' Campbell countered vehemently. He objected to being described as 'a bit of a wreck'.

Sim had gone on to be even more provocative. At various points in the conversation she'd compared Rory, in that flippant way of hers, to a smelly, runny cheese, a spreading stain and an airborne spore. Still, what did Campbell expect? He'd given Sim too much detail. He should never have told her about the costume elephants, so dedicated to their cause that they were willing to freeze all night in the Nappers' garden, or that Rory hadn't invited him to her party this weekend, the big thirtieth birthday bash to which all her other friends were invited. Campbell had successfully kept both these things from Sim until last week when, in return for an expert opinion on the state of Eve's feelings for Neil, she'd dragged them out of him.

Rory, Sim claimed, was a Midas in reverse: everything she touched turned to disaster. This assessment was too merciless for Campbell's liking, particularly in its implications about his present condition. By the end of their conversation, Campbell had been cross with Sim. He wondered, as he paid for his and Eve's drinks with a tenner from his mum that had arrived in this morning's post, whether to extend his annoyance or put it behind him.

As he approached the table sheepishly, he detected a fragile atmosphere. Nobody was speaking, not even Sim. 'Hi, folks,' he said. 'What's up?'

'I've got a cleaner!' Hazel announced. 'Ian's my cleaner. Everyone else knows, so you might as well.'

'I thought Ian was your boyfriend,' said Campbell. That was what Sim had led him to believe.

'He's both.' Sim grinned like a maniac and nodded, as if nothing could be more brilliant or more natural. She clutched a bottle of champagne with both hands. 'Now, let's open this,' she said firmly.

'Like *Chinatown*.' Vanessa laughed. 'He's my boyfriend *and* my cleaner. Nicholas won't let us have a cleaner, will you, darling? Even though we could have one for free. His principles won't allow it.'

'Come on, Nicholas,' said Hazel. 'I know you want to attack me.'

'What?' He blinked at her, as if he'd only just realised she was there.

'Why would Nicholas want to attack *you*?' asked Vanessa, in a tone that implied Hazel was unworthy even as an object of abuse.

'He said I should have changed Gatting's name because Gatting the cricketer went to South Africa.' Hazel turned to Nicholas. 'You didn't care how I felt, you just looked at things with your usual tunnel vision.'

'Nicholas?' Vanessa prompted him to defend himself.

'I don't care what you call your stupid cactus,' said Nicholas tonelessly, as if the proceedings were boring him rigid. 'I hardly know you.'

'That's not true,' Sim countered. 'You and Hazel have been friends for ages.'

'Gatting's not stupid.' Hazel's voice shook. 'Go on, carry on attacking me. I know you want to.' Campbell watched all this in disbelief. What on earth was going on? Had all his friends been touched by reverse Midases too? 'You disapprove of me having a cleaner, don't you?'

'Hazel, do what you want, okay?' Nicholas seemed oddly remote from the scene. Tension oozed from everybody else, but he sat outside the atmosphere, as if he'd been replaced by a hologram of himself. 'It's none of my business,' he said.

'You do disapprove, though,' Vanessa muttered. 'Or else why can't I have a cleaner? You've done sod all round the flat recently and I'm fed up of living in squalor.'

'Fine. Get a cleaner,' said Nicholas.

'What?' Vanessa looked worried. 'Nicholas! He does disapprove,' she assured everybody. 'He's just being polite.'

'That'd be a first,' Francis attempted a joke. 'Not like you to keep your disapproval quiet, Nicholas.'

'Look, I don't think it's fantastic to employ a servant to clean up after you when you're an able-bodied person, perfectly capable of doing your own dirty work. But . . . each to his own.'

'*Each to his own?*' Vanessa turned on him. 'I never thought I'd hear *you* say that.'

'I knew it!' said Hazel. 'Come on, then, what's wrong with it?' she demanded.

'Oh, for God's sake . . .'

'No, tell me. I demand to know!' Hazel's voice vibrated with restrained hysteria.

'Look, it's just crap, okay?' Nicholas snapped. 'No one

should be subservient in that way. People shouldn't have to clean other people's loos to earn a living.'

'Nicholas, you've no idea how busy Hazel is,' said Sim sternly. 'Sometimes she doesn't get in until ten o'clock at night.'

'Fine!' said Nicholas, sounding a bit more like himself at last. 'I really don't care, Sim. I didn't start this.'

'I'd get a cleaner like a shot if Francis wasn't so messy,' said Sim. 'There's no floor space in our flat for anyone to hoover.'

'We've got a cleaner,' Matt announced. 'What's the problem?'

Hazel was still staring accusingly at Nicholas. 'Why shouldn't I employ the services of a professional to help me out?' she asked.

'Dignify it with the status of a profession if it'll salve your conscience,' said Nicholas.

'Oh, cheers,' said Ian sarcastically.

'Nicholas! Apologise,' Sim instructed.

'No, I won't.' Nicholas waved her away. He stood up. 'I've had enough of this. I was just minding my own business, but ...' Evidently he didn't feel the sentence was worth finishing. Campbell knew how he felt, though it was strange for Nicholas to be so calm, apathetic even. It makes him seem more in the right, thought Campbell. Nicholas shrugged and walked out of the bar, hands in his pockets.

'Vanessa, go and get him back.' Sim frowned.

'You go. I'm fine here, thank you.' Vanessa couldn't bear to be seen running after a man.

'That was a bit unfair to him, Hazel,' said Eve. 'You can't bully him into saying what he thinks and then have a go at him when you don't like it.'

'Eve's got a point, Haze,' said Ian gently. 'He didn't want to say anything. You did kind of force it out of him.'

'Why are you all siding with him?' Hazel blinked back

tears. 'What about me?' She pointed at herself with both index fingers. 'What about my feelings?'

'Hazel, everything's fine,' Lucy assured her.

'No, it isn't! For the first time in my life I tell you all what I really think and everything is most definitely not fine!' The people at the next table had turned their chairs round to get a better view.

'Hazel . . .' Ian put a hand on her arm.

'No, I'm having my say. My mum and dad are in their sixties. All their lives they've worn themselves out doing full-time jobs and housework, even though they could afford a whole army of cleaners. But no, they'd rather suffer! There's no point in them having any leisure time; they don't know how to enjoy it. Well, I'm sorry, but I don't think it's immoral to do things to make life easier, or nicer. All I'm trying to do is break free of that . . . baggage and allow myself to be happy, and *shits* like Nicholas come along and ruin it!' She stood up to go. 'I'm sorry. I'm not in the mood for drinking and chatting any more.'

'Another one bites the dust,' said Matt, as Hazel brushed past him. 'This is fun.' Ian got up to follow her.

'Aah, there's true love for you!' Vanessa cooed.

'Vanessa, leave Ian alone,' said Eve. 'You've been getting at him since you arrived.'

'Excuse me? I think you've got it the wrong way round.'

'Can I just point out that in another forty years or so we'll all be dead?' said Francis, apropos nothing in particular. Everyone inspected him closely.

'And your point is?' Sim prompted.

'We're wasting time with these stupid arguments. It's sheer vandalism!'

'Some stag weekend this is,' said Matt. 'We haven't even opened the champagne. Why couldn't Nicholas keep his bloody trap shut?'

'You can't blame Nicholas,' said Eve. 'I can understand why he thinks having a cleaner's a bit dodgy.'

'I can blame who I want,' said Matt. 'It's my stag

weekend and nothing to do with you.' He tried to sound offhand but didn't quite pull it off.

'For God's sake, Matt!' Francis groaned.

'Oh, here we go,' said Eve. 'What's the problem, Matt?'

'You've got the problem, not me. Stealing our wedding day, ruining the most important event of our lives.'

'Matt, stop,' murmured Lucy.

'That's not fair.' Eve looked as if she'd been slapped. 'I asked Lucy if she minded.' Campbell found himself in the familiar predicament of not knowing what to do. He wanted to stick up for Eve, but not for her plan to marry Neil.

'Well, you didn't ask me,' said Matt. 'And I mind. Why can't you get married some other time? The truth is, you know your wedding's going to be a complete farce and you're scared no one'll turn up if you don't append it to ours.'

'Temper, temper.' Vanessa smirked.

The look on Eve's face reminded Campbell of when he'd first told her about Rory. Matt was a total bastard. Still, he was spot on.

'That's a terrible thing to say.' Lucy nudged him.

'How much have you had to drink, Matt?' asked Francis.

'Drink!' Vanessa gave a hollow laugh. 'It's like the Temperance Society headquarters around here.'

'Of course we'd all turn up, whenever Eve's wedding was,' said Sim.

'Yeah, it's a bit much,' Campbell contributed eventually.

'My wedding won't be a farce,' said Eve matter-of-factly. 'I'm marrying someone who would never do what you've just done, Matt. The only farce around here is that I thought you were my friend. Neil and I *are* getting married next Saturday, but don't worry, we wouldn't dream of coming to your party, or your wedding, so you can have them all to yourself! And now it's my turn to go off in a huff.' She made a swift, dignified exit.

'Matt, go after her,' said Lucy. 'I'm not prepared to lose one of my best friends over this. I'd rather share our party with them, if it's not too late for that. What difference does it make?'

'Campbell, go and see Eve,' Sim whispered.

'Why me? It was Matt who upset her.' Hadn't Eve just said she was marrying Neil next week, come what may? What was the point in going upstairs with her if that were true?

'What?' Matt asked Lucy irritably. 'What have I done? I didn't say anything that bad, did I?'

'Just do it.' Sim gave Campbell a meaningful look. He decided he'd better do as she suggested, just this once. Later he'd definitely be showing her who was boss.

2

'Sim, you're not doing it properly,' Francis hissed. It was midnight and they were in their hotel bedroom. It was the sort of symmetrical room Sim loved, with matching cabinets and lamps on either side of the bed and a mirror and desk in front of it. Eve and Campbell were in the adjacent room.

'Ssh!'

'Let me . . .'

'Sssshhh!' Sim pressed her ear against the wall. 'I can hear them talking.'

'You're so stubborn,' Francis whispered, climbing out of bed. 'You could eavesdrop more effectively.' He freed a clean glass from its plastic wrapper in the en suite bathroom and brought it into the bedroom. 'Look,' he said, pushing Sim out of the way. He placed the glass against the wall and pressed his ear to it. 'Let me try with this. And go back to bed. You're heavier than me, you'll make the floorboards creak.'

'Charming.' Sim tiptoed towards the bed. Maybe Francis had a point.

'I think I can hear something, but . . .'

'Does it sound like sex?'

'Shut it, will you?' He turned round, peeved. 'All experiments need time to work. If you analyse the results prematurely, you end up with the wrong conclusion. I'm not sure the glass is in its optimum position yet.'

'Oh, for heaven's sake.' Sim lay down on the bed and thought about the dreadful night they'd had. How could Matt have said those things to Eve? At least Lucy hadn't seconded them, that was something, but . . . Sim's mind struggled with what it was having to adjust to: the idea of Matt as someone who could hurt other people. She didn't like it at all. Francis was his best man. It made her feel dizzy. And then there was Hazel. And Nicholas. And Vanessa and Ian. Oh, God, the problems were stacking up all right and the weird thing was, Sim wasn't sure who was at fault in any of these spats, which made them harder to deal with.

It would be awful if Matt and Lucy's stag-hen week-end were totally ruined. Sim was a resolute optimist; she refused to believe it already had been. Tomorrow could still be salvaged, as long as everyone berried hat sheds in the morning. I would, she thought, if I were Eve, or Hazel, or Nicholas. Could she be sure, though, with her track record? It was all very well to believe that Gillian was different – worse – but the one time Sim had been attacked by a friend she'd ended the friendship. What did that say about her? She tried to call upon her world-view, but it didn't seem to want to talk to her tonight.

So Ian was Hazel's cleaner. Sim had guessed the truth would come out sooner or later, which was partly why she'd been so blasé about Ian's determination to withhold juicy gossip from her, its patron saint. It was good for the spirit to act out of character from time to time. One risked stagnation, otherwise. To be devoid of internal contradictions was no good for a person.

How ridiculous, she thought, that Hazel's big secret should turn out to be so harmless. Yet with people like Nicholas around, Sim could see why Hazel had wanted to keep it to herself. What hope was there for a better world, though, when such non-issues furred our ethical arteries? Sim smiled. That was a good phrase; someone in *Potters Court* would have to use it soon.

'Eve just laughed,' Francis whispered.

'What sort of a laugh was it?'

'I don't know. Are there different sorts?'

'Yes, of course. Laughs are as different as . . . weddings,' said Sim.

'You know, I won't be able to go to Eve's wedding if it's on the same day as Matt's. I'm Matt's best man. I have to spend the whole day sorting him out, don't I?'

'Yes.' Sim sighed deeply. 'Well done, Francis.'

'Why?'

'For anticipating a political crisis. Now we can think about how to defuse it.' She tried to sound more hopeful than she felt.

'Why don't we get married on that day too?' Francis suggested. 'Then we'll be legitimately busy and off the hook.'

'Yeah, right.' Sim laughed.

'I'm not joking.' He turned round. Looking at Sim's expectant face, he realised that, in spite of all his deliberation on the matter, he was utterly unprepared for this moment. 'Sim, you probably don't want to,' he said, 'but . . . well, you know.'

'What?'

He blushed. 'You *know*.'

'You mean . . . will I marry you?'

'Yes!'

Sim's inclination was still to laugh, but she resisted it. Francis, wanting to get married? 'Are you serious?' she asked.

'Shouldn't I be?' he said in a guarded tone.

'Don't be defensive, Francis. Are you serious?' Sim smiled at him encouragingly.

He pondered the matter for a few seconds. 'Yes,' he announced defiantly.

'Then, yes, I'll marry you.'

'Oh!' Francis looked surprised. 'Good. That's settled,

then.' He turned back to his eavesdropping, keen to conceal his pleasure and relief from Sim.

'Francis!'

'Sshh! What?'

'Are you really serious? Are we getting married?' Sim beamed.

'I thought we'd just dealt with that.' Francis's face clouded over. Was it too soon to mention the sort of wedding (or rather non-wedding) he wanted?

'Francis, there is one thing, though.' He knew it; it was too good to be true that Sim would marry him. She was going to change her mind. 'Can we do it quietly? You know, just us, a registrar and two witnesses?'

'What?' Francis's eyes lit up. 'I thought you'd want a big do. You've been raving about Matt and Lucy's wedding . . .'

'Matt and Lucy are different,' said Sim automatically, then wondered about it. Perhaps they weren't so different after all. 'I'm fed up with being the linking person,' she said. 'I mean, look what happened tonight. Why did Vanessa and Ian take against each other? Why was Matt so mean to Eve? Why didn't Eve know Matt and Lucy wouldn't want her to pinch their wedding day, even if they were too polite to say so? People should be able to anticipate how their close friends will feel about things. And Nicholas said he hardly knew Hazel – those were his very words: "I hardly know you," he said.'

'What are you driving at?' asked Francis.

'This: how come I know all of them inside out? I can anticipate how they'll react, how they feel; I instinctively know how not to antagonise any of them. Ask yourself why that is, Francis.'

'It's obvious. You're the centre of the group.'

'Is it that I'm at the centre, or is it that I've forced the group together?'

Francis considered this for a few moments. 'It's that you've forced the group together,' he said eventually.

375

'Oh, cheers.' Sim grinned. 'Well, I don't think it's quite that extreme, but the point is, I'm the linking person, the one with overall responsibility.'

'I thought you liked that,' said Francis.

'I didn't mind it when I thought we were a group of genuinely close friends. But if none of the others get on, I'd rather just have lots of separate friends and see them separately. I'm fed up of situations like tonight: everyone does and says what they want and stonks off to bed thinking only of themselves, and I lie awake worrying about the bigger picture.'

'But, Sim, you've set yourself up in that role. No one asked you to be the linking person.'

'Of course,' said Sim. 'Like all tragic heroines, I contain the seeds of my own downfall. That's why I've got to fight it. If we have a big wedding, I'll spend all day worrying about whether everyone's getting on. I mean, it's mad! Every social occasion is a political crisis for me. What with Vanessa's barbed comments about Hazel, Nicholas yelling at everyone, Eve and her often unwelcome common sense, Hazel's surreal streak, your tendency to leave the room if you're bored . . . there's no way I can smooth it all over.'

'You were the only one who ever thought you could,' Francis reminded her. 'You even tried with Gillian. She was always dodgy. Look how quickly she vanished from the scene as soon as you gave us all permission to drop her.' Sim sighed. Francis was right. She'd expected people first to be pro- then anti-Gillian. The reality was that no one cared. None of Sim's friends had the sense of community, of tribal belonging, that she had. She'd perceived Gillian as a threat to the group; no wonder the others hadn't if the group meant nothing to them. 'So what are you saying?' asked Francis. 'That you're a spent force?'

'Francis, you have a charming way of putting things.' Sim laughed. 'No, all I'm saying is that I want a small wedding. Our witnesses will have to be two strangers, too – you can imagine the complications otherwise. And Francis, not a word about us getting married to the others, not this weekend. There's enough wedding congestion as it is.'

'You're still doing it,' said Francis.

'What?'

'Thinking about the others. Being the linking person.'

'Well, I can't just stop, can I? There'd be chaos. If you give people total freedom too soon they don't know how to use it properly. There has to be a sort of handover period.'

'Hopeless.' Francis shook his head.

'Are we really getting married, then?' Sim jumped out of bed and ran over to hug him. 'Oh, Francis, it's so romantic!'

Hazel lay face down on her twin bed. Ian had given up trying to get her to look at him. 'It's over, it's all over,' she kept repeating.

'What is?' Ian had asked several times. 'Us? Me cleaning for you? What?'

'Both. Everything,' was what Ian thought he heard through the duvet muffle effect.

'Hazel, I'll stop cleaning for you if you want, but I'm not giving up on . . . well, on everything else. I love you. I thought you loved me.'

'But it's ruined,' Hazel sobbed. 'It'll never be the same. You heard Nicholas say those things. That'll always be between us. If we go through a bad patch, you'll remember what Nicholas said and you'll think he was right all along, that I exploited you . . .'

'Hazel, how many times . . . ! I won't.'

'I was mad to think I could mix our personal lives with a business transaction. It's as if I've bought you and you're a prostitute . . .'

'Oh, cheers.' Ian laughed, despite the pressure that was building up inside him. This was a crisis Hazel had been anticipating for months, one she'd had ample opportunity to prepare for. How would she cope if Ian told her the truth about himself? He'd have to tell her some time and that really would be an unexpected blow. Not the truth itself so much as the net of lies Ian had got himself caught up in. 'You really know how to flatter a person,' he said, hoping a joke would calm her down. 'First I'm Dale Dingley, then I'm a prostitute. The thing is, Hazel, you can say whatever you want and I'll still love you. And I'll never think you exploited me. If anything, it's the other way round.' He hadn't meant to add that last bit.

Hazel sat up, leaving a face-shaped wet patch on the duvet. 'What do you mean?' she asked.

Here goes, thought Ian. Hazel was miserable anyway. If he told her the truth now, at least he wouldn't have to watch her smile fade and know it was his fault. 'I'm the one who's exploited you,' he said. Why hadn't he done this a lot sooner? Habit was the only answer he could come up with. Secrets cluttered up the mind unnecessarily if you didn't review the case for their concealment on a regular basis.

'How have you exploited me?' Hazel looked frightened.

'I've been meaning to tell you something for a while,' said Ian. 'But the time never seemed right.'

'*What?*' Hazel clutched the duvet, as if tempted to dive under it for protection.

'I'm not a cleaner, not any more. I haven't been for a while. I still clean for you, but that's all. I've got another source of income, one you don't know about . . .'

'Oh my God! You're a heroin dealer.'

'No, it's nothing like that, nothing illegal. It's all above board.'

'What, then? Ian, tell me, I can't bear it.'

'I will,' Ian assured her. 'But I have to do it in my own way. The thing is, I've been working in your flat, using my key to get in. I arrive at quarter to nine, Monday to Friday, and leave at seven on the days when I'm not supposed to be there. I'm sorry, Hazel. I know it's an invasion of your space, breaking and entering, even. I do extra cleaning every day, though, to compensate, more than you know about. I make sure the flat's always spotless.' It was such a relief to be telling her this that Ian couldn't stop the words rushing out. 'I can't work at my mam and dad's, it's too noisy, and my dad'd take the piss out of what I do.'

'What do you do, Ian?' Hazel wailed. 'Please tell me, quickly. I'm scared.'

'I'm a writer.' This was absurd; Ian felt as if he were coming out of the closet.

'A writer?' Bafflement replaced fear on Hazel's face. 'But . . . I'm a literature development officer!'

'I know that, you dolt.' He smiled. 'You might have wondered why we had so much in common.'

'I didn't.' Hazel looked pained. 'I thought we were just . . . two people who got on well. Unlike Nicholas, I don't think cleaners are lower or subservient, or whatever it was he said.'

'My dad'd think writing was for girls. It was bad enough with the cleaning. He used to try and persuade me to call myself a floor technician, said it sounded more manly. But that's not the only reason I kept my writing quiet. I wanted to protect my first book from the . . . scrutiny of the people in my life at the time, my family, mates down the pub. That was before I knew you, Hazel. I didn't know any intelligent, sensitive people. I didn't believe they existed, to be honest.'

'You've published a book?' Hazel gasped. 'That's brilliant! Did it do well?'

'Well enough to fund me to write the next one. I gave up cleaning – you were the only client I kept. That was before we became such good friends, but I probably loved you even then. I certainly loved writing in your study. I knew if I told you I couldn't clean for you any more I'd have no excuse to carry on seeing you.'

'Oh, Ian!' Hazel started to bounce on the bed. 'All this time you've been a writer! Nicholas is wrong – you aren't an oppressed mass!'

'I wasn't when I was a cleaner, either,' said Ian. 'In fact, cleaning is about four times easier than writing novels, and it pays better. Most novelists don't even earn the minimum wage.'

'Novels. Oh. I'd assumed you were a poet.' Hazel frowned.

'Why?' Ian was reassured to see that her vivid imagination had sprung into action once again.

'I don't know. I bet you'd write good poems, though. Better than the Throat Parrot's. So . . . you must have a pseudonym.'

'Yes, but . . . do you forgive me for lying to you, for using your flat without your permission?'

'Of course,' said Hazel. 'You did my cleaning, didn't you? And you were there all day! I needn't have worried about Gatting getting lonely.'

'No,' Ian agreed. 'I chatted to him all the time.'

'I wish you'd told me. Why didn't you? You must have known I wouldn't have begrudged you the flat during the day.'

'I wish I'd told you too,' said Ian. 'I want you to trust me, Hazel. I know you don't, not fully, and it's my own fault. Sim told me you know about the *His and Hers* thing, that I ripped out that ad.'

Hazel's eyes widened. 'Is that to do with this?' she asked.

'Yes,' said Ian. 'And believe me, I've hated keeping it a secret from you for so long.'

'Then why did you?'

'Because I had to, if I wanted my writing to be a secret. It's odd, I don't give a stuff about that now that I've got you. I'm more confident about everything. But I wasn't then and our friendship was still at an early stage when I first started to use your flat to write in. Even if you hadn't minded, you wouldn't have been able to resist the urge to tell Sim I was also a certain writer she might have heard of.'

'Are you famous?' Hazel lowered her eyes in awe. 'Are you Danielle Steele?'

'Far from it. But your friends would still recognise my name.' Ian sighed heavily. 'Because one of them's my editor.'

'What?' Hazel's voice came out as a croak.

'Vanessa.'

'Oh, my God,' said Hazel slowly. '*His and Hers*!' She looked Ian up and down, as if she'd never seen him before. 'You're Greg Pendry, aren't you?' she said.

Eve lay fully clothed in bed beside Campbell, feeling like a block of lead. How could she have done this to herself? She was a laughing stock and everyone knew it. Matt and Lucy hated her. Neil would hate her when he found out she'd set off to Yorkshire hoping for a reconciliation with Campbell, and Campbell would hate her if she married Neil. The terrible irony was that all she'd ever wanted was to be loved, properly loved. She'd gone about it in such a cowardly, devious way, though. And now the game was up; enough was enough. She had to take a long, hard look at herself and her behaviour. Until she'd been through that process, she only knew one thing for certain. 'I can't marry Neil,' she said. 'Matt's right. I've been a right plonker.'

'Don't you love him, then?' asked Campbell hopefully.

'I don't know. Yes, I love him, but I still love you too. Oh, God, what am I going to do?'

'You could marry me,' Campbell suggested quietly. Neil had upped the stakes; this was the only way Campbell could beat him. It wasn't just about Eve, though Campbell was beginning to suspect he wanted her back. Mainly, however, he wanted to shirk responsibility. His actions had led directly to Eve's engagement to Neil. The damage had to be repaired, or the permanent loss of Eve would be Campbell's fault. He couldn't stand the thought of being responsible for something bad for ever, so his only choice was to undo it.

Campbell resented the unpleasantness and effort involved in bringing about a situation that, not too long ago, he had been in effortlessly, without having to put himself out. It had all been so unnecessary, so avoidable; to think Eve used to be unequivocally *his* and he didn't appreciate it. Campbell, who existed very much in the realm of ideas, knew this particular idea would torment him for the rest of his life if he didn't get Eve back.

'How can you say you want to marry me without saying anything about the Grimble?' Eve asked.

'What do you mean?'

'What if I said yes, I'll marry you? What would you do about her?'

Campbell considered this. It hadn't occurred to him that he'd need to do anything. If he was honest with himself – which he acknowledged he rarely was – things with the Grimble had been on the wane for a while. She'd never been serious about him, Campbell could see that now. Tomorrow was her birthday party and he was excluded, too common to go to the ball. Rory would end up with someone like herself – rich, privileged, a society person – and their wedding would be filmed by *Hello!* magazine. Campbell was disappointed that he would never be rich, but more disappointed that his grand passion had hit the ground snoozing. 'I'd end it,' he said.

'How?'

'Does that matter?'

'It matters to me.'

'I suppose I'd tell her I thought it was better for us just to be friends.'

'Of course you would.' Eve sighed.

Neil sat up in bed and turned on the lamp. What the hell was he doing, trying to fall asleep in what used to be Campbell's bed, while Eve and Campbell were in a hotel together in Yorkshire?

He squinted as his eyes adjusted to the light, then came

to rest on Imogen's envelope, which he'd brought up to bed with him. He pulled the small sheet of yellow paper out of the envelope and read what Imogen had written for the second time. The child was a genius. She'd given Neil a weapon; why wait until Eve got back to use it? So what if it was the middle of the night? Neil had become the sort of man who might well do things at unconventional hours if they were important enough.

Oddly, the act of wondering what Campbell was up to in Yorkshire with Eve had had a paralysing effect upon Neil this evening, almost as if he only had the capacity to be dominant and active when Campbell was dormant and passive, when Neil knew for sure that his rival was in remission. What am I, Neil asked himself in disgust, some fucking pod creature, like in *Invasion of the Body Snatchers*, who can only flourish while his original is asleep?

A vision of himself in his pre-Eve life flashed before Neil's eyes: a sad geek who wore slippers round the house and ate ready-made meals on a tray in front of the six o'clock news. He never wanted to go back to that.

Neil jumped out of bed and dressed quickly. Campbell was always passive, he assured himself; going to Yorkshire wouldn't change that. Besides, Campbell hadn't 'gone', he'd been taken by Eve, in Eve's car. Neil grabbed the yellow envelope, stuffed it in his pocket and ran downstairs. It was only when he was in his car, about to set off to Yorkshire in the dark, that he realised he'd forgotten something vital.

Eve had made him happy in the past few weeks, but it was Imogen who'd made Neil feel like a hero, Imogen whose words had spurred him into action. How could he go without her?

Francis's mobile phone rang as he made his way to the hotel restaurant the next morning to meet the others. Sim wasn't with him; Eve had banged on their door five minutes ago, saying that she needed to talk, so Francis had left Sim to work her magic unobserved. 'Hello?' he said quietly. Talking on a mobile in public made him feel ostentatious.

'Is that Francis Weir?'

'Yes.'

'This is Annette Wrigley.'

'Annette?' Francis's feet stopped, as if they'd obstinately overruled his brain's instruction to carry on walking. 'How did you get this number?'

'From your office. I told them it was urgent.'

'Right,' said Francis, preparing for the worst. It would be naïve to assume Annette had phoned him for a conciliatory chat.

'I thought I should let you know I've had a phone call.'

'From the Dingleys?' Christ, that was all Annette needed.

'No. From someone who knows where they are. An old woman. In Manchester. She . . . she heard them interviewed on your programme and recognised their voices. She seems to think they're holed up in the flat next door to hers.'

'Lots of people have Yorkshire accents, Annette.'

'That's what I said to her. But it wasn't just the accents. She's heard them refer to each other by name.'

'Oh.' Francis didn't want this. He'd had his brush with the Dingleys. What he wanted now was for no one to know where they were. No, that was wrong. He wanted them to be nowhere, to vanish.

'Her walls are thin,' said Annette.

'She might be a crank.'

'And she equally might not.'

'Of course. But . . . don't get your hopes up.'

'Hopes?' She emitted a low laugh. 'I don't have hopes any more.'

'No. But . . . no.' Why had Annette phoned him? What could he say?

'I'm intrigued. Why do you think I'd hope that this old woman is right?'

384

'Well . . . now that you mention it, I'm not sure.' Francis scratched his head. 'You sounded pleased when you told me, I suppose. Well, not pleased exactly, but . . . satisfied.'

'I am satisfied. It's a very sad and very minor victory, I know, but if they're in hiding, I'm glad their cover's been blown. It helps to know where they are.'

'And the fact that the old woman bothered to contact you . . . well, that's good too, isn't it? Not everyone's on the Dingleys' side, you see. Most people aren't.'

'And is it good that you went ahead with the interview, even though I asked you not to?' Annette challenged him.

'I didn't say that.'

'No. Still, something valuable has come out of it. That's why I rang you. Because the interview was your doing. So you should know what happens as a result of it.'

'I agree.'

'You realise I'm going to have to look into it, see whether it's true or not.'

'Annette, whatever you do, don't confront them.'

'Unarmed, you mean?'

'What?'

Annette laughed. 'I'm going to kill them, Francis.' Neither of them spoke for a few seconds. 'Ah. I see I've shocked you.'

Francis's mind worked furiously. 'It'll be harder than you imagine,' he said eventually.

'With all due respect,' said Annette with heavy irony, 'you are not the parent of a child who was raped and murdered.'

'Fair point. So why are you telling me this? Do you expect me to try to talk you out of it?'

'You wouldn't succeed. I'm telling you because, as you said, it's your business as well, not only mine. You're responsible too.'

'Right,' said Francis.

'So go to the police if you want to, tell them I'm going

to kill the Dingleys. How's that for shared ownership of the situation?' It was only as she said this that it hit Francis: this wasn't just anger talking. Annette Wrigley hated him. Francis wasn't even sure she made any great distinction between him and the Dingleys, which enraged him.

'There's no joint ownership here, Annette,' he said. 'There's only my choice and your choice, and they're entirely separate. I've already made mine – I'm not going to the police; I'm going to dismiss what you've told me as hysterical ravings. *Your* choice is between murdering Dale and Wayne Dingley and not murdering them, and you're the only person responsible for making it.'

'I've already told you I'm going to kill them.' Her words were almost inaudible.

'Yes, but you were hoping for a response from me that would act either as an egging-on or as a constraint. So you'd have an excuse, whatever you did. You're not sure enough to go ahead and do it, are you? You need an ally. You think your grief makes you a force that other people have to struggle to contain. Well, that's unreasonable. You're a responsible adult woman.'

'I'll tell you exactly when and how I'm going to do it,' Annette threatened. 'You could prevent it from happening.'

'Temporarily, perhaps, but not permanently. You're the only one who can prevent it, Annette. Goodbye.'

Francis switched off his phone so she couldn't ring back. He saw that his hands were shaking and sank into an armchair in the foyer. To calm himself, he sat very still and silently recited a list of the kings and queens of England: 'Two Williams, two Henries . . . Two Williams, two Henries . . .' That was as far as he could get.

Eventually his breathing steadied. Do I care if Dale and Wayne Dingley die, he asked himself. Shameful though it was, he had a feeling he didn't. Some people forfeited their right to life. But that didn't mean anyone else had a right to kill them, Francis was very certain of that. He hoped

Annette was merely consoling herself with a fantasy, but could he take the risk? If he told the police and they saved the Dingleys' lives, would Francis have contributed to justice or injustice?

This wasn't a decision he could make on his own; he needed to talk to Sim, who by now was likely to be in Heathcliff's, the hotel's main restaurant, having breakfast with the others. Francis got up and made his feet go in that direction, though there was no chance of his being able to eat anything.

He practised looking normal all the way to the restaurant. When he glanced in through the glass door, he was tempted to back away into the corridor again, so startled was he by what he saw.

It was too late. Ian had spotted him and was smiling in acknowledgement. Francis took a deep breath and approached the table. Matt, Nicholas and Campbell shuffled in their seats with varying degrees of discomfort, eyes downcast. Nicholas looked as if he'd spent the past nine hours on the night bus back from hell. But the most abnormal thing of all was that there was only one hen present at this stag-heavy gathering: that bloody harpie Gillian Kench. Beside her was a man Francis didn't know but assumed was her boyfriend (Jimmy? Johnny?). What the hell were they doing, bang in the middle of the breakfast table?

'His proposal had "last resort" written all over it,' said Eve tearfully, who was sitting cross-legged on Sim and Francis's king-sized hotel bed. 'It wasn't even a proposal. He said "You could marry me instead" and that was it. Talk about pathetic!'

'Are you sure you aren't confusing understatement with a lack of enthusiasm?' asked Sim, who was applying glittery mauve lipstick in front of the mirror.

'Rory's slept with someone else,' Eve addressed her friend's reflection. 'She hasn't invited Campbell to this big party she's having tonight. It's obvious: she's trying to shake him off and he knows it. If she was as keen on him as he is on her, there's no way he'd still be interested in me.'

Sim turned to face Eve, unsure how to respond. She was starving, keen to get down to the restaurant and see Francis (her fiancé!). Disconcertingly, her world-view appeared to be taking its annual leave. Eve's analysis had an uncomfortable ring of truth to it. On the other hand, Sim had always seen Campbell's attraction to Rory as a sort of virus, assuming that the core, healthy, original Campbell had never stopped loving Eve.

'Would I rather be the second choice of my first choice, or the first choice of my second?' said Eve. 'That's what it boils down to, isn't it?'

'You're amazing.' Sim laughed. 'In a good way, I mean. To be able to put it to yourself so . . . so starkly. I don't know, Eve. I can't decide for you.'

'Why not?' Eve smiled sadly. 'Don't stop meddling now, when I need your interference most. I thought you knew all the answers.'

'So did I,' said Sim. Perhaps getting engaged had sapped her of her powers. 'I tell you what, though,' she said, brightening as she realised she did have one insight to offer Eve. 'If Campbell thinks he can get you back and still be friends with old Cruelty-without-Beauty, he deserves instant demotion from first choice to second. The only way Campbell can make up for going off with Rory is by finishing with her in a fitting manner.'

'I know. Then I could get back with him and not feel that it's such a . . . I don't know, an anticlimax. Why can't he say, "Fuck off, Grimbelina – I never want to see your pimply face again"?' Eve giggled. 'Can you imagine it, Campbell saying that?'

Sim was about to say no and that therein lay his downfall, when the door burst open and Hazel stampeded into the room, looking radiant. 'Guess what,' she said, grinning and panting with joy. Sim and Eve exchanged a look. What could have happened between last night and now to bring about such a drastic change of mood? 'Guess who Ian is,' Hazel prompted.

'Your cleaner?' Eve offered.

'No! Well, yes, but guess who else he is.'

Sim sighed. 'Hazel, it's okay for him to be your cleaner, you know. I don't know why you . . .'

'He's Cal Raynard!' Hazel announced triumphantly. 'My favourite author!'

Sim and Eve stared at her, bemused. 'Hazel, don't be silly,' said Sim eventually.

'I'm *not* being silly. Ian is Cal Raynard. *Cloudy* and *Howdy* – you know, Sim, you read *Cloudy*.'

'Yes, but . . .'

'Well, Ian wrote it. He's Cal Raynard. He only told me last night; he didn't want Vanessa to find out . . .' Hazel tailed off as she heard the door swing open.

'Who didn't want me to find out what?' Vanessa stood in the doorway wearing a navy satin dressing gown. 'I overslept,' she said by way of explanation.

'Come in,' said Sim. 'Close the door behind you.'

'Is this a girly chat? I don't want to know about anyone's periods or orgasms, please. Well?' Vanessa gave Hazel a contemptuous look. 'What mustn't I find out?'

'Nothing, Vanessa.' Sim gave her a look. 'Hazel, come on, now, stop being silly. Just because I thought Ian was Dale Dingley . . .'

'You *what*?' said Eve.

'Dingley's sexier,' Vanessa contributed. She hadn't forgiven Hazel for driving Nicholas out of the bar last night.

'It's a long story,' said Sim.

Hazel turned to Vanessa. 'Ian is Cal Raynard,' she told her. 'Your author.'

Vanessa laughed. 'Yeah, right. Of course he is. And I'm Rabindranath Tagore.'

'I don't care if you don't believe me. It's true. Sim, you believe me, don't you?'

'Hazel . . .' Sim began tentatively. 'Presumably if this Cal Raynard's one of Vanessa's authors, she's met him.' She wished Hazel would backtrack before she embarrassed herself any further.

'I haven't, actually,' said Vanessa. 'He's a pseudonym. But you know that, I fucking told you,' she spat at Hazel. 'When you first started going on about him. And now you're weaving it into your sick little fantasy life.'

'Some of us have got real problems,' Eve reminded Hazel.

'It's true, Sim,' Hazel turned to the most sympathetic face in the room. 'He told me last night.' Sim felt awful for her. This had to be a reaction to the trauma of the night before. Where was Ian? Was he even aware of what Hazel was saying about him?

Vanessa wandered over to the window and lit a cigarette. '. . . fucking strait-jacket,' she muttered.

'Eve, I told Sim a while ago that Ian had torn a page out of my copy of *Howdy* and I didn't know why,' Hazel went on undaunted. 'Didn't I, Sim?' Sim nodded. 'Well, he told me why.'

'And?'

'His agent had specifically asked for there to be no books by other authors advertised in the back of *Howdy*. The publishers ignored . . .'

'What's Cal Raynard's agent's name?' asked Vanessa, a glint of triumph in her eyes.

'I don't know.' Hazel blushed. 'I didn't ask.'

'Hazel!' Eve snapped.

'Somebody's pants are on fire.' Vanessa smirked, then, looking Hazel up and down, she added, 'Unlikely though it sounds.' Sim shook her head. She couldn't believe this was happening. By now they should all have been having a serene, contented, vegetarian breakfast together.

'Call me whatever you want,' said Hazel. 'I don't care what anyone thinks of me any more.'

'Carry on, Hazel. Why did Ian tear out that page?' Sim

390

still didn't believe a word of it, but in the light of Eve's and Vanessa's reactions she felt obliged to pretend to.

'Because he was so furious that they'd advertised that shitty *His and Hers* in the back of his book without his permission. He felt as if *Howdy* had been contaminated by having an ad for such a lowbrow book in it.'

'Hazel, what's wrong with you?' Eve demanded. 'Why are you determined to be the centre of attention all the time? That story's so obviously made up. No one'd care about something like that. Would they, Sim?'

Sim was looking at Vanessa, whose lips were clamped, vice-like, around her cigarette. 'Vanessa?' she said. 'Is Eve right?' To Sim, this last titbit of information had rung oddly true. How would she feel, she asked herself, if the advert breaks in *Potters Court* were used to advertise *EastEnders*? She'd be bloody pissed off, was the short answer. It was a territorial issue and writers were vain creatures. 'Did Cal Raynard's agent ask you not to plug other authors' books in the back of his?'

Vanessa shrugged aggressively. 'How the fuck should I know? I never listen to a word those cretins say, do I?'

There was a rapping on the door. 'Come in,' Sim called.

Lucy's pale, worried face appeared. 'Oh, God, guys . . .' she said. 'You'd better come down, quickly. I don't know what to do. Gillian Kench is here.'

Neil was waiting with his jacket on and the car keys in his hand when the doorbell rang. He'd been unable to bring himself to phone Imogen in the middle of the night, so he'd waited until first thing this morning. He'd been awake all night, pacing, so tired that he couldn't risk sleeping in case he never woke up. He felt like someone who'd accidentally taken an overdose and had to drag himself around the room until the ambulance arrived.

'Are you ready?' Neil bumped into Imogen as he tried to leave the house and she tried to come in.

391

'Look.' She waved a piece of paper in front of his face, bobbing up and down on the doorstep.

'What? We haven't got time . . .'

'It's from school. Read it, quick.' Neil took the letter from her and began to read as Imogen hopped impatiently from one foot to the other. It was from Claire Morgan and had been printed on official school notepaper.

Dear Imogen

I am writing to inform you that it has been the unanimous decision of the judges of the school poetry competition this year to award joint first prize to your poem, 'Memories'. All three judges felt the poem was formally extremely adept, linguistically sophisticated and very moving. The prize-giving ceremony will take place on 12 May and it would be wonderful if you could attend. I hope you will continue to pursue creative writing as a hobby, as you so clearly have an aptitude for it. I enclose a ten-pound book token and congratulate you on your good work.

Yours sincerely

Claire Morgan.

'Well? What do you think?' said Imogen.

'Great.' Neil tried to look as happy as he could under the circumstances. 'You've got your prize at last.'

'But Miss Morgan's lying. It wasn't the unanimous decision of the judges. They only gave my poem a prize because of our made-up letter.'

'Imogen! They gave it a prize.' Neil couldn't believe she wasn't thrilled. 'We won.'

'Yes, but . . . I don't know.' Imogen frowned. 'It's not *perfect*. I wanted them to change their minds about my poem. Genuinely. Properly.'

'Life isn't very proper.' Neil sighed. 'This is still a victory, though.'

'But not a complete one!'

'Imogen, there's no such thing as a complete victory, I'm afraid. I wish there were, but . . .'

'What about if we got Eve back? Wouldn't that be a complete victory? We should go up to Campbell and say, "Your mam blows goats!"'

'Pardon?' Neil, putting his jacket on, did a double take. '"Your mam . . ."'

'No, no, I heard it the first time. Imogen! You're too young to be saying gross things like that.'

'Everyone says it.' Imogen waved away his concern. 'Anyway, I'm a prize-winning author and I reject censorship in all its forms.'

'Do you, indeed?' Neil held the door open. 'Come on! I thought you wanted to get Eve back. What are we waiting for?'

Francis was repelled by the sight of Gillian. Her skin was orange with make-up and her glossy pink lips had a black line round them. A limp mop of dyed blond hair was fixed to the top of her head with metal clips and a few loose strands fell over her face. She reminded Francis of a waxwork.

Where the hell was Sim? She'd go mad. Gillian wasn't invited, Francis knew that much. No one had been expecting her. 'Hello, Francis,' she said. 'I bet you got a right shock when you saw me!' She tittered flirtatiously. 'Me and Andrew thought we'd surprise you.'

On the table, several full English breakfasts lay untouched on plates, congealing. Sim's appeal for mass vegetarianism had been roundly ignored. 'Where are the hens?' Francis asked, hoping a joke would lighten the atmosphere. He should have phoned the police before going to breakfast, he realised. Now it would be awkward to get away; he wanted to be there to cushion the blow for Sim when she arrived and was confronted with this scene.

Francis wondered whether Gillian's presence alone could

account for the devastation he saw before him. No one had even had a stab at answering his question. Never had the sight of his friends been a sorrier one. Campbell's mouth was one large, gruesome blister; Francis suspected he'd spent much of the night picking at it. Nicholas's skin was grey and his eyes were hollow, as if he'd peered deep into the abyss, and Matt, pale and resentful, looked more like a snail than a stag. Gillian's boyfriend also looked extremely uncomfortable. Francis wondered whether he'd known all along that he and Gillian weren't invited or whether it had only just become apparent to him.

Loud female voices cut themselves off in mid-sentence as they approached the table. Francis turned round. Sim and Vanessa were staring at Gillian in disbelief. Hazel, Eve and Lucy hovered in their wake. How was Sim going to deal with this, Francis wondered.

'What are you doing here?' Vanessa asked Gillian.

'Charming!' Gillian twittered, looking around the table, trying to drum up support. 'Hi, Sim,' she said. 'Surprise surprise.'

'It's a surprise because you weren't invited,' said Vanessa in her most cutting voice. 'It wasn't an oversight, you know.'

This statement went uncontradicted and Gillian's boyfriend (Francis racked his brain for the man's name, but it eluded him) sighed heavily and blushed. 'Gillian,' he said under his breath. 'You lied . . .'

'God!' Gillian interrupted him. She looked wounded. 'You really find out who your friends are at times like this, don't you?' Francis wondered why Sim still hadn't spoken. What was she thinking? Did she have a plan? 'Well, I've got news for you: I *was* invited. Not by Matt and Lucy, even though I've bought them a really nice, expensive wedding present.' She paused for a moment to let the injustice of this sink in. Then she smiled and said triumphantly, 'Nicholas invited me. So there.'

'*So there?*' Matt echoed. 'How fucking old are you?'

'Oh, God, Gillian, please . . .' Her boyfriend, by the sound of it, had had more than he could take.

Vanessa marched over to the empty chair beside Nicholas and gripped its back with both hands. 'Is this true? Did you invite the village idiot?'

'*What* did you call me?'

'You heard.'

'Look, this isn't helping anything,' said Sim feebly. Francis wondered what was wrong with her. Normally she'd take charge of a situation like this. He couldn't believe she wasn't frogmarching Gillian to the door. Why the sudden neutrality, the moderation?

'Tell them, Nicholas. You invited me, didn't you? We're good mates, me and Nicholas. Aren't we?'

This Francis found impossible to believe. He nearly fell over when Nicholas replied, 'Yes. I invited her.' Vanessa stifled a gasp.

'For Christ's sake, you bloody know you didn't!' Gillian's boyfriend yelled at Nicholas. 'Why are you saying that? I can't take much more of this, I really can't.'

'Why don't you just say toodle-pip, then, like a good Toodle-pipster?' said Vanessa. 'And take Dufus Maximus with you.'

'What the hell is going on?' Eve asked. 'I'm completely lost.'

Francis frowned. Toodle-pipster – where had he heard that before? Sim. Sim on the phone. Phrases came back to him, analyses, discussions . . .

'Toodle-pipster?' Andrew blushed furiously and turned to look at Sim, who avoided his gaze. 'I see. So that's my nickname, is it?'

'Are you all right, Sim?' asked Gillian, smiling sweetly. 'You look a bit worried.'

Francis saw Nicholas flinch. It was clear from his body language that he loathed Gillian. There was no way he'd ever invite her to anything, so why was he lying? The Toodle-pipster. What was it Francis had overheard? He stood up and coughed to attract attention. 'I . . . er . . . I have to go and make a quick phone call. Work.' Sim nodded her approval. Was she a bit too approving, Francis wondered, a bit too keen to get him out of the way? He had to get out of there; the tension in the room was stifling. He needed to think. He needed to phone the police.

When he reached the door, he heard Andrew (that was his name!) say, 'Sim, can I have a word with you, please? In private.'

Feeling like a robot, Sim led the way out of the restaurant and into a small parlour by the side of reception. Behind her, she could hear the sound of Andrew's rubber soles squeaking as he walked. The room was empty, thank God. Sim had half expected to find Francis in there, making his phone call. Had he heard Andrew ask to speak to her in private?

In the centre of the room two navy sofas faced one another. Beside each one was a small mahogany coffee table on which neatly laid-out newspapers flashed their headlines. Sim wasn't sure if the hotel intended this as a place for formality or for casual lounging; it didn't seem to belong fully in either category. Normally she'd have appreciated the symmetrical layout of the furniture, but everything she'd once enjoyed about life now seemed an optional extra. She felt as if her character had been stripped, rubbed down with acid and sandpaper until only the bones were left. Her world-view was nowhere to be found and it was all she could do to survive from one moment to the next. How could she ever have been arrogant enough to plan beyond that?

She perched on the edge of one sofa, while Andrew shuffled uneasily on the other. 'I'm sorry we're here,' he said eventually. 'I'm not stupid, Sim. I can see we're not invited. I was crazy to believe Gillian. It's not as if . . .'

'What was all that about Nicholas?' Sim asked. It was odd, really. If she'd been asked to imagine this scenario and predict her feelings, she'd have guessed she'd loathe Andrew for putting her in this predicament. But he looked so dejected, so drained, that she couldn't help but take pity on him. She should have spoken to him sooner, properly spoken to him, instead of punishing him because she regretted their affair.

'Nicholas didn't invite Gillian,' said Andrew. 'Or if he did, it was only because he had no choice. I've been trying to tell you this for weeks, Sim, but you won't speak to me. She's been terrorising him. She's driven him out of his office and threatened to accuse him of raping her if he does anything about it. The poor guy's gone completely to pieces.'

'But . . . why?'

'There *is* no why where Gillian's concerned, you know that as well as I do. Nicholas's office used to be her office, and when their departments switched buildings she didn't want to give it up.'

'Fucking hell,' Sim muttered. She'd suspected something was wrong with Nicholas, but not this. Vanessa must have noticed that there was a serious problem; why hadn't she said anything?

'Sim, you know I wouldn't make this up, don't you?' Andrew's eyes pleaded with her.

I was once fond of this man, she thought. Poor Andrew. She'd used him for as long as it suited her, then coldly disposed of him. Ashamed of her betrayal of Francis, she'd erected a barrier in her mind, over which no thoughts of Andrew could hope to climb. But he was still a person. He'd needed Sim and she'd looked the other way. That he overused the phrase 'toodle-pip' was no excuse. Grow up, Sim told herself. 'Nicholas backed her up, though,' she said. 'He said he'd invited her, that they were friends.'

'Because he's embarrassed,' said Andrew. 'Think how humiliating it'd be for him to admit the truth with all his mates listening. He's been driven out of his own office. I won't go into detail about what she's done to him, but

397

believe me, if you knew you'd see why he doesn't want to talk about it. What man would want to admit to having been bullied by a mad bitch . . .'

'Your girlfriend,' Sim reminded him.

'No, she isn't.' Andrew put his head in his hands. 'At first I didn't know what to do. The only person I could talk to, the only one I thought'd understand was you, Sim, but you'd made it clear you wanted nothing more to do with me . . .'

'Hang on a minute.' Sim leaned forward. The emotional torpor in her mind began to clear as nosiness stirred within her. 'What are you saying?' She wondered where Francis was, what she'd do if he suddenly came into the room.

'Why do you think I can talk so confidently about what Nicholas is going through?' Andrew blurted out. 'Gillian did the same thing to me. I never wanted her to move in with me. We slept together once, that was all, and then she turned up one day with all her possessions in plastic bags. She . . . scared me into the relationship. She blackmailed me, threatened to accuse me of rape, just as she did with Nicholas. For ages I was too ashamed to admit it to myself, let alone anyone else. I should have done something about it but I was still so miserable. You'd dumped me and . . . I didn't have the energy to fight. At least worrying about Gillian stopped me thinking about you. But it was horrendous . . .' Andrew shuddered. 'She's done things to me that I wouldn't wish on my worst enemy.'

'What a nightmare,' said Sim, trying to digest all this information. 'But . . . did she tell you about Nicholas? Did she admit it?'

'No, of course not. I hear her on the phone to him. I've listened on the extension a few times. She writes him letters too. I've seen a couple of them lying around.'

'You say you slept with her once, when you first met her, but . . . surely you've slept with her since then. I mean, you live together.'

'No! Listen, will you? I'm in the same position as

Nicholas. Gillian's nothing to me, she's just a . . . a monster who's latched on to me for no reason I can think of. I can't get rid of her.' Andrew started to cry. 'You've got to help me, Sim. She's not my girlfriend, I swear! She's not my girlfriend.'

Hazel wondered whether she ought to worry about herself. The worse things got, objectively, the better she felt. Her secret was out, Ian's secret was out, they were still together, and she felt . . . happy was the only word she could think of. She didn't care a jot what Nicholas thought about her domestic arrangements. Who was he, anyway? What a fuss she'd made about having a cleaner. Hazel was thoroughly ashamed that she'd put herself and Ian through such contortions of concealment. So what if people disapproved? Was she so fragile, so pathetic, that she couldn't withstand a bit of criticism? She'd defended herself eloquently against Nicholas, and she didn't care that Sim, Eve, Lucy and Vanessa had all, with varying degrees of tactlessness, called her a liar when she told them Ian was Cal Raynard. For the first time in her adult life she felt no compulsion to invent weird and wonderful tales to attract other people's attention.

Look at this sorry bunch, she thought as she squeezed Ian's hand under the table. What a state they all looked. Hazel didn't understand anything that had happened so far this weekend, apart from the things that had happened directly to her. Where had Sim gone with Gillian's boyfriend? What could they possibly have to talk about in private? If Nicholas was Gillian's friend, why was he avoiding eye contact with her? Hazel couldn't believe, somehow, that Nicholas would have an affair with Gillian, but she supposed it was possible. Vanessa had to be wondering the same thing, surely. In which case, why wasn't she saying something, demanding to know the truth? It wasn't like her to be quiet. And what about Campbell and Eve; were they back together or not?

'Well,' Hazel broke the silence. 'Somebody say something.'

'Yeah, it's more like a funeral than a hen party,' Gillian agreed.

'Sorry if we've let you down,' said Lucy coldly.

'I'll say something,' said Eve. 'Matt, you'll be glad to hear I'm not marrying Neil on Saturday.' Matt shrugged.

'Or ever,' Campbell added quietly.

'I didn't say that,' Eve snapped. 'Just not yet, that's all.'

'Oo, who's Neil?' asked Gillian.

'You shut up,' Vanessa ordered.

Gillian stuck out her tongue and giggled. 'I wonder where Sim's run off to with that boyfriend of mine,' she said.

'Eve?' Lucy elbowed Matt. 'Matt's sorry for what he said last night, aren't you, Matt?'

'Yeah.' He looked at Eve dully. 'I was a bit tactless, but . . . you asked for it.'

'That's not an apology,' Eve pointed out.

'Come on, now, let's have no bickering,' said Gillian merrily. 'Me and Nicholas never bicker, do we, Nicholas? We're good old mates, good old china plates.'

Nicholas made a strangled noise that died in his throat. He was shaking, Hazel noticed. 'Are you okay, Nicholas?' she asked. 'You look awful.'

'You mind your own business, runt,' said Vanessa.

Ian stood up. 'If you speak to Hazel like that again, Vanessa, you'll have me to deal with.'

Vanessa sniggered. 'You ought to hear what she's been saying about you.'

'I told her you were Cal Raynard,' said Hazel. 'She didn't believe me. No one believed me.'

'It's true,' Ian told Vanessa.

'You're Cal Raynard?' Campbell chipped in. 'Hazel's favourite writer?'

'Yes.' Hazel beamed at Campbell, who seemed to believe

her and asked for no proof. Good old Campbell; she'd been way too hard on him.

'But ... how come?' he asked. 'Why didn't you tell us?'

'I only found out last night,' said Hazel.

'What utter shit!'

'Tell Vanessa your agent's name, Ian.'

'Yeah, go on, Cal!' Vanessa taunted him.

'My agent's name is Miff McGarvey,' said Ian. 'The manuscript of mine that you're reading at the moment is called *Considering Marmalade*, though you'd like to call it *Rowdy* because your chimpanzee of a cover designer can't spell any word that's longer than five letters. The main character's called Larry Kidd and his wife's called Martha. Satisfied?' Vanessa stared at him blankly for a few seconds. 'I've heard all about you from Hazel,' said Ian. 'I know what a low opinion you have of your authors, the names you call them. Me in particular.'

'Scum and vermin,' said Vanessa. 'Things like that?'

'Very amusing. Very witty,' said Ian. He loathed this woman. Even Gillian Kench was preferable.

'I'm not having this.' Vanessa stood up. 'I'm not being put on trial by a pair of wankers like you two.'

'Vanessa, where are you going?' Nicholas grabbed her wrist, but she shook him off and walked out of the restaurant.

So even when I'm found to be telling the truth, I'm still a wanker, thought Hazel. How was she to know that she shouldn't have passed on certain bits of information to Ian, when she'd had no idea that he was connected to Vanessa in any way? Before this weekend, the idea that she'd inadvertently caused a row would have made Hazel feel physically sick. How wrong she'd been to worry so much about pleasing other people. It was an impossible task, however hard one tried.

'Some fucking stag weekend this is,' said Matt.

*   *   *

If anyone had told Sim she'd be hugging Andrew Johnson, here, today, the weekend before Matt and Lucy's wedding, the day after Francis had proposed and she'd accepted, she'd have called them a lunatic. Yet hugging Andrew she was. 'You've got to call Gillian's bluff,' she told him. 'Throw her out. If she won't leave, you leave. Get another flat. Don't let her move into it. I can lend you money.' What was she saying? She couldn't lend him money, not without telling Francis, not unless she was prepared to tell more lies.

'I don't want money,' said Andrew. 'I've got enough.'

'So will you do it? There's nothing she can do, Andrew. She's not going to tell anyone you tried to rape her. If you stand up to her, if Nicholas does, she'll back down. No one's going to believe her if you and Nicholas both tell the truth.'

'You heard Nicholas! He has no intention of . . .'

'Let me talk to him. And to Vanessa. Between us, we'll be able to . . .'

'Sim, you must know that I'm in love with you. I didn't want to . . .'

'Don't!' Sim disentangled herself. 'The others don't know yet, but . . . I'm marrying Francis. He asked me last night.'

'Oh.'

'I'm really sorry, Andrew. I should never have gone anywhere near you when I was living with someone else. I've caused all this unnecessary pain . . .'

'Don't be silly. I knew you were attached, I knew what I was getting into . . .'

'Andrew, I've got to be on my own for a while. I need to think. Do you mind?'

'No.' He sighed and wiped his face. 'I should go, anyway.'

'What about Gillian?' Sim asked anxiously. Having told Andrew to shun his unsavoury cohabitee and to hell with the consequences, she could hardly ask him to take Gillian

402

with him back to Cambridge, but if Andrew left Hollins Hall alone Sim saw no way of ousting her. It was ironic, she thought. All this time she'd been furious with the Toodle-pipster for taking up with her ex-friend. Now she'd found out the truth, she almost wished they *were* a couple; then Gillian would be Andrew's responsibility. It was far scarier to think of her on the loose, as it were.

'I'll tell her I'm going with or without her. She'll come with me,' said Andrew. 'She'll . . . sense immediately that something's changed, as soon as she sees my face. She's got Nicholas exactly where she wants him, so she'll focus on me. There's no way she'll let me leave alone. She's not stupid. I could go home and change the locks, couldn't I?'

'Phone some of your friends,' said Sim gently. 'Get them to meet you in Cambridge and wait there while you pack some stuff. Leave Gillian in the flat. It's only rented anyway, isn't it?' Andrew nodded. 'You'll be fine. And on Monday, phone some of Gillian's colleagues.'

'Why?'

'I don't know. I've got a hunch that you'll find more support there. When you work with a person, you see them at their very worst, I reckon. For all you know Gillian blackmailed her way into that job by threatening to accuse everyone of all sorts. Speak to her boss, the other secretaries . . .'

'Oh, God, you're right.' Andrew started to cry again. 'I feel as if I've wasted so much of my life. It's like being in prison, it's too awful to describe.'

Sim winced. She'd always imagined that she'd be thrilled to have Gillian's rottenness confirmed, proven beyond all reasonable doubt, but there was no satisfaction in this, none whatsoever. It would have been nice to be wrong, just this once, to be able to salvage something, find good where she'd believed there was none. 'I'll ring you at work in a few days, see how things are going,' she heard herself promise Andrew. Meanwhile, where was Francis?

*　　*　　*

Campbell had never been in a steam room before. Hollins Hall's was large, curved at the corners and tiled from top to bottom. He could see the edge of a bench, which he guessed went all the way round the room, but nothing beyond that. The steam was as dense as thick fog. Campbell took a couple more steps, hoping he didn't trip over a prone body, then stepped back when a jet of steam burned his shin. He felt his way along the wall towards the bit of bench he'd seen and perched tentatively on its edge, wondering how, precisely, this sort of thing was supposed to do one good.

The door thwacked open and closed, and a welcome breeze cooled the room for a couple of seconds. Had someone peered in and decided against entering? No, Campbell could hear footsteps. How odd to be in the same room as someone yet unable to see them. Still, that worked both ways, and there was something immensely comforting about the idea of invisibility.

Campbell was glad to be out of the restaurant. The stag-hen weekend had disintegrated almost to breaking point; no one seemed to know what to say to anybody else. Campbell had no idea if and when Sim, Francis or Vanessa would reappear. Matt and Lucy had gone into Leeds to do some last-minute wedding shopping, they claimed, though it was more likely that they simply wanted to escape. Andrew had left, with Gillian running after him, ordering him to get back here, now. Campbell would count himself lucky if he never saw her again. He didn't know what was going on between Gillian and Nicholas but he sensed it was something deeply unpleasant and that Gillian was the cause of it.

The swift-exit-from-the-table bug was contagious. Hazel and Ian had crept out, holding hands and blushing, clearly on their way back to bed, and sitting in silence with a grumpy Eve and a shell-shocked Nicholas was so depressing that Campbell had mumbled something incoherent and sought refuge in the health club. After thirty seconds in the steam room he didn't feel any healthier and the blister on his lip was burning.

'Campbell?'

'Ah!' He gasped out loud, remembering the last time a disembodied voice had summoned him, at Leeds station. But this was only Sim. 'God, you gave me a shock. I can't see you at all.'

'I can't see you either,' said Sim, 'but I recognised your breathing. Where are the others?'

'They've all drifted off.'

'Including Gillian?'

'Yeah. I think she's gone back to Cambridge.'

'Good.'

'I think we should sack this weekend and go home. It's pointless carrying on.' This wasn't what Campbell really wanted; he hoped Sim would argue against him. Things with Eve were still so up in the air.

'I think carrying on might be our only hope.' Sim sighed.

'Sim?'

'Mm?'

'I asked Eve to marry me last night.'

'I know.'

'Oh. But . . . she didn't say yes or no. I thought she'd be pleased and say yes straight away, but this morning she told Matt that she still might marry Neil.'

'Campbell, are you sure you want Eve back?'

'Yes. I proposed to her, didn't I?'

'Why?'

'What do you mean, why?'

'I mean, do you want to marry Eve because you passionately love and adore her, or do you just want to outdo Neil?'

'Well . . .'

'If Rory hadn't had sex with someone else . . .'

Campbell swore under his breath. 'Isn't a person entitled to any privacy?'

'Minding one's own business is an overrated virtue,'

405

said Sim. 'It's not even a virtue, in fact; it's something that, over the years, has been elevated to that status by mediocrities who haven't got any genuine star qualities. The same applies to punctuality and being an early riser. Bloody hell, it's hot, isn't it? I might have to get out soon. Anyway, answer the question.'

'What? Do I only want Eve back because it hasn't worked out with Rory?'

'Yes.'

'No.' Motivation was a complex thing, though. There were many strands to it; surely Sim could understand that.

'Why don't I believe you?' she asked sharply.

'Look, I admit I don't know if I'd feel differently if things had gone better with Rory, but . . . you know, part of the reason that didn't work out is because I still have feelings for Eve.'

'Fine.' Sim still sounded dissatisfied. 'Well, if you want Eve back, you need to reject Rory. That's why Eve's pissed off.'

'What? She's pissed off with me? I thought it was Matt she was annoyed with.'

'You must reject Rory wholly and brutally,' said Sim. 'Nothing short of that will do, none of this still being friends crap. To win Eve back from Neil you've got to deserve her and that means cutting the Grimble out of your life altogether. The symbolism and aesthetics of the situation demand nothing less.'

'I can't be brutal,' said Campbell. 'I'm not a brutal person.'

'Says who?' Sim laughed. 'I see you're still suffering from wrongness wrongness. If Eve took you back and you stayed friends with Rory, that'd be a worse sort of brutality than if you told Rory to fuck off.'

'I disagree,' said Campbell huffily. 'Why? Why must I tell Rory to fuck off?' Women can be so barbaric, he thought.

'You don't have to do that necessarily,' said Sim, 'but . . . I don't know, something. A grand gesture. I can see that violence, verbal or physical, isn't your style, so do something else. Whatever it is, though, it has to be *final*, it has to represent the absolute end of Rory.'

'Like what?' asked Campbell, bewildered. How could something that wasn't violent put a final end to Rory? He didn't like the sound of this at all.

Sim groaned. 'I'm going to have to get out or I'll melt,' she said. 'Listen, I'll have a think about it, okay? But you think about it too. It'll be better if it's your idea, and frankly, Campbell . . .'

'What?' Sim sounded like a disappointed parent, like Campbell's mother used to sound when he got into trouble at school.

'I just hope I'm not throwing good wisdom after bad where you're concerned.'

Campbell was about to reply when he heard the thwack of the door. Sim had gone. Typical. She could keep her wisdom for all Campbell cared; he'd never asked for it in the first place. Then he thought to himself, hang on a minute: what bloody wisdom?

Sim sat cross-legged on the floor of the jacuzzi, letting the bubbles swallow her whole. She was trying to effect a sort of non-religious baptism. She'd made her decision. Now all she needed was to see Francis so that she could sort things out, assuming they could be sorted. Campbell wasn't the only one from whom a grand gesture was required.

When she emerged from the water, gasping for breath, Vanessa was sitting beside her in an Armani swimsuit. 'I thought you might be trying to drown yourself,' she said. 'I was considering doing the same.'

'Why, what's up?'

'Apart from Nicholas having an affair with Gillian Kench, you mean? Okay, let's see. Well, for starters,

Runtelstiltskin wasn't lying. That dog of a boyfriend of hers is Cal Raynard.'

'What?' Sim groaned. 'Oh, no!' She dunked her face in the water, covering it with bubbles to hide her distress. It wasn't a good idea to get tearful in front of Vanessa. Poor Hazel had been telling the truth. 'I didn't believe her,' she said miserably, feeling as if her willingness to stand by Hazel when she'd thought Ian was Dale Dingley had been cancelled out in a stroke. Ian had turned out to be someone utterly harmless and Sim had treated Hazel's confidence with utter disdain simply because it seemed improbable. So much for being the sole believer. What sort of a friend was she?

'I never want to see the runt again,' said Vanessa. 'I mean it, Sim. You'd better make sure our paths don't cross in future.'

'But what about Matt and Lucy's . . .'

'I don't care. You're the social secretary. Sort it out. I'm not going to the wedding if she's there.'

'Vanessa, I don't get it. Why are you so against Hazel all of a sudden? I know it must be a bit weird to find out that you're Ian's editor . . .'

'Not for long, I'm not. First thing Monday I'm handing him over to my assistant.' Vanessa's voice grew shrill. 'All this time I've been wondering why Cal Raynard acts like I don't exist and now I know. It's because the runt's been telling him, and I quote, "the sort of thing I say about my authors". For fuck's sake, talk about being misrepresented. You know I like to let off steam. I occasionally express myself in a colourful way, but I don't always mean it.'

'I know,' said Sim, 'but you can't blame Hazel. She wasn't to know. She only found out last night.'

'You always defend her.' Vanessa had no intention of voicing her true feelings if Sim was determined to be so dense. Of course Hazel couldn't be blamed; that was why Vanessa loathed her. Without even putting herself in the wrong, Hazel had taken something that belonged

408

to Vanessa – her idea of Cal Raynard – and smashed it up. She'd taken Vanessa's personal life and her professional life and mixed a lethal cocktail with them. The worst thing was that Vanessa knew she'd get no sympathetic bitching out of anyone because the runt, goodie-two-shoes that she was, had done nothing wrong.

All Vanessa had to do was be nice to Hazel and Ian, and she'd lose neither a friend nor an author. But that was the trouble: previously she could have risked one without the other. Now they were intertwined, and Vanessa felt she had to be on her best behaviour in both her social life and her working life because there were spies in one who could shop her in the other.

She didn't expect Sim to understand any of this. As usual, Vanessa would handle the problem in her own way, unaided. She would cut off both Hazel and Ian without further ado. It was the only way she could exercise her power.

'Are you sure you're not just upset about Nicholas?' Sim asked.

'I don't want to talk about that traitor.'

'Vanessa, he's not having an affair with Gillian.'

'What do you mean?' Vanessa picked up on the certainty in Sim's voice. 'You know something?'

Sim sighed. If she told Vanessa exactly what Andrew had told her it would reveal Nicholas to be weak, a victim, and Vanessa had no time for victims. Still, she couldn't let Vanessa believe Nicholas was sleeping with Gillian. 'I know something,' she amitted and prepared to lie.

Francis stood on the wide, sloping lawn in front of the country club part of the hotel, smoking a Marlboro Light. He felt dizzy, not having smoked for years until today. He'd seen the police, driven all the way to Leeds and back to speak to the officers he knew who had dealt with the Bethan Wrigley case at the time. DCI Schwartzmantel and DS Blaug seemed confident Annette wouldn't carry out her threat, but they were grateful to be alerted. Francis had missed lunch, but he didn't feel he needed food at the moment. Nicotine was enough to sustain him for the time being.

He wondered what everyone else had been up to. Had Sim spoken to the Toodle-pipster in private? Francis felt neither angry nor jealous; if anything, he was glad he'd worked it out. This was an opportunity to begin a new phase of his life. He'd only just realised that lives had phases and was quite happy about it.

'Francis!' He heard Sim's voice and turned to see her rushing towards him. 'Where have you been? I've been frantic.'

'Leeds,' he said.

'You're smoking. Francis!' She tutted. 'Give us one, will you?' Francis smiled and produced the packet. 'Why did you go to Leeds?'

'Long story,' said Francis, who didn't have the energy to go into it. He didn't want to spend any more of this weekend thinking about work-related matters, which was what the Dingleys were.

'Francis, will you come for a drive with me?'

'I've only just got back. I was planning on going for a sauna.'

'It's important. Please.'

'Why? Where to?'

'Eldwick. I've got to collect something and . . . there's something I have to tell you.'

'No, there isn't,' said Francis, grinning at Sim's puzzled expression. Outwitting her was fun.

'I'm being serious,' said Sim. 'It's something that might put you off marrying me.'

'No, it isn't.'

'But, Francis . . .'

'You had a fling with Andrew,' said Francis matter-of-factly, as if he were reciting his two-times table. 'It didn't mean anything to you. You quite fancied him at first, but

410

you never loved him. It was no threat to our relationship. You went off him as soon as the deed was done because he said "toodle-pip" all the time and was . . . how shall I put it? Not terribly well endowed. Am I right?'

'You already know,' Sim whispered, stunned. 'Vanessa! I'll *kill* her.'

'Kill yourself.' Francis smiled. 'You're the one with the big mouth, Simone. I heard it all from you, no one else.'

'What?'

'On the phone. You assume I don't listen to you prattling away to your mates, but I do sometimes. Vanessa called Andrew the Toodle-pipster this morning. I'd heard the two of you talking about him on the phone a few times, but I assumed it was a *Potters Court* plot line.'

'Oh, my God,' Sim muttered under her breath.

'I don't know why you're looking so aghast,' said Francis. 'You were just about to tell me, anyway.'

'I know, but . . .' That was different from having him tell her. 'Francis, I'm so sorry. I've got no excuse.'

'Let's just forget it. I'm not angry . . .'

'But . . . why not? Aren't you . . . I don't know, jealous?'

'Sim, I've heard the way you talk about this guy. You don't exactly paint a glamorous picture. I suppose I *could* say I've got a few qualms about your taste, but . . .' Francis grinned, but decided not to veer towards bitchiness. 'It doesn't sound as if I've got much to be jealous of. You can't stand him.'

'I've been unfair to him,' said Sim. 'He's in an awful state. It's too complicated to explain now. It's to do with Gillian. I'm afraid I'm going to have to keep in touch with Andrew.'

'That's fine, Sim. Look, I said I was fine about it and I am. You're engaged to me. That's all that matters now, isn't it?'

'I suppose,' said Sim doubtfully.

'Have you said anything to anyone?'

'Vanessa's the only person who knows,' said Sim. 'But I don't expect you to protect me, Francis. I planned to make a clean breast of it.'

'Well, if that means telling everyone, I'd rather you didn't. I don't want to be constantly inspected for my reaction. It'll put me on edge.'

'Of course,' said Sim. 'I'm so sorry, Francis. I know it sounds mad but . . . well, it didn't seem wrong while I was doing it. It seemed like . . . just the sort of thing I might do.'

'I don't blame you for it,' said Francis. 'I wasn't the best of boyfriends, was I?'

'Well . . .'

'I wasn't,' said Francis firmly. 'I was probably even worse than Nicholas or Campbell.' He smiled. 'Although now they're definitely both worse than me. Come on, let's go to Eldwick. What for, by the way?'

'Long story. Francis, if you ever want to have a fling – you know, to make things fair – just feel free.'

'Don't be ridiculous.' Francis smiled and kissed her. 'That'd involve far too much effort.'

'Or if you want to move back to Cambridge. I'd give up my job. I was so desperate to run away from Andrew . . .'

'Why would I want to move?' Francis looked down at the view from Hollins Hill. The squat, brown centre of Shipley crouched in the distance. 'I love it here,' he said.

'You should have told me.' Vanessa kept taking her eyes off the road to examine Nicholas's face. Why wouldn't he speak? 'I could have helped you, advised you.' Still nothing, not a word. 'That's if what Andrew told Sim was true. Well? Was it?'

'Yes.'

'Gillian kept a key to your office?'

'Yes.'

'She started letting herself in when you weren't there,

412

treating it as hers. You came in and found her one day and . . .'

'That's right.'

'What? What did you do? Sim said you hit her, but . . . was it a slap? Did you punch her, what?' Nicholas's face was inscrutable. He closed his eyes, signalling an end to the conversation. 'Nicholas, why won't you talk to me? Am I really so unreasonable, so unapproachable?' Of course I am, Vanessa answered her own question. If someone disagrees with me, I regard running them over as a reasonable tit-for-tat. 'Just answer one question: did you rape Gillian?'

'No!'

'So you just hit her? And then she threatened to tell the police you raped her unless you gave her your office? Nicholas? Is that what happened?'

'Yes,' said Nicholas quietly. Unless she got some corroboration from him, Vanessa might start to doubt the story. 'I slapped her quite hard, just once. I lost my temper, okay? But she was going to say I raped her and the police would have believed her.' He had no idea where this version of events had come from, but that didn't concern him. Who knew why Gillian had decided to tell Andrew that Nicholas had hit her when he'd never laid a finger on her? She distorted everything. The important thing was that she'd admitted to Andrew that Nicholas hadn't raped or tried to rape her. He was finally off the hook.

'First thing Monday we're going to your office,' said Vanessa. 'I'll speak to the porters, get your lock changed.'

'I can do that myself,' said Nicholas sharply. 'I don't need you to hold my hand.' He felt ashamed. Whatever he told anyone else, he knew the truth: he'd been incapable of handling the Gillian situation, of elevating himself, at any stage, above the status of her helpless prey. Why hadn't he slapped her? No one could deny she deserved it. Now he was clinging to a lie Gillian had told in order to salvage some shred of pride.

413

'Well, cheer up, then.' Vanessa tutted. 'Look, we're on our way home – you don't have to face anyone. Not that they'd even disapprove – that cow deserves a good beating. And on Monday it'll all be sorted. Sim says Andrew's throwing Gillian out of the house, so she'll have a lot else on her mind. There's no way she'll go to the police.'

Vanessa couldn't get over the coincidence. Both she and Nicholas had in some shape or form attacked another person. It was uncanny how much they had in common, though of course Nicholas was unaware of this new bond. Vanessa made a silent bargain with God, on the off-chance that He existed: make Nicholas normal again, make him want to stay in Cambridge, and I'll behave properly towards Red-tooth. She didn't quite know what that might involve and didn't like to think about it; would sending back Red-tooth's cheque when it arrived be sufficient, or would Vanessa also have to pay for the dentist and taxis? Would a letter of apology also be required, a full confession? Vanessa was so unused to behaving properly that she wasn't sure.

It struck her that if there were a God, He'd see through her ploy. It was all very well to say that she'd be good after He'd sorted out all her problems; anyone could promise that, then forget about it as soon as they had what they wanted. It would be more impressive to promise to be good first, before God had done anything. I'll make peace with Red-tooth, she resolved. Send her a cheque, the works. And then maybe, if she was lucky, Nicholas would stop turning away from her in bed.

Vanessa sighed. Whom was she trying to kid? Any God that existed would see that her contrition was no more than a bargaining tool. And she'd deliberately made no mention of Hazel and Ian in her negotiations with the Almighty. She was trying, though. Perhaps the best she could do, given that she wasn't a good person by nature, was pretend to be one as far as was possible.

I do love Nicholas, she assured God, then wondered if

she was telling the wrong person. 'Nicholas?' She cleared her throat.

'What?'

'I do love you, you know.' There. She'd said it. Nicholas's eyes widened in surprise.

The weekend ground on, as difficult weekends tend to. It was three o'clock. The remaining weary participants in Matt and Lucy's stag-hen festivities sat in the Long Weekend Café Bar, drinking gins and tonic. The overall mood was not a positive one. Lucy kept murmuring, 'I can't believe we flew back from Florida for this.' Campbell and Eve didn't appear to be talking to each other; both seemed lost in worlds of their own. Poor Ian looked simply fed up, as if he wished he'd been sensible enough to remain in a world of his own rather than enter this perplexing one. Hazel sat beside him with a proud hand on his knee. Sim suspected nothing could deflate Hazel's joy and she was pleased for her friend. At least someone was happy.

Matt had slumped into a moody silence, which he only broke every so often to say, 'I can't believe Nicholas and Vanessa just . . . went!' Sim had pretended to be as much in the dark as the others; she hadn't even told Francis what Andrew had told her. It was up to Nicholas if he wanted to tell Vanessa the truth or cling to Sim's lie. Would it be more important to him to hide his weakness from Vanessa or deny the charge of hitting a woman?

Sim had no idea whether she'd done the right thing; she'd told the best story that came to mind in an awkward moment in the jacuzzi. Doing the right thing, she'd discovered, was harder than most people imagined. What did it mean, to be a force for good? Was it enough to mean well, or were intentions irrelevant compared with the effect, the end result? Perhaps both intention and outcome mattered less than the symbolism involved. Sim hoped so; what she was about to do, the plan she was about to put to the others, relied almost entirely upon symbolism. It was risky

415

– there was a good chance of it leading to disaster of some sort – but it struck Sim, nevertheless, as a winning idea.

On the floor by her feet were eight polythene-wrapped bundles. 'Come on, everyone,' she said, forcing herself to sound jolly. It was hard, when both she and Francis knew what a flawed person she was. 'Guess what these are.'

'Who cares?' said Matt.

'What are they?' Hazel obliged. Good old Hazel.

'Yeah, come on, Sim.' Eve yawned. 'Enough suspense. Just tell us.'

'Go on,' said Francis encouragingly, who was in on the secret. The look on his face said, 'Anything to break the mood.'

Sim lifted the top bundle by the coat-hanger that protruded from one end of it and began to pull away the thick plastic wrapping bit by bit, tearing at it with her long turquoise fingernails. The others watched as, gradually, a pile of grey felt was revealed, flecked here and there with pink and white. A long dangly bit swayed above the table, narrowly missing a glass or two.

'An elephant costume?' asked Hazel.

'Correct!' Sim beamed. 'Courtesy of Dutton's in Eldwick. Matt, your fancy dress wish is granted. We're going to Rory Napper's thirtieth birthday party.'

'Are they all elephants?' asked Eve. Sim nodded.

'I don't want to be an elephant,' said Matt. 'I want to be a cowboy.'

'Sim, no way!' said Campbell. His face and neck glowed bright red.

'What's going on?' asked Ian.

'Campbell's girlfriend – shortly to become his ex – is Rory Napper,' Sim explained. 'Her father's an ivory trader.'

'I know, but . . .'

'Oh, wow!' Hazel giggled.

'What?' said Lucy.

Sim took a deep breath, still holding the droopy felt

elephant. Its trunk hovered in mid-air, seeming to point first at one person then another. 'Remember those protestors Campbell saw in Rory's garden? Come on, I must have told you all.'

'Oh, God!' Campbell buried his face in his hands. Eve smiled at his discomfort.

'They were dressed as elephants!' said Hazel.

'Will you stop fucking yelling?' Matt barked at her.

'They were dressed as elephants,' Sim confirmed. 'And they had a sign: "Business thrives means elephant lives". Sim dropped the cloth elephant. She reached beneath the pile of costumes and produced a long, rolled-up piece of green card. 'Here's something Francis and I prepared earlier,' she said, taking off the elastic band and unrolling it. She held up the banner.

'"Campbell for Eve! Rory must leave!"?' Lucy read aloud incredulously.

'Francis, mate, have you lost it?' asked Matt. Francis shrugged amiably.

'There's no way I'm going to Rory's party dressed as an elephant, with that sign,' said Campbell, still looking like a human lava lamp.

'Why not?' Sim threw herself into her role; here was her chance to cheer everyone up. 'You say you want Eve back – well, this is your opportunity to prove it. Do something public. It's Rory's thirtieth birthday party tonight,' she told the others. 'She didn't invite Campbell, being the thoughtful girlfriend that she is. Well, we're going to turn up anyway.'

'Sim, we can't do that,' said Ian. 'It's not fair on Campbell. Look, he's clearly not into the idea.'

'I think we should,' said Eve, who'd livened up considerably. 'It'd be a laugh.' The others still looked doubtful.

'Look, I've paid for the costumes,' said Sim solemnly, thinking of the large cheque she'd just written. Elephant attire was not cheap. 'Oh, come on, guys. I'm supposed to be the least political one of all of us.'

'What's it got to do with politics?' asked Francis.

'This is what politics is,' said Sim, as if it were obvious.

'What, dressing up as an elephant and standing in your mate's ex-girlfriend's garden?' asked Matt.

'Yes,' said Sim. 'The other sort of politics, the newsy, partyish sort, is just a spectator sport. What we do in our everyday lives, that's what counts. I've always thought this, you know – people get it the wrong way round.'

'How do you mean?' asked Ian.

'We've been indoctrinated into dividing life into two layers, the personal and the political, and we've turned the personal into a sort of discreet cesspit where anything goes as long as we put a sign up saying "private", while we get all worked up about this other, further removed realm, the political, that we know much less about, where it's easy to be black and white about stuff because some other poor sod – Bill Clinton – has to take responsibility and live with the consequences, not us.'

'Sim, what's this got to do with me dressing up as an elephant?' asked Campbell.

'I'm just saying, that's all. Most of us leave our personal lives unpatrolled. We're used to dealing in contingencies, making allowances. It's all wrong; the private sphere is our patch; it should be the focus for all our black-and-white moral energies. But we're too cowardly for that. We allow baddies to grow unchecked, until eventually they make headlines. Like Slobodan Milosevic. Once a baddy makes the news, then we come forward with our firm moral positions. We pretend to see these distant things in black and white when they're so far removed from our experience and area of expertise that they can only ever really be grey to us. More to the point, by then it's too late. Too much is at stake; often things have escalated to a life-and-death level. So we sit back and criticise politicians for being instrumental, but why shouldn't they be? We are. To a certain extent we can't help it. It's easy to say someone's evil when they've never been nice to us personally. It's easy for us to sit back and say Slobodan Milosevic is evil, or Saddam Hussein, because that doesn't actually require us to do anything. In the public sphere, we expect Tony Blair and Bill Clinton to do the difficult stuff for us, then we moan at them for not being morally pure. It's all a smokescreen, an attempt to pass the buck! Do you see what I mean?'

Everyone indicated that they did not.

'Think about it. Blair and Clinton have probably played Skittles with Milosevic a couple of times at Politicians' Holiday Camp. They probably remember the odd great joke Saddam Hussein made, or a time when he lent them his swimming trunks. The point is, they know these guys *personally*. No wonder they find it hard to deal with them when they get out of line, and sometimes make a hash of it. Who are we to criticise them? Don't we compromise our own principles daily, in exactly the same way? Imagine how hard it must be to bomb someone who's lent you his swimming trunks.'

'Swimming trunks?' Matt queried, looking utterly bemused.

'That's what they must wear at Politicians' Holiday Camp,' Ian muttered. Was this some sort of elaborate joke, he wondered, or was Sim madder than he'd thought?

'Don't get hung up on the details,' said Sim impatiently. 'We all want to be good and tackle evil, don't we? Let's do it in our own lives, where we're experts, where we can catch evil at an early stage. Damage limitation. Why wait until Rory's on the news having massacred loads of people when we can get to her now? Look, most people would agree that the world's a fairly shitty place – starvation, torture, all that Amnesty-ish stuff. Well, unless people start thinking like me, things'll never change. It takes a lot of energy to change the world and in order to have energy you need to care – care *deeply*, I mean. And the fact is, no one *really* cares about things that don't affect them personally. See what I mean?'

419

Sim's friends' inability to do so was unanimous. She sighed. 'All that stuff people do to kid themselves that they're making the world a better place, like voting and . . . swearing at Ann Widdecombe when she appears on the news – it's safe and meaningless, and it achieves nothing. The world is still just as crap, with just as much suffering. So you have to ask yourself why don't people do more? Because they haven't got the energy, that's why. Ann Widdecombe isn't impinging on their personal lives. They call her evil, but they don't really feel it, and in any case, unless you've met someone yourself, unless you *know* them, you can't properly know whether they're a good or a bad thing. So when someone does impinge on our private sphere, when we do care and have the energy, and when we know our facts from our hearsay, that's when it's our duty to do something. That's real political action. If we protest now, Rory might think twice about being so foul in future. *That's* why we're going to picket her party.'

'No, we aren't,' said Campbell in a panicky tone. 'Rory isn't evil.'

'She is,' countered Eve.

'Sim, surely you can't mean this,' said Ian.

'That's preposterous, to say that.' Campbell's face looked wobbly. 'What's she done that's so terrible?'

'Isn't it enough that she . . . wallows in the mire of her own warty consciousness?' Sim asked rhetorically. 'Reasonable definitions and all that.' She gave Campbell a sharp look and he deeply regretted educating her philosophically to the extent that he had. 'It's partly for her own good. If she's censured now, there might be some hope for her. That's why we have to do this, Campbell. All her friends are going to be at this party, aren't they, all the people she wants to think well of her? If we're there in her garden, in costume, with our banner, her friends'll see that we feel strongly enough to take a public stand against her.'

'Mightn't they be inclined to take her side?' asked Lucy. 'Against the costume elephants staking out her house?'

'At first, perhaps,' said Sim. 'But then they'll wonder . . .'

'Sim's right!' Matt cut in suddenly. 'It'll be a laugh. Come on, we need a change of scene – this is perfect! It's totally bonkers and I'm supposed to be doing totally bonkers things. It's my stag weekend. Ours,' he corrected himself quickly, looking at Lucy.

'It might be fun,' she said doubtfully.

'I think it would be.' Hazel looked anxiously at Ian. 'Ian? It wouldn't really do any harm, would it? It'd sort of be like . . . a joke.'

'Guys, it's crazy,' said Campbell desperately. 'Driving all the way to London and back in one day . . .'

'We could stay in a hotel overnight,' said Sim.

'Getting out of this place might do us good,' said Francis. For Sim's sake, because he loved her, he'd broken his golden rule about fancy dress and agreed to wear an elephant costume, after some persuasion. Sim had said his eventual capitulation was a sign that he'd matured.

'That's true,' said Lucy. 'I feel like I'm in prison here, after everything that's happened.'

'No way,' said Campbell fiercely. 'I'm not putting on that costume. I'll look like a complete tit.'

Sim cast her eyes heavenwards. 'Do you think Alexander the Great worried about looking a complete tit? Do you think Napoleon cared about his street cred?'

'Campbell, for God's sake,' said Eve. 'Do you want me back or not?'

Neil sank back in the driver's seat, exhausted. He and Imogen had finally arrived at Hollins Hall and he was trying very hard not to see it as a bad omen that a journey which normally took an hour and a half had taken more like five. One of the car's front tyres had exploded on the M62. Luckily no one was hurt; Neil managed to swerve on to the hard shoulder and avoid hitting anything. All he could think about, though, was that it could so easily have been otherwise; Imogen might

421

have been killed. He shuddered. The threat of permanent loss was everywhere; how could one simply get on with life and enjoy it, knowing that?

Neil had no spare tyre in the boot – he'd given his to a colleague who'd had a puncture the week before and hadn't yet replaced it, so he and Imogen had had to wait for a mechanic. Never had time moved so slowly. 'It won't matter,' Imogen had tried to console him. 'It just means Eve'll be even more sick of Campbell by the time we get there.'

Neil hoped she was right. 'Come on, let's get this over with,' he said. 'Have you got your poem?'

'Yes, in my pocket. Should I read it to Eve or give it to her to read herself?' asked Imogen as they got out of the car.

'I'm not sure. Either. No, read it.' Neil locked the car and strode towards the hotel's main entrance. In the foyer, two businessmen in suits were chatting and laughing, matching copies of the *Telegraph* flapping in their hands. Neil loathed them, unreasonably, for having no idea what he was going through and not bothering to imagine.

When he reached the door he stopped and turned round, realising that he hadn't heard Imogen's footsteps for a while. She was running towards him along the driveway. 'Guess what I just saw?' she said.

'What?'

'Four people dressed as elephants, in a car.'

'Yeah, right,' said Neil. 'Come on, stop messing about.' He walked towards reception, deciding to ask simply which room Eve was in, not whether she was sharing with anybody.

Imogen trailed after him. She *had* seen it, but she shouldn't have mentioned it now, when Neil had so many more important things on his mind. She wondered whether the four elephants had been grown-ups or children; she'd only seen them from behind. The elephant faces had been clearly visible, though, as the car drove down the hill.

They'd grinned at Imogen upside-down, through the back window, trunks drooping downwards. The four fancy dressers obviously would not pull up their head-hoods until they got to wherever the party was. Did elephants grin, she wondered.

'Imogen!' Neil hissed, pointing to two figures who were emerging from the lift. They too were dressed as elephants, for the time being unhooded. One was tall, male and thin apart from a bump of stomach, the other female, medium height and roundish.

Imogen was about to laugh and say 'Told you so', when she looked at the woman's face. 'That's Sim!' she blurted out loudly. 'I recognise her from that photo on the wall . . .' She stopped, realising that she'd been about to say 'at home'. Cromer Street wasn't her home, not properly. Soon it might not be Neil's any more either. It wasn't fair.

Spotting Neil and Imogen, the rounder elephant nudged her companion. 'I think that's Francis,' Imogen whispered to Neil.

'Where's Eve?' Neil demanded, marching over to where they stood. Had he even noticed the costumes, Imogen wondered.

'Neil and Imogen, right?' said Sim. 'Hi, I'm . . .'

'I know who you are.' Neil didn't smile. 'Where's Eve?'

Sim sighed. 'Look, come and have a drink and . . .'

'Where's Eve? I want a quick, straight answer. And where's Campbell?'

'They're on their way to London,' said Francis. Sim gave him a look that Imogen couldn't quite interpret. 'What?' he said defensively. 'He wants a quick, straight answer and I gave him one.'

'London? Why?' Neil ran his hands through his hair.

'It's a long story,' said Sim. 'You know it's Matt and Lucy's stag-hen weekend? Of course you do,' she hurried on. 'Well, an extra event was added to the schedule at short notice and . . .'

'Well . . . is she at the station?' Neil demanded.

'No, they've gone by car,' Francis told him.

'Who's in Eve's car?'

'Neil, I think we should . . .'

'Let me guess: Campbell, right?'

Sim and Francis nodded.

'Why are you dressed as elephants?' asked Imogen, but nobody answered.

Neil turned his back on them and strode away, then marched straight back. He didn't know what to do with himself; he felt like a boiling pot of nervous energy. And there was no release in sight. 'When will they be back?' he asked.

'Tomorrow,' said Sim.

'We can go too, Neil,' said Imogen.

'Look, before you decide anything, there are things you need to know,' said Francis firmly. 'Will you please *please* come and have a drink and we can talk properly?'

'I don't have much choice, do I?' said Neil coldly. He followed Francis into the Long Weekend Café Bar.

Imogen and Sim were left standing by the lift, staring at one another. 'I liked your poem, "Memories",' said Sim. 'It's brilliant.'

'It won joint first prize in the school competition,' Imogen told her.

'Did it? That's fantastic.' That must have been Neil's doing, thought Sim. She was killing time, talking to Imogen because it seemed easier. What could she say to Neil? He might be – very probably was – about to lose his fiancée and Sim had been a driving force behind the whole business. Oh, God, it was all more complicated than she'd imagined. She liked the look of Neil and guessed he was the sort of person who'd be fair, firm, a good ally. He had a nice face too: trustworthy. Christ, this was all Sim needed.

'Eve's going to go off with Campbell, isn't she?' said Imogen. Behind her tortoiseshell glasses, her eyes were wide, round and earnest.

'Erm . . .' Sim played for time, wondering if she should be having this sort of conversation with a twelve-year-old.

'I know she is. It's not fair! Neil worships Eve. He'd never leave her like Campbell did. You're Eve's friend, why can't you stop her?'

'It's not as simple as that.' Sim wanted to run away. Where was her world-view? It ought to be on hand to help her out; this situation was too tricky to negotiate on her own, especially now that she was a flawed person. What if she got it wrong?

'It is simple,' Imogen insisted, stamping her foot. 'Neil and Eve and me are a family. You've got to do something! Eve says you always do something.'

'Neil and Eve and I,' Sim said automatically. She could hardly bear the disappointment in Imogen's voice. Clearly she'd been billed as some kind of Wizard of Oz equivalent, and everyone knew what a let-down he'd turned out to be. 'Imogen, it's not . . . what about your real family?'

'Oh, they're no good,' said Imogen matter-of-factly. 'They don't love me. They don't even speak to me.'

'Oh.' Sim hardly knew where to look. She wasn't used to feeling socially or conversationally awkward.

'Don't worry about it.' Imogen saw Sim's expression. 'I don't. I only care about Neil and Eve. Well? What are you going to do?'

'I can't do anything . . .'

'That's rubbish! You can and you . . . you better had!' Great, thought Sim, I'm being threatened by a skinny schoolgirl.

Imogen was fumbling in her pocket. She pulled out a yellow envelope and thrust it at Sim. 'Read this,' she said. 'Then you'll know.' With one last hard, penetrating look, she turned and went to join Neil and Francis in the café bar.

Sim opened the envelope. On it, in neat handwriting, was a poem. Its title was underlined: 'Wedding Poem for

Neil and Eve'. 'Great,' Sim muttered to herself. She began to read:

> There is a school that love attends
> Once it has paid its fees.
> Two people can go in as friends
> Or even enemies.
>
> Some strangers who have never met
> Turn up and meet inside.
> There is a school where love can get
> Tutored and qualified.
>
> It's optional. Some never go.
> Others go more than twice.
> There is a school for love, although
> First love must pay the price:
>
> Fidelity and trust and hope.
> Love must be strong and good.
> There is a school where people cope
> Who never thought they would.
>
> To fail the first time and return
> Might not be such a shame.
> There is a school where love can learn
> And marriage is its name.
>
> True, there are lots of other schools,
> Ones where you're free to roam,
> With fewer standards, fewer rules,
> Cheaper and nearer home,
>
> But if you saw inside their doors
> I think you'd be appalled.
> There's just one school where love matures:
> Marriage is what it's called.

Sim gawped at the poem. To her embarrassment, she found there was a lump in her throat. Could this really be the unassisted work of a twelve-year-old, she thought, then felt immediately guilty. 'Read this and then you'll know,' Imogen had said. But Sim had read it. And she didn't.

The Nappers' street was wide and lined with trees, on the trunks of which Neighbourhood Watch notices competed for space with hygiene instructions for dog owners and the odd portrait of a missing cat. A quiet affluence hung in the air. Each house was set so far back from the road and had its privacy guarded by such a thick veil of greenery that the party of eight elephants was able to saunter along the pavement without attracting nearly as much attention as it would attract in, say, Rusholme. One man, washing the Saab that was parked at a jaunty angle on his gravel drive, looked up, smiled indulgently and waved. Campbell wondered whether the man had mistaken them for the other elephants, the ivory protestors. If so, he was obviously in sympathy with their cause.

Campbell was furious with Sim and with the others for supporting her. Why did he have to go through this hideously embarrassing ordeal in order to get Eve back? Sim had tried to present it as the inevitable last act of the drama, an essential rite of passage Campbell needed to go through in order to deserve Eve again, but it was so damned spurious. Couldn't he have taken Eve out for dinner, or bought her flowers or something? Eve had fallen for Sim's bullshit as she always did and Campbell, once again, was to be sacrificed for the greater good. This was a neat conclusion for everyone but him: Matt and Lucy's stag-hen do would be saved by this inspired feat of – ugh, Campbell loathed the word – *wackiness*, Sim and Eve would enjoy ruining Rory's party and gloating about it afterwards, and the rest of them would sit back and savour the spectacle.

'Here we are,' said Sim, stopping at the Nappers' gate-posts. 'Number fifteen. Everyone ready? Eve, Hazel, have you got the sign?'

'Sim, are you sure this is a good idea?' asked Ian.

'Shut up, man, and get a beer down you!' Matt slurred. He'd been drinking all the way to London while Lucy drove and could barely stand up.

As they crept on to the front lawn, a powerful spotlight came on and they found themselves temporarily blinded, standing squarely in its beam. 'Shit, Campbell, why didn't you tell us they had a security light?' said Francis, who'd dropped his can of beer and could feel its foamy liquid seeping into his sock through the foot of his elephant costume.

'They didn't when I last visited,' said Campbell, pleased that things weren't running as smoothly as his friends had hoped.

Sim ruined his moment of glee by saying 'Don't be silly, it's good. We want a spotlight. We're the forces of light, after all, fighting the forces of darkness.' Mad bitch, thought Campbell. Was Sim as naïve as she made out? It was clear to anyone who looked that light and dark forces were a myth; the only force he'd ever known was a blurred, greyish one. Elephant-coloured.

He heard the sound of music stopping, being abruptly switched off. Funny, he hadn't been aware a song was playing – he couldn't say, even now, which song it was, though he had a feeling it was one he knew – until it was replaced, suddenly, by silence. Embarrassment and regret had frozen his brain. It would be safer not to think at all, until all this was over.

A curtain twitched on the top floor and a face peered out of the window. 'It's the Grimble,' Sim squealed, delighted. 'Hold up the sign!'

Eve and Hazel lifted their banner. 'Let's . . . I dunno, chant something,' said Matt. 'It's a bit crap if we just stand here in silence.'

'Let's chant what's on the banner, then,' said Eve. A faint wail could be heard from the house. 'Come on, quick, before they shoo us away.'

'No, no, that's . . . let's choose something else,' said Sim. She wasn't sure she wanted to chant 'Campbell for Eve' now that she'd met Neil. Besides, Eve still hadn't decided if she wanted to go back to Campbell or not. 'What about "Rory thrives means more wrecked lives"?' Sim suggested. Imogen's wedding poem was still emblazoned on her memory. She was trying very hard not to think about it, but it was difficult to forget that the yellow envelope was in her cardigan pocket beneath her elephant costume. She wanted to show it to Eve, but it didn't seem fair to do that after orchestrating this little performance; it wasn't a good idea to confuse Eve while she was in the middle of such a highly charged situation. Sim told herself that whatever happened, whoever Eve ended up with, Rory needed to be taught a lesson and that was all tonight was: the Grimble's come-uppance. There'd be plenty of time later to show Eve the poem, to tell her that Neil and Imogen had turned up at Hollins Hall.

For an awful moment Sim had thought Neil was going to insist on following the stag-hen party to London, once he'd heard the story of the weekend so far from Francis. That would have been disastrous. 'I'll take the poem to London and show it to Eve,' Sim had promised him.

'It's lucky for you that I've got Imogen with me,' said Neil coldly. 'Otherwise I'd be coming with you.'

'I want to go!' Imogen squealed in protest.

'Well, you can't,' said Neil firmly. 'There might be trouble and I'm too exhausted to drive all the way to London safely. I don't mind risking my life, but I'm not risking yours. But if Eve's not back in Rusholme by tomorrow night . . .'

'Why lucky for me?' Sim interrupted him.

'Oh, come on! Don't pretend you don't want her and Campbell to get back together.'

'What I want is irrelevant.' Sim made up for dodging the issue by adding, 'I can tell you one thing: Eve and Campbell haven't . . . done anything. They haven't slept together.' This had mollified Neil slightly – Sim could tell he'd believed her – and he and Imogen had set off back to Manchester, leaving Sim with the poem and her confusion.

'Yeah, cool slogan!' said Matt. 'One, two, three: RORY THRIVES MEANS MORE WRECKED LIVES!' he yelled. Campbell cringed as the words came back to him as an echo in the still night air.

'Come on, Campbell,' said Eve. 'I can see you skulking in the background. Join in!'

'Look, we've done it now,' said Campbell. 'Let's go back to Yorkshire.'

'No way!' said Matt. 'This is fun. RORY THRIVES MEANS MORE WRECKED LIVES! RORY, RORY, WHAT'S THE STORY?'

'Matt, don't confuse the issue,' said Sim. 'We don't want her to respond; that makes it sound as if we're giving her a chance.'

'WHAT'S THE STORY, MORNING RORY?' Matt screamed at the top of his voice.

'Ssh!' Lucy elbowed him.

Eve wandered over to Sim. 'Doesn't Campbell look cute in his elephant costume,' she whispered.

'I need a little time to wake up, wake up,' Matt mumbled, before staggering off on a circuit of the garden.

'Yes. Eve, we need to talk later about . . .'

Eve waved Sim's words away. 'Come on, guys,' she shouted. 'On the count of three again. One, two, three . . .' The official slogan rang out several more times. Campbell moved his lips when he saw Eve looking in his direction; the rest of the time he stared at his elephant feet. Hazel's rendition of the slogan verged on the operatic; Ian glanced anxiously at the Nappers' windows. This all seemed highly unusual; he'd have to have words with Hazel about it later. He hoped her friends didn't always carry on in this manner. Ian had had strong reservations about Sim's plan, but didn't want to be the only killjoy when even Campbell

430

had agreed. And Sim had been willing to help him, even when she'd believed he was Dale Dingley. Ian smiled; he supposed he owed her one. Perhaps only one, though, if all her ideas were this bad.

The front door swung open and a balding middle-aged man in a tuxedo marched down the front path towards the elephant army. Campbell recognised him as Clive Terry, the Nappers' . . . he supposed butler was his official title.

'Hoods off, folks,' Sim ordered. 'Let's show our faces.'

Damn, thought Campbell. At least in full costume he could pretend he wasn't himself. Just as he was wondering if he could get away with leaving his hood up, he felt a sharp tug near the top of his neck as his grey felt defence was pulled down. The night air hit his face. Eve grinned at him. 'Don't hide,' she said. Is it any wonder I left her, when she behaves like this, Campbell thought angrily.

'Get out of it, or I'll call the police,' Clive Terry threatened Sim, who'd placed herself at the front of the line of elephants.

'Call them,' she said. 'This is a peaceful protest.' Giggling broke out behind her and Sim felt proud that she'd succeeded in uniting the group against a common enemy.

'You're trespassing!'

'We're making a protest,' Francis explained. 'I'm Francis Weir, deputy editor of *The North Today* . . .'

'Francis, you name-dropping tosser!' Matt laughed raucously.

'I don't care who you are,' said Clive Terry.

'We're Grimbelina's mates,' said Matt. 'Sorry, Rory's mates. She invited us to her parrrty.' He stumbled over the last word. Clive Terry curled his nose at the strong smell of alcohol that wafted towards him on Matt's breath. 'Honest, we're her pals. Let us in, go on!'

'I see.' The butler looked as if he was considering it. 'Well, you're a bit late. Rory thought no one had turned up. You're the first to arrive.'

'Ha ha!' Eve shrieked. 'The Grimble's got no friends!'

431

'Come on, let's go,' said Campbell. 'We've made our point.'

'Is that you, Mr Golightly?'

'Yes, erm . . .'

'Tell Rory that Campbell was here,' said Eve. 'Rory!' She shouted up at the top window. 'Rory-no-mates! Look who's here!'

'Let's go,' said Matt suddenly. 'I'm bored and we're out of booze. Let's find a pub or something.'

'Not yet,' said Sim. 'Call the cops,' she instructed Clive Terry.

'Sim, come on, don't start trouble,' said Ian.

'I never start trouble,' she corrected him. 'I merely respond fulsomely to trouble started by other people.'

The front door opened again and Rory ran outside, wearing a long green velvet evening dress with a slit up one side that revealed one of her legs. 'Ugh, look, she's got one of her tentacles out,' Eve said to Sim. It was weird, seeing Rory in the flesh after all this time. Here she was, though, the demon, right in front of her, within reach. 'Chant!' Sim instructed her elephant army, enough of whom obliged to make a substantial impact. 'RORY THRIVES MEANS MORE WRECKED LIVES!' rang out in the London air.

'Campbell, you bastard!' Rory enunciated clearly, as if she didn't want anyone to miss a word. Now the whole neighbourhood would be clear about precisely who was a bastard, thought Campbell. This was excruciating. In the well-lit hallway of the house, he could see the faces of some of the Nappers' other servants peering avidly into the garden, whispering to one another. He hadn't opened his mouth yet. The others were chanting but he wasn't, which made him the solitary non-bastard. Couldn't Rory see that, see how uncomfortable he was? If she'd only use her imagination, thought Campbell, it'd be obvious to her that I've been forced into this. She couldn't blame him.

Eve looked at Campbell looking at Rory. He was clearly

terrified, poor thing – of Rory, the stupid butler man, Sim, the police, life, everything. Tonight, this, was so much not his scene that Eve found it hilarious to see him here, in the thick of it. He seemed to be making a point of boycotting the chanting, sitting on the fence as usual. Still, he was here, and with Eve, not Rory. How could Eve refuse to give him a second chance after this? She pushed the uncomfortable thought of Neil out of her mind, thinking to herself, 'I'm too swept up in the moment to think about Neil.' She walked over to Campbell. 'This is your last chance,' she whispered in his ear. 'If you love me, chant.'

And Campbell, God help him, chanted.

(vi)

'Francis, phone Neil!'

1

'Francis.' Sim sat bolt upright in bed. It was Sunday night and they were at home in their flat. She'd been sound asleep. Dreaming. Something had woken her up. Was it . . . could it be . . . ? 'Francis!' she whispered urgently.

'Mm?'

'Sit up. Listen.' There was no doubt about it. Sim's world-view had returned. She could feel its presence as surely as if she'd heard it let itself into the flat with its own key and slam the door behind it.

'. . . middle of the night,' Francis mumbled sleepily.

'I know, but Francis, my world-view's come back! You've got to ring Neil.'

'What?'

'Phone Neil. Oh, thank God – I'm cured!'

'Are you crazy? He'll be asleep. As I was, only seconds ago.'

'He won't, he'll be lying awake, miserable. Eve will have gone home and told him the wedding's off, that she's leaving him for Campbell. They're probably screaming at each other right now.'

'And you expect me to phone in the middle of all that? No thanks!'

'You've got to phone him, Francis. Imogen's poem's a sign.' Sim reached for the yellow envelope, which was on her bedside table. She hadn't passed it on to Eve yet, wanting to choose her moment wisely. She could hardly do it when Campbell was there.

'A sign of what?'

'Doesn't it seem a bit funny to you, a girl of that age writing such a mature, intelligent poem?'

'Well . . . you said she wouldn't have pretended it was hers if it wasn't.'

'She didn't pretend.' Sim shook her head impatiently. Francis was slow sometimes. 'But that doesn't mean there couldn't have been something else, speaking through her.'

'Like what?'

'I don't know! Doesn't it strike you as odd, though? I mean, first Neil helps Imogen's poem – the one she wrote for the competition – then Imogen writes another poem which helps Neil by getting it through to me how much he and Eve mean to her. It's symmetrical, Francis.'

'Bully for it!' Francis groaned and rolled over on to his side.

'Francis, don't turn away. I can't ignore this, it's a sign. Neil needs us to help him get Eve back.'

'What?' Francis sat up and turned on his bedside lamp. 'What did you just say?'

'Look, I know it sounds mad . . .'

'You can say that again!'

'Oh, Francis. Neil's a decent guy. You liked him, didn't you? We have to help him.'

'Sim, have you gone insane? What about Campbell?'

'Campbell's in a position of strength now. He's got Eve back, he made a stand against Rory. He's doesn't need us any more.'

'Oh, for God's sake!'

'If Campbell and Eve's love is as good as I've been claiming it is all this time, it'll withstand our trying to get Eve and Neil back together. It's the perfect test. The best man will win. I need to know who the best man is, Francis. And there's Imogen to consider. The three of them are a family. I owe it to them to . . .'

438

'I refuse to consider anything or anyone. This is absurd!'

'Francis, don't be like that. That was how you used to be, before.'

'Very sensible, I must have been!'

'Francis . . .'

'No!' he wailed, pressing a pillow against his face.

'It wasn't a fair contest,' Sim tugged at his pyjama sleeve. 'Campbell had the benefit of my hard work, all my efforts on his behalf. Neil's never had that and until he does we won't know who deserves to win.'

'Look, can I make a suggestion? Why don't you stop inflicting your help on people? It doesn't do anyone any good.'

'Stop wasting time, Francis. Neil and Eve are booked into Cambridge Register Office on Saturday morning . . .'

'. . . oh, no, God, please!'

'. . . Neil's a pretty exceptional character, you've got to admit. We can't desert him now.'

'Oh, Christ!'

'Francis, phone Neil!'

Acknowledgements

Thanks to Lisanne Radice, Jane Gregory, Jane Barlow, Claire Morris, Terry Bland and Tom Santorelli of Gregory and Radice, and to Suzanne Amphlet. Thanks, also, to everyone at Random House, both then and now: Victoria Hipps, Lynne Drew, Natalie Fenton, Nicky Reynolds, Ron Beard, Kate Parkin, Thomas Wilson, Anna Dalton-Knott, everyone in the publicity and design departments and especially to Kate Elton for her dedicated and inspired editorial input at every stage.

I am also very grateful to the following people, all of whom helped with or inspired aspects of this book: Dan Jones, Morgan White, Claire, Martin and Lauren Chappell, Adèle, Norm and Jenny Geras, Suzanne Davies and Johnny Woodhams, Rosanna Keefe and Dominic Gregory, Emma Connelly and Kurt Haselwimmer, Chris Gribble, Ian, Rachel and Ben Tomlinson, Isabelle Thomas, Julian Murphet, Olivia Jones, Charlie Hall and Jigs Patel, Simon Rae and Sian Hughes, David and Sharon Williams, Natasha Hewitt and Rod Ellison, Michael Schmidt, Catherine Barnard and John Cary, Stephen Goode and Gina, Swithun Cooper and family, Isaac Zailer and Caroline Fletcher, Tony Weir, Tom and Rebecca Palmer, Peter Salt, Morris Szeftel.